THE BEST OF
philip josé farmer

THE BEST OF
philip josé farmer

Edited by Dorman T. Shindler

Subterranean Press • 2006

FIRST EDITION

ISBN
1-59606-036-0

Subterranean Press
P. O. Box 190106
Burton, MI 48519

e-mail:
info@subterraneanpress.com

website:
www.subterraneanpress.com

CONTENTS

Philip José Farmer:
♦ ♦ ♦ ♦ ♦ ♦ ♦ ♦ The Man with the Electric Brain

JOE R. LANSDALE

Philip José Farmer is a hero of mine. He has written much, and some might say too much, but I am not among them. Not all of his work has been sterling, but nearly all of it has been brave, and the bulk of it has been genius. He is, to my mind, the most underrated science fiction writer of all time, and considering he has received considerable praise for his work in that field, you will understand the intent of my statement.

He is even better than we think he is.

That's my story and I'm sticking to it. He's the writer with the electric brain.

Readers forget that without Farmer there might not be sex in science fiction. It would be stiff stuff about boy meets rocket and whips monster's ass, that would be the deal. Stories short on diddling of any kind, short on sexual metaphors that vault like track stars, short on adult viewpoints. In short, it would be, well, short.

Farmer gave science fiction sex, and it is the most important delivery package ever delivered to the field. It transformed it from boy's literature to a literature with adult potential.

I should also note that when he gave science fiction sex, he didn't give it conventional sex. He went even further, and when "The Lovers" was published, oh my, back then, it was a far jump indeed.

Some of this bears repeating.

Without Farmer, who just went for it, the arrival of sex in science fiction might have been stalled for many years. "The Lovers" is the story responsible for that. Before Farmer science fiction was a neutered field. Farmer opened the door, so to speak, and pretty soon others came through. But Farmer, he was there first, and the story still stands as one of the most unique stories in the literature of science fiction.

It should also be noted that Farmer is more than just a science fiction writer. That alone would be good enough, but in Farmer's case, it isn't. He is also a great fantasy writer, a writer of whimsy, and a great writer of literature. More often than not, he is all of these things simultaneously.

Sure, he wrote many books that are strictly adventure, in the vein of Edgar Rice Burroughs, a sentimental favorite of mine, but he brought to his books, even some of those in the aforementioned vein, an understanding of why books like those written by Burroughs continue to be effective. Farmer understands psychology. Freudian, Jungian, and some that have no name. There is an insight in his work that crawls through the backgrounds like some kind of beast. A wild beast that will do or say anything.

No one, absolutely no one, is braver than Philip José Farmer. He's willing to crawl out on most any limb. Like Tarzan, a name he was called as a child, he is willing to go where no one has gone before. At least as a writer. He'll crawl out on that limb, be it rickety and weak and disease ridden, and he'll not only crawl out there, he'll stand up and grin at you.

Sometimes the limb breaks, but because of Farmer's willingness to try anything, take any kind of chance, the results are often brilliant. Farmer is one of those handful of writers whose work, when it works, and on those rare occasions even when it doesn't, that strikes sparks off the mind and sends you reeling into worlds and thoughts you might never have thought to explore.

Hell. Sometimes I didn't even know those worlds were there, let alone thought to explore them. Not until Farmer showed them to me. Not until he ripped open the wall of my imagination, said, hey, man, did you know all this stuff was back there? This place has more than one room. And an attic. And a basement. And a backyard. A real large backyard. And, hey, we haven't even gone out front yet. And did you look in the dog house? How about the tool shed? Oh, and you should notice this too. Your imagination room. It has windows.

He's stunning.

And he's fun. It's not all stiff business here, not by a long shot. Farmer is never stiff, and he's certainly not above a great goof of a novel. Wonderful ideas thrown together to make a wild mixture of humor, adventure, war in the air, and, well, just about every damn thing you can think of. He's done it many times. Examples being one of my favorite hoots of a novel, *The Adventure of the Peerless Peer,* or his unique *Greatheart Silver,* which reads like a series of old pulp adventures, but better written than the bulk of those original pulp tales ever were. He rings the bells of nostalgia while moving the old concepts forward into new territory.

He does it time after time after time.

And what of the Riverworld story that inspired the series of novels of the same name, and its many sequels? In these books, the dead find they are brought to the banks of a world where all those who have died now live.

There are paddle wheels too, churning along on a great river with the dead on board. Or the once dead. The question is, why are they here? Are the alive, dead, in limbo? And why do they travel down a river not unlike the Mississippi? But more magical, by far.

Oh yeah, and there are all these nifty characters from history and sometimes you can almost see where this is going. But not exactly. Farmer's too smart for us. You never really know what he's up to. He doesn't follow the uniform idea of plot. He tries sometimes, but then, well, it steers off into Farmer territory. Thank goodness.

Any story by Farmer isn't just a good idea, it's chock full of ideas, more than most writers could pack into a lifetime of work, and Farmer sometimes has that many ideas in one book. And sometimes, now get this, in one short story.

He pops with ideas and notions while the rest of us are trying to form our first sentence.

I believe his genius is best represented in his short stories. They are his best work. I believe that in this form he has written some of the most influential and highly original stories ever written by anyone, science fiction or any kind of fiction.

Who else but Farmer would write about what happened after King Kong fell?

Who but Farmer would write a Tarzan story as if it were written by William S. Burroughs instead of Edgar Rice Burroughs? And though I'm uncertain if the story will appear in this collection due to space restrictions (Farmer has written way too many great stories), who else would write about Jesus Christ on a dude ranch? That's right. "J.C. on the Dude Ranch." The title alone makes the mind spin.

Farmer has written science fiction and he's written horror and he's written adventure and he's written fantasy and he's written.:.well, mostly, he's written Farmer stories. There is absolutely no one like him. Not enough of his work is in print. Why is that? Who is responsible for this travesty? If we can put a name to any one individual, then drawing and quartering and forcing them to watch *The Postman* over and over is just not good enough punishment. There is no punishment good enough for such a knave.

It is time this injustice was repaired. It is time Farmer's great and wonderful and highly original body of work was brought back into print.

And this book is a beginning. It's a great book. It is, in fact, the finest collection of Farmer short stories ever assembled. I am glad to be part of it, if in only a small way.

Take it.

Read it.

Farmer's electric brain is full of ideas and insight. It throws off sparks. When he's finished with you, your brain will spark as well. It might even be on fire.

Read him.

Be transformed.

Joe R. Lansdale,
Nacogdoches, Texas,

FOREWORD

During the day, the dreadnaught *Gabriel* squatted in a park in the center of the city of Siddo, on the planet Ozagen. From sunrise to sunset the *Gabriel*'s personnel ventured out among the Ozagenians — or wogglebugs, as they were familiarly and contemptuously called — learning all they could of Ozagen's history, customs, language and other things.

The "other things," though the Earthmen did not mention this to the wogglebugs, were Ozagen's technologies. As far as could be seen, the wogs had progressed, roughly speaking, to the level of Earth's early twentieth-century science. Logically, there should be nothing to fear from them. But the men of Earth's Haijac Union trusted no one. What if the wogs were hiding terrible weapons, waiting to catch the men unawares?

At nightfall, the spaceship rose to a height of fifty feet and poised there until the sun rose again. Then it sank back into the deep depression made by its own weight. Always a radar gig hovered in the stratosphere and probed for other spacecraft. Presumably, neither Earth's Israeli Republics nor its Bantu-Malay Federation knew of Ozagen...but if they found out!

Meanwhile the Terrans searched, studied, prowled and planned. Before they attacked the natives, before they began their decimation project to make room for the hordes that would follow, they must learn the wogs' potentialities.

And so it was that, a month after the appearance of the *Gabriel* above Siddo, two presumably friendly (to wogs) Terrans set out with two presumably friendly (to Terrans) wogglebugs on a trip. They were going to investigate the ruins of a city left by a dead humanoid race. They rode a vehicle fantastic to the men....

ONE

The motor hiccoughed and jerked. The Ozagenian sitting on the right side of the rear seat leaned over and shouted something. Hal Yarrow twisted his head and yelled, "*Quoi?*"

Fobo, sitting directly behind Hal, stuck his mouth against the Earthman's ear. He translated the gibberish into French:

"Zugu says and emphasizes that you should pump the throttle. That little rod to your right. It gives the carburetor more alcohol. Où quelque chose."

Fobo's antennae tickled Hal's ears. Hal said, "*Merci,*" and worked the throttle. To do so, he had to lean across the gapt, sitting at his right. "*Pardonnez-moi, monsieur Pornsen!*" he bellowed.

The gapt did not look at Yarrow; his hands, lying on his lap, were locked together. The knuckles showed white. Like his ward, he was having his first experience with an internal combustion motor. Unlike Hal, he was scared by the loud noise, the fumes, the bumps and bangs, and just the idea of riding in a manually controlled vehicle.

Hal grinned. He loved this quaint car, so reminiscent of Earth's early twentieth-century autos. It thrilled him to be able to twist the stiff-acting wheel and feel the heavy body obey his muscles. The four cylinders banging and the alcohol's reek excited him. As for the bouncing, that was fun. It was romantic, like putting out to sea in a sailboat — something else he hoped to do before they left Ozagen.

Also, anything that scared his gapt pleased Yarrow.

His pleasure ended. The cylinders popped, off-key. The car jerked and then rolled to a stop. At once, the two wogglebugs hopped over the side and raised the hood. Hal followed. Pornsen sat. He pulled a package of Merciful Seraphim from his uniform pocket, took one out and lit up.

He noted that it was the fourth time he'd seen Pornsen smoking since morning prayers. If Pornsen wasn't careful, he'd be going over his quota. That meant that the next time Hal got in trouble, he could blackmail the gapt into helping him. Judging by his troubles so far on this expedition, it wouldn't be long before he would have to.

Hal bent over the motor and watched. Zugu seemed to know what the matter was. He should, since he was the inventor and builder of the only — as far as the Terrans knew — native-made self-propelling vehicle on this planet.

Zugu used a wrench to unscrew a long narrow pipe from a round glass case. Yarrow remembered that this was a gravity feed system. The fuel ran from the tank into the glass case, which was a sediment chamber. From there it ran into the feed pipe, which in turn passed to the carburetor.

Pornsen called harshly, "Well, Yarrow, are we going to be stuck here all day?"

Though he still wore the hood and goggles the Ozagenians had equipped him with as windbreaks, the gapt's expression was clear enough. He would take out his annoyance in a report that would not be favorable to Hal. Unless, that is, his ward came across something so important in the humanoid ruins that it would justify this long trip.

The gapt—G.A.P.T., or Guardian Angel Pro Tempore—had wanted to wait the two days that would be needed until they could get a gig. The trip to the ruins could then have taken fifteen minutes, a soundless and comfortable ride through the air. But Hal had argued that driving through the countryside would be as valuable—if not more so, in detecting any hidden large industries—as reconnoitering by air. That superiors had agreed was another thing that had exasperated Pornsen. Where his ward went, he had to go. So he had sulked all day while the young Terran, coached by Zugu, wheeled the jalopy down the forest roads. The only times the gapt spoke was to remind Hal of the sacredness of the human self by telling him to slow down. Hal would nod and would ease his foot off the accelerator. But after a while he would roar and leap down the dirt road.

Zugu unscrewed both ends of the pipe, stuck one in his V-shaped mouth, and blew. Nothing came out the other end. Zugu shut his big blue eyes and blew again. Nothing happened, except that his already green-tinged face turned a dark green. Then he rapped the copper tubing against the hood and blew once more. No reaction.

Fobo reached into a large leather pouch slung from a belt around his big belly. His finger and thumb came out holding a tiny blue insect. Gently, he pushed the creature into one end of the pipe. In about five seconds a small red insect dropped out of the other end. Behind it, evidently in pursuit, came the blue. Fobo picked up his pet and put it back in the pouch. Zugu squashed the red thing beneath his bare heel.

"*Voilà. C'est un mangeur de l'alcool, monsieur,*" said Fobo. "It lives in the tank and imbibes freely and unmolested. It extracts the carbohydrates therein. A swimmer upon the golden seas of alcohol. What a life! But now and then it goes into the sediment chamber, eats and devours the filter, and passes into the feedpipe. *Voyez!* Zugu is even now replacing the filter. In a moment we will be on our way and road."

Fobo's breath had a strange and sickening odor. Hal wondered if the wog had been drinking liquor. He had never smelled alcohol on anybody's breath before, so he had no experience to go on. But even the thought of it made Hal nervous. If his gapt knew a bottle was being passed back and forth in the rear seat, he would not for a minute let Hal out of his sight.

The wogs climbed into the back seat. *"Allons!"*

Pornsen pursed his thin lips. He had meant to ask Zugu to drive, but he realized the wogs might think he lacked confidence in Yarrow. He did, but he could not admit that in front of an Ozagenian.

◆ ◆ ◆

Though Hal started slowly enough, he soon found his foot heavy. The trees began whizzing by. He glanced at Pornsen. The gapt's rigid back and set teeth showed that he was thinking of the report he would make to the chief Uzzite back in the spaceship. He looked mad enough to demand the 'Meter for his ward.

Yarrow breathed deeply the wind battering his face-mask. To H with Pornsen! To H with the 'Meter! The blood lurched in his veins. This planet's air was not stuffy Earth's. His lungs sucked it in like a happy bellows. At that moment he felt as if he could have snapped his fingers under the nose of the Sandalphon himself.

"Look out!" screamed Pornsen.

Hal glimpsed out of the corners of his eyes the large antelope-like beast that leaped from the forest onto the road. A half-second later, he twisted the wheel away from it. The jalopy skidded on the dirt. Its rear end swung around. Hal was not well enough grounded in the physics of driving to know that he should have turned the wheels in the direction of the skid to straighten the car out.

His lack of knowledge was not fatal, except to the beast, for its bulk struck the vehicle's side. Checked, the car quit trying to circle. Instead, it angled off the road and ran up a sloping ridge of earth. From there it leaped high into the air and landed with an all-at-once bang of four tires blowing.

Even that did not halt it. A big bush loomed. Hal jerked on the wheel. Too late.

His chest pushed hard against the wheel as if it were trying to telescope the steering shaft against the dashboard. Fobo slammed into Yarrow's back. Both cried out, and the wog fell off.

Then, except for a sharp hissing, there was silence. A pillar of steam from the broken radiator shot through the branches that held Hal's face in a rough barky embrace.

Yarrow stared through steamshapes into big brown eyes. He shook his head. Was he stunned? Eyes. And arms like branches. Or branches like arms. He thought he was in the grip of a brown-eyed nymph. Or were they called dryads? He couldn't ask anybody. He wasn't supposed to know about such creatures. *Nymph* and *dryad* had even been cut out of such books as Hack's edition of the Revised and Moral Milton. Only an unexpurgated *Paradise Lost* booklegged from Israel, had enabled Hal to learn of Greek mythology.

Thoughts flashed off and on like lights on a spaceship's pilotboard. Nymphs sometimes turned into trees to escape their pursuers. Was this one the fabled forest woman staring at him with large and beautiful eyes through the longest lashes he had ever seen?

He shut his lids and wondered if a head injury were responsible for the vision and if it were permanent. If it were, so what? Hallucinations like that were worth keeping.

He opened his eyes. The illusion was gone.

He thought, It was that antelope looking at me. It got away after all. It ran around the bush and looked back. Antelope eyes.

TWO

He forgot about the eyes. He was choking. A heavy nauseating odor hung around the car. The crash must have frightened the wogs very much, else they would not have released the sphincter muscles which controlled the neck of their "madbags." This organ, a bladder located near the small of their backs, had once been used by the prehumanoid ancestors of the Ozagenians as a powerful weapon of defense in much the same way as a bombardier beetle thwarts attackers. Now an almost vestigial structure, the madbag served as a means of relieving extreme nervous tension. Its function was effective, but is presented problems such as that of the wog psychiatrists, who either had to keep their windows open or else wear gasmasks during therapy.

Hal pushed aside the branches and struggled over the side. Why didn't wogs build doors in their vehicles?

Wong Af Pornsen, assisted by Zugu, crawled out from under the foliage. His big paunch, the color of his uniform, and the white nylon angel's wings sewed on the back of his jacket made him resemble a fat blue bug. When he stood up and took off his windmask, he showed a bloodless face. His shaking fingers fumbled over the crossed hourglass and sword, symbol of the Haijac Union, before they found the button he was searching for. He pulled out a pack of Merciful Cherubim. Once the cigarette was in his lips, he had a hard time holding the lighter to it.

Hal took out his own and held the glowing coil to the tobacco. It didn't waver.

Only thirty years of discipline could have shoved back the grin he felt deep inside his face muscles.

Pornsen accepted the light. A second later, a tremor of skin around his lips and eyes revealed that he knew he had lost much of his advantage over Yarrow. Trained in psychology, he realized you don't let a man do you a service—even one as slight as his ward's and then crack the whip on him.

He began formally, "Hal Shamshiel Yarrow…"

"Shib, *abba,* I hear."

"You're—uh—much too reckless."

Considering the offense, his voice was milder than it should have been. Now and then he stopped to draw in or puff out smoke.

"The hierarchy has had its eye (puff) upon you for a long time. Though you have not been suspected of any moral turpitude—as regards sex or liquor, that is—you have shown signs of a certain pride and independence. That is not shib, Yarrow. That is not real. It smacks of behavior that does not conform to the structure of the universe as we know it, as it has been revealed to mankind by the Forerunner, real be his name.

"I have (puff)—may the Forerunner forgive them!—sent two dozen men to H. I didn't like it, for I am a tenderhearted man, but it is the duty of the Guardian Angels Pro Tempore to watch out for the diseases of the self that may spread and infect the followers of Isaac Sigmen. Unreality must not be tolerated; the self is too weak and precious to be subjected to temptation.

"I have been your gapt since you were (puff) born. You always were a disobedient child, but you could be whipped into submissiveness, into seeing reality. Not until you were eighteen did you become hard to handle. That was when you decided to become a joat. I thought you'd make a very good specialist, and I warned you that as a joat you'd only get so high in our society. But you persisted. And since we have need of joats, and since I was overridden by my superior, I allowed you to become one.

"That wasn't too (puff) unshib, but when I picked out the woman most suitable to be your wife, I saw just how proud and rebellious you were. She was a woman whom the Urielites, selfdocs, and Sandalphons agreed was the ideal mate as set forth in the Western Talmud. And yet you argued and held out for a year before you consented to marry her. In that year of unreal behavior, you cost the Sturch one self...."

Hal's face had paled, and in so doing had revealed seven thin red marks that rayed out fanwise from the left corner of his lips and across his cheek to his ear. They were scars left by Pornsen's lash years before.

"I cost it nothing," blazed Hal. "Mary and I were married ten years, and she proved barren. And it was her fault, not mine, as the tests proved. When that came out, why didn't you insist on our divorce, as your duty required, instead of pigeonholing my petition?"

◆ ◆ ◆

Pornsen blew out smoke slowly enough, but his voice tensed. He dropped one shoulder lower than the other, a characteristic when he forgot himself, and said, "That's another thing. I was sure when you applied for this expedition that it was not out of desire to serve the Sturch in its quest for new lands for our overcrowded planets. (Puff) I was sure you signed up for one reason. To get away from your wife. Since barrenness, adultery, and space travel are the only legal grounds for divorce, and adultery means going to H, you took the only way out. You became legally dead. You—"

"You can't prove it!" Hal was shaking, and loathed himself because he could not hide his rage.

"Oh, I could have, if I had recommended you for the Elohimeter. But we needed scientists very much, and my superiors thought it best to overlook your possible motives. Besides, you had an excuse in that sterility report, which was lost through the inefficiency of my secretaries.

"However, the hierarchy has been slowly and regretfully, but surely, coming to the conclusion that you do not have a high enough regard for your self. Or that of others.

"The self, as defined by Isaac Sigmen, is sacred, sacred to God, to the angels both high and low, to the pre-Torah prophets..."

Hal listened with only a half-ear. Pornsen was repeating Moral Lecture PT19, which his ward knew by heart. Hal was looking at the beast's body crumpled on the road. Now he remembered the thump the jalopy had made when it struck it. But if it were dead, whose eyes had he seen through the bush?

Fobo, the empathist, was bending over it. He straightened up; large tears filled his blue eyes and ran down the long tubular nose. The antennae rising from his bald forehead waved. He made a circular sign with his index finger over the carcass.

Hal said to Pornsen, "Shut up!"

The gapt stiffened. The lower left shoulder drew level with the other. The cigarette fell from his slack thin lips. Red swarmed up his bull-neck and sagging jowls. His right hand shot to his belt and grabbed the crux ansata on the handle of his whip. He jerked it out and cracked it in the air.

The marks on Yarrow's cheek tingled in remembrance of that other time when the lashes, one for each of the Seven Deadly Unrealities, had cut the flesh.

The gapt said, "How dare you?"

Hal said in a low voice, swiftly, "A moment ago you said something in English. You know French is the only tongue we're allowed to speak under any circumstances."

The whip dropped.

"When — when was that?"

"When you screamed at me just before we struck that animal. Remember? And when you were yelling for help under the bush."

Pornsen stuck the whip back in his belt and lit up another Merciful Seraphim. His fifth that day. Another, and he'd be over his quota.

"You say nothing to the chief," he muttered. "And I'll keep quiet about your sibboleth recklessness."

"Shib," agreed Hal.

He tried to keep the contempt and elation out of his voice. Once a gapt cracked....

Pornsen rolled his small green eyes at the approaching Fobo. "Think he heard me?"

"I wouldn't know."

Fobo stopped and looked at them. His antennae became rigid. He said, "*Un argument, messieurs?*"

Fobo had wept as the dying beast's nervous discharges of grief and pain struck his overtrained, too receptive antennae. Now he smiled the ghastly V-in-V smile of a wogglebug. Though supersensitive, his nervous system was a hit and run one. Charge and discharge came easily.

"*Non!*" replied Hal. "No disagreement. We were just wondering how far we'd have to walk to get to the humanoid ruins. Your jalopy's wrecked. Tell Zugu I'm sorry."

"*Ca ne fait rien.* The walk will be pleasant and stimulating. It is only a mile. Or thereabouts."

"*Bien. Allons.*"

The ward turned away and threw his mask and goggles in the rear seat of the car, where the Ozagenians had laid theirs.

He picked up his suitcase, but left the gapt's on the floor. Let him carry his own.

He said, "Fobo, aren't you afraid the driving-clothes will be stolen?"

"Pardon? What does that mean?"

"*Voler. Voler.* To take an article of property from someone without their permission, and keep it for yourself. It is a crime, punishable by law."

"*Un crime?*"

Hal gave up. He shrugged and moved his long legs fast. Behind him the gapt, afraid of losing dignity if he trailed behind Hal, and angry because his ward was breaking etiquette by forcing him to carry his own case, shouted, "You'll pay for this, you—you joat!"

With which outburst he lost face.

Hal didn't turn. He plunged on ahead. The angry retort he was phrasing beneath his breath fizzed away. Out of the corner of his eye he had caught a flash of white skin in the green summer foliage.

But when he turned to look for it, it was gone. Nor did he see it or its owner the rest of the day.

THREE

"*Soo* Yarrow. *Soo* Yarrow. *B'swa. L'fvayfvoo, Soo* Yarrow."

Hal woke up. For a moment, he didn't remember where he was. Then he recalled that he was sleeping in one of the marble rooms of the mammal-humanoid ruins. The moonlight, brighter than Earth's, poured in through the doorway. It shone on a small shape on the floor near the entrance, and on a flying insect that passed above the shape. Something long and thin flickered up and wrapped itself around the flier and pulled it into a suddenly gaping mouth.

The lizard loaned by the ruins custodian was doing a fine job of keeping out pests.

Hal turned his head to look at the open window a foot above him. The bugcatcher there was busily sweeping the area clean of mosquitoes. From beyond that moonwashed square the voice had seemed to come. He listened. Silence. Then a snuffling and rattling jerked him upright. A thing the size of a raccoon stood by the doorway. It was one of the quasi-insects, the so called lungbugs, that prowled the forest at night. It represented a development of arthropod not found on Earth.

Unlike its Terran cousins, it no longer depended solely on tracheae, or breathing tubes, for oxygen. A pair of distensible sacs, like a frog's, swelled out and fell in behind its mouth, and enabled it to make the heavy breathing sound.

Though it was shaped like a praying mantis, Hal wasn't worried. Fobo had told him it would not attack without provocation.

A shrilling like that of an alarm clock suddenly filled the room. Pornsen, on the cot across the room, sat up. He saw the insect and yelled. It scurried off. The shrilling, which had come from the mechanism on Pornsen's wrist, stopped.

Pornsen lay down and groaned. "That makes the sixth time those bugs have woke me up."

"Turn off the wristbox," said Hal.

Pornsen did not answer. For about ten minutes he was restless and then he began snoring. Hal's lids felt heavy. He must have dreamed the soft low voice speaking in a tongue neither Terran nor Ozagenian. He must have, because it had been human; and he and the gapt were the only specimens of homo sapiens for at least two hundred miles.

It had been a woman's voice. God! To hear one again. Almost two years now!

And he knew it would probably be five years before he would hear another. That is, if he returned.

"*Soo Yarrow. L'fvayfvoo. Say mwa, zh'not w'stinvak.*"

Hal stood up. His neck was cased in ice. The whisper *was* coming from the window. He turned his head. The outline of a woman's head leaned into the solid box of moonlight that was the window. Moonwash fell off white shoulders. A pale finger crossed the black of mouth.

"*Poo lamoo d'b'tyu, soo. Seelahs. F'nay. Feet, seel-fvooplay.*"

Numbed, but obeying as if shot full of hypno-lipno, he threw aside the sheet over his legs. Slowly, he turned on his buttocks and moved his feet until they touched the stone floor. With a look to make sure Pornsen was still asleep, he rose.

For a second his training almost overcame him and forced him to wake the gapt up. But it was evident the woman was addressing him alone. Her urgency and suppressed fear decided him to take a chance. It also made him wonder if she might not be a member of one of the unreal sects that had fled the Haijac Union two hundred or more years ago —

No. That couldn't be. She spoke in no tongue he knew. For that same reason, it was improbable that she was a party to an expedition from one of the other Earth nations.

Her words had seemed to click something familiar, however—as if he ought to know the language. But he didn't. It wasn't the English or Icelandic or Caucasian of the Haijac Union, or the Hebrew of the Israeli Republics, or the Bazaar or Swahili of the Bantu-Malay Federation. Yet it had sounded like something he'd heard before. And recently.

He picked up his suitcase and shoved it under the sheet. He rolled up a blanket and packed it next to the case. His jacket he folded and laid on the pillow. If Pornsen woke up and took a quick look at the cot, he might be fooled into thinking the bulk under the sheet was Hal's.

Softly, on bare feet, he walked to the doorway. A cylinder the size of a tin can squatted on guard. If any object larger than a mouse came within two feet of the field radiating from the cylinder, it would set up a disturbance which would cause a signal to be transmitted to the small box mounted on a silver bracelet around the gapt's wrist. The box would shrill—as it had at the appearance of the lungbug and up would come Pornsen from the bottom of his ever-watchful sleep.

The watchcan was not only there to insure against trespassers. Its primary purpose was to make certain that Hal would not leave the room without Pornsen's knowledge. As the ruins had no working plumbing, the only permissible excuse to step outside would be to relieve bowel or bladder. The gapt would go along to see that that was what he intended.

Two things Pornsen was watching for. One was unsupervised contact with the wogs. The other was that unreal conduct, punishable by exile to H and cataloged in the *Sefer shel ha Chetim,* or the Book of Sins, as Onanism. The long space voyage had resulted in the arrest of five men for that very unreality.

Hal picked up one of the flyswatters given them by the ruins custodian. It had a three-foot-long handle made of some flexible wood. Its mass would not be enough to touch off the field. Though his hand trembled, he grasped the swatter-end and very gently pushed the cylinder to one side with the handle. He had to be careful not to upset it, for that, too, would trigger the alarm. Fortunately, the stone floor was smooth.

When he had stepped outside, he reached back in and slid the cylinder back to its former spot. Then, with his heart pounding under the double burden of tampering with the guard and of meeting a strange woman, he walked around the corner.

She had moved from the window into the shadow of a kneeling goddess' statue about sixty yards away. When Hal began striding toward her, he saw the reason for her hiding. Fobo was strolling towards him. Hal walked faster. He wanted to intercept the wog before he no-

ticed the girl and also before he came so close that their voices might
wake up Pornsen.

"*Bon soir,*" greeted Fobo. His antennae described little circles. "You
seem nervous. Is it that incident of the forenoon?"

"*Non.* I am just restless."

Hal looked at the empathist. Ozagen! What was the story? That the
discoverer of this planet, upon first seeing the natives, had exclaimed,
"Oz again!" because the aborigines had so much resembled Frank
Baum's Professor Wogglebug? Their bodies were rather round, and their
limbs were skinny in proportion. Their mouths were shaped like two
broad and shallow V's, one set inside the other. The lips were thick and
lobular. Actually, a wogglebug had four lips, each leg of the two V's
separated by a deep seam at the connection. Once, far back on the evolutionary path, those lips had been modified arms. Now they were rudimentary limbs, so disguised as true labial parts that no one who did
not know their history would have guessed their origin. When the wide
V-in-V mouths opened in a laugh, they startled the Terrans. The teeth
were quite human, true, but a fold of skin hung from the roof of the
mouth. Once the epipharynx, it was now a vestigial upper tongue, of
no use at all except to tell of the wogs' arthropodal ancestry.

Their skins were as unpigmented as Hal's redhead complexion, but
where the Earthman's epidermis was pink, theirs was a very faint green.
Copper, not iron, carried oxygen in their blood cells.

They had antennae, their forepates were bald, but a stiff corkscrew
fuzz rose from their backpates to form a corona. To complete the Oz
parallel, their noses were bridgeless and shot straight out from their
faces in projectile fashion.

The Terran who first saw them might have been justified by his
remark. However, the story wasn't true. Ozagen was the native name
for "Mother Earth."

FOUR

Wogglebug they were called, yet they were no more insects than
the Earthmen. It was true that millions of years ago their ancestors had
been a primitive unspecialized wormlike arthropod. But evolution follows parallel paths when aiming at intelligent beings. Realizing the
limitations of the anatomy, she had split Fobo's Nth-great-grandfather
from the arthropod phylum. When the crustacea, arachnida, and insecta
had formed exoskeletons and ventral nervous systems, Grandpa the
Nth had declined to go along with his cousins. He had refused to harden

his delicate cuticle-skin into chitin and had begun shifting the central nerves from chest and belly to the back and had also erected a skeleton inside the flesh. Both of the latter feats were equal to lifting oneself by the bootstraps.

As the price for that action, by the time the true arthropods were very developed, highly specialized creatures creeping, hopping, and flying by the billions over the hot new globe, Fobo's ancestors were still ugly, flatwormish things hiding from their beautiful, fully rounded-out relatives.

Becoming chordate arthropods—a contradiction in terms, by the way—was a deed that took many millions of years and much humility and self-denial.

Yet it had been worth it. The wogs' fathers had finally made the ventral to dorsal shift and sheathed their bones in muscle. Their cold blood became warm; they developed airsacs and then lungs. Their nerves ramified and grew intricate. The strata-shot eye of the epoch winked, and a monkeylike creature appeared. Another wink, and it was an ape. After a very long while, as years go, it came down from the trees. Once brachiate, it began walking on two feet. It passed through australopithecoid, pithecanthropoid, and neanderthaloid stages. It became Fobo.

One of the few arthropodal heritages left was the pair of antennae. Eras ago they might have been used, as some insects are supposed to use theirs, for communication. Now their function was rudimentary, but effective. They were so sensitive they could pick up nervous discharges from the skin of other beings. That gift, thought Hal, probably helped make the Ozagen society what it was. No wogglebug could fool another about his emotions. If he pretended friendliness, he would be betrayed. Hate, fear, rage, affection and love were easily read. A wog had to express what he felt, because he could not hide it. And once he had expressed, he had discharged his emotions, rebalanced his organism, and opened himself to rational talk and conduct.

At least, that was the theory. In actual practice, as Fobo said, it was not so easy.

Hal became aware that Fobo was talking to him:

" — this *joat* that *monsieur* Pornsen called you when he was so angry and furious. What does that mean?"

The Terran could not tell Fobo that the word was an initial combination, formed from the first letters of jack-of-all-trades. The wog would wonder how they deduced that combination from French.

"It means," he said carefully, "that I am not a specialist in any of the sciences, but one who knows, or is supposed to know, a great deal about all of them. Actually, I am a liaison officer between various scientists and the government. It is my business to summarize and integrate what is going on in science and then report to the hierarchy."

He glanced at the statue. The woman was not in sight.

"Science has become so specialized that intelligible communication even between scientists in the same field is very difficult. Each has a deep vertical knowledge of his own little field, but not much horizontal. The more he knows about his own subject, the less aware he is of what others are doing. It is so bad that a physicist, for instance, who deals in mercury anti-ions will find it hard to talk the same language as one whose study is radioactive isotopes. Or two doctors who specialize in nose dysfunctions. One treats the left nostril; the other, the right. Believe me, that's not exaggerated."

Fobo shrugged his shoulders and threw up his hands. He might have been French.

"But...science would come to a standstill!"

"Exactly."

Hal saw a head stick out from the base of the statue. It withdrew. Hal began sweating.

Fobo questioned the joat about the religion of the Forerunner. Hal was as taciturn as possible and replied to some questions not at all. The wog was nothing if not logical, and logic was the light that Hal had never turned upon what he had been taught by the Urielites.

Finally the empathist said, "I feel that this conversation is making you nervous. Perhaps we can pursue it some other time. Tell me, what do you think of these ruins?"

"Very interesting. What I cannot imagine is how these people, who you say once covered this huge continent, could entirely die out."

"Oh, there may be a few in the backwoods or jungles. But most died in the wars with us about five hundred years ago. Since then there's been peace on this planet. It's true we wiped them out, but they were very decadent, quarrelsome and greedy, and forced my ancestors to fight them."

Human, all right, thought Hal.

"I'll tell you later about their decline and fall," Fobo said. "In some ways it is a fantastic story. Right now, I think I'll go to bed."

"I'm restless. If you don't mind, I'll poke around. These ruins are fascinating in the moonlight."

"Reminds me of a poem by our great bard, Shamero. If I could remember it, I'd quote it." Fobo's V-in-V lips yawned. *"Bonne nuit."*

Hal watched him until he'd disappeared, then turned and walked toward the statue of the Great Mother. When he got to the shadows in its base, he saw the girl slipping into the darkness cast by a mountain-ous heap of rubble. He followed, only to see her thirty yards ahead, leaning against a monolith. Beyond was the lake, silvery and black in the moonpaint.

"*B'swa, soo Yarrow.*" Her voice was low and throaty.

"*Bon soir, mademoiselle,*" he said mechanically.... and then paused, struck.

Of course! Now he knew why it had had a familiar ring. *B'swa* was *bon soir!* Even though her words were a degraded form, they could not disguise their essential Latinity. *B'swa!* And *l'fvayfvoo* was *levez-vous,* which was French for "get up." How could he have missed it? It must have been because his mind wasn't expecting the familiar, and there-fore had not recognized it. *Say mwa. C'est moi.* It's I. And *soo* Yarrow. Could that be *mon-sieur* Yarrow? The initial m dropped. Final r also. Abandonment of nasalization plus vowel and consonant shifts in other words. Different, but still subtly Gallic.

"*Bon soir, mademoiselle.*"

How inadequate those words were. Here were two human beings meeting a thousand light-years from Earth, one a man who had not seen a woman for two years, the other a woman obviously hiding; per-haps the only woman left on the planet. And all he could say was "Good evening, miss."

He stepped closer. Suddenly he was flushed with heat. Her white skin was relieved only by two black, narrow strips of cloth, one across her breasts, the other diapered around the hips. In all his life he had seen only one woman who was not clad from neck to floor in thick cloth, and that had been in a semidarkness. She had been his wife.

The heat of his embarrassment was followed by a gasp of astonish-ment. She was lipsticked! Her lips were scarlet in the moonlight with the forbidden rouge.

His mind gave that problem a quick flip in the air and considered its other side. Cosmetics had gone out with the coming of the Forerun-ner. They were unreal, immoral. No woman dared...well, that wasn't true...it was just in the Haijac Union that they were not used. Israeli and Bantu women wore rouge; but then everybody knew what kind of women they were.

Another step, and Hal breathed hard again. He was close enough to see that the scarlet was natural. That meant that she was not Earthborn but was an Ozagen human being. The murals in the ruins showed red-lipped women, and Fobo had told him they were born with the flam-ing labile pigment.

But how could that be? She spoke a Terran dialect.

The next moment he forgot about his doubts and paradoxes. She was clinging to him and he had his arms around her, clumsily trying to comfort her. She was pouring out words, one so fast after the other that even though he knew they came from the French he could only make out a word here and a phrase there.

Hal asked her to slow down and go over what she had said. She paused, her head cocked slightly to the left, while he enunciated clearly his request. When he was through, she brushed back the hair over one ear, a gesture he was to find characteristic of her when she was thinking.

Then she repeated.

She began slowly enough. But as she progressed she speeded up, her full lips working like two bright-red things independent of her, packed with their own life and purpose.

Fascinated, Hal watched them. As they worked, they seemed to send stabs of desire into him, almost as if they were heliographing erotic messages.

With an effort he lifted his gaze from them and listened, trying to grasp her whole story.

She told it disconnectedly and with repetition and backtracking. But he could understand that her name was Jeannette, that she came from a plateau in the tropics of Ozagen, that she was one of the few human beings left on the planet, that she had been captured by an exploring party of wogs and taken to Siddo, that she had only recently escaped, that she had been hiding in the ruins and the nearby forest, that she was frightened because of the things that prowled the forest at night, that she lived on wild fruit and berries or on food stolen from wog farmhouses, that she had seen Hal when he crashed the jalopy, that she had followed him and listened to his conversations with the two wogs and with the gapt, that she could tell by her instincts — here she used a word that he did not understand but which he translated as "instincts" — that he was a man she could trust, that he had to do something for her.

That he had to save her.

Tears filled her big dark eyes, and her voice broke. She leaned against him; her shoulders were soft and smooth; her full breasts pressed against his ribs. What her words did not say, her body did.

Yarrow thought swiftly. He had to get back to the room in the ruins before Pornsen woke up. And he couldn't see her tomorrow, because a gig from the ship was picking the two Haijacs up in the morning. Whatever he was going to do would have to be told to her in the next few minutes.

Suddenly he had a plan; it unfolded in an instant from another idea, one he had long carried around buried in the fertile soil of his brain. Its seeds had been in him even before the ship had left Earth. But he hadn't had the courage to carry it out. Now, with the sudden appearance of this girl as a catalyst, he was thrown into action. She was what he needed to spark his guts and make him step onto a path that, once taken, could not be retraced.

"Jeannette," he said rapidly and fiercely, "listen to me! You'll have to wait here every night. No matter what things haunt the dark, you'll have to be here. I can't tell you just when I'll be able to get a gig and fly here. Sometime in the next three weeks, I think. If I'm not here by then, keep waiting. Keep waiting! I'll be here! And when I am, we'll be safe. Safe for a while, at least. Can you do that? Can you hide here? And wait?"

She nodded her head and said, "*Vi.*"

FIVE

Two weeks later, Yarrow flew from the spaceship *Gabriel* to the ruins. His needle-shaped gig gleamed in the big moon as it floated over the white marble buildings and settled to a stop. The city lay silent and bleached, great stone cubes and hexagons and cylinders and pyramids and statues like toys left scattered while the giant child went to bed and slept forever.

The Terran stepped out, glanced to left and right, and then strode to an enormous arch. His flashlight probed its darkness; his voice echoed from the faraway roof and walls.

"*Jeannette. C'est moi. Votre ami,* Hal Yarrow. *Jeannette. Ou êtes vous?*"

He walked down the fifty-yard-broad staircase that led to the crypts of the kings. The beam bounced up and down the steps and suddenly splashed against the black and white figure of the girl.

"Hal!" she cried, looking up at him. "Thank the Great Stone Mother! I've waited every night! But I knew you'd come!"

Tears trembled on the long lashes; her scarlet mouth was screwed up as if she were doing her best to keep from sobbing. He wanted to take her in his arms and comfort her, but a lifetime of "you-must-nots" stiffened his arms. It was a terrible thing even to look at a woman as unclothed as she was. To embrace her would be unthinkable. Nevertheless, that was exactly what he was thinking of.

The next minute, as if divining his paralysis, she moved to him and put her head on his chest. Her own shoulders hunched forward as she tried to burrow into him. He found his arms going around her. His muscles tightened, and heat stabbed from his stomach down into his loins.

He released her and looked away. "We'll talk later. We've no time to lose. Come."

She followed him, silently, until they came to the gig. Then she hesitated by the door. He gestured impatiently for her to climb in and sit down beside him.

"You will think I'm a coward," she said. "But I have never been in a flying machine. To leave this solid earth...."

Surprised, he could only stare at her. It was hard for him to understand the mental attitude of a person totally unaccustomed to airtravel. Such reactions did not fit into his culture.

"Get in!" he barked.

Obediently enough, she got in and sat down in the co-pilot's seat. She could not keep from trembling, however, or looking with huge brown eyes at the instruments before and around her.

Deciding the best thing to do was to ignore her fear, Hal glanced at his watchphone.

"Ten minutes to get to my apartment in the city. One minute to drop you off there. A half-minute to return to the ship. Fifteen minutes to report on my espionage among the wogs. Thirty seconds to return to the apartment. Not quite half an hour in all. Not bad."

He laughed. "I would have been here two days ago, but I had to wait until all the gigs that were on automatic were in use. Then I pretended that I was in a hurry, that I had forgotten some notes, and that I had to go back to my apartment to pick them up. So I borrowed one of the manually controlled gigs used for exploration outside the city. I never could have gotten permission from the O.D. for that, but he was overwhelmed by this."

Hal touched a large golden badge on his left chest. It bore a Hebrew L.

"That means I'm one of the Chosen. I've passed the 'Meter."

Jeannette had seemingly forgotten her terror and had been looking at Hal's face in the glow from the panel-light. She gave a little cry. "Hal Yarrow! What have they done to you?" Her fingers touched his face.

He looked at her. A deep purple ringed his eyes; his cheeks were sunken, and in one a muscle twitched; a rash spread ever his forehead; and the seven whipmarks stood out against a pale skin.

"Anybody would say I was crazy to do it," he said. "I stuck my head in the lion's mouth. And he didn't bite my head off. Instead, I bit his tongue."

"What do you mean?"

"Listen. Didn't you think it was strange that Pornsen wasn't with me tonight, breathing his sanctimonious breath down my neck? No? Well, you don't know our setup. There was only one way I could get permission to move out of my quarters in the ship and get an apartment in Siddo. That is, without having a gapt living with me to watch my every move. And without having to leave you out here in the forest. And I couldn't do that."

He shook his head. She ran her finger down the line from his nose to the corner of his lip. Ordinarily he would have shrunk from the touch, because he hated close contact with anybody. Now, he didn't shrink.

"Hal," she said softly. "*M' sheh.*"

"*Mon cher,*" he corrected

"*Mon cher,*" she repeated.

He felt a glow. *My dear.* Well, why not?

To stave off the headiness her touch gave, he said, "There was only one thing to do. Volunteer for the 'Meter."

"*Le Mètre? Keskasekasah?*"

"It's the only thing that can free you from the constant shadow of a gapt. Once you've passed it, you're pure, above suspicion — theoretically, at least.

"My petition caught the hierarchy off guard. They never expected any of the scientists — let alone me — to volunteer. Urielites and Uzzites have to take it if they hope to advance in the hierarchy — "

"Urielites? Uzzites?"

"To put it in ancient terminology, priests and cops. The Forerunner adopted those terms — the names of angels — for religious-governmental use — from the Talmud. See?"

"*Non.*"

"You'll be clearer about that later. Anyway, only the most zealous ask to face the 'Meter. It's true that many people do but the majority do it because they are compelled to. The Urielites were gloomy about my chances before it, but they were forced by law to let me try my chances. Besides, they were bored, and they wanted to be entertained — in their grim fashion.

He scowled a little at the memory. "So it was that a day later I was told to report to the psych lab at 2300 S.T. — Ship's Time, that is. I went into my cabin — Pornsen was out — opened my labcase, and took out a bottle labeled 'Prophetsfood.' It was supposed to contain a powder whose base was peyote. That's a drug that was once used by American Indian medicine-men."

"*Quoi?*"

"Just listen. You'll get the main points. Prophetsfood is taken by everybody during Purification Period. That's two days of locking yourself in a cell, fasting, praying, being flagellated by electric whips, and seeing visions induced by hunger and Prophetsfood. Also subjective time-traveling."

"*Quoi?*"

"Don't keep saying 'What?' I haven't got time to explain dunnology…It took me ten years of hard study to understand it and its mathematics. Even then, there were a lot of questions I had. But it's not wise to ask them. You might be thought to be doubting.

"Anyway, my bottle did not hold Prophetsfood. Instead it contained a substitute I'd secretly prepared just before the ship left Earth. That powder was the reason why I dared face the 'Meter. And why I was not as terrified as I should have been…though I was scared enough. Believe me."

"I do believe you. You were brave. You overcame your fear."

Hot blood crept beneath his face-skin. It was the first time in his life he had ever been complimented.

"A month before the expedition took off for Ozagen, I had noticed in one of the many scientific journals that passed under my nose an announcement that a certain drug had been synthesized. Its efficacy was in destroying the virus of the so-called Sirian 'rash.' What interested me was a footnote. It was in small print and in Hebrew, which showed that the biochemist must have realized its importance."

"*Poow kwa?*"

"Why? Well, I imagine it was in Hebrew in order to keep any layman from understanding it. If a secret like that became generally known.…

"The note commented briefly that it had been found that a man suffering from the 'rash' was temporarily immune to the effects of hypno-lipno. And that the Urielites should take care during any sessions with the 'Meter that their subject was healthy."

"I have trouble understanding you," she said.

"I'll go slower. Hypno-lipno is the most widely used truth-drug. I saw at once the implications in the note. The beginning of the article had described how the Sirian 'rash' was narcotically induced for experimental purposes. The drug used was not named, but it did not take me long to look it and its processing up in other journals. I thought: if the true 'rash' would make a man immune to hypno-lipno, why wouldn't the artificial?

"No sooner said than done. I prepared a batch, inserted a tape of questions about my personal life in a psychotester, injected the 'rash' drug, injected the truth drug, and swore that I would lie to the tester about my life. And I *could* lie, even though shot full of hypno-lipno!"

"You're so intelligent," she murmured.

She squeezed his biceps. He hardened them. It was a vain thing to do, but he wanted her to think he was strong.

"Nonsense!" he clipped. "A blind man would have seen what to do. In fact, I wouldn't be surprised if the Uzzites had arrested the chemist and put out orders for some other truth drug to be used. If they did, they were too late. Our ship left before any such news reached us.

"Anyway, the first day with the 'Meter was nothing to worry about. I took a twelve-hour written and oral test in serialism. That's Dunne's theories of time and Sigmen's amplifications on it. I've been taking that same test for years. Easy but tiring.

"The next day I rose early, bathed, injected what was supposed to be Prophetsfood, and, breakfastless, went into the Purification Cell. Alone, I lay two days on a cot. From time to time I took a drink of water or a shot of the false drug. Now and then I pressed the button that sent the mechanical scourge lashing against me. The more flagellations, you know, the higher your credit.

"I didn't see any visions. I did break out with the 'rash.' That didn't worry me. If anybody got suspicious, I could explain that I had an allergy to Prophetsfood. Some people do."

He looked below. Moonfrosted forest and an occasional square or hexagonal light from a farmhouse. Ahead was the high range of hills that shielded Siddo.

"So," he continued, unconsciously talking faster as the hills loomed closer, "at the end of my purification I rose, dressed, and ate the ceremonial dinner of locusts and honey."

"Ugh!"

"Locusts aren't so bad if you've been eating them since childhood."

"Locusts are delicious," she said. "I've eaten them many times. It's the combination with honey that sickens me."

He shrugged and said, "I'm turning out the cabin lights. Get down on the floor. And put on that cloak and nightmask. You can pass for a wog."

Obediently she slid off the seat. Before he flicked the lights off, he glanced down. She was leaning over while picking up the cloak, and he could not help getting a full glimpse of her superb breasts. Though he jerked his head away, he kept the image in his head. He felt both deeply aroused and ashamed.

He continued uncomfortably: "Then the hierarch came in. Macneff the Sandalphon, that is, the Archurielite, the theologians, and the dunnological specialists: the psychoneural parallelists, the intervention-ists, the substratumists, the chronentropists, the pseudotemporalists, the cosmobservists.

"I was seated on a chair. Wires were taped to my body. Needles were stuck in my arms and back. Hypno-lipno was injected. The lights were turned out. Prayers were said; readings from the Western Talmud and the Revised Scriptures were intoned. Then a spotlight shone down from the ceiling upon the Elohimeter...."

"*Keskasekasah?*"

"Elohim is Hebrew for God. Meter is Greek for — well, for those." He pointed at the instrument panel. "The Elohimeter is round and enor-mous, and its needle, as long as my arm, is straight up and down. The circumference of the dial's face is marked with Hebraic letters that are supposed to mean something to those giving the test.

"Most people are ignorant of what the dipping and rising needle shows. But I'm a joat. I've access to the books that describe the test."

"Then you knew the answers, *nespa?*"

"*Oui*. Though that means nothing, because hypno-lipno brings out the truth, the reality...unless, of course, you are suffering from Sirian 'rash,' natural or artificial."

His sudden laugh was a mirthless bark.

"Under the drug, Jeannette, all the dirty and foul things you've done and thought, all the hates you've had for your superiors, all the doubts about the realness of the Forerunner's doctrines — these rise up from your lower-level minds like soap released at the bottom of a dirty bathtub. Up it comes, slick and irresistibly buoyant and covered with all the layers of scum.

"But I sat there, and I watched the needle — it's just like watching the face of God, Jeannette — you can't understand that, can you? — and I lied. Oh, I didn't overplay it. I didn't pretend to be incredibly pure and faithful. I confessed to minor unrealities. Then the needle would flicker and go back around the circumference a few square letters. But on the big issues, I answered as if my life depended on them. Which it did.

"And I told them my dreams — my subjective time-traveling."

"*Subjectif?*"

"*Oui*. Everybody travels in time subjectively. But the Forerunner is the only man, except his first disciples and a few of the scriptural proph-ets, who has traveled objectively.

"Anyway, my dreams were beauties — architecturally speaking. Just what they liked to hear. My last, and crowning creation — or lie — was one in which the Forerunner himself appeared on Ozagen and spoke to the Sandalphon, Macneff. That event is supposed to take place a year from now.

"Oh, Hal!" she breathed. "Why did you tell them that?"

"Because now, *ma chère,* the expedition will not leave Ozagen until that year is up.. They couldn't go without giving up the chance of seeing Sigmen in the flesh as he voyages up and down the stream of time. Nor without making a liar of him. And of me. So, you see, that colossal lie will make sure that we have at least a year together..."

"And then?"

"We'll think of something else then." Her throaty voice murmured in the darkness by the seat: "And you would do all that for me...."

Hal did not reply. He was too busy keeping the gig close to the rooftop level. Clumps of buildings, widely separated by woods, flashed by. So fast was he going that he almost overshot Fobo's castlelike house. Three stories high, medieval-seeming with its crenellated towers and gargoyle heads of stone beasts and insects leering out from many niches, it was not nearer than a hundred yards to any other building. Wogs built their cities with plenty of elbow-room in mind.

Jeannette put on the long-snouted nightmask; the gig's door swung open; they ran across the sidewalk and into the building. After they dashed through the lobby and up on the steps to the second floor, they had to stop while Hal fumbled for the key. He had had a wog smith make the lock and a wog carpenter install it. He hadn't trusted the carpenter's mate from the ship, because there was too much chance of duplicate keys being made.

He finally found the key, had trouble inserting it. When the door opened, he was breathing hard. He almost pushed Jeannette through. She had taken her mask off.

"Wait, Hal," she said, leaning her weight against his. "Haven't you forgotten something?"

"Oh, *Forerunner!* What could it be? Something serious?"

"No. I only thought," and she smiled and then lowered her lids, "that it was the Terran custom for men to carry their brides across the threshold."

His jaw dropped. Bride! She was certainly taking a lot for granted!

He couldn't take time to argue. Without a word, he swept her up in his arms and carried her into the apartment. There he put her down and said, "Back as soon as possible. If anybody knocks or tries to get in, hide in that special closet I told you about. Don't make a sound or come out until you're sure it's me."

She suddenly put her arms around him and kissed him.

"*M'sheh, m'gwa foh.*"

Things were going too fast. He didn't say a word or even return her kiss. Vaguely he felt that her words, applied to him, were somewhat ridiculous. If he translated her degenerate French right, she had called him her dear, her strong man.

Turning, he closed the door; but not so quickly that he did not see the hall light shine on a white face haloed blackly by a hood. A red red mouth stained the whiteness.

He shook. He had a feeling that Jeannette was not going to be the frigid mate so much admired, officially, by the Sturch.

SIX

Hal was an hour late returning home from the *Gabriel*, because the Sandalphon asked for more details about the prophecy he'd made concerning Sigmen. Then Hal had to dictate his report on the day's espionage to a stenoservo. Afterwards, he ordered a sailor to pilot his gig back to the apartment. While he was walking toward the launching-rack, he met Pornsen.

"*Shalom, abba,*" greeted Hal.

He smiled and rubbed his knuckles against the raised lamech on the shield.

The gapt's left shoulder, always low, sagged even more, as if it were a flag dipping in surrender. His ward was now out of his reach. More, if there were any whipcuts to be given, they would be struck by Yarrow.

The joat puffed out his chest and started to walk on, but Pornsen said, "Just a minute, son. Are you going back to the city?"

"Shib."

"Shib. I'll ride back with you. I have an apartment in the same building. On the third floor, right next door to Fobo's.

Hal opened his mouth to protest, then closed it. It was Pornsen's turn to smile. He knew he had nettled the joat. He turned and led the way. Hal followed with tight lips. Had the gapt perhaps trailed him and seen his meeting with Jeannette? No. If he had, he would have had Hal arrested at once.

The thing was that the gapt was small-minded. He knew his presence would annoy Hal.

Under his breath Hal quoted an old proverb, "A gapt's teeth never let loose."

The sailor was waiting by the gig. They all got in and dropped silently into the night.

At the apartment building Hal strode into the doorway ahead of Pornsen. He felt a slight glow of satisfaction at thus breaking etiquette and expressing his contempt for the man.

Before opening his door, he paused. The guardian angel passed silently behind him. Hal, struck with a devilish thought, called out in French, *"Père!"*

Pornsen turned.

"What?"

"Would you care to inspect my rooms and see if I'm hiding a woman in there?"

The little man purpled. He closed his eyes and swayed, dizzy with sheer fury. When he opened them he shouted, "Yarrow! If ever I saw an unreal personality, you're it! I don't care how you stand with the hierarchy! I think you're — you're — just not simply shib!"

Hal looked blank. "I'm sure I don't know what you mean, Pornsen. I'm pure. I've proven there isn't an evil thought in my head."

His voice became strident, harsh. "Pornsen, you've just been talking in English! I'm sorry, but I have to report that in the morning. You know what that means!"

Pornsen's red face was suddenly drained of its blood. He opened his mouth, closed it, looked at Yarrow's merciless face, spun on his bootheels and walked away.

Hal leaned against the doorway. He felt both weak and triumphant. When he had recovered from the reaction of baiting his guardian, he turned the key in his lock. Around and around in his head flew the thought that it had taken this girl only a few hours to fill him with enough courage to overcome thirty years of fear and submissiveness.

He clicked on the front room lights. Looking beyond into the dining room, he could see the closed kitchen door. The rattling of pots came through it. He sniffed deeply.

Steak!

The pleasure was replaced by a frown. He'd told her to hide until he returned. What if he had been a wog or an Uzzite?

When he swung the door open, the hinges squeaked. Jeannette's back was to him. At the first protest of unoiled iron, she whirled. The spatula in her hand dropped; the other hand flew to her open mouth.

The angry words on his lips died. If he were to scold her now, she would probably break out in embarrassing tears.

"*M'tyuh!* You startled me!"

He grunted and went by her to lift the lids on the pots.

"You see," she said, her voice trembling as if she divined his anger and were defending herself, "I have lived such a life, being afraid of getting caught, that anything sudden scares me. I am always ready to run."

"How those wogs fooled me!" Hal said sourly. "I thought they were so kind and gentle, and now I find they've kept you prisoner for two years."

She glanced at him out of the side of her large eyes. Her color had come back; her red lips smiled.

"Oh, they weren't so bad. They really were kind. They gave me everything I wanted, except my freedom. They were afraid I'd make my way back to my aunts and sisters."

"What did they care?"

"Oh, they thought there might be some males of my race left in the jungle and that I might give them children. They are terribly frightened of my race becoming numerous and strong again and making war on them. They do not like war."

"Hm! Well, let's eat."

When they had finished, he sighed, patted his stomach, and said, "Ah, Jeannette, the soup was the best I tasted. The bread was fresh and hot. The salad was superb. The steak perfect."

"My aunts gave me very good training. Among my people the female is taught at an early age all that will please a man. All. By the time we've grown up, we do it almost instinctively."

Hal leaned back and lit a cigarette. She tried one, coughed, then drew in and blew out smoke like a veteran. She seemed to have an amazing facility for imitation. Show or tell her something once, and she never forgot it.

They smoked awhile, looking at each other. During the meal she had chattered lightly and amusingly about her life with her father and her relatives. She had the trick of raising her eyebrows as she laughed; he was fascinated by them. They were almost bracket-shaped. A thin line rose from the bridge of the nose, turned at right angles, curved slightly while going above the eyesockets, and then made a little hook downwards. He asked her if the shape was a trait of her mother's people. She laughed and said No, she got them from her father. Her laughter was low and musical. It did not get on his nerves, as his ex-wife's had. Lulled by it, he felt pleasant. She seemed to have a sixth sense that guessed his moods and thoughts and exactly what he needed to blunt any gloominess or sharpen any gaiety.

Finally he said, "We'll have to wash the dishes. It would never do for a visitor to see a table set for two. And another thing: we'll have to hide the cigarettes, and air out the rooms frequently. Now that I've been 'Metered, I'm supposed to have renounced such vices as smoking."

Jeannette would not let him help her do the dishes. He smoked and speculated about the chances of getting tobacco. She so enjoyed the cigarettes that he could not stand the idea of her missing out on them. One of the crewmen he knew did not smoke, but instead sold his ration to his mates. Maybe a wog could act as middleman; buy the stuff from the sailor, and pass it on to Hal. He'd have to be careful...maybe it wasn't worth it....

Hal sighed. Having Jeannette was wonderful, but she was beginning to complicate his life. Here he was, contemplating a criminal action as if it were the most natural thing in the world.

She was standing before him, hands on her hips, eyes shining.

"Now, Hal, *mon cher,* if we only had something to drink...it would make a perfect evening."

He got to his feet. "Sorry. I forgot you wouldn't know how to make coffee."

"*Non. Non.* It is the liquor I am thinking of. *L'alcool. Pas le café.*"

"Alcohol? Good God, girl, we don't *drink!* That'd be the most disgust—"

He stopped. She was hurt. He mastered himself. After all, she couldn't help it. She came from a different culture. She wasn't even, strictly speaking, all human.

"I'm sorry," he said. "It's a religious matter. Forbidden."

Tears filled her eyes. Her shoulders began to shake. She put her face into her hands and began to sob. "You don't understand. I have to have it. I have to."

"But why?"

She spoke from behind her fingers. "Because during my imprisonment I had little to do but entertain myself. My captors gave me liquor; it helped to pass the time and make me forget how utterly homesick I was. Before I knew it, I was an—an alcoholic."

Hal clenched his fists and growled, "Those sons of bugs!"

"So you see, I have to have a drink. It would make me feel better, just for the time being. And later, maybe later, I can try to overcome it. I know I can, if you'll help me."

He gestured emptily. "But—but where can I get you any?" His stomach revolted at the idea of trafficking in alcohol, but if she needed it, he'd try his best to get it.

Swiftly she said, "Fobo lives on the third floor. Perhaps he could give you some."

"But Fobo was one of your captors! Won't he suspect something if I come asking for alcohol?"

"He'll think it's for you."

"All right," he said, somewhat sullenly, and at the same time guiltily because he was sullen. "But I hate for anybody to think I drink. Even if he is just a wog."

She came up to him and seemed to flow against him. Her lips pressed softly and hotly. Her body tried to pass through his. He held her for a minute and then took his mouth away.

"Do I have to leave you?" he whispered. "Couldn't you pass up the liquor? Just for tonight? Tomorrow I'll get you some."

Her voice broke. "Oh, *m'namoow*, I wish I could. How I wish I could. But I can't. I just can't. Believe me...."

"I believe you."

He released her and walked into the front room, where he took a hood, cloak, and nightmask out of the closet. His head was bent; his shoulders sagged. Everything would be spoiled. He would not be able to get near her, not with her breath stinking with alcohol. And she'd probably wonder why he was cold, and he wouldn't have the nerve to tell how revolting she was, because that would hurt her feelings. To make it worse, she'd be hurt anyway, if he offered no explanation.

Before he left, she kissed him again on his now frozen lips.

"Hurry! I'll be waiting."

"Yeah."

SEVEN

Yarrow knocked lightly. Fobo's apartment was next door to Pornsen's. Tonight was not a good time for the gapt to see him visiting the empathist.

When the door opened, he stepped in and shut it quickly. Noise bounced off the walls of the room, large as a basketball court. Screaming, twelve wog children raced around. Abasa, Fobo's wife, was sitting in one corner and chattering with three female visitors. The empathist himself was at a table by the door, reading.

Hal shouted, "How can you concentrate?"

Fobo looked up. "Why, can't you cut out all unwanted noises with an effort of will? That is, turn off certain nerve paths? No? Well, we wogs can, though how, we don't know. That is one of the subjects for research at the nearby College of Empathology. And now, won't you sit down? I'd offer you a drink, but I'm fresh out."

Hal was sure that his dismay didn't show on his face, but Fobo's antennae must have picked it up.

"Anything wrong?"

Hal decided not to waste time. "Yes. Where can I get a quart of liquor?"

The wog took his night garments down from a hook, put them on, and then buckled on a broad leather belt with sheath and short rapier.

"I was just thinking of going out and getting some. You see, this empathology is very trying on the nerves. I run into so many people who need help; and since I must put myself into their shoes, feel their emotions as they feel them, and then must wrench myself out of their shoes and take an objective look at their problems, I am exhausted and shaken at the end of the day. I find that a drink or two relaxes me. You understand?"

The Terran didn't, but he shook his head yes. He wondered how he was going to explain that he was breaking the law by drinking. He'd have to stress the necessity of saying nothing to Pornsen.

Outside, Hal said, "Why the sword?"

"Oh, there isn't much danger, but it's best to be careful. You see, this is a world of insects whose development and specialization go even beyond your planet. You know the parasites and mimics that infest ant colonies, don't you? The beetles that look like ants and make an easy living from that resemblance? The pygmy ants and other tiny creatures that live in the walls and prey on the eggs and the young? Well, we have things analogous to them. Things that hide in sewers or basements or hollow trees and creep around the city at night. Our streets are well-lighted and patrolled, but they are often separated by wooded stretches...."

By the time Fobo had finished talking, they had passed through a park, zigzagged down a dozen blocks of a shopping district, now closed, and stopped before a building in front of which a big electric sign blazed.

"Duroku's Tavern," translated Fobo.

◆ ◆ ◆

It was in the basement. Hal, after stopping to shudder at the blast of liquor that came up the steps, followed the wog. In the entrance he paused to blink.

Loud odors of alcohol mingled with loud bars of a strange music and even louder talk. Wogs crowded the hexagonal-topped tables and leaned across big pewter stems to shout in each other's face. Antennae wiggled with drunken emotion. Somebody waved his hands uncoordinatedly and sent a stein crashing. A waitress, looking much like her Terran counterpart with her white apron and peaked cap, hurried up with a towel to mop up the mess. When she bent over, she was slapped resoundingly on the rump by a jovial, greenfaced, and very fat wogglebug. His tablemates howled with laughter, their broad V-in-V lips wide open. The waitress laughed, too, and said something to the fat one that must have been witty, for the tables roundabout guffawed.

On a platform at one end of the room a five-piece band slammed out fast and weird notes. Hal saw three instruments that looked Terranlike: a harp, a trumpet, and a drum. A fourth musician, however, was not himself producing any music, but was now and then prodding with a long stick a rabbit-sized locustoid insect in a cage. When so urged, the creature rubbed its hind wings over its back legs and gave four loud chirps followed by a long, nerve-scratching screech.

The fifth player was pumping away at a bellows connected to a bag and three short and narrow pipes. A thin squealing came out.

Fobo shouted, "You mustn't judge Ozagen by this place. It's a lower-class hangout. Especially, don't think that noise is typical of our music. It's cheap popular stuff. I'll take you to a symphony concert one of these days and you'll hear what great music is like."

The wog led the man to one of the curtained-off booths scattered along the walls. They sat down. A waitress came to them. Sweat ran off her forehead and down her tubular nose.

"Keep your mask on until we've gotten our drinks," said Fobo. "Then we can close the curtains."

The waitress said something in Wog. Fobo repeated in French, "Beer, wine, or alcohol à la beetle. Myself, I wouldn't touch the first two. They're for women and children."

The Terran didn't want to lose face. He said with a bravado he didn't feel, "The latter, of course."

"Double shot?"

Hal didn't know what that meant, but he nodded.

Fobo held up two fingers. The waitress returned quickly with two big steins. The wog leaned his nose into the fumes and breathed deeply. He closed his eyes in ecstasy, lifted the stein, and drank a long time. When he put the container down, he belched loudly and then smacked his lips.

"Tastes as good coming up as going down!" he bellowed.

The man felt queasy. Eructation was very frowned upon in the Haijac Union.

"*Mais, monsieur!* You are not drinking."

Yarrow said weakly, "*Damifaino*," the Ozagen equivalent of mud-in-your-eye, and drank.

Fire ran down his throat like lava down a volcano's slope. And, like a volcano, Hal erupted. He coughed and wheezed; liquor spurted out of his mouth; his eyes shut and squeezed out big tears.

"*Tres bonne, n'est-ce pas?*" said Fobo calmly.

"Yes, very good," croaked Yarrow from a throat that seemed to be permanently scarred. Though he had spat most of the stuff out, some of it must have dropped straight through his intestines and into his legs, for he felt a hot tide down there swinging back and forth as if pulled by some invisible moon circling around and around in his head, a big moon that bulged and brushed against the inside of his skull.

"Have another."

The second drink he managed better outwardly, at least, for he did not cough or sputter But inwardly he was not so unconcerned. His belly writhed, and he was sure he would disgrace himself. After a few deep breaths, he thought he would keep the liquor down. Then he belched. The lava got as far as his throat before he managed to stop it.

"Pardon me," he said, blushing.

"Why?" said Fobo.

Hal thought that was one of the funniest retorts he had ever heard. He laughed loudly and sipped at the stein. If he could empty it swiftly and then buy a quart for Jeannette, he could get back before the night was completely wasted.

♦ ♦ ♦

When the liquor had receded halfway down the stein, Hal heard Fobo, dimly and faroff as if he were at the end of a long tunnel, ask him if he cared to see where the alcohol was made.

"Shib," Hal agreed.

He rose, but had to put a hand on the table to steady himself. The wog told him to put his mask back on. "Earthmen are still objects of curiosity. We don't want to waste all evening answering questions. Or drinking drinks that'll be forced on us."

They threaded through the noisy crowd to a backroom. There Fobo gestured and said, "*Voilà. L'escarbot.*"

Hal looked. If he had not had some of his inhibitions washed away in the liquorish flood, he might have been overwhelmingly repulsed. As it was, he was curious.

The thing sitting on a chair by the table might at first glance have been taken for a wogglebug. It had the antennae, the blonde fuzz, the bald pate, the nose, and the V-shaped mouth. It also had the round body and enormous paunch of some of the Ozagens.

But a second look in the bright light from the unshaded bulb overhead showed a creature whose body was sheathed in a hard and lightly green-tinted chitin. And though it wore a long cloak, the legs and arms were naked. They were not smooth-skinned but were ringed, segmented with the edges of armor-sections, like stovepipes.

Fobo spoke to it in Wog. Yarrow understood some of the words; the others he was able to fill in.

"Ducko, this is Mr. Yarrow. Say hello to Mr. Yarrow, Ducko."

The big blue eyes looked at Hal. There was nothing about them to distinguish them from a wog's, yet they seemed inhuman, thoroughly arthropodal.

"Hello, Mr. Yarrow," Ducko said in a parrot's voice.

"Tell Mr. Yarrow what a fine night it is."

"It's a fine night, Mr. Yarrow."

"Tell him Ducko is happy to see him."

"Ducko is happy to see you."

"And serve him."

"And serve you."

"Show Mr. Yarrow how you make beetlejuice."

A wog standing by the table glanced at his wristwatch. He spoke in rapid Ozagen. Fobo translated.

"He says Ducko ate a half hour ago. He ahould be ready to serve. These creatures eat a big meal every half hour and then they — watch!"

Duroku hurried up with a huge earthenware bowl and set it on the table. Ducko leaned over it until a half-inch long tube, probably a modified tracheal opening, was poised above the edge. From the tube he shot a clear liquid into the bowl until it was filled to the brim. Duroku grabbed the bowl and carried it off. An Ozagen came from the kitchen with a plate of highly-sugared spaghetti. He set it down, and Ducko began eating from it with a big spoon.

Hal's brain was by then not working very fast, but he began to see what was going on. Frantically, he looked around for a place to throw up. Fobo shoved a drink under his nose. For lack of anything better to do, he swallowed some. Whole hog or none. Surprisingly, the fiery stuff settled his stomach. Or else burned away the rising tide.

"Exactly," replied Fobo to Hal's strangled question. "These creatures are a superb example of parasitical mimicry. Though quasi-insectal, they look much like us. They live among us and earn their board and room by furnishing us with a cheap and smooth alcoholic drink. You noticed its enormous belly, no? *Eh bien,* it is there that they so rapidly manufacture the alcohol and so easily upchuck it. Simple and natural, *oui?* Duroku has two others working for him, but it is their night off, and doubtless they are in some neighborhood tavern, getting drunk. A sailor's holiday...."

Hal burst out, "Can't we buy a quart and get out? I feel sick. It must be the closeness of the air. Or something."

"Something, probably," murmured Fobo.

He sent a waitress after two quarts. While they were waiting for her, they saw a short wog in a mask and blue cloak enter. The newcomer stood in the doorway, black boots widespread and the long tubular projection of the mask pointing this way and that like a sub's periscope peering for prey.

Hal gasped and said, "Pornsen!"

"*Oui,*" replied Fobo. "That drooping shoulder and the black boots and the lack of antennae give him away. Who does he think he's fooling?"

The joat looked wildly around. "I've got to get out of here!"

The waitress returned with the bottles. Fobo paid her and gave one to Hal, who automatically put it in the inside pocket of his cloak.

The gapt saw them through the doorway, but he must not have recognized them. Yarrow still wore his mask, while the empathist probably still looked to Pornsen like any other wog. Methodical as always, Pornsen evidently determined to make a thorough search. He brought up his sloping shoulder in a sudden gesture and began parting the curtains of the booths along the walls. Whenever he saw a wog with his or her mask on, he lifted the grotesque covering and looked behind.

Fobo chuckled. "He won't keep that up long. What does he think we Ozagens are? A bunch of rabbits?"

What he had been waiting for happened. A burly wog suddenly stood up as Pornsen reached for his mask and instead lifted the gapt's. Surprised at seeing a non-Ozagenians' features, the wog dropped his jaw and stared for a second. Then he gave a screech, yelled something, and punched the Earthman in the nose.

At once there was bedlam. Pornsen staggered back into a table, knocking it and its stems over, and fell to the floor. Two wogs jumped him. Another hit a fourth. The fourth struck back. Duroku, carrying a short club, hurried up and began thumping his fighting customers on the back and legs. Somebody threw beetlejuice in his face.

And at that moment Fobo threw the switch that plunged the tavern into darkness.

EIGHT

Hal stood bewildered. A hand seized his. "Follow me!" The hand tugged. Hal turned and allowed himself to be led, stumbling, toward what he thought was the back door.

Any number of others must have had the same idea. Hal was knocked down and trampled upon. Fobo's hand was torn from his. Yarrow cried out for the wog, but any possible answer was drowned out in a chorus of *Beat it! Get off my back, you dumb son-of-a-bug! Great Larva, we're piled up in the doorway!*

Sharp reports added to the noise. A foul stench choked Hal as the wogs, under nervous stress, released the gas in their madbags. Gasping, he fought his way through the door. A few seconds later his mad scrambling over twisting bodies got him his freedom. He lurched down an alleyway. Once on the street, he ran as fast as he could. He didn't know where he was going. His one thought was to put as much distance as possible between himself and Pornsen.

Arc-lights on top of tall slender iron poles flashed by. He ran with his shoulder almost scraping the buildings. He wanted to stay in the shadows thrown by the many balconies jutting out from the second stories. Presently, he slowed down at a narrow passageway. A glance showed him it wasn't a blind alley. He darted down it until he came to a large square can, one that by its odor must have been used for garbage. Squatting behind it, he tried to lessen his gaspings. After a minute his lungs regained their balance; he no longer had to sob for air. Then he could listen without having his heart thudding in his ears.

He heard no pursuer. After a while he decided it was safe to rise. He felt the bottle in his cloakpocket. Miraculously, it had not been broken. Jeannette would get her liquor. What a story he would have to tell her! After all he had gone through for her, he would surely get a just reward....

He shivered with goose pimples at the thought and began to walk briskly down the alley. Where he was he had no idea, but he carried a map of the city in his pocket. It had been printed in the ship and bore street names in Ozagen with French translations beneath. All he had to do was read the street signs under one of the many lamps, orient himself with the map, and return home. As for Pornsen, the fellow had no real evidence against him, and would not be able to accuse him until he got some. Hal's possession of the golden lamech made him above suspicion. Pornsen....

Pornsen! No sooner had he muttered the name than the flesh appeared. There was a click of hard bootheels behind him. He turned. A short, cloaked figure was coming down the alley. A lamp's glow outlined the droop of a shoulder and shone on black leather boots. His mask was off.

"Yarrow!" shrilled the gapt. "No use running! Wait!" Triumph was in the voice. "I saw you go in that tavern!"

He clickclacked up to his ward's tall rigid form. "Drinking! I know you were drinking!"

"Yeah?" Hal croaked. "What else?"

"Isn't that enough?" screamed the gapt. "Or are you hiding something in your apartment? Maybe you are! Maybe you've got the place filled with bottles. Come on. Come on. Let's get back to your apartment. We'll go over it and see what we see. I wouldn't be surprised to find all sorts of evidence of your unreal thinking."

Hal hunched his shoulders and clenched his fists, but he said nothing. When the gapt told him to precede him back to Fobo's building, he walked without a sign of resistance. Like conqueror and conquered, they marched from the alley into the street. Yarrow, however, spoiled the picture by reeling a little and having to put his hand to the wall to steady himself.

Pornsen sneered, "You drunken joat! You make me sick to my stomach!"

Hal pointed ahead. "I'm not the only one who's sick. Look at that fellow."

He was not really interested, but he had a wild hope that anything he said or did, however trivial, might put off the final and fatal moment when they would return to his apartment. What he indicated was a large and evidently intoxicated wogglebug hanging onto a lamppost to keep from falling on his tube-shaped nose. The picture might have been one of a nineteenth or twentieth century drunk, complete to top hat, cloak and lamppost. Now and then the creature groaned as if he were deeply disturbed.

"Perhaps we'd better stop and see if he's hurt?" said Hal.

He had to say anything, anything, to delay Pornsen. Before his captor could protest, he went up to the wog. He put his hand on the free arm—the other was wrapped around the post—and spoke in Ozagen.

"Can we help you?"

The big wog looked as if he, too, had been in a brawl. His cloak, besides being ripped down the back, was spotted with dried green blood. He kept his face away from Hal, so that the Earthman had a hard time understanding his muttering.

Pornsen jerked at his arm. "Come on, Yarrow. He'll get by all right. What's one sick bug more or less?"

"Shib," agreed Hal, tonelessly. He let his hand drop and started to walk on. Pornsen, behind, took one step...and then bumped into Hal as Hal stopped.

"What are you stopping for, Yarrow?" The gapt's voice was suddenly apprehensive.

And then the voice was screaming in agony.

Hal whirled...to see in grim actuality what had flashed across his mind and caused him to stop in his tracks. When he had put his hand on the wog's arm, he had felt, not warm skin, but hard and cool chitin. For a few seconds the meaning of that had not cleared the brain's switchboard. Then it had come through, and he had remembered the talk he and Fobo had had on the way to the tavern, and why Fobo wore a sword. Too late, he had wheeled to warn Pornsen.

Now the gapt was holding both hands to his eyes and shrieking. The big thing that had been leaning against the lamppost was advancing towards Hal. Its body seemed to grow huger with every step. A sac across its chest was swelled until it looked like a palpitating gray balloon; the hideous insectal face, with two vestigial arms waving on each side of its mouth and the funnel-shaped proboscis below the mouth, was pointed at him. It was that proboscis which Hal had mistakenly thought was a wog's nose. In reality, the thing must breath through tracheae and two slits below the enormous eyes.

Hal yelled with fury and as a means of discharging his fear. At the same time he grabbed his cloak and threw it up before his face. His mask might have saved him, but he did not care to take the chance.

Something burned the back of his hand. He yelped with pain, but leaped forward. Before the thing could breath in air to bloat the sac again and expel the acid through the funnel, Hal rammed his head against its paunch.

The thing said, "*Oof!*" and fell backward where it lay on its back and thrashed its legs and arms like a giant poisonous bug — which it was. Then, as it recovered from the shock and rolled over and tried to get back on its feet, Hal kicked hard. His leather toe drove with a crunching sound through the thin chitin.

The toe withdrew; a greenish blood oozed out; Hal kicked again in the open place. The thing screamed and tried to crawl away on all fours. The Terran leaped upon it with both feet and bore it sprawling to the cement. He pressed his heel against its thin neck and shoved with all the strength of his leg. The neck cracked. The thing lay still. Its lower jaw dropped open and exposed two rows of tiny needle-teeth. The mouth's rudimentary arms wigwagged feebly for a while and then drooped.

Hal's chest heaved in agony. He couldn't get enough air. His guts quivered and threatened to force their way through his throat. Then they did, and Hal bent over, retching.

All at once, he was sober. By that time Pornsen had quit screaming. He was lying huddled on his side in the gutter. Hal turned him over and shuddered at what he saw. The eyes were partly burned out, and the lips were gray with large blisters. The tongue, too, sticking from the mouth, was swollen and lumpy. Evidently Pornsen had swallowed some of the venom. According to Fobo, even a small part was fatal.

Hal straightened up and walked away. A wog patrol would find the gapt's body and turn it over to the Earthmen. Let the hierarchy figure out what had happened. Pornsen was dead, and now that he was, Yarrow admitted to himself what he had never allowed himself to admit before this time. He had hated Pornsen. And he was glad that he was dead. If Pornsen had suffered horribly, so what? His pains were brief, but the pain and grief he had caused Hal had lasted for almost thirty years.

In all that time Hal had kept unconscious his desire to kill the man. Now his feelings, anticlimactically, exploded. Tears ran down his cheeks; his shoulders shook with sobs; he staggered like a drunk. Something was reaching down into his intestines and tearing them apart. It wasn't grief. It was hate, working out like a poison, a swift poison leaving his body but boiling him alive. Still, it was coming out, and though he felt that he was dying while it lasted by the time he arrived at home he felt much better. Fatigue held his arms and legs down, and he could hardly make it up the steps. But inside, where the heart was, he was stronger than he had ever been in his life.

NINE

A tall ghost in a light blue shroud was waiting for the Terran in the false dawn. It was the empathist, standing in the hexagonal-shaped arch that led into his building. When Hal came close, Fobo threw back the hood and exposed a face that was scratched on one cheek and blacked around the right eye.

He chuckled and said, "Some son of a bug pulled my mask off and plowed me good. But it was fun. It helps if you blow off steam that way now and then. How did you come out? I was afraid you might have been picked up by the police. Normally that wouldn't worry me, but I know your colleagues at the ship would frown upon such activities."

Hal smiled wanly. "Frown misses it by a mile."

He wondered how Fobo knew what the hierarch's reaction would be. How much did these wogs know about the Terrestrials? Were they onto the Haijac game, and waiting to pounce? If so, with what? Their technology, as far as could be determined, was way behind Earth's. True, they seemed to know more of psychic functions than the Terrans did, but that was understandable. The Sturch had long ago decreed that the proper psychology had been perfected and that further research was unnecessary. The result had been a standstill in the psychical sciences.

He shrugged mentally. He was too tired to think of such things. All he wanted was to go to bed.

"I'll tell you later what happened," he said.

Fobo replied, "I can guess. Your hand. You'd better let me fix that burn. Nightlifer venom is nasty."

Like a little child, Hal followed to the wog's apartment and let him put a cooling salve on it.

"*Voilà*," said Fobo. "Go to bed. Tomorrow you can tell me all about it."

Hal thanked him and walked down to his floor. His hand fumbled with the key. Finally, after using Sigmen's name in vain, he inserted the key. When he had shut and locked the door, he called Jeannette. She must have been hiding in the closet-within-a-closet in the bedroom, for he heard two doors bang. In a moment she was running to him. She threw her arms around him.

"*Oh, mon homme, mon homme!* Hal, *mon amour,* what has happened? I was so worried. I thought I would scream when the night went by, and you didn't return."

Though he was sorry he had caused her pain, he could not help a prickling of pleasure because someone cared enough about him to worry. Nobody ever had before.

"There was a brawl," he said. He had decided not to say anything about the gapt or the nightlifer. Later, when the strain had passed, he'd talk.

She untied his cloak and hood and took off his mask. While she hung them up in the front-room closet, he sank into a chair and closed his eyes. A moment later they were pulled open by the sound of liquid pouring into a glass. She was standing in front of him and filling a large glass from the quart. The odor of beetlejuice began to turn his stomach, and the picture of a beautiful girl about to drink the nauseating stuff spun it all the way around.

She looked at him. The delicate brackets of her brows rose. "*Qu'y a-t-il?*"

"Nothing's the matter!" he groaned. "I'm all right."

She put down the glass, picked up his hand, and led him into the bedroom. There she gently sat him down, pressed on his shoulder until he laid down, and then took off his shoes. He didn't resist. After she unbuttoned his shirt, she stroked his hair.

"You're sure you're all right?"

"Shib. I could lick the world with one hand tied behind my back."

"Good."

The bed creaked as she got up and walked out of the room. Before he could fall asleep, she returned. Again, he opened his eyes. Again, she was standing with a glass in her hand.

She said, "Would you like a sip now, Hal?"

"Great Mind, girl, don't you understand?" he barked. Fury poured adrenalin into his tired blood. He sat up. "Why do you think I got sick? I can't stand the stuff! I can't stand to see you drink it. It makes me sick. You make me sick. What's the matter with you? Are you stupid?"

Jeannette's eyes widened. Blood drained from her face and left the pigment of her lips a crimson moon in a white lake. Her hand shook so that the liquor spilled.

"Why—why—" she gasped—"I thought you said you felt fine. I thought you were all right. I thought you wanted to go to bed with me."

Yarrow groaned. He shut his eyes and laid back down. Sarcasm was lost on her. She insisted on taking everything literally. She would have to be re-educated, not only in irony, but in other things. If he weren't so exhausted, he would have been shocked by her open proposal—so much like that of the Scarlet Woman in the Western Talmud when she had tried to seduce the Forerunner.

But he was past being shocked. Moreover, a voice on the edge of his conscience said that she had merely put into hard and unrecallable words what he had planned in his heart all this time. But when you spoke them!

A crash of glass shattered his thoughts. He jerked upright. She was standing there, face twisted, lovely red mouth quivering and tears flowing. Her hand was empty. A large wet patch against the wall, still dripping, showed what had become of the glass.

"I thought you loved me!" she yelled.

Unable to think of anything to say, he stared. She spun and walked away. He heard her go into the front room. Loud sobs forced him to jump out of bed and walk swiftly after her. These rooms were supposed to be soundproof, but one never knew. What if she were overheard?

Anyway, she was twisting something inside him, and he had to straighten it out.

When he entered the front room, she didn't look up. For a while he stood silent, wanting to say something but utterly unable to because he had never been forced to solve such a problem before. Haijac women didn't cry often, or if they did, they wept alone in privacy.

He sat down by her and put his hand on her soft shoulder.

"Jeannette."

She turned quickly and laid her dark hair against his chest and said, between sobs, "I thought maybe you didn't love me. And I couldn't stand it. Not after all I've been through!"

"Well, Jeannette, I didn't...I mean I wasn't...."

He paused. He had had no intention of saying he loved her. He'd never told any girl he loved her. Nor had any girl ever told him. And here was this girl on a faraway planet, only half-human at that, taking it for granted that he was hers, body and self.

He began speaking in a soft voice. Words came easily, because he was quoting Moral Lecture AT-16:

"...all beings with their hearts in the right place are brothers...Man and woman are brother and sister...Love is everywhere...but love should be on a higher plane...Man and woman should rightly loathe the beastly act as something the Great Mind, the Cosmic Observer, has not yet eliminated in man's evolutionary development...The time will come when children will be produced otherwise. Meanwhile we must recognize sex as outmoded, and necessary for only one reason: children..."

Slap! His head rang, and points of fire whirled off into the blackness before his eyes.

It was a moment before he could realize that Jeannette had leaped to her feet and slammed him hard with the palm of her hand. He saw her standing above him with her eyes slitted and her red mouth open and drawn back in a snarl.

Then she whirled and ran into the bedroom. He got up and followed her. She was lying on the bed, sobbing.

"Jeannette, you don't understand."

"*Va t'feh fut!*"

When he understood that, he blushed. Then he got mad. He grabbed her by the shoulder and turned her over so that she faced him. Suddenly he was saying, "But I do love you, Jeannette. I do."

He sounded strange, even to himself. The concept of love, as she meant it, was alien to him — rusty, perhaps, if it could be put that way. It would need a lot of polishing. But it would, he knew, be polished. Here in his arms was one whose nature and instinct and education were pointed toward love. He had thought he had drained himself of grief earlier that night, but now, as he forgot his resolve not to tell her what had happened, and as he recounted, step by step, the long and terrible night, tears ran down his face. Thirty years makes a deep well; it takes a long time to pump out all the weeping.

Jeannette, too, cried, and said that she was sorry that she had gotten angry at him. She promised never again to do so. He said it was all right. They kissed again and again until, like two babies who have wept themselves and loved themselves out of frustration and fury, they passed gently into sleep.

TEN

At dawn the Haijac ship, which had been suspended fifty feet high, settled to earth. All day long it would rest there in the middle of a big glade. At nightfall it would rise again. Even though the Terrans had so far seen no evidence of wog aerial flight, except for a few balloons, they took no chances of sudden attack. The sinking sun always saw the *Gabriel* poised above the treetops, radar probing, ready on the instant to accelerate into Ozagen's stratosphere, or, if necessary, into the safety of space.

At 0900 Ship's Time, Yarrow walked into the *Gabriel*, the smell of morning dew on grass in his nostrils. As he had a little time before the conference, he looked up Turnboy, the historian joat. Casually, he asked if Turnboy knew anything of a spaceflight emigration from France during the Forerunner's early days. Turnboy was delighted to show off his knowledge. Yes, the remnants of the Gallic nation had gathered in the Loire country after the Apocalyptic War and had formed the nucleus of what might have become a new France.

But the fast-growing colonies sent from Iceland to the northern part of France, and from Israel to the southern part, had surrounded the Loire. New France found itself squeezed economically and religiously. Sigmen's disciples invaded the Catholic territory in waves of missionaries. High tariffs had strangled the little state's trade. Finally a group of Frenchmen, seeing the inevitable absorption or conquest of their state, religion, and tongue, had left in six spaceships, three thousand strong, to find another Gaul rotating about some far-off star. Where they had landed, nobody knew.

Hal thanked Turnboy and walked to the conference room. He spoke to many; two years of flight had enabled him to recognize most of the personnel. Half of them, like him, had a Mongolian tinge to their features. They were the English-speaking descendants of Hawaiian and Australian survivors of the same war which had decimated France. Their many-times great-grandfathers had repopulated Australia, the Americas, and Japan.

Almost half of the crew spoke Icelandic. Their ancestors had sailed from the grim island to spread across northern Europe and Siberia and Manchuria.

About a sixteenth of the crew spoke Georgian when among their fellows from home. Their fathers had moved down from the Caucasus Mountains and resettled the depopulated plains of southern Russia. A minority in the Haijac Union, they were gradually abandoning their native tongue in favor of that of their closest neighbors — the Icelanders.

At 1200 Hal left the conference room. He felt wonderful. First, he had been moved from twentieth place to the Archurielite's left to sixth from his right. The lamech on his chest made the difference. Second, there was little difficulty about Pornsen's death. The gapt was considered as a casualty of war. Everyone was warned about the nightlifers and other things that sometimes prowled Siddo after dusk. It was not, however, suggested that the Haijacs quit their moonlit espionage.

Macneff, the Achurielite, ordered Hal, as the dead gapt's spiritual son, to arrange for the funeral the following day. Then he pulled down a huge map from a long roller on the wall. This was the representation of Earth that would be given to the wogs.

It was a good example of the Haijacs' subtlety and Chinese box-within-a-box thinking. The sheet bore two hemispheres of Earth with colored political boundaries. It was correct as far as the Bantu and Malay states were concerned. But the positions of the Israeli and Haijac nations had been reversed. The legend beneath the map said that green was the color of the Forerunner states and yellow was the Hebrews'. The green portion, however, was a ring around the Mediterranean, covering Palestine, Turkey, the Balkans, Italy, Austria, south Germany, lower France, Spain and northern Africa; it included the Sahara Sea, Arabia, Mesopotamia, and eastern Persia.

In other words, said Macneff, if by any inconceivable chance the Ozagenians were concealing spaceships, or captured the *Gabriel* and built ships with it as a model, and if they managed to find Sol, they would still attack the wrong country. They would think the Israeli Republic was the Union. Unless, that is, they took time to capture and question Terrans and thus found out the truth. But that was unlikely, for the essence of modern war was the surprise attack. The wogs would not want to give their enemies a chance to prepare.

As everyone knew, Macneff added, the deception might have been furthered by having the *Gabriel*'s members speak Hebrew. But since that was the holy tongue, not to be used by the lower classes except in religious rituals nor to be used at all in profane matters such as carrying on a war, it was forbidden.

However — due to the excellent suggestion of Yarrow, the linguistic joat — French was being spoken. If the wogs pierced the deception, they would think it was a ruse of the Israeli.

After the conference, still glowing from the Achurielite's compliment, Hal gave orders for the funeral arrangements. Other duties kept him till dark, when he returned home.

ELEVEN

When Yarrow locked the door behind him, he heard the shower running. He hung his coat up in the closet; the water quit splashing. As he went toward his bedroom door, Jeannette stepped out from the bathroom. She was drying her hair with a big towel, and she was naked.

She said, "*Bon jour, Hal,*" and walked on unselfconsciously into the bedroom.

Hal replied feebly. He turned and went back into the front room. He felt foolish, because of his timorousness, and at the same time vaguely wicked, unreal, because of the pounding of his heart, his heavy breathing, the hot and fluid fingers that wrapped themselves, half-pain, half-delight, around his loins.

She came out dressed in a pale green robe which he had purchased for her and which she had recut and resewed to fit her figure. Her heavy black hair was piled on her head in a Psyche knot. She kissed him and asked if he wanted to come into the kitchen while she cooked. He said that would be fine.

She began making a sort of spaghetti. He asked her to tell him about her life. Once started, she was not hard to keep going.

"...and so my father's people found a planet like Earth and settled there. It was a beautiful planet; that is why they called it *Luhbawpfey.*"

"Huh?"

"*Le Beau Pays,*" she enunciated more carefully. "The beautiful land. According to my father, there are about thirty million living there on one continent. My father was not content to live the life his grandfathers had—tilling the soil or running a shop and raising many children. He and some other young men like him took the only spaceship left of the original six that had come there, and they sailed off to the stars. They came to Ozagen. And crashed. No wonder. It was two hundred and fifty years old."

"The obsolete ion-beam drive. Is the wreck still around?"

"*Vi.* I mean *oui.* Close to where my sisters and aunts and cousins live."

"Your mother is dead?"

She hesitated, then nodded. "Yes. She died giving birth to me. And my sisters. Father died later. Or rather, we think he did. He went on a hunting-party and never came back."

Hal frowned. "Wait a minute. You told me that your mother and aunts were the last of the native human beings on Ozagen. And you said once before that Rastignac was the only Earthman to get out alive from the wreck. He was your mother's husband, naturally…and incredible as it sounds, their union—one of a terrestrial and an extraterrestrial—was fertile! That alone would rock my colleagues on their heels. Amazing! Completely contrary to accepted science, that their body chemistry and chromosomes should match! But—what I'm getting at is that your mother's sisters had children, too. If the last Ozagenian human male died years before Rastignac crashed, who was their father?"

"Jean Rastignac. He was the husband of my mother and my four aunts. They all say that he was a superb and very virile lover."

Hal said, "Oh."

Until she had the spaghetti and salad ready, he watched her in silence. By then he had regained some of his perspective. After all, the Frenchman was not too much worse than he himself was. Maybe not as bad. He chuckled. How easy it was to condemn somebody else for giving way to temptation until you yourself faced the same situation. He wondered what Pornsen would have done if Jeannette had contacted him.

"…and so it was easy to escape from the wogs," she was saying. "They did not watch me closely, and they were through examining me. *Mon Dieu,* the tests. Questions, questions! That Fobo asked me all sorts of things. Wanted to find out my intelligence, my personality, my etcetera. Put me under all kinds of machines. He and his fellows turned me inside out. Literally, my dear. They took pictures of my insides. Showed me my skeleton and organs and just simply everything. They said it was most interesting. Imagine that! I am exposed as no woman has ever been exposed, and to them I am just most interesting. Indeed!"

"Well," laughed Hal. "You can't expect arthropods to take the viewpoint of a mammal towards a female…that is…."

She looked archly at him. "And am I a mammal?"

"Obviously, unmistakably, indisputably, and enthusiastically."

"For that you get a kiss."

"Hmmm. I'll bet that was almost as good as the spaghetti is going to be."

"You eat your food, and then I will show you something that is much better than almost as good."

He was learning fast. He didn't even flush.

◆ ◆ ◆

After the meal he cut a pitcher of beetlejuice with water, poured in a purplish liquid which made the drink smell like grapes, and dropped sprigs of an orange plant on the surface. Poured into a glass of ice cubes, it was cool and even tasted like grapes. It did not gag him at all.

"Why did you pick me, instead of Pornsen?" he asked.

She sat on his lap, one arm around his neck, the other on the table, drink in hand. "Oh, you were so good-looking, and he was so ugly. Besides, I eavesdropped, and he sounded mean. You were nice. And I knew I had to be careful. My father had told me about Earthmen. He said they couldn't be trusted."

"How true. But you must have an instinct for doing the right thing, Jeannette. If you had antennae, I'd say you could detect nervous emanations. Here, let's see!" He went to run his fingers through her hair, but she ducked her head and laughed.

He laughed with her and dropped the hand to her shoulder, rubbing the smooth skin. "I was probably the only person on the ship who wouldn't have betrayed you. But I'm in a quandary now. You see, your presence here raises the devil. Here we Haijacs are, speaking French as a sort of camouflage for our real nationality, and all the time the wogs knew our language from the beginning. When we first came here, we were careless of what we said before them, because we figured it would take some time for them to learn French.

"Now our expedition may be in danger. And I can't tell Macneff that, because he would want to know how I knew. That'd give you away. And there's something else. You told me they have x-ray machines. So far we've seen none. Are the wogs hiding them? And if they are, what else are they concealing? And why? It's important that we know; but I can't tell Macneff they've got a hidden technology. So I'm on the horns of a dilemma."

"A dilemma? A beast I never heard of."

He hugged her. "I hope you never do. Listen, Jeannette, this is serious. Sooner or later, and probably sooner, we'll have to make up our minds to leave. Our specialists are working night and day on samples of wogglebug blood. They hope to make an artificial semivirus that will attach itself to the copper in the green blood-cells and change their electrophoretic properties."

"*Comment?*"

"Don't look so blank. Or giggle. It's deadly serious. It's what killed seven-eighths of Earth's people. Guided missiles by the tens of thousands circling high over the surface. Dropping little knots of protein molecules that locked onto the hemoglobin in the red blood cells and gave them a positive charge so that one end of a globin molecule would bind with the end of another. Which would make the molecules go into a sort of crystallization. Which would twist the doughnut shaped red cells into a scimitar, and cause an artificial sickle cell anemia.

"The lab-created anemia was much swifter and more certain than the natural kind, because every red cell would be affected, not just a small percentage. Every cell would soon break down. The blood would have no carriers of oxygen to various parts of the body. The body would die.

"The body did die, Jeannette—the body of humanity. Almost a planetful of human beings perished from lack of oxygen. Only by accident did any organized governments survive. Most of those were islands that weren't attacked because they were felt to be too small to bother with. Hawaii, and Iceland, and a city in Australia and Bali.

"Palestine got scotfree by sheer coincidence. An experiment with short radiowaves interfered with the missiles' guiding beams. None got to the Holy Land. By the time the enemy found out why, they were dead. All over the world—not only in the civilized parts, but in the arctic, the jungles, the mountains—they died. Everywhere the missiles circled; everywhere was the invisible rain of death, the skulls, the bones—"

"Hush!" Jeannette put her finger on his quivering lips. "I don't know what you mean by proteins and molecules and those—those electrofrenetic charges! They're way above my head. But I do know that the longer you've been talking, the more scared you've been getting. Your voice was getting higher, and your eyes were growing wider.

"Somebody has frightened you in the past. No! Don't interrupt! They've scared you, and you've been man enough to hide most of your fear; but they've done such a horribly efficient job that you haven't been able to get over it.

"Well —" and she put her soft lips to his ears and whispered — "I'm going to wipe that fear out, I'm going to lead you out of that valley of fright. No! Don't protest! I know it hurts your ego to think that a woman could know you're afraid. But I don't think any the less of you. I admire you all the more because you've conquered so much of it. I know what courage it took to face the 'Meter. I know you did it because of me. I'm proud that you did. I love you for it. And I know what courage it takes to keep me here, when any time a slip would send you to certain disgrace and death. I know what it all means. It's my nature and instinct and business and love to know.

"Now! Drink with me. We're not outside these walls where we have to worry ourselves about such things and be scared. We're in here. Away from everything except ourselves. Drink. And love me. I'll love you, Hal, and we'll not see the world outside nor need to. For the time being, forget in my arms."

They drank the purplish liquor. After a while he picked her up and carried her into the bedroom. There he forgot. The only disconcerting item was that she insisted upon keeping her eyes open, even during the climax, as if she were trying to photograph his features upon her mind.

TWELVE

On Earth, the alcoholics were not cured but were sent to H. Therefore no psychological or narcotic therapies had been worked out for addicts. Hal, dead-ended by this fact in his desire to wipe out Jeannette's alcoholism, went for medicine to the very people who had given her the disease. Only he pretended that the cure was for himself.

Fobo said, "There is widespread drinking on Ozagen, but it is light. Our few alcoholics are quickly empathized into normality. Why don't you let me empathize you?"

"Sorry. My government forbids that." He had given Fobo the same excuse for not inviting the wog home.

"You have the most forbidding government," said Fobo, and went into one of his long, howling laughs. When he recovered, he said, "You're forbidden to touch liquor, too, but that doesn't hold you back. Well, there's no accounting for inconsistency. Seriously, though, I have just the thing for you. It's called Easyglow. It's a stimulant which has an effect similar to alcohol's, but which is, in reality, however, depressing. We put it into the daily ration of liquor, increasing slowly the Easyglow and diminishing the alcohol. In two or three weeks the patient is drinking from a fluid 96 percent Easyglow. The taste is much the same; the drinker seldom suspects. Continued treatment eases the patient from his dependence on the alcohol. There is only one drawback."

He paused and said, "The drinker is now addicted to Easyglow!"

He whooped and slapped his thigh and wiggled his antennae and laughed until the tears came.

"Really, though, the peculiar effect of Easyglow is that it opens the patient for discharge of the strains that have driven him to drink. He may then be empathized and at the same time weaned from the stimulant. Since I have no opportunity to slip the stuff to you secretly, I'm taking the chance that you are seriously interested in curing yourself. When you're ready for therapy, tell me."

Hal took the bottle to his apartment. Every day its contents went quietly and carefully into the beetlejuice he got for Jeannette. He hoped that he was psychologist enough to cure her once the Easyglow took effect.

Although he didn't know it, he was himself being "cured" by Fobo. His almost daily talks with the empathist instilled doubts about the religion and science of the Haijacs — or, as their enemies termed them, the Highjackers. Fobo read the biographies of Isaac Sigmen and the Works: the Pre-Torah, the Western Talmud, the Revised Scriptures, the Foundations of Serialism, Time and Theology, The Self and the World-Line. Calmly sitting at his table with a glass of juice in his hand, the wog challenged the mathematics of the dunnologists. Hal proved; Fobo disproved. He pointed out that the math was mainly based on false-to-fact assumptions; that Dunne's and Sigmen's reasoning was buttressed by too many analogs, metaphors and strained interpretations. Remove the buttresses, and the structure fell.

And worse, far worse, he said that the Forerunner's biographies and theological writings revealed him, even through the censor's veil, as a sexually frigid and woman-hating man with a messiah complex and paranoid and schizophrenic tendencies which burst through his icy shell from time to time in religious-scientific frenzies and fantasies.

"Other men," Fobo said, "have stamped their personality and ideas upon their times. But Sigmen had an advantage over those great leaders who came before him. Because of Earth's rejuvenation serums he lived long enough, not only to set up his kind of society, but to consolidate it and weed out its weaknesses. He didn't die until the cement of his social form had hardened."

"But the Forerunner didn't die," protested Yarrow. "He left in time. He is still with us, traveling down the fields of presentation, skipping here and there, now to the past, now to the future. Always, wherever he is needed to turn pseudo-time into real time, he is there."

"Ah, yes," smiled Fobo. "That was the reason you went to the ruins, was it not? To check up on a mural which hinted that the Ozagen humans had once been visited by a man from outer space. You thought it might have been the Forerunner, didn't you?"

"Macneff did," said Hal, annoyed. "But my report showed that, though the man resembled Sigmen somewhat, the evidence was too inconclusive. The Forerunner may or may not have visited this planet a thousand years ago."

"Be that as it may, I maintain your theses are meaningless. You claim that his prophecies came true. I say, first, that they were couched ambiguously. Second, if they have been realized, it is because your powerful state-church — you may call it the Sturch — has made strenuous efforts to fulfill them.

"Furthermore, this pyramidal society of yours — this guardian-angel administration — where every ten families have a gapt to supervise their most intimate and minute details, and every ten family-gapts have a block-gapt at their head, and every fifty block-gapts are directed by a supervisor-gapt, and so on — this society is based on fear and ignorance and suppression."

Hal, shaken, angered, shocked, would get up to leave. Fobo would call him back and ask him to disprove what he'd said. Hal would let loose a flood of wrath. Sometimes, when he had finished, he would be asked to sit down and continue the discussion. Sometimes, Fobo would lose his temper; they would shout and scream insults; twice, they fought with fists; Hal got a bloody nose once and Fobo a black eye. Then the wog, weeping, would embrace Hal and ask for his forgiveness, and they would sit down and drink some more until their nerves were calmed.

Yarrow told Jeannette of these incidents. She encouraged him to tell them over and over again until he had talked away the stress and strain of grief and hate and doubt. Afterwards, there was always love such as he had never thought possible. For the first time he knew that man and woman could become one flesh. His wife and he had remained outside the circle of each other, but Jeannette knew the geometry that would take him in and the chemistry that would mix his substance with hers.

Always, too, there was the light and the drink. But they did not bother him. Unknown to her, she was now drinking a liquor almost entirely Easyglow. And he had gotten used to the light above their bed. It was one of her quirks. Fear of the dark wasn't behind it, because it was only while making love that she required a bulb be left on. He didn't understand it. Perhaps she wanted to impress his image on her memory, always to have it if she ever lost him. If so, let her keep the light. By its glow he explored her body with an interest that was part sexual and part anthropological. He was delighted and astonished at the many small differences between her and Terran women. There was a small appendage of skin on the roof of her mouth that might have been the rudiment of some organ whose function was long ago cast aside by evolution. There were two bumps of cartilage on the top of her head, hidden by her thick black hair. She had thirty teeth; the wisdom teeth were missing. That might or might not have been a characteristic of her mother's people.

He suspected that she either had an extra set of pectoral muscles or else an extraordinarily well-developed normal set. Her large and cone-shaped breasts did not sag. They were high and firm and pointed slightly upwards: the ideal of feminine beauty so often portrayed through the ages by male sculptors and painters and so seldom existing in nature.

She was not only a pleasure to look at; she was pleasing to be with. At least once a week she would greet him with a new garment. She loved to sew; out of the materials he gave her she fashioned slips, blouses, skirts and even gowns. Along with the change in dress went new hairdos. She was ever-new and ever-beautiful, and she made Hal realize for the first time that a thing of beauty was a joy, if not for forever, then for at least as long as it lasted.

Her imitativeness was another thing that delighted him. She had switched from her brand of French to his almost overnight. Within a week she was speaking it faster and more expressively than he. As she also knew Ozagen thoroughly, he decided the best way for him to learn it was to have her read wog books to him. He'd lie on the divan while she sat on a chair. Her accent and pronunciation were correct, and trained his ear. Where she saved him time was in his not having to look up each new word in a dictionary — she translated for him.

Jeannette loved to read to him, but she wearied of the dry and technical books he gave her. When he saw that she was tired, he softened and let her stop. He never did, for example, finish Weenai's monumental *Rise and Fall of Man on Ozagen*. That evening Jeannette began, as usual, bravely enough. Her low, throaty voice tried to simulate interest in what her eyes saw. She went through the first chapter, which described the formation of the planet and the beginnings of life. In the second she yawned quite openly and looked at Hal, but he closed his eyes and pretended not to notice. So she read of the rise of the wogs from an arthropod that had changed its mind and decided to become a chordate. Weenai made some heavy jests about the contrariness of the wogglebugs since that fateful day, and then took up, in the third chapter, the story of mammalian evolution on the other large continent of Ozagen. It climaxed in man.

She quoted: "But homo sapiens, like us, had its mimical parasites. One was a different species of the so-called tavern beetle. It, instead of resembling a wog, looked like a man. Like its counterpart, it could fool no intelligent person, but its gift of alcohol made it very acceptable to man. It, too, accompanied its host from primitive times, became an integral part of his civilization, and, finally, a large cause of man's downfall.

"Humanity's disappearance from the face of Ozagen is due not only to the tavern beetle. That creature can be controlled, and has been by us. Like most things, it has benefits to confer. Like most things, it can be abused or its purpose distorted so that it becomes a menace.

"That is what man did with it.

"He had, it must be noted, an ally to help him in the misuse of the insect. This was another parasite, one of a somewhat different kind; one that was, indeed, our cousin. That is, it is a so-called chordate arthropod.

"One thing, however, distinguishes it from us, and from man, and from any other animal on this planet with the exception of some very low species. That is, that from the very first fossil evidence we have of it, it was wholly —"

Jeannette put the book down. "I don't know the next word. Hal, do I have to read this? It's so boring."

"No. Forget it. Read me one of those comics that you and the crew like so much."

She smiled, a beautiful sight, and began Vol.1037, Book 56, of the *Adventures of Leif Magnus, Beloved Disciple of the Forerunner, When He Met the Horror from Arcturus.*

He listened to her translation of the French into vernacular Wog until he grew tired of the banalities and pulled her down to him.

Always, there was the light left on above them.

THIRTEEN

It was the following day that Yarrow, returning from the market with a large box, said, "You've sure been putting away the groceries lately. You're not eating for two? Or maybe three?"

She paled. "*Mon Dieu!* Do you know what you're saying?"

He put the box on a table and grabbed her shoulders.

"Shib. I do. Jeannette, I've been thinking about that very thing for a long time, but I haven't said anything. I didn't want to worry you. Tell me, are you?"

She looked him straight in the eye, but her body was shaking. "Oh, no. It is impossible!"

"Why should it be? We've used no preventives."

"*Oui.* But I know — don't ask me how — call it instinct, if you wish — that it cannot be. But you must never say things like that. Not even joking. I can't stand it."

He pulled her close and said over her shoulder, "Is it because you can't? Because you know you'll never bear my children?"

Her thick, faintly perfumed hair nodded. "I know. Don't ask me how I know."

He held her at arm's length again. "Listen, Jeannette. I'll tell you what's been troubling you. You and I are really of different species. Your mother and father were, too. Yet they had issue. But you're thinking that the ass and the mare have young, too, but the mule is sterile. The lion and the tigress may breed, but the liget or tigon can't. Isn't that right? You're afraid you're a mule!"

She put her head on his chest and sobbed.

He said, "Let's be real about this, honey. Maybe you are. So what? My God, our situation is bad enough without a baby to complicate it. We'll be lucky if you are...uh...well, we have each other, haven't we? That's all I want. You."

He couldn't keep from being reflective as he dried her tears and kissed her and helped her put the food in the refrigerator.

The quantities of groceries and milk she had been consuming were more than a normal amount, especially the milk. There had been no telltale change in her superb figure, true. But the stuff was going somewhere.

A month passed. He watched her closely. She ate enormously. Nothing happened.

Yarrow put it down to his ignorance of her alien metabolism.

FOURTEEN

Another month. Hal was just leaving the ship's library when Turnboy stopped him.

"The rumor is that the techs have finally made the globinlocking molecule," the historian said. "I think that this time the grapevine's right. A conference is called for 1500."

"Shib." Hal kept his despair out of his voice.

When the meeting broke up at 1650, it left him with sagging shoulders. The virus was already in production. In a week a large enough supply would be made to fill the disseminators of six prowler-torpedoes. The plan was to release them to wipe out the city of Siddo. A beachhead would be established there. While the *Gabriel* flew back to Earth, the beachhead would keep making the virus and would send prowlers out in spirals whose range would expand until a large territory would be covered. By the time a huge fleet returned, millions of wogs would be slain. The fleet would then deal with the rest of the planet.

When he got home, he found Jeannette lying in bed. She smiled weakly. Her hair was loose in a black corona on the pillow.

He forgot his mood in a thrill of concern.

"What's the matter, baby?"

He laid his hand on her forehead. The skin was dry and hot and rough.

"I don't know. I haven't been feeling really well for two weeks, but I didn't complain. I thought I'd get over it. Today I felt so bad I just had to go back to bed after breakfast."

"We'll get you well."

He sounded confident. Inside himself, he was lost. If she had contracted a serious disease, she could get no doctor, no medicine —

For the next few days she continued to lie in bed. Her temperature fluctuated from 99.5 in the morning to 100.2 at night. Hal attended her as well as he could. He put wet towels and ice-bags on her head and gave her aspirin. She had quit eating so much food; all she wanted was liquid. She seemed to be always asking for milk. Even the beetlejuice and the cigarettes were turned down.

Her illness was bad enough, but her silences stung Yarrow into a frenzy. As long as he had known her, she had chattered lightly, merrily, amusingly. She could be quiet, but it was with an interested wordlessness. Now she let him talk, and when he quit, she did not fill his silence with questions or comments.

In an effort to arouse her, he told her of his plan to steal a gig and take her back to her jungle home. A light came into her dulled eyes; the brown looked shiny for the first time. She even sat up while he put a map of the continent on her lap. She indicated the general area where she had lived, and then described the mountain range that rose from the green tropics, and the table-land on its top where her aunts and sisters lived in the ruins of a metropolis.

Hal sat down at the little octagonal-shaped table by the bed and worked out the coordinates from the maps. Now and then he glanced up. She was lying on her side, her white and delicate shoulder rising from her nightgown, her eyes large in the shadows that were beginning to stain rings around them.

"All I have to do is steal a little key," he said. "You see, the milometer on a gig is set at 0 before every flight from the field. The boat will run fifty miles on manual. That gives us leeway to go any place in Siddo and return. But once the tape passes fifty, the gig automatically stops and sends out a location signal. That's to keep anybody from running away. However, the autos can be unlocked and the signal turned off. A little key will do it. I can get it. Don't worry."

"You must love me very much."

"You bet I do!"

He rose and kissed her. Her mouth, once so soft and dewy, felt dry and hard. It was almost as if the skin were turning to horn.

He returned to his calculations. An hour later, a sigh from her made him look up. Her eyes were closed, and her lips were slightly open. Sweat ran down her face.

He hoped her fever had broken. No. The mercury stopped at 100.3.

She said something.

He bent down. "What?"

She was muttering in an unknown language. Delirious. Hal swore. He had to act. No matter what the consequences. He ran into the bathroom, shook from a bottle a ten grain rockabye tablet, went back and propped Jeannette up and got her to wash the pill down with a glass of water.

After he locked her bedroom door, he put on a hood and cloak and walked fast to the nearest pharmacy. There he purchased three 20-gauge needles, three syringes, and some anti-coagulant. Back in his apartment, he tried to insert the needle in an arm vein. The point refused to go in until the fourth attempt when, in a fit of exasperation, he pressed hard.

During none of the jabbings did she open her eyes or jerk her arm.

When the first fluid crept into the glass tube, he gasped with relief. Though he hadn't known it, he had been biting his lower lip and holding his breath. Suddenly he knew that he had for the last month been pushing a horrible suspicion back to the outlands of his mind. Now, he realized the thought had been ridiculous.

The blood was red.

He tried to arouse her in order to get a specimen of urine. She twisted her mouth over strange syllables, then lapsed back into sleep or a coma — he didn't know which. In an anguish of despair he slapped her face, again and again, hoping he could bring her to. He swore once more, for he realized all at once that he should have gotten the specimen before giving her the rockabye pill. How stupid could he get! He wasn't thinking straight; he was too excited over her condition and what he had to do at the ship.

He perked some very strong coffee and managed to get part of it down her. The rest dribbled down her chin and soaked her gown.

Either the caffeine or his desperate tone awoke her, for she opened her eyes long enough to look at him while he explained what he wanted her to do and where he was going afterwards. Once he'd gotten the urine into a previously boiled jar, he wrapped the syringes and jar in a handkerchief and dropped them into the cloak-pocket.

He had already wristphoned the *Gabriel* for a gig. A horn beeped outside. He took another look at Jeannette, locked the bedroom door, locked the apartment door, and ran down the stairs. The gig hovered above the curb. He entered, sat down, and punched the *Go* button. The boat rose to a thousand feet and then flashed at an 11-degree angle toward the park where the ship squatted.

FIFTEEN

The medical section was empty, except for one orderly. The fellow dropped his comic and jumped to his feet.

"Take it easy," said Hal. "I just want to use the Labtech. And I don't want to be bothered with making out triplicate forms. This is a little personal matter, see?"

Hal had taken off his cloak. The orderly looked at the bright golden lamech.

"Shib," he grunted.

Hal gave him two cigarettes.

"Geez, thanks." The orderly lit up, sat down, and picked up his *The Forerunner and Delilah in the Wicked City of Gaza.*

Yarrow went around the corner of the Labtech, where the orderly couldn't see him, and set the proper dials. After he inserted his specimens, he sat down. Almost at once he jumped up and began pacing back and forth. Meanwhile, the huge cube of the Labtech purred like a contented cat as it digested its strange food. A half-hour later, it rumbled once and then flashed a green light: ANALYSIS COMPLETE.

Hal pressed a button. Like a tongue out of a metal mouth, a long tape slid out. He read the code. Urine was normal. No infection there. Also normal was the pH and the blood count.

He hadn't been sure the "eye" would recognize the cells in her blood. However, the chances had been strong that her red cells would be Terranlike. Why not? Evolution follows parallel paths; the biconcave disk is the most efficient form for carrying the maximum of oxygen.

The machine chattered. More tape. Unknown hormone! Similar in molecular structure to the parathyroid hormone primarily concerned in the control of calcium metabolism.

What did that mean? Could the mysterious substance loosed in her bloodstream be the cause of her trouble?

More clicks. The calcium content of the blood was 40 mg. per cent.

Strange. Such an abnormally high percentage should mean that the renal threshold was passed and that an excess of calcium should be "spilling" into the urine. Where was it going?

The Labtech flashed a red light: FINISHED.

He took a Hematology book down from the shelf and opened it to the Ca section. When he quit reading, he straightened his shoulders. New hope? Perhaps. Her case sounded as if she had a form of hypercalcemia, which was manifested by any number of diseases ranging from rickets and steomalacia to chronic hypertrophic arthritis. Whatever she had, she was suffering from a malfunction of the parathyroid glands.

The next move was to the Pharm machine. He punched three buttons, dialed a number, stood for two minutes, and then lifted a little door at waist-level. A tray slid out. On it was a cellophane sheath containing a hypodermic needle and a tube holding 30 cc of a pale blue fluid. It was Jesper's serum, a "one-shot" readjustor of the parathyroid.

Hal put on his cloak, stuck the package in the inside pocket, and strode out. The orderly didn't even look up.

The next step was the weapons room. There he gave the storekeeper an order — made out in triplicate — for one .1 mm. automatic and a clip of one hundred cartridges. The keeper only glanced over the forged signatures — he, too, was awed by the lamech — and unlocked the door.

Hal took the gun, which he could easily hide in the palm of his hand, and stuck it in his pants pocket.

At the key room, two corridors away, he repeated the crime. Or rather, he tried to.

Moto, the officer on duty, looked at the papers, hesitated, and said, "I'm sorry. My orders are to check on any requests with the Chief Uzzite. That won't be possible for about an hour, though. He's in conference with the Archurielite."

Hal picked up his papers. "Never mind. My business'll hold. Be back in the morning."

On the way home, he planned what he'd do. After injecting Jesper's serum in Jeannette, he'd move her into the gig. The floor beneath the gig's control-panel would have to be ripped up, two wires would be unhooked, and one connected to another lead. That would remove the fifty-mile limit. Unfortunately, it would also set off an alarm back in the *Gabriel*. His hope was that he could take off straight up, level off, and dive behind the range of hills to the west of Siddo. The hills would deflect the radar. The autopilot could be set long enough for him to demolish the box that would be sending out the signal by which the *Gabriel* might track him down.

After that, with the gig hedgehopping, he could hope to be free until daybreak. Then he'd submerge in the nearest deep-enough lake or river until nightfall. During the darkness he could rise and speed towards the tropics; and if his radar showed any signs of pursuit, he could plunge again into a body of water.

◆ ◆ ◆

He left the long needle-shape parked by the curb. His feet pounded the stairs. The key missed the hole the first two tries. He slammed the door without bothering to lock it again.

"Jeannette!" he shouted. Suddenly he was afraid that she might have gotten up while delirious and somehow opened the doors and wandered out.

A low moan answered him. He unlocked the bedroom door and shoved it open. She was lying with her eyes wide.

"Jeannette. Do you feel better?"

"No. Worse. Much worse."

"Don't worry, baby. I've got just the medicine that'll put new life in you. In a couple of hours you'll be sitting up and yelling for steaks. And you won't even want to touch that milk. You'll be drinking Easyglow by the gallon. And then—"

He faltered as he saw her face. It was a stony mask of distress, like the grotesque and twisted wooden faces of the Greek tragedians.

"Oh, no...*no!* My God," she moaned. "What did you say? Easyglow?" Her voice rose. "Is that what you've been giving me?"

"Shib, Jeannette. Take it easy. You liked it. What's the difference? The point is that we're going—"

"Oh, Hal, Hal! What have you done?"

Her pitiful face tore at him. Tears were falling; if ever stone could weep, it was weeping now.

He turned and ran into the kitchen where he took out the sheath, removed the contents, and inserted the needle in the tube. He went back into the bedroom. She said nothing as he thrust the point into her vein. For a moment he was afraid the needle would break. The skin was almost brittle.

"This stuff cures Earth people in a jiffy," he said, with what he hoped was a cheery bedside manner.

"Oh, Hal, come here. It's—it's too late now."

He withdrew the needle, rubbed alcohol on the break and put a pad on it. Then he dropped to his knees by the bed and kissed her. Her lips were hard.

"Hal, do you love me?"

"Won't you ever believe me? How many times must I tell you?"

"No matter what you'll find out about me?"

"I know all about you."

"No, you don't. You can't. Oh, Great Mother, if only I'd told you, Hal! Maybe you'd have loved me just as much, anyway. Maybe..."

"Jeannette! What's the matter?"

Her lids had closed. Her body shook in a spasm. When the violent trembling passed, she whispered with stiff lips. He bent his head to hear her.

"What did you say? Jeannette! Speak!"

He shook her. The fever must have died, for her shoulder was cold. And hard.

The words came low and slurring.

"Take me to my aunts and sisters. They'll know what to do. Not for me...but for the..."

"What do you mean?"

"Hal, will you always love..."

"Yes, yes. You know that! We've got more important things to do now than talk about that."

If she heard him she gave no sign. Her head was tilted far back with her exquisite nose pointed at the ceiling. Her lids and mouth were closed, and her hands were by her side, palms up. The breasts were motionless. Whatever breath she might have was too feeble to stir them.

SIXTEEN

Hal ran upstairs to the third floor and pounded on Fobo's door until it opened.

The empathist's wife said, "Bugs, alive, Hal, you startled me!"

"Where's Fobo?"

"He's at a college board meeting."

"I've got to see him at once."

Abasa yelled after him, "If it's important, go ahead. Those meetings bore him, anyway."

By the time Yarrow had taken the steps three at a time and beelined across the nearby campus, his lungs were on fire. He didn't slacken his pace; he hurtled up the steps of the administration building and burst into the board room.

When he tried to speak, he had to stop and suck in deep breaths.

Fobo jumped out of his chair.

"What's up?"

"You — gasp — you've — got to come. Matter — life — death!"

"Excuse me, gentlemen," said Fobo. The ten wogs nodded their antennae and resumed the conference. The empathist put on his cloak and high-crowned, plumed hat and led Hal out.

"Now, what is it?"

"Listen. I've got to trust you. I know you can't promise me anything. But I think you won't turn me in to my people. You're a real person, Fobo. Not like the Haijac men."

"Get to the point, my friend."

"Listen. You wogs are as advanced as we are in endocrinology. And you've got an advantage. You know Jeannette inside out. You've examined her."

"Jeannette? Oh, Rastignac! The *lalitha*."

"Yes. I've been hiding her in my apartment."

"I know."

"You...know! How?"

"Never mind." The wog put his hand on Hal's shoulder. "Something bad has happened, or you'd not have come to me about her."

By the time Hal had told him, they were at their apartments. Fobo stopped him at the door.

"I may as well tell you. Your countrymen know you're up to something. For the last eight days a man has been living in that building down the street and spying on you. His name is Art Hunah Fedtof."

"An Uzzite!"

"*Oui*. He lives in the front room on the ground floor. His windows are darkened, but he is probably watching you right now."

"Forget about him!" Yarrow snarled. He bounded up the stairs. Fobo followed him into his rooms. The wog felt Jeannette's forehead and tried to lift her lid to look at her eye. It would not bend.

"Hmm! Calcification of the outer skin layer is far advanced."

With one hand he threw the sheet from her figure and with the other he grabbed her gown by the neckline and ripped the thin cloth down the middle. The two parts fell to either side. She lay nude, as silent and pale and beautiful as a sculptor's masterpiece.

Her lover gave a little cry at what seemed like a violation. But he shut up at once, because he knew that Fobo's move was medical. In any case, the wog would not have been sexually interested.

Puzzled, he watched. Fobo had tapped his fingertips against her flat belly and then put his ear against it. When he stood up, he shook his head.

"I won't deceive you, Hal. Though we'll do the best we can, we may not be good enough. She'll have to go to a surgeon. If we can cut her eggs out before they hatch, that, plus the serum you gave her, may reverse the effect and pull her out."

"Eggs?"

"I'll tell you later. Wrap her up. I'll run upstairs and phone Dr. Kuto."

Yarrow folded a blanket around her. When he rolled her over, she was as stiff as a show-window dummy. He covered her face. The stony look was too much for him.

His wristphone shrilled. Automatically he reached to flick the stud and just in time drew his hand back. It shrilled loudly, insistently. Finally he decided that if he didn't answer, he would stir up their suspicion far faster.

"Yarrow!"

"Shib!"

"Report to the Archurielite. You will be given fifteen minutes."

"Shib."

Fobo came back in and said, "What're you going to do?"

Hal squared his mouth and said, "You take her by the shoulders, and I'll carry her feet. Rigid as she is, we won't need a stretcher."

As they carried her down the steps, he said, "Can you hide us after the operation, Fobo? We won't be able to use the gig now."

"Don't worry," the wog said enigmatically over his shoulder. "The Earthmen are going to be too busy to run after you."

It took sixty seconds to get her in the gig, hop to the hospital, and get her out.

Hal said, "Let's put her on the ground for a minute. I've got to set the gig on auto and send her back to the *Gabriel*. That way, at least, they won't know where I'm at."

"No. Leave it here. You may be able to use it afterward."

"After what?"

"Later. Ah, there's Kuto."

♦ ♦ ♦

In the waiting room the joat paced back and forth and puffed Merciful Seraphim out in smoke. The empathist sat on a chair and rubbed his bald pate and the thick golden corkscrew fuzz on the back of his head.

"All this could have been avoided," he said unhappily. "But I didn't know until a week ago that the *lalitha* was living with you. I didn't think there was any hurry to tell you that I knew. Anyway, I was busy working on Project Earthman."

"What was that?" barked Yarrow.

"Oh, for some time we've had our electroencephalographs on you. You Terrans are far ahead of us in most of the physical sciences, but in the psychical sciences we've got you beaten. For instance, you haven't yet found out that below the level of the general brain-waves, which might be likened to 'static,' lie very weak but definite impulses.

"These we call the 'semantic' waves. Our instruments, built with our antennae and nervous system as a model, are so sensitive that they can pick them up at quite a distance and amplify them. The various heights of the semantic waves are then correlated with the spoken syllables of the language. In other words, we have a more or less efficient mind-reader.

"We trained them on you Terrans from the beginning. We thought we would have quite an advantage, because we had learned a type of French from the *lalitha*. To our consternation, however, we found that you talked to us in one language but tended to do your thinkng in, not one, but four different tongues."

"Those were Hebrew for the theological thinking of the Urielites and technical thinking of some of the scientists," snapped Hal. "English, Icelandic and Georgian for the everyday thoughts. Any other time

I'd be interested in this thinkpicker. But for Forerunner's sake, I want to hear about Jeannette!"

"Believe me, Hal, I can feel for and with you." He wiggled his antennae to indicate he was receiving grief and anxiety emanations. "It's necessary and justifiable that I take my explanation in order. Otherwise, I'll be confused and backtracking all the time, which I detest. As I was saying, we were stumped for a while because the semantic waves fluctuations did not match those of the spoken word. However, we kept picking up stray thoughts here and there in French. As well grounded as you all seem to have been in that language, it was inevitable that you would do a certain amount of private thinking in it, regardless of your native tongue. About two weeks ago we managed to work out the complete synchronization in the artificial tongue and also bind up a great many impulses with the other languages' words by comparing them with the French."

"Then you know we have perfected the globinlocker?"

Fobo smiled. "Yes, but we were suspicious of that from the beginning. When you asked us for samples of blood, your request was accompanied by too heavy a charge of what we call 'furtive' emanations. We gave you the blood, all right, but it was that of a barnyard creature which uses copper in its blood cells. We wogs use magnesium as the oxygen-carrying element in our cells."

"Our virus is useless!"

"Naturally. Now to get to the personal. My colleagues had their e.c.g's turned on you whenever you came into my room. They didn't think it was any use tapping your waves when you were in your room. You'd be likely to be thinking in the vernacular. About a week ago they did, however, just for experiment, and they were amazed to find the *lalitha* there. They told me. I was too engrossed with this business with the ship to put two and two together. Otherwise, I'd have known why you were pretending to be an alcoholic. I—"

A nurse entered and said, "Phone, Doctor."

Yarrow paced, and smoked another cigarette. Fobo came back.

He said, We're going to have company. One of my colleagues, who is watching the ship, tells me Macneff and two Uzzites left in a gig a minute ago. They should be arriving at the hospital any second now."

Yarrow stopped in midstride. His jaw dropped. "Here?"

"Don't be afraid."

Hal just stood there. The cigarette, unnoticed, burned until it seared his fingers. He dropped it and crushed it beneath his sole.

Bootheels clicked in the corridor.

Three men entered. One was a tall and gaunt ghost—Macneff, the Archurielite. The others were short and broad-shouldered and clad in black. Their meaty hands, though empty, were hooked, ready to dart into their pockets. Their heavy-lidded eyes stabbed at Fobo and then at Hal.

Macneff strode up to the joat. His pale blue eyes glared; his lipless mouth was drawn back in a skull's smile.

"You unspeakable degenerate!" he shouted.

His arm flashed, and the whip, jerked out of his belt, cracked. Thin red marks crawled out of Yarrow's white face and began oozing blood.

"You will be taken back to Earth in chains and there exhibited as an example of the worst pervert, traitor, and—and—!"

He drooled, unable to find words.

"You—who have passed the Elohimeter, who are supposed to be so pure—you have lusted after and lain with an insect!"

"What! What!"

"Yes. With a thing that is even lower than a beast of the field. What even Moses did not think of when he forbade union between man and beast, what even the Forerunner could not have guessed when he reaffirmed the law and set the death penalty for it, you have done. You, Hal Yarrow, the pure, the lamech wearer!"

Fobo rose and said in a deep voice, "Might I suggest and stress that you are not quite right in your zoological classification? It is not the class of insecta but the class of the chordata pseudarthropoda, or words to that effect."

The joat said, "What?" again. He could not think.

The wog growled, "Shut up, Hal. Let me talk."

He swung to face Macneff. "You know about her?"

"You are shib that I know her! Yarrow thought he was getting away with something. But no matter how clever these unrealists are, they're always tripped up. In this case, it was his asking Turnboy about those Frenchmen that fled Earth two and a half centuries ago. Turnboy, who is very zealous in his attitude towards the Sturch, reported the conversation. It lay among my papers for quite a while. When I came across it, I turned it over to the psychologists. They told me that the joat's question was a deviation from the pattern expected of him; a thing totally irrelevant unless it was connected to something we didn't know about him.

"A man was put on his trail. He saw Yarrow buying twice the groceries he should have. And much cloth and sewing equipment and silk stockings and perfume and earrings. Moreover, when you wogs learned the tobacco habit from us and began making cigarettes too, he bought them from you. The conclusion was obvious. He had a female in his apartment.

"We didn't think it'd be a wog female for she wouldn't have to stay hidden. Therefore she must be human. But we couldn't imagine how she got here on Ozagen. It was impossible for him to have stowed her away on the *Gabriel*. She must either have come here in a different ship, or be descended from people who had.

"It was Yarrow's talk with Turnboy that furnished the clue. Obviously, the French had landed here. She was a great-great-granddaughter. How the joat had found her, we didn't know. It wasn't important. We'll find out, anyhow."

"You're due to find out some other things, too," Fobo said calmly. "How did you discover she wasn't human?"

Yarrow muttered, "I've got to sit down."

SEVENTEEN

He swayed to the wall and sank into a chair. One of the Uzzites started to move toward him. Macneff waved the man back and said, "Turnboy had been reading the history of man on Ozagen. He came across so many references to the *lalitha* that the suspicion was bound to rise that the girl might be one.

"Last week one of the wog physicians, while talking to Turnboy, mentioned that he had once examined a *lalitha*. Later, he said, she had run away. It wasn't hard for us to guess where she had ended up!"

"My boy," said Fobo, turning to Hal, "didn't you read Weenai's book?"

Hal shook his head. "We started it, but Jeannette mislaid it."

"And doubtless saw to it that you had other things to think of...they are good at diverting a man's mind. Why not? That is their purpose in life.

"Well, Hal, I'll explain. The *lalitha* are the highest example of mimetic parasitism known. Also, they are unique among sentient beings. Unique in that all are female.

"You see, if you'd read on in Weenai, you'd have found that fossil evidence shows that about the time that Ozagenian man was still an insectivorous marmoset-like creature, he had in his family group not only his own females but the females of another class, perhaps another phylum. These animals looked and probably stank enough like the females of prehomo marmoset to be able to live and mate with them.

They seemed mammalian, but dissection would have indicated very strongly their pseudoarthropodal ancestry.

"It's reasonable to suppose that these precursors of the *lalitha* were man's parasites long before the marmosetoid stage. They may have met him when he first crawled out of the sea, and promptly adapted their shape, through an evolutionary process, to that of the lung-fish. And later to the amphibian's. And the reptile's and primitive mammal's. And so on.

"What we do know is that the *lalitha* were Nature's most amazing experiment in parasitism and parallel evolution. As man metamorphosed into higher forms, so she kept pace with him. All female, mind you, depending upon the male of another phylum for the continuance of the species.

"It is astonishing the way they became integrated into the prehuman cultures, the pithecanthropoid and neanderthaloid steps. Only when homo sapiens developed did their troubles begin. Some families and tribes accepted them; others killed them. So they resorted to artifice, and disguised themselves as human women. A thing not hard to do — unless they became pregnant.

"In which case they died."

Hal groaned and put his hands over his face.

"Painful but real, as our acquaintance Macneff would say," said Fobo. "Of course — such a condition required a secret sorority. In those societies where the *lalitha* was forced to camouflage, she would, once pregnant, have to leave. And perish in some hidden place among her kind, who would then take care of the nymphs — " here Hal shuddered — "until they were able to go into human cultures. Or else be introduced as foundlings or changelings.

"You'll find quite a tribal lore about them — fables and myths make them central or peripheral characters quite frequently. They were regarded as witches, demons, or worse.

"With the introduction of the alcohol beetle in primitive times, a change for the better came to the *lalitha*. Alcohol made them sterile. At the same time, barring accident, disease, or murder, it made them *immortal*.

Hal took his hands off his face. "You — you mean Jeannette would have lived — forever? That I cost her that?"

"She could have lived a thousand years, at least. We know that some did. What's more, they remained young. Let me explain. In due order. Some of what I'm going to say will distress you, Hal, but it must be said.

"The long life of the pseudo-woman, sometimes so long that they survived tribes and nations they had joined when first founded, led to their being worshipped as goddesses. They became the repositories of wisdom and wealth. Religions were established with *lalitha* as the focus and priests and beetles on the circumference as permanent marks of human civilizations. The priests and the kings were their lovers.

"Some cultures barred the *lalitha*. They could not, however, keep them out. The false women infiltrated. Being always very beautiful, they mated with the most powerful men — the leaders, the rich, the poets, the thinkers. They competed with women and beat them at their own game, hands down, because in the *lalitha* Nature wrought the complete female.

"You see, they had no male hormone, no male element. They were all woman, and they centered their lives on men. They were instinctively and consciously sensitive to their lovers' desires, whims and moods. Yet they were crafty enough not to be clinging vines. When the time demanded a quarrel, they produced it. They knew what few human females did: the time to speak and the time not to speak.

"You noticed that in Jeannette, didn't you, Hal? No wonder. As part of their arthropodal heritage they owned two rudimentary antennae — mere bumps on their heads, but still sensitive in detecting the grosser nervous emanations.

"And so they gained mastery over their lovers. Influenced unduly the governments. Caused widespread slavery and wholesale breeding of beetles and the resulting alcoholism which led to humankind's downfall.

"When we wogs came to this continent, half their cities were ruined. War, liquor, depraved religious rites, falling birth rate, graft, corruption — a hundred factors leveled once mighty man. Yet, though weakened, they fought us. The *lalitha* urged them to battle, for they saw in us their doom. We could not be influenced by them as their men were. War and disease slew half of them; the rest just seemed to lose interest in living...."

A wog nurse with a white mask over her long nose came out of the operating room. Hal sprang up and watched her as she said something to the empathist in a low voice.

Macneff had been pacing back and forth with his hands clutched behind him. Hal wondered, in the back of his mind, why he, Hal, had not been dragged away at once; why the priest had waited to hear Fobo. Then a flash of insight told him that Macneff had wanted the joat to hear all about Jeannette and realize the full enormity of his deeds.

The nurse went back into the operating room. The Archurielite said loudly, "Is the beast of the fields dead yet?"

Fobo, ignoring him, spoke to Hal, who had shaken as if at a blow when he heard the word "dead."

"Your larv — that is, your children, have been removed. They are in an incubator. They are — " he hesitated — "eating well. They will live."

Yarrow could tell from his tone that it was no use asking about the mother.

The wog twitched his antennae. Big tears rolled from his round blue eyes. He did not, however, offer any sympathy. He kept on talking:

"You won't understand, Hal, what has happened unless you comprehend the *lalitha's* unique method of reproduction. To begin, their ovaries furnish the matrix for the bodies of the embryo, all beautiful bodies, the apex of art as practiced by Nature. The male spermatozoa is in no way connected with the genes that lay out the pattern for the body.

"Two things the *lalitha* needs to reproduce. Those two things must occur simultaneously. They are, excitation from orgasm and the stimulation of the photokinetic nerve."

Fobo paused and seemed to cock an ear, as if he were listening for something outside. Hal, who had absorbed some of the empathy of the wog during his acquaintanceship, felt that he was waiting for something big. Really big. And whatever it was, it involved the fate of the Earthmen.

Suddenly he thrilled to hot and cold tinglings...and the knowledge that he was on the wog's side!

"What is this nerve?" Fobo went on. "It is a property of the *lalitha*, and runs from the retina of the eye, along with the optic nerve, to the back of the brain. From there it descends the spinal column and leaves the base to enter the uterus. Or, as we term it, the *camera obscura uteri*. The dark room of the womb. Where the photographs of the father's features are developed. And attached to the daughters' faces.

"Yes, that is one of their unique anatomical marks. The photogenes. A *lalitha's* chromosomes are connected to the photokinetic nerve. During intercourse, at the moment of the climax, an electrochemical change takes place in that nerve. By the light that the *lalitha* always requires — an arc-reflex makes it impossible for her to close her eyes at that time — the face of the male is photographed.

"Photographed is an inadequate word, but it is the only one we have for the process. Anyway, if his hair is light brown, that information passes down a string of genes, each of which controls a specific hair color from jet-black down through the hair-spectrum to orange-red. The genes work on a cybernetic parallel. A yes-no binary system. If the gene's color does not correspond to the photokinetic nerve's request, it does not respond. It says no. If it approximates most closely the request, it says yes.

"The same thing happens with the shape and thickness of the hair, the size and shape of the nose and lips, the cheekhones, and jaw, and chin, and the color of the eyes. The shape of the nose, for instance, might have to be turned down a hundred and fifty times before the right combination of genes were struck — "

"You hear that?" exulted Macneff. "You have begat larvae! Monsters of an unholy union. Insect children! And they will have your face as witness of this revolting carnality — "

"Of course, I am no connoisseur of human features," interrupted Fobo, "but the young man's strike me as vigorous and handsome. In a human way, you understand."

He turned to Yarrow. "Now you see why Jeannette desired light. And why she pretended alcoholism. As long as she drank a sufficient amount of liquor before copulation, she was sure that the workings of the delicate photokinetic nerve would be interfered with. No pregnancy that way. No death. But when...you cut the beetlejuice with Easyglow...unknowing, of course...."

Macneff burst into a high-pitched laughter. "What irony! Truly it has been said that the wages of unrealism are death!"

Fobo spoke loudly; "Go ahead, son. Cry, if you like. You'll feel better. You can't, eh? I wish you would.

"*Eh, bien. Je continue.* The *lalitha,* no matter how human she looks, cannot escape her arthropod heritage. The nymphs that develop from the larvae can easily pass for babies, but it would pain you to see the larvae themselves. Though they are not any uglier than a five months human embryo. Not to me, anyway.

"It is a sad thing that the *lalitha* mother must die. Hundreds of millions of years ago, when the primitive pseudo-arthropod was ready to hatch the eggs in her womb, a hormone was released in her body. It calcified the skin and turned her into a womb-tomb. She became a shell. Her larvae ate the organs and the bones, which were softened by the draining away of their calcium. When the young had fulfilled the function of the larva, which is to eat and grow, they rested and became nymphs. Then they broke the shell in its weak place in the belly.

"That weak point is the navel. It alone does not calcify with the epidermis, but remains soft. By the time the nymphs are ready to come out, the soft flesh of the navel has decayed. Its dissolution lets loose a chemical which decalcifies an area that takes in most of the abdomen. The nymphs, though weak as human babies and much smaller, are activated by instinct to kick out the thin and brittle covering.

"You must understand, Hal, that the navel itself is both functional and mimetic. Since the larvae are not connected to the mother by an umbilical cord, they would have no navel. But they grow an excrescence which resembles one.

"The breasts of the adult also have two functions. Like the human female's, they are both sexual and reproductive. They never produce milk, of course, but they are glands. At the time the larvae are ready to hatch from the eggs, the breasts act as two powerful pumps of the hormone which carries out the hardening of the skin.

"Nothing wasted, you see—Nature's economy. The things that enable her to survive in human society also carry out the death process.

"It is a sad thing, but it has not changed in all these epochs. The mothers must give their lives for their young. Yet Nature, as a sort of recompense, has given them a gift. On the analogy of reptiles, which do not stop growing larger as long as they aren't killed, the *lalitha* will not die if they remain unpregnant. And so—"

Hal leaped to his feet and shouted, "Stop it!"

"I'm sorry," Fobo said softly. "I'm just trying to make you see why Jeannette felt that she couldn't tell you what she truly was. She loved you, Hal; she possessed the three factors that make love: a genuine passion, a deep affection, and the feeling of being one flesh with you, male and female so inseparable it would be hard to tell where one began and the other ended. I know she did, believe me, for we empathists can put ourselves into somebody else's nervous system and think and feel as they do.

"And feel, despite all this, she must have had a bitter leaven in her love. The belief that if you knew she was of an utterly alien branch of the animal kingdom, separated by millions of years of evolution, barred by her ancestry and anatomy from the true completion of marriage—children—you would turn from her with horror. That belief must have shot with darkness even her brightest moments...."

"No! I would have loved her, anyway! It might have been a shock. But I'd have gotten over it. Why, she was human; she was more human than most of the women I've known!"

Macneff sounded as if he were going to retch. When he had recovered himself, he howled, "You absymal thing! How can you stand yourself, now you know what utterly filthy monster you have lain with! Why don't you try to tear out your eyes, which have seen that vile filth! Why don't you bite off your lips, which have kissed that insect mouth!

Why don't you cut off your hands, which have pawed with loathsome lust that mockery of a body! Why don't you tear out by the roots those organs of carnal—"

Fobo spoke through the storm of wrath. "Macneff! Macneff!"

The gaunt head swiveled towards the empathist. His eyes stared, and his lips had drawn back into what seemed to be an impossibly large smile; a smile of absolute fury.

"What? What?" he muttered, like a man waking from sleep.

"Macneff. Why don't you tell Yarrow what you were thinking about the other night? When you were alone in your cabin, and supposedly at your prayers. Why don't you tell him what you were planning to do if your agents brought in the *lalitha* alive? What were you thinking?"

The Sandalphon's jaw fell. Red flooded his face and became purple. The violent color faded, and a corpselike white replaced it.

He screeched like an owl.

"*Enough!* Uzzites, take this—this thing that calls itself a man to the gig!"

The two men in black circled to come at the joat from front and back. Their approach was based on training, not real caution. Years of taking prisoners had taught them to expect no resistance. The arrested always stood cowed and numb before the representatives of the Sturch. Now, despite the unusual circumstances, and the knowledge that Hal carried a gun, they saw nothing different in him.

Normally, they would have been right. They could not guess that they had met a man whose basically rebellious character was on the point of bursting the lifelong cocoon of repression. He stood with bowed head and hunched shoulders and dangling arms, the typical arrestee.

That was one second; the next, he was a tiger striking.

The agent in front of him reeled back, blood flowing from his mouth and spilling on his black jacket. When he bumped into the wall, he paused to spit out three teeth.

By then Yarrow had whirled and rammed a fist into the big soft belly of the man behind him.

"*Whoof!*" went the Uzzite.

He folded. As he did so, Hal brought his knee up against the unguarded chin. There was a crack of bone breaking, and the agent fell to the floor.

"Watch him!" yelled Macneff. "He's got a gun!"

The Uzzite by the wall shoved his hand under his jacket, feeling for the weapon in his armpit holster. Simultaneously a heavy bronze bookend, thrown by Fobo, struck his temple. He crumpled.

Macneff screamed, "You are resisting, Yarrow! You are resisting!"

Hal bellowed, "You're damn shib I am!"

Head down like a mad bull's, he plunged at the Archurielite.

Macneff slashed with his whip at his attacker's skull. Hal rammed into the grayclad form and knocked it to the floor. When Macneff got to his knees, Yarrow seized him by the throat and squeezed. Macneff turned purple and clutched at the terrible hands.

At that moment a tremendous *boom!* rattled the hospital windows. On its heels came another shock wave. Somewhere outside, the night became day for a second.

Hal unclenched his hands and let Macneff fall.

"What was that?" he demanded.

"I imagine it was the *Gabriel* falling from a height of fifty feet," Fobo said. "Not very far, of course, but the ship is tremendous. Something must have exploded. I hope the damage wasn't too serious, for we want to use the ship as a model to build some for ourselves."

Macneff groaned. Hal, standing over him and breathing hard, stared at the wog.

"We don't have mechanical flying missiles, Hal. But we do have hordes of winged and poisonous insects whose flight may be directed, within limits, by painful or pleasing super or subsonic waves. And who also may be conditioned by the sweat-impregnated clothing of Terrans to bite any Earthmen that come within their sense of smell.

"What happened a moment ago was that our fierce little fighters were sent through the open ports and ventilators of the *Gabriel*. Once inside, it is probable that they stung everybody on the ship, and that those stung colapsed with half-paralyzed nervous systems. Naturally, I don't know why the ship fell and then exploded. However, that makes it unnecessary for us to board the ship from a balloon which Zugu had powered with a motor."

"You wogs think of everything, don't you?"

Fobo shrugged. "We are peaceful but, unlike you Terrans, we are really 'realists.' If we have to take action against vermin, we exterminate them. On this insect-ridden planet we have had a long history of battling vermin."

He looked at Macneff, who was on all fours, eyes glazed, shaking his head like a wounded bear.

Fobo said, "I do not include you in that vermin, Hal. You are free to go where you want."

Hal sat down again and croaked, "What is there left for me?"

"Plenty, man." Tears ran down Fobo's nose and collected at the end. "You have your daughters to care for, to love. In a few days they will be through with their feeding in the incubator — they survived the

Caesarean quite well — and will be beautiful babies. They will be yours as much as any human infants could be. After all, they look like you — in a modified feminine way, of course. Your genes are theirs. What's the difference whether genes act by cellular or photonic means? Genes are genes.

"And there will be women for you. You forget that she has aunts and sisters. All young and beautiful."

"Thanks, Fobo, but that's not for me." He buried his face in his hands.

A nurse stuck her head out of the door of the operating room.

"Doctor Fobo, we are bringing the body out. Does the man care to look?"

Without removing his hands, Hal shook his head.

Two nurses wheeled the carrier out. A white sheet was draped over the form. It clung to the superb curves of the shell beneath.

Hal did not look up.

He moaned, "Jeannette! Jeannette!"

Friar Sparks sat wedged between the wall and the realizer. He was motionless except for his forefinger and his eyes. From time to time his finger tapped rapidly on the key upon the desk, and now and then his irises, gray-blue as his native Irish sky, swiveled to look through the open door of the *toldilla* in which he crouched, the little shanty on the poop deck. Visibility was low.

Outside was dusk and a lantern by the railing. Two sailors leaned on it. Beyond them bobbed the bright lights and dark shapes of the *Niña* and the *Pinta*. And beyond them was the smooth horizon-brow of the Atlantic, edged in black and blood by the red dome of the rising moon.

The single carbon filament bulb above the monk's tonsure showed a face lost in fat — and in concentration.

The luminiferous ether crackled and hissed tonight, but the phones clamped over his ears carried, along with them, the steady dots and dashes sent by the operator at the Las Palmas station on the Grand Canary.

"*Zzisss!* So you are out of sherry already....*Pop!*...Too bad... *Crackle*...you hardened old winebutt...*Zzz*...May God have mercy on your sins....

"Lots of gossip, news, et cetera....*Hisses!*...Bend your ear instead of your neck, impious one....The Turks are said to be gathering... *crackle*...an army to march on Austria. It is rumored that the flying sausages, said by so many to have been seen over the capitals of the Christian world, are of Turkish origin. The rumor goes they have been invented by a renegade Rogerian who was converted to the Muslim religion....I say...*zziss*...to that. No one of us would do that. It is a falsity spread by our enemies in the Church to discredit us. But many people believe that....

"How close does the Admiral calculate he is to Cipangu now?

"Flash! Savonarola today denounced the Pope, the wealthy of Florence, Greek art and literature, and the experiments of the disciples of Saint Roger Bacon...*Zzz!*...The man is sincere but misguided and

dangerous....I predict he'll end up at the stake he's always prescribing
for us....

"*Pop*....This will kill you....Two Irish mercenaries by the name of
Pat and Mike were walking down the street of Granada when a beautiful Saracen lady leaned out of a balcony and emptied a pot
of...*hiss!*...and Pat looked up and...*Crackle*....Good, hah? Brother Juan
told that last night....

"PV...PV...Are you coming in?...PV...PV...Yes, I know it's dangerous to bandy such jests about, but nobody is monitoring us tonight....Zzz....I think they're not, anyway...."

And so the ether bent and warped with their messages. And presently Friar Sparks tapped out the PV that ended their talk — the "Pax
vobiscum." Then he pulled the plug out that connected his earphones
to the set and, lifting them from his ears, clamped them down forward
over his temples in the regulation manner.

After sidling bent-kneed from the *toldilla,* punishing his belly
against the desk's hard edge as he did so, he walked over to the railing. De Salcedo and de Torres were leaning there and talking in low
tones. The big bulb above gleamed on the page's red-gold hair and on
the interpreter's full black beard. It also bounced pinkishly off the
priest's smooth-shaven jowls and the light scarlet robe of the Rogerian
order. His cowl, thrown back, served as a bag for scratch paper, pens,
an ink bottle, tiny wrenches and screwdrivers, a book of cryptogra-
phy, a slide rule, and a manual of angelic principles.

"Well, old rind," said young de Salcedo familiarly, "what do you
hear from Las Palmas?"

"Nothing now. Too much interference from that." He pointed to
the moon riding the horizon ahead of them. "What an orb!" bellowed
the priest. "It's as big and red as my revered nose!"

The two sailors laughed, and de Salcedo said, "But it will get smaller
and paler as the night grows, Father. And your proboscis will, on the
contrary, become larger and more sparkling in inverse proportion according to the square of the ascent — "

He stopped and grinned, for the monk had suddenly dipped his
nose, like a porpoise diving into the sea, raised it again, like the same
animal jumping from a wave, and then once more plunged it into the
heavy currents of their breath. Nose to nose, he faced them, his twin-
kling little eyes seeming to emit sparks like the realizer in his *toldilla.*

Again, porpoiselike, he sniffed and snuffed several times, quite
loudly. Then satisfied with what he had gleaned from their breaths, he
winked at them. He did not, however, mention his findings at once,
preferring to sidle toward the subject.

He said, "This Father Sparks on the Grand Canary is so entertaining. He stimulates me with all sorts of philosophical notions, both valid and fantastic. For instance, tonight, just before we were cut off by that" — he gestured at the huge bloodshot eye in the sky — "he was discussing what he called worlds of parallel time tracks, an idea originated by Dysphagius of Gotham. It's his idea there may be other worlds in coincident but not contacting universes, that God, being infinite and of unlimited creative talent and ability, the Master Alchemist, in other words, has possibly — perhaps necessarily — created a plurality of continua in which every probable event has happened."

"Huh?" grunted de Salcedo.

"Exactly. Thus, Columbus was turned down by Queen Isabella, so this attempt to reach the Indies across the Atlantic was never made. So we could not now be standing here plunging ever deeper into Oceanus in our three cockle-shells, there would be no booster buoys strung out between us and the Canaries, and Father Sparks at Las Palmas and I on the *Santa Maria* would not be carrying on our fascinating conversations across the ether.

"Or, say, Roger Bacon was persecuted by the Church, instead of being encouraged and giving rise to the order whose inventions have done so much to insure the monopoly of the Church on alchemy and its divinely inspired guidance of that formerly pagan and hellish practice."

De Torres opened his mouth, but the priest silenced him with a magnificent and imperious gesture and continued.

"Or, even more ridiculous, but thought-provoking, he speculated just this evening on universes with different physical laws. One, in particular, I thought very droll. As you probably don't know, Angelo Angelei has proved, by dropping objects from the Leaning Tower of Pisa, that different weights fall at different speeds. My delightful colleague on the Grand Canary is writing a satire which takes place in a universe where Aristotle is made out to be a liar, where all things drop with equal velocities, no matter what their size. Silly stuff, but it helps to pass the time. We keep the ether busy with our little angels."

De Salcedo said, "Uh, I don't want to seem too curious about the secrets of your holy and cryptic order, Friar Sparks. But these little angels your machine realizes intrigue me. Is it a sin to presume to ask about them?"

The monk's bull roar slid to a dove cooing. "Whether it's a sin or not depends. Let me illustrate, young fellows. If you were concealing a bottle of, say, very scarce sherry on you, and you did not offer to share it with a very thirsty old gentleman, that would be a sin. A sin of omission. But if you were to give that desert-dry, that pilgrim-weary, that devout, humble, and decrepit old soul a long, soothing, refreshing, and stimulating draught of lifegiving fluid, daughter of the vine, I would find it in my heart to pray for you for that deed of loving-kindness, of encompassing charity. And it would please me so much I might tell you a little of our realizer. Not enough to hurt you, just enough so you might gain more respect for the intelligence and glory of my order."

De Salcedo grinned conspiratorially and passed the monk the bottle he'd hidden under his jacket. As the friar tilted it, and the chug-chug-chug of vanishing sherry became louder, the two sailors glanced meaningfully at each other. No wonder the priest, reputed to be so brilliant in his branch of the alchemical mysteries, had yet been sent off on this half-baked voyage to devil-knew-where. The Church had calculated that if he survived, well and good. If he didn't, then he would sin no more.

The monk wiped his lips on his sleeve, belched loudly as a horse, and said, "*Gracias,* boys. From my heart, so deeply buried in this fat, I thank you. An old Irishman, dry as a camel's hoof, choking to death with the dust of abstinence, thanks you. You have saved my life."

"Thank rather that magic nose of yours," replied de Salcedo. "Now, old rind, now that you're well greased again, would you mind explaining as much as you are allowed about that machine of yours?"

Friar Sparks took fifteen minutes. At the end of that time, his listeners asked a few permitted questions.

"...and you say you broadcast on a frequency of eighteen hundred k.c.?" the page asked. "What does 'k.c.' mean?"

"K stands for the French *kilo,* from a Greek word meaning thousand. And c stands for the Hebrew *cherubim,* the 'little angels.' Angel comes from the Greek *angelos,* meaning messenger. It is our concept that the ether is crammed with these cherubim, these little messengers. Thus, when we Friar Sparkses depress the key of our machine, we are able to realize some of the infinity of 'messengers' waiting for just such a demand for service.

"So, eighteen hundred k.c. means that in a given unit of time one million, eight hundred thousand cherubim line up and hurl themselves across the ether, the nose of one being brushed by the feathertips of the cherub's wings ahead. The height of the wing crests of each little creature is even, so that if you were to draw an outline of the whole train, there would be nothing to distinguish one cherub from the next, the whole column forming that grade of little angels known as C. W."

"C. W.?"

"Continuous wingheight. My machine is a C. W. realizer."

Young de Salcedo said, "My mind reels. Such a concept! Such a revelation! It almost passes comprehension. Imagine, the aerial of your realizer is cut just so long, so that the evil cherubim surging back and forth on it demand a predetermined and equal number of good angels to combat them. And this seduction coil on the realizer crowds 'bad' angels into the left-hand, the sinister, side. And when the bad little cherubim are crowded so closely and numerously that they can't bear each other's evil company, they jump the spark gap and speed around the wire to the 'good' plate. And in this racing back and forth they call themselves to the attention of the 'little messengers,' the yea-saying cherubim. And you, Friar Sparks, by manipulating your machine thus and so, and by lifting and lowering your key, you bring these invisible and friendly lines of carriers, your etheric and winged postmen, into reality. And you are able, thus, to communicate at great distances with your brothers of the order."

"Great God!" said de Torres.

It was not a vain oath but a pious exclamation of wonder. His eyes bulged; it was evident that he suddenly saw that man was not alone, that on every side, piled on top of each other, flanked on every angle, stood a host. Black and white, they presented a solid chessboard of the seemingly empty cosmos, black for the naysayers, white for the yea-sayers, maintained by a Hand in delicate balance and subject as the fowls of the air and the fish of the sea to exploitation by man.

Yet de Torres, having seen such a vision as has made a saint of many a man, could only ask, "Perhaps you could tell me how many angels may stand on the point of a pin?"

Obviously, de Torres would never wear a halo. He was destined, if he lived, to cover his bony head with the mortar-board of a university teacher.

De Salcedo snorted. "I'll tell you. Philosophically speaking, you may put as many angels on a pinhead as you want to. Actually speaking, you may put only as many as there is room for. Enough of that. I'm interested in facts, not fancies. Tell me, how could the moon's rising interrupt your reception of the cherubim sent by the Sparks at Las Palmas?"

"Great Caesar, how would I know? Am I a repository of universal knowledge? No, not I! A humble and ignorant friar, I! All I can tell you is that last night it rose like a bloody tumor on the horizon, and that when it was up I had to quit marshaling my little messengers in their short and long columns. The Canary station was quite overpowered, so that both of us gave up. And the same thing happened tonight."

"The moon sends messages?" asked de Torres.

"Not in a code I can decipher. But it sends, yes."

"Santa Maria!"

"Perhaps," suggested de Salcedo, "there are people on that moon, and they are sending."

Friar Sparks blew derision through his nose. Enormous as were his nostrils, his derision was not smallbore. Artillery of contempt laid down a barrage that would have silenced any but the strongest of souls.

"Maybe"—de Torres spoke in a low tone—"maybe, if the stars are windows in heaven, as I've heard said, the angels of the higher hierarchy, the big ones, are realizing—uh—the smaller? And they only do it when the moon is up so we may know it is a celestial phenomenon?"

He crossed himself and looked around the vessel.

"You need not fear," said the monk gently. "There is no Inquisitor leaning over your shoulder. Remember, I am the only priest on this expedition. Moreover, your conjecture has nothing to do with dogma. However, that's unimportant. Here's what I don't understand: how can a heavenly body broadcast? Why does it have the same frequency as the one I'm restricted to? Why—"

"I could explain," interrupted de Salcedo with all the brashness and impatience of youth. "I could say that the Admiral and the Rogerians are wrong about the earth's shape. I could say the earth is not round but is flat. I could say the horizon exists, not because we live upon a globe, but because the earth is curved only a little ways, like a greatly flattened-out hemisphere. I could also say that the cherubim are coming, not from Luna, but from a ship such as ours, a vessel which is hanging in the void off the edge of the earth."

"What?" gasped the other two.

"Haven't you heard," said de Salcedo, "that the King of Portugal secretly sent out a ship after he turned down Columbus' proposal? How do we know he did not, that the messages are from our predecessor, that he sailed off the world's rim and is now suspended in the air and becomes exposed at night because it follows the moon around Terra—is, in fact, a much smaller and unseen satellite?"

The monk's laughter woke many men on the ship. "I'll have to tell the Las Palmas operator your tale. He can put it in that novel of his. Next you'll be telling me those messages are from one of those fire-shooting sausages so many credulous laymen have been seeing flying around. No, my dear de Salcedo, let's not be ridiculous. Even the ancient Greeks knew the earth was round. Every university in Europe teaches that. And we Rogerians have measured the circumference. We know for sure that the Indies lie just across the Atlantic. Just as we know for sure, through mathematics, that heavier-than-air machines are impossible. Our Friar Ripskulls, our mind doctors, have assured us these flying creations are mass hallucinations or else the tricks of heretics or Turks who want to panic the populace.

"That moon radio is no delusion, I'll grant you. What it is, I don't know. But it's not a Spanish or Portuguese ship. What about its different code? Even if it came from Lisbon, that ship would still have a Rogerian operator. And he would, according to our policy, be of a different nationality from the crew so he might the easier stay out of political embroilments. He wouldn't break our laws by using a different code in order to communicate with Lisbon. We disciples of Saint Roger do not stoop to petty boundary intrigues. Moreover, that realizer would not be powerful enough to reach Europe, and must, therefore, be directed at us."

"How can you be sure?" said de Salcedo. "Distressing though the thought may be to you, a priest could be subverted. Or a layman could learn your secrets and invent a code. I think that a Portuguese ship is sending to another, a ship perhaps not too distant from us."

De Torres shivered and crossed himself again. "Perhaps the angels are warning us of approaching death? Perhaps?"

"Perhaps? Then why don't they use our code? Angels would know it as well as I. No, there is no perhaps. The order does not permit perhaps. It experiments and finds out; nor does it pass judgment until it knows."

"I doubt we'll ever know," said de Salcedo gloomily. "Columbus has promised the crew that if we come across no sign of land by evening tomorrow, we shall turn back. Otherwise" — he drew a finger across his throat — "*kkk!* Another day, and we'll be pointed east and getting away from that evil and bloody-looking moon and its incomprehensible messages."

"It would be a great loss to the order and to the Church," sighed the friar. "But I leave such things in the hands of God and inspect only what He hands me to look at."

With which pious statement Friar Sparks lifted the bottle to ascertain the liquid level. Having determined in a scientific manner its existence, he next measured its quantity and tested its quality by putting all of it in that best of all chemistry tubes, his enormous belly.

Afterward, smacking his lips and ignoring the pained and disappointed looks on the faces of the sailors, he went on to speak enthusiastically of the water screw and the engine which turned it, both of which had been built recently at the St. Jonas College at Genoa. If Isabella's three ships had been equipped with those, he declared, they would not have to depend upon the wind. However, so far, the fathers had forbidden its extended use because it was feared the engine's fumes might poison the air and the terrible speeds it made possible might be fatal to the human body. After which he plunged into a tedious description of the life of his patron saint, the inventor of the first cherubim realizer and receiver, Jonas of Carcassonne, who had been martyred when he grabbed a wire he thought was insulated.

The two sailors found excuses to walk off. The monk was a good fellow, but hagiography bored them. Besides, they wanted to talk of women....

If Columbus had not succeeded in persuading his crews to sail one more day, events would have been different.

At dawn the sailors were very much cheered by the sight of several large birds circling their ships. Land could not be far off; perhaps these winged creatures came from the coast of fabled Cipangu itself, the country whose houses were roofed with gold.

The birds swooped down. Closer, they were enormous and very flattish and almost saucer-shaped and small in proportion to the wings, which had a spread of at least thirty feet. Nor did they have legs. Only a few sailors saw the significance of that fact. These birds dwelt in the air and never rested upon land or sea.

While they were meditating upon that, they heard a slight sound as of a man clearing his throat. So gentle and far off was the noise that nobody paid any attention to it, for each thought his neighbor had made it.

A few minutes later, the sound had become louder and deeper, like a lute string being twanged.

Everybody looked up. Heads were turned west.

Even yet they did not understand that the noise like a finger plucking a wire came from the line that held the earth together, and that the line was stretched to its utmost, and that the violent finger of the sea was what had plucked the line.

It was some time before they understood. They had run out of horizon.

When they saw that, they were too late.

The dawn had not only come up *like* thunder, it *was* thunder. And though the three ships heeled over at once and tried to sail close-hauled on the port tack, the suddenly speeded-up and relentless current made beating hopeless.

Then it was the Rogerian wished for the Genoese screw and the wood-burning engine that would have made them able to resist the terrible muscles of the charging and bull-like sea. Then it was that some men prayed, some raved, some tried to attack the Admiral, some jumped overboard, and some sank into a stupor.

Only the fearless Columbus and the courageous Friar Sparks stuck to their duties. All that day the fat monk crouched wedged in his little shanty, dot-dashing to his fellow on the Grand Canary. He ceased only when the moon rose like a huge red bubble from the throat of a dying giant. Then he listened intently all night and worked desperately, scribbling and swearing impiously and checking cipher books.

When the dawn came up again in a roar and a rush, he ran from the *toldilla*, a piece of paper clutched in his hand. His eyes were wild, and his lips were moving fast, but nobody could understand that he had cracked the code. They would not hear him shouting, "It is the Portuguese! It is the Portuguese!"

Their ears were too overwhelmed to hear a mere human voice. The throat clearing and the twanging of a string had been the noises preliminary to the concert itself. Now came the mighty overture; as compelling as the blast of Gabriel's horn was the topple of Oceanus into space.

ONE

"Look, Mother. The clock is running backwards."

Eddie Fetts pointed to the hands on the pilot room dial.

Dr. Paula Fetts said, "The crash must have reversed it."

"How could it do that?"

"I can't tell you. I don't know everything, son."

"Oh!"

"Well, don't look at me so disappointedly. I'm a pathologist, not an electronician."

"Don't be so cross, Mother. I can't stand it. Not now."

He walked out of the pilot room. Anxiously, she followed him. The burial of the crew and her fellow scientists had been very trying for him. Spilled blood had always made him dizzy and sick; he could scarcely control his hands enough to help her sack the scattered bones and entrails.

He had wanted to put the corpses in the nuclear furnace, but she had forbidden that. The Geigers amidships were ticking loudly, warning that there was invisible death in the stern.

The meteor that struck the moment the ship came out of Translation into normal space had probably wrecked the engine room. So she had understood from the incoherent highpitched phrases of a colleague before he fled to the pilot room. She had hurried to find Eddie. She feared his cabin door would still be locked, as he had been making a tape of the aria "Heavy Hangs the Albatross" from Gianelli's *Ancient Mariner*.

Fortunately, the emergency system had automatically thrown out the locking circuits. Entering, she had called out his name in fear he'd been hurt. He was lying half-unconscious on the floor, but it was not the accident that had thrown him there. The reason lay in the corner, released from his lax hand; a quart freefall thermos, rubber-nippled.

From Eddie's open mouth charged a breath of rye that not even Nodor pills had been able to conceal.

Sharply she had commanded him to get up and onto the bed. Her voice, the first he had ever heard, pierced through the phalanx of Old Red Star. He struggled up, and she, though smaller, had thrown every ounce of her weight into getting him up and onto the bed.

There she had lain down with him and strapped them both in. She understood that the lifeboat had been wrecked also, and that it was up to the captain to bring the yacht down safely to the surface of this charted but unexplored planet, Baudelaire. Everybody else had gone to sit behind the captain, strapped in crashchairs, unable to help except with their silent backing.

Moral support had not been enough. The ship had come in on a shallow slant. Too fast. The wounded motors had not been able to hold her up. The prow had taken the brunt of the punishment. So had those seated in the nose.

Dr. Fetts had held her son's head on her bosom and prayed out loud to her God. Eddie had snored and muttered. Then there was a sound like the clashing of the gates of doom — a tremendous bong as if the ship were a clapper in a gargantuan bell tolling the most frightening message human ears may hear — a blinding blast of light and darkness and silence.

A few moments later Eddie began crying out in a childish voice, "Don't leave me to die, Mother! Come back! Come back!"

Mother was unconscious by his side, but he did not know that. He wept for a while, then he lapsed back into his rye-fogged stupor — if he had ever been out of it — and slept. Again, darkness and silence.

♦ ♦ ♦

It was the second day since the crash, if "day" could describe that twilight state on Baudelaire. Dr. Fetts followed her son wherever he went. She knew he was very sensitive and easily upset. All his life she had known it and had tried to get between him and anything that would cause trouble. She had succeeded, she thought, fairly well until three months ago when Eddie had eloped.

The girl was Polina Fameux, the ash-blonde long-legged actress whose tridi image, taped, had been shipped to frontier stars where a small acting talent meant little and a large and shapely bosom much. Since Eddie was a well-known Metro tenor, the marriage made a big splash whose ripples ran around the civilized galaxy.

Dr. Fetts had felt very bad about the elopement, but she had, she hoped, hidden her grief very well beneath a smiling mask. She didn't regret having to give him up; after all, he was a full-grown man, no longer her little boy. But, really, aside from the seasons at the Met and his tours, he had not been parted from her since he was eight.

That was when she went on a honeymoon with her second husband. And then she and Eddie had not been separated long, for Eddie had gotten very sick, and she'd had to hurry back and take care of him, as he had insisted she was the only one who could make him well.

Moreover, you couldn't count his days at the opera as a total loss, for he vised her every noon and they had a long talk — no matter how high the vise bills ran.

The ripples caused by her son's marriage were scarcely a week old before they were followed by even bigger ones. They bore the news of the separation of Eddie and his wife. A fortnight later, Polina applied for divorce on grounds of incompatibility. Eddie was handed the papers in his mother's apartment. He had come back to her the day he and Polina had agreed they "couldn't make a go of it," or, as he phrased it to his mother, "couldn't get together."

Dr. Fetts was, of course, very curious about the reason for their parting, but, as she explained to her friends, she "respected" his silence. What she didn't say was that she had told herself the time would come when he would tell her all.

Eddie's "nervous breakdown" started shortly afterward. He had been very irritable, moody, and depressed, but he got worse the day a so-called friend told Eddie that whenever Polina heard his name mentioned, she laughed loud and long. The friend added that Polina had promised to tell someday the true story of their brief merger.

That night his mother had to call in a doctor.

In the days that followed, she thought of giving up her position as research pathologist at De Kruif and taking all her time to help him "get back on his feet." It was a sign of the struggle going on in her mind that she had not been able to decide within a week's time. Ordinarily given to swift consideration and resolution of a problem, she could not agree to surrender her beloved quest into tissue regeneration.

Just as she was on the verge of doing what was for her the incredible and the shameful, tossing a coin, she had been vised by her superior. He told her she had been chosen to go with a group of biologists on a research cruise to ten preselected planetary systems.

Joyfully, she had thrown away the papers that would turn Eddie over to a sanatorium. And, since he was quite famous, she had used her influence to get the government to allow him to go along. Ostensibly, he was to make a survey of the development of opera on planets colonized by Terrans. That the yacht was not visiting any colonized globes seemed to have been missed by the bureaus concerned. But it was not the first time in the history of a government that its left hand knew not what its right was doing.

Actually, he was to be "rebuilt" by his mother, who thought herself much more capable of curing him than any of the prevalent A, F, J, R, S, K, or H therapies. True, some of her friends reported amazing results with some of the symbol-chasing techniques. On the other hand, two of her close companions had tried them all and had gotten no benefits from any of them. She was his mother; she could do more for him than any of those "alphabatties;" he was flesh of her flesh, blood of her blood. Besides, he wasn't so sick. He just got awfully blue sometimes and made theatrical but insincere threats of suicide or else just sat and stared into space. But she could handle him.

TWO

So now it was that she followed him from the backward-running clock to his room. And saw him step inside, look for a second, and then turn to her with a twisted face.

"Neddie is ruined, Mother. Absolutely ruined."

She glanced at the piano. It had torn loose from the wallracks at the moment of impact and smashed itself against the opposite wall. To Eddie it wasn't just a piano; it was Neddie. He had a pet name for everything he contacted for more than a brief time. It was as if he hopped from one appellation to the next, like an ancient sailor who felt lost unless he was close to the familiar and designated points of the shoreline. Otherwise, Eddie seemed to be drifting helplessly in a chaotic ocean, one that was anonymous and amorphous.

Or, analogy more typical of him, he was like the nightclubber who feels submerged, drowning, unless he hops from table to table, going from one well-known group of faces to the next, avoiding the featureless and unnamed dummies at the strangers' tables.

He did not cry over Neddie. She wished he would. He had been so apathetic during the voyage. Nothing, not even the unparalleled splendor of the naked stars nor the inexpressible alienness of strange planets had seemed to lift him very long. If he would only weep or laugh loudly or display some sign that he was reacting violently to what was happening. She would even have welcomed his striking her in anger or calling her "bad" names.

But no, not even during the gathering of the mangled corpses, when he looked for a while as if he were going to vomit, would he give way to his body's demand for expression. She understood that if he were to throw up, he would be much better for it, would have gotten rid of much of the psychic disturbance along with the physical.

He would not. He had kept on raking flesh and bones into the large plastic bags and kept a fixed look of resentment and sullenness.

She hoped now that the loss of his piano would bring tears and shaking shoulders. Then she could take him in her arms and give him sympathy. He would be her little boy again, afraid of the dark, afraid of the dog killed by a car, seeking her arms for the sure safety, the sure love.

"Never mind, baby," she said. "When we're rescued, we'll get you a new one."

"When —!"

He lifted his eyebrows and sat down on the bed's edge.

"What do we do now?"

She became very brisk and efficient.

"The ultrad automatically started working the moment the meteor struck. If it's survived the crash, it's still sending SOS's. If not, then there's nothing we can do about it. Neither of us knows how to repair it.

"However, it's possible that in the last five years since this planet was located, other expeditions may have landed here. Not from Earth but from some of the colonies. Or from nonhuman globes. Who knows? It's worth taking a chance. Let's see."

A single glance was enough to wreck their hopes. The ultrad had been twisted and broken until it was no longer recognizable as the machine that sent swifter-than-light waves through the no-ether.

Dr. Fetts said with false cheeriness, "Well, that's that! So what? It makes things too easy. Let's go into the storeroom and see what we can see."

Eddie shrugged and followed her. There she insisted that each take a panrad. If they had to separate for any reason, they could always communicate and also, using the DF's — the built-in direction finders — locate each other. Having used them before, they knew the instruments' capabilities and how essential they were on scouting or camping trips.

The panrads were lightweight cylinders about two feet high and eight inches in diameter. Crampacked, they held the mechanisms of two dozen different utilities. Their batteries lasted a year without recharging, they were practically indestructible and worked under almost any conditions.

Keeping away from the side of the ship that had the huge hole in it, they took the panrads outside. The long wave bands were searched by Eddie while his mother moved the dial that ranged up and down the shortwaves. Neither really expected to hear anything, but to search was better than doing nothing.

Finding the modulated wave-frequencies empty of any significant noises, he switched to the continuous waves. He was startled by a dot-dashing.

"Hey, Mom! Something in the 1000 kilocycles! Unmodulated!"

"Naturally, son," she said with some exasperation in the midst of her elation. "What would you expect from a radio-telegraphic signal?"

She found the band on her own cylinder. He looked blankly at her. "I know nothing about radio, but that's not Morse."

"What? You must be mistaken!"

"I—I don't think so."

"Is it or isn't it? Good god, son, can't you be certain of *anything!*"

She turned the amplifier up. As both of them had learned Galacto-Morse through sleeplearn techniques, she checked him at once.

"You're right. What do you make of it?"

His quick ear sorted out the pulses.

"No simple dot and dash. Four different time-lengths."

He listened some more.

"They've got a certain rhythm, all right. I can make out definite groupings. Ah! That's the sixth time I've caught that particular one. And there's another. And another."

Dr. Fetts shook her ash-blonde head. She could make out nothing but a series of zzt-zzt-zzt's.

Eddie glanced at the DF needle.

"Coming from NE by E. Should we try to locate?"

"Naturally," she replied. "But we'd better eat first. We don't know how far away it is, or what we'll find there. While I fix a hot meal, you get your field trip stuff ready."

"O.K.," he said with more enthusiasm than he had shown for a long time.

When he came back he ate everything in the large dish his mother had prepared on the unwrecked galley stove.

"You always did make the best stew," he said.

"Thank you. I'm glad you're eating again, son. I am surprised. I thought you'd be sick about all this."

He waved vaguely but energetically.

"The challenge of the unknown. I have a sort of feeling this is going to turn out much better than we thought. Much better."

She came close and sniffed his breath. It was clean, innocent even of stew. That meant he'd taken Nodor, which probably meant he'd been sampling some hidden rye. Otherwise, how to explain his reckless disregard of the possible dangers? It wasn't like him.

She said nothing, for she knew that if he tried to hide a bottle in his clothes or field sack while they were tracking down the radio signals, she would soon find it. And take it away. He wouldn't even protest, merely let her lift it from his limp hand while his lips swelled with resentment.

THREE

They set out. Both wore knapsacks and carried the panrads. He carried a gun over his shoulder, and she had snapped onto her sack her small black bag of medical and lab supplies.

High noon of late autumn was topped by a weak red sun that barely managed to make itself seen through the eternal double layer of clouds. Its companion, an even smaller blob of lilac, was setting on the northwestern horizon. They walked in a sort of bright twilight, the best that Baudelaire ever achieved. Yet, despite the lack of light, the air was warm. It was a phenomenon common to certain planets behind the Horsehead Nebula, one being investigated but as yet unexplained.

The country was hilly, with many deep ravines. Here and there were prominences high enough and steep-sided enough to be called embryo mountains. Considering the roughness of the land, however, there was a surprising amount of vegetation. Pale green, red, and yellow bushes, vines, and little trees clung to every bit of ground, horizontal or vertical. All had comparatively broad leaves that turned with the sun to catch the light.

From time to time, as the two Terrans strode noisily through the forest, small multicolored insect-like and mammal-like creatures scuttled from hiding place to hiding place. Eddie decided to carry his gun in the crook of his arm. Then, after they were forced to scramble up and down ravines and hills and fight their way through thickets that became unexpectedly tangled, he put it back over his shoulder, where it hung from a strap.

Despite their exertions, they did not tire quickly. They weighed about twenty pounds less than they would have on Earth and, though the air was thinner, it was richer in oxygen.

Dr. Fetts kept up with Eddie. Thirty years the senior of the twenty-three-year-old, she passed even at close inspection for his older sister. Longevity pills took care of that. However, he treated her with all the courtesy and chivalry that one gave one's mother and helped her up the steep inclines, even though the climbs did not appreciably cause her deep chest to demand more air.

They paused once by a creek bank to get their bearings.

"The signals have stopped," he said.

"Obviously," she replied.

At that moment the radar-detector built into the panrad began to ping. Both of them automatically looked upward.

"There's no ship in the air."

"It can't be coming from either of those hills," she pointed out. "There's nothing but a boulder on top of each one. Tremendous rocks."

"Nevertheless, it's coming from there, I think. Oh! Oh! Did you see what I saw? Looked like a tall stalk of some kind being pulled down behind that big rock."

She peered through the dim light. "I think you were imagining things, son. I saw nothing."

Then, even as the pinging kept up, the zzting started again. But after a burst of noise, both stopped.

"Let's go up and see what we shall see," she said.

"Something screwy," he commented. She did not answer.

They forded the creek and began the ascent. Halfway up, they stopped to sniff in puzzlement at a gust of some heavy odor coming downwind.

"Smells like a cageful of monkeys," he said.

"In heat," she added. If his was the keener ear, hers was the sharper nose.

They went on up. The RD began sounding its tiny hysterical gonging. Nonplussed, Eddie stopped. The DF indicated the radar pulses were not coming from the top of the hill they were climbing, as formerly, but from the other hill across the valley. Abruptly, the panrad fell silent.

"What do we do now?"

"Finish what we started. This hill. Then we go to the other one."

He shrugged and then hastened after her tall slim body in its long-legged coveralls. She was hot on the scent, literally, and nothing could stop her. Just before she reached the bungalow-sized boulder topping the hill, he caught up with her. She had stopped to gaze intently at the DF needle, which swung wildly before it stopped at neutral. The monkey-cage odor was very strong.

"Do you suppose it could be some sort of radio-generating mineral?" she asked, disappointedly.

"No. Those groupings were semantic. And that smell...."

"Then what—?"

He didn't know whether to feel pleased or not that she had so obviously and suddenly thrust the burden of responsibility and action on him. Both pride and a curious shrinking affected him. But he did feel exhilarated. Almost, he thought, he felt as if he were on the verge of discovering what he had been looking for for a long time. What the object of his search had been, he could not say. But he was excited and not very much afraid.

He unslung his weapon, a two-barreled combination shotgun and rifle. The panrad was still quiet.

"Maybe the boulder is camouflage for a spy outfit," he said. He sounded silly, even to himself.

Behind him, his mother gasped and screamed. He whirled and raised his gun, but there was nothing to shoot. She was pointing at the hilltop across the valley, shaking, and saying something incoherent.

He could make out a long slim antenna seemingly projecting from the monstrous boulder crouched there. At the same time, two thoughts struggled for first place in his mind: one, that it was more than a coincidence that both hills had almost identical stone structures on their brows, and, two, that the antenna must have been recently stuck out, for he was sure he had not seen it the last time he looked.

He never got to tell her his conclusions, for something thin and flexible and irresistible seized him from behind. Lifted into the air, he was borne backwards. He dropped the gun and tried to grab the bands or tentacles around him and tear them off with his bare hands. No use.

He caught one last glimpse of his mother running off down the hillside. Then a curtain snapped down, and he was in total darkness.

FOUR

Eddie sensed himself, still suspended, twirled around. He could not know for sure, of course, but he thought he was facing in exactly the opposite direction. Simultaneously, the tentacles binding his legs and arms were released. Only his waist was still gripped. It was pressed so tightly that he cried out with pain.

Then, boot-toes bumping on some resilient substance, he was carried forward. Halted, facing he knew not what horrible monster, he was suddenly assailed — not by a sharp beak or tooth or knife or some other cutting or mangling instrument — but by a dense cloud of that same monkey perfume.

In other circumstances, he might have vomited. Now his stomach was not given the time to consider whether it should clean house or not. The tentacle lifted him higher and thrust him against something soft and yielding — something fleshlike and womanly — almost breastlike in texture and smoothness and warmth and in its hint of gentle curving.

He put his hands and feet out to brace himself, for he thought for a moment he was going to sink in and be covered up — enfolded — ingested. The idea of a gargantuan amoeba-thing hiding within a hollow rock — or a rocklike shell — made him writhe and yell and shove at the protoplasmic substance.

But nothing of the kind happened. He was not plunged into a smothering and slimy jelly that would strip him of his skin and then his flesh and then dissolve his bones. He was merely shoved repeatedly against the soft swelling. Each time, he pushed or kicked or struck at it. After a dozen of these seemingly purposeless acts, he was held away, as if whatever was doing it was puzzled by his behavior.

He had quit screaming. The only sounds were his harsh breathing and the zzzts and pings from the panrad. Even as he became aware of them, the zzzts changed tempo and settled into a recognizable pattern of bursts — three units that crackled out again and again.

"Who are you? Who are you?"

Of course it could just as easily have been "What are you?" or "What the hell!" or "Nov smoz ka pop?"

Or nothing — semantically speaking.

But he didn't think the latter. And when he was gently lowered to the floor, and the tentacle went off to only-God-knew-where in the dark, he was sure that the creature was communicating — or trying to — with him.

It was this thought that kept him from screaming and running around in the lightless and fetid chamber, brainlessly seeking an outlet. He mastered his panic and snapped open a little shutter in the panrad's side and thrust in his right-hand index finger. There he poised it above the key and in a moment, when the thing paused in transmitting, he sent back, as best he could, the pulses he had received. It was not necessary for him to turn on the light and spin the dial that would put him on the 1000 kc. band. The instrument would automatically key that frequency in with the one he had just received.

The oddest part of the whole procedure was that his whole body was trembling almost uncontrollably — one part excepted. That was his index finger, his one unit that seemed to him to have a definite function in this otherwise meaningless situation. It was the section of him that was helping him to survive — the only part that knew how — at that moment. Even his brain seemed to have no connection with his finger. That digit was himself, and the rest just happened to be linked to it.

When he paused, the transmitter began again. This time the units were unrecognizable. There was a certain rhythm to them, but he could not know what they meant. Meanwhile, the RD was pinging. Something somewhere in the dark hole had a beam held tightly on him.

He pressed a button on the panrad's top, and the built-in flashlight illuminated the area just in front of him. He saw a wall of reddish-gray rubbery substance. On the wall was a roughly circular, light gray swelling about four feet in diameter. Around it, giving it a Medusa appearance, were coiled twelve very long, very thin tentacles.

Though he was afraid that if he turned his back to them the tentacles would seize him once more, his curiosity forced him to wheel about and examine his surroundings with the bright beam. He was in an egg-shaped chamber about thirty feet long, twelve wide, and eight to ten high in the middle. It was formed of a reddish-gray material, smooth except for irregular intervals of blue or red pipes. Veins and arteries?

A door-sized portion of the wall had a vertical slit running down it. Tentacles fringed it. He guessed it was a sort of iris and that it had opened to drag him inside. Starfish-shaped groupings of tentacles were scattered on the walls or hung from the ceiling. On the wall opposite the iris was a long and flexible stalk with a cartilaginous ruff around its free end. When Eddie moved, it moved, its blind point following him as a radar antenna tracks the thing it is locating. That was what it was. And unless he was wrong, the stalk was also a C.W. transmitter-receiver.

He shot the light around. When it reached the end farthest from him, he gasped. Ten creatures were huddled together facing him! About the size of half-grown pigs, they looked like nothing so much as unshelled snails; they were eyeless, and the stalk growing from the forehead of each was a tiny duplicate of that on the wall. They didn't look dangerous. Their open mouths were little and toothless, and their rate of locomotion must be slow, for they moved like snails, on a large pedestal of flesh — a foot-muscle.

Nevertheless, if he were to fall asleep they could overcome him by force of numbers, and those mouths might drip an acid to digest him, or they might carry a concealed poisonous sting.

His speculations were interrupted violently. He was seized, lifted, and passed on to another group of tentacles. He was carried beyond the antenna-stalk and toward the snail-beings. Just before he reached them, he was halted, facing the wall. An iris, hitherto invisible, opened. His light shone into it, but he could see nothing but convolutions of flesh.

His panrad gave off a new pattern of dit-dot-deet-dats. The iris widened until it was large enough to admit his body, if he were shoved in head first. Or feet first. It didn't matter. The convolutions straightened out and became a tunnel. Or a throat. From thousands of little pits emerged thousands of tiny, razor sharp teeth. They flashed out and sank back in, and before they had disappeared thousands of other wicked little spears darted out and past the receding fangs.

Meat-grinder.

Beyond the murderous array, at the end of the throat, was a huge pouch of water. Steam came from it, and with it an odor like that of his mother's stew. Dark bits, presumably meat, and pieces of vegetables floated on the seething surface.

Then the iris closed, and he was turned around to face the slugs. Gently, but unmistakably, a tentacle spanked his buttocks. And the panrad zzzted a warning.

Eddie was not stupid. He knew now that the ten creatures were not dangerous unless he molested them. In which case he had just seen where he would go if he did not behave.

Again he was lifted and carried along the wall until he was shoved against the light gray spot. The monkey-cage odor, which had died out, became strong again. Eddie identified its source with a very small hole which appeared in the wall.

When he did not respond — he had no idea yet how he was supposed to act — the tentacles dropped him so unexpectedly that he fell on his back. Unhurt by the yielding flesh, he rose.

What was the next step? Exploration of his resources. Itemization: The panrad. A sleeping bag, which he wouldn't need as long as the present too-warm temperature kept up. A bottle of Old Red Star capsules. A freefall thermos with attached nipple. A box of A-2-Z rations. A Foldstove. Cartridges for his double-barrel, now lying outside the creature's boulderish shell. A roll of toilet paper. Toothbrush. Paste.

Soap. Towel. Pills: Nodor, hormone, vitamin, longevity, reflex, and sleeping. And a thread-thin wire, a hundred feet long when uncoiled, that held prisoner in its molecular structure a hundred symphonies, eighty operas, a thousand different types of musical pieces, and two thousand great books ranging from Sophocles and Dostoyevsky to the latest bestseller. It could be played inside the panrad.

He inserted it, pushed a button, and spoke, "Eddie Fetts's recording of Puccini's *Che gelida manina,* please."

And while he listened approvingly to his own magnificent voice, he zipped open a can he had found in the bottom of the sack. His mother had put into it the stew left over from their last meal in the ship.

Not knowing what was happening, yet for some reason sure he was for the present safe, he munched meat and vegetables with a contented jaw. Transition from abhorrence to appetite sometimes came easily for Eddie.

He cleaned out the can and finished with some crackers and a chocolate bar. Rationing was out. As long as the food lasted, he would eat well. Then, if nothing turned up, he would…But then, he reassured himself as he licked his fingers, his mother, who was free, would find some way to get him out of his trouble.

She always had.

FIVE

The panrad, silent for a while, began signaling. Eddie spotlighted the antenna and saw it was pointing at the snail-beings, which he had, in accordance with his custom, dubbed familiarly. Sluggos he called them.

The Sluggos crept toward the wall and stopped close to it. Their mouths, placed on the tops of their heads, gaped like so many hungry young birds. The iris opened, and two lips formed into a spout. Out of it streamed steaming-hot water and chunks of meat and vegetables. Stew! Stew that fell exactly into each waiting mouth.

That was how Eddie learned the second phrase of Mother Polyphema's language. The first message had been, "What are you?" This was, "Come and get it!"

He experimented. He tapped out a repetition of what he'd last heard. As one, the Sluggos — except the one then being fed — turned to him and crept a few feet before halting, puzzled.

Inasmuch as Eddie was broadcasting, the Sluggos must have had some sort of built-in DF. Otherwise they wouldn't have been distinguish between his pulses and their Mother's.

Immediately after, a tentacle smote Eddie across the shoulders and knocked him down. The panrad zzzted its third intelligible message: "Don't ever do that!"

And then a fourth, to which the ten young obeyed by wheeling and resuming their former positions.

"This way, children."

Yes, they were the offspring, living, eating, sleeping, playing, and learning to communicate in the womb of their mother — the Mother. They were the mobile brood of this vast immobile entity that had scooped up Eddie as a frog scoops up a fly. This Mother. She who had once been just such a Sluggo until she had grown hog-size and had been pushed out of her Mother's womb. And who, rolled into a tight ball, had free-wheeled down her natal hill, straightened out at the bottom, inched her way up the next hill, rolled down, and so on. Until she found the empty shell of an adult who had died. Or, if she wanted to be a first class citizen in her society and not a prestigeless *occupée,* she found the bare top of a tall hill — or any eminence that commanded a big sweep of territory — and there squatted.

And there she put out many thread-thin tendrils into the soil and into the cracks in the rocks, tendrils that drew sustenance from the fat of her body and grew and extended downwards and ramified into other tendrils. Deep underground the rootlets worked their instinctive chemistry; searched for and found the water, the calcium, the iron, the copper, the nitrogen, the carbons, fondled earthworms and grubs and larvae, teasing them for the secrets of their fats and proteins; broke down the wanted substance into shadowy colloidal particles; sucked them up the thready pipes of the tendrils and back to the pale and slimming body crouching on a flat space atop a ridge, a hill, a peak.

There, using the blueprints stored in the molecules of the cerebellum, her body took the building blocks of elements and fashioned them into a very thin shell of the most available material, a shield large enough so she could expand to fit it while her natural enemies — the keen and hungry predators that prowled twilighted Baudelaire — nosed and clawed it in vain.

Then, her evergrowing bulk cramped, she would resorb the hard covering. And if no sharp tooth found her during that process of a few days, she would cast another and a larger. And so on through a dozen or more.

Until she had become the monstrous and much reformed body of an adult and virgin female. Outside would be the stuff that so much resembled a boulder, that was, actually, rock: either granite, diorite, marble, basalt, or maybe just plain limestone. Or sometimes iron, glass, or cellulose.

Within was the centrally located brain, probably as large as a man's. Surrounding it, the tons of organs: the nervous system, the mighty heart, or hearts, the four stomachs, the microwave and longwave generators, the kidneys, bowels, tracheae, scent and taste organs, the perfume factory which made odors to attract animals and birds close enough to be seized, and the huge womb. And the antennae—the small one inside for teaching and scanning the young, and a long and powerful stalk on the outside, projecting from the shelltop, retractable if danger came.

The next step was from virgin to Mother, lowercase to uppercase as designated in her pulse-language by a longer pause before a word. Not until she was deflowered could she take a high place in her society. Immodest, unblushing, she herself made the advances, the proposals, and the surrender.

After which, she ate her mate.

The clock in the panrad told Eddie he was in his thirtieth day of imprisonment when he found out that little bit of information. He was shocked, not because it offended his ethics, but because he himself had been intended to be the mate. And the dinner.

His finger tapped, "Tell me, Mother, what you mean."

He had not wondered before how a species that lacked males could reproduce. Now he found that, to the Mothers, all creatures except themselves were male. Mothers were immobile and female. Mobiles were male. Eddie had been mobile. He was, therefore, a male.

He had approached this particular Mother during the mating season, that is, midway through raising a litter of young. She had scanned him as he came along the creek banks at the valley bottom. When he was at the foot of the hill, she had detected his odor. It was new to her. The closest she could come to it in her memory banks was that of a beast similar to him. From her description, he guessed it to be an ape. So she had released from her repertoire its rut stench. When he seemingly fell into the trap, she had caught him.

He was supposed to attack the conception-spot, that light gray swelling on the wall. After he had ripped and torn it enough to begin the mysterious workings of pregnancy, he would have been popped into her stomach-iris.

Fortunately, he had lacked the sharp beak, the fang, the claw. And she had received her own signals back from the panrad.

Eddie did not understand why it was necessary to use a mobile for mating. A Mother was intelligent enough to pick up a sharp stone and mangle the spot herself.

He was given to understand that conception would not start unless it was accompanied by a certain titillation of the nerves — a frenzy and its satisfaction. Why this emotional state was needed, Mother did not know.

Eddie tried to explain about such things as genes and chromosomes and why they had to be present in highly developed species.

Mother did not understand.

Eddie wondered if the number of slashes and rips in the spot corresponded to the number of young. Or if there were a large number of potentialities in the heredity-ribbons spread out under the conception-skin. And if the haphazard irritation and consequent stimulation of the genes paralleled the chance combining of genes in human male-female mating. Thus resulting in offspring with traits that were combinations of their parents.

Or did the inevitable devouring of the mobile after the act indicate more than an emotional and nutritional reflex? Did it hint that the mobile caught up scattered gene-nodes, like hard seeds, along with the torn skin, in its claws and tusks, that these genes survived the boiling in the stew-stomach, and were later passed out in the feces? Where animals and birds picked them up in beak, tooth, or foot, and then, seized by other Mothers in this oblique rape, transmitted the heredity-carrying agents to the conception-spots while attacking them, the nodules being scraped off and implanted in the skin and blood of the swelling even as others were harvested? Later, the mobiles were eaten, digested, and ejected in the obscure but ingenious and never-ending cycle? Thus ensuring the continual, if haphazard, recombining of genes, chances for variations in offspring, opportunities for mutations, and so on?

Mother pulsed that she was nonplussed.

Eddie gave up. He'd never know. After all, did it matter?

He decided not, and rose from his prone position to request water. She pursed up her iris and spouted a tepid quartful into his thermos. He dropped in a pill, swished it around till it dissolved, and drank a reasonable facsimile of Old Red Star. He preferred the harsh and powerful rye, though he could have afforded the smoothest. Quick results were what he wanted. Taste didn't matter, as he disliked all liquor tastes. Thus he drank what the Skid Row bums drank and shuddered even as they did, renaming it Old Rotten Tar and cursing the fate that had brought them so low they had to gag such stuff down.

The rye glowed in his belly and spread quickly through his limbs and up to his head, chilled only by the increasing scarcity of the capsules. When he ran out—then what? It was at times like this that he most missed his mother.

Thinking about her brought a few large tears. He snuffled and drank some more and when the biggest of the Sluggos nudged him for a back-scratching, he gave it instead a shot of Old Red Star. A slug for Sluggo. Idly, he wondered what effect a taste for rye would have on the future of the race when these virgins became Mothers.

At that moment he was shaken by what seemed a life-saving idea. These creatures could suck up the required elements from the earth and with them duplicate quite complex molecular structures. Provided, of course, they had a sample of the desired substance to brood over in some cryptic organ.

Well, what easier to do than give her one of the cherished capsules? One could become any number. Those, plus the abundance of water pumped up through hollow underground tendrils from the nearby creek, would give enough to make a master-distiller green!

He smacked his lips and was about to key her his request when what she was transmitting penetrated his mind.

Rather cattily, she remarked that her neighbor across the valley was putting on airs because she, too, held prisoner a communicating mobile.

SIX

The Mothers had a society as hierarchical as table-protocol in Washington or peck-order in a barnyard. Prestige was what counted, and prestige was determined by the broadcasting power, the height of the eminence on which the Mother sat, which governed the extent of her radar-territory, and the abundance and novelty and wittiness of her gossip. The creature that had snapped Eddie up was a queen. She had precedence over thirty-odd of her kind; they all had to let her broadcast first, and none dared start pulsing until she quit. Then, the next in order began, and so on down the line. Any of them could be interrupted at any time by Number One, and if any of the lower echelon had something interesting to transmit, she could break in on the one then speaking and get permission from the queen to tell her tale.

Eddie knew this, but he could not listen in directly to the hilltop-gabble. The thick pseudo-granite shell barred him from that and made him dependent upon her womb-stalk for relayed information.

Now and then Mother opened the door and allowed her young to crawl out. There they practiced beaming and broadcasting at the Sluggos of the Mother across the valley. Occasionally that Mother deigned herself to pulse the young, and Eddie's keeper reciprocated to her offspring.

Turnabout.

The first time children had inched through the exit-iris, Eddie had tried, Ulysses-like, to pass himself off as one of them and crawl out in the midst of the flock. Eyeless, but no Polyphemus, Mother had picked him out with her tentacles and hauled him back in.

It was following that incident that he had named her Polyphema.

He knew she had increased her own already powerful prestige tremendously by possession of that unique thing—a transmitting mobile. So much had her importance grown that the Mothers on the fringes of her area passed on the news to others. Before he had learned her language, the entire continent was hooked-up. Polyphema had become a veritable gossip columnist; tens of thousands of hillcrouchers listened in eagerly to her accounts of her dealings with the walking paradox: a semantic male.

That had been fine. Then, very recently, the Mother across the valley had captured a similar creature. And in one bound she had become Number Two in the area and would, at the slightest weakness on Polyphema's part, wrest the top position away.

Eddie became wildly excited at the news. He had often daydreamed about his mother and wondered what she was doing. Curiously enough, he ended many of his fantasies with lip-mutterings, reproaching her almost audibly for having left him and for making no try to rescue him. When he became aware of his attitude, he was ashamed. Nevertheless, the sense of desertion colored his thoughts.

Now that he knew she was alive and had been caught, probably while trying to get him out, he rose from the lethargy that had lately been making him doze the clock around. He asked Polyphema if she would open the entrance so he could talk directly with the other captive. She said yes. Eager to listen in on a conversation between two mobiles, she was very cooperative. There would be a mountain of gossip in what they would have to say. The only thing that dented her joy was that the other Mother would also have access.

Then, remembering she was still Number One and would broad-cast the details first, she trembled so with pride and ecstasy that Eddie felt the floor shaking.

Iris open, he walked through it and looked across the valley. The hillsides were still green, red, and yellow, as the plants on Baudelaire did not lose their leaves during winter. But a few white patches showed that winter had begun. Eddie shivered from the bite of cold air on his naked skin. Long ago he had taken off his clothes. The womb-warmth had made garments too uncomfortable; moreover, Eddie, being hu-man, had had to get rid of waste products. And Polyphema, being a Mother, had had periodically to flush out the dirt with warm water from one of her stomachs. Every time the tracheae-vents exploded streams that swept the undesirable elements out through her door-iris, Eddie had become soaked. When he abandoned dress, his clothes had gone floating out. Only by sitting on his pack did he keep it from a like fate.

Afterward, he and the Sluggos had been dried off by warm air pumped through the same vents and originating from the mighty bat-tery of lungs. Eddie was comfortable enough—he'd always liked show-ers—but the loss of his garments had been one more thing that kept him from escaping. He would soon freeze to death outside unless he found the yacht quickly. And he wasn't sure he remembered the path back.

So now, when he stepped outside, he retreated a pace or two and let the warm air from Polyphema flow like a cloak from his shoulders.

Then he peered across the half-mile that separated him from his mother, but he could not see her. The twilight state and the dark of the unlit interior of her captor hid her.

He tapped in Morse, "Switch to the talkie, same frequency." Paula Fetts did so. She began asking him frantically if he were all right.

He replied he was fine.

"Have you missed me terribly, son?"

"Oh, very much."

Even as he said this he wondered vaguely why his voice sounded so hollow. Despair at never again being able to see her, probably.

"I've almost gone crazy, Eddie. When you were caught I ran away as fast as I could. I had no idea what horrible monster it was that was attacking us. And then, halfway down the hill, I fell and broke my leg...."

"Oh, no, Mother!"

"Yes. But I managed to crawl back to the ship. And there, after I'd set it myself, I gave myself B.K. shots. Only, my system didn't react like it's supposed to. There are people that way, you know, and the healing took twice as long.

"But when I was able to walk, I got a gun and a box of dynamite. I was going to blow up what I thought was a kind of rock-fortress, an outpost for some kind of extee. I'd no idea of the true nature of these beasts. First, though, I decided to reconnoiter. I was going to spy on the boulder from across the valley. But I was trapped by this thing.

"Listen, son. Before I'm cut off, let me tell you not to give up hope. I'll be out of here before long and over to rescue you."

"How?"

"If you remember, my lab kit holds a number of carcinogens for field work. Well, you know that sometimes a Mother's conception-spot when it is torn up during mating, instead of begetting young, goes into cancer—the opposite of pregnancy. I've injected a carcinogen into the spot and a beautiful carcinoma has developed. She'll be dead in a few days."

"Mom! You'll be buried in that rotting mass!"

"No. This creature has told me that when one of her species dies, a reflex opens the labia. That's to permit their young—if any—to escape. Listen, I'll—"

A tentacle coiled about him and pulled him back through the iris, which shut.

When he switched back to C.W., he heard, "Why didn't you communicate? What were you doing? Tell me! Tell me!"

Eddie told her. There was a silence that could only be interpreted as astonishment. After Mother had recovered her wits, she said, "From now on, you will talk to the other male through me."

Obviously, she envied and hated his ability to change wavebands, and, perhaps, had a struggle to accept the idea.

"Please," he persisted, not knowing how dangerous were the waters he was wading in, "please let me talk to my mother di—"

For the first time, he heard her stutter.

"Wha-wha-what? Your Mo-Mo-Mother?"

"Yes. Of course."

The floor heaved violently beneath his feet. He cried out and braced himself to keep from falling and then flashed on the light. The walls were pulsating like shaken jelly, and the vascular columns had turned from red and blue to gray. The entrance-iris sagged open, like a lax mouth, and the air cooled. He could feel the drop in temperature in her flesh with the soles of his feet.

It was some time before he caught on.

Polyphema was in a state of shock.

What might have happened had she stayed in it, he never knew. She might have died and thus forced him out into the winter before his mother could escape. If so, and he couldn't find the ship, he would die. Huddled in the warmest corner of the egg-shaped chamber, Eddie contemplated that idea and shivered to a degree for which the outside air couldn't account.

SEVEN

However, Polyphema had her own method of recovery. It consisted of spewing out the contents of her stew-stomach, which had doubtless become filled with the poisons draining out of her system from the blow. Her ejection of the stuff was the physical manifestation of the psychical catharsis. So furious was the flood that her foster son was almost swept out in the hot tide, but she, reacting instinctively, had coiled tentacles about him and the Sluggos. Then she followed the first upchucking by emptying her other three water-pouches, the second hot and the third lukewarm and the fourth, just filled, cold.

Eddie yelped as the icy water doused him.

Polyphema's irises closed again. The floor and walls gradually quit quaking; the temperature rose; and her veins and arteries regained their red and blue. She was well again. Or so she seemed.

But when, after waiting twenty-four hours, he cautiously approached the subject, he found she not only would not talk about it, she refused to acknowledge the existence of the other mobile.

Eddie, giving up hope of conversation, thought for quite a while. The only conclusion he could come to, and he was sure he'd grasped enough of her psychology to make it valid, was that the concept of a mobile female was utterly unacceptable.

Her world was split into two: mobile and her kind, the immobile. Mobile meant food and mating. Mobile meant — male. The Mothers were — female.

How the mobiles reproduced had probably never entered the hillcrouchers' minds. Their science and philosophy were on the instinctive body-level. Whether they had some notion of spontaneous generation or amoebalike fission being responsible for the continued population of mobiles, or they'd just taken for granted they "growed," like Topsy, Eddie never found out. To them, they were female and the rest of the protoplasmic cosmos was male.

That was that. Any other idea was more than foul and obscene and blasphemous. It was — unthinkable.

Polyphema had received a deep trauma from his words. And though she seemed to have recovered, somewhere in those tons of unimaginably complicated flesh a bruise was buried. Like a hidden flower, dark purple, it bloomed, and the shadow it cast was one that cut off a certain memory, a certain tract, from the light of consciousness. That bruise-stained shadow covered that time and event which the Mothers, for reasons unfathomable to the human being, found necessary to mark KEEP OFF.

Thus, though Eddie did not word it, he understood in the cells of his body, he felt and knew, as if his bones were prophesying and his brain did not hear, what came to pass.

Sixty-six hours later by the panrad clock, Polyphema's entrance-lips opened. Her tentacles darted out. They came back in, carrying his helpless and struggling mother.

Eddie, roused out of a doze, horrified, paralyzed, saw her toss her lab kit at him and heard an inarticulate cry from her. And saw her plunged, headforemost, into the stomach-iris.

Polyphema had taken the one sure way of burying the evidence.

Eddie lay face down, nose mashed against the warm and faintly throbbing flesh of the floor. Now and then his hands clutched spasmodically as if he were reaching for something that someone kept putting just within his reach and then moving away.

How long he was there he didn't know, for he never again looked at the clock.

Finally, in the darkness, he sat up and giggled inanely, "Mother always did make good stew."

That set him off. He leaned back on his hands and threw his head back and howled like a wolf under a full moon.

Polyphema, of course, was dead-deaf, but she could radar his posture, and her keen nostrils deduced from his body-scent that he was in terrible fear and anguish.

A tentacle glided out and gently enfolded him.

"What is the matter?" zzted the panrad.

He stuck his finger in the keyhole.

"I have lost my mother!"

"?"

"She's gone away, and she'll never come back!"

"I don't understand. *Here I am.*"

Eddie quit weeping and cocked his head as if he were listening to some inner voice. He snuffled a few times and wiped away the tears, slowly disengaged the tentacle, patted it, walked over to his pack in a corner, and took out the bottle of Old Red Star capsules. One he popped

into the thermos; the other he gave to her with the request she duplicate it, if possible. Then he stretched out on his side, propped on one
elbow like a Roman in his sensualities, sucked the rye through the
nipple, and listened to a medley of Beethoven, Moussorgsky, Verdi,
Strauss, Porter, Feinstein, and Waxworth.

So the time — if there were such a thing there — flowed around Eddie.
When he was tired of music or plays or books, he listened in on the
area hookup. Hungry, he rose and walked — or often just crawled — to
the stew-iris. Cans of rations lay in his pack; he had planned to eat
those until he was sure that — what was it he was forbidden to eat?
Poison? Something had been devoured by Polyphema and the Sluggos.
But sometime during the music-rye orgy, he had forgotten. He now
ate quite hungrily and with thought for nothing but the satisfaction of
his wants.

Sometimes the door-iris opened, and Billy Greengrocer hopped in.
Billy looked like a cross between a cricket and a kangaroo. He was the
size of a collie, and he bore in a marsupialian pouch vegetables and
fruit and nuts. These he extracted with shiny green, chitinous claws
and gave to Mother in return for meals of stew. Happy symbiote, he
chirruped merrily while his many-faceted eyes, revolving independently of each other, looked one at the Sluggos and the other at Eddie.

Eddie, on impulse, abandoned the 1000 kc. band and roved the
frequencies until he found that both Polyphema and Billy were emitting a 108 wave. That, apparently, was their natural signal. When Billy
had his groceries to deliver, he broadcast. Polyphema, in turn, when
she needed them, sent back to him. There was nothing intelligent on
Billy's part; it was just his instinct to transmit. And the Mother was,
aside from the "semantic" frequency, limited to that one band. But it
worked out fine.

EIGHT

Everything was fine. What more could a man want? Free food,
unlimited liquor, soft bed, air-conditioning, shower-baths, music, intellectual works (on the tape), interesting conversation (much of it was
about him), privacy, and security.

If he had not already named her, he would have called her Mother
Gratis.

Nor were creature comforts all. She had given him the answers to
all his questions, all....

Except one.

That was never expressed vocally by him. Indeed, he would have been incapable of doing so. He was probably unaware that he had such a question.

But Polyphema voiced it one day when she asked him to do her a favor.

Eddie reacted as if outraged.

"One does not —! One does not —!"

He choked, and then he thought, how ridiculous! She is not —

And looked puzzled, and said, "But she is."

He rose and opened the lab kit. While he was looking for a scalpel, he came across the carcinogens. He threw them through the half-opened labia far out and down the hillside.

Then he turned and, scalpel in hand, leaped at the light gray swelling on the wall. And stopped, staring at it, while the instrument fell from his hand. And picked it up and stabbed feebly and did not even scratch the skin. And again let it drop.

"What is it? What is it?" crackled the panrad hanging from his wrist.

Suddenly, a heavy cloud of human odor — mansweat — was puffed in his face from a nearby vent.

"? ? ? ?"

And he stood, bent in a half-crouch, seemingly paralyzed. Until tentacles seized him in fury and dragged him toward the stomach-iris, yawning man-sized.

Eddie screamed and writhed and plunged his finger in the panrad and tapped, "All right! All right!"

And once back before the spot, he lunged with a sudden and wild joy; he slashed savagely; he yelled. "Take that! And that, P..." and the rest was lost in a mindless shout.

He did not stop cutting, and he might have gone on and on until he had quite excised the spot had not Polyphema interfered by dragging him toward her stomach-iris again. For ten seconds he hung there, helpless and sobbing with a mixture of fear and glory.

Polyphema's reflexes had almost overcome her brain. Fortunately, a cold spark of reason lit up a corner of the vast, dark, and hot chapel of her frenzy.

The convolutions leading to the steaming, meat-laden pouch closed and the foldings of flesh rearranged themselves. Eddie was suddenly hosed with warm water from what he called the "sanitation" stomach. The iris closed. He was put down. The scalpel was put back in the bag.

For a long time Mother seemed to be shaken by the thought of what she might have done to Eddie. She did not trust herself to transmit until her nerves were settled. When they were, she did not refer to his narrow escape. Nor did he.

He was happy. He felt as if a spring, tight-coiled against his bowels since he and his wife had parted, was now, for some reason, released. The dull vague pain of loss and discontent, the slight fever and cramp in his entrails, and the apathy that sometimes afflicted him, were gone. He felt fine.

Meanwhile, something akin to deep affection had been lighted, like a tiny candle under the drafty and overtowering roof of a cathedral. Mother's shell housed more than Eddie; it now curved over an emotion new to her kind. This was evident by the next event that filled him with terror.

For the wounds in the spot healed and the swelling increased into a large bag. Then the bag burst and ten mouse-sized Sluggos struck the floor. The impact had the same effect as a doctor spanking a newborn baby's bottom; they drew in their first breath with shock and pain; their uncontrolled and feeble pulses filled the ether with shapeless SOS's.

When Eddie was not talking with Polyphema or listening in or drinking or sleeping or eating or bathing or running off the tape, he played with the Sluggos. He was, in a sense, their father. Indeed, as they grew to hog-size, it was hard for their female parent to distinguish him from her young. As he seldom walked anymore, and was often to be found on hands and knees in their midst, she could not scan him too well. Moreover, something in the heavywet air or in the diet had caused every hair on his body to drop off. He grew very fat. Generally speaking, he was one with the pale, soft, round, and bald offspring. A family likeness.

There was one difference. When the time came for the virgins to be expelled, Eddie crept to one end, whimpering, and stayed there until he was sure Mother was not going to thrust him out into the cold, hard, and hungry world.

That final crisis over, he came back to the center of the floor. The panic in his breast had died out, but his nerves were still quivering. He filled his thermos and then listened for a while to his own tenor singing the "Sea Things" aria from his favorite opera, Gianelli's *Ancient Mariner*. Suddenly, he burst out and accompanied himself, finding himself thrilled as never before by the concluding words.

> And from my neck so free
> The Albatross fell off, and sank
> Like lead into the sea.

Afterwards, voice silent but heart singing, he switched off the wire and cut in on Polyphema's broadcast.

Mother was having trouble. She could not precisely describe to the continent-wide hook-up this new and almost inexpressible emotion she felt about the mobile. It was a concept her language was not prepared for. Nor was she helped any by the gallons of Old Red Star in her bloodstream.

Eddie sucked at the plastic nipple and nodded sympathetically and drowsily at her search for words. Presently, the thermos rolled out of his hand.

He slept on his side, curled in a ball, knees on his chest and arms crossed, neck bent forward. Like the pilot room chronometer whose hands reversed after the crash, the clock of his body was ticking backwards, ticking backwards...

In the darkness, in the moistness, safe and warm, well fed, much loved.

It was the first time that the U.S. Marines had ever been routed with water pistols.

The screen flickered. Another scene replaced the first. But the afterimage had burned itself on my mind.

A distorted sun that had no business in a mid-Illinois sky made the scene bright for the long-range cameras. A regiment of Marines, helmeted, wearing full packs, toting rifles with bayonets and automatic weapons, were stumbling backward in full retreat before a horde of naked men and women. The nudists, laughing and capering, were aiming toy cowboy-sixshooters and Captain Orbit rayguns. These sprayed streams of liquid from tiny muzzles, streams that arched over desperately upraised guns and squirted off the faces under the helmets.

Then, the tough veterans were throwing their weapons down and running away. Or else standing foolishly, blinking, running their tongues over wet lips. And the victors were taking the victims by the hand and leading them away behind their own uneven lines.

Why didn't the Marines shoot? Simple. Their cartridges *refused* to explode.

Flamethrowers, burpguns, recoilless cannon? They might as well have been shillelaghs.

The screen went white. Lights flashed on. Major Alice Lewis, WHAM, put down her baton.

"Well, gentlemen, any questions? None? Mr. Temper, perhaps *you'd* like to tell us why you expect to succeed where so many others have failed. Mr. Temper, gentlemen, will give us the *bald* facts."

I rose. My face was flushed; my palms, sticky. I'd have been wiser to laugh at the major's nasty crack about my lack of hair, but a quarter century hadn't killed my self-consciousness over the eggishness of my head. When I was twenty, I came down with a near-fatal fever the doctors couldn't identify. When I rose from bed, I was a shorn lamb, and I'd stayed fleeced. Furthermore, I was allergic to toupées. So it was a trifle embarrassing to get up before an audience just after the beautiful Major Lewis had made a pun at the expense of my shining pate.

I walked to the table where she stood, pert and, dammit, pretty. Not until I got there did I see that the hand holding the stick was shaking. I decided to ignore her belligerent attitude. After all, the two of us were going to be together on our mission, and she couldn't help it any more than I. Moreover, she had reason to be nervous. These were trying times for everybody, and especially for the military.

I faced a roomful of civilians and officers, all V.I.P. or loud brass. Through the window at the back, I could see a segment of snow-covered Galesburg, Illinois. The declining sun was perfectly normal. People were moving about as if it were customary for fifty thousand soldiers to be camped between them and the valley of the Illinois, where strange creatures roamed through the fantastically luxuriant vegetation.

I paused to fight down the wave of reluctance which invariably inundated me when I had to speak in public. For some reason, my upper plate always went into a tap dance at such crucial moments.

"Ladie-s-s and gentlemen, I s-s-saw S-s-susie on the s-s-seashore yes-s-sterday." You know what I mean. Even if you're describing the plight of the war orphans in Azerbaijan, you watch your listeners smile and cover their lower faces, and you feel like a fool.

I shouldn't have taken so long to summon my nerve, for the major spoke again. Her lip curled. It was a very pretty lip, but I didn't think even a nonpermanent wave improved its appearance at the moment.

"Mr. Temper believes he has the key to our problem. Perhaps he does. I must warn you, however, that his story combines such unrelated and unlikely events as the escape of a bull from the stockyards, the drunken caperings of a college professor who was noted for his dedicated sobriety, to say nothing of the disappearance of said professor of classical literature and two of his students on the same night."

I waited until the laughter died down. When I spoke, I said nothing about two other improbably connected facts. I did not mention the bottle I had purchased in an Irish tavern and shipped to the professor two years before. Nor did I say what I thought one of the camera shots taken by an Army balloon over the city of Onaback meant. This photograph had shown a huge red brick statue of a bull astride the football field of Traybell University.

"Gentlemen," I said, "before I say much about myself, I'll tell you why the Food and Drug Administration is sending a lone agent into an area where, so far, the combined might of the Army, Air Force, Coast Guard, and Marines have failed."

Red faces blossomed like flowers in springtime.

"The F.D.A. necessarily takes a part in the *affaire à l'Onaback*. As you know, the Illinois River, from Chillicothe to Havana, now runs with beer."

Nobody laughed. They'd long ago quit being amused by that. As for me, I loathed any alcoholic drink or drug. With good reason.

"I should modify that. The Illinois has an odor of hops, but those of our volunteers who have drunk from the river where the stuff begins to thin out don't react to it as they would to a regular alcoholic drink. They report a euphoria, plus an almost total lack of inhibition, which lasts even after all alcohol is oxidized from their bloodstream. And the stuff acts like a stimulant, not a depressant. There is no hangover. To add to our mystification, our scientists can't find any unknown substance in the water to analyze.

"However, you all know this, just as you know why the F.D.A. is involved. The main reason I'm being sent in, aside from the fact that I was born and raised in Onaback, is that my superiors, including the President of the United States, have been impressed with my theory about the identity of the man responsible for this whole fantastic mess.

"Besides," I added with a not entirely unmalicious glance at Major Lewis, "they believe that, since I first thought of psychologically conditioning an agent against the lure of the river-water, I should be the agent sent in.

"After this situation had come to the notice of the F.D.A. authorities, I was assigned to the case. Since so many Federal Agents had disappeared in Onabagian territory, I decided to do some checking from the outside. I went to the Congressional Library and began reading the Onaback *Morning Star* and *Evening Journal* backwards, from the day the Library quit receiving copies of them. Not until I came across the January 13 issues of two years ago, did I find anything significant."

I stopped. Now that I had to put my reasonings in spoken words before these hardheaded bigshots, I could weigh their reception. Zero. Nevertheless, I plunged ahead. I did have an ace-in-the-hole. Or, to be more exact, a monkey-in-a-cage.

"Gentlemen, the January 13 issues related, among other things, the disappearance on the previous night of Dr. Boswell Durham of Traybell University, along with two of his students in his survey course on classical literature. The reports were conflicting, but most of them agreed on the following. One, that during the day of the 13th, a male student, Andrew Polivinosel, made some slighting remark about classical literature. Dr. Durham, a man noted for his mildness and forbearance, called Polivinosel an ass. Polivinosel, a huge football player, rose and said he'd toss Durham out of the building by the seat of his pants. Yet, if we are to believe the witnesses, the timid, spindly, and middle-aged Durham took the husky Polivinosel by one hand and literally threw him out of the door and down the hall.

"Whereupon, Peggy Rourke, an extremely comely coed and Polivinosel's 'steady,' persuaded him not to attack the professor. The athlete, however, didn't seem to need much persuasion. Dazed, he made no protest when Miss Rourke led him away.

"The other students in the class reported that there had been fric-tion between the two and that the athlete bugged Dr. Durham in class. Durham now had an excellent opportunity for getting Polivinosel kicked out of school, even though Polivinosel was Little All-Ameri-can. The professor didn't, however, report the matter to the Dean of Men. He was heard to mutter that Polivinosel was an ass and that this was a fact anyone could plainly see. One student said he thought he detected liquor on the professor's breath, but believed he must have been mistaken, since it was campus tradition that the good doctor never even touched Cokes. His wife, it seems, had a great deal to do with that. She was an ardent temperance worker, a latter-day disciple of Frances Willard.

"This may seem irrelevant, gentlemen, but I assure you it isn't. Consider two other students' testimony. Both swore they saw the neck of a bottle sticking from the professor's overcoat pocket as it hung in his office. It was uncapped. And, though it was freezing outside, the professor, a man famed for his aversion to cold, had both windows open. Perhaps to dispel the fumes from the bottle.

"After the fight, Peggy Rourke was asked by Dr. Durham to come into his office. An hour later, Miss Rourke burst out with her face red and her eyes full of tears. She told her roommate that the professor had acted like a madman. That he had told her he had loved her since the day she'd walked into his classroom: That he had known he was too old and ugly even to think of eloping with her. But, now that 'things' had changed, he wanted to run away with her. She told him she had always been fond of him, but she was by no stretch of the imagination in love with him. Whereupon, he had promised that by that same evening he would be a changed man, and that she would find him irresistible.

"Despite all this, everything seemed to be smooth that evening when Polivinosel brought Peggy Rourke to the Sophomore Frolic. Durham, a chaperon, greeted them as if nothing had happened. His wife did not seem to sense anything wrong. That in itself was strange, for Mrs. Durham was one of those faculty wives who has one end of the campus grapevine grown permanently into her ear. Moreover, a highly nervous woman, she was not one to conceal her emotions. Nor was she subdued by the doctor. He was the butt of many a joke behind his back because he was so obviously henpecked. Mrs. Durham often made a monkey of him and led him around like a bull with a ring in his nose. Yet that night..."

Major Lewis cleared her throat. "Mr. Temper, streamline the details, will you please? These gentlemen are very busy, and they'd like the bald facts. The *bald* facts, mind you."

I continued, "The bare facts are these. Late that night, shortly after the ball broke up, a hysterical Mrs. Durham called the police and said her husband was out of his mind. Never a word that he might be drinking. Such a thing to her was unthinkable. He wouldn't dare..."

Major Lewis cleared her throat again. I shot her a look of annoyance. Apparently, she failed to realize that some of the details were necessary.

"One of the policemen who answered her call reported later that the professor was staggering around in the snow, dressed only in his pants with a bottle sticking out of his hip pocket, shooting red paint at everybody with a spray gun. Another officer contradicted him. He said the doctor did all the damage with a bucket of paint and a brush.

"Whatever he used, he covered his own house and some of his neighbors' houses from roof to base. When the police appeared, he plastered their car with the paint and blinded them. While they were trying to clear their eyes, he walked off. A half-hour later, he streaked the girls' dorm with red paint and scared a number of the occupants into hysteria. He entered the building, pushed past the scandalized housemother, raced up and down the halls, threw paint over anybody who showed his head, seemingly from a bottomless can, and then, failing to find Peggy Rourke, disappeared.

"I might add that all this time he was laughing like a madman and announcing loudly to all and sundry that tonight he was painting the town red.

"Miss Rourke had gone with Polivinosel and some of his fraternity brothers and dates to a restaurant. Later, the couple dropped the others off at their homes and then proceeded, theoretically, to the girls' dormitory. Neither got there. Nor were they or the professor seen again during the two years that elapsed between that incident and the time the Onaback papers quit publishing. The popular theory was that the love-crazed professor had killed and buried them and then fled to parts unknown. But I choose, on good evidence, to believe otherwise."

Hurriedly, for I could see they were getting restless, I told them of the bull that had appeared from nowhere at the foot of Main Street. The stockyards later reported that none of their bulls was missing. Nevertheless, too many people saw the bull for the account to be denied. Not only that, they all testified that the last they saw of it, it was swimming across the Illinois River with a naked woman on its back. She was waving a bottle in her hand. It, and the woman, then plunged into the forest on the bluffs and disappeared.

At this there was an uproar. A Coast Guard Commander said "Are you trying to tell me that Zeus and Europa have come to life, Mr. Temper?"

There was no use in continuing. These men didn't believe unless they saw with their own eyes. I decided it was time to let them see.

I waved my hand. My assistants pushed in a large cage on wheels. Within it crouched a very large ape, wearing a little straw hat, a sour expression, and a pair of pink nylon panties. A hole cut in the bottom of the latter allowed her long tail to stick through. Strictly speaking, I suppose, she couldn't be classified as an ape. Apes have no tails.

An anthropologist would have seen at once that this wasn't a monkey, either. It was true that she did have a prognathous muzzle, long hair that covered her whole body, long arms, and a tail. But no monkey ever had such a smooth, high brow, or such a big hooked nose, or legs so long in proportion to her trunk.

When the cage had come to rest beside the platform, I said, "Gentlemen, if everything I've said seemed irrelevant, I'm sure that the next few minutes will convince you I have not been barking up the wrong tree."

I turned to the cage, caught myself almost making a bow, and said, "Mrs. Durham, will you please tell these gentlemen what happened to you?"

Then I waited, in full expectation of the talk, torrential and disconnected but illuminating, that had overwhelmed me the previous evening after my buddies had captured her on the edge of the area. I was very proud, because I'd made a discovery that would shock and rock these gentlemen from their heads of bone to their heels of leather and show them that one little agent from the F.D.A. had done what the whole armed forces had not. Then they wouldn't snicker and refer to me as Out-of-Temper by Frothing-at-the-Mouth.

I waited...

And I waited...

And Mrs. Durham refused to say a word. Not one, though I all but got down on my knees and pleaded with her. I tried to explain to her what giant forces were in balance and that she held the fate of the world in the hollow of her pink hairless palm. She would not open her mouth. Somebody had injured her dignity, and she would do nothing but sulk and turn her back on all of us and wave her tail above her pink panties.

She was the most exasperating female I'd ever known. No wonder that her husband made a monkey of her.

Triumph had become fiasco. Nor did it convince the big shots when I played the recording of my last night's conversation with her. They still thought I had less brains than hair, and they showed it when they replied to my request for questions with silence. Major Alice Lewis smiled scornfully.

Well, it made no difference in my mission. I was under orders they hadn't power to countermand.

At 7:30 that evening, I was outside the area with a group of officers and my boss. Though the moon was just coming up, its light was bright enough to read by. About ten yards from us, the whiteness of snow and cold ended, and the green and warmth began.

General Lewis, Major Lewis' father, said, "We'll give you two days to contact Durham, Mr. Temper. Wednesday, 1400, we attack. Marines, equipped with bows and arrows and airguns, and wearing oxygen masks, will be loaded into gliders with pressurized cabins. These will be released from their tow-planes at high altitude. They will land upon U.S. Route 24 just south of the city limits, where there are now two large meadows. They will march up South Adams Street until they come to the downtown district. By then, I hope, you will have located and eliminated the source of this trouble."

For "eliminated," read "assassinated." By his expression, he thought I couldn't do it. General Lewis disliked me, not only because I was a civilian with authority, backed by the President himself, but because the conditions of my assignment with his daughter were unorthodox, to say the least. Alice Lewis was not only a major and a woman—she was a mightily attractive one and young for her rank.

She stood there, shivering, in her bra and panties, while I was stripped down to my own shorts. Once we were safely in the woods, we would take off the rest of our clothes. When in Rome...

Marines with bows and arrows and BB guns—no wonder the military was miserable. But, once inside the Area controlled by my former professor and his Brew, firearms simply refused to work. And the Brew *did* work, making addicts of all who tasted it.

All but me.

I was the only one who had thought to have myself conditioned against it.

Dr. Duerf asked me a few questions while someone strapped a three-gallon tank of distilled water to my back. The doctor was the Columbia psychiatrist who had conditioned me against the Brew.

Suddenly, in the midst of a casual remark, he grabbed the back of my head. A glass seemed to appear from nowhere in his fist. He tried to force its contents past my lips. I took just one sniff and knocked the glass from his grip and struck him with the other fist.

He danced back, holding the side of his face. "How do you feel now?" he asked.

"I'm all right," I said, "but I thought for a moment I'd choke. I wanted to kill you for trying to do that to me."

"I had to give you a final test. You passed it with a big A. You're thoroughly conditioned against the Brew."

The two Lewises said nothing. They were irked because I, a civilian, had thought of this method of combating the allure of the Brew. The thousand Marines, scheduled to follow me in two days, would have to wear oxygen masks to save them from temptation. As for my companion, she had been hastily put under hypnosis by Duerf, but he didn't know how successfully. Fortunately, her mission would not take as long as mine. She was supposed to go to the source of the Brew and bring back a sample. If, however, I needed help, I was to call on her. Also, though it was unstated, I was to keep her from succumbing to the Brew.

We shook hands all around, and we walked away. Warm air fell over us like a curtain. One moment, we were shivering; the next, sweating. That was bad. It meant we'd be drinking more water than we had provided ourselves with.

I looked around in the bright moonlight. Two years had changed the Illinois-scape. There were many more trees than there had been, trees of a type you didn't expect to see this far north. Whoever was responsible for the change had had many seeds and sprouts shipped in, in preparation for the warmer climate. I knew, for I had checked in Chicago on various shipments and had found that a man by the name of Smith—Smith!—had, two weeks after Durham's disappearance, begun ordering from tropical countries. The packages had gone to an Onaback house and had ended up in the soil hereabouts. Durham must have realized that this river-valley area couldn't support its customary 300,000 people, once the railroads and trucks quit shipping in cans of food and fresh milk and provisions. The countryside would have been stripped by the hungry hordes.

But when you looked around at the fruit trees, bananas, cherries, apples, pears, oranges, and others, most of them out of season and flourishing in soils thought unfavorable for their growth—when you noted the blackberry, blueberry, gooseberry, and raspberry bushes, the melons and potatoes and tomatoes on the ground—all large enough to have won county fair first prizes in any pre-Brew age—then you realized there was no lack of food. All you had to do was pick it and eat.

"It looks to me," whispered Alice Lewis, "like the Garden of Eden."

"Stop talking treason, Alice!" I snapped.

She iced me with a look. "Don't be silly. And don't call me Alice. I'm a major in the Marines."

"Pardon," I said. "But we'd better drop the rank. The natives might wonder. What's more, we'd better shed these clothes before we run into somebody."

She wanted to object, but she had her orders. Even though we were to be together at least thirty-six hours, and would be mother-naked all that time, she insisted we go into the bushes to peel. I didn't argue.

I stepped behind a tree and took off my shorts. At the same time, I smelled cigar smoke. I slipped off the webbing holding the tank to my back and walked out onto the narrow trail. I got a hell of a shock.

A monster leaned against a tree, his short legs crossed, a big Havana sticking from the side of his carnivorous mouth, his thumbs tucked in an imaginary vest.

I shouldn't have been frightened. I should have been amused. This creature had stepped right out of a very famous comic strip. He stood seven feet high, had a bright green hide and yellow-brown plates running down his chest and belly. His legs were very short; his trunk, long. His face was half-man, half-alligator. He had two enormous bumps on top of his head and big dish-sized eyes. The same half-kindly, half-stupid, and arrogant look was upon his face. He was complete, even to having four fingers instead of five.

My shock came not only from the unexpectedness of his appearance. There is a big difference between something seen on paper and that seen in the flesh. This thing was cute and humorous and lovable in the strip. Transformed into living color and substance, it was monstrous.

"Don't get scared," said the apparition. "I grow on you after a while."

"Who are you?" I asked.

At that moment, Alice stepped out from behind a tree. She gasped, and she grabbed my arm.

He waved his cigar. "I'm the Allegory on the Banks of the Illinois. Welcome, strangers, to the domain of the Great Mahrud."

I didn't know what he meant by those last few words. And it took a minute to figure out that his title was a pun derived from the aforesaid cartoonist and from Sheridan's Mrs. Malaprop.

"Albert Allegory is the full name," he said. "That is, in this metamorph. Other forms, other names, you know. And you two, I suppose, are outsiders who wish to live along the Illinois, drink from the Brew, and worship the Bull."

He held out his hand with the two inside fingers clenched and the thumb and outside finger extended.

"This is the sign that every true believer makes when he meets another," he said. "Remember it, and you'll be saved much trouble."

"How do you know I'm from the outside?" I asked. I didn't try to lie. He didn't seem to be bent on hurting us.

He laughed, and his vast mouth megaphoned the sound. Alice, no longer the cocky WHAM officer, gripped my hand hard.

He said, "I'm sort of a demigod, you might say. When Mahrud, bull be his name, became a god, he wrote a letter to me — using the U.S. mails of course — and invited me to come here and demigod for him. I'd never cared too much for the world as it was so I slipped in past the Army cordon and took over the duties that Mahrud, bull be his name, gave me."

I, too, had received a letter from my former professor. It had arrived before the trouble developed, and I had not understood his invitation to come live with him and be his demigod. I'd thought he'd slipped a gear or two.

For lack of anything pertinent to say, I asked, "What are your duties?"

He waved his cigar again. "My job, which is anything but onerous, is to meet outsiders and caution them to keep their eyes open. They are to remember that not everything is what it seems, and they are to look beyond the surface of the deed for the symbol."

He puffed on his cigar and then said, "I have a question for you. I don't want you to answer it now, but I want you to think about it and give me an answer later." He blew smoke again. "My question is this — where do you want to go now?"

He didn't offer to expand his question. He said, "So long," and strolled off down a side-path, his short legs seeming to move almost independently of his elongated saurian torso. I stared for a moment, still shaking from the encounter. Then I returned to the tree behind which I'd left my water-tank and strapped it back on.

We walked away fast. Alice was so subdued that she did not seem conscious of our nudity. After a while, she said, "Something like that frightens me. How could a man assume a form like that?"

"We'll find out," I said with more optimism than I felt. "I think we'd better be prepared for just about anything."

"Perhaps the story Mrs. Durham told you back at Base was true."

I nodded. The professor's wife had said that, shortly before the Area was sealed off, she had gone to the bluffs across the river, where she knew her husband was. Even though he had announced himself a god by then, she was not afraid of him.

Mrs. Durham had taken two lawyers along, just in case. She was highly incoherent about what happened across the river. But some strange force, apparently operated by Dr. Durham, had turned her into a large tailed ape, causing her to flee. The two lawyers, metamorphosed into skunks, had also beaten a retreat.

Considering these strange events, Alice said, "What I can't understand is how Durham could do these things. Where's his power? What sort of gadget does he have?"

Hot as it was, my skin developed gooseflesh. I could scarcely tell her that I was almost certainly responsible for this entire situation. I felt guilty enough without actually telling the truth. Moreover, if I *had* told her what I believed to be the truth, she'd have *known* I was crazy. Nevertheless, that was the way it was, and that was why I had volunteered for this assignment. I'd started it; I had to finish it.

"I'm thirsty," she said. "What about a drink, Pops? We may not get a chance at another for a long time."

"Damn it," I said as I slipped off the tank, "don't call me Pops! My name is Daniel Temper, and I'm not so old that I could be..."

I stopped. I was old enough to be her father. In the Kentucky mountains, at any rate.

Knowing what I was thinking, she smiled and held out the little cup she had taken from the clip on the tank's side. I growled, "A man's only as old as he feels, and I don't feel over thirty."

At that moment I caught the flicker of moonlight on a form coming down the path. "Duck!" I said to Alice.

She just had time to dive into the grass. As for me, the tank got in my way, so I decided to stay there and brazen things out.

When I saw what was coming down the path, I wished I had taken off the tank. Weren't there *any* human beings in this Godforsaken land? First it was the Allegory. Now it was the Ass.

He said, "Hello, brother," and before I could think of a good come-back, he threw his strange head back and loosed tremendous laughter that was half *ha-ha!* and half *hee-haw!*

I didn't think it was funny. I was far too tense to pretend amusement. Moreover, his breath stank of Brew. I was half-sick before I could back up to escape it.

He was tall and covered with short blonde hair, unlike most asses, and he stood upon two manlike legs that ended in broad hoofs. He had two long hairy ears, but, otherwise, he was as human as anybody else you might meet in the woods — or on the street. And his name, as he wasn't backward in telling me, was Polivinosel.

He said, "Why are you carrying that tank?"

"I've been smuggling the Brew to the outside."

His grin revealed long yellow horselike teeth. "Bootlegging, eh? But what do they pay you with? Money's no good to a worshiper of the All-Bull."

He held up his right hand. The thumb and two middle fingers were bent. The index finger and little finger were held straight out. I didn't respond immediately, and he looked hard. I imitated his gesture, and he relaxed a little.

"I'm bootlegging for the love of it," I said. "And also to spread the gospel."

Where that last phrase came from, I had no notion. Perhaps from the reference to "worshiper" and the vaguely religious-looking sign that Polivinosel had made.

He reached out a big hairy hand and turned the spigot on my tank. Before I could move, he had poured out enough to fill his cupped palm. He raised his hand to his lips and slurped loudly. He blew the liquid out so it sprayed all over me. "Whee-oo! That's *water!*"

"Of course," I said. "After I get rid of my load of Brew, I fill the tank with ordinary water. If I'm caught by the border patrol, I tell them I'm smuggling pure water into our area."

Polivinosel went *hoo-hah-hah* and slapped his thigh so hard, it sounded like an axe biting into a tree.

"That's not all," I said. "I even have an agreement with some of the higher officers. They allow me to slip through if I bring them back some Brew."

He winked and brayed and slapped his thigh again. "Corruption, eh, brother? Even brass will rust. I tell you, it won't be long until the Brew of the Bull spreads everywhere."

Again he made that sign, and I did so almost at the same time.

He said, "I'll walk with you a mile or so. My worshipers — the local Cult of the Ass — are holding a fertility ceremony down the path a way. Care to join us?"

I shuddered. "No, thank you," I said fervently.

I had witnessed one of those orgies through a pair of fieldglasses one night. The huge bonfire had been about two hundred yards inside the forbidden boundary. Against its hellish flame, I could see the white and capering bodies of absolutely uninhibited men and women. It was a long time before I could get that scene out of my mind. I used to dream about it.

When I declined the invitation, Polivinosel brayed again and slapped me on the back, or where my back would have been if my tank hadn't been in the way. As it was, I fell on my hands and knees in a patch of tall grass. I was furious. I not only resented his too-high spirits, I was afraid he had bent the thin-walled tank and sprung a leak in its seams.

But that wasn't the main reason I didn't get up at once. I couldn't move because I was staring into Alice's big blue eyes.

Polivinosel gave a loud whoop and leaped through the air and landed beside me. He got down on his hands and knees and stuck his big ugly mule-eared face into Alice's and bellowed, "How now, white cow! How high browse thou?"

He grabbed Alice by the waist and lifted her up high, getting up himself at the same time. There he held her in the moonlight and turned her around and over and over, as if she were a strange-looking bug he had caught crawling in the weeds.

She squealed and gasped, "Damn you, you big jackass, take your filthy paws off me!"

"I'm Polivinosel, the local god of fertility!" he brayed. "It's my duty — and privilege — to inspect your qualifications. Tell me, daughter, have you prayed recently for a son or daughter? Are your crops coming along? How are your cabbages growing? What about your onions and your parsnips? Are your hens laying enough eggs?"

Instead of being frightened, Alice got angry. "All right, Your Asininity, would you please let me down? And quit looking at me with those big lecherous eyes. If you want what I think you do, hurry along to your own orgy. Your worshippers are waiting for you."

He opened his hands so she fell to the ground. Fortunately, she was quick and lithe and landed on her feet. She started to walk away, but he reached out and grabbed her by the wrist.

"You're going the wrong way, my pretty little daughter. The infidels are patrolling the border only a few hundred yards away. You wouldn't want to get caught. Then you'd not be able to drink the divine Brew anymore. You wouldn't want that, would you?"

"I'll take care of myself, thank you," she said huskily. "Just leave me alone. It's getting so a girl can't take a snooze by herself in the grass without some minor deity or other wanting to wrestle!"

Alice was picking up the local lingo fast.

"Well, now, daughter, you can't blame us godlings for that. Not when you're built like a goddess yourself."

He gave that titanic bray that should have knocked us down, then grabbed both of us by the wrists and dragged us along the path.

"Come along, little ones. I'll introduce you around. And we'll all have a ball at the Feast of the Ass." Again, the loud offensive bray. I could see why Durham had metamorphosed this fellow into his present form.

That thought brought me up short. The question was, how had he done it? I didn't believe in supernatural powers, of course. If there were any, they weren't possessed by man. And anything that went on in this physical universe had to obey physical laws.

Take Polivinosel's ears and hoofs. I had a good chance to study them more closely as I walked with him. His ears may have been changed, like Bottom's, into a donkey's, but whoever had done it had not had an accurate picture in his mind. They were essentially human ears, elongated and covered over with tiny hairs.

As for the legs, they were human, not equine. It was true he had no feet. But his pale, shiny hoofs, though cast into a good likeness of a horse's, were evidently made of the same stuff as toenails. And there was still the faintest outline and curve of five toes.

It was evident that some biological sculptor had had to rechisel and then regrow the basic human form.

I looked at Alice to see what she thought of him. She was magnificent in her anger. As Polivinosel had been uncouth enough to mention, she had a superb figure. She was the sort of girl who is always president of her college sorority, queen of the Senior Prom, and engaged to a senator's son. The type I had never had a chance with when I was working my way through Traybell University.

Polivinosel suddenly stopped and roared, "Look, you, what's your name?"

"Daniel Temper," I said.

"Daniel Temper? D.T? Ah, *hah, hoo, hah, hah!* Listen, Old D.T., throw that tank away. It burdens you down, and you look like an ass, a veritable beast of burden, with it on your back. And I won't have anybody going around imitating me, see? *Hoohah-heehaw!* Get it?"

He punched me in the ribs with a big thumb as hard as horn. It was all I could do to keep from swinging at him. I never hated a man—or deity—so much. Durham had failed if he had thought to punish him. Polivinosel seemed to be proud of his transformation and had, if I understood him correctly, profited enough by his experience to start a cult. Of course, he wasn't the first to make a religion of his infirmity.

"How will I be able to bootleg the Brew out?" I asked.

"Who cares?" he said. "Your piddling little operations won't help the spread of the divine Drink much. Leave that up to the rivers of the world and to Mahrud, bull be his name."

He made that peculiar sign again.

I couldn't argue with him. He'd have torn the tank off my back. Slowly, I unstrapped it. He helped me by grabbing it and throwing it off into the darkness of the woods.

Immediately, I became so thirsty, I could hardly stand it.

"You don't want that filthy stuff!" Polivinosel brayed. "Come with me to the Place of the Ass! I have a nice little temple there—nothing fancy, understand, like the Flower Palace of Mahrud, may he be all bull—but it will do. And we do have a good time."

All this while, he was ogling Alice shamelessly and projecting more than his thoughts. Like all the degenerates in this area, he had absolutely no inhibitions. If I had had a gun, I think I would have shot him then and there. That is, if the cartridges could have exploded.

"Look here," I said, abandoning caution in my anger. "We're going where we damn well please." I grabbed the girl's wrist. More wrist-grabbing going on lately. "Come on, Alice, let's leave this glorified donkey."

Polivinosel loomed in our way. The slightly Mongolian tilt of his eyes made him look more Missouri-mulish than ever. Big and mean and powerful, with the accent on mean.

"Don't think for a minute," he bellowed, "that you're going to get me mad enough to harm you so you can go tell your prayerman to report me to Mahrud! You can't tempt me into wrath! That would be a mortal sin, mortals!"

Shouting about my not being able to disturb his Olympian aloofness, he put his arm around my neck and with the other hand reached into my mouth and yanked out my upper plate.

"You and your mushmouthing annoy me!" he cried.

He released his choking grip around my neck and threw the plate into the shadows of the forest. I rushed toward the bush where I thought I'd seen the white teeth land. I got down on my hands and knees and groped frantically around, but I couldn't find them.

Alice's scream brought me upward. Too fast, for I bumped my head hard against a branch. Despite the pain, I turned back to see what was the trouble and charged through the brush. And I banged my shins hard against some object and fell flat on my face, knocking my breath out.

When I rose, I saw I'd tripped over my own watertank. I didn't stop to thank whatever gods might be for my good fortune. Instead, I picked the tank up and, running up to them, brought it crashing down against the back of his head. Soundlessly, he crumpled. I threw the container to one side and went to Alice.

"You all right?" I asked.

"Yes-s," she said, sobbing, and put her head on my shoulder.

I judged she was more frightened and mad than hurt. I patted her shoulder — she had beautifully smooth skin — and stroked her long black hair. But she wouldn't quit weeping.

"That filthy creep! First he ruins my sister, and now he tries to do the same to me."

"Huh?"

She raised her head to look at me. Look down at me, rather — she was an inch or two taller.

"Peggy was my half-sister, daughter by my father's first marriage. Her mother married a Colonel Rourke. But we were always close."

I wanted to hear more, but the immediate situation demanded my attention.

I turned Polivinosel over. His heart was still beating. Blood flowed from the gash in the back of his scalp, not the clear ichor you expect from a god's veins.

"Type O," said Alice. "Same as it was before. And don't worry about him. He deserves to die. He's a big stupid jerk of a Don Juan who got my sister in trouble and wouldn't..."

She stopped and gasped. I followed her stricken gaze and water had spilled into the dirt. And again I felt that sudden wrench of thirst. It was purely mental, of course, but that knowledge didn't make me less dry.

She put her hand to her throat and croaked, "All of a sudden, I'm thirsty."

"There's nothing we can do about it unless we find a source of uncontaminated water," I said. "And the longer we stand around talking about it, the thirstier we'll get."

The tank was empty. Stopping to check this sad fact, I saw light flash on something beneath a bush. I retrieved my upper plate. With my back toward Alice, I inserted the teeth and, feeling a little more assured, told her we'd better start walking on.

We did, but she still had the water problem on her mind. "Surely, there are wells and creeks that aren't infected. Only the river is filled with the Brew, isn't it?"

"If I were sure of that I'd not have taken the watertank," I was unkind enough to point out.

She opened her mouth to reply. But just then we heard voices down the path and saw the flare of approaching torches. Quickly, we stepped into the brush and hid.

The newcomers were singing. Their song owed its music to *The Battle Hymn of the Republic,* but the words were Latin. It was wretched Latin, for their accent paid allegiance to the beat of the original English meter. It didn't bother them at all. I doubt if many even knew what they were singing.

> "Orientis partibus
> Adventavit Asinus,
> Pulcher et Fortissimus,
> Sarcinis aptissimus.
> Orientis partibus
> Adventavit…Eeeeek!"

They had rounded the trail's bend and discovered their god, bleeding and unconscious.

Alice whispered, "Let's get out of here. If that mob catches us, they'll tear us apart."

I wanted to watch, to learn from their behavior how we should act when among the natives. I told her so, and she nodded. Despite our antagonism, I had to admit that she was intelligent and brave. If she was a little nervous, she had good reason to be.

These people didn't act at all as I'd thought they would. Instead of wailing and weeping, they stood away from him, huddled together, not quite sure what to do. I didn't see at first what caused their attitude. Then I realized from their expressions and whispers that they were afraid to interfere in the affairs of a demigod — even one as demi as Polivinosel.

The thing that italicized their indecision was their youthfulness. There wasn't a man or woman in the group who looked over twenty-five, and all were of superb physique.

Something made a loud cracking noise down the path behind us. Alice and I jumped, as did the whole group. They took off like a bunch of scared rabbits. I felt like joining them, but I stayed. I did, however, pray that this wouldn't be another nerve-rocking monster.

It was merely a naked native, a tall lean one with a long thin nose, who looked as if he ought to be teaching in some college. The effect was intensified by the fact that he had his nose in a book. As I've said, the moonlight was strong enough for reading, but I hadn't really expected anyone to take advantage of it.

His scholarly appearance was somewhat marred by the dead squirrel, large as a collie, which hung around his neck and over his shoulders. He had been hunting, I suppose, though I'd never heard of hunting squirrels in the dark. Moreover, he carried no weapons.

All of this, except for the squirrel's size, was surprising. I'd seen camera shots of the great beasts taken along the Area's edge.

I watched him closely to see what he'd do when he saw Polivinosel. He disappointed me. When he came to the prostrate form, he did not hesitate or give any sign that he had seen the god except to lift his feet over the outstretched legs. His nose remained dipped in the book.

I took Alice's hand. "Come on. We're following him."

We walked behind the reader for perhaps a half-mile. When I thought it was safe to stop him, I called out to him. He halted and put his squirrel on the ground and waited for me.

I asked him if he had noticed Polivinosel lying on the path.

Puzzled, he shook his head.

"I saw you step over him," I said.

"I stepped over nothing," he insisted. "The path was perfectly clear." He peered closely at me. "I can see you're a newcomer. Perhaps you've had your first taste of the Brew. Sometimes, at first, it gives strange sensations and visions. Takes a little time to get adjusted to it, you know."

I said nothing about that, but I did argue with him about Polivinosel. Not until I mentioned the name, however, did he look enlightened. He smiled in a superior manner and looked down his long nose.

"Ah, my good man, you mustn't believe everything you hear, you know. Just because the majority, who have always been ignorami and simpletons, choose to explain the new phenomena in terms of ancient superstition is no reason for an intelligent man such as yourself to put any credence in them. I suggest you discard anything you hear — with the exception of what I tell you, of course — and use the rational powers that you were lucky enough to be born with and to develop in some university, providing, that is, you didn't go to some institution which is merely a training ground for members of the Chamber of

Commerce, Rotary, Odd Fellows, Knights of Columbus, Shriners, or the Lions, Moose, Elk, and other curious beasts. I scarcely — "

"But I *saw* Polivinosel!" I said, exasperated. "And if you hadn't lifted your feet, you'd have fallen over him!"

Again, he gave a superior smile. "Tut, tut! Self-hypnotism, mass delusion, something of that sort. Perhaps you are a victim of suggestion. Believe me, there are many unsettling things in this valley. You mustn't allow yourself to be bamboozled by the first charlatan who comes along and has an easy — if fantastic — explanation for all this."

"What's yours?" I challenged.

"Dr. Durham invented some sort of machine that generates the unknown chemical with which he is now infecting the Illinois River. And eventually, we hope, the waters of the world. One of its properties is a destruction of many of the sociologically and psychologically conditioned reflexes which some term inhibitions, mores, or neuroses. And a very good thing, too. It also happens to be a universal antibiotic and tonic — such a combination! — besides a number of other things, not all of which I approve.

"However, he has, I must admit, done away with such societal and politico-economic structurologies and agents as factories, shops, doctors, hospitals, schools — which have hitherto devoted most of their time and energy to turning out half-educated morons — bureaucracies, automobiles, churches, movies, advertising, distilleries, soap operas, armies, prostitutes, and innumerable other institutions until recently considered indispensable.

"Unfortunately, the rationalizing instinct in man is very hard to down, as is the power-drive. So you have charlatans posing as prophets and setting up all sorts of new churches and attracting the multitudes in all their moronic simplicity and pathetic eagerness to grasp at some explanation for the unknown."

I wanted to believe him, but I knew that the professor had neither ability nor money enough to build such a machine.

"What is the peasants' explanation for the Brew?" I asked.

"They have none except that it comes from the Bottle," said the Rational Man. "They swear that Durham derives his powers from this Bottle, which, by description, is nothing more than a common everyday beer bottle. Some declare, however, that it bears, *in stiacciato*, the image of a bull."

Guilt brought sweat out on my forehead. So, it *had* been my gift! And I'd thought I was playing a harmless little hoax on my likable but daffy old Classical-Lit prof!

"That story is probably derived from his name," I said hastily. "After all, his students used to call him 'Bull.' It wasn't only the fact that his name was Durham. His wife led him around with a ring in his nose, and—"

"In which case, he fooled his students," said the Rational Man. "For he was, beneath that mild and meek exterior, a prize bull, a veritable stallion, a lusty old goat. As you may or may not know, he has any number of nymphs stabled in his so-called Flower Palace, not to mention beautiful Peggy Rourke, now known as the—"

Alice gasped. "Then she *is* living! And with Durham!"

He raised his eyebrows. "Well that depends upon whether or not you listen to these charlatans. Some of them would have it that she has become transfigured in some mystical-muddled manner—*multiplied*, they call it—and is each and every one of those nymphs in Mahrud's seraglio, yet is in some way none of them and exists in essence only."

He shook his head and said, "Oh, the rationalizing species that must invent gods and dogmas!"

"Who's Mahrud?" I asked.

"Why, Durham spelled backward, of course. Don't you know that there is a tendency in every religion to avoid pronouncing the True Name? However, I believe that those fakers, the Scrambled Men, invented the name, mainly because they couldn't say it right. They insisted the predeity name be distinguished from the Real One. It caught on fast, probably because it sounded so Oriental and, therefore, in the minds of these peons, mystical."

I was getting so much data all at once that I was more mixed up than ever.

"Haven't you ever seen Mahrud?" I asked.

"No, and I never shall. Those so-called gods just don't exist, any more than the Allegory or the Ass. Nobody with a rational mind could believe in them. Unfortunately, the Brew, despite its many admirable qualities, does have a strong tendency to make one illogical, irrational, and susceptible to suggestion."

He tapped his high forehead and said, "But I accept all the good things and reject the others. I'm quite happy."

Shortly after this, we came out on a country road I recognized.

The Rational Man said, "We'll be coming soon to my house. Would you two care to stop? We'll have this squirrel to eat and lots of Brew from the well in the backyard. Some of my friends will be there, and we'll have a nice intellectual talk before the orgy starts. You'll find them congenial—they're all atheists or agnostics."

I shuddered at the idea of being asked to drink the hated Liquor. "Sorry," I said. "We must be going. But tell me, as a matter of curiosity, how you caught that squirrel. You're not carrying any weapon."

"Can't," he replied, waving his book.

"Can't? Why not?"

"No, not can't. K-a-n-t. Kant. You see, the Brew has had this extraordinary effect on stimulating certain animals' growth. More than that, it has, I'm sure, affected their cerebral systems. They seem much more intelligent than before. A combination of increase in size of brain and change in organization of neurons, probably. Whatever the effect, the change has been most remarkable in rodents. A good thing, too. Wonderful source of meat, you know.

"Anyway," he continued, as he saw my increasing impatience, "I've found that one doesn't need a gun, which no longer explodes in this area, anyway, nor a bow and arrow. All one has to do is locate an area abundant in squirrels and sit down and read aloud. While one is both enjoying and educating oneself, the squirrel, attracted by one's monotonous voice, descends slowly from his tree and draws nearer.

"One pays no attention to him — one reads on. The beast sits close to one, slowly waving its bushy tail, its big black eyes fixed on one. After a while, one rises, closes the book, and picks up the squirrel, which is by now completely stupefied and never comes out of its state, not even when one takes it home and cuts it throat.

"I've found by experiment that one gets the best results by reading *The Critique of Pure Reason*. Absolutely stuns them. However, rabbits, for some reason, are more easily seduced by my reading Henry Miller's *Tropic of Capricorn*. In the French translation, of course. Friend of mine says that the best book for the birds is Hubbard's *Dianetics*, but one ought to take pride in one's tools, you know. I've always caught my pheasants and geese with *Three Contributions to the Theory of Sex*."

We came to his estate and said good-by to him. Stepping up our pace, we walked for several miles past the many farmhouses along the gravel road. Some of these had burned down, but their occupants had simply moved into the barn. Or, if that had gone up in flames, had erected a lean-to.

"Photographs from Army balloons have shown that a good many houses in the city have burned down," I said. "Not only that, the grass is literally growing in the streets again. I've been wondering where the burned-out people were living, but this shows how they manage. They live like savages."

"Well, why not?" asked Alice. "They don't seem to have to work very hard to live in abundance. I've noticed we haven't been bitten by mosquitoes, so noxious insects must have been exterminated. Sanitation shouldn't bother them—the Brew kills all diseases, if we're to believe that squirrel-reader. They don't have much refuse in the way of tin cans, paper, and so on to get rid of. They all seem very happy and hospitable. We've had to turn down constant invitations to stop and eat and drink some Brew. And even," she added with a malicious smile, "to participate in orgies afterward. That seems to be quite a respectable word now. I noticed that beautiful blonde back at the last farm tried to drag you off the road. You'll have to admit that that couldn't have happened Outside."

"Maybe I *am* bald," I snarled, "but I'm not so damned repulsive that no good-looking girl could fall in love with me. I wish I had a photo of Bernadette to show you. Bernadette and I were just on the verge of getting engaged. She's only thirty and—"

"Has she got all her teeth?"

"Yes, she has," I retorted. "She didn't get hit in the mouth by a mortar fragment and then lose the rest of her upper teeth through an infection, with no antibiotics available because enemy fire kept her in a foxhole for five days."

I was so mad I was shaking.

Alice answered softly, "Dan, I'm sorry I said that. I didn't know."

"Not only that," I plunged on, ignoring her apology. "What have you got against me besides my teeth and hair and the fact that I thought of this conditioning idea and my superiors—including the President—thought enough of my abilities to send me into this area without ten thousand Marines paving the way for me? As far as that goes, why were you sent with me? Was it because your father happens to be a general and wanted to grab some glory for you and him by association with me? If that isn't militaristic parasitism, what is? And furthermore..."

I raved on, and every time she opened her mouth, I roared her down. I didn't realize how loud I was until I saw a man and a woman standing in the road ahead of us, watching intently. I shut up at once, but the damage was done.

As soon as we were opposite them, the man said, "Newcomer, you're awfully grumpy." He held out a bottle to me. "Here, drink. It's good for what ails you. We don't have any harsh words in Mahrudland."

I said, "No, thanks," and tried to go around them, but the woman, a brunette who resembled a cross between the two Russells, Jane and Lillian, grabbed me around my neck and said, "Aw, come on, skinhead, I think you're cute. Have a drink and come along with us. We're going to a fertility ceremony at Jonesy's farm. Polivinosel himself'll be there. He's deigning to mix with us mortals for tonight. And you can make love with me and ensure a good crop. I'm one of Poli's nymphs, you know."

"Sorry," I said. "I've got to go."

I felt something wet and warm flooding over my scalp. For a second, I couldn't guess what it was. But when I smelled the hop-like Brew, I knew! And I responded with all the violence and horror the stuff inspired in me. Before the man could continue pouring the liquid over my head, I tore the woman's grip loose and threw her straight into the face of her companion. Both went down.

Before they could rise, I grabbed Alice's hand and fled with her down the road.

After we had run about a quarter of a mile, I had to slow to a walk. My heart was trying to beat its way out of my chest, and my head was expanding to fill the dome of the sky. Even my setting-up exercises hadn't fitted me for this.

However, I didn't feel so bad when I saw that Alice, young and fit as she was, was panting just as hard.

"They're not chasing us," I said. "Do you know, we've penetrated this area so easily, I wonder how far a column of Marines could have gone if they'd come in tonight. Maybe it would have been better to try an attack this way."

"We've tried four already," said Alice. "Two by day, two by night. The first three marched in and never came back, and you saw what happened to the last."

We walked along in silence for a while. Then I said, "Look, Alice, I blew my top a while ago, and we almost got into trouble. So why don't we agree to let bygones be bygones and start out on a nice fresh foot?"

"Nothing doing! I will refrain from quarreling, but there'll be none of this buddy-buddy stuff. Maybe, if we drank this Brew, I might get to liking you. But I doubt if even that could do it."

I said nothing, determined to keep my mouth shut if it killed me.

Encouraged by my silence—or engaged—she said, "Perhaps we might end up by drinking the Brew. Our water is gone, and if you're as thirsty as I am, you're on fire. We'll be at least fourteen hours without water, maybe twenty. And we'll be walking all the time. What happens when we just have to have water and there's nothing but the river to drink from? It won't be as if the stuff was poison.

"As a matter of fact, we know we'll probably be very happy. And that's the worst of it. That X substance, or Brew, or whatever you want to call it, is the most insidious drug ever invented. Its addicts not only seem to be permanently happy, they benefit in so many other ways from it."

I couldn't keep silent any longer. "That's dangerous talk!"

"Not at all, *Mister* Temper. Merely the facts."

"I don't like it!"

"What are *you* so vehement about?"

"Why?" I asked, my voice a little harder. "There's no reason why I should be ashamed. My parents were hopheads. My father died in the state hospital. My mother was cured, but she burned to death when the restaurant she was cooking in caught fire. Both are buried in the old Meltonville cemetery just outside Onaback. When I was younger, I used to visit their graves at night and howl at the skies because an unjust God had allowed them to die in such a vile and beastly fashion. I..."

Her voice was small but firm and cool. "I'm sorry, Dan, that that happened to you. But you're getting a little melodramatic aren't you?"

I subsided at once. "You're right. It's just that you seem to needle me so I want to —"

"Bare your naked soul? No, thanks, Dan. It's bad enough to have to bare our bodies. I don't want to make you sore, but there's not much comparison between the old narcotics and this Brew."

"There's no degeneration of the body of the Brewdrinker? How do you *know* there isn't? Has this been going on long enough to tell? And if everybody's so healthy and harmless and happy, why did Polivinosel try to rape you?"

"I'm certainly not trying to defend that Jackass," she said. "But, Dan, can't you catch the difference in the psychic atmosphere around here? There seem to be no barriers between men and women doing what they want with each other. Nor are they jealous of each other. Didn't you deduce, from what that Russell-type woman said, that Polivinosel had his choice of women and nobody objected? He probably took it for granted that I'd want to roll in the grass with him."

"All right, all right," I said. "But it's disgusting, and I can't understand why Durham made him a god of fertility when he seems to have hated him so."

"What do you know about Durham?" she countered.

I told her that Durham had been a short, bald, and paunchy little man with a face like an Irish leprechaun, with a wife who henpecked him till the holes showed, with a poet's soul, with a penchant for quoting Greek and Latin classics, with a delight in making puns, and with an unsuppressed desire to get his book of essays, *The Golden Age*, published.

"Would you say he had a vindictive mind?" she asked.

"No, he was very meek and forbearing. Why?"

"Well, my half-sister Peggy wrote that her steady, Polivinosel, hated Durham because he had to take his course to get a credit in the Humanities. Not only that, it was evident that Durham was sweet on Peggy. So, Polivinosel upset the doctor every time he got a chance. In fact, she mentioned that in her last letter to me just before she disappeared. And when I read in the papers that Durham was suspected of having murdered them, I wondered if he hadn't been harboring his hate for a long time."

"Not the doc," I protested. "He might get mad, but not for long."

"There you are," she said triumphantly. "He changed Polivinosel into a jackass, and then he got soft-hearted and forgave him. Why not? He had Peggy."

"But why wasn't Polivinosel changed back to a man then?"

"All I know is that he was majoring in Agriculture, and, if I'm to believe Peggy's letters, he was a Casanova."

"No wonder you were a little sarcastic when I gave my lecture," I said. "You knew more about those two than I did. But that doesn't excuse your reference to my baldness and false teeth."

She turned away. "I don't know why I said that. All I do know is that I hated you because you were a civilian and were being given such authority and entrusted with such an important mission."

I wanted to ask her if she'd changed her mind. Also I was sure that wasn't all there was to it, but I didn't press the point. I went on to tell her all I knew about Durham. The only thing I kept back was the most important. I had to sound her out before I mentioned that.

"Then the way you see it," she said, "is that everything that's been happening here fits this Doctor Boswell Durham's description of the hypothetical Golden Age?"

"Yes," I said. "He often used to lecture to us on what an opportunity the ancient gods lost. He said that if they'd taken the trouble to look at their mortal subjects, they'd have seen how to do away with disease, poverty, unhappiness, and war. But he maintained the ancient gods were really men who had somehow or other gotten superhuman powers and didn't know how to use them because they weren't versed in philosophy, ethics, or science.

"He used to say he could do better, and he would then proceed to give us his lecture entitled *How to Be a God and Like It*. It used to make us laugh, because you couldn't imagine anyone less divine than Durham."

"I know that," she said. "Peggy wrote me about it. She said that was what irked Polivinosel so. He didn't understand that the doctor was just projecting his dream world into classroom terms. Probably he dreamed of such a place so he could escape from his wife's nagging. Poor little fellow."

"Poor little fellow, my foot!" I snorted. "He's done just what he said he wanted to do, hasn't he? How many others can say the same, especially on such a scale?"

"No one," she admitted. "But tell me, what was Durham's main thesis in *The Golden Age*?"

"He maintained that history showed that the so-called common man, Mr. Everyman, is a guy who wants to be left alone and is quite pleased if only his mundane life runs fairly smoothly. His ideal is an existence with no diseases, plenty of food and amusement and sex and affection, no worry about paying bills, just enough work to keep from getting bored with all play and someone to do his thinking for him. Most adults want a god of some sort to run things for them while they do just what they please."

"Why," exclaimed Alice, "he isn't any better than Hitler or Stalin!"

"Not at all," I said. "He *could* bring about Eden as we can see by looking around us. And he didn't believe in any particular ideology or in using force. He..."

I stopped, mouth open. I'd been defending the professor!

Alice giggled. "Did you change your mind?"

"No," I said. "Not at all. Because the professor, like my dictator, must have changed *his* mind. He *is* using force. Look at Polivinosel."

"He's no example. He always was an ass, and he still is. And how do we know he doesn't *like* being one?"

I had no chance to reply. The eastern horizon was lit up by a great flash of fire. A second or two later, the sound of the explosion reached us.

We were both shocked. We had come to accept the idea that such chemical reactions just didn't take place in this valley.

Alice clutched my hand and said sharply. "Do you think the attack has started ahead of schedule? Or is that one we weren't told about?"

"I don't think so. Why would an attack be launched around here? Let's go and see what's up."

"You know, I'd have thought that was lightning, except that — well, it was just the opposite of lightning."

"The negative, you mean?" I asked her.

She nodded. "The streak was — black."

"I've seen lightning streaks that branched out like trees," I said. "But this is the first tree that I ever..." I stopped and murmured. "No, that's crazy. I'll wait until I get there before I make any more comments."

We left the gravel road and turned right onto a paved highway. I recognized it as the state route that ran past the airfield and into Meltonville, about a mile and a half away. Another explosion lit up the eastern sky, but this time we saw it was much closer than we had first thought.

We hurried forward, tense, ready to take to the woods if danger threatened. We had traveled about half a mile when I stopped so suddenly that Alice bumped into me. She whispered, "What is it?"

"I don't remember that creekbed ever being there," I replied slowly. "In fact, I *know* it wasn't there. I took a lot of hikes along here when I was a Boy Scout."

And there it was. It came up from the east, from Onaback's general direction, and cut southwest, away from the river. It slashed through the state highway, leaving a thirty-foot gap in the road. Somebody had dragged two long tree trunks across the cut and laid planks between them to form a rough bridge.

We crossed it and walked on down the highway, but another explosion to our left told us we were off the trail. This one, very close, came from the edge of a large meadow that I remembered had once been a parking lot for a trucking company

Alice sniffed and said, "Smell that burning vegetation?"

"Yes." I pointed to the far side of the creek where the moon shone on the bank. "Look at those."

Those were the partly burned and shattered stalks and branches of plants about the size of pine trees. They were scattered about forty feet apart. Some lay against the bank; some were stretched along the bottom of the creekbed.

What did it mean? The only way to find out was to investigate. So, as we came abruptly to the creek's end, which was surrounded by a ring of about a hundred people, we tried to elbow through to see what was so interesting.

We never made it, for at that moment a woman screamed, "He put in too much Brew!"

A man bellowed, "Run for your lives!"

The night around us was suddenly gleaming with bodies and clamorous with cries. Everybody was running and pushing everybody else to make room. Nevertheless, in spite of their reckless haste, they were laughing as if it was all a big joke. It was a strange mixture of panic and disdain for the panic.

I grabbed Alice's hand and started running with them. A man came abreast of us and I shouted, "What's the danger?"

He was a fantastic figure, the first person I had seen with any clothing on. He wore a red fez with a tassel and a wide green sash wound around his waist. A scimitar was stuck through it at such an angle it looked like a ducktail-shaped rudder. The illusion was furthered by the speed at which he was traveling.

When he heard my shout, he gave me a wild look that contributed to the weirdness of his garb and shouted something.

"Huh?"

Again he yelled at me and sped on.

"What'd he say?" I panted at Alice. "I'll swear he said 'Horatio Hornblower.'"

"Sounded more like 'Yorassiffencornblows,'" she replied.

That was when we found out why the crowd was running like mad. A lion the size of a mountain roared behind us — a blast knocked us flat on our faces — a wave of hot air succeeded the shock — a hail of rocks and clods of dirt pelted us. I yelped as I was hit in the back of one leg. For a moment, I could have sworn my leg was broken.

Alice screamed and grabbed me around the neck. "Save me!"

I'd have liked to, but who was going to save *me?*

Abruptly, the rocks quit falling, and the yells stopped. Silence, except for the drawing of thankful breaths. Then, giggles and yelps of pure delight and calls back and forth and white bodies were shining in the moonlight as they rose like ghosts from the grass. Fear among these uninhibited people could not last long. They were already joshing each other about the way they'd run and then were walking back to the cause of their flight.

I stopped a woman, a beautiful buxom wench of twenty-five — all the adult female Brew addicts, I later found, were pretty and well-shaped and looked youthful — and I said, "What happened?"

"Ah, the fool Scrambler put too much Brew in the hole," she replied, smiling. "Anybody could see what'd happen. But he wouldn't listen to us, and his own buddies are as scrambled as he is, thanks to Mahrud."

When she uttered *that* name, she made *that* sign. These people, no matter how lightly and irreverently they behaved in other matters, were always respectful toward their god Mahrud.

I was confused. "He? Who?" I said, inelegantly.

"He *haw?*" she brayed and my body turned cold as I thought she was referring to Polivinosel. But she was merely mocking the form of my question. "The Scrambled Men, of course, Baldy." Looking keenly at me in a single sweep that began at my feet and ended at the top of my head, she added, "If it weren't for that, I'd think you hadn't tasted the Brew yet."

I didn't know what she meant by *that*. I looked upward, because she had pointed in that direction. But I couldn't see anything except the clear sky and the huge distorted moon.

I didn't want to continue my questioning and expose myself as such a newcomer. I left the woman and, with Alice, followed the crowd back. Their destination was the end of the creek, a newly blasted hole which showed me in a glance how the dry bed had so suddenly come into existence. Somebody has carved it out with a series of the tremendous blasts we'd heard.

A man brushed by me. His legs pumped energetically, his body was bent forward, and one arm was crooked behind his back. His right hand clutched the matted hair on his chest. Jammed sideways on his head was one of those plumed cocked hats you see the big brass of men's lodges wear during parades. A belt around his otherwise naked waist supported a sheathed sword. High-heeled cowboy boots completed his garb. He frowned deeply and carried, in the hand behind his back, a large map.

"Uh — Admiral," I called out.

He paid no attention but plowed ahead.

"General!"

Still he wouldn't turn his head.

"Boss. Chief. Hey, *you!*"

He looked up. "*Winkled tupponies?*" he queried.

"Huh?"

Alice said, "Close your mouth before your plate falls out, and come along."

We got to the excavation's edge before the crowd became too thick to penetrate. It was about thirty feet across and sloped steeply down to the center, which was about twenty feet deep. Exactly in the middle reared an enormous, blackened, and burning plant. Talk about Jack and your beanstalk. This *was* a cornstalk, ears, leaves, and all, and it was at least fifty feet high. It leaned perilously and would, if touched with a finger, fall flaming to the ground. Right on top of us, too, if it happened to be toppling our way. Its roots were as exposed as the plumbing of a half-demolished tenement.

The dirt had been flung away from the roots and piled up around the hole to complete the craterlike appearance of the excavation. It looked as if a meteor had plowed into the ground.

That's what I thought at first glance. Then I saw from the way the dirt scattered that the meteor must have come up from below.

There was no time to think through the full implication of what I saw, for the huge cornstalk began its long-delayed fall. I was busy, along with everybody else, in running away. After it had fallen with a great crash, and after a number of the oddly dressed men had hitched it up to a ten-horse team and dragged it away to one side, I returned with Alice. This time I went down into the crater. The soil was hard and dry under my feet. Something had sucked all the water out and had done it fast, too, for the dirt in the adjoining meadow was moist from a recent shower.

Despite the heat contained in the hole, the Scrambled Men swarmed in and began working with shovels and picks upon the western wall. Their leader, the man with the admiral's hat, stood in their middle and held the map before him with both hands, while he frowned blackly at it. Every once in a while he'd summon a subordinate with a lordly gesture, point out something on the map, and then designate a spot for him to use his shovel.

"*Olderen croakish richbags,*" he commanded.

"*Eniatipac nom, iuo, iuo,*" chanted the subordinate.

But the digging turned up nothing they were looking for. And the people standing on the lip of the crater—like the big city crowds that watch steam-shovel excavating—hooted and howled and shouted unheeded advice at the Scrambled Men. They passed bottles of Brew back and forth and had a good time, though I thought some of their helpful hints to the workers were definitely in bad taste.

Suddenly, the semi-Napoleon snorted with rage and threw his hands up so the map fluttered through the air.

"*Shimsham the rodtammed shipshuts!*" he howled.

"*Rerheuf niem, lohwaj!*" his men shouted.

"*Frammistab the wormbattened frigatebarns!*"

The result of all this was that everybody quit digging except for one man. He was dressed in a plug hat and two dozen slave bracelets. He dropped a seed of some sort within a six-foot-deep hole cut almost horizontally into the bank. He filled this with dirt, tamped it, then drove a thin wire down through the soil. Another man, wearing harlequin spectacles in which the glass had been knocked out, and a spiked Prussian officer's helmet from the First World War, withdrew the wire and poured a cascade of Brew from a huge vase. The thirsty soil gulped it eagerly.

There was silence as the Scrambled Men and the spectators intently watched the ceremony. Suddenly a woman on the excavation's edge shouted, "He's putting in too much again! Stop the fool!"

The Napoleon looked up fiercely and reprimanded, "*Fornicoot the onus squeered.*"

Immediately, the ground rumbled, the earth shook, the crust quivered. Something was about to pop, and it was going to pop loud!

"Run for the hills! This time he's really done it!"

I didn't know what he'd done, but it didn't seem a time to be standing around asking questions.

We ran up the slope and out onto the meadow and across it. When we were halfway to the road, I overcame the contagious panic long enough to risk a glance over my shoulder. And I saw *it*.

You've heard of explosions flowering? Well, this was the first time I had ever seen the reverse — a colossal sunflower exploding, energized and accelerated fantastically in its growth by an overdose of that incredible stimulant, the Brew. It attained the size of a Sequoia within a split-second, its stalk and head blasting the earth in a hurry to get out. It was reaching high into the sky and burning, because of the tremendous energy poured out in its growth.

And then, its lower parts having been denied a grip because its foundations had been thrust aside, it was toppling, toppling, a flaming tower of destruction.

Alice and I got out of the way. But we barely made it and, for a second, I was sure that that titanic blazing hulk would smash us like beetles beneath a hard leather heel.

It went *whoosh!* And then *karoomp!* And we fell forward, stunned, unable to move. Or so we thought. The next instant we both leaped from our paralysis, bare rumps blistered.

Alice screamed. "Oh, God, Dan! It hurts!"

I knew that, for I had been burned too in that region. I think our expedition would have come to a bad end right then and there, for we needed immediate medical attention and would have had to go back to HQ to get it. These primitives had evidently forgotten all knowledge of up-to-date healing.

True enough — but they had forgotten because they no longer needed the knowledge. Attracted by our pitiful plight, two men, before I could object, had thrown the contents of two buckets over our backs.

I yelped with terror, but I had no place to run except back into the fire. Even the Brew was better than that. And I didn't get any in or even near my mouth.

Nevertheless, I was going to protest angrily at this horse-play while we were in such agony. But before I could say anything, I no longer felt pain.

I couldn't see what was happening to me, but I could see Alice's reaction. Her back was toward me, and she had quit whimpering.

Beneath the moist film of Brew, the blisters had fallen off, and a new healthy pink shone through.

Alice was so overcome, she even forgot her feud with me long enough to put her head on my chest and weep, "Oh, Dan, Dan, isn't it wonderful?"

I didn't want to give this evil drug too much credit. After all, like any narcotic, it had its beneficial effects if used correctly, but it could be horribly vicious if mishandled.

I said, "Come on, we have to go back," and I took her hand and led her to the new crater. I felt I *must* solve the puzzle of the Scrambled Men. And I thought of the credit I'd get for suggesting a new method of warfare — dropping bombcases filled with Brew and seeds from balloons. And what about cannon shooting shells whose propulsive power would also be seed and Brew? Only — how would you clean the cannon out afterward? You'd have to have a tree surgeon attached to every artillery team. Of course, you could use the rocket principle for your missiles. Only — wouldn't a Brobdingnagian pansy or cornstalk trailing out behind create an awful drag and a suddenly added weight? Wouldn't you have to train botanists to be aerodynamicists, or vice versa, and...?

I rejected the whole idea. The brass at HQ would never believe me.

The Scrambled Men worked quickly and efficiently and with all the added vigor Brew-drinking gave. Inside of fifteen minutes, they had put out the fire and had then pulled the smoldering trunk out of the way. They at once began digging into the slopes and bottom of the excavation.

I watched them. They seemed to be obeying the orders of the man in the admiral's hat, and were continually conferring with him and their fellow workers. But not a single one could understand what the other was saying. All effective communication was done by facial expressions and gestures. Yet none would admit that to any of the others.

Well, I thought, this was scarcely a novelty, though I had never seen it carried out on such a thorough scale. And what — or who — was responsible?

Again, wearily this time, I asked a spectator what was going on. These people seemed to be incapable of making a serious statement, but there was always the chance that I'd find somebody who was an exception.

"I'll tell you, stranger. These men are living evidences of the fact that it doesn't pay to corrupt religion for your own purposes."

He drank from a flask he carried on a chain around his neck and then offered me a slug. He looked surprised at my refusal but took no offense.

"These were the leaders of the community just before Mahrud manifested himself as the Real Bull. You know — preachers, big and little businessmen, newspaper editors, gamblers, lawyers, bankers, union business agents, doctors, book reviewers, college professors. The men who are supposed to know how to cure your diseases social, economic, financial, administrative, psychological, spiritual, and so on, into the deep dark night. They knew the Right Word, comprehend? The Word that'd set Things straight, understand?

"The only trouble was that after the Brew began to flow freely, nobody who'd drunk from the Holy Bottle would pay any attention to these pillars of the community. They tried hard for a long time. Then, seeing which way the tide was inevitably foaming, they decided that maybe they'd better get in on a good thing. After all, if everybody was doing it, it must be the correct thing to do.

"So, after drinking enough Brew to give them courage, but not enough to change them into ordinary fun-loving but Mahrud-fearing citizens, they announced they were the prophets of a new religion. And from then on, according to their advertisements, none but them was fit to run the worship of the Big Bull. Of course, Sheed the Weather Prophet and Polivinosel and the Allegory ignored them, and so were denounced as false gods.

"Makes you laugh, doesn't it? But that's the way it goes. And that's the way it went until Mahrud — bibulous be his people forever — got mad. He announced, through Sheed, that these pillars of the community were just dummy-prophets, fakes. As punishment, he was going to give them a gift, as he had earlier done to the Dozen Diapered Darlings.

"So he said, in effect, 'You've been telling the people that you, and only you, have possession of the Real Bull, the Right Word. Well, you'll have it. Only it'll be the Word that nobody but you can understand, and to every other man it'll be a strange tongue. Now — scram!'

"But after he'd watched these poor characters stumbling around trying to talk to each other and the people and getting madder than the hops in the Brew or else sadder than the morning-after, Mahrud felt sorry. So he said, 'Look, I'll give you a chance. I've hidden the key to your troubles somewhere in this valley. Search for it. If you find it, you'll be cured. And everybody will understand you, understand?'

"So he gave them a map — all of them, mind you — but this half-dressed Napoleon here grabbed the map, and he kept it by virtue of being the most un-understandable of the bunch. And, ever since, he's been directing the search for the key that'll unscramble them."

"That's why they're doing all this blasting and digging?" I asked, dazed.

"Yes, they're following the map," he said, laughing.

I thanked him and walked up behind the man with the admiral's hat and sword. I looked over his shoulder. The map was covered with long squiggly lines and many shorter branches. These, I supposed, were the lines he was following in his creekbed-making.

He looked around at me. "*Symfrantic gangleboys?*"

"You said it," I choked, and then I had to turn and walk away. "That map is a chart of the human nervous system," I gasped to Alice. "And he's following one of the branches of the vagus nerve."

"The *wandering* nerve," murmured Alice. "Or is it the *wondering* nerve? But what could all this mean?"

As we began our climb from the pit, I said, "I think we're seeing the birth-pangs of a new mythology. One of the demigods is based upon a famous comic strip character. Another is formed in the image of a pun on the translation of his name — though his new form does correspond to his lustful, asinine character. And we see that the chief deity bases his worship — and at least one of his epiphanies — on his mortal nickname. All this makes me wonder upon what foundations the old-time pantheons and myth were built. Were they also originally based on such incongruous and unlikely features?"

"Daniel Temper!" Alice snapped. "You talk as if you believed the old pagan gods once existed and as if this Mahrud actually is a god!"

"Before I came here, I'd have laughed at any such theory," I said. "How do *you* explain what you've seen?"

We climbed up in silence. At the edge, I turned for one more glimpse of the Scrambled Men, the object lesson designed by Mahrud. They were digging just as busily as ever paying no attention to the ribald comments of the spectators. The funny thing about this, I thought, was

that these unscrambled men had not yet caught on to the fact that the
Scrambled Men were more than a wacky sect, that they were symbols
of what the spectators must themselves do if they wished to travel
beyond their own present carefree and happy but unprogressive state.

As plainly as the ears on the head of the Ass-God, the plight of
these frantically digging sons of Babel said to everybody, "Look within
yourselves to find the key."

That advice was probably uttered by the first philosopher among
the cavemen.

I caught the glint of something metallic almost buried in the dirt of
the slope. I went back and picked it up. It was a long-handled silver
screwdriver.

If I hadn't known my old teacher so well, I don't think I ever would
have understood its presence. But I'd been bombarded in his classes
with his bizarre methods of putting things over. So I knew that I held
in my hand another of his serious jokes—a utensil designed to take its
place in the roster of myths springing up within this Valley Olympus.

You had the legend of Pandora's Box, of Philemon and Baucis'
Pitcher, Medusa's Face, Odin's Pledged Eye. Why not the Silver Screwdriver?

I explained to Alice. "Remember the gag about the boy who was
born with a golden screw in his navel? How all his life he wondered
what it was for? How *ashamed* he was because he was different from
anybody else and had to keep it hidden? Remember how he finally
found a psychiatrist who told him to go home and dream of the fairy
queen? And how Queen Titania slid down on a moonbeam and gave
him a silver screwdriver? And how, when he'd unscrewed the golden
screw from his navel, he felt so happy about being normal and being
able to marry without making his bride laugh at him? Remember, he
then forgot all his vain speculations upon the purpose of that golden
screw? And how, very happy, he got up from his chair to reach for a
cigarette? And his derrière, deprived of its former fastening, dropped
off?"

"You don't mean it?" she breathed.

"But I do! How do we know the tale of the Golden Apples or the
Golden Fleece didn't have their origin in jokes and that they later ac-
quired a symbolic significance?"

She had no answer to that, any more than anybody did.

"Aren't you going to give it to the Scrambled Men?" she asked.
"It'd save them all this blasting and digging. And they could settle
down and quit talking gibberish."

"I imagine they've stumbled over it a hundred times before and kicked it to one side, refusing to recognize its meaning."

"Yes, but what does it mean?"

Exasperatedly, I said, "It's another clue to the fact that they ought to look within themselves, that they ought to consider the nature of their punishment and the lesson to be derived from it."

We walked away. The whole incident had left me plunged in gloom. I seemed to be getting deeper and deeper into a murk furnished by a being who, in the far dim background, mocked me. Was it mere coincidence that we'd been met by the Allegory, that he'd given us his vaguely ominous advice?

I didn't have much time to think, for we came to the side road — which led to the State Hospital. I could look down it and see the white stones of the cemetery outside the high wire fence. I must have stood there longer than I thought, because Alice said, "What's the matter?"

"The State Hospital cemetery is just inside the fence. The Meltonville cemetery is on the other side. My father is buried in the state grounds; my mother lies in the village's cemetery. They are separated in death, as they were in life."

"Dan," she said softly, "we ought to get a few hours' sleep before we go on. We've walked a long way. Why don't we visit your parents' graves and then sleep there? Would you like that?"

"Very much. Thank you for the thought, Alice." The words came hard. "You're a pretty wonderful person."

"Not so much. It's merely the decent thing to do."

She would have to say that just when I was beginning to feel a little warmer toward her.

We went down the road. A big red-haired man walked toward us. He was all eyes for Alice, so much so that I expected the same sort of trouble we'd had with Polivinosel. But when he looked at me, he stopped, grinned, and burst into loud howls of laughter. As he passed me, I smelled his breath. It was loaded with the Brew.

"What's the matter with *him?*"

"I don't know," said Alice, looking at me. "Wait a minute! Of course! Polivinosel and the others must have known all the time that you were an Outsider!"

"Why?"

"Because you're bald! Have we seen any bald men? No! That's why this fellow laughed!"

"If that's so, I'm marked! All Polivinosel has to do is have his worshipers look for a skinhead."

"Oh, it's not that bad," she said. "You have to remember that Outsiders are constantly coming in, and that any number of ex-soldiers are in the process of changing. You could pass for one of those." She grabbed my hand. "Oh well, come along, let's get some sleep. Then we can think about it."

We came to the cemetery entrance. The shrubbery on either side of the stone arch had grown higher than my head. The iron gate in the arch was wide open and covered with rust. Inside, however, I did not see the expected desolate and wild expanse of tall weeds. They were kept trimmed by the goats and sheep that stood around like silvery statues in the moonlight.

I gave a cry and ran forward.

My mother's grave gaped like a big brown mouth. There was black water at the bottom, and her coffin was tilted on end. Evidently, it had been taken out and then slid carelessly back in. Its lid was open. It was empty.

Behind me, Alice said, "Easy, Dan. There's no cause for looking so alarmed."

"So *this* is your splendid people, Alice, the gods and nymphs of the New Golden Age. Grave-robbers! *Ghouls!*"

"I don't think so. They'd have no need or desire for money and jewels. Let's look around. There must be some other explanation."

We looked. We found Weepenwilly.

He was sitting with his back against a tombstone. He was so large and dark and quiet that he seemed to be cast out of bronze, a part of the monument itself. He looked like Rodin's *Thinker* — a *Thinker* wearing a derby hat and white loincloth. But there was something alive about him and, when he raised his head, we saw tears glistening in the moonlight.

"Could you tell me," I asked excitedly, "why all these graves are dug up?"

"Bless you, my bhoy," he said in a slight brogue. "Sure, now, and have you a loved one buried here?"

"My mother," I said.

His tears flowed faster. "Faith, bhoy, and is it so? Then you'll be happy when I tell you the glorious news. Me own dear wife was buried here, you know."

I didn't see anything about that to make me happy, but I kept quiet and waited.

"Yes, me bhoy — you'll pardon my calling you that, won't you? After all, I was a veteran o' the Spanish-American War, and I outrank you by quite a few years. In fact, if it hadn't been for the blessed ascent o'

Mahrud — may he stub his divine toe and fall on his glorious face, bless him — I would now be dead of old age and me bones resting in the boat along with me wife's, and so — "

"What boat?" I interrupted.

"What *boat?* Where have you been? Ah, yes, you're new." He pointed his finger at his head, to indicate my baldness, I suppose.

"Faith, bhoy, you must hurry to Onaback in the morning and see the boatload o'bones leave. Twill be big doings then, you can count on that, with lots o' Brew and barbecued beef and pork and enough love-making to last you for a week."

After repeated questioning, I learned that Mahrud had had the remains of the dead in all the graveyards of the Area dug up and trans-ported to Onaback. The next day, a boat carrying the bones would cross the Illinois and deposit the load upon the eastern shore. What would happen after that, not even the minor gods knew — or else would not tell — but everybody was sure that Mahrud intended to bring the dead back to life. And everybody was thronging into the city to witness such an event.

That news made me feel better. If there were to be many people on the roads and in the city itself, then it would be easy to stay lost in the crowds.

The man with the derby said, "As sure as they call me Weepenwilly, children, the All-Bull is going too far. He'll try to raise the dead, and he won't be able to do it. And then where will the people's faith in him be? Where will I be?"

He sobbed, "I'll be out o'work again, me position lost — me that served the Old God faithfully until I saw He was losing ground and that Mahrud was the up-and-coming deity nowadays. A God such as they had in the ancient days in Erin when gods was gods and men was giants. But now Mahrud — bull be his name, curse him — will lose face, and he'll never get it back. Then I'll be that most miserable o' all things, a prophet without honor. What's worse, I was just about to be pro-moted to a hemi-semi-demigod — I've been coming up fast all on ac-count o' me faithful and hard work and keeping me mouth shut — when this big promotional stunt has to enter the All-Bull's head. Why can't he leave well enough alone?"

At last, I got out of him that he wasn't so much afraid Mahrud would fail as he was that he might succeed.

"If Mahrud does clothe the old bones with new flesh, me everloving wife will be out looking for me, and me life won't be worth a pre-Brew nickel. She'll never forget nor forgive that 'twas me who pushed her down those steps ten years ago and broke her stringy neck. 'Twill make no difference to her that she'll come back better than ever, with a lovely new figure and a pretty face instead o' that hatchet. Not her, the black-hearted, stone-livered wrath o' God!

"Sure, and I've had an unhappy life ever since the day I opened me innocent blue eyes — untainted except for the old original sin, but Mahrud says that's no dogma o' his — and first saw the light o' day. Unhappy I've been, and unhappy I'll live. I can't even taste the sweet sting o' death — because, as sure as the sun rises in the east, as sure as Durham became a bull and swam the Illinois with the lovely Peggy on his back and made her his bride upon the high bluffs — I can't even die because me everloving wife would search out me bones and ship them to Mahrud and be standing there facing me when I arose."

I was getting weary of listening to this flow of hyperbole, interminable as the Illinois itself. I said, "Thank you, Mr. Weepenwilly, and good night. We've got a long trip ahead of us."

"Sure, me bhoy, and that's not me given name. 'Tis a nickname given me by the bhoys down at the town hall because..."

I heard no more. I went back to my mother's grave and lay down by it. I couldn't get to sleep, because Alice and Weepenwilly were talking. Then, just as I'd managed almost to drop off, Alice sat down by me. She insisted on retelling me the story Weepenwilly had just told her.

I'd seen his white loincloth, hadn't I? Well, if Weepenwilly had stood up, I'd have perceived the three-cornered fold of it. And I'd have seen its remarkable resemblance to early infant apparel. That resemblance was not coincidental, for Weepenwilly was one of the Dozen Diapered Darlings.

Moreover, if he had stood up, I'd have noticed the yellow glow that emanated from his posterior, the nimbus so much like a firefly's in color and position.

It seemed that, shortly after the Brew began taking full effect, when the people of Onaback had turned their backs to the outside world, numerous self-styled prophets had tried to take advantage of the new religion. Each had presented his own variation of an as-yet-misunderstood creed. Among them had been twelve politicians who had long been bleeding the city's treasury dry. Because it was some time before the Bottle's contents began affecting the nature of things noticeably, they had not been aware at first of what was happening.

The wheels of industry slowed by degrees. Grass and trees subtly encroached upon pavement. People gradually lost interest in the cares of life. Inhibitions were imperceptibly dissolved. Enmities and bitternesses and diseases faded. The terrors, burdens, and boredoms of life burned away as magically as the morning mist under the rising sun.

A time came when people quit flying to Chicago for business or pleasure. When nobody went to the library to take out books. When the typographers and reporters of the daily newspapers failed to show up for work. When the Earthgripper Diesel Company and Myron Malker's Distillery — biggest on earth of their kind, both of them — blew the final whistle. When people everywhere seemed to realize that all had been wrong with the world, but that it was going to be fine and dandy in the future.

About then, the mail-carriers quit. Frantic telegrams and letters were sent to Washington and the state capital — though from other towns, because the local operators had quit. This was when the Food and Drug Administration, and the Internal Revenue Bureau, and the F.B.I. sent agents into Onaback to investigate. These agents did not come back and others were sent in, only to succumb to the Brew.

The Brew had not yet reached its full potency, when Durham had just revealed himself, through the prophet Sheed, as Mahrud. There was still some opposition, and the most vigorous came from the twelve politicians. They organized a meeting in the courthouse square and urged the people to follow them in an attack on Mahrud. First they would march on Traybell University, where Sheed lived in the Meteorological Building.

"Then," said one of the twelve, shaking his fist at the long thin line of Brew geysering from the Bottle up on the hills, "we'll lynch this mad scientist who calls himself Mahrud, this lunatic we know is a crazy university professor and a reader of poetry and philosophy. Friends, citizens, Americans, if this Mahrud is indeed a god, as Sheed, another mad scientist claims, let him strike me with lightning! My friends and I dare him to!"

The dozen were standing on a platform in the courthouse yard. They could look down Main Street and across the river to the hills. They faced the east defiantly. No bellowings came, no lightnings. But in the next instant, the dozen were forced to flee ignominiously, never again to defy the All-Bull.

Alice giggled. "They were struck by an affliction which was not as devastating as lightning nor as spectacular. But it was far more demoralizing. Mahrud wished on them a disability which required them to wear diapers for much the same reason babies have to. Of course, this convinced the Dozen Diapered Darlings. But that brassy-nerved bunch of ex-ward-heelers switched right around and said they'd known all along that Mahrud was the Real Bull. They'd called the meeting so they could make a dramatic announcement of their change of heart. Now he'd given them a monopoly on divine revelation. If anybody wanted to get in touch with him, let them step up and pay on the line. They still hadn't realized that money was no good anymore.

"They even had the shortsightedness and the crust to pray to Mahrud for a special sign to prove their prophethood. And the All-Bull did send them signs of their sanctity. He gave them permanent halos, blazing yellow lights."

Sitting up and hugging her knees, Alice rocked back and forth with laughter. "Of course, the Dozen should have been ecstatically happy. But they weren't. For Mahrud had slyly misplaced their halos, locating them in a place where, if the Darlings wished to demonstrate their marks of sainthood, they would be forced to stand up.

"And, would you believe it, this thick-headed Dozen refuses to admit that Mahrud has afflicted them. Instead, they brag continually about their halos' location, and they attempt to get everybody else to wear diapers. They say a towel around the middle is as much a sign of a true believer in Mahrud as a turban or fez is that of a believer in Allah.

"Naturally, their real reason is that they don't want to be conspicuous. Not that they mind being outstanding. It's just that they don't want people to be reminded of their disability or their original sin."

Tears ran from her eyes. She choked with laughter.

I failed to see anything funny about it, and I told her so.

"You don't get it, Temper," she said. "This condition is curable. All the Darlings have to do is pray to Mahrud to be relieved of it, and they will be. But their pride won't let them. They insist it's a benefit and a sign of the Bull's favor. They suffer, yes, but they like to suffer. Just as Weepenwilly likes to sit on his wife's tombstone—as if that'd keep her under the ground—and wail about his misfortune. He and his kind wouldn't give up their punishment for the world—literally!"

She began laughing loudly again. I sat up and grabbed her shoulders and pulled her close to smell her breath. There was no hint of the Brew, so she hadn't been drinking from Weepenwilly's bottle. She was suffering from hysteria, plain and simple.

The normal procedure for bringing a woman back to normality is to slap her resoundingly upon the cheek. But in this case Alice turned the tables by slapping me first—resoundingly. The effect was the same. She quit laughing and glared at me.

I held my stinging cheek. "What was that for?"

"For trying to take advantage of me," she said.

I was so angry and taken aback that I could only stutter, "Why, I—, why, I—"

"Just keep your hands to yourself," she snapped. "Don't mistake my sympathy for love. Or think, because these Brew-bums have no inhibitions or discrimination, that I've also succumbed."

I turned my back on her and closed my eyes. But the longer I lay there, and the more I thought of her misinterpretation, the madder I became. Finally, boiling within, I sat up and said tightly, "Alice!"

She must not have been sleeping either. She raised up at once and stared at me, her eyes big. "What—what is it?"

"I forgot to give you this." I let her have it across the side of her face. Then, without waiting to see the effect of my blow, I lay down and turned my back again. For a minute, I'll admit, my spine was cold and tense, waiting for the nails to rake down my naked skin.

But nothing like that happened. First, there was the sort of silence that breathes. Then, instead of the attack, came a racking breath, followed by sobs, which sloped off into snifflings and the wiping of tears.

I stood it as long as I could. Then I sat up again and said, "All right, so maybe I shouldn't have hit you. But you had no business taking it for granted that I was trying to make love to you. Look, I know I'm repulsive to you, but that's all the more reason why I wouldn't be making a pass at you. I have some pride. And you don't exactly drive me out of my mind with passion, you know. What makes you think you're any Helen of Troy or Cleopatra?"

There I went. I was always trying to smooth things over, and every time I ended by roughing them up. Now she was mad and she showed it by getting up and walking off. I caught her as she reached the cemetery gate.

"Where do you think you're going?" I asked.

"Down to the foot of Main Street, Onaback, Illinois, and I'm bottling a sample of the Brew there. Then I'm reporting to my father as soon as possible."

"You little fool, you can't do that. You're supposed to stick with me."

She tossed her long black hair. "My orders don't say I have to. If, in my opinion, your presence becomes a danger to my mission, I may leave you. And I think you're a definite danger—if not to my mission, at least to me!"

I grabbed her wrist and whirled her around. "You're acting like a little girl, not like a major in the U.S. Marines. What's the matter with you?"

She tried to jerk her wrist loose. That made me madder, but when her fist struck me, I saw red. I wasn't so blinded that I couldn't find her cheek again with the flat of my hand. Then she was on me with a hold that would have broken my arm if I hadn't applied the counterhold. Then I had her down on her side with both her arms caught behind her back. This was where a good little man was better than a good big girl.

"All right," I gritted, "what is it?"

She wouldn't reply. She twisted frantically, though she knew she couldn't get loose and groaned with frustration

"Is it the same thing that's wrong with me?"

She quit struggling and said, very softly. "Yes, that's it."

I released her arms. She rolled over on her back, but she didn't try to get up. "You mean," I said, still not able to believe it, "that you're in love with me, just as I am with you?"

She nodded again. I kissed her with all the pent-up desire that I'd been taking out on her in physical combat a moment ago.

I said, "I still can't believe it. It was only natural for me to fall in love with you, even if you did act as if you hated my guts. But why did you fall in love with me? Or, if you can't answer that, why did you ride me?"

"You won't like this," she said. "I could tell you what a psychologist would say. We're both college graduates, professional people, interested in the arts and so on. That wouldn't take in the differences, or course. But what does that matter? It happened.

"I didn't want it to. I fought against it. And I used the reverse of the old Jamesian principle that, if you pretend to be something or to like something, you will be that something. I tried to act as if I loathed you."

"Why?" I demanded. She turned her head away, but I took her chin and forced her face to me. "Let's have it."

"You know I was nasty about your being bald. Well, I didn't really dislike that. Just the opposite—I loved it. And that was the whole trouble. I analyzed my own case and decided I loved you because I had an Electra complex. I—"

"You mean," I said, my voice rising, "that because I was bald like your father and somewhat older than you, you fell for me?"

"Well, no, not really. I mean that's what I told myself so I'd get over it. That helped me to pretend to hate you so that I might end up doing so."

Flabbergasted was no word for the way I felt. If I hadn't been lying on the ground, I'd have been floored. Alice Lewis was one of those products of modern times, so psychology-conscious that she tended to regard an uninhibited affection of parent and child as a sign that both ought to rush to the nearest psychoanalyst.

"I'm in a terrible fix," said Alice. "I don't know if you fulfill my father-image or if I'm genuinely in love with you. I think I am, yet…"

She put her hand up to stroke my naked scalp. Knowing what I did, I resented the caress. I started to jerk my head away, but she clamped her hand on it and exclaimed, "Dan, your scalp's *fuzzy!*"

I said, "Huh?" and ran my own palm over my head. She was right. A very light down covered my baldness.

"So," I said, delighted and shocked at the same time, "that's what the nymph meant when she pointed at my head and said that if it weren't for *that*, she'd think I hadn't tasted the Brew yet! The Brew that fellow poured on my head — *that's* what did it!"

I jumped up and shouted, "Hooray!"

And scarcely had the echoes died down than there was an answering call, one that made my blood chill. This was a loud braying laugh from far off, a bellowing hee-haw!

"Polivinosel!" I said. I grabbed Alice's hand, and we fled down the road. Nor did we stop until we had descended the hill that runs down into U.S. Route 24. There, puffing and panting from the half-mile run and thirstier than ever, we walked toward the city of Onaback, another half-mile away.

I looked back from time to time, but I saw no sign of the Ass. There was no guarantee he wasn't on our trail, however. He could have been lost in the great mass of people we'd encountered. These carried baskets and bottles and torches and were, as I found out from conversation with a man, latecomers going to view the departure of the bone-boat from the foot of Main Street.

"Rumor says that Mahrud — may his name be bull — will raise the dead at the foot of the hill the Fountain of the Bottle spurts from. Whether that's so or not, we'll all have fun. Barbecue, Brew, and bundling make the world go round."

I couldn't argue with that statement. They certainly were the principal amusements of the natives.

During our progress down Adams Street, I learned much about the valley's setup. My informant was very talkative, as were all his fellow Brew-drinkers. He told me that the theocracy began on the lowest plane with his kind, Joe Doe. Then there were the prayermen. These received the petitions of the populace, sorted them out, and passed on those that needed attention to prophets like the Forecaster Sheed, who screened them. Then these in turn were relayed to demigods like

Polivinosel, Albert Allegory, and a dozen others I had not heard of before then. They reported directly to Mahrud or Peggy.

Mahrud handled godhood like big business. He had delegated various departments to his vice-presidents such as the Ass, who handled fertility, and Sheed, who was probably the happiest forecaster who'd ever lived. Once a professor of physics at Traybell and the city's meteorologist, Sheed was now the only weatherman whose prophecies were one hundred percent correct. There was a good reason for that. He made the weather.

All this was very interesting, but my mind wasn't as intent on the information as it should have been. For one thing, I kept looking back to see if Polivinosel was following us. For another, I worried about Alice's attitude toward me. Now that I had hair, would she stop loving me? Was it a — now I was doing it — fixation that attracted her to me or was it a genuine affection?

If my situation hadn't been so tense, I'd have laughed at myself. Who would have thought that some day I might not leap with joy at the possibility of once again having a full head of hair and a beautiful girl in love with me?

The next moment, I did leap. It was not from joy, however. Somebody behind me had given a loud braying laugh. There was no mistaking the Ass's hee-haw. I whirled and saw, blazing golden in both the light of the moon and the torches, the figure of Polivinosel galloping toward us. There were people in the way, but they ran to get out of his path, yelling as they did so. His hoofs rang on the pavement even above their cries. Then he was on us and bellowing, "What now, little man? What now?"

Just as he reached us, I fell flat on my face. He was going so fast, he couldn't stop. His hoofs didn't help him keep his balance either, nor did Alice when she shoved him. Over he went, carrying with him bottles and baskets of fruit and corn and little cages of chickens. Women shrieked, baskets flew, glass broke, chickens squawked and shot out of sprung doors — Polivinosel was buried in the whole mess.

Alice and I burst through the crowd, turned a corner and raced down to Washington Street, which ran parallel to Adams. There was a much smaller parade of pilgrims here, but it was better than nothing. We ducked among these while, a block away, the giant throat of the Ass called again and again, "Little man, what now? What now, little man?"

I could have sworn he was galloping toward us. Then his voice, mighty as it was, became smaller, and the fast cloppety-clop died away.

Panting, Alice and I walked down Washington. We saw that the three bridges across the Illinois had been destroyed. A native told us that Mahrud had wrecked them with lightning one stormy night.

"Not that he needed to worry about crossing to the other side," he said, swiftly making the sign of the bull. "All of what used to be East Onaback is now sacred to the owner of the Bottle."

His attitude verified what I had noticed already. These people, though uninhibited by the Brew in other respects, retained enough awe to give the higher gods plenty of privacy. Whatever the priests relayed to them was enough to keep them happy.

When we came to the foot of Main Street, which ran right into the Illinois, we looked for a place to rest. Both of us were bone-weary. It was almost dawn. We had to have some sleep, if we wanted to be at all efficient for our coming work.

First, though, we had to watch the Fountain. This was a thin arc of the Brew which rose from the Bottle, set on the top of the bluffs across the river from Onaback, and ended in the middle of the waters. The descending moon played a rainbow of wavering and bright colors along it. How that trick was done, I didn't know, but it was one of the most beautiful sights I've ever seen.

I studied it and concluded that some force was being exerted linearly to keep the winds from scattering it into fine spray. And I saw how easy it would be to locate the Bottle. Follow the fountain to its source, a mile and a half away. Then destroy it, so the power of the Bull would be gone. After that, sit back and watch the Marines glide in and begin the conquest of Onaback.

It was as simple as that.

We looked around some more and found a place on the riverside park to lie down. Alice, snuggled in my arms, said, "Dan, I'm awfully thirsty. Are you?"

I admitted that I was, but that we'd have to stand it. Then I said, "Alice, after you get your sample, are you going to hike right back to H.Q.?"

"No," she said, kissing my chest, "I'm not. I'm sticking with you. After all, I want to see if your hair turns out curly or straight. And don't tell me!"

"I won't. But you're going to get awfully thirsty before this assignment. is over."

Secretly, I was pleased. If she wanted to be with me, then my returning hair wasn't putting a roadblock in the course of true love. Maybe it was the real thing, not just something laid by a trauma and hatched by a complex. Maybe...

◆ ◆ ◆

There I was in the tavern in the little town of Croncruachshin. I'd just fulfilled my mother's deathbed wish that I visit her mother, who was living when I stepped aboard the plane for Ireland and died the day I set foot on the green sod.

After the funeral, I'd stopped in Bill O'basean's for a bite, and Bill, who was wearing horns like a Texas steer's, picked the bottle off the shelf where he kept his other curios, and bellowed, "Danny Temper, look at the bull on the side o' that piece of glass! Know what that means? 'Tis the bottle that Goibniu, the smith o' the gods, fashioned. 'Twill run forever with magical brew for him that knows the words, for him that has a god hidden within himself."

"What happened to the owner?" I said, and he answered, "Sure and bejasus, all the Old Ones – Erse and Greek and Dutch and Rooshian and Chinee and Indian – found they was crowdin' each other, so they had a trooce and left Airth and went elsewhere. Only Pan stayed here for a few centuries, and he flew away on the wings o' light when the New Ones came. He didn't die as the big mouths claim.

"And then, in the eighteenth century, the New Ones, who'd become Old Ones now, thought that, begorry, they'd better be leavin', too, now that they was crowdin' each other and makin' a mess o' things. But the Bottle o' Goibniu has been lyin' around here collectin' dust and stories and here ye are, my bhoy, for ten American dollars, and what do ye intend doin' with it?"

So I said, "I'll wrap if up and send it on to my old professor as a joke. It'll tickle him when I tell him it's for sure the genuine everflowing bottle o' Goibniu."

And Bill O'basean winked and said, "And him a teetotaller. What'll his wife, the old hag and wicked witch, say to that?"

And I said, "Wouldn't it be funny if the old prof thought this really was Goibniu's bottle?"

And Bill, who had now become the Rational Man, looked severely at me and said to the squirrel crouched on his shoulder, "O Nuciferous One, what this simpleton don't know nohow! Hasn't he intellect enough, begorry, to see that the bottle was destined from its making for Boswell Durham? 'Bos,' which is Latin for the bovine species, and 'well,' a combination of the Anglo-Saxon 'wiella,' meaning fountain or well-spring 'wiellan' or 'wellen,' meaning to pour forth, and the Anglo-Saxon adverb 'wel,' meaning worthily or abundantly, and the adjective, meaning healthy. Boswell – the fountaining, abundantly healthy bovine. And of course, Durham. Everybody knows that that is sign and symbol for a bull."

"And he was born under Taurus too," I said.

And then the bartender, who was bald Alice by now — bald alas! — handed me the Bottle. "Here, have a drink on the house." And then I was on the steeply sloping rooftop and sliding fast toward the edge. "Drink, drink, drink!" screamed Alice. "Or you're lost, lost, lost!"

♦ ♦ ♦

But I wouldn't do it, and I awoke moaning, with the sun in my eyes and Alice shaking me and saying, "Dan, Dan, what's the matter?"

I told her about my dream and how it was mixed up with things that had actually happened. I told her how I had bought this bottle from O'basean and sent it to the professor as a hoax. But she didn't pay much attention because, like me, she had one thing uppermost in the cells of both body and mind. Thirst. Thirst was a living lizard that, with a hot rough skin, forced its swelling body down our throats and pulsed there, sucking moisture from us with every breath.

She licked her dry, cracked lips and then, glancing wistfully toward the river, where bathers shouted and plunged with joy, asked, "I don't suppose it'd hurt me if I sat in it, do you?"

"Be careful," I said, my words rattling like pebbles in a dried gourd. I ached to join her, but I couldn't even get near the water. I was having trouble enough combatting the panic that came with the odor of the Brew blowing from the river on the morning breeze.

While she waded out until the water was hip-deep and cupped it in her hands and poured it over her breasts, I examined my surroundings in the daylight. To my left was a warehouse and a wharf. Tied alongside the latter was an old coal barge that had been painted bright green. A number of men and women, ignoring the festivities, were busy carrying bags and long mummy-shaped bundles from the warehouse to the boat. These were the bones that had been dug up recently. If my information was correct, they'd be ferried across to the other side after the ceremonies.

That was fine. I intended to go over with them. As soon as Alice came back out of the water, I'd unfold my plans to her and if she thought she could go through with it, we'd...

A big grinning head emerged from the water just behind Alice. It belonged to one of those jokers on every beach who grabs you from behind and pulls you under. I opened my mouth to yell a warning, but it was too late. I don't suppose I'd have been heard above the crowd's noise, anyway.

After sputtering and blowing the water out, she stood there with the most ecstatic expression, then bent over and began drinking great mouthfuls. That was enough for me. I was dying within, because she was now on the enemy's side, and I'd wanted so badly to do something for her that I hurt. But I had to get going before she saw me and yelled, "Come on in, Dan, the beer's fine!"

I trotted through the crowd, moaning to myself at losing her, until I came to the far end of the warehouse, where she couldn't possibly see me enter. There, under the cool cavernous roof, I paused until I saw a lunch-basket sitting by a pile of rags. I scooped it up, untied one of the bags, put the basket inside, and hoisted the bag over my shoulder. I stepped, unchallenged, into the line of workers going out to the barge. As if I belonged there, I briskly carried my burden over the gangplank.

But instead of depositing it where everybody else was, I walked around the mountain of bags. Out of view on the riverside, I took the basket out and dumped the bones inside the bag over the railing into the river. I took one peek around my hiding place. Alice was nowhere to be seen.

Satisfied she would not be able to find me, and glad that I'd not disclosed my plans to her last night, I took the basket and crawled backward into the bag.

Once there, I succumbed to the three things that had been fighting within me — grief, hunger, and thirst. Tears ran as I thought of Alice. At the same time, I greedily devoured, in rapid succession, an orange, a leg and breast of chicken, a half-loaf of fresh bread, and two great plums.

The fruit helped my thirst somewhat, but there was only one thing that could fully ease that terrible ache in my throat — water. Moreover, the bag was close and very hot. The sun beat down on it and, though I kept my face as close to the open end as I dared, I suffered. But as long as I kept sweating and could draw some fresh air now and then, I knew I'd be all right. I wasn't going to give up when I'd gotten this far.

I crouched within the thick leather bag like — I couldn't help thinking — an embryo within its sac. I was sweating so much that I felt as if I were floating in amniotic fluid. The outside noises came through dimly; every once in a while I'd hear a big shout.

When the workers quit the barge, I stuck my head out long enough to grab some air and look at the sun. It seemed to be about eleven o'clock, although the sun, like the moon, was so distorted that I couldn't be sure. Our scientists had said the peculiar warmth of the valley and the elongation of the sun and moon were due to some "wave-focusing force field" hanging just below the stratosphere. This had no more meaning than calling it a sorcerer's spell, but it had satisfied the general public and the military.

About noon, the ceremonies began. I ate the last two plums in the basket, but I didn't dare open the bottle at its bottom. Though it felt like a wine-container, I didn't want to chance the possibility that the Brew might be mixed in it.

From time to time, I heard, intermingled with band music, snatches of chants. Then, suddenly, the band quit playing and there was a mighty shout of, "Mahrud is Bull—Bull is all—and Sheed is the prophet!"

The band began playing the Semiramis overture. When it was almost through, the barge trembled with an unmistakable motion. I had not heard any tug, nor did I think there was one. After all I'd seen, the idea of a boat moving by itself was just another miracle.

The overture ended in a crash of chords. Somebody yelled, "Three cheers for Albert Allegory!" and the crowd responded.

The noises died. I could hear, faintly, the slapping of the waves against the side of the barge. For a few minutes, that was all. Then heavy footsteps sounded close by. I ducked back within the bag and lay still. The steps came very near and stopped.

The rumbling unhuman voice of The Allegory said, "Looks as if somebody forgot to tie up this bag."

Another voice said, "Oh, Al, leave it. What's the difference?"

I would have blessed the unknown voice except for one thing—it sounded so much like Alice's.

I'd thought that was a shock, but a big green four-fingered hand appeared in the opening of the bag's mouth and seized the cords, intending to draw them close and tie them up. At the same time, the tag, which was strung on the cord, became fixed in my vision long enough for me to read the name.

Mrs. Daniel Temper.

I had thrown my mother's bones into the river!

For some reason, this affected me more than the fact that I was now tied into a close and suffocating sack, with no knife to cut my way out.

The voice of The Allegory, strange in its saurian mouth-structure, boomed out. "Well, Peggy, was your sister quite happy when you left her?"

"Alice'll be perfectly happy as soon as she finds this Dan Temper," said the voice, which I now realized was Peggy Rourke's. "After we'd kissed, as sisters should who haven't seen each other for three years, I explained everything that had happened to me. She started to tell me of her adventures, but I told her I knew most of them. She just couldn't believe that we'd been keeping tabs on her and her lover ever since they crossed the border."

"Too bad we lost track of him after Polivinosel chased them down Adams Street," said Allegory. "And if we'd been one minute earlier, we'd have caught him, too. Oh, well, we know he'll try to destroy the Bottle — or steal it. He'll be caught there."

"If he does get to the Bottle," said Peggy, "he'll be the first man to do so. That F.B.I. agent only got as far as the foot of the hill, remember."

"If anybody can do it," chuckled Allegory, "Dan H. Temper can. Or so says Mahrud, who should know him well enough."

"Won't Temper be surprised when he finds out that his every move since he entered Mahrudland has been not only a reality, but a symbol of reality? And that we've been leading him by the nose through the allegorical maze?"

Allegory laughed with all the force of a bull-alligator's roar.

"I wonder if Mahrud isn't asking too much of him by demanding that he read into his adventures a meaning outside of themselves? For instance, could he see that he entered this valley as a baby enters the world, bald and toothless? Or that he met and conquered the ass that is in all of us? But that, in order to do so, he had to lose his outer strength and visible burden — the water-tank? And then operate upon his own strength with no source of external strength to fall back on? Or that, in the Scrambled Men, he met the living punishment of human self-importance in religion?"

Peggy said, "He'll die when he finds out that the real Polivinosel was down South and that you were masquerading as him."

"Well," rumbled Allegory, "I hope Temper can see that Mahrud kept Polivinosel in his asinine form as an object lesson to everybody that, if Polivinosel could become a god, then anybody could. If he can't, he's not very smart."

I was thinking that I had, strangely enough, thought that very thing about the Ass. And then the cork in the bottle in the basket decided to pop, and the contents — Brew — gushed out over my side.

I froze, afraid that the two would hear it. But they went on talking as if they hadn't noticed. It was no wonder — the Allegory's voice thundered on.

"He met Love, Youth, and Beauty — which are nowhere to be found in abundance except in this valley — in the form of Alice Lewis. And she, like all three of those qualities, was not won easily, nor without a change in the wooer. She rejected him, lured him, teased him, almost drove him crazy. She wanted him, yet she didn't. And he had to conquer some of his faults—such as shame of his baldness and toothlessness—before he could win her, only to find out his imagined faults were, in her eyes, virtues."

"Do you think he'll know the answer to the question you, in your metamorphosis, asked him?" Peggy said.

"I don't know. I wish I'd first taken the form of the Sphinx and asked him her questions, so he'd have had a clue to what was expected of him. He'd have known, of course, that the answer to the Sphinx is that man himself is the answer to all the old questions. Then he might have seen what I was driving at when I asked him where Man—Modern Man—was going."

"And when he finds the answer to that, then he too will be a god."

"If!" said Allegory. "*If!* Mahrud says that Dan Temper is quite a few cuts above the average man of this valley. He is the reformer, the idealist who won't be happy unless he's tilting his lance against some windmill. In his case, he'll not only have to defeat the windmills within himself—his neuroses and traumas—he'll have to reach deep within himself and pull up the drowned god in the abyss of himself by the hair. If he doesn't, he'll die."

"Oh, no, not that!" gasped Peggy. "I didn't know Mahrud *meant* that!"

"Yes," thundered the Allegory, "he does! He says that Temper will have to find himself or die. Temper himself would want it that way. He'd not be satisfied with being one of the happy-go-lucky, let-the-gods-do-it Brew-bums who loaf beneath this uninhibited sun. He'll either be first in this new Rome, or else he'll die."

The conversation was interesting, to say the least, but I lost track of the next few sentences because the bottle had not quit gushing. It was spurting a gentle but steady stream against my side. And, I suddenly realized that the bag would fill and the bottle's contents would run out the mouth of the bag and reveal my presence.

Frantically, I stuck my finger in the bottle's neck and succeeded in checking the flow.

"So," said Allegory, "he fled to the cemetery, where he met Weepenwilly. Weepenwilly who mourns eternally yet would resent the dead being brought back. Who refuses to take his cold and numbed posterior from the gravestone of his so-called beloved. That man was the living symbol of himself, Daniel Temper, who grieved himself into baldness at an early age, though he blamed his mysterious sickness and fever for it. Yet who, deep down, didn't want his mother back, because she'd been nothing but trouble to him."

The pressure in the bottle suddenly increased and expelled my finger. The Brew in it burst over me despite my efforts to plug it up again, gushing out at such a rate that the bag would fill faster than its narrow mouth could let it out. I was facing two dangers—being discovered and being drowned.

As if my troubles weren't enough, somebody's heavy foot descended on me and went away. A voice succeeded it. I recognized it, even after all these years. It was that of Doctor Boswell Durham, the god now known as Mahrud. But it had a basso quality and richness it had not possessed in his predeity days.

"All right, Dan Temper, the masquerade is over!"

Frozen with terror, I kept silent and motionless.

"I've sloughed off the form of the Allegory and taken my own," Durham went on. "That was really I talking all the time. I was the Allegory you refused to recognize. Myself—your old teacher. But then you always did refuse to see any of the allegories I pointed out to you.

"How's this one, Danny? Listen! You crawled aboard Charon's ferry—this coal barge—and into the sack which contained your mother's bones. Not only that, but as a further unconscious symbol of your rejection of the promise of life for your mother, you threw her bones overboard. Didn't you notice her name on the tag? Why not? Subconsciously on purpose?

"Well, Dan my boy, you're right back where you started—in your mother's womb where, I suspect, you've always wanted to be. How do I know so much? Brace yourself for a real shock. I was Doctor Duerf, the psychologist who conditioned you. Run that name backward and remember how I love a pun or an anagram."

I found all this hard to believe. The professor had always been kindly, gentle, and humorous. I would have thought he was pulling my leg if it hadn't been for one thing! That was the Brew, which was about to drown me. I really thought he was carrying his joke too far.

I told him so, as best I could in my muffled voice.

He yelled back, "'Life is real—life is earnest!' You've always said so, Dan. Let's see now if you meant it. All right, you're a baby due to be born. Are you going to stay in this sac, and die, or are you going to burst out from the primal waters into life?

"Let's put it another way, Dan. I'm the midwife, but my hands are tied. I can't assist in the accouchement directly. I have to coach you via long distance, symbolically, so to speak. I can tell you what to do to some extent, but you, being an unborn infant, may have to guess at the meaning of some of my words."

I wanted to cry out a demand that he quit clowning around and let me out. But I didn't. I had my pride.

Huskily, weakly, I said, "What do you want me to do?"

"Answer the questions I, as Allegory and Ass, asked you. Then you'll be able to free yourself. And rest assured, Dan, that I'm not opening the bag for you."

What was it he had said? My mind groped frantically; the rising tide of the Brew made thinking difficult. I wanted to scream and tear at the leather with my naked hands. But if I did that, I'd go under and never come up again.

I clenched my fists, forced my mind to slow down, to go back over what Allegory and Polivinosel had said.

What was it? What was it?

The Allegory had said, "Where do you want to go now?"

And Polivinosel, while chasing me down Adams Street — *Adam's Street?* — had called out, "Little man, what now?"

The answer to the *Sphinx's* question was:

Man.

Allegory and Ass had proposed *their* questions in the true scientific manner so that they contained their own answer.

That answer was that man was *more* than man.

In the next second, with that realization acting like a powerful motor within me, I snapped the conditioned reflex as if it were a wishbone. I drank deeply of the Brew, both to quench my thirst and to strip myself of the rest of my predeity inhibitions. I commanded the bottle to stop fountaining. And with an explosion that sent Brew and leather fragments flying over the barge, I rose from the bag.

Mahrud was standing there smiling. I recognized him as my old prof, even though he was now six and a half feet tall, had a thatch of long black hair, and had pushed his features a little here and there to make himself handsome. Peggy stood beside him. She looked like her sister, Alice, except that she was red-haired. She was beautiful, but I've always preferred brunettes — specifically, Alice.

"Understand everything now?" he asked.

"Yes," I said, "including the fact that much of this symbolism was thought up on the spur of the moment to make it sound impressive. Also, that it wouldn't have mattered if I *had* drowned, for you'd have brought me back to life."

"Yes, but you'd never have become a god. Nor would you have succeeded me."

"What do you mean?" I asked blankly.

"Peggy and I deliberately led you and Alice toward this dénouement so we could have somebody to carry on our work here. We're a little bored with what we've done, but we realize that we can't just leave. So I've picked you as a good successor. You're conscientious, you're an idealist, and you've discovered your potentialities. You'll probably do better than I have at this suspension of 'natural' laws. You'll make a better world than I could. After all, Danny, my godling, I'm the Old Bull, you know, the one for having fun.

"Peggy and I want to go on a sort of Grand Tour to visit the former gods of Earth, who are scattered all over the Galaxy. They're all young gods, you know, by comparison with the age of the Universe. You might say they've just got out of school — this Earth — and are visiting the centers of genuine culture to acquire polish."

"What about me?"

"You're a god now, Danny. You make your own decisions. Meanwhile, Peggy and I have places to go."

He smiled one of those long slow smiles he used to give us students when he was about to quote a favorite line of his.

> "'...listen: there's a hell
> of a good universe next door.
> Let's go.'"

Peggy and he did go. Like thistles, swept away on the howling winds of space, they were gone.

And after they had vanished, I was left staring at the river and the hills and the sky and the city, where the assembled faithful watched, awestruck. It was mine, all mine.

Including one black-haired figure — and *what* a figure — that stood on the wharf and waved at me.

Do you think I stood poised in deep reverie and pondered on my duty to mankind or the shape of teleology now that I was personally turning it out on my metaphysical potter's wheel?

Not I. I leaped into the air and completed sixteen entrechats of pure joy before I landed. Then I walked across the water — *on* the water — to Alice.

The next day, I sat upon the top of a hill overlooking the valley. As the giant troop-carrying gliders soared in, I seized them with psychokinesis, or what-have-you, and dunked them one by one in the river. And as the Marines threw away their arms and swam toward shore, I plucked away their oxygen masks and thereafter forgot about them, unless they seemed to be having trouble swimming. Then I was kind enough to pick them up and deposit them on shore.

I do think it was rather nice of me. After all, I wasn't in too good a mood. That whole night and morning, my legs and my upper gums had been very sore. They were making me somewhat irritable, despite liberal potions of Brew.

But there was a good reason.

I had growing pains, and I was teething.

$\mathbf{T}$he man from the puzzle factory was here this morning," said Gummy. "While you was out fishin."

She dropped the piece of wiremesh she was trying to tie with string over a hole in the rusty window screen. Cursing, grunting like a hog in a wallow, she leaned over and picked it up. Straightening, she slapped viciously at her bare shoulder.

"Figurin skeeters! Must be a million outside, all tryin to get away from the burnin garbage."

"Puzzle factory?" said Deena. She turned away from the battered kerosene-burning stove over which she was frying sliced potatoes and perch and bullheads caught in the Illinois River, half a mile away.

"Yeah!" snarled Gummy. "You heard Old Man say it. Nuthouse. Booby hatch. So...this cat from the puzzle factory was named John Elkins. He gave Old Man all those tests when they had him locked up last year. He's the skinny little guy with a moustache 'n never lookin you in the eye 'n grinnin like a skunk eatin a shirt. The cat who took Old Man's hat away from him 'n woun't give it back to him until Old Man promised to be good. Remember now?"

Deena, tall, skinny, clad only in a white terrycloth bathrobe, looked like a surprised and severed head stuck on a pike. The great purple birthmark on her cheek and neck stood out hideously against her paling skin.

"Are they going to send him back to the state hospital?" she asked.

Gummy, looking at herself in the cracked full-length mirror nailed to the wall, laughed and showed her two teeth. Her frizzy hair was a yellow brown, chopped short. Her little blue eyes were set far back in tunnels beneath two protruding ridges of bone; her nose was very long, enormously wide, and tipped with a broken-veined bulb. Her chin was not there, and her head bent forward in a permanent crook. She was dressed only in a dirty once-white slip that came to her swollen knees. When she laughed, her huge breasts, resting on her distended belly, quivered like bowls of fermented cream. From her expression, it was evident that she was not displeased with what she saw in the broken glass.

Again she laughed. "Naw, they din't comb to haul him away. Elkins just wanted to interduce this chick he had with him. A cute little brunette with big brown eyes behind real thick glasses. She looked just like a collidge girl, 'n she was. This chick has got a B.M. or somethin in sexology...."

"Psychology?"

"Maybe it was societyology...."

"Sociology?"

"Umm. Maybe. Anyway, this four-eyed chick is doin a study for a foundation. She wants to ride aroun with Old Man, see how he collects his junk, what alleys he goes up 'n down, what his, uh, habit patterns is, 'n learn what kinda bringin up he had...."

"Old Man'd never do it!" burst out Deena. "You know he can't stand the idea of being watched by a False Folker!"

"Umm. Maybe. Anyway, I tell em Old Man's not goin to like their slummin on him, 'n they say quick they're not slummin, it's for science. 'N they'll pay him for his trouble. They got a grant from the foundation. So I say maybe that'd make Old Man take another look at the color of the beer, 'n they left the house...."

"You *allowed* them in the house? Did you hide the birdcage?"

"Why hide it? His hat wasn't in it."

Deena turned back to frying her fish, but over her shoulder she said, "I don't think Old Man'll agree to the idea, do you? It's rather degrading."

"You *kiddin?* Who's lower'n Old Man? A snake's belly, maybe. Sure, he'll agree. He'll have an eye for the four-eyed chick, sure."

"Don't be absurd," said Deena. "He's a dirty stinking one-armed middle-aged man, the ugliest man in the world."

"Yeah, it's the uglies he's got, for sure. 'N he smells like a goat that fell in a outhouse. But it's the smell that gets em. It got me, it got you, it got a whole stewpotful a others, includin that high society dame he used to collect junk off of...."

"Shut up!" spat Deena. "This girl must be a highly refined and intelligent girl. She'd regard Old Man as some sort of ape."

"You know them apes," said Gummy, and she went to the ancient refrigerator and took out a cold quart of beer.

Six quarts of beer later, Old Man had still not come home. The fish had grown cold and greasy, and the big July moon had risen. Deena, like a long lean dirty-white nervous alley cat on top of a backyard fence, patrolled back and forth across the shanty. Gummy sat on the bench made of crates and hunched over her bottle. Finally, she lurched to her feet and turned on the battered set. But, hearing a rattling and pounding of a loose motor in the distance, she turned it off.

The banging and popping became a roar just outside the door. Abruptly, there was a mighty wheeze, like an old rusty robot coughing with double pneumonia in its iron lungs. Then, silence.

But not for long. As the two women stood paralyzed, listening apprehensively, they heard a voice like the rumble of distant thunder.

"Take it easy, kid."

Another voice, soft, drowsy, mumbling.

"Where...we?"

The voice like thunder, "Home, sweet home, where we rest our dome."

Violent coughing.

"It's this smoke from the burnin garbage, kid. Enough to make a maggot puke, ain't it? Lookit! The smoke's risin t'ward the full moon like the ghosts a men so rotten even their spirits're carryin the con- tamination with em. Hey, li'l chick, you din't know Old Man knew them big words like contamination, didja? That's what livin on the city dump does for you. I hear that word all a time from the big shots that come down inspectin the stink here so they kin get away from the stink a City Hall. I ain't no illiterate. I got a TV set. Hor, hor, hor!"

There was a pause, and the two women knew he was bending his knees and tilting his torso backward so he could look up at the sky.

"Ah, you lovely lovely moon, bride a The Old Guy In The Sky! Some day to come, rum-a-dum-a-dum, one day I swear it, Old Woman a The Old Guy In The Sky, if you help me find the longlost headpiece a King Paley that I and my fathers been lookin for for fifty thousand years, so help me, Old Man Paley'll spread the freshly spilled blood a a virgin a the False Folkers out acrosst the ground for you, so you kin lay down in it like a red carpet or a new red dress and wrap it aroun you. And then you won't have to crinkle up your lovely shinin nose at me and spit your silver spit on me. Old Man promises that, just as sure as his good arm is holdin a daughter a one a the Falsers, a virgin, I think, and bringin her to his home, however humble it be, so we shall see...."

"Stoned out a his head," whispered Gummy.

"My God, he's bringing a girl in here!" said Deena. "*The* girl!"

"Not the *collidge* kid?"

"Does the idiot want to get lynched?"

The man outside bellowed, "Hey, you wimmen, get off your fat asses and open the door 'fore I kick it in! Old Man's home with a fistful a dollars, a armful a sleepin lamb, and a gutful a beer! Home like a conquerin hero and wants service like one, too!"

Suddenly unfreezing, Deena opened the door.

Out of the darkness and into the light shuffled something so squat and blocky it seemed more a tree trunk come to life than a man. It stopped, and the eyes under the huge black homburg hat blinked glazedly. Even the big hat could not hide the peculiar lengthened-out bread-loaf shape of the skull. The forehead was abnormally low; over the eyes were bulging arches of bone. These were tufted with eyebrows like Spanish moss that made even more cavelike the hollows in which the little blue eyes lurked. Its nose was very long and very wide and flaring-nostriled. The lips were thin but pushed out by the shoving jaws beneath them. Its chin was absent, and head and shoulders joined almost without intervention from a neck, or so it seemed. A corkscrew forest of rusty-red hairs sprouted from its open shirt front.

Over his shoulder, held by a hand wide and knobbly as a coral branch, hung the slight figure of a young woman.

He shuffled into the room in an odd bent-kneed gait, walking on the sides of his thick-soled engineer's boots. Suddenly, he stopped again, sniffed deeply, and smiled, exposing teeth thick and yellow, dedicated to biting.

"Jeez, that smells good. It takes the old garbage stink right off. Gummy! You been sprinklin yourself with that perfume I found in a ash heap up on the bluffs?"

Gummy, giggling, looked coy.

Deena said, sharply, "Don't be a fool, Gummy. He's trying to butter you up so you'll forget he's bringing this girl home."

Old Man Paley laughed hoarsely and lowered the snoring girl upon an Army cot. There she sprawled out with her skirt around her hips. Gummy cackled, but Deena hurried to pull the skirt down and also to remove the girl's thick shell-rimmed glasses.

"Lord," she said, "how did this happen? What'd you do to her?"

"Nothin," he growled, suddenly sullen.

He took a quart of beer from the refrigerator, bit down on the cap with teeth thick and chipped as ancient gravestones, and tore it off. Up went the bottle, forward went his knees, back went his torso and he leaned away from the bottle, and down went the amber liquid, gurgle, gurgle, glub. He belched, then roared. "There I was, Old Man Paley, mindin my own figurin business, packin a bunch a papers and magazines I found, and here comes a blue fifty-one Ford sedan with Elkins, the doctor jerk from the puzzle factory. And this little four-eyed chick here, Dorothy Singer. And..."

"Yes," said Deena. "We know who they are, but we didn't know they went after you."

"Who asked you? Who's tellin this story? Anyway, they tole me what they wanted. And I was gonna say no, but this little collidge broad says if I'll sign a paper that'll agree to let her travel aroun with me and even stay in our house a couple a evenins, with us actin natural, she'll pay me fifty dollars. I says yes! Old Guy In The Sky! That's a hundred and fifty quarts a beer! I got principles, but they're washed away in a roarin foamin flood of beer.

"I says yes, and the cute little runt give me the paper to sign, then advances me ten bucks and says I'll get the rest seven days from now. Ten dollars in my pocket! So she climbs up into the seat a my truck. And then this figurin Elkins parks his Ford and says he thinks he ought a go with us to check on if everythin's gonna be OK."

"He's not foolin Old Man. He's after Little Miss Four-eyes. Everytime he looks at her, the lovejuice runs out a his eyes. So, I collect junk for a couple a hours, talkin all the time. And she is scared a me at first because I'm so figurin ugly and strange. But after a while she busts out laughin. Then I pulls the truck up in the alley back a Jack's Tavern on Ames Street. She asks me what I'm doin. I says I'm stoppin for a beer, just as I do every day. And she says she could stand one, too. So…"

"You actually went inside with her?" asked Deena.

"Naw. I was gonna try, but I started gettin the shakes. And I hadda tell her I coun't do it. She asks me why. I say I don't know. Ever since I quit bein a kid, I kin't. So she says I got a…somethin like a fresh flower, what is it?"

"Neurosis?" said Deena.

"Yeah. Only I call it a taboo. So Elkins and the little broad go into Jack's and get a cold six-pack, and brin it out, and we're off…."

"So?"

"So we go from place to place, though always stayin in alleys, and she thinks it's funnier'n hell gettin loaded in the backs a taverns. Then I get to seein double and don't care no more and I'm over my fraidies, so we go into the Circle Bar. And get in a fight there with one a the hillbillies in his sideburns and leather jacket that hangs out there and tries to take the four-eyed chick home with him."

Both the women gasped, "Did the cops come?"

"If they did, they was late to the party. I grab this hillbllly by his leather jacket with my one arm — the strongest arm in this world — and throw him clean acrosst the room. And when his buddies come after me, I pound my chest like a figurin gorilla and make a figurin face at em, and they all of a sudden get their shirts up their necks and go back to listenin to their hillbilly music. And I pick up the chick—she's laughin so hard she's chokin—and Elkins, white as a sheet out a the Laundromat, after me, and away we go, and here we are."

"Yes, you fool, here you are!" shouted Deena. "Bringing that girl here in that condition! She'll start screaming her head off when she wakes up and sees you!"

"Go figure yourself!" snorted Paley. "She was scared a me a first, and she tried to stay upwind a me. But she got to *liken* me. I could tell. And she got so she liked my smell, too. I knew she would. Don't all the broads? These False wimmen kin't say no once they get a whiff of us. Us Paleys got the gift in the blood."

Deena laughed and said, "You mean you have it in the head. Honest to God, when are you going to quit trying to forcefeed me with that bull? You're insane!"

Paley growled. "I tole you not never to call me nuts, not never!" and he slapped her across the cheek.

She reeled back and slumped against the wall, holding her face and crying, "You ugly stupid stinking ape, you hit me, the daughter of people whose boots you aren't fit to lick. *You* struck *me!*"

"Yeah, and ain't you glad I did," said Paley in tones like a complacent earthquake. He shuffled over to the cot and put his hand on the sleeping girl.

"Uh, feel that. No sag there, you two flabs."

"You beast!" screamed Deena. "Taking advantage of a helpless little girl!"

Like an alley cat, she leaped at him with claws out.

Laughing hoarsely, he grabbed one of her wrists and twisted it so she was forced to her knees and had to clench her teeth to keep from screaming with pain. Gummy cackled and handed Old Man a quart of beer. To take it, he had to free Deena. She rose, and all three, as if nothing had happened, sat down at the table and began drinking.

♦ ♦ ♦

About dawn a deep animal snarl awoke the girl. She opened her eyes but could make out the trio only dimly and distortedly. Her hands, groping around for her glasses, failed to find them.

Old Man, whose snarl had shaken her from the high tree of sleep, growled again. "I'm tellin you, Deena, I'm tellin you, don't laugh at Old Man, don't laugh at Old Man, and I'm tellin you again, three times, don't laugh at Old Man!"

His incredible bass rose to a high-pitched scream of rage.

"Whassa matter with your figurin brain? I show you proof after proof, and you sit there in all your stupidity like a silly hen that sits down too hard on its eggs and breaks em but won't get up and admit she's squattin on a mess. I—I—Paley—Old Man Paley—kin prove I'm what I say I am, a Real Folker."

Suddenly, he propelled his hand across the table toward Deena.

"Feel them bones in my lower arm! Them two bones ain't straight and dainty like the arm bones a you False Folkers. They're thick as flagpoles, and they're curved out from each other like the backs a two tomcats outbluffin each other over a fishhead on a garbage can. They're built that way so's they kin be real strong anchors for my muscles, which is bigger'n False Folkers'. Go ahead, feel em.

"And look at them brow ridges. Like the tops a those shellrimmed spectacles all them intelleckchooalls wear. Like the spectacles this collidge chick wears.

"And feel the shape a my skull. It ain't a ball like yours but a loaf a bread."

"Fossilized bread!" sneered Deena. "Hard as a rock, through and through."

Old Man roared on, "Feel my neck bones if you got the strength to feel through my muscles! They're bent forward, not—"

"Oh, I know you're an ape. You can't look overhead to see if that was a bird or just a drop of rain without breaking your back."

"Ape, hell! I'm a Real Man! Feel my heel bone! Is it like yours? No, it ain't! It's built diff'runt, and so's my whole foot!"

Is that why you and Gummy and all those brats of yours have to walk like chimpanzees?"

"Laugh, laugh, laugh!"

"I am laughing, laughing, laughing. Just because you're a freak of nature, a monstrosity whose bones all went wrong in the womb, you've dreamed up this fantastic myth about being descended from the Neanderthals...."

"Neanderthals!" whispered Dorothy Singer. The walls whirled about her, looking twisted and ghostly in the halflight, like a room in Limbo.

"...all this stuff about the lost hat of Old King," continued Deena, "and how if you ever find it you can break the spell that keeps you so-called Neanderthals on the dumpheaps and in the alleys, is garbage, and not very appetizing...."

"And you," shouted Paley, "are headin for a beatin!"

"Thass what she wants," mumbled Gummy. "Go ahead. Beat her. She'll get her jollies off, 'n quit needlin you. 'N we kin all get some shuteye. Besides, you're gonna wake up the chick."

"That chick is gonna get a wakin up like she never had before when Old Man gets his paws on her," rumbled Paley. "Guy In The Sky, ain't it somethin she should a met me and be in this house? Sure as an old shirt stinks, she ain't gonna be able to tear herself away from me.

"Hey, Gummy, maybe she'll have a kid for me, huh? We ain't had a brat aroun here for ten years. I kinda miss my kids. You gave me six that was Real Folkers, though I never was sure about that Jimmy, he looked too much like O'Brien. Now you're all dried up, dry as Deena always was, but you kin still raise em. How'd you like to raise the collidge chick's kid?"

Gummy grunted and swallowed beer from a chipped coffee mug. After belching loudly, she mumbled, "Don't know. You're crazier'n even I think you are if you think this cute little Miss Four-eyes'd have anythin to do with you. 'N even if she was out of her head enough to do it, what kind a life is this for a brat? Get raised in a dump? Have a ugly old maw 'n paw? Grow up so ugly nobody'd have nothin to do with him 'n smellin so strange all the dogs'd bite him?"

Suddenly, she began blubbering.

"It ain't only Neanderthals has to live on dumpheaps. It's the crippled 'n sick 'n the stupid 'n the queer in the head that has to live here. 'N they become Neanderthals just as much as us Real Folk. No diff'runce, no diff'runce. We're all ugly 'n hopeless 'n rotten. We're all Neander…"

Old Man's fist slammed the table.

"Name me no names like that! That's a *G'yaga* name for us Paleys — Real Folkers. Don't let me never hear that other name again! It don't mean a man; it means somethin like a high-class gorilla."

"Quit looking in the mirror!" shrieked Deena.

There was more squabbling and jeering and roaring and confusing and terrifying talk, but Dorothy Singer had closed her eyes and fallen asleep again.

♦ ♦ ♦

Some time later, she awoke. She sat up, found her glasses on a little table beside her, put them on, and stared about her.

She was in a large shack built of odds and ends of wood. It had two rooms, each about ten feet square. In the corner of one room was a large kerosene-burning stove. Bacon was cooking in a huge skillet; the heat from the stove made sweat run from her forehead and over her glasses.

After drying them off with her handkerchief, she examined the furnishings of the shack. Most of it was what she had expected, but three things surprised her. The bookcase, the photograph on the wall, and the birdcage.

The bookcase was tall and narrow and of some dark wood, badly scratched. It was crammed with comic books, Blue Books, and Argosies, some of which she supposed must be at least twenty years old. There were a few books whose ripped backs and waterstained covers indicated they'd been picked out of ash heaps. Haggard's *Allan and the Ice Gods*, Wells's *Outline of History, Vol. I,* and his *The Croquet Player*. Also *Gog and Magog, A Prophecy of Armageddon* by the Reverend Caleb G. Harris. Burroughs' *Tarzan the Terrible* and *In the Earth's Core*. Jack London's *Beyond Adam*.

The framed photo on the wall was that of a woman who looked much like Deena and must have been taken around 1890. It was very large, tinted in brown, and showed an aristocratic handsome woman of about thirty-five in a high-busted velvet dress with a high neckline. Her hair was drawn severely back to a knot on top of her head. A diadem of jewels was on her breast.

The strangest thing was the large parrot cage. It stood upon a tall support which had nails driven through its base to hold it to the floor. The cage itself was empty, but the door was locked with a long narrow bicycle lock.

Her speculation about it was interrupted by the two women calling to her from their place by the stove.

Deena said, "Good morning, Miss Singer. How do you feel?"

"Some Indian buried his hatchet in my head," Dorothy said. "And my tongue is molting. Could I have a drink of water, please?"

Deena took a pitcher of cold water out of the refrigerator, and from it filled up a tin cup.

"We don't have any running water. We have to get our water from the gas station down the road and bring it here in a bucket."

Dorothy looked dubious, but she closed her eyes and drank.

"I think I'm going to get sick," she said. "I'm sorry."

"I'll take you to the outhouse," said Deena, putting her arm around the girl's shoulder and heaving her up with surprising strength.

"Once I'm outside," said Dorothy faintly, "I'll be all right."

"Oh, I know," said Deena. "It's the odor. The fish, Gummy's cheap perfume, Old Man's sweat, the beer. I forgot how it first affected me. But it's no better outside."

Dorothy didn't reply, but when she stepped through the door, she murmured, "Ohh!"

"Yes, I know," said Deena. "It's awful, but it won't kill you...."

Ten minutes later, Deena and a pale and weak Dorothy came out of the ramshackle outhouse.

They returned to the shanty, and for the first time Dorothy noticed that Elkins was sprawled face-up on the seat of the truck. His head hung over the end of the seat and the flies buzzed around his open mouth.

"This is horrible," said Deena. "He'll be very angry when he wakes up and finds out where he is. He's such a respectable man."

"Let the heel sleep it off," said Dorothy. She walked into the shanty, and a moment later Paley clomped into the room, a smell of stale beer and very peculiar sweat advancing before him in a wave.

"How you feel?" he growled in a timbre so low the hairs on the back of her neck rose.

"Sick. I think I'll go home."

"Sure. Only try some a the hair."

He handed her a half-empty pint of whiskey. Dorothy reluctantly downed a large shot chased with cold water. After a brief revulsion, she began feeling better and took another shot. She then washed her face in a bowl of water and drank a third whiskey.

"I think I can go with you now," she said. "But I don't care for breakfast."

"I ate already," he said. "Let's go. It's ten-thirty accordin to the clock on the gas station. My alley's prob'ly been cleaned out by now. Them other ragpickers are always moochin in on my territory when they think I'm stayin home. But you kin bet they're scared out a their pants every time they see a shadow cause they're afraid it's Old Man and he'll catch em and squeeze their guts out and crack their ribs with this one good arm."

Laughing a laugh so hoarse and unhuman it seemed to come from some troll deep in the caverns of his bowels, he opened the refrigerator and took another beer.

"I need another to get me started, not to mention what I'll have to give that damn balky bitch, Fordiana."

As they stepped outside, they saw Elkins stumble toward the outhouse and then fall headlong through the open doorway. He lay motionless on the floor, his feet sticking out of the entrance. Alarmed, Dorothy wanted to go after him, but Paley shook his head.

"He's a big boy; he kin take care a hisself. We got to get Fordiana up and goin."

Fordiana was the battered and rusty pickup truck. It was parked outside Paley's bedroom window so he could look out at any time of the night and make sure no one was stealing parts or even the whole truck.

"Not that I ought a worry about her," grumbled Old Man. He drank three-fourths of the quart in four mighty gulps, then uncapped the truck's radiator and poured the rest of the beer down it.

"She knows nobody else'll give her beer, so I think that if any a these robbin figurers that live on the dump or at the shacks aroun the bend was to try to steal anythin off'n her, she'd honk and backfire and throw rods and oil all over the place so's her Old Man could wake up and punch the figurin shirt off a the thievin figurer. But maybe not. She's a female. And you kin't trust a figurin female."

He poured the last drop down the radiator and roared, "There! Now don't you dare *not* turn over. You're robbin me a the good beer I could be havin! If you so much as backfire, Old Man'll beat hell out a you with a sledgehammer!"

Wide-eyed but silent, Dorothy climbed onto the ripped open front seat beside Paley. The starter whirred, and the motor sputtered.

"No more beer if you don't work!" shouted Paley.

There was a bang, a fizz, a sput, a *whop, whop, whop,* a clash of gears, a monstrous and triumphant showing of teeth by Old Man, and they were bumpbumping over the rough ruts.

"Old Man knows how to handle all them bitches, flesh or tin, two-legged, four-legged, wheeled. I sweat beer and passion and promise em a kick in the tailpipe if they don't behave, and that gets em all. I'm so figurin ugly I turn their stomachs. But once they get a whiff a the out-a-this-world stink a me, they're done for, they fall prostrooted at my big hairy feet. That's the way it's always been with us Paley men and the *G'yaga* wimmen. That's why their menfolks fear us, and why we get into so much trouble."

Dorothy did not say anything, and Paley fell silent as soon as the truck swung off the dump and onto U.S. Route 24. He seemed to fold up into himself, to be trying to make himself as inconspicuous as possible. During the three minutes it took the truck to get from the shanty to the city limits, he kept wiping his sweating palm against his blue workman's shirt.

But he did not try to release the tension with oaths. Instead, he muttered a string of what seemed to Dorothy nonsense rhymes.

"Eenie, meenie, minie, moe. Be a good Guy, help me go. Hoola boola, teenie weenie, ram em, damn em, figure em, duck em, watch me go, don't be a shmoe. Stop em, block em, sing a go go go."

Not until they had gone a mile into the city of Onaback and turned from 24 into an alley did he relax.

"Whew! That's torture, and I been doin it ever since I was sixteen, some years ago. Today seems worsen ever, maybe cause you're along. G'yaga men don't like it if they see me with one a their wimmen, specially a cute chick like you."

Suddenly, he smiled and broke into a song about being covered all over "with sweet violets, sweeter than all the roses." He sang other songs, some of which made Dorothy turn red in the face though at the same time she giggled. When they crossed a street to get from one alley to another, he cut off his singing, even in the middle of a phrase, and resumed it on the other side.

Reaching the west bluff, he slowed the truck to a crawl while his little blue eyes searched the ash heaps and garbage cans at the rears of the houses. Presently, he stopped the truck and climbed down to inspect his find.

"Guy In The Sky, we're off to a flyin start! Look!—some old grates from a coal furnace. And a pile a Coke and beer bottles, all redeemable. Get down, Dor'thy—if you want to know how us ragpickers make a livin, you gotta get in and sweat and cuss with us. And if you come acrosst any hats, be sure to tell me."

Dorothy smiled. But when she stepped down from the truck, she winced.

"What's the matter?"

"Headache."

"The sun'll boil it out. Here's how we do this collectin, see? The back end a the truck is boarded up into five sections. This section here is for the iron and the wood. This, for the paper. This, for the cardboard. You get a higher price for the cardboard. This, for rags. This, for bottles we kin get a refund on. If you find any int'restin books or magazines, put em on the seat. I'll decide if I want to keep em or throw em in with the old paper."

They worked swiftly, and then drove on. About a block later, they were interrupted at another heap by a leaf of a woman, withered and blown by the winds of time. She hobbled out from the back porch of a large three-storied house with diamond-shaped panes in the windows and doors and cupolas at the corners. In a quavering voice she explained that she was the widow of a wealthy lawyer who had died fifteen years ago. Not until today had she made up her mind to get rid of his collection of law books and legal papers. These were all neatly cased in cardboard boxes not too large to be handled.

Not even, she added, her pale watery eyes flickering from Paley to Dorothy, not even by a poor one-armed man and a young girl.

Old Man took off his homburg and bowed.

"Sure, ma'am, my daughter and myself'd be glad to help you out in your housecleanin."

"Your daughter?" croaked the old woman.

"She don't look like me a tall," he replied. "No wonder. She's my foster daughter, poor girl, she was orphaned when she was still fillin her diapers. My best friend was her father. He died savin my life, and as he laid gaspin his life away in my arms, he begged me to take care a her as if she was my own. And I kept my promise to my dyin friend, may his soul rest in peace. And even if I'm only a poor ragpicker, ma'am, I been doin my best to raise her to be a decent Godfearin obedient girl."

Dorothy had to run around to the other side of the truck where she could cover her mouth and writhe in an agony of attempting to smother her laughter. When she regained control, the old lady was telling Paley she'd show him where the books were. Then she started hobbling to the porch.

But Old Man, instead of following her across the yard, stopped by the fence that separated the alley from the backyard. He turned around and gave Dorothy a look of extreme despair.

"What's the matter?" she said. "Why're you sweating so? And shaking? And you're so pale."

"You'd laugh if I tole you, and I don't like to be laughed at."

"Tell me. I won't laugh."

He closed his eyes and began muttering. "Never mind, it's in the mind. Never mind, you're just fine." Opening his eyes, he shook himself like a dog just come from the water.

"I kin do it. I got the guts. All them books're a lotta beer money I'll lose if I don't go down into the bowels a hell and get em. Guy In The Sky, give me the guts a a goat and the nerve a a pork dealer in Palestine. You know Old Man ain't got a yellow streak. It's the wicked spell a the False Folkers workin on me. Come on, let's go, go, go."

And sucking in a deep breath, he stepped through the gateway. Head down, eyes on the grass at his feet, he shuffled toward the cellar door where the old lady stood peering at him.

Four steps away from the cellar entrance, he halted again. A small black spaniel had darted from around the corner of the house and begun yapyapping at him.

Old Man suddenly cocked his head to one side, crossed his eyes, and deliberately sneezed.

Yelping, the spaniel fled back around the corner, and Paley walked down the steps that led to the cool dark basement. As he did so, he muttered, "That puts the evil spell on em figurin dogs."

When they had piled all the books in the back of the truck, he took off his homburg and bowed again.

"Ma'am, my daughter and myself both thank you from the rockbottom a our poor but humble hearts for this treasure trove you give us. And if ever you've anythin else you don't want, and a strong back and a weak mind to carry it out...well, please remember we'll be down this alley every Blue Monday and Fish Friday about time the sun is three-quarters acrosst the sky. Providin it ain't rainin cause The Old Guy In The Sky is cryin in his beer over us poor mortals, what fools we be."

Then he put his hat on, and the two got into the truck and chugged off. They stopped by several other promising heaps before he announced that the truck was loaded enough. He felt like celebrating; perhaps they should stop off behind Mike's Tavern and down a few quarts. She replied that perhaps she might manage a drink if she could have a whiskey. Beer wouldn't set well.

"I got some money," rumbled Old Man, unbuttoning with slow clumsy fingers his shirt pocket and pulling out a roll of worn tattered bills while the truck's wheels rolled straight in the alley ruts.

"You brought me luck, so Old Man's gonna pay today through the hose, I mean, nose, har, har, har!"

♦ ♦ ♦

He stopped Fordiana behind a little neighborhood tavern. Dorothy, without being asked, took the two dollars he handed her and went into the building. She returned with a can opener, two quarts of beer, and a half pint of V.O.

"I added some of my money. I can't stand cheap whiskey."

They sat on the running board of the truck, drinking, Old Man doing most of the talking. It wasn't long before he was telling her of the times when the Real Folk, the Paleys, had lived in Europe and Asia by the side of the woolly mammoths and the cave lion.

"We worshiped The Old Guy In The Sky who says what the thunder says and lives in the east on the tallest mountain in the world. We faced the skulls a our dead to the east so they could see The Old Guy when he came to take them to live with him in the mountain.

"And we was doin fine for a long long time. Then, out a the east come them motherworshipin False Folk with their long straight legs and long straight necks and flat faces and thundermug round heads and their bows and arrows. They claimed they was sons a the goddess Mother Earth, who was a virgin. But we claimed the truth was that a crow with stomach trouble sat on a stump and when it left the hot sun hatched em out.

"Well, for a while we beat em hands-down because we was stronger. Even one a our wimmen could tear their strongest man to bits. Still, they had that bow and arrow, they kept pickin us off, and movin in and movin in, and we kept movin back slowly, till pretty soon we was shoved with our backs against the ocean.

"Then one day a big chief among us got a bright idea. 'Why don't we make bows and arrows, too?' he said. And so we did, but we was clumsy at makin and shootin em cause our hands was so big, though we could draw a heavier bow'n em. So we kept gettin run out a the good huntin grounds.

"There was one thin might a been in our favor. That was, we bowled the wimmen a the Falsers over with our smell. Not that we smell good. We stink like a pig that's been makin love to a billy goat on a manure pile. But, somehow, the wimmen folk a the Falsers was all mixed up in their chemistry, I guess you'd call it, cause they got all excited and developed roundheels when they caught a whiff a us. If we'd been left alone with em, we could a Don Juan'd them Falsers right off a the face a the earth. We would a mixed our blood with theirs so much that after a while you coun't tell the diff'runce. Specially since the kids lean to their pa's side in looks, Paley blood is so much stronger.

"But that made sure there would always be war tween us. Specially after our king, Old King Paley, made love to the daughter a the Falser king, King Raw Boy, and stole her away.

"Gawd, you should a seen the fuss then! Raw Boy's daughter flipped over Old King Paley. And it was her give him the bright idea a callin in every able-bodied Paley that was left and organizin em into one big army. Kind a puttin all our eggs in one basket, but it seemed a good idea. Every man big enough to carry a club went out in one big mob on Operation False Folk Massacre. And we ganged up on every little town a them motherworshipers we found. And kicked hell out a em. And roasted the men's hearts and ate em. And every now and then took a snack off the wimmen and kids, too.

"Then, all of a sudden, we come to a big plain. And there's a army a them False Folk, collected by Old King Raw Boy. They outnumber us, but we feel we kin lick the world. Specially since the magic strength a the *G'yaga* lies in their wimmen folk, cause they worship a woman god, The Old Woman In The Earth. And we've got their chief priestess, Raw Boy's daughter.

"All our own personal power is collected in Old King Paley's hat — his magical headpiece. All a us Paleys believed that a man's strength and his soul was in his headpiece.

"We bed down the night before the big battle. At dawn there's a cry that'd wake up the dead. It still sends shivers down the necks a us Paley's fifty thousand years later. It's King Paley roarin and cryin. We ask him why. He says that that dirty little sneakin little hoor, Raw Boy's daughter, has stole his headpiece and run off with it to her father's camp.

"Our knees turn weak as nearbeer. Our manhood is in the hands a our enemies. But out we go to battle, our witch doctors out in front rattlin their gourds and whirlin their bullroarers and prayin. And here comes the G'yaga medicine men doin the same. Only thing, their hearts is in their work cause they got Old King's headpiece stuck on the end a a spear.

"And for the first time they use dogs in war, too. Dogs never did like us any more'n we like em.

"And then we charge into each other. Bang! Wallop! Crash! Smash! Whack! Owwwrrroooo! And they kick hell out a us, do it to us. And we're never again the same, done forever. They had Old King's headpiece and with it our magic, cause we'd all put the soul a us Paleys in that hat.

"The spirit and power a us Paleys was prisoners cause that headpiece was. And life became too much for us Paleys. Them as wasn't slaughtered and eaten was glad to settle down on the garbage heaps a the conquerin Falsers and pick for a livin with the chickens, sometimes comin out second best.

"But we knew Old King's headpiece was hidden somewhere, and we organized a secret society and swore to keep alive his name and to search for the headpiece if it took us forever. Which it almost has, it's been so long.

"But even though we was doomed to live in shantytowns and stay off the streets and prowl the junkpiles in the alleys, we never gave up hope. And as time went on some a the nocounts a the G'yaga came down to live with us. And we and they had kids. Soon, most a us had disappeared into the bloodstream a the lowclass G'yaga. But there's always been a Paley family that tried to keep their blood pure. No man kin do no more, kin he?"

He glared at Dorothy. "What d'ya think a that?"

Weakly, she said, "Well, I've never heard anything like it."

"Gawdamighty!" snorted Old Man. "I give you a history longer'n a hoor's dream, more'n fifty thousand years a history, the secret story a a longlost race. And all you kin say is that you never heard nothin like it before."

He leaned toward her and clamped his huge hand over her thigh.

"Don't flinch from me!" he said fiercely. "Or turn your head away. Sure, I stink, and I offend your dainty figurin nostrils and upset your figurin delicate little guts. But what's a minute's whiff a me on your part compared to a lifetime on my part a havin all the stinkin garbage in the universe shoved up my nose, and my mouth filled with what you woun't say if your mouth was full a it? What do you say to that, huh?"

Coolly, she said, "Please take your hand off me."

"Sure, I din't mean nothin by it. I got carried away and forgot my place in society."

"Now, look here," she said earnestly. "That has nothing at all to do with your so-called social position. It's just that I don't allow anybody to take liberties with my body. Maybe I'm being ridiculously Victorian, but I want more than just sensuality. I want love, and —"

"OK, I get the idea."

Dorothy stood up and said, "I'm only a block from my apartment. I think I'll walk on home. The liquor's given me a headache."

"Yeah," he growled. "You sure it's the liquor and not me?"

She looked steadily at him. "I'm going, but I'll see you tomorrow morning. Does that answer your question?"

"OK," he grunted. "See you. Maybe."

She walked away very fast.

♦ ♦ ♦

Next morning, shortly after dawn, a sleepy-eyed Dorothy stopped her car before the Paley shanty. Deena was the only one home. Gummy had gone to the river to fish, and Old Man was in the outhouse. Dorothy took the opportunity to talk to Deena, and found her, as she had suspected, a woman of considerable education. However, although she was polite, she was reticent about her background. Dorothy, in an effort to keep the conversation going, mentioned that she had phoned her former anthropology professor and asked him about the chances of Old Man being a genuine Neanderthal. It was then that Deena broke her reserve and eagerly asked what the professor had thought.

"Well," said Dorothy, "he just laughed. He told me it was an absolute impossibility that a small group, even an inbred group isolated in the mountains, could have kept their cultural and genetic identity for fifty thousand years.

"I argued with him. I told him Old Man insisted he and his kind had existed in the village of Paley in the mountains of the Pyrenees until Napoleon's men found them and tried to draft them. Then they fled to America, after a stay in England. And his group was split up during the Civil War, driven out of the Great Smokies. He, as far as he knows, is the last purebreed, Gummy being a half or quarter-breed.

"The professor assured me that Gummy and Old Man were cases of glandular malfunctioning, of acromegaly. That they may have a superficial resemblance to the Neanderthal man, but a physical anthropologist could tell the difference at a glance. When I got a little angry and asked him if he wasn't taking an unscientific and prejudiced attitude, he became rather irritated. Our talk ended somewhat frostily.

"But I went down to the university library that night and read everything on what makes *Homo Neanderthalensis* different from *Homo sapiens.*"

"You almost sound as if you believe Old Man's private little myth is the truth," said Deena.

"The professor taught me to be convinced only by the facts and not to say anything is impossible," replied Dorothy. "If he's forgotten his own teachings, I haven't."

"Well, Old Man is a persuasive talker," said Deena. "He could sell the devil a harp and halo."

Old Man, wearing only a pair of blue jeans, entered the shanty. For the first time Dorothy saw his naked chest, huge, covered with long redgold hairs so numerous they formed a matting almost as thick as an orangutan's. However, it was not his chest but his bare feet at which she looked most intently. Yes, the big toes were widely separated from the others, and he certainly tended to walk on the outside of his feet.

His arm, too, seemed abnormally short in proportion to his body.

Old Man grunted a good morning and didn't say much for a while. But after he had sweated and cursed and chanted his way through the streets of Onaback and had arrived safely at the alleys of the west bluff, he relaxed. Perhaps he was helped by finding a large pile of papers and rags.

"Well, here we go to work, so don't you dare to shirk. Jump, Dor'thy! By the sweat a your brow, you'll earn your brew!"

When that load was on the truck, they drove off. Paley said, "How you like this life without no strife? Good, huh? You like alleys, huh?"

Dorothy nodded. "As a child, I liked alleys better than streets. And they still preserve something of their first charm for me. They were more fun to play in, so nice and cozy. The trees and bushes and fences leaned in at you and sometimes touched you as if they had hands and liked to feel your face to find out if you'd been there before, and they remembered you. You felt as if you were sharing a secret with the alleys and the things of the alleys. But streets, well, streets were always the same, and you had to watch out the cars didn't run you over, and the windows in the houses were full of faces and eyes, poking their noses in your business, if you can say that eyes had noses."

Old Man whopped and slapped his thigh so hard it would have broke if it had been Dorothy's.

"You must be a Paley! We feel that way, too! We ain't allowed to hang aroun streets, so we make our alleys into little kingdoms. Tell me, do you sweat just crossin a street from one alley to the next?"

He put his hand on her knee. She looked down at it but said nothing, and he left it there while the truck putputted along, its wheels following the ruts of the alley.

"No, I don't feel that way at all."

"Yeah? Well, when you was a kid, you wasn't so ugly you hadda stay off the streets. But I still wasn't too happy in the alleys because a them figurin dogs. Forever and forever they was barkin and bitin at me. So I took to beatin the bejesus out a them with a big stick I always carried. But after a while I found out I only had to look at em in a certain way. Yi, yi, yi, they'd run away yapping, like that old black spaniel did yesterday. Why? Cause they knew I was sneezin evil spirits at em. It was then I began to know I wasn't human. A course, my old man had been tellin me that ever since I could talk.

"As I grew up I felt every day that the spell a the *G'yaga* was gettin stronger. I was gettin dirtier and dirtier looks from em on the streets. And when I went down the alleys, I felt like I really *belonged* there. Finally, the day came when I coun't cross a street without gettin sweaty hands and cold feet and a dry mouth and breathin hard. That was cause I was becomin a full-grown Paley, and the curse a the *G'yaga* gets more powerful as you get more hair on your chest."

"Curse?" said Dorothy. "Some people call it a neurosis."

"It's a curse."

Dorothy didn't answer. Again, she looked down at her knee, and this time he removed his hand. He would have had to do it, anyway, for they had come to a paved street.

On the way down to the junk dealer's, he continued the same theme. And when they got to the shanty, he elaborated upon it.

During the thousands of years the Paley lived on the garbage piles of the *G'yaga,* they were closely watched. So, in the old days, it had been the custom for the priests and warriors of the False Folk to descend on the dumpheap dwellers whenever a strong and obstreperous Paley came to manhood. And they had gouged out an eye or cut off his hand or leg or some other member to ensure that he remembered what he was and where his place was.

"That's why I lost this arm," Old Man growled, waving the stump. "Fear a the *G'yaga* for the Paley did this to me."

Deena howled with laughter and said, "Dorothy, the truth is that he got drunk one night and passed out on the railroad tracks, and a freight train ran over his arm."

"Sure, sure, that's the way it was. But it coun't a happened if the Falsers din't work through their evil black magic. Nowadays, stead a cripplin us openly, they use spells. They ain't got the guts anymore to do it themselves."

Deena laughed scornfully and said, "He got all those psychopathic ideas from reading those comics and weird tale magazines and those crackpot books and from watching that TV program, *Alley Oop and the Dinosaur*. I can point out every story from which he's stolen an idea."

"You're a liar!" thundered Old Man.

He struck Deena on the shoulder. She reeled away from the blow, then leaned back toward him as if into a strong wind. He struck her again, this time across her purple birthmark. Her eyes glowed, and she cursed him. And he hit her once more, hard enough to hurt but not to injure.

Dorothy opened her mouth as if to protest, but Gummy lay a fat sweaty hand on her shoulder and lifted her finger to her own lips.

Deena fell to the floor from a particularly violent blow. She did not stand up again. Instead, she got to her hands and knees and crawled toward the refuge behind the big iron stove. His naked foot shoved her rear so that she was sent sprawling on her face, moaning, her long stringy black hair falling over her face and birthmark.

Dorothy stepped forward and raised her hand to grab Old Man. Gummy stopped her, mumbling, "'S all right. Leave em alone."

"Look at that figurin female bein happy!" snorted Old Man. "You know why I have to beat the hell out a her, when all I want is peace and quiet? Cause I look like a figurin caveman, and they're supposed to beat their hoors silly. That's why she took up with me."

"You're an insane liar," said Deena softly from behind the stove, slowly and dreamily nursing her pain like the memory of a lover's caresses. "I came to live with you because I'd sunk so low you were the only man that'd have me."

"She's a retired high society mainliner, Dor'thy," said Paley. "You never seen her without a longsleeved dress on. That's cause her arms're full a holes. It was me that kicked the monkey off a her back. I cured her with the wisdom and magic a the Real Folk, where you coax the evil spirit out by talkin it out. And she's been livin with me ever since. Kin't get rid a her.

"Now, you take that toothless bag there. I ain't never hit her. That shows I ain't no woman-beatin bastard, right? I hit Deena cause she likes it, wants it, but I don't ever hit Gummy.... Hey, Gummy, that kind a medicine ain't what you want, is it?"

And he laughed his incredibly hoarse, *hor, hor, hor.*

"You're a figurin liar," said Gummy, speaking over her shoulder because she was squatting down, fiddling with the TV controls. "You're the one knocked most a my teeth out."

"I knocked out a few rotten stumps you was gonna lose anyway. You had it comin cause you was runnin aroun with that O'Brien in his green shirt."

Gummy giggled and said, "Don't think for a minute I quit goin with that O'Brien in his green shirt just cause you slapped me aroun a little bit. I quit cause you was a better man 'n him."

Gummy giggled again. She rose and waddled across the room toward a shelf which held a bottle of her cheap perfume. Her enormous brass earrings swung, and her great hips swung back and forth.

"Look at that," said Old Man. "Like two bags a mush in a windstorm."

But his eyes followed them with kindling appreciation, and, on seeing her pour that reeking liquid over her pillow-sized bosom, he hugged her and buried his huge nose in the valley of her breasts and sniffed rapturously.

"I feel like a dog that's found an old bone he buried and forgot till just now," he growled, "Arf, arf, arf!"

Deena snorted and said she had to get some fresh air or she'd lose her supper. She grabbed Dorothy's hand and insisted she take a walk with her. Dorothy, looking sick, went with her.

◆ ◆ ◆

The following evening, as the four were drinking beer around the kitchen table, Old Man suddenly reached over and touched Dorothy affectionately. Gummy laughed, but Deena glared. However, she did not say anything to the girl but instead began accusing Paley of going too long without a bath. He called her a flatchested hophead and said that she was lying, because he had been taking a bath every day. Deena replied that, yes he had, ever since Dorothy had appeared on the scene. An argument raged. Finally, he rose from the table and turned the photograph of Deena's mother so it faced the wall.

Wailing, Deena tried to face it outward again. He pushed her away from it, refusing to hit her despite her insults — even when she howled at him that he wasn't fit to lick her mother's shoes, let alone blaspheme her portrait by touching it.

Tired of the argument, he abandoned his post by the photograph and shuffled to the refrigerator.

"If you dare turn her aroun till I give the word, I'll throw her in the creek. And you'll never see her again."

Deena shrieked and crawled onto her blanket behind the stove and there lay sobbing and cursing him softly.

Gummy chewed tobacco and laughed while a brown stream ran down her toothless jaws. "Deena pushed him too far that time."

"Ah, her and her figurin mother," snorted Paley. "Hey, Dor'thy, you know how she laughs at me cause I think Fordiana's got a soul. And I put the evil eye on em hounds? And cause I think the salvation a us Paleys'll be when we find out where Old King's hat's been hidden?

"Well, get a load a this. This here intellekchooall purple-faced dragon, this retired mainliner, this old broken-down nag for a monkey-jockey, she's the sooperstishus one. She thinks her mother's a god. And she prays to her and asks forgiveness and asks what's gonna happen in the future. And when she thinks nobody's aroun, she talks to her. Here she is, worshipin her mother like The Old Woman In The Earth, who's The Old Guy's enemy. And she knows that makes The Old Guy sore. Maybe that's the reason he ain't allowed me to find the longlost headpiece a Old King, though he knows I been lookin in every ash heap from here to Godknowswhere, hopin some fool *G'yaga* would throw it away never realizin what it was.

"Well, by all that's holy, that pitcher stays with its ugly face on the wall. Aw, shut up, Deena, I wanna watch *Alley Oop.*"

Shortly afterward, Dorothy drove home. There she again phoned her sociology professor. Impatiently, he went into more detail. He said that one reason Old Man's story of the war between the Neanderthals and the invading *Homo sapiens* was very unlikely was that there was evidence to indicate that *Homo sapiens* might have been in Europe before the Neanderthals — it was very possible the *Homo Neanderthalensis* was the invader.

"Not invader in the modern sense," said the professor. "The influx of a new species or race or tribe into Europe during the Paleolithic would have been a sporadic migration of little groups, an immigration which might have taken a thousand to ten thousand years to complete.

"And it is more than likely that *Neanderthalensis* and *sapiens* lived side by side for millennia with very little fighting between them because both were too busy struggling for a living. For one reason or another, probably because he was outnumbered, the Neanderthal was absorbed by the surrounding peoples. Some anthropologists have speculated that the Neanderthals were blondes and that they had passed their light hair directly to North Europeans.

"Whatever the guesses and surmises," concluded the professor, "it would be impossible for such a distinctly different minority to keep its special physical and cultural characteristics over a period of half a hundred millennia. Paley has concocted this personal myth to compensate for his extreme ugliness, his inferiority, his feelings of rejection. The elements of the myth came from the comic books and TV.

"However," concluded the professor, "in view of your youthful enthusiasm and naïveté, I will consider my judgment if you bring me some physical evidence of his Neanderthaloid origin. Say you could show me that he had a taurodont tooth. I'd be flabbergasted, to say the least."

"But, Professor," she pleaded, "why can't you give him a personal examination? One look at Old Man's foot would convince you, I'm sure."

"My dear, I am not addicted to wild-goose chases. My time is valuable."

That was that. The next day, she asked Old Man if he had ever lost a molar tooth or had an X-ray made of one.

"No," he said. "I got more sound teeth than brains. And I ain't gonna lose em. Long as I keep my headpiece, I'll keep my teeth and my digestion and my manhood. What's more, I'll keep my good sense, too. The loose-screw tighteners at the State Hospital really gave me a good goin-over, fore and aft, up and down, in and out, all night long, don't never take a hotel room right by the elevator. And they proved I wasn't hatched in a cuckoo clock. Even though they tore their hair and said somethin must be wrong. Specially after we had that row about my hat. I woun't let them take my blood for a test, you know, because I figured they was going to mix it with water—G'yaga magic—and turn my blood to water. Somehow, that Elkins got wise that I hadda wear my hat—cause I woun't take it off when I undressed for the physical, I guess—and he snatched my hat. And I was done for. Stealin it was stealin my soul; all Paleys wears their souls in their hats. I hadda get it back. So I ate humble pie; I let em poke and pry all over and take my blood."

There was a pause while Paley breathed in deeply to get power to launch another verbal rocket. Dorothy, who had been struck by an idea, said, "Speaking of hats, Old Man, what does this hat that the daughter of Raw Boy stole from King Paley look like? Would you recognize it if you saw it?"

Old Man stared at her with wide blue eyes for a moment before he exploded.

"Would I recognize it? Would the dog that sat by the railroad tracks recognize his tail after the locomotive cut it off? Would you recognize your own blood if somebody stuck you in the guts with a knife and it pumped out with every heartbeat? Certainly, I would recognize the hat a Old King Paley! Every Paley at his mother's knees get a detailed description a it. You want to hear about the hat? Well, hang on, chick, and I'll describe every hair and bone a it."

Dorothy told herself more than once that she should not be doing this. If she was trusted by Old Man, she was, in one sense, a false friend. But, she reassured herself, in another sense she was helping him. Should he find the hat, he might blossom forth, actually tear himself loose from the taboos that bound him to the dumpheap, to the alleys, to fear of dogs, to the conviction he was an inferior and oppressed citizen. Moreover, Dorothy told herself, it would aid her scientific studies to record his reactions.

The taxidermist she hired to locate the necessary materials and fashion them into the desired shape was curious, but she told him it was for an anthropological exhibit in Chicago and that it was meant to represent the headpiece of the medicine man of an Indian secret society dedicated to phallic mysteries. The taxidermist sniggered and said he'd give his eyeteeth to see those ceremonies.

Dorothy's intentions were helped by the run of good luck Old Man had in his alleypicking while she rode with him. Exultant, he swore he was headed for some extraordinary find; he could feel his good fortune building up.

"It's gonna hit," he said, grinning with his huge widely spaced gravestone teeth. "Like lightnin."

Two days later, Dorothy rose even earlier than usual and drove to a place behind the house of a well-known doctor. She had read in the society column that he and his family were vacationing in Alaska, so she knew they wouldn't be wondering at finding a garbage can already filled with garbage and a big cardboard box full of cast-off clothes. Dorothy had brought the refuse from her own apartment to make it seem as if the house were occupied. The old garments, with one exception, she had purchased at a Salvation Army store.

About nine that morning, she and Old Man drove down the alley on their scheduled route.

Old Man was first off the truck; Dorothy hung back to let him make the discovery.

Old Man picked the garments out of the box one by one.

"Here's a velvet dress Deena kin wear. She's been complainin she hasn't had a new dress in a long time. And here's a blouse and skirt big enough to wrap aroun an elephant. Gummy kin wear it. And here..."

He lifted up a tall conical hat with a wide brim and two balls of felted horsemane attached to the band. It was a strange headpiece, fashioned of roan horsehide over a ribwork of split bones. It must have been the only one of its kind in the world, and it certainly looked out of place in the alley of a mid-Illinois city.

Old Man's eyes bugged out. Then they rolled up, and he fell to the ground, as if shot. The hat, however, was still clutched in his hand.

Dorothy was terrified. She had expected any reaction but this. If he had suffered a heart attack, it would, she thought, be her fault.

Fortunately, Old Man had only fainted. However, when he regained consciousness, he did not go into ecstasies as she had expected. Instead, he looked at her, his face gray and said, "It kin't be! It must be a trick The Old Woman In The Earth's playing on me so she kin have the last laugh on me. How could it be the hat a Old King Paley's? Woun't the *G'yaga* that been keepin it in their famley all these years know what it is?"

"Probably not," said Dorothy. "After all, the *G'yaga*, as you call them, don't believe in magic anymore. Or it might be that the present owner doesn't even know what it is."

"Maybe. More likely it was thrown out by accident durin housecleanin. You know how stupid them wimmen are. Anyway, let's take it and get goin. The Old Guy In The Sky might a had a hand in fixin up this deal for me, and if he did, it's better not to ask questions. Let's go."

♦ ♦ ♦

Old Man seldom wore the hat. When he was home, he put it in the parrot cage and locked the cage door with the bicycle lock. At nights, the cage hung from the stand; days, it sat on the seat of the truck. Old Man wanted it always where he could see it.

Finding it had given him a tremendous optimism, a belief he could do anything. He sang and laughed even more than he had before, and he was even able to venture out onto the streets for several hours at a time before the sweat and shakings began.

Gummy, seeing the hat, merely grunted and made a lewd remark about its appearance. Deena smiled grimly and said, "Why haven't the horsehide and bones rotted away long ago?"

"That's just the kind a question a *G'yaga* dummy like you'd ask," said Old Man, snorting. "How kin the hat rot when there's a million Paley souls crowded into it, standin room only? There ain't even elbow room for germs. Besides, the horsehide and the bones're jampacked with the power and the glory a all the Paleys that died before our battle with Raw Boy, and all the souls that died since. It's seethin with soul-energy, the lid held on it by the magic a the *G'yaga*."

"Better watch out it don't blow up 'n wipe us all out," said Gummy, sniggering.

"Now you have the hat, what are you going to do with it?" asked Deena.

"I don't know. I'll have to sit down with a beer and study the situation."

Suddenly, Deena began laughing shrilly.

"My God, you've been thinking for fifty thousand years about this hat, and now you've got it, you don't know what to do about it! Well, I'll tell you what you'll do about it! You'll get to thinking big, all right! You'll conquer the world, rid it of all False Folk, all right! You fool! Even if your story isn't the raving of a lunatic, it would still be too late for you! You're alone! The last! One against two billion! Don't worry, World, this ragpicking Rameses, this alley Alexander, this junkyard Julius Caesar, he isn't going to conquer you! No, he's going to put on his hat, and he's going forth! To do what?

"To become a wrestler on TV, that's what! That's the height of his halfwit ambition—to be billed as the One-Armed Neanderthal, the Awful Apeman. That is the culmination of fifty thousand years, ha, ha, ha!"

The others looked apprehensively at Old Man, expecting him to strike Deena. Instead, he removed the hat from the cage, put it on, and sat down at the table with a quart of beer in his hand.

"Quit your cacklin, you old hen," he said. "I got my thinkin cap on!"

The next day Paley, despite a hangover, was in a very good mood. He chattered all the way to the west bluff and once stopped the truck so he could walk back and forth on the street and show Dorothy he wasn't afraid.

Then, boasting he could lick the world, he drove the truck up an alley and halted it by the backyard of a huge but somewhat rundown mansion. Dorothy looked at him curiously. He pointed to the jungle-thick shrubbery that filled a corner of the yard.

"Looks like a rabbit coun't get in there, huh? But Old Man knows thins the rabbits don't. Folly me."

Carrying the caged hat, he went to the shrubbery, dropped to all threes, and began inching his way through a very narrow passage. Dorothy stood looking dubiously into the tangle until a hoarse growl came from its depths.

"You scared? Or is your fanny too broad to get through here?"

"I'll try anything once," she announced cheerfully. In a short time she was crawling on her belly, then had come suddenly into a little clearing. Old Man was standing up. The cage was at his feet, and he was looking at a red rose in his hand.

She sucked in her breath. "Roses! Peonies! Violets!"

"Sure, Dor'thy" he said, swelling out his chest. "Paley's Garden a Eden, his secret hothouse. I found this place a couple a years ago, when I was lookin for a place to hide if the cops was lookin for me or I just wanted a place to be alone from everybody, including myself.

"I planted these rosebushes in here and these other flowers. I come here every now and then to check on em, spray em, prune em. I never take any home, even though I'd like to give Deena some. But Deena ain't no dummy, she'd know I was gettin em out a a garbage pail. And I just din't want to tell her about this place. Or anybody."

He looked directly at her as if to catch every twitch of a muscle in her face, every repressed emotion.

"You're the only person besides myself knows about this place." He held out the rose to her. "Here. It's yours."

"Thank you. I am proud, really proud, that you've shown this place to me."

"Really are? That makes me feel good. In fact, great."

"It's amazing. This, this spot of beauty. And...and..."

"I'll finish it for you. You never thought the ugliest man in the world, a dumpheaper, a man that ain't even a man or a human bein, a—I hate the word—a Neanderthal, could appreciate the beauty of a rose. Right? Well, I growed these because I love em.

"Look, Dor'thy. Look at this rose. It's round, not like a ball but a flattened roundness...."

"Oval."

"Sure. And look at the petals. How they fold in on one another, how they're arranged. Like one ring a red towers protectin the next ring a red towers. Protectin the gold cup on the inside, the precious source a life, the treasure. Or maybe that's the golden hair a the princess a the castle. Maybe. And look at the bright green leaves under the rose. Beautiful, huh? The Old Guy knew what he was doin when he made these. He was an artist then.

"But he must a been sufferin from a hangover when he shaped me, huh? His hands was shaky that day. And he gave up after a while and never bothered to finish me but went on down to the corner for some a the hair a the dog that bit him."

Suddenly; tears filled Dorothy's eyes.

"You shouldn't feel that way. You've got beauty, sensitivity, a genuine feeling, under..."

"Under this?" he said, pointing his finger at his face. "Sure. Forget it. Anyway, look at these green buds on these baby roses. Pretty, huh? Fresh with promise a the beauty to come. They're shaped like the breasts a young virgins."

He look a step toward her and put his arm around her shoulders.

"Dor'thy."

She put her hands on his chest and gently tried to shove herself away.

"Please," she whispered, "please, don't. Not after you've shown me how fine you really can be."

"What do you mean?" he said, not releasing her. "Ain't what I want to do with you just as fine and beautiful a thin as this rose here? And if you really feel for me, you'd want to let your flesh say what your mind thinks. Like the flowers when they open up for the sun."

She shook her head. "No. It can't be. Please. I feel terrible because I can't say yes. But I can't. I — you — there's too much diff — "

"Sure, we're diff'runt. Goin in diff'runt directions and then, comin roun the corner — bam! — we run into each other, and we wrap our arms aroun each other to keep from fallin."

He pulled her to him so her face was pressed against his chest.

"See!" he rumbled. "Like this. Now, breathe deep. Don't turn your head. Sniff away. Lock yourself to me, like we was glued and nothin could pull us apart. Breathe deep. I got my arm aroun you, like these trees roun these flowers. I'm not hurtin you: I'm givin you life and protectin you. Right? Breathe deep."

"Please," she whimpered. "Don't hurt me. Gently..."

"Gently it is. I won't hurt you. Not too much. That's right, don't hold yourself stiff against me, like you're stone. That's right, melt like butter. I'm not forcin you, Dor'thy, remember that. You want this, don't you?"

"Don't hurt me," she whispered. "You're so strong, oh my God, so strong."

♦ ♦ ♦

For two days, Dorothy did not appear at the Paleys'. The third morning, in an effort to fire her courage, she downed two double shots of V.O. before breakfast. When she drove to the dumpheap, she told the two women that she had not been feeling well. But she had returned because she wanted to finish her study, as it was almost at an end and her superiors were anxious to get her report.

Paley, though he did not smile when he saw her, said nothing. However, he kept looking at her out of the corners of his eyes when he thought she was watching him. And though he took the hat in its cage with him, he sweated and shook as before while crossing streets. Dorothy sat staring straight ahead, unresponsing to the few remarks he did make. Finally, cursing under his breath, he abandoned his effort to work as usual and drove to the hidden garden.

"Here we are," he said. "Adam and Eve returnin to Eden."

He peered from beneath the bony ridges of his brows at the sky. "We better hurry in. Looks as if The Old Guy got up on the wrong side a the bed. There's gonna be a storm."

"I'm not going in there with you," said Dorothy. "Not now or ever."

"Even after what we did, even if you said you loved me, I still make you sick?" he said. "You sure din't act then like Old Ugly made you sick."

"I haven't been able to sleep for two nights," she said tonelessly. "I've asked myself a thousand times why I did it. And each time I could only tell myself I didn't know. Something seemed to leap from you to me and take me over. I was powerless."

"You certainly wasn't paralyzed," said Old Man, placing his hand on her knee. "And if you was powerless, it was because you wanted to be."

"It's no use talking," she said. "You'll never get a chance again. And take your hand off me. If makes my flesh crawl."

He dropped his hand.

"All right. Back to business. Back to pickin people's piles a junk. Let's get out a here. Forget what I said. Forget this garden, too. Forget the secret I told you. Don't tell nobody. The dumpheapers'd laugh at me. Imagine Old Man Paley, the one-armed candidate for the puzzle factory, the fugitive from the Old Stone Age, growin peonies and roses! Big laugh, huh?"

Dorothy did not reply. He started the truck and, as they emerged onto the alley, they saw the sun disappear behind the clouds. The rest of the day, it did not come out, and Old Man and Dorothy did not speak to each other.

As they were going down Route 24 after unloading at the junkdealer's, they were stopped by a patrolman. He ticketed Paley for not having a chauffeur's license and made Paley follow him downtown to court. There Old Man had to pay a fine of twenty-five dollars. This, to everybody's amazement, he produced from his pocket.

As if that weren't enough, he had to endure the jibes of the police and the courtroom loafers. Evidently he had appeared in the police station before and was known as *King Kong, Alley Oop,* or just plain Chimp. Old Man trembled, whether with suppressed rage or nervousness Dorothy could not tell. But later, as Dorothy drove him home, he almost frothed at the mouth in a tremendous outburst of rage. By the time they were within sight of his shanty, he was shouting that his life savings had been wiped out and that it was all a plot by the *G'yaga* to beat him down to starvation.

It was then that the truck's motor died. Cursing, Old Man jerked the hood open so savagely that one rusty hinge broke. Further enraged by this, he tore the hood completely off and threw it away into the ditch by the roadside. Unable to find the cause of the breakdown, he took a hammer from the toolchest and began to beat the sides of the truck.

"I'll make her go, go, go!" he shouted. "Or she'll wish she had! Run, you bitch, purr, eat gasoline, rumble your damn belly and eat gasoline but run, run, run! Or your ex-lover, Old Man, sells you for junk, I swear it!"

Undaunted, Fordiana did not move.

Eventually, Paley and Dorothy had to leave the truck by the ditch and walk home. And as they crossed the heavily traveled highway to get to the dumpheap, Old Man was forced to jump to keep from getting hit by a car.

He shook his fist at the speeding auto.

"I know you're out to get me!" he howled. "But you won't! You been tryin for fifty thousand years, and you ain't made it yet! We're still fightin!"

At that moment, the black sagging bellies of the clouds overhead ruptured. The two were soaked before they could take four steps. Thunder bellowed, and lightning slammed into the earth on the other end of the dumpheap.

Old Man growled with fright, but seeing he was untouched, he raised his fist to the sky.

"OK, OK, so you got it in for me, too. I get it. OK, OK!"

Dripping, the two entered the shanty, where he opened a quart of beer and began drinking. Deena took Dorothy behind a curtain and gave her a towel to dry herself with and one of her white terrycloth robes to put on. By the time Dorothy came out from behind the curtain, she found Old Man opening his third quart. He was accusing Deena of not frying the fish correctly, and when she answered him sharply, he began accusing her of every fault, big or small, real or imaginary, of which he could think. In fifteen minutes, he was nailing the portrait of her mother to the wall with its face inward. And she was whimpering behind the stove and tenderly stroking the spots where he had struck her. Gummy protested, and he chased her out into the rain.

Dorothy at once put her wet clothes on and announced she was leaving. She'd walk the mile into town and catch the bus.

Old Man snarled, "Go! You're too snotty for us, anyway. We ain't your kind, and that's that."

"Don't go," pleaded Deena. "If you're not here to restrain him, he'll be terrible to us."

"I'm sorry," said Dorothy. "I should have gone home this morning."

"You sure should," he growled. And then began weeping, his pushed-out lips fluttering like a bird's wings, his face twisted like a gargoyle's.

"Get out before I forget myself and throw you out," he sobbed.

Dorothy, with pity on her face, shut the door gently behind her.

♦ ♦ ♦

The following day was Sunday. That morning, her mother phoned her she was coming down from Waukegan to visit her. Could she take Monday off?

Dorothy said yes, and then, sighing, she called her supervisor. She told him she had all the data she needed for the Paley report and that she would begin typing it out.

Monday night, after seeing her mother off on the train, she decided to pay the Paleys a farewell visit. She could not endure another sleepless night filled with fighting the desire to get out of bed again and again, to scrub herself clean, and the pain of having to face Old Man and the two women in the morning. She felt that if she said goodbye to the Paleys, she could say farewell to those feelings, too, or, at least, time would wash them away more quickly.

The sky had been clear, star-filled, when she left the railroad station. By the time she had reached the dumpheap clouds had swept out from the west, and a blinding rainstorm was deluging the city. Going over the bridge, she saw by the lights of her headlamps that the Kickapoo Creek had become a small river in the two days of heavy rains. Its muddy frothing current roared past the dump and on down to the Illinois River, a half mile away.

So high had it risen that the waters lapped at the doorsteps of the shanties. The trucks and jalopies parked outside them were piled high with household goods, and their owners were ready to move at a minute's notice.

Dorothy parked her car a little off the road, because she did not want to get it stuck in the mire. By the time she had walked to the Paley shanty, she was in stinking mud up to her calves, and night had fallen.

In the light streaming from a window stood Fordiana, which Old Man had apparently succeeded in getting started. Unlike the other vehicles, it was not loaded.

Dorothy knocked on the door and was admitted by Deena. Paley was sitting in the ragged easy chair. He was clad only in a pair of faded and patched blue jeans. One eye was surrounded by a big black, blue, and green bruise. The horsehide hat of Old King was firmly jammed onto his head, and one hand clutched the neck of a quart of beer as if he were choking it to death.

Dorothy looked curiously at the black eye but did not comment on it. Instead, she asked him why he hadn't packed for a possible flood.

Old Man waved the naked stump of his arm at her.

"It's the doins a The Old Guy In The Sky. I prayed to the old idiot to stop the rain, but it rained harder'n ever. So I figure it's really The Old Woman In The Earth who's kickin up this rain. The Old Guy's too feeble to stop her. He needs strength. So…I thought about pouring out the blood a a virgin to him, so he kin lap it up and get his muscles back with that. But I give that up, cause there ain't no such thin anymore, not within a hundred miles a here, anyway.

"So...I been thinkin about goin outside and doin the next best thing, that is pouring a quart or two a beer out on the ground for him. What the Greeks call pourin a liberation to the Gods...."

"Don't let him drink none a that cheap beer," warned Gummy. "This rain fallin on us is bad enough. I don't want no god pukin all over the place."

He hurled the quart at her. It was empty, because he wasn't so far gone he'd waste a full or even half-full bottle. But it was smashed against the wall, and since it was worth a nickel's refund, he accused Gummy of malicious waste.

"If you'd a held still, it woun't a broke."

Deena paid no attention to the scene. "I'm pleased to see you, child," she said. "But it might have been better if you had stayed home tonight."

She gestured at the picture of her mother, still nailed face inward. "He's not come out of his evil mood yet."

"You kin say that again," mumbled Gummy. "He got a pistol-whippin from that young Limpy Doolan who lives in that packinbox house with the Jantzen bathin suit ad pasted on the side, when Limpy tried to grab Old King's hat off a Old Man's head just for fun."

"Yeah, he tried to grab it," said Paley. "But I slapped his hand hard. Then he pulls a gun out a his coat pocket with the other hand and hit me in this eye with its butt. That don't stop me. He sees me comin at him like I'm late for work, and he says he'll shoot me if I touch him again. My old man din't raise no silly sons, so I don't charge him. But I'll get him sooner or later. And he'll be limpin in both legs, if he walks at all.

"But I don't know why I never had nothing but bad luck ever since I got this hat. It ain't supposed to be that way. It's supposed to be bringin me all the good luck the Paleys ever had."

He glared at Dorothy and said, "Do you know what? I had good luck until I showed you that place, you know, the flowers. And then, after you know what, everythin went sour as old milk. What did you do, take the power out a me by doin what you did? Did The Old Woman In The Earth send you to me so you'd draw the muscle and luck and life out a me if I found the hat when Old Guy placed it in my path?"

He lurched up from the easy chair, clutched two quarts of beer from the refrigerator to his chest, and staggered toward the door.

"Kin't stand the smell in here. Talk about *my* smell. I'm sweet violets, compared to the fish a some a you. I'm goin out where the air's fresh. I'm goin out and talk to The Old Guy In The Sky, hear what the thunder has to say to me. He understands me; he don't give a damn if I'm a ugly old man that's ha'f-ape."

Swiftly, Deena ran in front of him and held out her claws at him like a gaunt, enraged alley cat.

"So that's it! You've had the indecency to insult this young girl! You evil beast!"

Old Man halted, swayed, carefully deposited the two quarts on the floor. Then he shuffled to the picture of Deena's mother and ripped it from the wall. The nails screeched; so did Deena.

"What are you going to do?"

"Somethin I been wantin to do for a long long time. Only I felt sorry for you. Now I don't. I'm gonna throw this idol a yours into the creek. Know why? Cause I think she's a delegate a The Old Woman In The Earth, Old Guy's enemy. She's been sent here to watch on me and report to Old Woman on what I was doin. And you're the one brought her in this house."

"Over my dead body you'll throw that in the creek!" screamed Deena.

"Have it your way," he growled, lurching forward and driving her to one side with his shoulder.

Deena grabbed at the frame of the picture he held in his hand, but he hit her over the knuckles with it. Then he lowered it to the floor, keeping it from falling over with his leg while he bent over and picked up the two quarts in his huge hand. Clutching them, he squatted until his stump was level with the top part of the frame. The stump clamped down over the upper part of the frame, he straightened, holding it tightly, lurched toward the door, and was gone into the driving rain and crashing lightning.

Deena stared into the darkness for a moment, then ran after him.

Stunned, Dorothy watched them go. Not until she heard Gummy mumbling, "They'll kill each other," was Dorothy able to move.

She ran to the door, looked out, turned back to Gummy.

"What's got into him?" she cried. "He's so cruel, yet I know he has a soft heart. Why must he be this way?"

"It's you," said Gummy. "He thought it din't matter how he looked, what he did, he was still a Paley. He thought his sweat would get you like it did all em chicks he was braggin about, no matter how uppity the sweet young thin was. 'N you hurt him when you din't dig him. Specially cause he thought more a you 'n anybody before.

"Why'd you think life's been so miserable for us since he found you? What the hell, a man's a man, he's always got the eye for the chicks, right? Deena din't see that. Deena hates Old Man. But Deena kin't do without him, either...."

"I have to stop them," said Dorothy, and she plunged out into the black and white world.

Just outside the door, she halted, bewildered. Behind her, light streamed from the shanty, and to the north was a dim glow from the city of Onaback. But elsewhere was darkness. Darkness, except when the lightning burned away the night for a dazzling, frightening second.

She ran around the shanty toward the Kickapoo, some fifty yards away — she was sure that they'd be somewhere by the back of the creek. Halfway to the stream, another flash showed her a white figure by the bank.

It was Deena in her terrycloth robe, Deena now sitting up in the mud, bending forward, shaking with sobs.

"I got down on my knees," she moaned. "To him, to him. And I begged him to spare my mother. But he said I'd thank him later for freeing me from worshipping a false goddess. He said I'd kiss his hand."

Deena's voice rose to a scream. "And then he did it! He tore my blessed mother to bits! Threw her in the creek! I'll kill him! I'll kill him!"

Dorothy patted Deena's shoulder. "There, there. You'd better get back to the house and get dry. It's a bad thing he's done, but he's not in his right mind. Where'd he go?"

"Toward that clump of cottonwoods where the creek runs into the river."

"You go back," said Dorothy. "I'll handle him. I can do it."

Deena seized her hand.

"Stay away from him. He's hiding in the woods now. He's dangerous, dangerous as a wounded boar. Or as one of his ancestors when they were hurt and hunted by ours."

"Ours?" said Dorothy. "You mean you believe his story?"

"Not all of it. Just part. That tale of his about the mass invasion of Europe and King Paley's hat is nonsense. Or, at least it's been distorted through God only knows how many thousands of years. But it's true he's at least part Neanderthal. Listen! I've fallen low, I'm only a junkman's whore. Not even that, now — Old Man never touches me anymore, except to hit me. And that's not his fault, really. I ask for it; I want it.

"But I'm not a moron. I got books from the library, read what they say about the Neanderthal. I studied Old Man carefully. And I know he must be what he says he is. Gummy, too—she's at least a quarter-breed."

Dorothy pulled her hand out of Deena's grip.

"I have to go. I have to talk to Old Man, tell him I'm not seeing him anymore."

"Stay away from him," pleaded Deena, again seizing Dorothy's hand. "You'll go to talk, and you'll stay to do what I did. What a score of others did. We let him make love to us because he isn't human. Yet, we found Old Man as human as any man, and some of us stayed after the lust was gone because love had come in."

Dorothy gently unwrapped Deena's fingers from her hand and began walking away.

Soon she came to the group of cottonwood trees by the bank where the creek and the river met and there she stopped.

"Old Man!" she called in a break between the rolls of thunder. "Old Man! It's Dorothy!"

A growl as of a bear disturbed in his cave answered her, and a figure like a tree trunk come to life stepped out of the inkiness between the cottonwoods.

"What you come for?" he said, approaching so close to her that his enormous nose almost touched hers. "You want me just as I am, Old Man Paley, descendant a the Real Folk—Paley, who loves you? Or you come to give the batty old junkman a tranquilizer so you kin take him by the hand like a lamb and lead him back to the slaughterhouse, the puzzle factory, where they'll stick a ice pick back a his eyeball and rip out what makes him a man and not an ox."

"I came..."

"Yeah?"

"For this!" she shouted, and she snatched off his hat and raced away from him, toward the river.

Behind her rose a bellow of agony so loud she could hear it even above the thunder. Feet splashed as he gave pursuit.

Suddenly, she slipped and sprawled facedown in the mud. At the same time, her glasses fell off. Now it was her turn to feel despair, for in this halfworld she could see nothing without her glasses except the lightning flashes. She must find them. But if she delayed to hunt for them, she'd lose her headstart.

She cried out with joy, for her groping fingers found what they sought. But the breath was knocked out of her, and she dropped the glasses again as a heavy weight fell upon her back and half stunned her. Vaguely, she was aware that the hat had been taken away from her. A moment later, as her senses came back into focus, she realized she was being raised into the air. Old Man was holding her in the crook of his arm, supporting part of her weight on his bulging belly.

"My glasses. Please, my glasses. I need them."

"You won't be needin em for a while. But don't worry about em. I got em in my pants pocket. Old Man's takin care a you."

His arm tightened around her so she cried out with pain.

Hoarsely, he said, "You was sent down by the *G'yaga* to get that hat, wasn't you? Well, it din't work cause The Old Guy's stridin the sky tonight, and he's protectin his own."

Dorothy bit her lip to keep from telling him that she had wanted to destroy the hat because she hoped that that act would also destroy the guilt of having made it in the first place. But she couldn't tell him that. If he knew she had made a false hat, he would kill her in his rage.

"No. Not again," she said. "Please. Don't. I'll scream. They'll come after you. They'll take you to the State Hospital and lock you up for life. I swear I'll scream."

"Who'll hear you? Only The Old Guy, and he'd get a kick out a seein you in this fix cause you're a Falser and you took the stuffin right out a my hat and me with your Falser Magic. But I'm gettin back what's mine and his, the same way you took it from me. The door swings both ways."

He stopped walking and lowered her to a pile of wet leaves. "Here we are. The forest like it was in the old days. Don't worry. Old Man'll protect you from the cave bear and the bull a the woods. But who'll protect you from Old Man, huh?"

Lightning exploded so near that for a second they were blinded and speechless. Then Paley shouted, "The Old Guy's whoopin it up tonight, just like he used to do! Blood and murder and wickedness're ridin the howlin night air!"

He pounded his immense chest with his huge fist.

"Let The Old Guy and The Old Woman fight it out tonight. They ain't goin to stop us, Dor'thy. Not unless that hairy old god in the clouds is going to fry me with his lightnin, jealous a me cause I'm havin what he kin't."

Lightning rammed against the ground from the charged skies, and lightning leaped up to the clouds from the charged earth. The rain fell harder than before, as if it were being shot out of a great pipe from a mountain river and pouring directly over them. But for some time the flashes did not come close to the cottonwoods. Then, one ripped apart the night beside them, deafened and stunned them.

And Dorothy, looking over Old Man's shoulder, thought she would die of fright because there was a ghost standing over them. It was tall and white, and its shroud flapped in the wind, and its arms were raised in a gesture like a curse.

But it was a knife that it held in its hand.

Then, the fire that rose like a cross behind the figure was gone, and night rushed back in.

Dorothy screamed. Old Man grunted, as if something had knocked the breath from him.

He rose to his knees, gasped something unintelligible, and slowly got to his feet. He turned his back to Dorothy so he could face the thing in white. Lightning flashed again. Once more Dorothy screamed, for she saw the knife sticking out of his back.

Then the white figure had rushed toward Old Man. But instead of attacking him, it dropped to its knees and tried to kiss his hand and babbled for forgiveness.

No ghost. No man. Deena, in her white terrycloth robe.

"I did it because I love you!" screamed Deena.

Old Man, swaying back and forth, was silent.

"I went back to the shanty for a knife, and I came here because I knew what you'd be doing, and I didn't want Dorothy's life ruined because of you, and I hated you, and I wanted to kill you. But I don't really hate you."

Slowly, Paley reached behind him and gripped the handle of the knife. Lightning made everything white around him, and by its brief glare the women saw him jerk the blade free of his flesh.

Dorothy moaned, "It's terrible, terrible. All my fault, all my fault."

She groped through the mud until her fingers came across the Old Man's jeans and its backpocket, which held her glasses. She put the glasses on, only to find that she could not see anything because of the darkness. Then, and not until then, she became concerned about locating her own clothes. On her hands and knees she searched through the wet leaves and grass. She was about to give up and go back to Old Man when another lightning flash showed the heap to her left. Giving a cry of joy, she began to crawl to it.

But another stroke of lightning showed her something else. She screamed and tried to stand up but instead slipped and fell forward on her face.

Old Man, knife in hand, was walking slowly toward her.

"Don't try to run away!" he bellowed. "You'll never get away! The Old Guy'll light thins up for me so you kin't sneak away in the dark. Besides, your white skin shines in the night, like a rotten toadstool. You're done for. You snatched away my hat so you could get me out here defenseless, and then Deena could stab me in the back. You and her are Falser witches, I know damn well!"

"What do you think you're doing?" asked Dorothy. She tried to rise again but could not. It was as if the mud had fingers around her ankles and knees.

"The Old Guy's howlin for the blood a G'yaga wimmen. And he's gonna get all the blood he wants. It's only fair. Deena put the knife in me, and The Old Woman got some a my blood to drink. Now it's your turn to give The Old Guy some a yours."

"Don't!" screamed Deena. "Don't! Dorothy had nothing to do with it! And you can't blame me, after what you were doing to her!"

"She'd done everythin to me. I'm gonna make the last sacrifice to Old Guy. Then they kin do what they want to me. I don't care. I'll have had one moment a bein a real Real Folker."

Deena and Dorothy both screamed. In the next second, lightning broke the darkness around them. Dorothy saw Deena hurl herself on Old Man's back and carry him downward. Then, night again.

There was a groan. Then, another blast of light. Old Man was on his knees, bent almost double but not bent so far Dorothy could not see the handle of the knife that was in his chest.

"Oh, Christ!" wailed Deena. "When I pushed him, he must have fallen on the knife. I heard the bone in his chest break. Now he's dying!"

Paley moaned. "Yeah, you done it now, you sure paid me back, din't you? Paid me back for my takin the monkey off a your back and supportin you all these years."

"Oh, Old Man," sobbed Deena, "I didn't mean to do it. I was just trying to save Dorothy and save you from yourself. Please! Isn't there anything I can do for you?"

"Sure you kin. Stuff up the two big holes in my back and chest. My blood, my breath, my real soul's flowin out a me. Guy In the Sky, what a way to die! Kilt by a crazy woman!"

"Keep quiet," said Dorothy. "Save your strength. Deena, you run to the service station. It'll still be open. Call a doctor."

"Don't go, Deena," he said. "It's too late. I'm hangin onto my soul by its big toe now; in a minute I'll have to let go, and it'll jump out a me like a beagle after a rabbit.

"Dor'thy, Dor'thy, was it the wickedness a The Old Woman put you up to this? I must a meant something to you...under the flowers...maybe it's better...I felt like a god, then...not what I really am...a crazy old junkman...a alley man....Just think a it...fifty thousand years behint me...older'n Adam and Eve by far...now, this...."

Deena began weeping. He lifted his hand, and she seized it.

"Let loose," he said faintly. "I was gonna knock hell outta you for blubberin...just like a Falser bitch...kill me...then cry...you never did 'preciate me...like Dorothy...."

"His hand's getting cold," murmured Deena.

"Deena, bury that damn hat with me...least you kin do....Hey, Deena, who you goin to for help when you hear that monkey chitterin outside the door, huh? Who...?"

Suddenly, before Dorothy and Deena could push him back down, he sat up. At the same time, lightning hammered into the earth nearby and it showed them his eyes, looking past them out into the night.

He spoke, and his voice was stronger, as if life had drained back into him through the holes in his flesh.

"Old Guy's given me a good send-off. Lightnin and thunder. The works. Nothin cheap about him, huh? Why not? He knows this is the end a the trail for me. The last a his worshipers...last a the Paleys...."

He sank back and spoke no more.

◆ ◆ ◆ ◆ ◆ ◆ ◆ ◆ ◆ ◆ ◆ ◆ ◆ ◆ My Sister's Brother

The sixth night on Mars, Lane wept.

He sobbed loudly while tears ran down his cheeks. He smacked his right fist into the palm of his left hand until the flesh burned. He howled with loneliness. He swore the most obscene and blasphemous oaths he knew.

After a while, he quit weeping. He dried his eyes, downed a shot of Scotch, and felt much better.

He wasn't ashamed because he had bawled like a woman. After all, there had been a Man who had not been ashamed to weep. He could dissolve in tears the grinding stones within; he was the reed that bent before the wind, not the oak that toppled, roots and all.

Now, the weight and the ache in his breast gone, feeling almost cheerful, he made his scheduled report over the transceiver to the circum-Martian vessel five hundred and eight miles overhead. Then he did what men must do any place in the universe. Afterward, he lay down in the bunk and opened the one personal book he had been allowed to bring along, an anthology of the world's greatest poetry.

He read here and there, running, pausing for only a line or two, then completing in his head the thousand-times murmured lines. Here and there he read, like a bee tasting the best of the nectar....

> It is the voice of my beloved that knocketh, saying,
> Open to me, my sister, my love; my dove, my undefiled...

> We have a little sister,
> And she hath no breasts;
> What shall we do for our sister
> In the day when she shall be spoken for?

> Yea, though I walk through the valley of the shadow of death,
> I will fear no evil for Thou art with me...

Come live with me and be my love
And we shall all the pleasures prove...

It lies not in our power to love or hate
For will in us is over-ruled by fate...

With thee conversing, I forget all time,
All seasons, and their change, all please alike...

He read on about love and man and woman until he had almost forgotten his troubles. His lids drooped; the book fell from his hand. But he roused himself, climbed out of the bunk, got down on his knees, and prayed that he be forgiven and that his blasphemy and despair be understood. And he prayed that his four lost comrades be found safe and sound. Then he climbed back into the bunk and fell asleep.

At dawn he woke reluctantly to the alarm clock's ringing. Nevertheless, he did not fall back into sleep but rose, turned on the transceiver, filled a cup with water and instant, and dropped in a heat pill. Just as he finished the coffee, he heard Captain Stroyansky's voice from the 'ceiver. Stroyansky spoke with barely a trace of Slavic accent.

"Cardigan Lane? You awake?"

"More or less. How are you?"

"If we weren't worried about all of you down there, we'd be fine."

"I know. Well, what are your orders?"

"There is only one thing to do, Lane. You must go look for the others. Otherwise, you cannot get back up to us. It takes at least two more men to pilot the rocket."

"Theoretically, one man can pilot the beast," replied Lane. "But it's uncertain. However, that doesn't matter. I'm leaving at once to look for the others. I'd do that even if you ordered otherwise."

Stroyansky chuckled. Then he barked like a seal. "The success of the expedition is more important than the fate of four men. Theoretically, anyway. But if I were in your shoes, and I'm glad I'm not, I would do the same. So, good luck, Lane."

"Thanks," said Lane. "I'll need more than luck. I'll also need God's help. I suppose He's here, even if the place does look God forsaken."

He looked through the transparent double plastic walls of the dome.

"The wind's blowing about twenty-five miles an hour. The dust is covering the tractor tracks. I have to get going before they're covered up entirely. My supplies are all packed; I've enough food, air, and water to last me six days. It makes a big package, the air tanks and the sleeping tent bulk large. It's over a hundred Earth pounds, but here only about forty. I'm also taking a rope, a knife, a pickax, a flare pistol, half a dozen flares. And a walkie-talkie.

"It should take me two days to walk the thirty miles to the spot where the tracs last reported. Two days to look around. Two days to get back."

"You be back in five days!" shouted Stroyansky. "That's an order! It shouldn't take you more than one day to scout around. Don't take chances. Five days!"

And then, in a softer voice, "Good luck, and, if there is a God, may He help you!"

Lane tried to think of things to say, things that might perhaps go down with the *Doctor Livingstone, I presume*, category. But all he could say was, "So long."

Twenty minutes later, he closed behind him the door to the dome's pressure lock. He strapped on the towering pack and began to walk. But when he was about fifty yards from the base, he felt compelled to turn around for one long look at what he might never see again. There, on the yellow-red felsite plain, stood the pressurized bubble that was to have been the home of the five men for a year. Nearby squatted the glider that had brought them down, its enormous wings spreading far, its skids covered with the forever-blowing dust.

Straight ahead of him was the rocket, standing on its fins, pointing toward the blue-black sky, glittering in the Martian sun, shining with promise of power, escape from Mars, and return to the orbital ship. It had come down to the surface of Mars on the back of the glider in a hundred-and-twenty-mile an hour landing. After it had dropped the two six-ton caterpillar tractors it carried, it had been pulled off the glider and tilted on end by winches pulled by those very tractors. Now it waited for him and for the other four men.

"I'll be back," he murmured to it. "And if I have to, I'll take you up by myself."

He began to walk, following the broad double tracks left by the tank. The tracks were faint, for they were two days old, and the blowing silicate dust had almost filled them. The tracks made by the first tank, which had left three days ago, were completely hidden.

The trail led northwest. It left the three-mile wide plain between two hills of naked rock and entered the quarter-mile corridor between two rows of vegetation. The rows ran straight and parallel from horizon to horizon, for miles behind him and miles ahead.

Lane, on the ground and close to one row, saw it for what it was. Its foundation was an endless three-foot high tube, most of whose bulk, like an iceberg's, lay buried in the ground. The curving sides were covered with blue-green lichenoids that grew on every rock or projection. From the spine of the tube, separated at regular intervals, grew the trunks of plants. The trunks were smooth shiny blue-green pillars two feet thick and six feet high. Out of their tops spread radially many pencil-thin branches, like bats' fingers. Between the fingers stretched a blue-green membrane, the single tremendous leaf of the umbrella tree.

When Lane had first seen them from the glider as it hurtled over them, he had thought they looked like an army of giant hands uplifted to catch the sun. Giant they were, for each rib-supported leaf measured fifty feet across. And hands they were, hands to beg for and catch the rare gold of the tiny sun. During the day, the ribs on the side nearest the moving sun dipped toward the ground, and the furthest ribs tilted upward. Obviously, the daylong maneuver was designed to expose the complete area of the membrane to the light, to allow not an inch to remain in shadow.

It was to be expected that strange forms of plant life would be found here. But structures built by animal life were not expected. Especially when they were so large and covered an eighth of the planet.

These structures were the tubes from which rose the trunks of the umbrella trees. Lane had tried to drill through the rocklike side of the tube. So hard was it, it had blunted one drill and had done a second no good before he had chipped off a small piece. Contented for the moment with that, he had taken it to the dome, there to examine it under a microscope. After an amazed look, he had whistled. Embedded in the cementlike mass were plant cells. Some were partially destroyed; some, whole.

Further tests had shown him that the substance was composed of cellulose, a ligninlike stuff, various nucleic acids, and unknown materials.

He had reported his discovery and also his conjecture to the orbital ship. Some form of animal life had, at some time, chewed up and partially digested wood and then had regurgitated it as a cement. The tubes had been fashioned from the cement.

The following day he intended to go back to the tube and blast a hole in it. But two of the men had set out in a tractor on a field exploration. Lane, as radio operator for that day, had stayed in the dome. He was to keep in contact with the two, who were to report to him every fifteen minutes.

The tank had been gone about two hours and must have been about thirty miles away, when it had failed to report. Two hours later, the other tank, carrying two men, had followed the prints of the first party

They had gone about thirty miles from base and were maintaining continuous radio contact with Lane.

"There's a slight obstacle ahead," Greenberg had said. "It's a tube coming out at right angles from the one we've been paralleling. It has no plants growing from it. Not much of a rise, not much of a drop on the other side, either. We'll make it easy."

Then he had yelled.

That was all.

Now, the day after, Lane was on foot, following the fading trail. Behind him lay the base camp, close to the junction of the two *canali* known as Avernus and Tartarus. He was between two of the rows of vegetation which formed Tartarus, and he was traveling northeastward, toward the Sirenum Mare, the so-called Siren Sea. The Mare, he supposed, would be a much broader group of treebearing tubes.

He walked steadily while the sun rose higher and the air grew warmer. He had long ago turned off his suit-heater. This was summer and close to the equator. At noon the temperature would be around seventy degrees Fahrenheit.

But at dusk, when the temperature had plunged through the dry air to zero, Lane was in his sleeping tent. It looked like a cocoon, being sausage-shaped and not much larger than his body. It was inflated so he could remove his helmet and breathe while he warmed himself from the battery-operated heater and ate and drank. The tent was also very flexible; it changed its cocoon shape to a triangle while Lane sat on a folding chair from which hung a plastic bag and did that which every man must do.

During the daytime he did not have to enter the sleeping tent for this. His suit was ingeniously contrived so he could unflap the rear section and expose the necessary area without losing air or pressure from the rest of his suit. Naturally, there was no thought of tempting the teeth of the Martian night. Sixty seconds at midnight were enough to get a severe frostbite where one sat down.

Lane slept until half an hour after dawn, ate, deflated the tent, folded it, stowed it, the battery, heater, food-box, and folding chair into his pack, threw away the plastic sack, shouldered the pack, and resumed his walk.

By noon the tracks faded out completely. It made little difference, for there was only one route the tanks could have taken. That was the corridor between the tubes and the trees.

Now he saw what the two tanks had reported. The trees on his right began to look dead. The trunks and leaves were brown, and the ribs drooped.

He began walking faster, his heart beating hard. An hour passed, and still the line of dead trees stretched as far as he could see.

"It must be about here," he said out loud to himself.

Then he stopped. Ahead was an obstacle.

It was the tube of which Greenberg had spoken, the one that ran at right angles to the other two and joined them.

Lane looked at it and thought that he could still hear Greenberg's despairing cry.

That thought seemed to turn a valve in him so that the immense pressure of loneliness, which he had succeeded in holding back until then, flooded in. The blue-black of the sky became the blackness and infinity of space itself, and he was a speck of flesh in an immensity as large as Earth's land area, a speck that knew no more of this world than a newborn baby knows of his.

Tiny and helpless, like a baby....

No, he murmured to himself, not a baby. Tiny, yes. Helpless, no. Baby, no. I am a man, a man, an Earthman....

Earthman: Cardigan Lane. Citizen of the U.S.A. Born in Hawaii, the fiftieth state. Of mingled German, Dutch, Chinese, Japanese, Negro, Cherokee, Polynesian, Portuguese, Russian-Jewish, Irish, Scotch, Norwegian, Finnish, Czech, English, and Welsh ancestry. Thirty-one years old. Five foot six. One hundred and sixty pounds. Brown-haired. Blue-eyed. Hawkfeatured, M. D. and Ph.D. Married. Childless. Methodist. Sociable mesomorphic mesovert. Radio ham. Dog breeder. Deer hunter. Skin diver. Writer of first-rate but far from great poetry. All contained in his skin and his pressure suit, plus a love of companionship and life, an intense curiosity, and a courage. And now very much afraid of losing everything except his loneliness.

For some time he stood like a statue before the three-foot high wall of the tube. Finally, he shook his head violently, shook off his fear like a dog shaking off water. Lightly, despite the towering pack on his back, he leaped up onto the top of the tube and looked on the other side, though there was nothing he had not seen before jumping.

The view before him differed from the one behind in only one respect. This was the number of small plants that covered the ground. Or rather, he thought, after taking a second look, he had never seen these plants this size before. They were foot-high replicas of the huge umbrella trees that sprouted from the tubes. And they were not scattered at random, as might have been expected if they had grown from seeds blown by the wind. Instead, they grew in regular rows, the edges of the plants in one row separated from the other by about two feet.

His heart beat even faster. Such spacing must mean they were planted by intelligent life. Yet intelligent life seemed very improbable, given the Martian environment.

Possibly some natural condition might have caused the seeming artificiality of this garden. He would have to investigate.

Always with caution, though. So much depended on him: the lives of the four men, the success of the expedition. If this one failed, it might be the last. Many people on Earth were groaning loudly because of the cost of Space Arm and crying wildly for results that would mean money and power.

The field, or garden, extended for about three hundred yards. At its far end there was another tube at right angles to the two parallel ones. And at this point the giant umbrella plants regained their living and shining blue-green color.

The whole setup looked to Lane very much like a sunken garden. The square formation of the high tubes kept out the wind and most of the felsite flakes. The walls held the heat within the square.

Lane searched the top of the tube for bare spots where the metal plates of the caterpillar tractors' treads would have scraped off the lichenoids. He found none but was not surprised. The lichenoids grew phenomenally fast under the summertime sun.

He looked down at the ground on the garden side of the tube, where the tractors had presumably descended. Here there were no signs of the tractors' passage, for the little umbrellas grew up to within two feet of the edge of the tube, and they were uncrushed. Nor did he find any tracks at the ends of the tube where it joined the parallel rows.

He paused to think about his next step and was surprised to find himself breathing hard. A quick check of his air gauge showed him that the trouble wasn't an almost empty tank. No, it was the apprehension, the feeling of eeriness, of something *wrong*, that was causing his heart to beat so fast, to demand more oxygen.

Where could two tractors and four men have gone? And what could have caused them to disappear?

Could they have been attacked by some form of intelligent life? If that had happened, the unknown creatures had either carried off the six-ton tanks, or driven them away, or else forced the men to drive them off.

Where? How? By whom?

The hairs on the back of his neck stood up.

"Here is where it must have happened," he muttered to himself. "The first tank reported seeing this tube barring its way and said it would report again in another ten minutes. That was the last I heard from it. The second was cut off just as it was on top of the tube. Now, what happened? There are no cities on the surface of Mars, and no indications of underground civilization. The orbital ship would have seen openings to such a place through its telescope...."

He yelled so loudly that he was deafened as his voice bounced off the confines of his helmet. Then he fell silent, watching the line of basketball-size blue globes rise from the soil at the far end of the garden and swiftly soar into the sky.

He threw back his head until the back of it was stopped by the helmet and watched the rising globes as they left the ground, swelling until they seemed to be hundreds of feet across. Suddenly, like a soap bubble, the topmost one disappeared. The second in line, having reached the height of the first, also popped. And the others followed.

They were transparent. He could see some white cirrus clouds through the blue of the bubbles.

Lane did not move but watched the steady string of globes spurt from the soil. Though startled, he did not forget his training. He noted that the globes, besides being semitransparent, rose at a right angle to the ground and did not drift with the wind. He counted them and got to forty-nine when they ceased appearing.

He waited for fifteen minutes. When it looked as if nothing more would happen, he decided that he must investigate the spot where the globes seemed to have popped out of the ground. Taking a deep breath, he bent his knees and jumped out into the garden. He landed lightly about twelve feet out from the edge of the tube and between two rows of plants.

For a second he did not know what was happening, though he realized that something was wrong. Then he whirled around. Or tried to do so. One foot came up, but the other sank deeper.

He took one step forward, and the forward foot also disappeared into the thin stuff beneath the red-yellow dust. By now the other foot was too deep in to be pulled out.

Then he was hip-deep and grabbing at the stems of the plants to both sides of him. They uprooted easily, coming out of the soil, one clenched in each hand.

He dropped them and threw himself backward in the hope he could free his legs and lie stretched out on the jellylike stuff. Perhaps, if his body presented enough of an area, he could keep from sinking. And, after a while, he might be able to work his way to the ground near the tube. There, he hoped, it would be firm.

His violent effort succeeded. His legs came up out of the sticky semiliquid. He lay spread-eagled on his back and looked up at the sky through the transparent dome of his helmet. The sun was to his left; when he turned his head inside the helmet he could see the sun sliding down the arc from the zenith. It was descending at a slightly slower pace than on Earth, for Mars's day was about forty minutes longer. He hoped that, if he couldn't regain solid ground, he could remain suspended until evening fell. By then this quagmire would be frozen enough for him to rise and walk up on it. Provided that he got up before he himself was frozen fast.

Meanwhile, he would follow the approved method of saving oneself when trapped in quicksand. He would roll over quickly, once, and then spread-eagle himself again. By repeating this maneuver, he might eventually reach that bare strip of soil at the tube.

The pack on his back prevented him from rolling. The straps on his shoulders would have to be loosened.

He did so, and at the same time felt his legs sinking. Their weight was pulling them under, whereas the air tanks in the pack, the air tanks strapped to his chest, and the bubble of his helmet gave buoyancy to the upper part of his body

He turned over on his side, grabbed the pack, and pulled himself up on it. The pack, of course, went under. But his legs were free, though slimy with liquid and caked with dust. And he was standing on top of the narrow island of the pack.

The thick jelly rose up to his ankles while he considered two courses of action.

He could squat on the pack and hope that it would not sink too far before it was stopped by the permanently frozen layer that must exist....

How far? He had gone down hip-deep and felt nothing firm beneath his feet. And...He groaned. The tractors! Now he knew what had happened to them. They had gone over the tube and down into the garden, never suspecting that the solid-seeming surface covered this quagmire. And down they had plunged, and it had been Greenberg's horrified realization of what lay beneath the dust that had made him cry out, and then the stuff had closed over the tank and its antenna, and the transmitter, of course, had been cut off.

He must give up his second choice because it did not exist. To get to the bare strip of soil at the tube would be useless. It would be as unfirm as the rest of the garden. It was at that point that the tanks must have fallen in.

Another thought came to him: that the tanks must have disturbed the orderly arrangement of the little umbrellas close to the tube. Yet there was no sign of such a happening. Therefore, somebody must have rescued the plants and set them up again.

That meant that somebody might come along in time to rescue him.

Or to kill him, he thought.

In either event, his problem would be solved.

Meanwhile, he knew it was no use to make a jump from the pack to the strip at the tube. The only thing to do was to stay on top of the pack and hope it didn't sink too deeply.

However, the pack did sink. The jelly rose swiftly to his knees, then his rate of descent began slowing. He prayed, not for a miracle but only that the buoyancy of the pack plus the tank on his chest would keep him from going completely under.

Before he had finished praying, he had stopped sinking. The sticky stuff had risen no higher than his breast and had left his arms free.

He gasped with relief but did not feel overwhelmed with joy. In less than four hours the air in his tank would be exhausted. Unless he could get another tank from the pack, he was done for.

He pushed down hard on the pack and threw his arms up in the air and back in the hope his legs would rise again and he could spreadeagle. If he could do that, then the pack, relieved of his weight, might rise to the surface. And he could get another tank from it.

But his legs, impeded by the stickiness, did not rise far enough, and his body, shooting off in reaction to the kick, moved a little distance from the pack. It was just far enough so that when the legs inevitably sank again, they found no platform on which to be supported. Now he had to depend entirely on the lift of his air tank.

It did not give him enough to hold him at his former level; this time he sank until his arms and shoulders were nearly under, and only his helmet stuck out.

He was helpless.

Several years from now the second expedition, if any, would perhaps see the sun glinting off his helmet and would find his body stuck like a fly in glue.

If that does happen, he thought, I will at least have been of some use; my death will warn them of this trap. But I doubt if they'll find me. I think that Somebody or Something will have removed me and hidden me.

Then, feeling an inrush of despair, he closed his eyes and murmured some of the words he had read that last night in the base, though he knew them so well it did not matter whether he had read them recently or not.

Yea, though I walk through the valley of the shadow of death, I will fear no evil; for Thou art with me.

Repeating that didn't lift the burden of hopelessness. He felt absolutely alone, deserted by everybody, even by his Creator. Such was the desolation of Mars.

But when he opened his eyes, he knew he was not alone. He saw a Martian.

A hole had appeared in the wall of the tube to his left. It was a round section about four feet across, and it had sunk in as if it were a plug being pulled inward, as indeed it was.

A moment later a head popped out of the hole. The size of a Georgia watermelon, it was shaped like a football and was as pink as a baby's bottom. Its two eyes were as large as coffee cups and each was equipped with two vertical lids. It opened its two parrotlike beaks, ran out a very long tubular tongue, withdrew the tongue, and snapped the beak shut. Then it scuttled out from the hole to reveal a body also shaped like a football and only three times as large as its head. The pinkish body was supported three feet from the ground on ten spindly spidery legs, five on each side. Its legs ended in broad round pads on which it ran across the jelly-mire surface, sinking only slightly. Behind it streamed at least fifty others.

These picked up the little plants that Lane had upset in his struggles and licked them clean with narrow round tongues that shot out at least two feet. They also seemed to communicate by touching their tongues, as insects do with antennae.

As he was in the space between two rows, he was not involved in the setting up of the dislodged plants. Several of them ran their tongues over his helmet, but these were the only ones that paid him any attention. It was then that he began to stop dreading that they might attack him with their powerful-looking beaks. Now he broke into a sweat at the idea that they might ignore him completely.

That was just what they did. After gently embedding the thin roots of the plantlets in the sticky stuff, they raced off toward the hole in the tube.

Lane, overwhelmed with despair, shouted after them, though he knew they couldn't hear him through his helmet and the thin air even if they had hearing organs.

"Don't leave me here to die!"

Nevertheless, that was what they were doing. The last one leaped through the hole, and the entrance stared at him like the round black eye of Death itself.

He struggled furiously to lift himself from the mire, not caring that he was only exhausting himself.

Abruptly, he stopped fighting and stared at the hole.

A figure had crawled out of it, a figure in a pressure-suit.

Now he shouted with joy. Whether the figure was Martian or not, it was built like a member of *Homo sapiens*. It could be presumed to be intelligent and therefore curious.

He was not disappointed. The suited being stood up on two hemispheres of shiny red metal and began walking toward him in a sliding fashion. Reaching him, it handed him the end of a plastic rope it was carrying under its arm.

He almost dropped it. His rescuer's suit was transparent. It was enough of a shock to see clearly the details of the creature's body, but the sight of the two heads within the helmet caused him to turn pale.

The Martian slidewalked to the tube from which Lane had leaped. It jumped lightly from the two bowls on which it had stood, landed on the three-foot high top of the tube, and began hauling Lane out from the mess. He came out slowly but steadily and soon was scooting forward, gripping the rope. When he reached the foot of the tube, he was hauled on up until he could get his feet in the two bowls. It was easy to jump from them to a place beside the biped.

It unstrapped two more bowls from its back, gave them to Lane, then lowered itself on the two in the garden. Lane followed it across the mire.

Entering the hole, he found himself in a chamber so low he had to crouch. Evidently, it had been constructed by the dekapeds and not by his companion for it, too, had to bend its back and knees.

Lane was pushed to one side by some dekapeds. They picked up the thick plug, made of the same gray stuff as the tube walls, and sealed the entrance with it. Then they shot out of their mouths strand after strand of gray spiderwebby stuff to seal the plug.

The biped motioned Lane to follow, and it slid down a tunnel which plunged into the earth at a forty-five degree angle. It illuminated the passage with a flashlight which it took from its belt. They came into a large chamber which contained all of the fifty dekapeds. These were waiting motionless. The biped, as if sensing Lane's curiosity, pulled off its glove and held it before several small vents in the wall. Lane removed his glove and felt warm air flowing from the holes.

Evidently this was a pressure chamber, built by the ten-legged things. But such evidence of intelligent engineering did not mean that these things had the individual intelligence of a man. It could mean group intelligence such as Terrestrial insects possess.

After a while, the chamber was filled with air. Another plug was pulled; Lane followed the dekapeds and his rescuer up another forty-five degree tunnel. He estimated that he would find himself inside the tube from which the biped had first come. He was right. He crawled through another hole into it.

And a pair of beaks clicked as they bit down on his helmet!

Automatically, he shoved at the thing, and under the force of his blow the dekaped lost its bite and went rolling on the floor, a bundle of thrashing legs.

Lane did not worry about having hurt it. It did not weigh much, but its body must be tough to be able to plunge without damage from the heavy air inside the tube into the almost-stratospheric conditions outside.

However, he did reach for the knife at his belt. But the biped put its hand on his arm and shook one of its heads.

Later, he was to find out that the seeming bite must have been an accident. Always — with one exception — the leggers were to ignore him.

He was also to find that he was lucky. The leggers had come out to inspect their garden because, through some unknown method of detection, they knew that the plantlets had been disturbed. The biped normally would not have accompanied them. However, today, its curiosity aroused because the leggers had gone out three times in three days, it had decided to investigate.

The biped turned out its flashlight and motioned to Lane to follow. Awkwardly, he obeyed. There was light, but it was dim, a twilight. Its source was the many creatures that hung from the ceiling of the tube. These were three feet long and six inches thick, cylindrical, pinkish-skinned, and eyeless. A dozen frondlike limbs waved continuously, and their motion kept air circulating in the tunnel.

Their cold firefly glow came from two globular pulsing organs which hung from both sides of the round loose-lipped mouth at the free end of the creature. Slime drooled from the mouth, and dripped onto the floor or into a narrow channel which ran along the lowest part of the sloping floor. Water ran in the six-inch deep channel, the first native water he had seen. The water picked up the slime and carried it a little way before it was gulped up by an animal that lay on the bottom of the channel.

Lane's eyes adjusted to the dimness until he could make out the water-dweller. It was torpedo-shaped and without eyes or fins. It had two openings in its body; one obviously sucked in water, the other expelled it.

He saw at once what this meant. The water at the North Pole melted in the summertime and flowed into the far end of the tube system. Helped by gravity and by the pumping action of the line of animals in the channel, the water was passed from the edge of the Pole to the equator.

Leggers ran by him on mysterious errands. Several, however, halted beneath some of the downhanging organisms. They reared up on their hind five legs and their tongues shot out and into the open mouths by the glowing balls. At once, the fireworm — as Lane termed it — its cilia waving wildly, stretched itself to twice its former length. Its mouth met the beak of the legger, and there was an exchange of stuff between their mouths.

Impatiently, the biped tugged at Lane's arm. He followed it down the tube. Soon they entered a section where pale roots came down out of holes in the ceiling and spread along the curving walls, gripping them, then becoming a network of many thread-thin rootlets that crept across the floor and into the water of the channel.

Here and there a dekaped chewed at a root and then hurried off to offer a piece to the mouths of the fireworms.

After walking for several minutes, the biped stepped across the stream. It then began walking as closely as possible to the wall, meanwhile looking apprehensively at the other side of the tunnel, where they had been walking.

Lane also looked but could see nothing at which to be alarmed. There was a large opening at the base of the wall which evidently led into a tunnel. This tunnel, he presumed, ran underground into a room or rooms, for many leggers dashed in and out of it. And about a dozen, larger than average, paced back and forth like sentries before the hole.

When they had gone about fifty yards past the opening, the biped relaxed. After it had led Lane along for ten minutes, it stopped. Its naked hand touched the wall. He became aware that the hand was small and delicately shaped, like a woman's.

A section of the wall swung out. The biped turned and bent down to crawl into the hole, presenting buttocks and legs femininely rounded, well shaped. It was then that he began thinking of it as a female. Yet the hips, though padded with fatty tissue, were not broad. The bones were not widely separated to make room to carry a child. Despite their curving, the hips were relatively as narrow as a man's.

Behind them, the plug swung shut. The biped did not turn on her flashlight, for there was illumination at the end of the tunnel. The floor and walls were not of the hard gray stuff nor of packed earth. They seemed vitrified, as if glassed by heat.

She was waiting for him when he slid off a three-foot high ledge into a large room. For a minute he was blinded by the strong light. After his eyes adjusted, he searched for the source of light but could not find it. He did observe that there were no shadows in the room.

The biped took off her helmet and suit and hung them in a closet. The door slid open as she approached and closed when she walked away.

She signaled that he could remove his suit. He did not hesitate. Though the air might be poisonous, he had no choice. His tank would soon be empty. Moreover, it seemed likely that the atmosphere contained enough oxygen. Even then he had grasped the idea that the leaves of the umbrella plants, which grew out of the top of the tubes, absorbed sunlight and traces of carbon dioxide. Inside the tunnels, the roots drew up water from the channel and absorbed the great quantity of carbon dioxide released by the dekapeds. Energy of sunlight converted gas and liquid into glucose and oxygen, which were given off in the tunnels.

Even here, in this deep chamber which lay beneath and to one side of the tube, a thick root penetrated the ceiling and spread its thin white web over the walls. He stood directly beneath the fleshy growth as he removed his helmet and took his first breath of Martian air. Immediately afterward, he jumped. Something wet had dropped on his forehead. Looking up, he saw that the root was excreting liquid from a large pore. He wiped the drop off with his finger and tasted it. It was sticky and sweet.

Well, he thought, the tree must normally drop sugar in water. But it seemed to be doing so abnormally fast, because another drop was forming.

Then it came to him that perhaps this was so because it was getting dark outside and therefore cold. The umbrella trees might be pumping the water in their trunks into the warm tunnels. Thus, during the bitter subzero night, they'd avoid freezing and swelling up and cracking wide open.

It seemed a reasonable theory.

He looked around. The place was half living quarters, half biological laboratory. There were beds and tables and chairs and several unidentifiable articles. One was a large black metal box in a corner. From it, at regular intervals, issued a stream of tiny blue bubbles. They rose to the ceiling, growing larger as they did so. On reaching the ceiling they did not stop or burst but simply penetrated the vitrification as if it did not exist.

Lane now knew the origin of the blue globes he had seen appear from the surface of the garden. But their purpose was still obscure.

He wasn't given much time to watch the globes. The biped took a large green ceramic bowl from a cupboard and set it on a table. Lane eyed her curiously, wondering what she was going to do. By now he had seen that the second head belonged to an entirely separate creature. Its slim four-foot length of pinkish skin was coiled about her neck and torso; its tiny flat-faced head turned toward Lane; its snaky light blue eyes glittered. Suddenly, its mouth opened and revealed toothless gums, and its bright red tongue, mammalian, not at all reptilian, thrust out at him.

The biped, paying no attention to the worm's actions, lifted it from her. Gently, cooing a few words in a soft many-voweled language, she placed it in the bowl. It settled inside and looped around the curve, like a snake in a pit.

The biped took a pitcher from the top of a box of red plastic. Though the box was not connected to any visible power source, it seemed to be a stove. The pitcher contained warm water which she poured into the bowl, half filling it. Under the shower, the worm closed its eyes as if it were purring soundless ecstasy.

Then the biped did something that alarmed Lane.

She leaned over the bowl and vomited into it.

He stepped toward her. Forgetting the fact that she couldn't understand him, he said, "Are you sick?"

She revealed human-looking teeth in a smile meant to reassure him, and she walked away from the bowl. He looked at the worm, which had its head dipped into the mess. Suddenly, he felt sick, for he was sure that it was feeding off the mixture. And he was equally certain that she fed the worm regularly with regurgitated food.

It didn't cancel his disgust to reflect that he shouldn't react to her as he would to a Terrestrial. He knew that she was totally alien and that it was inevitable that some of her ways would repel, perhaps even shock him. Rationally, he knew this. But if his brain told him to understand and forgive, his belly said to loathe and reject.

His aversion was not much lessened by a close scrutiny of her as she took a shower in a cubicle set in the wall. She was about five feet tall and slim as a woman should be slim, with delicate bones beneath rounded flesh. Her legs were human; in nylons and high heels they would have been exciting—other things being equal. However, if the shoes had been toeless, her feet would have caused much comment. They had four toes.

Her long beautiful hands had five fingers. These seemed nailless, like the toes, though a closer examination later showed him they did bear rudimentary nails.

She stepped from the cubicle and began toweling herself, though not before she motioned to him to remove his suit and also to shower. He stared intently back at her until she laughed a short embarrassed laugh. It was feminine, not at all deep. Then she spoke.

He closed his eyes and was hearing what he had thought he would not hear for years: a woman's voice. Hers was extraordinary: husky and honeyed at the same time.

But when he opened his eyes, he saw her for what she was. No woman. No man. What? It? No. The impulse to think *her, she,* was too strong.

This, despite her lack of mammaries. She had a chest, but no nipples, rudimentary or otherwise. Her chest was a man's, muscled under the layer of fat which subtly curved to give the impression that beneath it...budding breasts?

No, not this creature. She would never suckle her young. She did not even bear them alive, if she *did* bear. Her belly was smooth, undimpled with a navel.

Smooth also was the region between her legs, hairless, unbroken, as innocent of organ as if she were a nymph painted for some Victorian children's book.

It was that sexless joining of the legs that was so horrible. Like the white belly of a frog, thought Lane, shuddering.

At the same time, his curiosity became even stronger. How did this thing mate and reproduce?

Again she laughed and smiled with fleshy pale-red humanly everted lips and wrinkled a short, slightly uptilted nose and ran her hand through thick straight red-gold fur. It was fur, not hair, and it had a slightly oily sheen, like a water-dwelling animal's.

The face itself, though strange, could have passed for human, but only passed. Her cheekbones were very high and protruded upward in an unhuman fashion. Her eyes were dark blue and quite human. This meant nothing. So were an octopus's eyes.

She walked to another closet, and as she went away from him he saw again that though the hips were curved like a woman's they did not sway with the pelvic displacement of the human female.

The door swung momentarily open, revealed the carcasses of several dekapeds, minus their legs, hanging on hooks. She removed one, placed it on a metal table, and out of the cupboard took a saw and several knives and began cutting.

Because he was eager to see the anatomy of the dekaped, he approached the table. She waved him to the shower. Lane removed his suit. When he came to the knife and ax he hesitated, but, afraid she might think him distrustful, he hung up the belt containing his weapons beside the suit. However, he did not take off his clothes because he was determined to view the inner organs of the animal. Later, he would shower.

The legger was not an insect, despite its spidery appearance. Not in the Terrestrial sense, certainly. Neither was it a vertebrate. Its smooth hairless skin was an animal's, as lightly pigmented as a blonde Swede's. But, though it had an endoskeleton, it had no backbone. Instead, the body bones formed a round cage. Its thin ribs radiated from a cartilaginous collar which adjoined the back of the head. The ribs curved outward, then in, almost meeting at the posterior. Inside the cage were ventral lung sacs, a relatively large heart, and liverlike and kidneylike organs. Three arteries, instead of the mammalian two, left the heart. He couldn't be sure with such a hurried examination, but it looked as if the dorsal aorta, like some Terrestrial reptiles, carried both pure and impure blood.

There were other things to note. The most extraordinary was that, as far as he could discern, the legger had no digestive system. It seemed to lack both intestines and anus unless you would define as an intestine a sac which ran straight through from the throat halfway into the body. Further, there was nothing he could identify as reproductive organs, though this did not mean that it did not possess them. The creature's long tubular tongue, cut open by the biped, exposed a canal running down the length of tongue from its open tip to the bladder at its base. Apparently these formed part of the excretory system.

Lane wondered what enabled the legger to stand the great pressure differences between the interior of the tube and the Martian surface. At the same time he realized that this ability was no more wonderful than the biological mechanism which gave whales and seals the power to endure without harm the enormous pressures a half mile below the sea's surface.

The biped looked at him with round and very pretty blue eyes, laughed, and then reached into the chopped open skull and brought out the tiny brain.

"*Hauaimi,*" she said slowly. She pointed to her head, repeated, "*Hauaimi,*" and then indicated his head. "*Hauaimi.*"

Echoing her, he pointed at his own head. "*Hauaimi.* Brain."

"Brain," she said, and she laughed again.

She proceeded to call out the organs of the legger which corresponded to hers. Thus, the preparations for the meal passed swiftly as he proceeded from the carcass to other objects in the room. By the time she had fried the meat and boiled strips of the membranous leaf of the umbrella plant, and also added from cans various exotic foods, she had exchanged at least forty words with him. An hour later, he could remember twenty.

There was one thing yet to learn. He pointed to himself and said, "Lane."

Then he pointed to her and gave her a questioning look.

"Mahrseeya," she said.

"Martia?" he repeated. She corrected him, but he was so struck by the resemblance that always afterward he called her that. After a while, she would give up trying to teach him the exact pronunciation.

Martia washed her hands and poured him a bowlful of water. He used the soap and towel she handed him, then walked to the table where she stood waiting. On it was a bowl of thick soup, a plate of fried brains, a salad of boiled leaves and some unidentifiable vegetables, a plate of ribs with thick dark legger meat, hardboiled eggs, and little loaves of bread.

Martia gestured for him to sit down. Evidently her code did not allow her to sit down before her guest did. He ignored his chair, went behind her, put his hand on her shoulder, pressed down, and with the other hand slid her chair under her. She turned her head to smile up at him. Her fur slid away to reveal one lobeless pointed ear. He scarcely noticed it, for he was too intent on the half-repulsive, half heart-quickening sensation he got when he touched her skin. It had not been the skin itself that caused that, for she was soft and warm as a young girl. It had been the *idea* of touching her.

Part of that, he thought as he seated himself, came from her nakedness. Not because it revealed her sex but because it revealed her lack of it. No breasts, no nipples, no navel, no pubic fold or projection. The absence of these seemed wrong, very wrong, unsettling. It was a shameful thing that she had nothing of which to be ashamed.

That's a queer thought, he said to himself. And for no reason, he became warm in the face.

Martia, unnoticing, poured from a tall bottle a glassful of dark wine. He tasted it. It was exquisite, no better than the best Earth had to offer but as good.

Martia took one of the loaves, broke it into two pieces, and handed him one. Holding the glass of wine in one hand and the bread in the other, she bowed her head, closed her eyes, and began chanting.

He stared at her. This was a prayer, a grace-saying. Was it the prelude to a sort of communion, one so like Earth's it was startling?

Yet, if it were, he needn't be surprised. Flesh and blood, bread and wine: the symbolism was simple, logical, and might even be universal.

However, it was possible that he was creating parallels that did not exist. She might be enacting a ritual whose origin and meaning were like nothing of which he had ever dreamed.

If so, what she did next was equally capable of misinterpretation. She nibbled at the bread, sipped the wine, and then plainly invited him to do the same. He did so. Martia took a third and empty cup, spat a piece of wine-moistened bread into the cup, and indicated that he was to imitate her.

After he did, he felt his stomach draw in on itself. For she mixed the stuff from their mouths with her finger and then offered it to him. Evidently, he was to put the finger in his mouth and eat from it.

So the action was both physical and metaphysical. The bread and the wine were the flesh and blood of whatever divinity she worshiped. More, she, being imbued with the body and the spirit of the god, now wanted to mingle hers and that of the god's with his.

What I eat of the god's, I become. What you eat of me, you become. What I eat of you, I become. Now we three are become one.

Lane, far from being repelled by the concept, was excited. He knew that there were probably many Christians who would have refused to share in the communion because the ritual did not have the same origins or conform to theirs. They might even have thought that by sharing they were subscribing to an alien god. Such an idea Lane considered to be not only narrow-minded and inflexible, but illogical, uncharitable, and ridiculous. There could be but one Creator; what names the creature gave to the Creator did not matter.

Lane believed sincerely in a personal god, one who took note of him as an individual. He also believed that mankind needed redeeming and that a redeemer had been sent to Earth. And if other worlds needed redeeming, then they too would have gotten or would get a redeemer. He went perhaps further than most of his fellow religionists, for he actually made an attempt to practice love for mankind. This had given him somewhat of a reputation as a fanatic among his acquaintances and friends. However, he had been restrained enough not to make himself too much of a nuisance, and his genuine warmheartedness had made him welcome in spite of his eccentricity.

Six years before, he had been an agnostic. His first trip into space had converted him. The overwhelming experience had made him realize shatteringly what an insignificant being he was, how awe-inspiringly complicated and immense was the universe, and how much he needed a framework within which to be and to become.

The strangest feature about his conversion, he thought afterward, was that one of his companions on that maiden trip had been a devout believer who, on returning to Earth, had renounced his own sect and faith and become a complete atheist.

He thought of this as he took her proffered finger in his mouth and sucked the paste off it.

Then obeying her gestures, he dipped his own finger into the bowl and put it between her lips.

She closed her eyes and gently mouthed the finger. When he began to withdraw it, he was stopped by her hand on his wrist. He did not insist on taking the finger out, for he wanted to avoid offending her. Perhaps a long time interval was part of the rite.

But her expression seemed so eager and at the same time so ecstatic, like a hungry baby just given the nipple, that he felt uneasy. After a minute, seeing no indication on her part that she meant to quit, he slowly but firmly pulled the finger loose. She opened her eyes and sighed, but she made no comment. Instead, she began serving his supper.

The hot thick soup was delicious and invigorating. Its texture was somewhat like the plankton soup that was becoming popular on hungry Earth, but it had no fishy flavor. The brown bread reminded him of rye. The legger meat was like wild rabbit, though it was sweeter and had an unidentifiable tang. He took only one bite of the leaf salad and then frantically poured wine down his throat to wash away the burn. Tears came to his eyes, and he coughed until she spoke to him in an alarmed tone. He smiled back at her but refused to touch the salad again. The wine not only cooled his mouth, it filled his veins with singing. He told himself he should take no more. Nevertheless, he finished his second cup before he remembered his resolve to be temperate.

By then it was too late. The strong liquor went straight to his head; he felt dizzy and wanted to laugh. The events of the day, his near-escape from death, the reaction to knowing his comrades were dead, his realization of his present situation, the tension caused by his encounters with the dekapeds, and his unsatisfied curiosity about Martia's origins and the location of others of her kind, all these combined to produce in him a half-stupor, half-exuberance.

He rose from the table and offered to help Martia with the dishes. She shook her head and put the dishes in a washer. In the meantime, he decided that he needed to wash off the sweat, stickiness, and body odor left by two days of travel. On opening the door to the shower cubicle, he found that there wasn't room enough to hang his clothes in it. So, uninhibited by fatigue and wine, also mindful that Martia, after all, was *not* a female, he removed his clothes.

Martia watched him, and her eyes became wider with each garment shed. Finally, she gasped and stepped back and turned pale.

"It's not that bad," he growled, wondering what had caused her reaction. "After all, some of the things I've seen around here aren't too easy to swallow."

She pointed with a trembling finger and asked him something in a shaky voice.

Perhaps it was his imagination, but he could swear she used the same inflection as would an English speaker.

"Are you sick? Are the growths malignant?"

He had no words with which to explain, nor did he intend to illustrate function through action. Instead, he closed the door of the cubicle after him and pressed the plate that turned on the water. The heat of the shower and the feel of the soap, of grime and sweat being washed away, soothed him somewhat, so that he could think about matters he had been too rushed to consider.

First, he would have to learn Martia's language or teach her his. Probably both would happen at the same time. Of one thing he was sure. That was that her intentions toward him were, at least at present, peaceful. When she had shared communion with him, she had been sincere. He did not get the impression that it was part of her cultural training to share bread and wine with a person she intended to kill.

Feeling better, though still tired and a little drunk, he left the cubicle. Reluctantly; he reached for his dirty shorts. Then he smiled. They had been cleaned while he was in the shower. Martia, however, paid no attention to his smile of pleased surprise but, grim-faced, she motioned to him to lie down on the bed and sleep. Instead of lying down herself, however, she picked up a bucket and began crawling up the tunnel. He decided to follow her, and, when she saw him, she only shrugged her shoulders.

On emerging into the tube, Martia turned on her flashlight. The tunnel was in absolute darkness. Her beam playing on the ceiling, showed that the glowworms had turned out their lights. There were no leggers in sight.

She pointed the light at the channel so he could see that the jetfish were still taking in and expelling water. Before she could turn the beam aside, he put his hand on her wrist and with his other hand lifted a fish from the channel. He had to pull it loose with an effort, which was explained when he turned the torpedo-shaped creature over and saw the column of flesh hanging from its belly. Now he knew why the reaction of the propelled water did not shoot them backward. The ventral-foot acted as a suction pad to hold them to the floor of the channel.

Somewhat impatiently, Martia pulled away from him and began walking swiftly back up the tunnel. He followed her until she came to the opening in the wall which had earlier made her so apprehensive. Crouching, she entered the opening, but before she had gone far she had to move a tangled heap of leggers to one side. These were the large great-beaked ones he had seen guarding the entrance. Now they were asleep at the post.

If so, he reasoned, then the thing they guarded against must also be asleep.

What about Martia? How did she fit into their picture? Perhaps she didn't fit into their picture at all. She was absolutely alien, something for which their instinctual intelligence was not prepared and which, therefore, they ignored. That would explain why they had paid no attention to him when he was mired in the garden.

Yet there must be an exception to that rule. Certainly Martia had not wanted to attract the sentinels' notice the first time she had passed the entrance.

A moment later he found out why. They stepped into a huge chamber which was at least two hundred feet square. It was as dark as the tube, but during the waking period it must have been very bright because the ceiling was jammed with glowworms.

Martia's flash raced around the chamber, showing him the piles of sleeping leggers. Then, suddenly, it stopped. He took one look, and his heart raced, and the hairs on the back of his neck rose.

Before him was a worm three feet high and twenty feet long.

Without thinking, he grabbed hold of Martia to keep her from coming closer to it. But even as he touched her, he dropped his hand. She must know what she was doing.

Martia pointed the flash at her own face and smiled as if to tell him not to be alarmed. And she touched his arm with a shyly affectionate gesture.

For a moment, he didn't know why. Then it came to him that she was glad because he had been thinking of her welfare. Moreover, her

reaction showed she had recovered from her shock at seeing him unclothed.

He turned from her to examine the monster. It lay on the floor,
asleep, its great eyes closed behind vertical slits. It had a huge head,
football-shaped like those of the little leggers around it. Its mouth was
big, but the beaks were very small, horny warts on its lips. The body,
however, was that of a caterpillar worm's, minus the hair. Ten little
useless legs stuck out of its side, too short even to reach the floor. Its
side bulged as if pumped full of gas.

Martia walked past the monster and paused by its posterior. Here
she lifted up a fold of skin. Beneath it was a pile of a dozen leathery-
skinned eggs, held together by a sticky secretion.

"Now I've got it," muttered Lane. "Of course. The egg-laying queen.
She specializes in reproduction. That is why the others have no repro-
ductive organs, or else they're so rudimentary I couldn't detect them.
The leggers are animals, all right, but in some things they resemble
Terrestrial insects.

"Still, that doesn't explain the absence also of a digestive system."

Martia put the eggs in her bucket and started to leave the room.
He stopped her and indicated he wanted to look around some more.
She shrugged and began to lead him around. Both had to be careful
not to step on the dekapeds, which lay everywhere.

They came to an open bin made of the same gray stuff as the walls.
Its interior held many shelves, on which lay hundreds of eggs. Strands
of the spiderwebby stuff kept the eggs from rolling off.

Nearby was another bin that held water. At its bottom lay more
eggs. Above them minnow-sized torpedo shapes flitted about in the
water.

Lane's eyes widened at this. The fish were not members of another
genus but were the larvae of the leggers. And they could be set in the
channel not only to earn their keep by pumping water which came
down from the North Pole but to grow until they were ready to metamorphose into the adult stage.

However, Martia showed him another bin which made him partially revise his first theory. This bin was dry, and the eggs were laid on
the floor. Martia picked one up, cut its tough skin open with her knife,
and emptied its contents into one hand.

Now his eyes did get wide. This creature had a tiny cylindrical
body, a suction pad at one end, a round mouth at the other, and two
globular organs hanging by the mouth. A young glowworm.

Martia looked at him to see if he comprehended. Lane held out his
hands and hunched his shoulders with an I-don't-get-it air. Beckon-

ing, she walked to another bin to show him more eggs. Some had been ripped from within, and the little fellows whose hard beaks had done it were staggering around weakly on ten legs.

Energetically, Martia went through a series of charades. Watching her, he began to understand.

The embryos that remained in the egg until they fully developed went through three main metamorphoses: the jetfish stage, the glowworm stage, and finally the baby dekaped stage. If the eggs were torn open by the adult nurses in one of the first two stages, the embryo remained fixed in that form, though it did grow larger.

What about the queen? he asked her by pointing to the monstrously egg-swollen body.

For answer, Martia picked up one of the newly hatched. It kicked its many legs but did not otherwise protest, being, like all its kind, mute. Martia turned it upside down and indicated a slight crease in its posterior. Then she showed him the same spot on one of the sleeping adults. The adult's rear was smooth, innocent of the crease.

Martia made eating gestures. He nodded. The creatures were born with rudimentary sexual organs, but these never developed. In fact, they atrophied completely unless the young were given a special diet, in which case they matured into egg-layers.

But the picture wasn't complete. If you had females, you had to have males. It was doubtful if such highly developed animals were self-fertilizing or reproduced parthenogenetically.

Then he remembered Martia and began doubting. She gave no evidence of reproductive organs. Could her kind be self-reproducing? Or was she a martin, her natural fulfillment diverted by diet?

It didn't seem likely, but he couldn't be sure that such things were not possible in her scheme of Nature.

Lane wanted to satisfy his curiosity. Ignoring her desire to get out of the chamber, he examined each of the five baby dekapeds. All were potential females.

Suddenly Martia, who had been gravely watching him, smiled and took his hand, and led him to the rear of the room. Here, as they approached another structure, he smelled a strong odor which reminded him of clorox.

Closer to the structure, he saw that it was not a bin but a hemispherical cage. Its bars were of the hard gray stuff, and they curved up from the floor to meet at the central point. There was no door. Evidently the cage had been built around the thing in it, and its occupant must remain until he died.

Martia soon showed him why this thing was not allowed freedom.
It—he—was sleeping, but Martia reached through the bars and struck
it on the head with her fist. The thing did not respond until it had been
hit five more times. Then, slowly, it opened its sidewise lids to reveal
great staring eyes, bright as fresh arterial blood.

Martia threw one of the eggs at the thing's head. Its beak opened
swiftly, the egg disappeared, the beak closed, and there was a noisy
gulp.

Food brought it to life. It sprang up on its ten long legs, clacked its
beak, and lunged against the bars again and again.

Though in no danger, Martia shrank back before the killer's lust in
the scarlet eyes. Lane could understand her reaction. It was a giant, at
least two feet higher than the sentinels. Its back was on a level with
Martia's head; its beaks could have taken her head in between them.

Lane walked around the cage to get a good look at its posterior.
Puzzled, he made another circuit without seeing anything of maleness
about it except its wild fury, like that of a stallion locked in a barn
during mating season. Except for its size, red eyes, and a cloaca, it
looked like one of the guards.

He tried to communicate to Martia his puzzlement. By now, she
seemed to anticipate his desires. She went through another series of
pantomimes, some of which were so energetic and comical that he had
to smile.

First, she showed him two eggs on a nearby ledge. These were
larger than the others and were speckled with red spots. Supposedly,
they held male embryos.

Then she showed him what would happen if the adult male got
loose. Making a face which was designed to be ferocious but only
amused him, clicking her teeth and clawing with her hands, she imitated the male running amok. He would kill everybody in sight. Everybody, the whole colony, queen, workers, guards, larvae, eggs, bite
off their heads, mangle them, eat them all up, all, all. And out of the
slaughterhouse he would charge into the tube and kill every legger he
met, devour the jetfish, drag down the glowworms from the ceiling,
rip them apart, eat them, eat the roots of the trees. Kill, kill, kill, eat,
eat, eat!

That was all very well, sighed Lane. But how did...?

Martia indicated that, once a day, the workers rolled, literally rolled
the queen across the room to the cage. There they arranged her so that
she presented her posterior some few inches from the bars and the
enraged male. And the male, though he wanted to do nothing but get

his beak into her flesh and tear her apart, was not master of himself. Nature took over; his will was betrayed by his nervous system.

Lane nodded to show he understood. In his mind was a picture of the legger that had been butchered. It had had one sac at the internal end of the tongue. Probably the male had two, one to hold excretory matter, the other to hold seminal fluid.

Suddenly Martia froze, her hands held out before her. She had laid the flashlight on the floor so she could act freely; the beam splashed on her paling skin.

"What is it?" said Lane, stepping toward her,

Martia retreated, holding out her hands before her. She looked horrified.

"I'm not going to harm you," he said. However, he stopped so she could see he didn't mean to get any closer to her.

What was bothering her? Nothing was stirring in the chamber itself besides the male, and he was behind her.

Then she was pointing, first at him and then at the raging dekaped. Seeing this unmistakable signal of identification, he comprehended. She had perceived that he, like the thing in the cage, was male, and now she perceived structure and function in him.

What he didn't understand was why that should make her so frightened of him. Repelled, yes. Her body, its seeming lack of sex, had given him a feeling of distaste bordering on nausea. It was only natural that she should react similarly to his body. However, she had seemed to have gotten over her first shock.

Why this unexpected change, this horror of him?

Behind him, the beak of the male clicked as it lunged against the bars.

The click echoed in his mind.

Of course, the monster's lust to kill!

Until she had met him, she had known only one male creature. That was the caged thing. Now, suddenly, she had equated him with the monster. A male was a killer.

Desperately, because he was afraid that she was about to run in panic out of the room, he made signs that he was not like this monster; he shook his head no, no, no. He wasn't, he wasn't, he wasn't!

Martia, watching him intently, began to relax. Her skin regained its pinkish hue. Her eyes became their normal size. She even managed a strained smile.

To get her mind off the subject, he indicated that he would like to know why the queen and her consort had digestive systems, though the workers did not. For answer, she reached up into the downhanging mouth of the worm suspended from the ceiling. Her hand, withdrawn, was covered with secretion. After smelling her fist, she gave it to him to sniff also. He took it, ignoring her slight and probably involuntary flinching when she felt his touch.

The stuff had an odor such as you would expect from predigested food.

Martia then went to another worm. The two light organs of this one were not colored red, like the others, but had a greenish tint. Martia tickled its tongue with her finger and held out her cupped hands. Liquid trickled into the cup.

Lane smelled the stuff. No odor. When he drank the liquid, he discovered it to be a thick sugar water.

Martia pantomimed that the glowworms acted as the digestive systems for the workers. They also stored food away for them. The workers derived part of their energy from the glucose excreted by the roots of the trees. The proteins and vegetable matter in their diet originated from the eggs and from the leaves of the umbrella plant. Strips of the tough membranous leaf were brought into the tubes by harvesting parties which ventured forth in the daytime. The worms partially digested the eggs, dead leggers, and leaves and gave it back in the form of a soup. The soup, like the glucose, was swallowed by the workers and passed through the walls of their throats or into the long straight sac which connected the throat to the larger blood vessels. The waste products were excreted through the skin or emptied through the canal in the tongue.

Lane nodded and then walked out of the room. Seemingly relieved, Martia followed him. When they had crawled back into her quarters, she put the eggs in a refrigerator and poured two glasses of wine. She dipped her finger in both, then touched the finger to her lips and to his. Lightly, he touched the tip with his tongue. This, he gathered, was one more ritual, perhaps a bedtime one, which affirmed that they were at one and at peace. It might be that it had an even deeper meaning, but if so, it escaped him.

Martia checked on the safety and comfort of the worm in the bowl. By now it had eaten all its food. She removed the worm, washed it, washed the bowl, half filled it with warm sugar water, placed it on the table by the bed, and put the creature back in. Then she lay down on the bed and closed her eyes. She did not cover herself and apparently did not expect him to expect a cover.

Lane, tired though he was, could not rest. Like a tiger in its cage, he paced back and forth. He could not keep out of his mind the enigma of Martia nor the problem of getting back to base and eventually to the orbital ship. Earth must know what had happened.

After half an hour of this, Martia sat up. She looked steadily at him as if trying to discover the cause of his sleeplessness. Then, apparently sensing what was wrong, she rose and opened a cabinet hanging down from the wall. Inside were a number of books.

Lane said, "Ah, maybe I'll get some information now!" and he leafed through them all. Wild with eagerness, he chose three and piled them on the bed before sitting down to peruse them.

Naturally he could not read the texts, but the three had many illustrations and photographs. The first volume seemed to be a child's world history.

Lane looked at the first few pictures. Then he said, hoarsely, "My God, you're no more Martian than I am!"

Martia, startled by the wonder and urgency in his voice, came over to his bed and sat down by him. She watched while he turned the pages over until he reached a certain photo. Unexpectedly, she buried her face in her hands, and her body shook with deep sobs.

Lane was surprised. He wasn't sure why she was in such grief. The photo was an aerial view of a city on her home planet — or some planet on which her people lived. Perhaps it was the city in which she had — somehow — been born.

It wasn't long, however, before her sorrow began to stir a response in him. Without any warning he, too, was weeping.

Now he knew. It was loneliness, appalling loneliness, of the kind he had known when he had received no more word from the men in the tanks and he had believed himself the only human being on the face of this world.

After a while, the tears dried. He felt better and wished she would also be relieved. Apparently she perceived his sympathy, for she smiled at him through her tears. And in an irresistible gust of rapport and affection she kissed his hand and then stuck two of his fingers in her mouth. This, he thought, must be her way of expressing friendship. Or perhaps it was gratitude for his presence. Or just sheer joy. In any event, he thought, her society must have a high oral orientation.

"Poor Martia," he murmured. "It must be a terrible thing to have to turn to one as alien and weird as I must seem. Especially to one who, a little while ago, you weren't sure wasn't going to eat you up."

He removed his fingers but, seeing her rejected look, he impulsively took hers in his mouth.

Strangely, this caused another burst of weeping. However, he quickly saw that it was happy weeping. After it was over, she laughed softly, as if pleased.

Lane took a towel and wiped her eyes and held it over her nose while she blew.

Now, strengthened, she was able to point out certain illustrations and by signs give him clues to what they meant.

This child's book started with an account of the dawn of life on her planet. The planet revolved around a star that, according to a simplified map, was in the center of the galaxy.

Life had begun there much as it had on Earth. It had developed in its early stages on somewhat the same lines. But there were some rather disturbing pictures of primitive fish life. Lane wasn't sure of his interpretation, however, for these took much for granted.

They did show plainly that evolution there had picked out biological mechanisms with which to advance different from those on Earth.

Fascinated, he traced the passage from fish to amphibian to reptile to warm-blooded but non-mammalian creature to an upright ground-dwelling apelike creature to beings like Martia.

Then the pictures depicted various aspects of this being's prehistoric life. Later, the invention of agriculture, working of metals, and so on.

The history of civilization was a series of pictures whose meaning he could seldom grasp. One thing was unlike Earth's history. There was a relative absence of warfare. The Rameseses, Genghis Khans, Attilas, Caesars, Hitlers, seemed to be missing.

But there was more much more. Technology advanced much as it had on Earth, despite a lack of stimulation from war. Perhaps, he thought, it had started sooner than on his planet. He got the impression that Martia's people had evolved to their present state much earlier than Homo sapiens.

Whether that was true or not, they now surpassed man. They could travel almost as fast as light, perhaps faster, and had mastered interstellar travel.

It was then that Martia pointed to a page which bore several photographs of Earth, obviously taken at various distances by a spaceship.

Behind them an artist had drawn a shadowy figure, half-ape, half-dragon.

"Earth means this to you?" Lane said. *"Danger? Do not touch?"*

He looked for other photos of Earth. There were many pages dealing with other planets but only one of his home. That was enough.

"Why are you keeping us under distant surveillance?" said Lane. "You're so far ahead of us that, technologically speaking, we're Australian aborigines. What're you afraid of?"

Martia stood up, facing him. Suddenly, viciously, she snarled and clicked her teeth and hooked her hands into claws.

He felt a chill. This was the same pantomime she had used when demonstrating the mindless kill-craziness of the caged male legger.

He bowed his head. "I can't really blame you. You're absolutely correct. If you contacted us, we'd steal your secrets. And then, look out! We'd infest all of space!"

He paused, bit his lip, and said, "Yet we're showing some signs of progress. There's not been a war or a revolution for fifteen years; the UN has been settling problems that would once have resulted in a world war; Russia and the U.S. are still armed but are not nearly as close to conflict as they were when I was born. Perhaps...?

"Do you know, I bet you've never seen an Earthman in the flesh before. Perhaps you've never seen a picture of one, or if you did, they were clothed. There are no photos of Earth people in these books. Maybe you knew we were male and female, but that didn't mean much until you saw me taking a shower. And the suddenly revealed parallel between the male dekaped and myself horrified you. And you realized that this was the only thing in the world that you had for companionship. Almost as if I'd been shipwrecked on an island and found the other inhabitant was a tiger.

"But that doesn't explain what you are doing here, alone, living in these tubes among the indigenous Martians. Oh, how I wish I could talk to you!

"*With thee conversing,*" he said, remembering those lines he had read the last night in the base.

She smiled at him, and he said, "Well, at least you're getting over your scare. I'm not such a bad fellow, after all, heh?"

She smiled again and went to a cabinet and from it took paper and pen. With them, she made one simple sketch after another. Watching her agile pen, he began to see what had happened.

Her people had had a base for a long time — a long long time — on the side of the Moon the Terrestrials could not see. But when rockets from Earth had first penetrated into space, her people had obliterated all evidences of the base. A new one had been set up on Mars.

Then, as it became apparent that a Terrestrial expedition would be sent to Mars, that base had been destroyed and another one set up on Ganymede.

However, five scientists had remained behind in these simple quarters to complete their studies of the dekapeds. Though Martia's people had studied these creatures for some time, they still had not found out how their bodies could endure the differences between tube pressure and that in the open air. The four believed that they were breathing hot on the neck of this secret and had gotten permission to stay until just before the Earthmen landed.

Martia actually was a native, in the sense that she had been born and raised here. She had been seven years here, she indicated, showing a sketch of Mars in its orbit around the sun and then holding up seven fingers.

That made her about fourteen Earth years old, Lane estimated. Perhaps these people reached maturity a little faster than his. That is, if she were mature. It was difficult to tell.

Horror twisted her face and widened her eyes as she showed him what had happened the night before they were to leave for Ganymede.

The sleeping party had been attacked by an uncaged male legger.

It was rare that a male got loose. But he occasionally managed to escape. When he did, he destroyed the entire colony, all life in the tube wherever he went. He even ate the roots of the trees so that they died, and oxygen ceased to flow into that section of the tunnel.

There was only one way a forewarned colony could fight a rogue male—a dangerous method. That was to release their own male. They selected the few who would stay behind and sacrifice their lives to dissolve the bars with an acid secretion from their bodies while the others fled. The queen, unable to move, also died. But enough of her eggs were taken to produce another queen and another consort elsewhere.

Meanwhile, it was hoped that the males would kill each other or that the victor would be so crippled that he could be finished off by the soldiers.

Lane nodded. The only natural enemy of the dekapeds was an escaped male. Left unchecked, they would soon crowd the tubes and exhaust food and air. Unkind as it seemed, the escape of a male now and then was the only thing that saved the Martians from starvation and perhaps extinction.

However that might be, the rogue had been no blessing in disguise for Martia's people. Three had been killed in their sleep before the other two awoke. One had thrown herself at the beast and shouted to Martia to escape.

Almost insane with fear, Martia had nevertheless not allowed panic to send her running. Instead, she had dived for a cabinet to get a weapon.

— A weapon, thought Lane. I'll have to find out about that.

Martia acted out what had happened. She had gotten the cabinet door open and reached in for the weapon when she felt the beak of the rogue fastening on her leg. Despite the shock, for the beak cut deeply into the blood vessels and muscles, she managed to press the end of the weapon against the male's body The weapon did its work, for the male dropped on the floor. Unfortunately, the beaks did not relax but held their terrible grip on her thigh, just above the knee.

Here Lane tried to interrupt so he could get a description of what the weapon looked like and of the principle of its operation. Martia, however, ignored his request. Seemingly, she did not understand his question, but he was sure that she did not care to reply. He was not entirely trusted, which was understandable. How could he blame her? She would be a fool to be at ease with such an unknown quantity as himself. That is, if he were unknown. After all, though she did not know him well personally, she knew the kind of people from whom he came and what could be expected from them. It was surprising that she had not left him to die in the garden, and it was amazing that she had shared that communion of bread and wine with him.

Perhaps, he thought, it is because she was so lonely and any company was better than nothing. Or it might be that he acted on a higher ethical plane than most Earthmen and she could not endure the idea of leaving a fellow sentient being to die, even if she thought him a bloodthirsty savage.

Or she might have other plans for him, such as taking him prisoner.

Martia continued her story. She had fainted and some time later had awakened. The male was beginning to stir, so she had killed him this time.

One more item of information, thought Lane. The weapon is capable of inflicting degrees of damage.

Then, though she kept passing out, she had dragged herself to the medicine chest and treated herself. Within two days she was up and hobbling around, and the scars were beginning to fade.

They must be far ahead of us in everything, he thought. According to her, some of her muscles had been cut. Yet they grew together in a day.

Martia indicated that the repair of her body had required an enormous amount of food during the healing. Most of her time had been spent in eating and sleeping. Reconstruction, even if it took place at a normal accelerated rate, still required the same amount of energy.

By then the bodies of the male and of her companions were stinking with decay. She had to force herself to cut them up and dispose of them in the garbage burner.

Tears welled in her eyes as she recounted this, and she sobbed.

Lane wanted to ask her why she had not buried them, but he reconsidered. Though it might not be the custom among her kind to bury the dead, it was more probable that she wanted to destroy all evidence of their existence before Earthmen came to Mars.

Using signs, he asked her how the male had gotten into the room despite the gate across the tunnel. She indicated that the gate was ordinarily closed only when the dekapeds were awake or when her companions and she were sleeping. But it had been the turn of one of their number to collect eggs in the queen's chamber. As she reconstructed it, the rogue had appeared at that time and killed the scientist there. Then, after ravening among the still-sleeping colony, it had gone down the tube and there had seen the light shining from the open tunnel. The rest of the story he knew.

Why, he pantomimed, why didn't the escaped male sleep when all his fellows did? The one in the cage evidently slept at the same time as his companions. And the queen's guards also slept in the belief they were safe from attack.

Not so, replied Martia. A male who had gotten out of a cage knew no law but fatigue. When he had exhausted himself in his eating and killing, he lay down to sleep. But it did not matter if it was the regular time for it or not. When he was rested, he raged through the tubes and did not stop until he was again too tired to move.

So then, thought Lane, that explains the area of dead umbrella plants on top of the tube by the garden. Another colony moved into the devastated area, built the garden on the outside, and planted the young umbrellas.

He wondered why neither he nor the others of his group had seen the dekapeds outside during their six days on Mars. There must be at least one pressure chamber and outlet for each colony, and there should be at least fifteen colonies in the tubes between this point and that near his base. Perhaps the answer was that the leaf-croppers only ventured out occasionally. Now that he remembered it, neither he nor anyone else had noticed any holes on the leaves. That meant that the trees must have been cropped some time ago and were now ready for an-

other harvesting. If the expedition had only waited several days before sending out men in tracs, it might have seen the dekapeds and
investigated. And the story would have been different.

There were other questions he had for her. What about the vessel
that was to take them to Ganymede? Was there one hidden on the outside, or was one to be sent to pick them up? If one was to be sent, how
would the Ganymedan base be contacted? Radio? Or some — to him —
inconceivable method?

The blue globes! he thought. Could they be means of transmitting
messages?

He did not know or think further about them because fatigue overwhelmed him, and he fell asleep. His last memory was that of Martia
leaning over him and smiling at him.

When he awoke reluctantly, his muscles ached, and his mouth was
as dry as the Martian desert. He rose in time to see Martia drop out of
the tunnel, a bucket of eggs in her hand. Seeing this, he groaned. That
meant she had gone into the nursery again, and that he had slept the
clock around.

He stumbled up and into the shower cubicle. Coming out much
refreshed, he found breakfast hot on the table. Martia conducted the
communion rite, and then they ate. He missed his coffee. The hot soup
was good but did not make a satisfactory substitute. There was a bowl
of mixed cereal and fruit, both of which came out of a can. It must
have had a high energy content, for it made him wide awake.

Afterward, he did some setting-up exercises while she did the
dishes. Though he kept his body busy, he was thinking of things un-
connected with what he was doing.

What was to be his next move?

His duty demanded that he return to the base and report. What
news he would send to the orbital ship! The story would flash from
the ship back to Earth. The whole planet would be in an uproar.

There was one objection to his plan to take Martia back with him.
She would not want to go.

Halfway in a deep knee bend, he stopped. What a fool he was! He
had been too tired and confused to see it. But if she had revealed that
the base of her people was on Ganymede, she did not expect him to
take the information back to his transmitter. It would be foolish on her
part to tell him unless she were absolutely certain that he would be
able to communicate with no one.

That must mean that a vessel was on its way and would arrive
soon. And it would not only take her but him. If he was to be killed, he
would be dead now.

Lane had not been chosen to be a member of the first Mars expedition because he lacked decision. Five minutes later, he had made up his mind. His duty was clear. Therefore, he would carry it out, even if it violated his personal feelings toward Martia and caused her injury.

First, he'd bind her. Then he would pack up their two pressure suits, the books, and any tools small enough to carry so they might later be examined on Earth. He would make her march ahead of him through the tube until they came to the point opposite his base. There they would don their suits and go to the dome. And as soon as possible the two would rise on the rocket to the orbital ship. This step was the most hazardous, for it was extremely difficult for one man to pilot the rocket. Theoretically, it could be done. It had to be done.

Lane tightened his jaw and forced his muscles to quit quivering. The thought of violating Martia's hospitality upset him. Still, she had treated him so well for a purpose not altogether altruistic. For all he knew, she was plotting against him.

There was a rope in one of the cabinets, the same flexible rope with which she had pulled him from the mire. He opened the door of the cabinet and removed it. Martia stood in the middle of the room and watched him while she stroked the head of the blue-eyed worm coiled about her shoulders. He hoped she would stay there until he got close. Obviously, she carried no weapon on her nor indeed anything except the pet. Since she had removed her suit, she had worn nothing.

Seeing him approaching her, she spoke to him in an alarmed tone. It didn't take much sensitivity to know that she was asking him what he intended to do with the rope. He tried to smile reassuringly at her and failed. This was making him sick.

A moment later, he was violently sick. Martia had spoken loudly one word, and it was as if it had struck him in the pit of his stomach. Nausea gripped him, his mouth began salivating, and it was only by dropping the rope and running into the shower that he avoided making a mess on the floor.

Ten minutes later, he felt thoroughly cleaned out. But when he tried to walk to the bed, his legs threatened to give way. Martia had to support him.

Inwardly, he cursed. To have a sudden reaction to the strange food at such a crucial moment! Luck was not on his side.

That is, if it was chance. There had been something so strange and forceful about the manner in which she pronounced that word. Was it possible that she had set up in him—hypnotically or otherwise—a reflex to that word? It would, under the conditions, be a weapon more powerful than a gun.

He wasn't sure, but it did seem strange that his body had accepted the alien food until that moment. Hypnotism did not really seem to be the answer. How could it be so easily used on him since he did not know more than twenty words of her language?

Language? Words? They weren't necessary. If she had given him a hypnotic drug in his food, and then had awakened him during his sleep, she could have dramatized how he was to react if she wanted him to do so. She could have given him the key word, then have allowed him to go to sleep again.

He knew enough hypnotism to know that that was possible. Whether his suspicions were true or not, it was a fact that he had laid flat on his back. However, the day was not wasted. He learned twenty more words, and she drew many more sketches for him. He found out that when he had jumped into the mire of the garden he had literally fallen into the soup. The substance in which the young umbrella trees had been planted was a zoogloea, a glutinous mass of one-celled vegetables and somewhat larger anaerobic animal life that fed on the vegetables. The heat from the jam-packed water-swollen bodies kept the garden soil warm and prevented the tender plants from freezing even during the forty degrees below zero Fahrenheit of the midsummer nights.

After the trees were transplanted into the roof of the tube to replace the dead adults, the zoogloea would be taken piecemeal back to the tube and dumped into the channel. Here the jetfish would strain out part and eat part as they pumped water from the polar end of the tube to the equatorial end.

Toward the end of the day, he tried some of the zoogloea soup and managed to keep it down. A little later, he ate some cereal.

Martia insisted on spooning the food for him. There was something so feminine and tender about her solicitude that he could not protest.

"Martia," he said, "I may be wrong. There can be good will and rapport between our two kinds. Look at us. Why, if you were a real woman, I'd be in love with you.

"Of course, you may have made me sick in the first place. But if you did, it was a matter of expediency, not malice. And now you are taking care of me, your enemy. Love thy enemy. Not because you have been told you should but because you do."

She, of course, did not understand him. However, she replied in her own tongue, and it seemed to him that her voice had the same sense of sympatico.

As he fell asleep, he was thinking that perhaps Martia and he would be the two ambassadors to bring their people together in peace. After all, both of them were highly civilized, essentially pacifistic, and devoutly religious. There was such a thing as the brotherhood, not only of man, but of all sentient beings throughout the cosmos, and...

Pressure on his bladder woke him up. He opened his eyes. The ceiling and walls expanded and contracted. His wristwatch was distorted. Only by extreme effort could he focus his eyes enough to straighten the arms on his watch. The piece, designed to measure the slightly longer Martian day, indicated midnight.

Groggily, he rose. He felt sure that he must have been drugged and that he would still be sleeping if the bladder pain hadn't been so sharp. If only he could take something to counteract the drug, he could carry out his plans now. But first he had to get to the toilet.

To do so, he had to pass close to Martia's bed. She did not move but lay on her back, her arms flung out and hanging over the sides of the bed, her mouth open wide.

He looked away, for it seemed indecent to watch when she was in such a position.

But something caught his eye—a movement, a flash of light like a gleaming jewel in her mouth.

He bent over her, looked, and recoiled in horror.

A head rose from between her teeth.

He raised his hand to snatch at the thing but froze in the posture as he recognized the tiny pouting round mouth and little blue eyes. It was the worm.

At first, he thought Martia was dead. The thing was not coiled in her mouth. Its body disappeared into her throat.

Then he saw her chest was rising easily and that she seemed to be in no difficulty.

Forcing himself to come close to the worm, though his stomach muscles writhed and his neck muscles quivered, he put his hand close to its lips.

Warm air touched his fingers, and he heard a faint whistling.

Martia was breathing through it!

Hoarsely, he said, "God!" and he shook her shoulder. He did not want to touch the worm because he was afraid that it might do something to injure her. In that moment of shock he had forgotten that he had an advantage over her, which he should use.

Mania's lids opened; her large gray-blue eyes stared blankly.

"Take it easy," he said soothingly.

She shuddered. Her lids closed, her neck arched back, and her face contorted.

He could not tell if the grimace was caused by pain or something else.

"What is this—this monster?" he said. "Symbiote? Parasite?"

He thought of vampires, of worms creeping into one's sleeping body and there sucking blood.

Suddenly, she sat up and held out her arms to him. He seized her hands, saying, "What is it?"

Martia pulled him toward her, at the same time lifting her face to his.

Out of her open mouth shot the worm, its head pointed toward his face, its little lips formed into an O.

It was reflex, the reflex of fear that made Lane drop her hands and spring back. He had not wanted to do that, but he could not help himself.

Abruptly, Martia came wide awake. The worm flopped its full length from her mouth and fell into a heap between her legs. There it thrashed for a moment before coiling itself like a snake, its head resting on Martia's thigh, its eyes turned upward to Lane.

There was no doubt about it. Martia looked disappointed, frustrated.

Lane's knees, already weak, gave way. However, he managed to continue to his destination. When he came out, he walked as far as Martia's bed, where he had to sit down. His heart was thudding against his ribs, and he was panting hard.

He sat behind her, for he did not want to be where the worm could touch him.

Martia made motions for him to go back to his bed and they would all sleep. Evidently, he thought, she found nothing alarming in the incident.

But he knew he could not rest until he had some kind of explanation. He handed her paper and pen from the bedside table and then gestured fiercely. Martia shrugged and began sketching while Lane watched over her shoulder. By the time she had used up five sheets of paper, she had communicated her message.

His eyes were wide, and he was even paler.

So—Martia *was* a female. Female at least in the sense that she carried eggs—and, at times, young—within her.

And there was the so-called worm. So called? What could he call it? It could not be designated under one category. It was many things in one. It was a larva. It was a phallus. It was also her offspring, of her flesh and blood.

But not of her genes. It was not descended from her.

She had given birth to it, yet she was not its mother. She was neither one of its mothers.

The dizziness and confusion he felt was not caused altogether by his sickness. Things were coming too fast. He was thinking furiously, trying to get this new information clear, but his thoughts kept going back and forth, getting nowhere.

"There's no reason to get upset," he told himself. "After all, the splitting of animals into two sexes is only one of the ways of reproduction tried on Earth. On Martia's planet Nature—God—has fashioned another method for the higher animals. And only He knows how many other designs for reproduction He has fashioned on how many other worlds."

Nevertheless, he was upset.

This worm, no, this larva, this embryo outside its egg and its secondary mother...well, call it, once and for all, larva, because it did metamorphose later.

This particular larva was doomed to stay in its present form until it died of old age.

Unless Martia found another adult of the Eeltau.

And unless she and this other adult felt affection for each other.

Then, according to the sketch she'd drawn, Martia and her friend, or lover, would lie down or sit together. They would, as lovers do on Earth, speak to each other in endearing, flattering, and exciting terms. They would caress and kiss much as Terrestrial man and woman do, though on Earth it was not considered complimentary to call one's lover Big Mouth.

Then, unlike the Terran custom, a third would enter the union to form a highly desired and indeed indispensable and eternal triangle.

The larva, blindly, brainlessly obeying its instincts, aroused by mutual fondling by the two, would descend tail first into the throat of one of the two Eeltau. Inside the body of the lover a fleshy valve would open to admit the slim body of the larva. Its open tip would touch the ovary of the host. The larva, like an electric eel, would release a tiny current. The hostess would go into an ecstasy, its nerves stimulate electrochemically. The ovary would release an egg no larger than a pencil dot. It would disappear into the open tip of the larva's tail, there to begin a journey up a canal toward the center of its body, urged on by the contraction of muscle and whipping of cilia.

Then the larva slid out of the first hostess's mouth and went tail first into the other, there to repeat the process. Sometimes the larva garnered eggs, sometimes not, depending upon whether the ovary had a fully developed one to release.

When the process was successful, the two eggs moved toward each other but did not quite meet.

Not yet.

There must be other eggs collected in the dark incubator of the larva, collected by pairs, though not necessarily from the same couple of donors.

These would number anywhere from twenty to forty pairs.

Then, one day, the mysterious chemistry of the cells would tell the larva's body that it had gathered enough eggs.

A hormone was released, the metamorphosis begun. The larva swelled enormously, and the mother, seeing this, placed it tenderly in a warm place and fed it plenty of predigested food and sugar water.

Before the eyes of its mother, the larva then grew shorter and wider. Its tail contracted; its cartilaginous vertebrae, widely separated in its larval stage, shifted closer to each other and hardened, a skeleton formed, ribs, shoulders. Legs and arms budded and grew and took humanoid shape. Six months passed, and there lay in its crib something resembling a baby of *Homo sapiens*.

From then until its fourteenth year, the Eeltau grew and developed much as its Terran counterpart.

Adulthood, however, initiated more strange changes. Hormone released hormone until the first pair of gametes, dormant these fourteen years, moved together.

The two fused, the chromatin of one uniting with the chromatin of the other. Out of the two—a single creature, wormlike, four inches long, was released into the stomach of its hostess.

Then, nausea. Vomiting. And so, comparatively painlessly, the bringing forth of a genetically new being.

It was this worm that would be both fetus and phallus and would give ecstasy and draw into its own body the eggs of loving adults and would metamorphose and become infant, child, and adult.

And so on and so on.

He rose and shakily walked to his own bed. There he sat down, his head bowed, while he muttered to himself.

"Let's see now. Martia gave birth to, brought forth, or up, this larva. But the larva actually doesn't have any of Martia's genes. Martia was just the hostess for it.

"However, if Martia has a lover, she will, by means of this worm, pass on her heritable qualities. This worm will become an adult and bring forth, or up, Martia's child."

He raised his hands in despair.

"How do the Eeltau reckon ancestry? How keep track of their relatives? Or do they care? Wouldn't it be easier to consider your foster mother, your hostess, your real mother? As, in the sense of having borne you, she is!

"And what kind of sexual code do these people have? It can't, I would think, be much like ours. Nor is there any reason why it should be.

"But who is responsible for raising the larva and child? Its pseudomother? Or does the lover share in the duties? And what about property and inheritance laws? And, and..."

Helplessly, he looked at Martia.

Fondly stroking the head of the larva, she returned his stare.

Lane shook his head.

"I was wrong. Eeltau and Terran couldn't meet on a friendly basis. My people would react to yours as to disgusting vermin. Their deepest prejudices would be aroused, their strongest taboos would be violated. They could not learn to live with you or consider you even faintly human.

"And as far as that goes, could you live with us? Wasn't the sight of me naked a shock? Is that reaction a part of why you don't make contact with us?"

Martia put the larva down and stood up and walked over to him and kissed the tips of his fingers. Lane, though he had to fight against visibly flinching, took her fingers and kissed them. Softly, he said to her, "Yet...individuals could learn to respect each other, to have affection for each other. And masses are made of individuals."

He lay back on the bed. The grogginess, pushed aside for a while by excitement, was coming back. He couldn't fight off sleep much longer.

"Fine noble talk," he murmured. "But it means nothing. Eeltau don't think they should deal with us. And we are, unknowingly, pushing out toward them. What will happen when we are ready to make the interstellar jump? War? Or will they be afraid to let us advance even to that point and destroy us before then? After all, one cobalt bomb..."

He looked again at Martia, at the not-quite-human yet beautiful face, the smooth skin of the chest, abdomen, and loins, innocent of nipple, navel, or labia. From far off she had come, from a possibly terrifying place across terrifying distances. About her, however, there was little that was terrifying and much that was warm, generous, companionable, attractive.

As if they had waited for some key to turn, and the key had been turned, the lines he had read before falling asleep the last night in the base came again to him.

> *It is the voice of my beloved that knocketh, saying,*
> *Open to me, my sister, my love, my dove, my undefiled...*

> *We have a little sister,*
> *And she hath no breasts:*
> *What shall we do for our sister*
> *In the day when she shall be spoken for?*

> *With thee conversing, I forget all time,*
> *All seasons, and their change, all please alike.*

"With thee conversing," he said aloud. He turned over so his back was to her, and he pounded his fist against the bed.

"Oh dear God, why couldn't it be so?"

A long time he lay there, his face pressed into the mattress. Something had happened; the overpowering fatigue was gone; his body had drawn strength from some reservoir. Realizing this, he sat up and beckoned to Martia, smiling at the same time.

She rose slowly and started to walk to him, but he signaled that she should bring the larva with her. At first, she looked puzzled. Then her expression cleared, to be replaced by understanding. Smiling delightedly, she walked to him, and though he knew it must be a trick of his imagination, it seemed to him that she swayed her hips as a woman would.

She halted in front of him and then stooped to kiss him full on the lips. Her eyes were closed.

He hesitated for a fraction of a second. She—no, it, he told himself—looked so trusting, so loving, so womanly, that he could not do it.

"For Earth!" he said fiercely and brought the edge of his palm hard against the side of her neck.

She crumpled forward against him, her face sliding into his chest. Lane caught her under the armpits and laid her facedown on the bed. The larva, which had fallen from her hand onto the floor, was writhing about as if hurt. Lane picked it up by its tail and, in a frenzy that owed its violence to the fear he might not be able to do it, snapped it like a whip. There was a crack as the head smashed into the floor and blood spurted from its eyes and mouth. Lane placed his heel on the head and stepped down until there was a flat mess beneath his foot.

Then, quickly, before she could come to her senses and speak any words that would render him sick and weak, he ran to a cabinet. Snatching a narrow towel out of it, he ran back and gagged her. After that he tied her hands behind her back with the rope.

"Now, you bitch!" he panted. "We'll see who comes out ahead! You would do that with me, would you! You deserve this; your monster deserves to die!"

Furiously he began packing. In fifteen minutes he had the suits, helmets, tanks, and food rolled into two bundles. He searched for the weapon she had talked about and found something that might conceivably be it. It had a butt that fitted to his hand, a dial that might be a rheostat for controlling degrees of intensity of whatever it shot, and a bulb at the end. The bulb, he hoped, expelled the stunning and killing energy. Of course, he might be wrong. It could be fashioned for an entirely different purpose.

Martia had regained consciousness. She sat on the edge of the bed, her shoulders hunched, her head drooping, tears running down her cheeks and into the towel around her mouth. Her wide eyes were focused on the smashed worm by her feet.

Roughly, Lane seized her shoulder and pulled her upright. She gazed wildly at him, and he gave her a little shove. He felt sick within him, knowing that he had killed the larva when he did not have to do so and that he was handling her so violently because he was afraid, not of her, but of himself. If he had been disgusted because she had fallen into the trap he set for her, he was so because he, too, beneath his disgust, had wanted to commit that act of love. Commit, he thought, was the right word. It contained criminal implications.

Martia whirled around, almost losing her balance because of her tied hands. Her face worked, and sounds burst from the gag.

"Shut up!" he howled, pushing her again. She went sprawling and only saved herself from falling on her face by dropping on her knees. Once more, he pulled her to her feet, noting as he did so that her knees were skinned. The sight of the blood, instead of softening him, enraged him even more.

"Behave yourself, or you'll get worse!" he snarled.

She gave him one more questioning look, threw back her head, and made a strange strangling sound. Immediately, her face took on a bluish tinge. A second later, she fell heavily on the floor.

Alarmed, he turned her over. She was choking to death.

He tore off the gag and reached into her mouth and grabbed the root of her tongue. It slipped away and he seized it again, only to have it slide away as if it were a live animal that defied him.

Then he had pulled her tongue out of her throat; she had swallowed it in an effort to kill herself.

Lane waited. When he was sure she was going to recover, he replaced the gag around her mouth. Just as he was about to tie the knot at the back of her neck, he stopped. What use would it be to continue this? If allowed to speak, she would say the word that would throw him into retching. If gagged, she would swallow her tongue again.

He could save her only so many times. Eventually, she would succeed in strangling herself.

The one way to solve his problem was the one way he could not take. If her tongue were cut off at the root, she could neither speak nor kill herself. Some men might do it; he could not.

The other way to keep her silent was to kill her.

"I can't do it in cold blood," he said aloud. "So, if you want to die, Martia, then you must do it by committing suicide. That, I can't help. Up you go. I'll get your pack, and we'll leave."

Martia turned blue and sagged to the floor.

"I'll not help you this time!" he shouted, but he found himself frantically trying to undo the knot.

At the same time, he told himself what a fool he was. Of course! The solution was to use her own gun on her. Turn the rheostat to a stunning degree of intensity and knock her out whenever she started to regain consciousness. Such a course would mean he'd have to carry her and her equipment, too, on the thirty-mile walk down the tube to an exit near his base. But he could do it. He'd rig up some sort of travois. He'd do it! Nothing could stop him. And Earth...

At that moment, hearing an unfamiliar noise, he looked up. There were two Eeltau in pressure suits standing there, and another crawling out of the tunnel. Each had a bulb-tipped handgun in her hand.

Desperately, Lane snatched at the weapon he carried in his belt. With his left hand he twisted the rheostat on the side of the barrel, hoping that this would turn it on full force. Then he raised the bulb toward the group...

He woke flat on his back, clad in his suit, except for the helmet, and strapped to a stretcher. His body was helpless, but he could turn his head. He did so, and saw many Eeltau dismantling the room. The one who had stunned him with her gun before he could fire was standing by him.

She spoke in English that held only a trace of foreign accent. "Settle down, Mr. Lane. You're in for a long ride. You'll be more comfortably situated once we're in our ship."

He opened his mouth to ask her how she knew his name but closed it when he realized she must have read the entries in the log at the base. And it was to be expected that some Eeltau would be trained in Earth languages. For over a century their sentinel spaceships had been tuning in to radio and TV.

It was then that Martia spoke to the captain. Her face was wild and reddened with weeping and marks where she had fallen.

The interpreter said to Lane, "*Mahrseeya* asks you to tell her why you killed her...baby. She cannot understand why you thought you had to do so."

"I cannot answer," said Lane. His head felt very light, almost as if it were a balloon expanding. And the room began slowly to turn around.

"I will tell her why," answered the interpreter. "I will tell her that it is the nature of the beast."

"That is not so!" cried Lane. "I am no vicious beast. I did what I did because I had to! I could not accept her love and still remain a man! Not the kind of man..."

"*Mahrseeya*," said the interpreter, "will pray that you be forgiven the murder of her child and that you will someday, under our teaching, be unable to do such a thing. She herself, though she is stricken with grief for her dead baby, forgives you. She hopes the time will come when you will regard her as a—sister. She thinks there is some good in you."

Lane clenched his teeth together and bit the end of his tongue until it bled while they put his helmet on. He did not dare to try to talk, for that would have meant he would scream and scream. He felt as if something had been planted in him and had broken its shell and was growing into something like a worm. It was eating him, and what would happen before it devoured all of him he did not know.

♦ UPROAR IN ACHERON ♦

INTRODUCTION

This is the only fictional tale which is not science-fiction. I include it because a book which samples the spectrum of my writings should have one non-s-f work and also because of its curious history.

When I wrote it in 1961, while living in Scottsdale, Arizona, I thought that the basic idea, that from which the plot derived, had never been used in fiction before then. As far as I know, that's still true.

I could have set the story almost anywhere on Earth, but, since I was living in Arizona, I used that locale.

At that time, I considered the story to be only one of a series which would be collected for a book. Or perhaps the stories would be rewritten to make a novel about the great conman of the Old West, Doc Grandtoul. Doc, as his name suggests—Grandtoul = Grand Tool—was also a great lover.

I still might write this book someday, but since I've started fifteen series and not as yet finished any, and since I keep getting new ideas at the rate of about three per week, I doubt that I'll finish this long-ago-conceived project. But you never know.

The story here will be extensively and somewhat differently written if I do decide to write a series for a collection.

As it was, I wrote it, and it was published in the May 1962 issue of *The Saint Mystery Magazine*. It was my first printed Western, though I had, during the '40s, written two or three Western short stories which had been rejected and got one-fourth of the way through a novel based on the Johnston County rancher-squatter war.

Two years later, on May 8, 1964, I sat down before the TV set to watch a *Twilight Zone* show. This was "Garrity and the Graves," a telecast on CBS, teleplay by Rod Serling, based on a story by Nike Korologos. The play had not gone long, perhaps five minutes, when I started swearing, and I told Bette, my wife, "You won't believe this. I can't. But that's based on 'Uproar in Acheron.'" Or something like that. I probably said something stronger.

Having watched it to the end, I rose and wrote a letter to my agent. And later I talked to him on the phone. I gave him all the details of the telecast and of my story. He commiserated with me but said there wasn't much to do about it. I could send a photocopy of the story and a letter to CBS, but he doubted that it would do any good.

I did a lot of fuming but at that time I was having some deep personal problems which made the *Twilight Zone* affair appear minor. Also, my agent, the agent's representative, rather, had not at all encouraged me to pursue the matter.

Then I found out later that my agent was also Rod Serling's. And I quit the agency. I also noticed that after talking to my agent, "Garrity and the Graves" seemed to have been dropped from the reruns. At least, though I looked for it during the reruns, I never saw that it was advertised.

When I moved to Beverly Hills in late 1965, I told several science-fiction and TV writers about my story and the telecast. And I found out that I was not the only writer who had been watching the series and experienced the same trauma.

And now, just this moment, while I was writing this foreword, I experienced an amazing coincidence—or synchronicity, if you prefer that term. I got a phone call from George Scheetz, a friend, fan, and publisher of the *Farmerage* fanzine, of a forthcoming bibliography of my works, and of *Wheelwrightings,* the irregular periodical of the local Sherlock Holmes Scion Society, The Hansoms of John Clayton. He'd just returned from a trip to the West, and he'd found out that, if "Garrity and the Graves" had been dropped from the series, it had been picked up again. It was now included in the reruns.

I suggest to the reader that he compare this story to "Garrity and the Graves." Consider the basic idea, which had not been used until this story appeared, the locale, the characters, the development of plot.

Everybody in the town of Acheron had been wondering for two weeks whom Linda Beeman favored. Now there was no doubt. The smoke of the revolvers had just thinned away when Linda ran into the Lucky Lode saloon and threw herself, sobbing, on the body of Johnny Addeson.

Skeeter Patton, the Colt still in his hand, stood blinking at her like a cat that'd been suddenly awakened. He was pale and shaking, and no wonder. He'd put two bullets into the chest of his best friend and lost forever his chance of marrying Linda. Yet he could have done nothing to stop what had happened.

The two young men had dropped in at the Lucky Lode after work to have a few. Johnny had been moody for about a week, but tonight he was laughing and joking. That is, he was until Skeeter said that he had to leave soon. He had a date to take Linda for a buggy ride.

Johnny's eyes had widened, and he had said, "Quit your fooling! She has a date with me!"

The men along the bar laughed and watched to see who would win the argument. They didn't expect the argument to be anything except the friendly pretend-mad joshing the two gave each other all the time. Johnny and Skeeter had come into Acheron only three weeks ago on the same stagecoach. They had not known each other before that day. Johnny had come from Tucson, where he'd been studying under a horse doctor. He'd opened his own business next door to the livery stable. Skeeter was fresh into the territory of Arizona from New Orleans, where he'd been a printer's devil. The two had struck it off together like flint and steel. Sparks flew sometimes, but their disputes always ended up with them laughing and backslapping each other. They'd even been agreeable about both courting Linda Beeman, the daughter of the owner of the Beeman Stables.

But Skeeter must have suddenly become serious about Linda. He swore at Johnny and said, "No call for that! And I'm not a liar!"

"This says you are!" shouted Johnny, and he drew his Smith and Wesson .45.

Skeeter struck Johnny's gun upwards with one hand and started to draw his own with the other hand. But Johnny brought his pistol down and fired. He was so close he couldn't have missed. But his bullet struck the far wall.

Skeeter fired his Colt .44 twice at point-blank range. And Johnny jerked backward from the force of the slugs and fell, face up, on the floor. Blood from the two wounds spread outwards on his chest.

There was uproar and confusion. Everybody was paralyzed with shock. A nice young man like Johnny going berserk was the last thing anybody would've thought of.

Old Doc Evans, Acheron's medico, coroner, and undertaker, finished his drink at the bar. Then he felt Johnny's pulse and pulled back one of Johnny's eyelids. When he rose from the body, Doc Evans shook his head.

"Right through the heart," he said. "Deader'n last week's newspaper."

Pedro, the Lucky Lode's janitor, ran to get Linda. He didn't take long. The stables, over which she lived with her father, were only the throw of a horseshoe away. In two minutes she was sobbing over Johnny's body.

Skeeter hadn't said a word. He was too dazed. Even when Sheriff Douglas said, "Don't worry, son. It was a clear case of self-defense," Skeeter didn't talk. Once, he put his hand out towards Linda and then, as if knowing it would do no good, withdrew his hand.

Old Doc Evans gave a few orders. Two men picked up Johnny's body and carried it out of the Lucky Lode. They were headed for the doc's house, which was also the undertaking parlor. But they had not gotten halfway across the street before they stopped.

Everybody else stopped, too, for down the main street was a blaze of lanterns, a squeak of wheels, and the high-walled bulk of a van. It was the kind of van a snake-oil man drives around in and lives in and carries his snake oil and fever pills and tonics in. But this van had no big signs on the side or anything to tell what the owner was selling.

The van pulled up just by the two men carrying the body, and the driver looked down from his high seat.

"Had a shooting, friends?" the man said. "Did this young fellow just die? Perhaps I can do something for him."

It was a strange thing to say, and the man who said it was even stranger. He was dressed in a rusty black suit and wore a black bowler from which hair black as stove polish hung. His face was as pale as if he'd just seen Death. He had a handsome face, though it was bony with high cheekbones and a Roman nose and deep hollow eyes and dark rims under the eyes. His neck, sticking out of his white collar, was thin as a colt's leg, and his shoulders were narrow as a cat's.

"I am Doctor Grandtoul," he said in a voice that surprised everybody because it was so deep.

"Always nice to meet another M.D. in this unpopulated territory," said old Doc Evans. He took off his Stetson and placed it over his heart. "But there ain't much you can do for Johnny Addeson. He breathed his last five minutes ago, and his soul has winged on to its reward."

Doctor Grandtoul raised a slim pale hand and pointed a slim pale finger. "Ah, my friend," he said, "that is where you are wrong."

He looked around at the crowd, which was rubbernecking as if they knew something out of the ordinary was coming and they weren't sure they were going to like it.

"Yes," said Doctor Grandtoul, "no discredit to you, my worthy Hippocratian comrade. But perhaps you have not heard of the latest scientific advancement.

"Advancement!" he repeated explosively. "No! Miracle, rather! The miracle of electricity, which is both the stuff of lightning and of life itself!"

He swung down off the seat of van and landed on his feet as lightly as a catamount.

"Bring the late departed to the back of my van," he said, "and help me place the body on my bed. Then I'll do what I can."

He walked around to the back of the van, opened the doors, and leaped into the van like a long lean black cat. Then he took Johnny from the two men who handed him up, and, with a strength amazing in a man with such pipe-cleaner arms, carried Johnny to the bed on one side of the van. Once he'd placed Johnny there, he ripped off Johnny's shirt. Then he cleaned the wounds and from a jar on a shelf he poured out some powder into his hand.

He turned to the buzzing gaping crowd, bowed, flashed white teeth, and said, "Friends, we can't leave an ugly hole in the departed's chest, can we? I think not, for he'd have trouble breathing, what with the air whistling in and out, a ghastly rune. So we'll just place this *soodoplazum*, a secret of the ancient Tibetan lamas, in the wounds. And, once the lightning of the revitalizing machine surges through the body, the *soodoplazum* will become real flesh."

There weren't many who really heard him, and those who heard didn't understand him. The were too busy staring at the big batteries that lined one side of the van. The batteries looked just like the monsters the telegraph companies used to provide electricity for their copper lines. There were many copper wires, very thin wires, that sprouted out of the main cables from the battery terminals. Doc Grandtoul took the wires, one by one, and attached them to Johnny's wrists and ankles and waist and head with thin copper bands.

Then he paused and said, "Would you gentlemen allow your doctor — Evans, is it? — to come up here? I want him to examine the late departed once more and make absolutely certain the ghost is gone."

"Ain't no need," grumbled Doc Evans, tugging at his white walrus moustache and swaying back and forth because, like always, he had a snootful. But at Doc Grandtoul's insistence Doc Evans climbed into the van and felt Johnny's pulse again and looked into his eyes. Then he said, "I'll stake my professional reputation that Johnny's dead as Julius Caesar's mule."

"Wanta buy a drink if he ain't?" somebody called, and the crowd hooted with laughter because they knew how tight old Doc Evans was when it came to buying a drink for anybody except himself.

Nevertheless, not a man or woman there — and everybody in Acheron except the kids and sick in bed was there — didn't believe Johnny was dead. Old Doc Evans might be closefisted, ornery, and too much a tippler, but he'd seen enough corpses to know a dead ringer from a live one.

Doc Grandtoul took a hypodermic syringe from a box, wiped the needle with alcohol, and plunged it into Johnny's chest. After taking the needle out, he said, "The late departed has just been injected with a serum which, coupled with the electricity coursing through his body, should bring the life back."

The crowd gasped. The doctor grinned at them and pulled a huge goldplated watch from his vest pocket. His black eyebrows rose knowingly, and he said, "Three minutes should do it, my friends. The combination of serum and electrical juice in a strong young body as recently deceased as this takes only a short time to accomplish its mission."

Afterwards, there were some that said those were the longest and most terrifying three minutes of their lives. Something about the scene, Johnny's body lying so still in the bed, dimly lit by the kerosene lamp inside the van, the copper wires sprouting from him and running to the huge black batteries, and the calm certain bearing of the mysterious stranger convinced them they were going to see something they'd never seen before, maybe something they shouldn't be seeing.

There wasn't a sound except the hard breathing of the men and women pressing together so they could get closer to the van for a good look.

Then—there was one big gasp, one loud scream, and the sound of running feet. Doc Grandtoul was calling after them, "Come back! There's nothing to be afraid of!"

But he was alone. Even old Doc Evans had bolted.

Not quite alone. Johnny was sitting up in the bed and saying, "What in blue blazes is going on?"

♦ ♦ ♦

Later, much later, Johnny Addeson, Skeeter Patton, and Doc Grandtoul left the Lucky Lode. Johnny had invited the doctor to stay at the room he shared with Skeeter in Mrs. Lundgren's hotel. The men of Acheron followed the three out of the saloon, for they still hadn't gotten over the wonder of seeing Johnny raised from the dead. They kept touching him and saying, "How was it while you was dead, Johnny?"

And Johnny kept saying, "Just like I was sleeping. I didn't know nothing until I woke up with a strange face looking down at me."

He would laugh and say, "At first I thought it was the devil," and he would whoop with laughter to show how glad he was to be alive.

Skeeter Patton, after making sure that Johnny wasn't still mad at him, was buddies with Johnny again. He swore he didn't have any real interest in Linda Beeman. As far as he was concerned, Johnny could have her all to himself.

That was the strangest thing of all. Linda should have been over-joyed, should have been hanging on to Johnny for all she was worth, shouldn't have wanted him out of her sight. But she hadn't seen Johnny since he sat up and she ran away with the others. Old Doc Evans was with her in her father's house taking care of her. He didn't leave her until Johnny and Skeeter and Doc Grandtoul left the Lucky Lode. He met them just as they crossed the street towards the hotel.

"Doc," said Johnny, "how is Linda? Does she want to see me now?"

Doc Evans shook his head. "Sorry, son. She seems scared to death of you; keeps saying it ain't right you should be living. A dead man ought to stay dead."

"I don't understand that at all," said Johnny, scratching his curly head. "You'd think she'd be thanking God I'm up and jumping."

"She's in a state of shock, son," said Doc Evans. "Why don't you try to see her tomorrow, when she'll probably be recovering? After all, it ain't every day a tender young girl sees her boyfriend rise from his death bed."

Doc Evans spoke to Doc Grandtoul. "You've created quite a sensation, to put it mildly. How do you plan to cap what you did tonight?"

Grandtoul lifted his hands, and the crowd fell silent. He looked impressive as Lucifer himself with the light streaming out from a window of the Lucky Lode on his pale handsome face and glistening off his hair and eyes, which were black as malapai rock. His rich baritone boomed out, "Friends, I came to you out of the desert with this miraculous means of revitalizing the dead. I intend eventually to go East. I expect to find fame and fortune there. But I'm in no hurry for it. I don't want to sound like a preacher, but I really am more interested in benefiting mankind than in gaining all the wealth of the world. It makes me happier to think about reuniting you with your beloved dead than in making personal gains. Your happiness is mine.

"So, tomorrow, after I've rested, I'll explain more of what I intend to do. I can't promise you all the dead in your cemetery will be brought back to life. That depends on how they died and how long they've been dead. But I can assure you that if any of those who were taken away from you can be brought back by my revitalizing machine, they will walk once more among you.

"And, to show you my heart is in the right place, I assure you that I will not take one red cent for doing this. I will do everything for free. So you can see that I am not some charlatan who intends to take you for all you have. Good night!"

He walked away with Johnny and Skeeter, leaving behind him, not wild shouts of joy but a silence. Even then, some of the people in Acheron were beginning to see what emptying the graveyard might mean to them.

♦ ♦ ♦

Late next morning Linda Beeman walked into the lobby of Mrs. Lundgren's hotel. She wanted to speak to Johnny Addeson, but she was told by Mrs. Lundgren she'd have to wait her turn. Johnny was busy working as Doc Grandtoul's secretary. He and Skeeter were ushering in people who wanted to see the doctor. The doctor had rented a room next to Johnny's and was giving interviews to those who wanted to speak to him in private.

Linda spoke to everybody in the crowded lobby. Half of Acheron seemed to be waiting to talk to the doctor. All seemed to be very nervous. As Linda was the last to come, she wasn't called upstairs until noon.

When she entered Johnny's room, she found Johnny and Skeeter and Doc Grandtoul seated around a table. A large carpetbag was by the doctor's feet.

"Johnny," said Linda, "I'd like to speak to you alone."

"You're not desperate to talk to me?" said Doc Grandtoul. "You're the first."

He rose. "Come along, Skeeter. We'll wet our whistles at the Lucky Lode. Watch that bag, Johnny. It contains all our worldly wealth."

Linda spoke before the doctor could close the door behind him. "Is it true that tomorrow you're going to raise the dead?"

"I'm no miracle-maker," he answered. "Those who are well-preserved will benefit by the scientific means I use. Those who are not, well"—he bowed his head for a second and then continued—"tomorrow I will bring life to the departed and joy into the hearts of the bereaved."

He smiled, bowed, and left. Johnny said, "How're you feeling now, Linda?"

"I'm all over the shock now," she said. She paused, breathed deeply as if to gain strength for what she was going to say, and then spoke. "Johnny, do you think Doctor Grandtoul is doing right by raising the dead?"

"Right?" he said. "Of course! Why, if it wasn't for him I'd be six feet under! You wouldn't like that, would you?"

"No," she said. "Only..."

"Only what? What's eating you? I thought you loved me!"

Linda sat down and frowned as if she were thinking deeply. Finally, she said, "Of course I love you. Didn't I tell you so a week ago? And weren't we going to announce our engagement this Sunday after church? But...well, Johnny, you didn't know this, but I was engaged to Roy Canton only six months ago. We were going to be married, and..."

"What about it?" he said. "You didn't marry him. And you're going to marry me, right?"

"Roy Canton is dead," she said quietly, her wide blue eyes fixed on his face. "He died of fever less than a week after we announced our engagement. He's buried in the cemetery here."

Johnny paled. He swallowed several times and then managed to find his voice. "You don't mean you want him back?"

Suddenly, Linda began weeping. "I don't know what I want!" she sobbed. "When Roy died, I thought I'd die, too. Then I met you. And I fell in love. I wasn't being unfaithful to Roy. You can't be unfaithful to the dead. They're gone; they're never coming back. You're living and can't go on acting as if the dead were just away on a short visit and will be home next week. But now, now, I don't know! I love you, but I never quit loving Roy. And if he comes back, then I won't know what to do! I'll have two living men that I love. And…and I don't know what to do!"

Johnny, choking, said, "Maybe I could talk Doc into not raising Roy."

"No, you don't!" said Linda fiercely. "That wouldn't be fair!"

"What am I supposed to do?" said Johnny. "Wait around while you make up your mind? Who *do* you love, Roy or me?"

"If somebody had asked me that yesterday I'd have told him I love you as I love the living. And Roy as I love the dead. But now…"

"In other words," said Johnny bitterly, "you'll wait until Roy can ask you again, and then you'll make up your mind which of us you want."

Linda began crying again. Johnny's face twisted as if somebody had stuck a knife in him.

And then he shouted, "There's no use crying, Linda! Roy isn't going to come back from the dead!"

Linda rose from the chair and took a step towards Johnny.

"What do you mean?"

Johnny bit his lip and started to turn away. But Linda caught him by the shoulder and, with a strength surprising for such a small woman, spun him around to face her.

"What do you mean by saying he isn't going to come back from the dead?"

"I'll give it to you straight, Linda." said Johnny. "Doc Grandtoul can't any more put life into a corpse than you or I can!"

Linda gave a little shriek and swayed back and forth for a minute. Johnny caught her in his arms and pulled her to him.

"Oh, Linda, darling, don't be mad at me! I'm a cheat, a liar, a crook! And Skeeter and Doc Grandtoul are cheats, liars, and crooks, too! This whole business is a fraud!"

He dropped his arms from around her and began pacing around the room while he talked loudly and furiously. He would not look directly at her. He seemed to be ashamed and to be afraid he might see scorn on her face.

"I met Doc and Skeeter about six months ago," he said. "In Jumpoff, Nevada. I'd been prospecting and hadn't had any luck. I was broke and hungry. Doc took me in, fed me, clothed me, taught me to be a good poker player. He and Skeeter were dealing for the house in the poker games at the High Stepper Saloon. But Doc wasn't satisfied. He wanted to make more money and faster. He's a great reader, is Doc, well educated. In fact, he's a real doctor, got his M.D. from an Eastern university, though he comes from an old New Orleans family.

"Doc had read something in one of his history books that gave him an idea. It seems that in the Middle Ages there was a band of sharpers that traveled from village to village, announcing they intended to raise the dead from the local cemetery. And things happened there and then just like they did here and now. Nobody was anxious for the dead to come back. In fact, they were determined they wouldn't come back. Why? Because they'd cause too much consternation and turmoil, make too many problems.

"Doc said people hadn't changed a bit since the 13th century. We have gunpowder and steam trains and telegraph and gas lights. But people are just as superstitious and gullible as in the old days. They don't want their lives disrupted any more than can be helped.

"So Doc, who's a smart man even if he is as crooked as a snake's path, made some hollow wax bullets with red dye in the hollows. When they're fired, the wax doesn't hurt the man it hits, just stings. And the wax just spreads out and splatters the red dye so it looks like a bullet wound."

Linda had seated herself on a chair. She had been staring at him as if she could not understand what he was telling her. But when he paused for breath, she said, "What about Doc Evans? He pronounced you dead. How'd you fool him?"

Johnny, still not looking at her, grinned crookedly: He said, "Skeeter and I always travel ahead of Doc Grandtoul. We stop in a town and look it over. If the local doctor can be bribed or if there ain't no doctors, we stay. Acheron was a setup for us. Old Doc Evans hasn't much money, and he likes his whiskey too well. He agreed to go along with us if we gave him a good cut of the loot. He said he could send his grandson through medical school with the money and have enough to retire on, too."

"Then the whole quarrel over me was arranged by you and Skeeter?"

For the first time since he had started talking, Johnny looked directly at her. Desperately, he said, "Yes! But I wasn't fooling when I said I loved you! I do love you!"

"And just what did you expect me to do when you had to leave town before everybody found out you were a fraud?" she said scornfully. "Go with you? A cheat and a liar!"

"Now, honey," said Johnny, "if you'll think about it, you'll remember that Doc said he'd raise only those that the revitalizing machine can raise. And since it can't raise anybody, well....And he also said he wouldn't take a red cent for raising anybody. He won't, either. He's just taken money not to raise certain dead people. Nothing really dishonest in that. Like Doc says, you can't cheat an honest man."

"I don't know what you mean," she said.

"Here's what I mean," said Johnny angrily as he picked up the carpetbag and dumped its contents on the top of the table. "See all this money? Piles and piles of money? This all comes from the people that saw Doc this morning.

"Here's five hundred from rich Mr. Baggs, the banker. Who'd think he was so anxious to make sure his dead partner didn't climb out of the grave and demand his half of the bank back, hah?

"And here's a hundred from Mrs. Tanner. Her first husband, I understand, died under rather mysterious circumstances. And it wasn't much later that she married her foreman. She must have good reason not to want the old boy to appear and clear up just how he did die.

"And here's two hundred from old Mr. Krank. He's about ready to be buried himself, but he wants his last few days to be peaceful and quiet. Which they wouldn't be if Mrs. Krank's tongue was freed from the silence of the tomb. She was quite a shrew.

"And here's five hundred, a contribution of a hundred each from the sons and daughters of Silas Johnson. He was a tyrant and a hypochondriac. Besides, he might want the inheritance back.

"And here's…well, why go on? It's the same story in every town we've come to."

"It's not a very nice story," Linda said. "But you've not answered me. What did you expect me to do when you had to leave town?"

"I was going to tell you as soon as I could get the nerve. But I was afraid you wouldn't want anything to do with me when I told you the truth."

"What about Doc Grandtoul and Skeeter?" she said. "Did they know you were going to tell me?"

"No. I supposed they'd be mad at me. However, they couldn't do much about it. Anyway, they've got about as much money as they'll get out of Acheron. They could go on and get another partner somewhere else."

"And how," she said sarcastically, "did you expect to keep from being lynched when people found out they'd been cheated?"

"Well," he said slowly, "I was hoping you'd go with me to some other town. We could get a fresh start there. I can't stay here. We'll have to leave tomorrow. Maybe tonight."

"You must be crazy!" she said. "I can't just run off and leave my father like that! I might go away with you, but not before I explain to my father. But I don't think he'd like me to marry a man like you. You might want to go back to cheating people."

"Don't say that, Linda. I'll admit I made a mistake. But Doc was so nice to me, and I really didn't know we'd be hurting people so much."

Linda walked up to Johnny and stood in front of him and looked him in the eye.

"Johnny, if you'll tell everybody in Acheron what you've done, and say you're sorry, and give them their money back, I'll marry you. But if you don't, we're through!"

"Use your horse sense," said Johnny. "If I did that, I couldn't ever settle down here. Who'd trust his horses to a man like me? And you couldn't hold your head high in this town, because you'd be the wife of that sharper Johnny Addeson. Give me a chance to straighten this out. I'll go talk with Doc and Skeeter. We'll fix this up somehow. I swear it! And you and I'll be able to live here the rest of our lives. And I'll be good to you, Linda. Good to you and good for this town. You'll be proud of me."

"All right," said Linda. "I'll give you a chance. I do want to live here. And I don't want anybody scorning you or me. Or our children."

Johnny smiled like a kid who's been given a sackful of candy for free. He picked up the bag and scooped the money into it and said, "I think Doc'll be able to help me out of this jam. He's a sharper, and he likes to take a dishonest sucker. But he isn't mean. He really does have a good heart. If anybody's smart enough to figure this out, he is."

He kissed Linda lightly on the lips and then ran out of the room.

Linda sat down again and waited. After a while she rose and went to the window to look out. She was just in time to see Johnny and Skeeter and Doc Grandtoul come out of the saloon across the street. Johnny was still holding the bag of money, and all three looked grim. Linda couldn't hear what they were saying, but they seemed to be arguing. They were talking and waving their hands when they walked into the livery stable.

Linda didn't leave the window. In about half an hour Johnny and Skeeter came out of the stable. Johnny was grinning. Neither of the two had the bag of money. They walked down the street and stopped in front of the Lucky Lode to talk to Doc Evans. The three talked earnestly for about ten minutes, but when some men joined them they quit talking to each other and joined in the general conversation.

The sound of a shot reached Linda through the half-opened window. The men on the street looked startled, milled around for a moment, and then ran towards the stable. Linda raced down the hall and down the steps to the street. When she was halfway to the stable, she heard what the whole town of Acheron knew by then.

Doc Grandtoul was dead. He had accidentally shot himself.

♦ ♦ ♦

Some stories have happy endings. Any story of young love should have a happy ending. It means two young citizens settling down in a town and raising more happy young citizens. And this was what happened in Acheron after the uproar over Doc Grandtoul's sudden and sad demise had quieted down. Doc Grandtoul was pronounced dead by Doc Evans, and the burial took place next day.

Only Linda thought it was peculiar that, when the coffin lid was closed over Doc Grandtoul, Doc Evans was the sole person present. And she noticed that Skeeter left town the same day. She didn't think it was so peculiar that not a word was said about the money paid to Doc Grandtoul. Those who had paid were not going to raise a fuss. Everybody pulled a long face and said what a pity it was that only Doc Grandtoul knew how to operate his machine. But very few moped around because of what had happened.

For a long time Linda never opened her mouth to Johnny about the incident of the revitalizing machine. She was satisfied that the result had been to make her happy. However, one thing bothered her.

And one night, years later, when she and Johnny were sitting before the fireplace, after putting the kids to bed, Linda said, unexpectedly, "Johnny, what happened to those people who pronounced you dead in all those towns you three scoundrels fleeced? Weren't they left to face everybody and be branded as sharpers just as Doc Evans would have been if Doc Grandtoul hadn't been killed?"

Johnny was startled, but after coughing a few times he managed to say, "I'm sorry to say that we didn't worry about them."

"If Doc Grandtoul had had an 'accident' in every town," she said, "nobody would have been left holding the bag."

Johnny was silent.

Linda looked into the fireplace a moment, and then she said, "I wonder where Doc Grandtoul is now?"

Johnny pretended to misunderstand her.

"I don't know, darling. I'll bet he went to the Good Place. After all, he brought us together, didn't he?"

The biologist was showing the distinguished visitor through the zoo and laboratory.

"Our budget," he said, "is too limited to re-create all known extinct species. So we bring to life only the higher animals, the beautiful ones that were wantonly exterminated. I'm trying, as it were, to make up for brutality and stupidity. You might say that man struck God in the face every time he wiped out a branch of the animal kingdom."

He paused, and they looked across the moats and the force fields. The quagga wheeled and galloped, delight and sun flashing off his flanks. The sea otter poked his humorous whiskers from the water. The gorilla peered from behind bamboo. Passenger pigeons strutted. A rhinoceros trotted like a dainty battleship. With gentle eyes a giraffe looked at them, then resumed eating leaves.

"There's the dodo. Not beautiful but very droll. And very helpless. Come, I'll show you the re-creation itself."

In the great building, they passed between rows of tall and wide tanks. They could see clearly through the windows and the jelly within.

"Those are African Elephant embryos," said the biologist. "We plan to grow a large herd and then release them on the new government preserve."

"You positively radiate," said the distinguished visitor. "You really love the animals, don't you?"

"I love all life."

"Tell me," said the visitor, "where do you get the data for re-creation?"

"Mostly, skeletons and skins from the ancient museums. Excavated books and films that we succeeded in restoring and then translating. Ah, see those huge eggs? The chicks of the giant moa are growing within them. There, almost ready to be taken from the tank, are tiger cubs. They'll be dangerous when grown but will be confined to the preserve."

The visitor stopped before the last of the tanks.

"Just one?" he said. "What is it?"

"Poor little thing," said the biologist, now sad. "It will be so alone. But I shall give it all the love I have."

"Is it so dangerous?" said the visitor. "Worse than elephants, tigers, and bears?"

"I had to get special permission to grow this one," said the biologist. His voice quavered.

The visitor stepped sharply back from the tank. He said, "Then it must be...But you wouldn't dare!"

The biologist nodded.

"Yes. It's a man."

ONE

The klaxon cleared its plastic throat and began to whoop. Alternate yellows and reds pulsed on the consoles wrapped like bracelets around the wrists of the captain and the navigator. The huge auxiliary screens spaced on the bulkheads of the bridge also flashed red and yellow.

Captain Grettir, catapulted from his reverie, and from his chair, stood up. The letters and numerals 20-G-DZ-R hung burning on a sector of each screen and spurted up from the wrist-console, spread out before his eyes, then disappeared, only to rise from the wrist-console again and magnify themselves and thin into nothing. Over and over again. 20-G-DZ-R. The code letters indicating that the alarm originated from the corridor leading to the engine room.

He turned his wrist and raised his arm to place the lower half of the console at the correct viewing and speaking distance.

"20-G-DZ-R, report!"

The flaming, expanding, levitating letters died out, and the long high-cheekboned face of MacCool, chief engineer, appeared as a tiny image on the sector of the console. It was duplicated on the bridge bulkhead screens. It rose and grew larger, shooting towards Grettir, then winking out to be followed by a second ballooning face.

Also on the wrist-console's screen, behind MacCool, were Comas, a petty officer, and Drinker, a machinist's mate. Their faces did not float up because they were not in the central part of the screen. Behind them was a group of Marines and an 88-K cannon on a floating sled.

"It's the Wellington woman," MacCool said. "She used a photer, lowpower setting, to knock out the two guards stationed at the engine-room port. Then she herded us — me, Comas, Drinker — out. She said she'd shoot us if we resisted. And she welded the grille to the bulkhead so it can't be opened unless it's burned off."

"I don't know why she's doing this. But she's reconnected the drive wires to a zander bridge so she can control the acceleration herself. We can't do a thing to stop her unless we go in after her."

He paused, swallowed and said, "I could send men outside and have them try to get through the engine room airlock or else cut through the hull to get her. While she was distracted by this, we could make a frontal attack down the corridor. But she says she'll shoot anybody that gets too close. We could lose some men. She means what she says."

"If you cut a hole in the hull, she'd be out of air, dead in a minute," Grettir said.

"She's in a spacesuit," MacCool replied. "That's why I didn't have this area sealed off and gas flooded in."

Grettir hoped his face was not betraying his shock. Hearing an exclamation from Wang, seated near him, Grettir turned his head. He said, "How in the hell did she get out of sick bay?"

He realized at the same time that Wang could not answer that question. MacCool said, "I don't know, sir. Ask Doctor Wills."

"Never mind that now!"

Grettir stared at the sequence of values appearing on the navigator's auxiliary bulkhead-screen. The 0.5 of light speed had already climbed to 0.96. It changed every 4 seconds. The 0.96 became 0.97, then 0.98, 0.99 and then 1.0. And then 1.1 and 1.2.

Grettir forced himself to sit back down. If anything was going to happen, it would have done so by now; the TSN-X cruiser *Sleipnir*, 280 million tons, would have been converted to pure energy.

A nova, bright but very brief, would have gouted in the heavens. And the orbiting telescopes of Earth would see the flare in 20.8 light-years.

"What's the state of the *emc* clamp and acceleration-dissipaters?" Grettir said.

"No strain—yet," Wang said. "But the power drain...if it continues...5 megakilowatts per 2 seconds, and we're just beginning."

"I think," Grettir said slowly, "that we're going to find out what we intended to find out. But it isn't going to be under the carefully controlled conditions we had planned."

♦ ♦ ♦

The Terran Space Navy experimental cruiser *Sleipnir* had left its base on Asgard, eighth planet of Altair (alpha Aquilae), 28 shipdays ago. It was under orders to make the first attempt of a manned ship to exceed the velocity of light. If its mission was successful, men could travel between Earth and the colonial planets in weeks instead of years. The entire galaxy might be opened to Earth.

Within the past two weeks, the *Sleipnir* had made several tests at 0.8 times the velocity of light, the tests lasting up to two hours at a time.

The *Sleipnir* was equipped with enormous motors and massive clamps, dissipaters, and space-time structure expanders ("hole-openers") required for near-lightspeeds and beyond. No ship in Terrestrial history had ever had such power or the means to handle such power.

The drive itself — the cubed amplification of energy produced by the controlled mixture of matter, antimatter and half-matter — gave an energy that could eat its way through the iron core of a planet. But part of that energy had to be diverted to power the energy-mass conversion "clamp" that kept the ship from being transformed into energy itself. The "hole-opener" also required vast power. This device — officially the Space-Time Structure Expander, or Neutralizer — "unbent" the local curvature of the universe and so furnished a "hole" through which the *Sleipnir* traveled. This hole nullified 99.3 percent of the resistance the *Sleipnir* would normally have encountered.

Thus the effects of speeds approaching and even exceeding lightspeed would be modified, even if not entirely avoided. The *Sleipnir* should not contract along its length to zero nor attain infinite mass when it reached the speed of light. It contracted, and it swelled, yes, by only 1/777,777th what it should have. The ship would assume the shape of a disk — but much more slowly than it would without its openers, clamps and dissipaters.

Beyond the speed of light, who knew what would happen? It was the business of the *Sleipnir* to find out. But, Grettir thought, not under these conditions. Not willy-nilly.

♦ ♦ ♦

"Sir!" MacCool said, "Wellington threatens to shoot anybody who comes near the engine room."

He hesitated, then said, "Except you. She wants to speak to you. But she doesn't want to do it over the intercom. She insists that you come down and talk to her face to face." Grettir bit his lower lip and made a sucking sound.

"Why me?" he said, but he knew why, and MacCool's expression showed that he also knew.

"I'll be down in a minute. Now, isn't there any way we can connect a bypass, route a circuit around her or beyond her and get control of the drive again?"

"No, sir!"

"Then she's cut through the engine-room deck and gotten to the redundant circuits also?"

MacCool said, "She's crazy, but she's clear-headed enough to take all precautions. She hasn't overlooked a thing."

Grettir said, "Wang! What's the velocity now?"

"2.3 sl/pm, sir!"

Grettir looked at the huge starscreen on the "forward" bulkhead of the bridge. Black except for a few glitters of white, blue, red, green, and the galaxy called XD-2 that lay dead ahead. The galaxy had been the size of an orange, and it still was. He stared at the screen for perhaps a minute, then said, "Wang, am I seeing right? The red light from XD-2 is shifting towards the blue, right?"

"Right, sir!"

"Then...why isn't XD-2 getting bigger? We're overhauling it like a fox after a rabbit."

Wang said, "I think it's getting closer, sir. But we're getting bigger."

TWO

Grettir rose from the chair. "Take over while I'm gone. Turn off the alarm; tell the crew to continue their normal duties. If anything comes up while I'm in the engine area, notify me at once."

The exec saluted. "Yes, sir!"

Grettir strode off the bridge. He was aware that the officers and crewmen seated in the ring of chairs in the bridge were looking covertly at him. He stopped for a minute to light up a cigar. He was glad that his hands were not shaking, and he hoped that his expression was confident. Slowly, repressing the impulse to run, he continued across the bridge and into the jump-shaft. He stepped off backward into the shaft and nonchalantly blew out smoke while he sank out of sight of the men in the bridge. He braced himself against the quick drop and then the thrusting deceleration. He had set the controls for Dock 14; the doors slid open; he walked into a corridor where a g-car and operator waited for him. Grettir climbed in, sat down and told the crewman where to drive.

Two minutes later, he was with MacCool. The chief engineer
pointed down the corridor. Near its end, on the floor, were two still
unconscious Marines. The door to the engine room was open. The secondary door, the grille, was shut. The lights within the engine room
had been turned off. Something white on the other side of the grille
moved. It was Donna Wellington's face, visible through the helmet.

"We can't keep this acceleration up," Grettir said. "We're already
going far faster than even unmanned experimental ships have been
allowed to go. There are all sorts of theories about what might happen
to a ship at these speeds, all bad."

"We've disproved several by now," MacCool said. He spoke evenly,
but his forehead was sweaty and shadows hung under his eyes.

MacCool continued, "I'm glad you got here, sir. She just threatened to cut the *emc* clamp wires if you didn't show up within the next
two minutes."

He gestured with both hands to indicate a huge and expanding
ball of light.

"I'll talk to her," Grettir said. "Although I can't imagine what she
wants."

MacCool looked dubious. Grettir wanted to ask him what the hell
he was thinking but thought better of it. He said, "Keep your men at
this post. Don't even look as if you're coming after me."

"And what do we do, sir, if she shoots you?"

Grettir winced. "Use the cannon. And never mind hesitating if I
happen to be in the way. Blast her! But make sure you use a beam short
enough to get her but not long enough to touch the engines."

"May I ask why we don't do that before you put your life in danger?" MacCool said.

Grettir hesitated, then said, "My main responsibility is to the ship
and its crew. But this woman is very sick; she doesn't realize the implications of her actions. Not fully anyway. I want to talk her out of this,
if I can."

◆ ◆ ◆

He unhooked the communicator from his belt and walked down
the corridor toward the grille and the darkness behind it and the whiteness that moved. His back prickled. The men were watching him intently. God knew what they were saying, or at least thinking, about
him. The whole crew had been amused for some time by Donna
Wellington's passion for him and his inability to cope with her. They

had said she was mad about him, not realizing that she really was mad. They had laughed. But they were not laughing now.

Even so, knowing that she was truly insane, some of them must be blaming him for this danger. Undoubtedly, they were thinking that if he had handled her differently, they would not now be so close to death.

He stopped just one step short of the grille. Now he could see Wellington's face, a checkerboard of blacks and whites. He waited for her to speak first. A full minute passed, then she said, "Robert!"

The voice, normally low-pitched and pleasant, was now thin and strained.

"Not Robert. Eric," he said into the communicator. "Captain Eric Grettir, Mrs. Wellington."

There was a silence. She moved closer to the grille. Light struck one eye, which gleamed bluely.

"Why do you hate me so, Robert?" she said plaintively. "You used to love me. What did I do to make you turn against me?"

"I am *not* your husband," Grettir said. "Look at me. Can't you see that I am not Robert Wellington? I am Captain Grettir of the *Sleipnir*. You *must* see who I *really* am, Mrs. Wellington. It is very important."

"You don't love me!" she screamed. "You are trying to get rid of me by pretending you're another man! But it won't work! I'd know you anywhere, you beast! You beast! I hate you, Robert!"

Involuntarily, Grettir stepped back under the intensity of her anger. He saw her hand come up from the shadows and the flash of light on a handgun. It was too late then; she fired; a beam of whiteness dazzled him.

Light was followed by darkness.

Ahead, or above, there was a disk of grayness in the black. Grettir traveled slowly and spasmodically towards it, as if he had been swallowed by a whale but was being ejected towards the open mouth, the muscles of the Leviathan's throat working him outwards.

Far behind him, deep in the bowels of the whale, Donna Wellington spoke.

"Robert?"

"Eric!" he shouted. "I'm *Eric!*"

♦ ♦ ♦

The *Sleipnir*, barely on its way out from Asgard, dawdling at 6200 kilometers per second, had picked up the Mayday call. It came from a spaceship midway between the 12th and 13th planet of Altair. Although Grettir could have ignored the call without reprimand from his superiors, he altered course, and he found a ship wrecked by a meteorite. Inside the hull was half the body of a man. And a woman in deep shock.

Robert and Donna Wellington were second-generation Asgardians, Ph.D.'s in biotatology, holding master's papers in astrogation. They had been searching for specimens of "space plankton" and "space hydras," forms of life born in the regions between Altair's outer planets.

The crash, the death of her husband and the shattering sense of isolation, dissociation and hopelessness during the eighty-four hours before rescue had twisted Mrs. Wellington. Perhaps twisted was the wrong word. Fragmented was a better description.

From the beginning of what at first seemed recovery, she had taken a superficial resemblance of Grettir to her husband for an identity. Grettir had been gentle and kind with her at the beginning and had made frequent visits to sick bay. Later, advised by Doctor Wills, he had been severe with her.

And so the unforeseen result.

Donna Wellington screamed behind him and, suddenly, the twilight circle ahead became bright, and he was free. He opened his eyes to see faces over him. Doctor Wills and MacCool. He was in sick bay.

MacCool smiled and said, "For a moment, we thought..."

"What happened?" Grettir said. Then, "I know what she did. I mean—"

"She fired full power at you," MacCool said. "But the bars of the grille absorbed most of the energy. You got just enough to crisp the skin off your face and to knock you out. Good thing you closed your eyes in time."

Grettir sat up. He felt his face; it was covered with a greasy ointment, pain-deadening and skin-growing *resec.*

"I got a hell of a headache."

Doctor Wills said, "It'll be gone in a minute."

"What's the situation?" Grettir said. "How'd you get me away from her?"

MacCool said, "I had to do it, Captain. Otherwise, she'd have taken another shot at you. The cannon blasted what was left of the grille. Mrs. Wellington—"

"She's dead?"

"Yes. But the cannon didn't get her. Strange. She took her suit off, stripped to the skin. Then she went out through the airlock in the engine room. Naked, as if she meant to be the bride of Death. We almost got caught in the outrush of air, since she fixed the controls so that the inner port remained open. It was close, but we got the port shut in time."

Grettir said, "I...never mind. Any damage to the engine room?"

"No. And the wires are reconnected for normal operation. Only —"

"Only what?"

MacCool's face was so long he looked like a frightened bloodhound.

"Just before I reconnected the wires, a funny...peculiar...thing happened. The whole ship, and everything inside the ship, went through a sort of distortion. Wavy, as if we'd all become wax and were dripping. Or flags flapping in a wind. The bridge reports that the fore of the ship seemed to expand like a balloon, then became ripply, and the entire effect passed through the ship. We all got nauseated while the waviness lasted."

There was silence, but their expressions indicated that there was more to be said.

"Well?"

MacCool and Wills looked at each other. MacCool swallowed and said, "Captain, we don't know where in hell we are!"

THREE

On the bridge, Grettir examined the forward EXT. screen. There were no stars. Space everywhere was filled with a light as gray and as dull as that of a false dawn on Earth. In the gray glow, at a distance as yet undetermined, were a number of spheres. They looked small, but if they were as large as the one immediately aft of the *Sleipnir*, they were huge.

The sphere behind them, estimated to be at a distance of fifty kilometers, was about the size of Earth's moon, relative to the ship. Its surface was as smooth and as gray as a ball of lead.

Darl spoke a binary code into her wrist-console, and the sphere on the starscreen seemed to shoot towards them. It filled the screen until Darl changed the line-of-sight. They were looking at about 20 degrees of arc of the limb of the sphere.

"There it is!" Darl said. A small object floated around the edge of the sphere and seemed to shoot towards them. She magnified it, and it became a small gray sphere.

"It orbits round the big one," she said.

Darl paused, then said, "We—the ship—came *out* of that small sphere. *Out* of it. *Through* its skin."

"You mean we had been inside it?" Grettir said. "And now we're outside it?"

"Yes, sir! Exactly!"

She gasped and said, "Oh, oh — sir!"

Around the large sphere, slightly above the plane of the orbit of the small sphere but within its sweep in an inner orbit, sped another object. At least fifty times as large as the small globe, it caught up with the globe, and the two disappeared together around the curve of the primary.

"Wellington's body!" Grettir said.

He turned away from the screen, took one step, and turned around again. "It's not right! She should be trailing along behind us or at least parallel with us, maybe shooting off at an angle but still moving in our direction.

"But she's been grabbed by the big sphere! She's in orbit! And her size, Gargantuan! It doesn't make sense! It shouldn't be!"

"Nothing should," Wang said.

"Take us back," Grettir said. "Establish an orbit around the primary, on the same plane as the secondary but further out, approximately a kilometer and a half from it."

Darl's expression said, "Then what?"

Grettir wondered if she had the same thought as he. The faces of the others on the bridge were doubtful. The fear was covered but leaking out. He could smell the rotten bubbles. Had they guessed, too?

"What attraction does the primary have on the ship?" he said to Wang.

"No detectable influence whatsoever, sir. The *Sleipnir* seems to have a neutral charge, neither positive nor negative in relation to any of the spheres. Or to Wellington's...body."

Grettir was slightly relieved. His thoughts had been so wild that he had not been able to consider them as anything but hysterical fantasies. But Wang's answer showed that Grettir's idea was also his. Instead of replying in terms of gravitational force, he had talked as if the ship were a subatomic particle.

But if the ship was not affected by the primary, why had Wellington's corpse been attracted by the primary?

"Our velocity in relation to the primary?" Grettir said.

"We cut off the acceleration as soon as the wires were reconnected," Wang said. "This was immediately after we came out into this...this space. We didn't apply any retrodrive. Our velocity, as indicated by power consumption, is ten megaparsecs per minute. That is," he added after a pause, "what the instruments show. But our radar, which should be totally ineffective at this velocity, indicates 50 kilometers per minute, relative to the big sphere."

Wang leaned back in his chair as if he expected Grettir to explode into incredulity. Grettir lit up another cigar. This time, his hands shook. He blew out a big puff of smoke and said, "Obviously, we're operating under different quote laws unquote *out here.*"

Wang sighed softly. "So you think so, too, Captain? Yes, different laws. Which means that, every time we make a move through this space, we can't know what the result will be. May I ask what you plan to do, sir?"

♦ ♦ ♦

By this question, which Wang would never have dared to voice before, though he had doubtless often thought it, Grettir knew that the navigator shared his anxiety. Beneath that apparently easy manner and soft voice was a pain just beneath the navel. The umbilical had been ripped out; Wang was hurting and bleeding inside. Was he, too, beginning to float away in a gray void? Bereft as no man had ever been bereft?

It takes a special type of man or woman to lose himself or herself from Earth or his native planet, to go out among the stars so far that the natal sun is not even a faint glimmer. It also takes special conditioning for the special type of man. He has to believe, in the deepest part of his unconscious, that his ship is a piece of Mother Earth. He has to believe; otherwise, he goes to pieces.

It can be done. Hundreds do it. But nothing had prepared even these farfarers for absolute divorce from the universe itself.

Grettir ached with the dread of the void. The void was coiling up inside him, a gray serpent, a slither of nothingness. Coiling. And what would happen when it uncoiled?

And what would happen to the crew when they were informed — as they must be — of the utter dissociation?

There was only one way to keep their minds from slipping their moorings. They must believe that they could get back into the world. Just as he must believe it.

"I'll play it by ear," Grettir said.

"What? Sir?"

"Play it by ear!" Grettir said more harshly than he had intended. "I was merely answering your question. Have you forgotten you asked me what I meant to do?"

"Oh, no, sir," Wang said. "I was just thinking..."

"Keep your mind on the job," Grettir said. He told Darl he would take over. He spoke the code to activate the ALL-STATIONS; a low rising-falling sound went into every room of the *Sleipnir*, and all screens flashed a black-and-green checked pattern. Then the warnings, visual and audible, died out, and the captain spoke.

He talked for two minutes. The bridgemen looked as if the lights had been turned off in their brains. It was almost impossible to grasp the concept of their being outside their universe. As difficult was thinking of their unimaginably vast native cosmos as only an "electron" orbiting around the nucleus of an "atom." If what the captain said was true (how could it be?), the ship was in the space between the superatoms of a supermolecule of a superuniverse.

Even though they knew that the *Sleipnir* had ballooned under the effect of nearly 300,000 times the speed of light, they could not wrap the fingers of their minds around the concept. It turned to smoke and drifted away.

◆ ◆ ◆

It took ten minutes, ship's time, to turn and to complete the maneuvers which placed the *Sleipnir* in an orbit parallel to but outside the secondary, or, as Grettir thought of it, "our universe." He gave his chair back to Darl and paced back and forth across the bridge while he watched the starscreen.

If they were experiencing the sundering, the cutting-off, they were keeping it under control. They had been told by their captain that they *were* going back in, not that they would make a *try* at re-entry. They had been through much with him, and he had never failed them. With this trust, they could endure the agony of dissolution.

As the *Sleipnir* established itself parallel to the secondary, Wellington's body curved around the primary again and began to pass the small sphere and ship. The arms of the mountainous body were extended stiffly to both sides, and her legs spread out. In the gray light, her skin was bluish-black from the ruptured veins and arteries below the skin. Her red hair, coiled in a Psyche knot, looked black. Her eyes, each of which was larger than the bridge of the *Sleipnir*, were open, bulging clots of black blood. Her lips were pulled back in a grimace, the teeth like a sootstreaked portcullis.

Cartwheeling, she passed the sphere and the ship.

Wang reported that there were three "shadows" on the surface of the primary. Those were keeping pace with the secondary, the corpse and the ship. Magnified on the bridge-bulkhead screen, each "shadow" was the silhouette of one of the three orbiting bodies. The shadows were only about one shade darker than the surface and were caused by a shifting pucker in the primary skin. The surface protruded along the edges of the shadows and formed a shallow depression within the edges.

If the shadow of the *Sleipnir* was a true indication of the shape of the vessel, the *Sleipnir* had lost its needle shape and was a spindle, fat at both ends and narrow-waisted.

When Wellington's corpse passed by the small sphere and the ship, her shadow or "print" reversed itself in shape. Where the head of the shadow should have been, the feet now were, and vice versa.

She disappeared around the curve of the primary and, on returning on the other side, her shadow had again become a "true" reflection. It remained so until she passed the secondary, after which the shadow once more reversed itself.

Grettir had been informed that there seemed to be absolutely no matter in the space outside the spheres. There was not one detectable atom or particle. Moreover, despite the lack of any radiation, the temperature of the hull, and ten meters beyond the hull, was a fluctuating 70° plus-or-minus 20° F.

FOUR

Three orbits later, Grettir knew that the ship had diminished greatly in size. Or else the small sphere had expanded. Or both changes occurred. Moreover, on the visual screen, the secondary had lost its spherical shape and become a fat disk during the first circling of the ship to establish its orbit.

Grettir was puzzling over this and thinking of calling Van Voorden, the physicist chief, when Wellington's corpse came around the primary again. The body caught up with the other satellites, and for a moment the primary, secondary, and the *Sleipnir* were in a line, strung on an invisible cord.

Suddenly, the secondary and the corpse jumped toward each other. They ceased their motion when within a quarter kilometer of each other. The secondary regained its globular form as soon as it had attained its new orbit. Wellington's arms and legs, during this change in position, moved in as if she had come to life. Her arms folded themselves across her breasts, and her legs drew up so that her thighs were against her stomach.

Grettir called Van Voorden. The physicist said, "Out here, the cabin boy — if we had one — knows as much as I do about what's going on or what to expect. The data, such as they are, are too inadequate, too confusing. I can only suggest that there was an interchange of energy between Wellington and the secondary."

"A quantum jump?" Grettir said. "If that's so, why didn't the ship experience a loss or gain?"

Darl said, "Pardon, sir. But it did. There was a loss of 50 megakilowatts in 0.8 second."

Van Voorden said, "The *Sleipnir* may have decreased in relative size because of decrease in velocity. Or maybe velocity had nothing to do with it or only partially, anyway. Maybe the change in spatial interrelationships among bodies causes other changes. In shape, size, energy transfer and so forth. I don't know. Tell me, how big is the woman — corpse — relative to the ship now?"

"The radar measurements say she's eighty-three times as large. She increased. Or we've decreased."

Van Voorden's eyes grew even larger. Grettir thanked him and cut him off. He ordered the *Sleipnir* to be put in exactly the same orbit as the secondary but ten dekameters ahead of it.

Van Voorden called back. "The jump happened when we were in line with the other three bodies. Maybe the *Sleipnir* is some sort of *geometrical catalyst* under certain conditions. That's only an analogy, of course."

Wang verbally fed the order into the computer-interface, part of his wrist-console. The *Sleipnir* was soon racing ahead of the sphere. Radar reported that the ship and secondary were now approximately equal in size. The corpse, coming around the primary again, was still the same relative size as before.

Grettir ordered the vessel turned around so that the nose would be facing the sphere. This accomplished, he had the velocity reduced. The retrodrive braked them while the lateral thrusts readjusted forces to keep the ship in the same orbit. Since the primary had no attraction for the *Sleipnir*, the ship had to remain in orbit with a constant rebalancing of thrusts. The sphere, now ballooning, inched towards the ship.

"Radar indicates we're doing 26.6 dekameters per second relative to the primary," Wang said. "Power drain indicates we're making 25,000 times the speed of light. That, by the way, is not proportionate to what we were making when we left our world."

"More braking," Grettir said. "Cut it down to 15 dm."

The sphere swelled, filled the screen, and Grettir involuntarily braced himself for the impact, even though he was so far from expecting one that he had not strapped himself into a chair. There had been none when the ship had broken through the "skin" of the universe.

Grettir had been told of the distorting in the ship when it had left the universe and so was not entirely surprised. Nevertheless, he could not help being both frightened and bewildered when the front part of the bridge abruptly swelled and then rippled. Screen, bulkheads, deck and crew waved as if they were cloth in a strong wind. Grettir felt as if he were being folded into a thousand different angles at the same time.

♦ ♦ ♦

Then Wang cried out, and the others repeated his cry. Wang rose from his seat and put his hands out before him. Grettir, standing behind and to one side of him, was frozen as he saw dozens of little objects, firefly-size, burning brightly, slip *through* the starscreen and bulkhead and drift towards him. He came out of his paralysis in time to dodge one tiny whitely glowing ball. But another struck his forehead, causing him to yelp.

A score of the bodies passed by him. Some were white; some blue; some green; one was topaz. They were at all levels, above his head, even with his waist, one almost touching the deck. He crouched down to let two pass over him, and as he did so, he saw Nagy, the communications officer, bent over and vomiting. The stuff sprayed out of his mouth and caught a little glow in it and snuffed it out in a burst of smoke.

Then the forepart of the bridge had reasserted its solidity and constancy of shape. There were no more burning objects coming through.

Grettir turned to see the aft bulkheads of the bridge quivering in the wake of the wave. And they, too, became normal. Grettir shouted the "override" code so that he could take control from Wang, who was screaming with pain. He directed the ship to change its course to an "upward vertical" direction. There was no "upward" sensation, because the artificial g-field within the ship readjusted. Suddenly, the forward part of the bridge became distorted again, and the waves reached through the fabric of the ship and the crew.

The starscreen, which had been showing nothing but the blackness of space, speckled by a few stars, now displayed the great gray sphere in one corner and the crepuscular light. Grettir, fighting the pain in his forehead and the nausea, gave another command. There was a delay of possibly thirty seconds, and then the *Sleipnir* began the turn that would take it back into a parallel orbit with the secondary.

Grettir, realizing what was happening shortly after being burned, had taken the *Sleipnir* back out of the universe. He put in a call for corpsmen and Doctor Wills and then helped Wang from his chair. There was an odor of burned flesh and hair in the bridge which the air-conditioning system had not as yet removed. Wang's face and hands were burned in five or six places, and part of the long coarse black hair on the right side of his head was burned.

Three corpsmen and Wills ran into the bridge. Wills started to apply a pseudoprotein jelly on Grettir's forehead, but Grettir told him to take care of Wang first. Wills worked swiftly and then, after spreading the jelly over Wang's burns and placing a false-skin bandage over the burns, treated the captain. As soon as the jelly was placed on his forehead, Grettir felt the pain dissolve.

"Third degree," Wills said. "It's lucky those things — whatever they are — weren't larger."

Grettir picked up his cigar, which he had dropped on the deck when he had first seen the objects racing towards him. The cigar was still burning. Near it lay a coal, swiftly blackening. He picked it up gingerly. It felt warm but could be held without too much discomfort.

Grettir extended his hand, palm up, so that the doctor could see the speck of black matter in it. It was even smaller than when it had floated into the bridge through the momentarily "opened" interstices of the molecules composing the hull and bulkheads.

"This is a *galaxy*," he whispered.

♦ ♦ ♦

Doc Wills did not understand. "A galaxy of our universe," Grettir added.

Doc Wills paled, and he gulped loudly.

"You mean...?"

Grettir nodded.

Wills said, "I hope...not our...Earth's...galaxy!"

"I doubt it," Grettir said. "We were on the edge of the star fields farthest out, that is, the closest to the — skin? — of our universe. But if we had kept on going..."

Wills shook his head. Billions of stars, possibly millions of inhabitable, hence inhabited, planets, were in that little ball of fire, now cool and collapsed. Trillions of sentient beings and an unimaginable number of animals had died when their world collided with Grettir's forehead.

Wang, informed of the true cause of the burns, became ill again. Grettir ordered him to sick bay and replaced him with Gomez. Van Voorden entered the bridge. He said, "I suppose our main objective has to be our reentry. But why couldn't we make an attempt to penetrate the primary, the nucleus? Do you realize what an astounding...?"

Grettir interrupted. "I realize. But our fuel supply is low, very low. If — I mean, *when* we get back through the 'skin,' we'll have a long way to go before we can return to Base. Maybe too long. I don't dare exceed a certain speed during reentry because of our size. It would be too dangerous....I don't want to wipe out any more galaxies. God knows the psychological problems we are going to have when the guilt really hits. Right now, we're numbed. *No!* We're not going to do any exploring!"

"But there may be no future investigations permitted!" Van Voorden said. "There's too much danger to the universe itself to allow any more research by ships like ours!"

"Exactly," Grettir said. "I sympathize with your desire to do scientific research. But the safety of the ship and crew comes first. Besides, I think that if I were to order an exploration, I'd have mutiny on my hands. And I couldn't blame my men. Tell me, Van Voorden, don't you feel a sense of...dissociation?"

Van Voorden nodded and said, "But I'm willing to fight it. There is so much..."

"So much to find out," Grettir said. "Agreed. But the authorities will have to determine if that is to be done."

Grettir dismissed him. Van Voorden marched off. But he did not give the impression of a powerful anger. He was, Grettir thought, secretly relieved at the captain's decision. Van Voorden had made his protest for Science's sake. But as a human being, Van Voorden must want very much to get "home."

FIVE

At the end of the ordered maneuver, the *Sleipnir* was in the same orbit as the universe but twenty kilometers ahead and again pointed toward it. Since there was no attraction between ship and primary, the *Sleipnir* had to use power to maintain the orbit; a delicate readjustment of lateral thrust was constantly required.

Grettir ordered braking applied. The sphere expanded on the starscreen, and then there was only a gray surface displayed. To the viewers the surface did not seem to spin, but radar had determined that the globe completed a revolution on its polar axis once every 33 seconds.

Grettir did not like to think of the implications of this. Van Voorden undoubtedly had received the report, but he had made no move to notify the captain. Perhaps, like Grettir, he believed that the fewer who thought about it, the better.

The mockup screen showed, in silhouette form, the relative sizes of the approaching spheres and the ship. The basketball was the universe; the toothpick, the *Sleipnir*. Grettir hoped that this reduction would be enough to avoid running into any more galaxies. Immediately after the vessel penetrated the "skin," the *Sleipnir* would be again braked, thus further diminishing it. There should be plenty of distance between the skin and the edge of the closest star fields.

"Here we go," Grettir said, watching the screen which indicated in meters the gap between ship and sphere. Again he involuntarily braced himself.

There was a rumble, a groan. The deck slanted upwards, then rolled to port. Grettir was hurled to the deck, spun over and over and brought up with stunning impact against a bulkhead. He was in a daze for a moment, and by the time he had recovered, the ship had reasserted its proper attitude. Gomez had placed the ship into "level" again. He had a habit of strapping himself into the navigator's chair although regulations did not require it unless the captain ordered it.

Grettir asked for a report on any damage and, while waiting for it, called Van Voorden. The physicist was bleeding from a cut on his forehead.

"Obviously," he said, "it requires a certain force to penetrate the outer covering or energy shield or whatever it is that encloses the universe. We didn't have it. So —"

"Presents quite a problem," Grettir said. "If we go fast enough to rip through, we're too large and may destroy entire galaxies. If we go too slow, we can't get through."

He paused, then said, "I can think of only one method. But I'm ignorant of the consequences, which might be disastrous. Not for us but for the universe. I'm not sure I should even take such a chance."

He was silent so long that Van Voorden could not restrain himself. "Well?"

"Do you think that if we could make a hole in the skin, the rupture might result in some sort of collapse or cosmic disturbance?"

"You want to beam a hole in the skin?" Van Voorden said slowly. His skin was pale, but it had been that color before Grettir asked him the question. Grettir wondered if Van Voorden was beginning to crumble under the "dissociation."

"Never mind," Grettir said. "I shouldn't have asked you. You can't know what the effects would be any more than anyone else. I apologize. I must have been trying to make you share some of the blame if anything went wrong. Forget it."

◆ ◆ ◆

Van Voorden stared, and he was still looking blank when Grettir cut off his image. He paced back and forth, once stepping over a tiny black object on the deck and then grimacing when he realized that it was too late for care. Millions of stars, billions of planets, trillions of creatures. All cold and dead. And if he experimented further in trying to get back into the native cosmos, then what? A collapsing universe?

But the *Sleipnir* had passed through the skin twice, and the rupture had not seemed to cause harm. The surface of the sphere was smooth and unbroken. It must be self-regulating and self-repairing.

Grettir stopped pacing and said aloud, "We came through the skin twice without harm to it. So we're going to try the beam!"

Nobody answered him, but the look on their faces was evidence of their relief. Fifteen minutes later, the *Sleipnir* was just ahead of the sphere and facing it. After an unvarying speed and distance from the sphere had been maintained for several minutes, laser beams measured the exact length between the tip of the cannon and the surface of the globe.

The chief gunnery officer, Abdul White Eagle, set one of the fore cannons. Grettir delayed only a few seconds in giving the next order. He clenched his teeth so hard he almost bit the cigar in two, groaned slightly then said, "Fire!"

Darl transmitted the command. The beam shot out, touched the skin and vanished.

The starscreen showed a black hole in the gray surface at the equator of the sphere. The hole moved away and then was gone around the curve of the sphere. Exactly 33 seconds later, the hole was in its original position. It was shrinking. By the time four rotations were completed, the hole had closed in on itself.

Grettir sighed and wiped the sweat off his forehead. Darl reported that the hole would be big enough for the ship to get through by the second time it came around. After that, it would be too small.

"We'll go through during the second rotation," Grettir said. "Set up the compigator for an automatic entry; tie the cannon in with the compigator. There shouldn't be any problem. If the hole shrinks too fast, we'll enlarge it with the cannon."

He heard Darl say, "Operation begun, sir!" as Gomez spoke into his console. The white beam spurted out in a cone, flicked against the "shell" or "skin" and disappeared. A circle of blackness three times the diameter of the ship came into being and then moved to one side of the screen. Immediately, under the control of the compigator, the retrodrive of the *Sleipnir* went into action. The sphere loomed; a gray wall filled the starscreen. Then the edge of the hole came into view, and a blackness spread over the screen.

"We're going to make it," Grettir thought. "The compigator can't make a mistake."

He looked around him. The bridgemen were strapped to their chairs now. Most of the faces were set, they were well disciplined and brave. But if they felt as he did — they must — they were shoving back a scream far down in them. They could not endure this "homesickness" much longer. And after they got through, were back in the womb, he would have to permit them a most unmilitary behavior. They would laugh, weep, shout, whoop. And so would he.

The nose of the *Sleipnir* passed through the hole. Now, if anything went wrong, the fore cannon could not be used. But it was impossible that...

♦ ♦ ♦

The klaxon whooped. Darl screamed, "Oh, my God! Something's wrong! The hole's shrinking too fast!"

Grettir roared, "Double the speed! No! Halve it!"

Increasing the forward speed meant a swelling in size of the *Sleipnir* but a contraction of the longitudinal axis and a lengthening of the lateral. The *Sleipnir* would get through the hole faster, but it would also narrow the gap between its hull and the edges of the hole.

Halving the speed, on the other hand, though it would make the ship smaller in relation to the hole, would also make the distance to be traversed greater. This might mean that the edges would still hit the ship.

Actually, Grettir did not know what order should be given or if any order would have an effect upon their chance to escape. He could only do what seemed best.

The grayness spread out from the perimeter of the starscreen. There was a screech of severed plastic running through the ship, quivering the bulkheads and decks, a sudden push forward of the crew as they

felt the inertia, then a release as the almost instantaneous readjustment of the internal g-field canceled the external effects.

Everybody in the bridge yelled. Grettir forced himself to cut off his
shout. He watched the starscreen. They were out in the gray again.
The huge sphere shot across the screen. In the corner was the secondary and then a glimpse of a giant blue-black foot. More grayness. A
whirl of other great spheres in the distance. The primary again. The
secondary. Wellington's hand, like a malformed squid of the void.

When Grettir saw the corpse again, he knew that the ship had been
deflected away from the sphere and was heading towards the corpse.
He did not, however, expect a collision. The orbital velocity of the dead
woman was greater than that of the secondary or of the *Sleipnir*.

Grettir, calling for a damage report, heard what he expected. The
nose of the ship had been sheared off. Bearing 45 crewmen with it, it
was now inside the "universe," heading toward a home it would never
reach. The passageways leading to the cut-off part had been automatically sealed, of course, so that there was no danger of losing air.

But the retrodrives had also been sliced off. The *Sleipnir* could drive
forward but could not brake itself unless it was first turned around to
present its aft to the direction of motion.

SIX

Grettir gave the command to stabilize the ship first, then to reverse
it. MacCool replied from the engine room that neither maneuver was,
at the moment, possible. The collision and the shearing had caused
malfunctions in the control circuits. He did not know what the trouble
was, but the electronic trouble-scanner was searching through the circuits. A moment later, he called back to say that the device was itself
not operating properly and that the troubleshooting would have to be
done by his men until the device had been repaired.

MacCool was disturbed. He could not account for the breakdown
because, theoretically, there should have been none. Even the impact
and loss of the fore part should not have resulted in loss of circuit
operation.

Grettir told him to do what he could. Meanwhile, the ship was
tumbling and was obviously catching up with the vast corpse. There
had been another unexplainable interchange of energy, position and
momentum, and the *Sleipnir* and Mrs. Wellington were going to collide.

Grettir unstrapped himself and began walking back and forth across the bridge. Even though the ship was cartwheeling, the internal g-field neutralized the effect for the crew. The vessel seemed level and stable unless the starscreen was looked at. When Grettir watched the screen, he felt slightly queasy because he was, at times, standing upside down in relation to the corpse.

Grettir asked for a computation of when the collision would take place and of what part of the body the *Sleipnir* would strike. It might make a difference whether it struck a soft or hard part. The difference would not result in damage to the ship, but it would affect the angle and velocity of the rebound path. If the circuits were repaired before the convergence, or just after, Grettir would have to know what action to take.

Wang replied that he had already asked the compigator for an estimate of the area of collision if conditions remained as they were. Even as he spoke, a coded card issued from a slot in the bulkhead. Wang read it, handed it to Grettir.

Grettir said, "At any other time, I'd laugh. So we will return—literally—to the womb."

The card had also indicated that, the nearer the ship got to Wellington, the slower was its velocity. Moreover, the relative size of the ship, as reported by radar, was decreasing in direct proportion to its proximity to the body.

Gomez said, "I think we've come under the influence of that…woman, as if she's become a planet and had captured a satellite. Us. She doesn't have any gravitational attraction or any charge in relation to us. But—"

"But there are other factors," Grettir said to her. "Maybe they are spatial relations, which, in this 'space,' may be the equivalent of gravity."

◆ ◆ ◆

The *Sleipnir* was now so close that the body entirely filled the starscreen when the ship was pointed towards it. First, the enormous head came into view. The blood-clotted and bulging eyes stared at them. The nose slid by like a Brobdingnagian guillotine; the mouth grinned at them as if it were to enjoy gulping them down. Then the neck, a diorite column left exposed by the erosion of softer rock; the cleavage of the blackened Himalayan breasts; the navel, the eye of a hurricane.

Then she went out of sight, and the secondary and primary and the gray-shrouded giants far off wheeled across the screen.

Grettir used the All-Stations to tell the nonbridge personnel what was happening. "As soon as MacCool locates the trouble, we will be on our way out. We have plenty of power left, enough to blast our way out of a hundred corpses. Sit tight. Don't worry. It's just a matter of time."

He spoke with a cheerfulness he did not feel, although he had not lied to them. Nor did he expect any reaction, positive or negative. They must be as numb as he. Their minds, their entire nervous systems, were boggling.

Another card shot out from the bulkhead-slot, a corrected impact prediction. Because of the continuing decrease in size of the vessel, it would strike the corpse almost dead-center in the navel. A minute later, another card predicted impact near the coccyx. A third card revised that to a collision with the top of the head. A fourth changed that to a strike on the lower part on the front of the right leg.

Grettir called Van Voorden again. The physicist's face shot up from the surface of Grettir's wrist-console but was stationary on the auxiliary bulkhead-screen. This gave a larger view and showed Van Voorden looking over his wrist-console at a screen on his cabin-bulkhead. It offered the latest impact report in large burning letters.

"Like the handwriting on the wall in the days of King Belshazzar," Van Voorden said. "And I am Daniel come to judgment. So we're going to hit her leg, heh, *Many, many tickle up her shin.* Hee, hee!"

Grettir stared uncomprehendingly at him, then cut him off. A few seconds later, he understood Van Voorden's pun. He did not wonder at the man's levity at a moment so grave. It was a means of relieving his deep anxiety and bewilderment. It might also mean that he was already cracking up, since it was out of character for him. But Grettir could do nothing for him at that moment.

As the *Sleipnir* neared the corpse, it continued to shrink. However, the dwindling was not at a steady rate nor could the times of shrinkage be predicted. It operated in spurts of from two to thirty seconds duration at irregular intervals. And then, as the 300th card issued from the slot, it became evident that, unless some new factor entered, the *Sleipnir* would spin into the gaping mouth. While the head rotated "downward," the ship would pass through the great space between the lips.

♦ ♦ ♦

And so it was. On the starscreen, the lower lip, a massive ridge, wrinkled with mountains and pitted with valleys, appeared. Flecks of lipstick floated by, black-red Hawaiis. A tooth like a jagged skyscraper dropped out of sight.

The *Sleipnir* settled slowly into the darkness. The walls shot away and upwards. The blackness outside knotted. Only a part of the gray "sky" was visible during that point of the cartwheel when the fore part of the starscreen was directed upwards. Then the opening became a thread of gray, a strand, and was gone.

Strangely — or was it so odd? — the officers and crew lost their feeling of dissociation. Grettir's stomach expanded with relief; the dreadful fragmenting was gone. He now felt as if something had been attached, or reattached, to his navel. Rubb, the psychology officer, reported that he had taken a survey of one out of fifty of the crew, and each described similar sensations.

Despite this, the personnel were free of only one anxiety and were far from being out of danger. The temperature had been slowly mounting ever since the ship had been spun off the secondary and had headed towards the corpse. The power system and air-conditioning had stabilized at 80° F for a while. But the temperature of the hull had gone upwards at a geometric progression, and the outer hull was now 2500 K. There was no danger of it melting as yet; it could resist up to 56,000 K. The air-conditioning demanded more and more power, and after thirty minutes ship's time, Grettir had had to let the internal temperature rise to 98.2° F to ease the load.

Grettir ordered everybody into spacesuits, which could keep the wearers at a comfortable temperature. Just as the order was carried out, MacCool reported that he had located the source of malfunction.

"The Wellington woman did it!" he shouted. "She sure took care of us! She inserted a monolith subparticle switch in the circuits; the switch had a timer which operated the switch after a certain time had elapsed. It was only coincidence that the circuits went blank right after we failed to get back into our world!"

SEVEN

"So she wanted to be certain that we'd be wrecked if she was frustrated in her attempts in the engine room," Grettir said. "You'd better continue the search for other microswitches or sabotage devices."

MacCool's face was long.

"We're ready to operate now...hell! We can't spare any power now because we need all we can get to keep the temperature down. I can spare enough to cancel the tumble. But that's all."

"Forget it for now," Grettir said. He had contacted Van Voorden, who seemed to have recovered. He confirmed the captain's theory about the rise in temperature. It was the rapid contraction of the ship that was causing the emission of heat.

"How is this contraction possible?" Grettir said. "Are the atoms of the ship, and of our bodies, coming closer together? If so, what happens when they come into contact with each other?"

"We've already passed that point of diminishment," Van Voorden said. "I'd say that our own atoms are shrinking also."

"But that's not possible," Grettir replied. Then, "Forget about that remark. What is possible? Whatever happens is possible."

Grettir cut him off and strode back and forth and wished that he could smoke a cigar. He had intended to talk about what the *Sleipnir* would find if it had managed to break back into its native universe. It seemed to Grettir that the universe would have changed so much that no one aboard the ship would recognize it. Every time the secondary — the universe — completed a revolution on its axis, trillions of Earth years, maybe quadrillions, might have passed. The Earth's sun might have become a lightless clot in space or even have disappeared altogether. Man, who might have survived on other planets, would no longer be homo sapiens.

Moreover, when the *Sleipnir* attained a supercosmic mass on its way out of the universe, it might have disastrously affected the other masses in the universe.

Yet none of these events would necessarily have occurred. It was possible that time inside that sphere was absolutely independent of time outside it. The notion was not so fantastic. God Almighty! Less than seventy minutes ago, Donna Wellington had been inside the ship. Now the ship was inside her.

And when the electrons and the nuclei of the atoms composing the ship and the crew came into contact, what then? Explosion?

Or were the elements made up of divisible subelements, and collapse would go on towards the inner infinity? He thought of the 20th-century stories of a man shrinking until the molecules became clusters of suns and the nuclei were the suns and the electrons were the planets. Eventually, the hero found himself on an electron-planet with atmosphere, seas, rivers, plains, mountains, trees, animals and aboriginal sentients.

These stories were only fantasies. Atomic matter was composed of wavicles, stuff describable in terms of both waves and particles. The parahomunculus hero would be in a cosmos as bewildering as that encountered by the crew of the *Sleipnir* on breaking into the extra-universe space.

That fantasy galloping across the sky of his mind, swift as the original *Sleipnir*, eight-legged horse of All-Father Odin of his ancestors' religion, would have to be dismissed. Donna Wellington was not a female Ymir, the primeval giant out of whose slain corpse was formed the world, the skull the sky, the blood the sea, the flesh the Earth, the bones the mountains.

No, the heat of contraction would increase until the men cooked in their suits. What happened after that would no longer be known to the crew and hence of no consequence.

♦ ♦ ♦

"Captain!"

MacCool's face was on the auxiliary screen, kept open to the engine room. "We'll be ready to go in a minute."

Sweat mingled with tears to blur the image of the engineer's face. "We'll make it then," Grettir said.

Four minutes later, the tumble was stopped, the ship was pointed upwards and was on its way out. The temperature began dropping inside the ship at one degree F per 30 seconds. The blackness was relieved by a gray thread. The thread broadened into ribbon, and then the ribbon became the edges of two mountain ridges, one below and the one above hanging upside down.

"This time," Grettir said, "we'll make a hole more than large enough."

Van Voorden entered the bridge as the *Sleipnir* passed through the break. Grettir said, "The hole repairs itself even more quickly than it did the last time. That's why the nose was cut off. We didn't know that the bigger the hole, the swifter the rate of reclosure."

Van Voorden said, "Thirty-six hundred billion years old or even more! Why bother to go home when home no longer exists?"

"Maybe there won't be that much time gone," Grettir said. "Do you remember Minkowski's classical phrase? *From henceforth space in itself and time in itself sink to mere shadows, and only a kind of union of the two preserves an independent existence.*

"That phrase applied to the world inside the sphere, our world. Perhaps *out here* the union is somehow dissolved, the marriage of space and time is broken. Perhaps no time, or very little, has elapsed in our world."

"It's possible," Van Voorden said. "But you've overlooked one thing, Captain. If our world has not been marked by time while we've been gone, *we* have been marked. Scarred by unspace and untime. I'll never believe in cause and effect and order throughout the cosmos again. I'll always be suspicious and anxious. I'm a ruined man."

Grettir started to answer but could not make himself heard. The men and women on the bridge were weeping, sobbing, or laughing shrilly. Later, they would think of that *out there* as a nightmare and would try not to think of it at all. And if other nightmares faced them here, at least they would be nightmares they knew.

Riders of the Purple Wage
or
♦ ♦ ♦ ♦ ♦ ♦ ♦ ♦ ♦ ♦ ♦ ♦ ♦ ♦ ♦ The Great Gavage

If Jules Verne could really have looked into the future, say 1966 A.D.,
he would have crapped in his pants. And 2166, oh, my!

—from Grandpa Winnegan's unpublished Ms. *How
I Screwed Uncle Sam & Other Private Ejaculations*

THE COCK THAT CROWED BACKWARDS

Un and Sub, the giants, are grinding him for bread.

Broken pieces float up through the wine of sleep. Vast treadings crush abysmal grapes for the incubus sacrament.

He as Simple Simon fishes in his soul as pail for the leviathan.

He groans, half-wakes, turns over, sweating dark oceans, and groans again. Un and Sub, putting their backs to their work, turn the stone wheels of the sunken mill, muttering Fie, fye, fo, fum. Eyes glittering orange-red as a cat's in a cubbyhole, teeth dull white digits in the murky arithmetic.

Un and Sub, Simple Simons themselves, busily mix metaphors non-self-consciously.

Dunghill and cock's egg: up rises the cockatrice and gives first crow, two more to come, in the flushrush of blood of dawn of I-am-the-erection-and-the-strife.

It grows out and out until weight and length merge to curve it over, a not-yet weeping willow or broken reed. The one-eyed red head peeks over the edge of bed. It rests its chinless jaw, then, as body swells, slides over and down. Looking monocularly this way and those, it sniffs archaically across the floor and heads for the door, left open by the lapsus linguae of malingering sentinels.

A loud braying from the center of the room makes it turn back. The three-legged ass, Baalim's easel, is heehawing. On the easel is the "canvas," an oval shallow pan of irradiated plastic, specially treated. The canvas is two meters high and forty-four centimeters deep. Within the painting is a scene that must be finished by tomorrow.

As much sculpture as painting, the figures are in alto-relief, rounded, some nearer the back of the pan than others. They glow with light from outside and also from the self-luminous plastic of the "canvas." The light seems to enter the figures, soak awhile, then break loose. The light is pale red, the red of dawn, of blood watered with tears, of anger, of ink on the debit side of the ledger.

This is one of his Dog Series: *Dogmas from a Dog, The Aerial Dogfight, Dog Days, The Sundog, Dog Reversed, The Dog of Flinders, Dog Berries, Dog Catcher, Lying Doggo, The Dog of the Right Angle,* and *Improvisations on a Dog.*

Socrates, Ben Jonson, Cellini, Swedenborg, Li Po, and Hiawatha are roistering in the Mermaid Tavern. Through a window, Daedalus is seen on top of the battlements of Cnossus, shoving a rocket up the ass of his son, Icarus, to give him a jet-assisted takeoff for his famous flight. In one corner crouches Og, Son of Fire. He gnaws on a sabertooth bone and paints bison and mammoths on the mildewed plaster. The barmaid, Athena, is bending over the table where she is serving nectar and pretzels to her distinguished customers. Aristotle, wearing goat's horns, is behind her. He has lifted her skirt and is tupping her from behind. The ashes from the cigarette dangling from his smirking lips have fallen onto her skirt, which is beginning to smoke. In the doorway of the men's room, a drunken Batman succumbs to a long-repressed desire and attempts to bugger the Boy Wonder. Through another window is a lake on the surface of which a man is walking, a green-tarnished halo hovering over his head. Behind him a periscope sticks out of the water.

Prehensile, the penisnake wraps itself around the brush and begins to paint. The brush is a small cylinder attached at one end to a hose which runs to a dome-shaped machine. From the other end of the cylinder extends a nozzle. The aperture of this can be decreased or increased by rotation of a thumb-dial on the cylinder. The paint which the nozzle deposits in a fine spray or in a thick stream or in whatever color or hue desired is controlled by several dials on the cylinder.

Furiously, proboscisean, it builds up another figure layer by layer: Then, it sniffs a musty odor of must and drops the brush and slides out the door and down the bend of wall of oval hall, describing the scrawl of legless creatures, a writing in the sand which all may read but few understand. Blood pumppumps in rhythm with the mills of Un and Sub to feed and swill the hot-blooded reptile. But the walls, detecting intrusive mass and extrusive desire, glow.

He groans, and the glandular cobra rises and sways to the fluting of his wish for cuntcealment. Let there not be light! The lights must be his cloaka. Speed past mother's room, nearest the exit. Ah! Sighs softly in relief but air whistles through the vertical and tight mouth, announcing the departure of the exsupress for Desideratum.

The door has become archaic; it has a keyhole. Quick! Up the ramp and out of the house through the keyhole and out onto the street. One person abroad a broad, a young woman with phosphorescent silver hair and snatch to match.

Out and down the street and coiling around her ankle. She looks down with surprise and then fear. He likes this; too willing were too many. He's found a diamond in the ruff.

Up around her kitten-ear-soft leg, around and around, and sliding across the dale of groin. Nuzzling the tender corkscrewed hairs and then, self-Tantalus, detouring up the slight convex of belly, saying hello to the bellybutton, pressing on it to ring upstairs, around and around the narrow waist and shyly and quickly snatching a kiss from each nipple. Then back down to form an expedition for climbing the mons veneris and planting the flag thereon.

Oh, delectation tabu and sickersacrosanct! There's a baby in there, ectoplasm beginning to form in eager preanticipation of actuality. Drop, egg, and shoot the chuty-chutes of flesh, hastening to gulp the lucky Micromoby Dick, outwriggling its million million brothers, survival of the fightingest.

A vast croaking fills the hall. The hot breath chills the skin. He sweats. Icicles coat the tumorous fuselage, and it sags under the weight of ice, and fog rolls around, whistling past the struts, and the ailerons and elevators are locked in ice, and he's losing altiattitude fast. Get up, get up! Venusberg somewhere ahead in the mists; Tannhäuser, blow your strumpets, send up your flares, I'm in a nose-dive.

Mother's door has opened. A toad squatfills the ovoid doorway. Its dewlap rises and falls bellows-like; its toothless mouth gawps. Ginungagap. Forked tongue shoots out and curls around the boar cuntstrictor. He cries out with both mouths and jerks this way and those. The waves of denial run through. Two webbed paws bend and tie the flopping body into a knot—a runny shape-shank, of course.

The woman strolls on. Wait for me! Out the flood roars, crashes into the knot, roars back, ebb clashing with flood. Too much and only one way to go. He jerkspurts, the firmament of waters falling, no Noah's ark or arc; he novas, a shatter of millions of glowing wriggling meteors, flashes in the pan of existence.

Thigh kingdom come. Groin and belly encased in musty armor, and he cold, wet, and trembling.

GOD'S PATENT ON DAWN EXPIRES

...the following spoken by Alfred Melophon Voxpopper, of the Aurora Pushups and Coffee Hour, Channel 69B. Lines taped during the 50th Folk Art Center Annual Demonstration and Competition, Beverly Hills, level 14. Spoken by Omar Bacchylides Runic, extemporaneously if you discount some forethought during the previous evening at the nonpublic tavern, The Private Universe, and you may because Runic did not remember a thing about that evening. Despite which he won First Laurel Wreath A, there being no Second, Third, etc., wreaths classified as A through Z, God bless our democracy.

> A gray-pink salmon leaping up the falls of night
> Into the spawning pool of another day.
>
> Dawn — the red roar of the heliac bull
> Charging over the horizon.
>
> The photonic blood of bleeding night,
> Stabbed by the assassin sun.

and so on for fifty lines punctuated and fractured by cheers, handclaps, boos, hisses, and yelps.

Chib is half-awake. He peeps down into the narrowing dark as the dream roars off into the subway tunnel. He peeps through barely opened lids at the other reality: consciousness.

"Let my peeper go!" he groans with Moses and so, thinking of long beards and horns (courtesy of Michelangelo), he thinks of his great-great-grandfather.

The will, a crowbar, forces his eyelids open. He sees the fido which spans the wall opposite him and curves up over half the ceiling. Dawn, the paladin of the sun, is flinging its gray gauntlet down.

Channel 69B, YOUR FAVORITE CHANNEL, LA's own, brings you dawn. (Deception in depth. Nature's false dawn shadowed forth with electrons shaped by devices shaped by man.)

Wake up with the sun in your heart and a song on your lips! Thrill to the stirring lines of Omar Runic! See dawn as the birds in the trees, as God, see it!

Voxpopper chants the lines softly while Grieg's *Anitra* wells softly. The old Norwegian never dreamed of this audience and just as well. A young man, Chibiabos Elgreco Winnegan, has a sticky wick, courtesy of a late gusher in the oilfield of the unconscious.

"Off your ass and onto your steed," Chib says. "Pegasus runs to-day."

He speaks, thinks, lives in the present tensely.

Chib climbs out of bed and shoves it into the wall. To leave the bed sticking out, rumpled as an old drunkard's tongue, would fracture the aesthetics of his room, destroy that curve that is the reflection of the basic universe, and hinder him in his work.

The room is a huge ovoid and in a corner is a small ovoid, the toilet and shower. He comes out of it looking like one of Homer's god-like Achaeans, massively thighed, great-armed, golden-brown-skinned, blue-eyed, auburn-haired — although beardless. The phone is simulating the tocsin of a South American tree frog he once heard over Channel 122.

"Open O sesame!"

INTER CAECOS REGNAT LUSCUS

The face of Rex Luscus spreads across the fido, the pores of skin like the cratered fields of a World War I battlefield. He wears a black monocle over the left eye, ripped out in a brawl among art critics during the *I Love Rembrandt Lecture Series,* Channel 109. Although he has enough pull to get a priority for eye-replacement, he has refused.

"*Inter caecos regnat luscus,*" he says when asked about it and quite often when not. "Translation: among the blind, the one-eyed man is king. That's why I renamed myself Rex Luscus, that is, King One-eyed."

There is a rumor, fostered by Luscus, that he will permit the bioboys to put in an artificial protein eye when he sees the works of an artist great enough to justify focal vision. It is also rumored that he may do so soon, because of his discovery of Chibiabos Elgreco Winnegan.

Luscus looks hungrily (he swears by adverbs) at Chib's tomentum and outlying regions. Chib swells, not with tumescence but with anger.

Luscus says, smoothly, "Honey, I just want to reassure myself that you're up and about the tremendously important business of this day.

You must be ready for the showing, must! But now I see you, I'm reminded I've not eaten yet. What about breakfast with me?"

"What're we eating?" Chib says. He does not wait for a reply. "No. I've too much to do today. Close O sesame!"

Rex Luscus' face fades away, goatlike, or, as he prefers to describe it, the face of Pan, a Faunus of the arts. He has even had his ears trimmed to a point. Real cute.

"Baa-aa-aa!" Chib bleats at the phantom. "Ba! Humbuggery! I'll never kiss your ass, Luscus, or let you kiss mine. Even if I lose the grant!"

The phone bells again. The dark face of Rousseau Red Hawk appears. His nose is as the eagle's, and his eyes are broken black glass. His broad forehead is bound with a strip of red cloth, which circles the straight black hair that glides down to his shoulders. His shirt is buckskin; a necklace of beads hangs from his neck. He looks like a Plains Indian, although Sitting Bull, Crazy Horse, or the noblest Roman Nose of them all would have kicked him out of the tribe. Not that they were anti-Semitic, they just could not have respected a brave who broke out into hives when near a horse.

Born Julius Applebaum, he legally became Rousseau Red Hawk on his Naming Day. Just returned from the forest reprimevalized, he is now reveling in the accursed fleshpots of a decadent civilization.

"How're you, Chib? The gang's wondering how soon you'll get here?"

"Join you? I haven't had breakfast yet, and I've a thousand things to do to get ready for the showing. I'll see you at noon!"

"You missed out on the fun last night. Some goddam Egyptians tried to feel the girls up, but we salaamed them against the walls."

Rousseau vanished like the last of the red men.

Chib thinks of breakfast just as the intercom whistles. Open O sesame! He sees the living room. Smoke, too thick and furious for the air-conditioning to whisk away, roils. At the far end of the ovoid, his little half-brother and half-sister sleep on a flato. Playing Mama-and-friend, they fell asleep, their mouths open in blessed innocence, beautiful as only sleeping children can be. Opposite the closed eyes of each is an unwinking eye like that of a Mongolian Cyclops.

"Ain't they cute?" Mama says. "The darlings were just too tired to toddle off."

The table is round. The aged knights and ladies are gathered around it for the latest quest of the ace, king, queen, and jack. They are armored only in layer upon layer of fat. Mama's jowls hang down like banners on a windless day. Her breasts creep and quiver on the table, bulge, and ripple.

"A gam of gamblers," he says aloud, looking at the fat faces, the tremendous tits, the rampant rumps. They raise their eyebrows. What the hell's the mad genius talking about now?

"Is your kid really retarded?" says one of Mama's friends, and they laugh and drink some more beer. Angela Ninon, not wanting to miss out on this deal and figuring Mama will soon turn on the sprayers anyway, pisses down her leg. They laugh at this, and William Conqueror says, "I open."

"I'm always open," Mama says, and they shriek with laughter.

Chib would like to cry. He does not cry, although he has been encouraged from childhood to cry any time he feels like it.

> —It makes you feel better and look at the Vikings, what men they were and they cried like babies whenever they felt like it.
>
> —Courtesy of Channel 202 on the popular program
> *What's a Mother Done?*

He does not cry because he feels like a man who thinks about the mother he loved and who is dead but who died a long time ago. His mother has been long buried under a landslide of flesh. When he was sixteen, he had a lovely mother.

Then she cut him off.

THE FAMILY THAT BLOWS IS THE FAMILY THAT GROWS

> —from a poem by Edgar A. Grist, via Channel 88

"Son, I don't get much out of this. I just do it because I love you."

Then, fat, fat, fat! Where did she go? Down into the adipose abyss. Disappearing as she grew larger.

"Sonny, you could at least wrestle with me a little now and then."

"You cut me off, Mama. That was all right. I'm a big boy now. But you haven't any right to expect me to want to take it up again."

"You don't love me any more!"

"What's for breakfast, Mama?" Chib says.

"I'm holding a good hand, Chibby," Mama says. "As you've told me so many times, you're a big boy. Just this once, get your own breakfast."

"What'd you call me for?"

"I forgot when your exhibition starts. I wanted to get some sleep before I went."

"14:30, Mama, but you don't have to go."

Rouged green lips part like a gangrened wound. She scratches one rouged nipple. "Oh, I want to be there. I don't want to miss my own son's artistic triumphs. Do you think you'll get the grant?"

"If I don't, it's Egypt for us," he says.

"Those stinking Arabs!" says William Conqueror.

"It's the Bureau that's doing it, not the Arabs," Chib says. "The Arabs moved for the same reason we may have to move."

From Grandpa's unpublished Ms.:
Whoever would have thought that Beverly Hills would become anti-Semitic?

"I don't want to go to Egypt!" Mama wails. "You got to get that grant, Chibby. I don't want to leave the clutch. I was born and raised here, well, on the tenth level, anyway, and when I moved all my friends went along. I won't go!"

"Don't cry, Mama," Chib says, feeling distress despite himself. "Don't cry. The government can't force you to go, you know. You got your rights."

"If you want to keep on having goodies, you'll go," says Conqueror. "Unless Chib wins the grant, that is. And I wouldn't blame him if he didn't even try to win it. It ain't his fault you can't say no to Uncle Sam. You got your purple and the yap Chib makes from selling his paintings. Yet it ain't enough. You spend faster than you get it."

Mama screams with fury at William, and they're off. Chib cuts off fido. Hell with breakfast; he'll eat later. His final painting for the Festival must be finished by noon. He presses a plate, and the bare egg-shaped room opens here and there, and painting equipment comes out like a gift from the electronic gods. Zeuxis would flip and Van Gogh would get the shakes if they could see the canvas and palette and brush Chib uses.

The process of painting involves the individual bending and twisting of thousands of wires into different shapes at various depths. The wires are so thin they can be seen only with magnifiers and manipulated with exceedingly delicate pliers. Hence, the goggles he wears and the long almost-gossamer instrument in his hand when he is in the first stages of creating a painting. After hundreds of hours of slow and patient labor (of love), the wires are arranged.

Chib removes his goggles to perceive the overall effect. He then uses the paint-sprayer to cover the wires with the colors and hues he desires. The paint dries hard within a few minutes. Chib attaches electrical leads to the pan and presses a button to deliver a tiny voltage through the wires. These glow beneath the paint and, Lilliputian fuses, disappear in blue smoke.

The result is a three-dimensional work composed of hard shells of paint on several levels below the exterior shell. The shells are of varying thicknesses and all are so thin that light slips through the upper to the inner shell when the painting is turned at angles. Parts of the shells are simply reflectors to intensify the light so that the inner images may be more visible.

When being shown the painting is on a self-moving pedestal which turns the painting 12 degrees to the left from the center and then 12 degrees to the right from the center.

The fido tocsins. Chib, cursing, thinks of disconnecting it. At least, it's not the intercom with his mother calling hysterically. Not yet, anyway. She'll call soon enough if she loses heavily at poker.

Open O sesame!

SING, O MEWS, OF UNCLE SAM

Grandpa writes in his *Private Ejaculations:* Twenty-five years after I fled with twenty billion dollars and then supposedly died of a heart attack, Falco Accipiter is on my trail again. The IRB detective who named himself Falcon Hawk when he entered his profession. What an egotist! Yet, he is as sharp-eyed and relentless as a bird of prey, and I would shiver if I were not too old to be frightened by mere human beings. Who loosed the jesses and hood? How did he pick up the old and cold scent?

♦ ♦ ♦

Accipiter's face is that of an overly suspicious peregrine that tries to look everywhere while it soars, that peers up its own anus to make sure that no duck has taken refuge there. The pale blue eyes fling glances like knives shot out of a shirtsleeve and hurled with a twist of the wrist. They scan all with sherlockian intake of minute and significant detail. His head turns back and forth, ears twitching, nostrils expanding and collapsing, all radar and sonar and odar.

"Mr. Winnegan, I'm sorry to call so early. Did I get you out of bed?"

"It's obvious you didn't!" Chib says. "Don't bother to introduce yourself. I know you. You've been shadowing me for three days."

Accipiter does not redden. Master of control, he does all his blushing in the depths of his bowels, where no one can see. "If you know me, perhaps you can tell me why I'm calling you?"

"Would I be dumbshit enough to tell you?"

"Mr. Winnegan, I'd like to talk to you about your great-great-grandfather."

"He's been dead for twenty-five years!" Chib cries. "Forget him. And don't bother me. Don't try for a search warrant. No judge would give you one. A man's home is his hassle...I mean castle."

He thinks of Mama and what the day is going to be like unless he gets out soon. But he has to finish the painting.

"Fade off, Accipiter," Chib says. "I think I'll report you to the BPHR. I'm sure you got a fido inside that silly-looking hat of yours."

Accipiter's face is as smooth and unmoving as an alabaster carving of the falcon-god Horus. He may have a little gas bulging his intestines. If so, he slips it out unnoticed.

"Very well, Mr. Winnegan. But you're not getting rid of me that easily. After all..."

"Fade out!"

The intercom whistles thrice. What I tell you three times is Grandpa. "I was eavesdropping," says the 120-year-old voice, hollow and deep as an echo from a Pharaoh's tomb. "I want to see you before you leave. That is, if you can spare the Ancient of Daze a few minutes."

"Always, Grandpa," Chib says, thinking of how much he loves the old man. "You need any food?"

"Yes, and for the mind, too."

Der Tag. Dies Irae. Götterdämmerung. Armageddon. Things are closing in. Make-or-break day. Go-no-go time. All these calls and a feeling of more to come. What will the end of the day bring?

THE TROCHE SUN SLIPS INTO THE SORE THROAT OF NIGHT

—from Omar Runic

Chib walks towards the convex door, which rolls into the interstices between the walls. The focus of the house is the oval family room. In the first quadrant, going clockwise, is the kitchen, separated from the family room by six-meter-high accordion screens, painted with scenes from Egyptian tombs by Chib, his too subtle comment on modern food. Seven slim pillars around the family room mark the borders of room and corridor. Between the pillars are more tall accordion screens, painted by Chib during his Amerind mythology phase.

The corridor is also oval-shaped; every room in the house opens onto it. There are seven rooms, six bedroom-workroom-study-toilet-shower combinations. The seventh is a storeroom.

Little eggs within bigger eggs within great eggs within a megamonolith on a planetary pear within an ovoid universe, the latest cosmogony indicating that infinity has the form of a hen's fruit. God broods over the abyss and cackles every trillion years or so.

Chib cuts across the hall, passes between two pillars, carved by him into nymphet caryatids, and enters the family room. His mother looks sidewise at her son, who she thinks is rapidly approaching insanity if he has not already overshot his mark. It's partly her fault; she shouldn't have gotten disgusted and in a moment of wackiness called It off. Now, she's fat and ugly, oh, God, so fat and ugly. She can't reasonably or even unreasonably hope to start up again.

It's only natural, she keeps telling herself, sighing, resentful, teary, that he's abandoned the love of his mother for the strange, firm, shapely delights of young women. But to give them up, too? He's not a bisex. He quit all that when he was thirteen. So what's the reason for his chastity? He isn't in love with the fornixator, either, which she would understand, even if she did not approve.

Oh, God, where did I go wrong? And then, There's nothing wrong with me. He's going crazy like his father — Raleigh Renaissance, I think his name was — and his aunt and his great-great-grandfather. It's all that painting and those radicals, the Young Radishes, he runs around with. He's too artistic, too sensitive. Oh, God, if something happens to my little boy, I'll have to go to Egypt.

Chib knows her thoughts since she's voiced them so many times and is not capable of having new ones. He passes the round table without a word. The knights and ladies of the canned Camelot see him through a beery veil.

In the kitchen, he opens an oval door in the wall. He removes a tray with food in covered dishes and cups, all wrapped in plastic.

"Aren't you going to eat with us?"

"Don't whine, Mama," he says and goes back to his room to pick up some cigars for his Grandpa. The door, detecting, amplifying, and transmitting the shifting but recognizable eidolon of epidermal electrical fields to the activating mechanism, balks. Chib is too upset. Magnetic maelstroms rage over his skin and distort the spectral configuration. The door half-rolls out, rolls in, changes its minds again, rolls out, rolls in.

Chib kicks the door and it becomes completely blocked. He decides he'll have a video or vocal sesame put in. Trouble is, he's short of units and coupons and can't buy the materials. He shrugs and walks along the curving, one-walled hall and stops in front of Grandpa's door, hidden from view of those in the living room by the kitchen screens.

> "For he sang of peace and freedom,
> Sang of beauty, love, and longing;
> Sang of death, and life undying
> In the Islands of the Blessed,
> In the kingdom of Ponemah,
> In the land of the Hereafter.
> Very dear to Hiawatha
> Was the gentle Chibiabos."

Chib chants the passwords; the door rolls back.

Light glares out, a yellowish red-tinged light that is Grandpa's own creation. Looking into the convex oval door is like looking into the lens of a madman's eyeball. Grandpa, in the middle of the room, has a white beard falling to midthigh and white hair cataracting to just below the back of his knees. Although beard and headhair conceal his nakedness, and he is not out in public, he wears a pair of shorts. Grandpa is somewhat old-fashioned, forgivable in a man of twelve decadencies.

Like Rex Luscus, he is one-eyed. He smiles with his own teeth, grown from buds transplanted thirty years ago. A big green cigar sticks out of one corner of his full red mouth. His nose is broad and smeared as if time had stepped upon it with a heavy foot. His forehead and cheeks are broad, perhaps due to a shot of Ojibway blood in his veins, though he was born Finnegan and even sweats celtically, giving off an aroma of whiskey. He holds his head high, and the blue-gray eye is like a pool at the bottom of a prediluvian pothole, remnant of a melted glacier.

All in all, Grandpa's face is Odin's as he returns from the Well of Mimir, wondering if he paid too great a price. Or it is the face of the windbeaten, sandblown Sphinx of Gizeh.

"Forty centuries of hysteria look down upon you, to paraphrase Napoleon," Grandpa says. "The rockhead of the ages. *What, then, is Man?* sayeth the New Sphinx, Oedipus having resolved the question of the Old Sphinx and settling nothing because She had already delivered another of her kind, a smartass kid with a question nobody's been able to answer yet. And perhaps just as well it can't be."

"You talk funny," Chib says. "But I like it."

He grins at Grandpa, loving him.

"You sneak into here every day, not so much from love for me as to gain knowledge and insight. I have seen all, heard everything, and thought more than a little. I voyaged much before I took refuge in this room a quarter of a century ago. Yet confinement here has been the greatest Odyssey of all.

THE ANCIENT MARINATOR

I call myself. A marinade of wisdom steeped in the brine of oversalted cynicism and too long a life."

"You smile so, you must have just had a woman," Chib teases.

"No, my boy. I lost the tension in my ramrod thirty years ago. And I thank God for that, since it removes from me the temptation of fornication, not to mention masturbation. However, I have other energies left, hence, scope for other sins, and these are even more serious.

"Aside from the sin of sexual commission, which paradoxically involves the sin of sexual emission, I had other reasons for not asking that Old Black Magician Science for shots to starch me out again. I was too old for young girls to be attracted to me for anything but money. And I was too much a poet, a lover of beauty, to take on the wrinkled blisters of my generation or several just before mine.

"So now you see, my son. My clapper swings limberly in the bell of my sex. Ding, dong, ding, dong. A lot of dong, but not much ding."

Grandpa laughs deeply, a lion's roar with a spray of doves.

"I am but the mouthpiece of the ancients, a shyster pleading for long-dead clients. Come not to bury but to praise and forced by my sense of fairness to admit the faults of the past, too. I'm a queer crabbed old man, pent like Merlin in his tree trunk. Samolxis, the Thracian bear god, hibernating in his cave. The Last of the Seven Sleepers."

Grandpa goes to the slender plastic tube depending from the ceiling and pulls down the folding handles of the eyepiece.

"Accipiter is hovering outside our house. He smells something rotten in Beverly Hills, level 14. Could it be that Win-again Winnegan isn't dead? Uncle Sam is like a diplodocus kicked in the ass. It takes twenty-five years for the message to reach its brain."

Tears appear in Chib's eyes. He says, "Oh, God, Grandpa, I don't want anything to happen to you."

"What can happen to a 120-year-old man besides failure of brain or kidneys?"

"With all due respect, Grandpa," Chib says, "you do rattle on."

"Call me Id's mill," Grandpa says. "The flour it yields is baked in the strange oven of my ego — or half-baked, if you please."

Chib grins through his tears and says, "They taught me at school that puns are cheap and vulgar."

"What's good enough for Homer, Aristophanes, Rabelais, and Shakespeare is good enough for me. By the way, speaking of cheap and vulgar, I met your mother in the hall last night, before the poker party started. I was just leaving the kitchen with a bottle of booze. She almost fainted. But she recovered fast and pretended not to see me. Maybe she did think she'd seen a ghost. I doubt it. She'd have been blabbing all over town about it."

"She may have told her doctor," Chib says. "She saw you several weeks ago, remember? She may have mentioned it while she was bitching about her so-called dizzy spells and hallucinations."

"And the old sawbones, knowing the family history, called the IRB. Maybe."

Chib looks through the periscope's eyepiece. He rotates it and turns the knobs on the handle-ends to raise and lower the cyclops on the end of the tube outside. Accipiter is stalking around the aggregate of seven eggs, each on the end of a broad thin curved branchlike walk projecting from the central pedestal. Accipiter goes up the steps of a branch to the door of Mrs. Applebaum's. The door opens.

"He must have caught her away from the fornixator," Chib says. "And she must be lonely; she's not talking to him over fido. My God, she's fatter than Mama!"

"Why not?" Grandpa says. "Mr. and Mrs. Everyman sit on their asses all day, drink, eat, and watch fido, and their brains run to mud and their bodies to sludge. Caesar would have had no trouble surrounding himself with fat friends these days. You ate, too, Brutus?"

Grandpa's comment, however, should not apply to Mrs. Applebaum. She has a hole in her head, and people addicted to fornication seldom get fat. They sit or lie all day and part of the night, the needle in the fornix area of the brain delivering a series of minute electrical jolts. Indescribable ecstasy floods through their bodies with every impulse, a delight far surpassing any of food, drink, or sex. It's illegal, but the government never bothers a user unless it wants to get him for something else, since a fornic rarely has children. Twenty percent of LA have had holes drilled in their heads and tiny shafts inserted for access of the needle. Five per cent are addicted; they waste away, seldom eating, their distended bladders spilling poisons into the bloodstream.

Chib says, "My brother and sister must have seen you sometimes when you were sneaking out to mass. Could they...?"

"They think I'm a ghost, too. In this day and age! Still, maybe it's a good sign that they can believe in something, even a spook."

"You better stop sneaking out to church."

"The Church, and you, are the only things that keep me going. It was a sad day, though, when you told me you couldn't believe. You would have made a good priest—with faults, of course—and I could have had private mass and confession in this room."

Chib says nothing. He's gone to instruction and observed services just to please Grandpa. The Church was an egg-shaped seashell which, held to the ear, gave only the distant roar of God receding like an ebb tide.

THERE ARE UNIVERSES BEGGING FOR GODS

yet He hangs around this one looking for work.

—from Grandpa's Ms.

Grandpa takes over the eyepiece. He laughs. "The Internal Revenue Bureau! I thought it'd been disbanded! Who the hell has an income big enough to report on any more? Do you suppose it's still active just because of me? Could be."

He calls Chib back to the scope, directed towards the center of Beverly Hills. Chib has a lane of vision between the seven-egged clutches on the branched pedestals. He can see part of the central plaza, the giant ovoids of the city hall, the federal bureaus, the Folk Center, part of the massive spiral on which set the houses of worship, and the dora (from pandora) where those on the purple wage get their goods and those with extra income get their goodies. One end of the big artificial lake is visible; boats and canoes sail on it and people fish.

The irradiated plastic dome that enfolds the clutches of Beverly Hills is sky-blue. The electronic sun climbs towards the zenith. There are a few white genuine-looking images of clouds and even a V of geese migrating south, their honks coming down faintly. Very nice for those who have never been outside the walls of LA. But Chib spent two years in the World Nature Rehabilitation and Conservation Corps—the WNRCC—and he knows the difference. Almost, he decided to desert with Rousseau Red Hawk and join the neo-Amerinds. Then, he was going to become a forest ranger. But this might mean he'd end up shooting or arresting Red Hawk. Besides, he didn't want to become a sammer. And he wanted more than anything to paint.

"There's Rex Luscus," Chib says. "He's being interviewed outside the Folk Center. Quite a crowd."

THE PELLUCIDAR BREAKTHROUGH

Luscus' middle name should have been Upmanship. A man of great erudition, with privileged access to the Library of Greater LA computer, and of Ulyssean sneakiness, he is always scoring over his colleagues.

He it was who founded the Go-Go School of Criticism.

Primalux Ruskinson, his great competitor, did some extensive research when Luscus announced the title of his new philosophy. Ruskinson triumphantly announced that Luscus had taken the phrase from obsolete slang, current in the mid-twentieth century.

Luscus, in the fido interview next day, said that Ruskinson was a rather shallow scholar, which was to be expected.

Go-go was taken from the Hottentot language. In Hottentot, *go-go* meant to examine, that is, to keep looking until something about the object—in this case, the artist and his works—has been observed.

The critics got in line to sign up at the new school. Ruskinson thought of committing suicide, but instead accused Luscus of having blown his way up the ladder of success.

Luscus replied on fido that his personal life was his own, and Ruskinson was in danger of being sued for violation of privacy. However, he deserved no more effort than a man striking at a mosquito.

"What the hell's a mosquito?" say millions of viewers. "Wish the bighead would talk language we could understand."

Luscus' voice fades off for a minute while the interpreters explain, having just been slipped a note from a monitor who's run off the word through the station's encyclopedia.

Luscus rode on the novelty of the Go-Go School for two years.

Then he re-established his prestige, which had been slipping somewhat, with his philosophy of the Totipotent Man.

This was so popular that the Bureau of Cultural Development and Recreation requisitioned a daily one-hour slot for a year-and-a-half in the initial program of totipotentializing.

◆ ◆ ◆

Grandpa Winnegan's penned comment in his *Private Ejaculations:* What about The Totipotent Man, that apotheosis of individuality and complete psychosomatic development, the democratic Übermensch, as recommended by Rex Luscus, the sexually one-sided? Poor old Uncle Sam! Trying to force the proteus of his citizens into a single stabilized shape so he can control them. And at the same time trying to encourage each and every to bring to flower his inherent capabilities — if any! The poor old long-legged, chin-whiskered, milk-hearted, flint-brained schizophrenic! Verily, the left hand knows not what the right hand is doing. As a matter of fact, the right hand doesn't know what the right hand is doing.

♦ ♦ ♦

"What about the totipotent man?" Luscus replied to the chairman during the fourth session of the *Luscan Lecture Series.* "How does he conflict with the contemporary Zeitgeist? He doesn't. The totipotent man is the imperative of our times. He must come into being before the Golden World can be realized. How can you have a Utopia without utopians, a Golden World with humans of brass?"

It was during this Memorable Day that Luscus gave his talk on The Pellucidar Breakthrough and thereby made Chibiabos Winnegan famous. And more than incidentally gave Luscus his biggest score over his competitors.

"Pellucidar? Pellucidar?" Ruskinson mutters. "Oh, God, what's Tinker Bell doing now?"

"I'll take me some time to explain why I use this phrase to describe Winnegan's stroke of genius," Luscus continues. "First, let me seem to detour

FROM THE ARCTIC TO ILLINOIS

"Now, Confucius once said that a bear could not fart at the North Pole without causing a big wind in Chicago.

"By this he meant that all events, therefore, all men, are interconnected in an unbreakable web. What one man does, no matter how seemingly insignificant, vibrates through the strands and affects every man."

♦ ♦ ♦

Ho Chung Ko, before his fido on the 30th level of Lhasa, Tibet, says to his wife, "That white prick has got it all wrong. Confucius didn't say that. Lenin preserve us! I'm going to call him up and give him hell."

His wife says, "Let's change the channel. Pai Ting Place is on now, and..."

♦ ♦ ♦

Ngombe, 10th level, Nairobi: "The critics here are a bunch of black bastards. Now you take Luscus; he could see my genius in a second. I'm going to apply for emigration in the morning."

Wife: "You might at least ask me if I want to go! What about the kids...mother...friends...dog...?" and so on into the lionless night of self-luminous Africa.

♦ ♦ ♦

"...ex-president Radinoff," Luscus continues, "once said that this is the 'Age of the Plugged-In Man.' Some rather vulgar remarks have been made about this, to me, insighted phrase. But Radinoff did not mean that human society is a daisy chain. He meant that the current of modern society flows through the circuit of which we are all part. This is the Age of Complete Interconnection. No wires can hang loose; otherwise we all short-circuit. Yet, it is undeniable that life without individuality is not worth living. Every man must be a *hapax legomenon*..."

Ruskinson jumps up from his chair and screams, "I know that phrase! I got you this time, Luscus!"

He is so excited he falls over in a faint, symptom of a widespread hereditary defect. When he recovers, the lecture is over. He springs to the recorder to run off what he missed. But Luscus has carefully avoided defining The Pellucidar Breakthrough. He will explain it at another lecture.

♦ ♦ ♦

Grandpa, back at the scope, whistles, "I feel like an astronomer. The planets are in orbit around our house, the sun. There's Accipiter, the closest, Mercury, although he's not the god of thieves but their nemesis. Next, Benedictine, your sad-sack Venus. Hard, hard, hard! The sperm would batter their heads flat against the stony ovum. You sure she's pregnant?

"Your Mama's out there, dressed fit to kill and I wish someone would. Mother Earth headed for the perigee of the gummint store to waste your substance."

Grandpa braces himself as if on a rolling deck, the blue-black veins on his legs thick as strangling vines on an ancient oak. "Brief departure from the role of Herr Doktor Sternscheissdreckschnuppe, the great astronomer, to that of der Unterseeboot Kapitan von Schooten die Fischen in der Barrel. Ach! I zee yet das tramp schteamer, Deine Mama, yawing, pitching, rolling in the seas of alcohol. Compass lost; rhumb dumb. Three sheets to the wind. Paddlewheels spinning in the air. The black gang sweating their balls off, stoking the furnaces of frustration. Propeller tangled in the nets of neurosis. And the Great White Whale a glimmer in the black depths but coming up fast, intent on broaching her bottom, too big to miss. Poor damned vessel, I weep for her. I also vomit with disgust.

"Fire one! Fire two! Baroom! Mama rolls over, a jagged hole in her hull but not the one you're thinking of. Down she goes, nose first, as befits a devoted fellationeer, her huge aft rising into the air. Blub, blub! Full fathom five!

"And so back from undersea to outer space. Your sylvan Mars, Red Hawk, has just stepped out of the tavern. And Luscus, Jupiter, the one-eyed All-Father of Art, if you'll pardon my mixing of Nordic and Latin mythologies, is surrounded by his swarm of satellites."

EXCRETION IS THE BITTER PART OF VALOR

Luscus says to the fido interviewers, "By this I mean that Winnegan, like every artist, great or not, produces art that is, first, secretion, unique to himself, then excretion. Excretion in the original sense of 'sifting out.' Creative excretion or discrete excretion. I know that my distinguished colleagues will make fun of this analogy, so I hereby challenge them to a fido debate whenever it can be arranged.

"The valor comes from the courage of the artist in showing his inner products to the public. The bitter part comes from the fact that the artist may be rejected or misunderstood in his time. Also from the terrible war that takes place in the artist with the disconnected or chaotic elements, often contradictory, which he must unite and then mold into a unique entity. Hence my 'discrete excretion' phrase."

Fido interviewer: "Are we to understand that everything is a big pile of shit but that art makes a strange seachange, forms it into something golden and illuminating?"

"Not exactly: But you're close. I'll elaborate and expound at a later date. At present, I want to talk about Winnegan. Now, the lesser artists give only the surface of things; they are photographers. But the great ones give the interiority of objects and beings. Winnegan, however, is the first to reveal more than one interiority in a single work of art. His invention of the alto-relief multilevel technique enables him to epiphanize — show forth — subterranean layer upon layer."

Primalux Ruskinson, loudly, "The Great Onion Peeler of Painting!"

Luscus, calmly after the laughter has died: "In one sense, that is well put. Great art, like an onion, brings tears to the eyes. However, the light on Winnegan's paintings is not just a reflection; it is sucked in, digested, and then fractured forth. Each of the broken beams makes visible, not various aspects of the figures beneath, but whole figures. Worlds, I might say.

"I call this The Pellucidar Breakthrough. Pellucidar is the hollow interior of our planet, as depicted in a now forgotten fantasy-romance of the twentieth-century writer, Edgar Rice Burroughs, creator of the immortal Tarzan."

Ruskinson moans and feels faint again. "Pellucid! Pellucidar! Luscus, you punning exhumist bastard!"

"Burroughs' hero penetrated the crust of Earth to discover another world inside. This was, in some ways, the reverse of the exterior, continents where the surface seas are, and vice versa. Just so, Winnegan has discovered an inner world, the obverse of the public image Everyman projects. And, like Burroughs' hero, he has returned with a stunning narrative of psychic dangers and exploration.

"And just as the fictional hero found his Pellucidar to be populated with stone-age men and dinosaurs, so Winnegan's world is, though absolutely modern in one sense, archaic in another. Abysmally pristine. Yet, in the illumination of Winnegan's world, there is an evil and inscrutable patch of blackness, and that is paralleled in Pellucidar by the tiny fixed moon which casts a chilling and unmoving shadow.

"Now, I did intend that the ordinary 'pellucid' should be part of Pellucidar. Yet 'pellucid' means 'reflecting light evenly from all surfaces' or 'admitting maximum passage of light without diffusion or distortion.' Winnegan's paintings do just the opposite. But — under the broken and twisted light, the acute observer can see a primeval luminosity, even and straight. This is the light that links all the fractures and multilevels, the light I was thinking of in my earlier discussion of the 'Age of the Plugged-In Man' and the polar bear.

"By intent scrutiny, a viewer may detect this, feel, as it were, the photonic fremitus of the heartbeat of Winnegan's world."

Ruskinson almost faints. Luscus' smile and black monocle make him look like a pirate who has just taken a Spanish galleon loaded with gold.

♦ ♦ ♦

Grandpa, still at the scope, says, "And there's Maryam bint Yusuf, the Egyptian backwoodswoman you were telling me about. Your Saturn, aloof, regal, cold, and wearing one of those suspended whirling manycolored hats that're all the rage. Saturn's rings? Or a halo?"

"She's beautiful, and she'd make a wonderful mother for my children," Chib says.

"The chic of Araby. Your Saturn has two moons, mother and aunt. Chaperones! You say she'd make a good mother! How good a wife! Is she intelligent?"

"She's as smart as Benedictine."

"A dumbshit then. You sure can pick them. How do you know you're in love with her? You've been in love with twenty women in the last six months."

"I love her. This is it."

"Until the next one. Can you really love anything but your painting? Benedictine's going to have an abortion, right?'

"Not if I can talk her out of it," Chib says. "To tell the truth, I don't even like her any more. But she's carrying my child."

"Let me look at your pelvis. No, you're male. For a moment, I wasn't sure, you're so crazy to have a baby."

"A baby is a miracle to stagger sextillions of infidels."

"It beats a mouse. But don't you know that Uncle Sam has been propagandizing his heart out to cut down on propagation? Where've you been all your life?"

"I got to go, Grandpa."

Chib kisses the old man and returns to his room to finish his latest painting. The door still refuses to recognize him, and he calls the gummint repair shop, only to be told that all technicians are at the Folk Festival. He leaves the house in a red rage. The bunting and balloons are waving and bobbing in the artificial wind, increased for this occasion, and an orchestra is playing by the lake.

Through the scope, Grandpa watches him walk away.

"Poor devil! I ache for his ache. He wants a baby, and he is ripped up inside because that poor devil Benedictine is aborting their child. Part of his agony, though he doesn't know it, is identification with the doomed infant. His own mother has had innumerable — well, quite a few — abortions. But for the grace of God, he would have been one of them, another nothingness. He wants this baby to have a chance, too. But there is nothing he can do about it, nothing.

"And there is another feeling, one which he shares with most of humankind. He knows he's screwed up his life, or something has twisted it. Every thinking man and woman knows this. Even the smug and dimwitted realize this unconsciously. But a baby, that beautiful being, that unsmirched blank tablet, unformed angel, represents a new hope. Perhaps it won't screw up. Perhaps it'll grow up to be a healthy confident reasonable good-humored unselfish loving man or woman. 'It won't be like me or my next-door neighbor,' the proud, but apprehensive, parent swears.

"Chib thinks this and swears that his baby will be different. But, like everybody else, he's fooling himself. A child has one father and mother, but it has trillions of aunts and uncles. Not only those that are its contemporaries; the dead, too. Even if Chib fled into the wilderness and raised the infant himself, he'd be giving it his own unconscious assumptions. The baby would grow up with beliefs and attitudes that the father was not even aware of. Moreover, being raised in isolation, the baby would be a very peculiar human being indeed.

"And if Chib raises the child in this society, it's inevitable that it will accept at least part of the attitudes of its playmates, teachers, and so on ad nauseam.

"So, forget about making a new Adam out of your wonderful potential-teeming child, Chib. If it grows up to become at least half-sane, it's because you gave it love and discipline and it was lucky in its social contacts and it was also blessed at birth with the right combination of genes. That is, your son or daughter is now both a fighter and a lover.

ONE MAN'S NIGHTMARE IS ANOTHER MAN'S WET DREAM

Grandpa says.

♦ ♦ ♦

"I was talking to Dante Alighieri just the other day, and he was telling me what an inferno of stupidity, cruelty, perversity, atheism, and outright peril the sixteenth century was. The nineteenth left him gibbering, hopelessly searching for adequate enough invectives.

"As for this age, it gave him such high-blood pressure, I had to slip him a tranquilizer and ship him out via time machine with an attendant nurse. She looked much like Beatrice and so should have been just the medicine he needed — maybe."

Grandpa chuckles, remembering that Chib, as a child, took him seriously when he described his time-machine visitors, such notables as Nebuchadnezzar, King of the Grass-Eaters; Samson, Bronze Age Riddler and Scourge of the Philistines; Moses, who stole a god from his Kenite father-in-law and who fought against circumcision all his life; Buddha, the Original Beatnik; No-Moss Sisyphus, taking a vacation from his stone-rolling; Androcles and his buddy, the Cowardly Lion of Oz; Baron von Richthofen, the Red Knight of Germany; Beowulf; Al Capone; Hiawatha; Ivan the Terrible; and hundreds of others.

The time came when Grandpa became alarmed and decided that Chib was confusing fantasy with reality. He hated to tell the little boy that he had been making up all those wonderful stories, mostly to teach him history. It was like telling a kid there wasn't any Santa Claus.

And then, while he was reluctantly breaking the news to his grandson, he became aware of Chib's barely suppressed grin and knew that it was his turn to have his leg pulled. Chib had never been fooled or else had caught on without any shock. So, both had a big laugh and Grandpa continued to tell of his visitors.

"There are no time machines," Grandpa says. "Like it or not, Miniver Cheevy, you have to live in this your time.

"The machines work in the utility-factory levels in a silence broken only by the chatter of a few mahouts. The great pipes at the bottom of the seas suck up water and bottom sludge. The stuff is automatically carried through pipes to the ten production levels of LA. There the inorganic chemicals are converted into energy and then into the matter of food, drink, medicines, and artifacts. There is very little agriculture or animal husbandry outside the city walls, but there is superabundance for all. Artificial but exact duplication of organic stuff, so who knows the difference?

"There is no more starvation or want anywhere, except among the self-exiles wandering in the woods. And the food and goods are shipped to the pandoras and dispensed to the receivers of the purple wage. *The purple wage.* A Madison-Avenue euphemism with connotations of royalty and divine right. Earned by just being born.

"Other ages would regard ours as a delirium, yet ours has benefits others lacked. To combat transiency and rootlessness, the megalopolis is compartmented into small communities. A man can live all his life in one place without having to go elsewhere to get anything he needs. With this has come a provincialism, a small-town patriotism and hostility towards outsiders. Hence, the bloody juvenile gang-fights between towns. The intense and vicious gossip. The insistence on conformity to local mores.

"At the same time, the small-town citizen has fido, which enables him to see events anywhere in the world. Intermingled with the trash and the propaganda, which the government thinks is good for the people, is any amount of superb programs. A man may get the equivalent of a Ph.D. without stirring out of his house.

"Another Renaissance has come, a fruition of the arts comparable to that of Pericles' Athens and the city-states of Michelangelo's Italy or Shakespeare's England. Paradox. More illiterates than ever before in the world's history. But also more literates. Speakers of classical Latin outnumber those of Caesar's day. The world of aesthetics bears a fabulous fruit. And, of course, fruits.

"To dilute the provincialism and also to make international war even more unlikely, we have the world policy of *homogenization*. The voluntary exchange of a part of one nation's population with another's. Hostages to peace and brotherly love. Those citizens who can't get along on just the purple wage or who think they'll be happier elsewhere are induced to emigrate with bribes.

"A Golden World in some respects; a nightmare in others. So what's new with the world? It was always thus in every age. Ours has had to deal with overpopulation and automation. How else could the problem be solved? It's Buridan's ass (actually, the ass was a dog) all over again, as in every time Buridan's ass, dying of hunger because it can't make up its mind which of two equal amounts of food to eat.

"History: *a pons asinorum* with men the asses on the bridge of time.

"No, those two comparisons are not fair or right. It's Hobson's horse, the only choice being the beast in the nearest stall. Zeitgeist rides tonight, and the devil take the hindmost!

"The mid-twentieth-century writers of the Triple Revolution document forecast accurately in some respects. But they deemphasized what lack of work would do to Mr. Everyman. They believed that all men have equal potentialities in developing artistic tendencies, that all could busy themselves with arts, crafts, and hobbies or education for education's sake. They wouldn't face the 'undemocratic' reality that only about ten per cent of the population — if that — are inherently capable of producing anything worthwhile, or even mildly interesting, in the arts. Crafts, hobbies, and a lifelong academic education pale after a while, so back to the booze, fido, and adultery.

"Lacking self-respect, the fathers become free-floaters, nomads on the steppes of sex. Mother, with a capital M, becomes the dominant figure in the family. She may be playing around, too, but she's taking care of the kids; she's around most of the time. Thus, with father a lower-case figure, absent, weak, or indifferent, the children often become homosexual or ambisexual. The wonderland is also a fairyland.

"Some features of this time could have been predicted. Sexual permissiveness was one, although no one could have seen how far it would go. But then no one could have foreknown of the Panamorite sect, even if America has spawned lunatic-fringe cults as a frog spawns tadpoles. Yesterday's monomaniac is tomorrow's messiah, and so Sheltey and his disciples survived through years of persecution and today their precepts are embedded in our culture."

Grandpa again fixes the cross-reticules of the scope on Chib.

"There he goes, my beautiful grandson, bearing gifts to the Greeks. So far, that Hercules has failed to clean up his psychic Augean stable. Yet, he may succeed, that stumblebum Apollo, that Edipus Wrecked. He's luckier than most of his contemporaries. He's had a permanent father, even if a secret one, a zany old man hiding from so-called justice. He has gotten love, discipline, and a superb education in this starred chamber. He's also fortunate in having a profession.

"But Mama spends far too much and also is addicted to gambling, a vice which deprives her of her full guaranteed income. I'm supposed to be dead, so I don't get the purple wage. Chib has to make up for all this by selling or trading his paintings. Luscus has helped him by publicizing him, but at any moment Luscus may turn against him. The money from the paintings is still not enough. After all, money is not the basic of our economy; it's a scarce auxiliary. Chib needs the grant but won't get it unless he lets Luscus make love to him.

"It's not that Chib rejects homosexual relations. Like most of his contemporaries, he's sexually ambivalent. I think that he and Omar Runic still blow each other occasionally. And why not? They love each other. But Chib rejects Luscus as a matter of principle. He won't be a whore to advance his career. Moreover, Chib makes a distinction which is deeply embedded in this society. He thinks that uncompulsive homosexuality is natural (whatever that means?) but that compulsive homosexuality is, to use an old term, queer. Valid or not, the distinction is made.

"So, Chib may go to Egypt. But what happens to me then?

"Never mind me or your mother, Chib. No matter what. Don't give in to Luscus. Remember the dying words of Singleton, Bureau of Relocation and Rehabilitation Director, who shot himself because he couldn't adjust to the new times.

"'What if a man gain the world and lose his ass?'"

At this moment, Grandpa sees his grandson, who has been walking along with somewhat drooping shoulders, suddenly straighten them. And he sees Chib break into a dance, a little improvised shuffle followed by a series of whirls. It is evident that Chib is whooping. The pedestrians around him are grinning.

Grandpa groans and then laughs. "Oh, God, the goatish energy of youth, the unpredictable shift of spectrum from black sorrow to bright orange joy! Dance, Chib, dance your crazy head off! Be happy, if only for a moment! You're young yet, you've got the bubbling of unconquerable hope deep in your springs! Dance, Chib, dance!"

He laughs and wipes a tear away.

SEXUAL IMPLICATIONS OF THE CHARGE OF THE LIGHT BRIGADE

is so fascinating a book that Doctor Jespersen Joyce Bathymens, psycholinguist for the federal Bureau of Group Reconfiguration and Intercommunicability, hates to stop reading. But duty beckons.

"A radish is not necessarily reddish," he says into the recorder. "The Young Radishes so named their group because a radish is a radicle, hence, radical. Also, there's a play on roots and on red-ass, a slang term for anger, and possibly on ruttish and rattish. And undoubtedly on rude-ickle, Beverly Hills dialectical term for a repulsive, unruly, and socially ungraceful person.

"Yet the Young Radishes are not what I would call Left Wing; they represent the current resentment against Life-in-General and advocate no radical policy of reconstruction. They howl against Things As They Are, like monkeys in a tree, but never give constructive criticism. They want to destroy without any thought of what to do after the destruction.

"In short, they represent the average citizen's grousing and bitching, being different in that they are more articulate. There are thousands of groups like them in LA and possibly millions all over the world. They had normal lives as children. In fact, they were born and raised in the same clutch, which is one reason why they were chosen for this study. What phenomenon produced ten such creative persons, all mothered in the seven houses of Area 69-14, all about the same time, all practically raised together, since they were put together in the playpen on top of the pedestal while one mother took her turn baby-sitting and the others did whatever they had to do, which...where was I?

"Oh, yes, they had a normal life, went to the same school, palled around, enjoyed the usual sexual play among themselves, joined the juvenile gangs and engaged in some rather bloody warfare with the

Westwood and other gangs. All were distinguished however, by an intense intellectual curiosity and all became active in the creative arts.

"It has been suggested — that might be true — that that mysterious stranger, Raleigh Renaissance, was the father of all ten. This IS possible but can't be proved. Raleigh Renaissance was living in the house of Mrs. Winnegan at the time, but he seems to have been unusually active in the clutch, and, indeed, all over Beverly Hills. Where this man came from, who he was, and where he went are still unknown despite intensive search by various agencies. He had no ID or other cards of any kind yet he went unchallenged for a long time. He seems to have had something on the Chief of Police of Beverly Hills and possibly on some of the federal agents stationed in Beverly Hills.

"He lived for two years with Mrs. Winnegan, then dropped out of sight. It is rumored that he left LA to join a tribe of white neo-Amerinds, sometimes called the Seminal Indians.

"Anyway, back to the Young (pun on Jung?) Radishes. They are revolting against the Father Image of Uncle Sam, whom they both love and hate. Uncle is, of course, linked by their subconsciouses with *unco*, a Scottish word meaning strange, uncanny, weird, this indicating that their own fathers were strangers to them. All come from homes where the father was missing or weak, a phenomenon regrettably common in our culture.

"I never knew my own father...Tooney, wipe that out as irrelevant. *Unco* also means news or tidings, indicating that the unfortunate young men are eagerly awaiting news of the return of their fathers and perhaps secretly hoping for reconciliation with Uncle Sam, that is, their fathers.

"Uncle Sam. Sam is short for Samuel, from the Hebrew *Shemu'el*, meaning Name of God. All the Radishes are atheists, although some, notably Omar Runic and Chibiabos Winnegan, were given religious instruction as children (Panamorite and Roman Catholic, respectively).

"Young Winnegan's revolt against God, and against the Catholic Church, was undoubtedly reinforced by the fact that his mother forced strong cathartics upon him when he had a chronic constipation. He probably also resented having to learn his catechism when he preferred to play. And there is the deeply significant and traumatic incident in which a catheter was used on him. (This refusal to excrete when young will be analyzed in a later report.)

"Uncle Sam, the Father Figure. *Figure* is so obvious a play that I won't bother to point it out. Also perhaps on *figger*, in the sense of 'a fig on thee!' — look this up in Dante's *Inferno*, some Italian or other in Hell said, 'A fig on thee, God!' biting his thumb in the ancient gesture of defiance and disrespect. Hmm? Biting the thumb—an infantile characteristic?

"Sam is also a multileveled pun on phonetically, orthographically, and semisemantically linked words. It is significant that young Winnegan can't stand to be called *dear;* he claims that his mother called him that so many times it nauseates him. Yet the word has a deeper meaning to him. For instance, *sambar* is an Asiatic *deer* with *three*-pointed antlers. (Note the *sam*, also.) Obviously, the three points symbolize, to him, the Triple Revolution document, the historic dating point of the beginning of our era, which Chib claims to hate so. The three points are also archetypes of the Holy Trinity, which the Young Radishes frequently blaspheme against.

"I might point out that in this the group differs from others I've studied. The others expressed an infrequent and mild blasphemy in keeping with the mild, indeed pale, religious spirit prevalent nowadays. Strong blasphemers thrive only when strong believers thrive.

"Sam also stands for *same,* indicating the Radishes' subconscious desire to conform.

"Possibly, although this particular analysis may be invalid, Sam corresponds to Samekh, the fifteenth letter of the Hebrew alphabet. (Sam! Ech!?) In the old style of English spelling, which the Radishes learned in their childhood, the fifteenth letter of the Roman alphabet is O. In the Alphabet Table of my dictionary, Webster's 128th New Collegiate, the Roman O is in the same horizontal column as the Arabic Dad. Also with the Hebrew Mem. So we get a double connection with the missing and longed for Father (or Dad) and with the over-dominating Mother (or Mem).

"I can make nothing out of the Greek Omicron, also in the same horizontal column. But give me time; this takes study.

"Omicron. The little O! The lower-case omicron has an egg shape. The little egg is their father's sperm fertilized? The womb? The basic shape of modern architecture?

"Sam Hill, an archaic euphemism for Hell. Uncle Sam is a Sam Hill of a father? Better strike that out, Tooney. It's possible that these highly educated youths have read about this obsolete phrase, but it's not confirmable. I don't want to suggest any connections that might make me look ridiculous.

"Let's see. Samisen. A Japanese musical instrument with *three* strings. The Triple Revolution document and the Trinity again. Trinity? Father, Son, and Holy Ghost. Mother the thoroughly despised figure, hence, the Wholly Goose? Well, maybe not. Wipe that out, Tooney.

"Samisen. Son of Sam? Which leads naturally to Samson, who pulled down the temple of the Philistines on them and on himself. These boys talk of doing the same thing. Chuckle. Reminds me of myself when I was their age, before I matured. Strike out that last remark, Tooney.

"Samovar. The Russian word means, literally, self-boiler. There's no doubt the Radishes are boiling with revolutionary fervor. Yet their disturbed psyches know, deep down, that Uncle Sam is their everloving Father-Mother, that he has only their best interests at heart. But they force themselves to hate him, hence, they self-boil.

"A samlet is a young salmon. Cooked salmon is a yellowish pink or pale red, near to a radish in color, in their unconsciouses, anyway. Samlet equals Young Radish; they feel they're being cooked in the great pressure cooker of modern society.

"How's that for a trinely furned phase — I mean, finely turned phrase, Tooney? Run this off, edit as indicated, smooth it out, you know how, and send it off to the boss. I got to go. I'm late for lunch with Mother; she gets very upset if I'm not there on the dot.

"Oh, postscript! I recommend that the agents watch Winnegan more closely. His friends are blowing off psychic steam through talk and drink, but he has suddenly altered his behavior pattern. He has long periods of silence, he's given up smoking, drinking, and sex."

A PROFIT IS NOT WITHOUT HONOR

even in this day. The gummint has no overt objection to privately owned taverns, run by citizens who have paid all license fees, passed all examinations, posted all bonds, and bribed the local politicians and police chief. Since there is no provision made for them, no large buildings available for rent, the taverns are in the homes of the owners themselves.

The Private Universe is Chib's favorite, partly because the proprietor is operating illegally. Dionysus Gobrinus, unable to hew his way through the roadblocks, prise-de-chevaux, barbed wire, and booby-traps of official procedure, has quit his efforts to get a license.

Openly, he paints the name of his establishment over the mathematical equations that once distinguished the exterior of the house. (Math prof at Beverly Hills U. 14, named Al-Khwarizmi Descartes Lobachevsky, he has resigned and changed his name again.) The atrium and several bedrooms have been converted for drinking and carousing. There are no Egyptian customers, probably because of their supersensitivity about the flowery sentiments painted by patrons on the inside walls.

A BAS, ABU
MOHAMMED WAS THE SON OF A VIRGIN DOG
THE SPHINX STINKS
REMEMBER THE RED SEA!
THE PROPHET HAS A CAMEL FETISH

Some of those who wrote the taunts have fathers, grandfathers, and great-grandfathers who were themselves the objects of similar insults. But their descendants are thoroughly assimilated, Beverly Hillsians to the core. Of such is the kingdom of men.

Gobrinus, a squat cube of a man, stands behind the bar, which is square as a protest against the ovoid. Above him is a big sign:

ONE MAN'S MEAD IS ANOTHER MAN'S POISSON

Gobrinus has explained this pun many times, not always to his listener's satisfaction. Suffice it that Poisson was a mathematician and that Poisson's frequency distribution is a good approximation to the binomial distribution as the number of trials increases and probability of success in a single trial is small.

When a customer gets too drunk to be permitted one more drink, he is hurled headlong from the tavern with furious combustion and utter ruin by Gobrinus, who cries, "Poisson! Poisson!"

Chib's friends, the Young Radishes, sitting at a hexagonal table, greet him, and their words unconsciously echo those of the federal psycholinguist's estimate of his recent behavior.

"Chib, monk! Chibber as ever! Looking for a chibbie, no doubt! Take your pick!"

Madame Trismegista, sitting at a little table with a Seal-of-Solomon-shape top, greets him. She has been Gobrinus' wife for two years, a record, because she will knife him if he leaves her. Also, he believes that she can somehow juggle his destiny with the cards she deals. In this age of enlightenment, the soothsayer and astrologer flourish. As science pushes forward, ignorance and superstition gallop around the flanks and bite science in the rear with big dark teeth.

Gobrinus himself, a Ph.D., holder of the torch of knowledge (until lately, anyway), does not believe in God. But he is sure the stars are marching towards a baleful conjunction for him. With a strange logic, he thinks that his wife's cards control the stars; he is unaware that card-divination and astrology are entirely separate fields.

What can you expect of a man who claims that the universe is asymmetric?

Chib waves his hand at Madame Trismegista and walks to another table. Here sits

A TYPICAL TEEMAGER

Benedictine Serinus Melba. She is tall and slim and has narrow lemurlike hips and slender legs but big breasts. Her hair, black as the pupils of her eyes, is parted in the middle, plastered with perfumed spray to the skull, and braided into two long pigtails. These are brought over her bare shoulders and held together with a golden brooch just below her throat. From the brooch, which is in the form of a musical note, the braids part again, one looping under each breast. Another brooch secures them, and they separate to circle behind her back, are brooched again, and come back to meet on her belly. Another brooch holds them, and the twin waterfalls flow blackly over the front of her bell-shaped skirt.

Her face is thickly farded with green, aquamarine, a shamrock beauty mark, and topaz. She wears a yellow bra with artificial pink nipples; frilly lace ribbons hang from the bra. A demicorselet of bright green with black rosettes circles her waist. Over the corselet, half-concealing it, is a wire structure covered with a shimmering pink quilty material. It extends out in back to form a semifuselage or a bird's long tail, to which are attached long yellow and crimson artificial feathers.

An ankle-length diaphanous skirt billows out. It does not hide the yellow and dark-green striped lace-fringed garter-panties, white thighs, and black net stockings with green clocks in the shape of musical notes. Her shoes are bright blue with topaz high heels.

Benedictine is costumed to sing at the Folk Festival; the only thing missing is her singer's hat. Yet, she came to complain, among other things, that Chib has forced her to cancel her appearance and so lose her chance at a great career.

She is with five girls, all between sixteen and twenty-one, all drinking P (for popskull).

"Can't we talk in private, Benny?" Chib says.

"What for?" Her voice is a lovely contralto ugly with inflection.

"You got me down here to make a public scene," Chib says.

"For God's sake, what other kind of scene is there?" she shrills. "Look at him! He wants to talk to me alone!"

It is then that he realizes she is afraid to be alone with him. More than that, she is incapable of being alone. Now he knows why she insisted on leaving the bedroom door open with her girlfriend, Bela, within calling distance. And listening distance.

"You said you was just going to use your finger!" she shouts. She points at the slightly rounded belly. "I'm going to have a baby! You rotten smooth-talking sick bastard!"

"That isn't true at all," Chib says. "You told me it was all right, you loved me."

"'Love! Love!' he says! What the hell do I know what I said, you got me so excited! Anyway, I didn't say you could stick it in! I'd never say that, never! And then what you *did! What* you did! My God, I could hardly walk for a week, you bastard, you!"

Chib sweats. Except for Beethoven's Pastoral welling from the fido, the room is silent. His friends grin. Gobrinus, his back turned, is drinking scotch. Madame Trismegista shuffles her cards, and she farts with a fiery conjunction of beer and onions. Benedictine's friends look at their Mandarin-long fluorescent fingernails or glare at him. Her hurt and indignity is theirs and vice versa.

"I can't take those pills. They make me break out and give me eye trouble and screw up my monthlies! You know that! And I can't stand those mechanical uteruses! And you lied to me anyway! You said you took a pill!"

Chib realizes she's contradicting herself, but there's no use trying to be logical. She's furious because she's pregnant; she doesn't want to be inconvenienced with an abortion at this time, and she's out for revenge.

Now how, Chib wonders, how could she get pregnant that night? No woman, no matter how fertile, could have managed that. She must have been knocked up before or after. Yet she swears that it was that night, the night he was

THE KNIGHT OF THE BURNING PESTLE OR FOAM, FOAM ON THE RANGE

"No, no!" Benedictine cries.

"Why not? I love you," Chib says. "I want to marry you."

Benedictine screams, and her friend Bela, out in the hall, yells, "What's the matter? What happened?"

Benedictine does not reply. Raging, shaking as if in the grip of a fever, she scrambles out of bed, pushing Chib to one side. She runs to the small egg of the bathroom in the corner, and he follows her.

"I hope you're not going to do what I think...?" he says.

Benedictine moans, "You sneaky no-good son of a bitch!"

In the bathroom, she pulls down a section of wall, which becomes a shelf. On its top, attached by magnetic bottoms to the shelf, are many containers. She seizes a long thin can of spermatocide, squats, and inserts it. She presses the button on its bottom, and it foams with a hissing sound even its cover of flesh cannot silence.

Chib is paralyzed for a moment. Then he roars.

Benedictine shouts, "Stay away from me, you rude-ickle!"

From the door to the bedroom comes Bela's timid, "Are you all right, Benny?"

"I'll all-right her!" Chib bellows.

He jumps forward and takes a can of tempoxy glue from the shelf. The glue is used by Benedictine to attach her wigs to her head and will hold anything forever unless softened by a specific defixative.

Benedictine and Bela both cry out as Chib lifts Benedictine up and then lowers her to the floor. She fights, but he manages to spray the glue over the can and the skin and hairs around it.

"What're you doing?" she screams.

He pushes the button on the bottom of the can to full-on position and then sprays the bottom with glue. While she struggles, he holds her arms tight against her body and keeps her from rolling over and so moving the can in or out. Silently, Chib counts to thirty, then to thirty more to make sure the glue is thoroughly dried. He releases her.

The foam is billowing out around her groin and down her legs and spreading out across the floor. The fluid in the can is under enormous pressure in the indestructible unpunchable can, and the foam expands vastly if exposed to open air.

Chib takes the can of defixative from the shelf and clutches it in his hand, determined that she will not have it. Benedictine jumps up and swings at him. Laughing like a hyena in a tentful of nitrous oxide, Chib blocks her fist and shoves her away. Slipping on the foam, which is ankle-deep by now, Benedictine falls and then slides backward out of the bedroom on her buttocks, the can clunking.

She gets to her feet and only then realizes fully what Chib has done. Her scream goes up, and she follows it. She dances around, yanking at the can, her screams intensifying with every tug and resultant pain. Then she turns and runs out of the room or tries to. She skids; Bela is in her way; they cling together and both ski out of the room, doing a half-turn while going through the door. The foam swirls out so that the two look like Venus and friend rising from the bubble-capped waves of the Cyprian Sea.

Benedictine shoves Bela away but not without losing some flesh to Bela's long sharp fingernails. Bela shoots backwards through the door toward Chib. She is like a novice ice skater trying to maintain her balance. She does not succeed and shoots by Chib, wailing, on her back, her feet up in the air.

Chib slides his bare feet across the floor gingerly, stops at the bed to pick up his clothes, but decides he'd be wiser to wait until he's outside before he puts them on. He gets to the circular hall just in time to see Benedictine crawling past one of the columns that divides the corridor from the atrium. Her parents, two middle-aged behemoths, are still sitting on a flato, beer cans in hand, eyes wide, mouths open, quivering.

Chib does not even say goodnight to them as he passes along the hall. But then he sees the fido and realizes that her parents had switched it from EXT. to INT. and then to Benedictine's room. Father and mother have been watching Chib and daughter and it is evident from father's not-quite dwindled condition that father was very excited by this show, superior to anything seen on exterior fido.

"You peeping bastards!" Chib roars.

Benedictine has gotten to them and on her feet and she is stammering, weeping, indicating the can and then stabbing her finger at Chib. At Chib's roar, the parents heave up from the flato as two leviathans from the deep. Benedictine turns and starts to run towards him, her arms outstretched, her longnailed fingers curved, her face a medusa's. Behind her streams the wake of the livid witch and father and mother on the foam.

Chib shoves up against a pillar and rebounds and skitters off, helpless to keep himself from turning sidewise during the maneuver. But he keeps his balance. Mama and Papa have gone down together with a crash that shakes even the solid house. They are up, eyes rolling and bellowing like hippos surfacing. They charge him but separate, Mama shrieking now, her face, despite the fat, Benedictine's. Papa goes around one side of the pillar; Mama, the other. Benedictine has rounded another pillar, holding to it with one hand to keep her from slipping. She is between Chib and the door to the outside.

Chib slams against the wall of the corridor, in an area free of foam. Benedictine runs towards him. He dives across the floor, hits it, and rolls between two pillars and out into the atrium.

Mama and Papa converge in a collision course. The Titanic meets the iceberg, and both plunge swiftly. They skid on their faces and bellies towards Benedictine. She leaps into the air, trailing foam on them as they pass beneath her.

By now it is evident that the government's claim that the can is good for 40,000 shots of death-to-sperm, or for 40,000 copulations, is justified. Foam is all over the place ankle-deep — knee-high in some places — and still pouring out.

Bela is on her back now and on the atrium floor, her head driven into the soft folds of the flato.

Chib gets up slowly and stands for a moment, glaring around him, his knees bent, ready to jump from danger but hoping he won't have to since his feet will undoubtedly fly away from under him.

"Hold it, you rotten son of a bitch!" Papa roars. "I'm going to kill you! You can't do this to my daughter!"

Chib watches him turn over like a whale in a heavy sea and try to get to his feet. Down he goes again, grunting as if hit by a harpoon. Mama is no more successful than he.

Seeing that his way is unbarred — Benedictine having disappeared somewhere — Chib skis across the atrium until he reaches an unfoamed area near the exit. Clothes over his arm, still holding the defixative, he struts towards the door.

At this moment Benedictine calls his name. He turns to see her sliding from the kitchen at him. In her hand is a tall glass. He wonders what she intends to do with it. Certainly, she is not offering him the hospitality of a drink.

Then she scoots into the dry region of the floor and topples forward with a scream. Nevertheless, she throws the contents of the glass accurately.

Chib screams when he feels the boiling hot water, painful as if he had been circumcised unanesthetized.

Benedictine, on the floor, laughs. Chib, after jumping around and shrieking, the can and clothes dropped, his hands holding the scalded parts, manages to control himself. He stops his antics, seizes Benedictine's right hand, and drags her out into the streets of Beverly Hills. There are quite a few people out this night, and they follow the two. Not until Chib reaches the lake does he stop and there he goes into the water to cool off the burn, Benedictine with him.

The crowd has much to talk about later, after Benedictine and Chib have crawled out of the lake and then run home. The crowd talks and laughs quite a while as they watch the sanitation department people clean the foam off the lake surface and the streets.

◆ ◆ ◆

"I was so sore I couldn't walk for a month!" Benedictine screams.

"You had it coming," Chib says. "You've got no complaints. You said you wanted my baby, and you talked as if you meant it."

"I must've been out of my mind!" Benedictine says. "No, I wasn't! I never said no such thing! You lied to me! You forced me!"

"I would never force anybody," Chib said. "You know that. Quit your bitching. You're a free agent, and you consented freely. You have free will."

Omar Runic, the poet, stands up from his chair. He is a tall thin red-bronze youth with an aquiline nose and very thick red lips. His kinky hair grows long and is cut into the shape of the *Pequod*, that fabled vessel which bore mad Captain Ahab and his mad crew and the sole survivor Ishmael after the white whale. The coiffure is formed with a bowsprit and hull and three masts and yardarms and even a boat hanging on davits.

Omar Runic claps his hands and shouts, "Bravo! A philosopher! Free will it is; free will to seek the Eternal Verities — if any — or Death and Damnation! I'll drink to free will! A toast, gentlemen! Stand up, Young Radishes, a toast to our leader!" And so begins

THE MAD P PARTY

Madame Trismegista calls, "Tell your fortune, Chib! See what the stars tell through the cards!"

He sits down at her table while his friends crowd around.

"O.K., Madame. How do I get out of this mess?"

She shuffles and turns over the top card.

"Jesus! The ace of spades!"

"You're going on a long journey!"

"Egypt!" Rousseau Red Hawk cries. "Oh, no, you don't want to go there, Chib! Come with me to where the buffalo roam and..."

Up comes another card.

"You will soon meet a beautiful dark lady."

"A goddam Arab! Oh, no, Chib, tell me it's not true!"

"You will win great honors soon."

"Chib's going to get the grant!"

"If I get the grant, I don't have to go to Egypt," Chib says. "Madame Trismegista, with all due respect, you're full of crap."

"Don't mock, young man. I'm not a computer. I'm tuned to the spectrum of psychic vibrations."

Flip. "You will be in great danger, physically and morally."

Chib says, "That happens at least once a day."

Flip. "A man very close to you will die twice."

Chib pales, rallies, and says, "A coward dies a thousand deaths."

"You will travel in time, return to the past."

"Zow!" Red Hawk says. "You're outdoing yourself, Madame. Careful! You'll get a psychic hernia, have to wear an ectoplasmic truss!"

"Scoff if you want to, you dumbshits," Madame says. "There are more worlds than one. The cards don't lie, not when I deal them."

"Gobrinus!" Chib calls. "Another pitcher of beer for the Madame."

The Young Radishes return to their table, a legless disc held up in the air by a graviton field. Benedictine glares at them and goes into a huddle with the other teemagers. At a table nearby sits Pinkerton Legrand, a gummint agent, facing them so that the fido under his one-way window of a jacket beams in on them. They know he's doing this. He knows they know and has reported so to his superior. He frowns when he sees Falco Accipiter enter. Legrand does not like an agent from another department messing around on his case. Accipiter does not even look at Legrand. He orders a pot of tea and then pretends to drop into the teapot a pill that combines with tannic acid to become P.

Rousseau Red Hawk winks at Chib and says, "Do you really think it's possible to paralyze all of LA with a single bomb?"

"Three bombs!" Chib says loudly so that Legrand's fido will pick up the words. "One for the control console of the desalinization plant, a second for the backup console, the third for the nexus of the big pipe that carries the water to the reservoir on the 20th level."

Pinkerton Legrand turns pale. He downs all the whiskey in his glass and orders another, although he has already had too many. He presses the plate on his fido to transmit a triple top-priority. Lights blink redly in HQ; a gong clangs repeatedly; the chief wakes up so suddenly he falls off his chair.

Accipiter also hears, but he sits stiff, dark, and brooding as the diorite image of a Pharaoh's falcon. Monomaniac, he is not to be diverted by talk of inundating all LA, even if it will lead to action. On Grandpa's trail, he is now here because he hopes to use Chib as the key to the house. One "mouse" — as he thinks of his criminals — one "mouse" will run to the hole of another.

"When do you think we can go into action?" Huga Wells-Erb Heinsturbury, the science-fiction authoress, says.

"In about three weeks," Chib says.

At HQ, the chief curses Legrand for disturbing him. There are thousands of young men and women blowing off steam with these plots of destruction, assassination, and revolt. He does not understand why the young punks talk like this, since they have everything handed them free. If he had his way, he'd throw them into jail and kick them around a little or more than.

"After we do it, we'll have to take off for the big outdoors," Red Hawk says. His eyes glisten. "I'm telling you, boys, being a free man in the forest is the greatest. You're a genuine individual, not just one of the faceless breed."

Red Hawk believes in this plot to destroy LA. He is happy because, though he hasn't said so, he has grieved while in Mother Nature's lap for intellectual companionship. The other savages can hear a deer at a hundred yards, detect a rattlesnake in the bushes, but they're deaf to the footfalls of philosophy, the neigh of Nietzsche, the rattle of Russell, the honkings of Hegel.

"The illiterate swine!" he says aloud. The others say, "What?"

"Nothing. Listen, you guys must know how wonderful it is. You were in the WNRCC."

"I was 4-F," Omar Runic says. "I got hay fever."

"I was working on my second M.A.," Gibbon Tacitus says.

"I was in the WNRCC band," Sibelius Amadeus Yehudi says. "We only got outside when we played the camps, and that wasn't often."

"Chib, you were in the Corps. You loved it, didn't you?"

Chib nods but says, "Being a neo-Amerind takes all your time just to survive. When could I paint? And who would see the paintings if I did get time? Anyway, that's no life for a woman or a baby."

Red Hawk looks hurt and orders a whiskey mixed with P.

Pinkerton Legrand doesn't want to interrupt his monitoring, yet he can't stand the pressure in his bladder. He walks towards the room used as the customers' catch-all. Red Hawk, in a nasty mood caused by rejection, sticks his leg out. Legrand trips, catches himself, and stumbles forward. Benedictine puts out her leg. Legrand falls on his face. He no longer has any reason to go to the urinal except to wash himself off.

Everybody except Legrand and Accipiter laughs. Legrand jumps up, his fists doubled. Benedictine ignores him and walks over to Chib, her friends following. Chib stiffens. She says, "You perverted bastard! You told me you were just going to use your finger!"

"You're repeating yourself," Chib says. "The important thing is, what's going to happen to the baby?"

"What do you care?" Benedictine says. "For all you know, it might not even be yours!"

"That'd be a relief," Chib says, "if it weren't. Even so, the baby should have a say in this. He might want to live—even with you as his mother."

"In this miserable life!" she cries. "I'm going to do it a favor. I'm going to the hospital and get rid of it. Because of you, I have to miss out on my big chance at the Folk Festival! There'll be agents from all over there, and I won't get a chance to sing for them!"

"You're a liar," Chib says. "You're all dressed up to sing."

Benedictine's face is red; her eyes, wide; her nostrils, flaring.

"You spoiled my fun!"

She shouts, "Hey, everybody, want to hear a howler! This great artist, this big hunk of manhood, Chib the divine, he can't get a hard-on unless he's gone down on!"

Chib's friends look at each other. What's the bitch screaming about? So what's new?

> From Grandpa's *Private Ejaculations:* Some of the features of the Panamorite religion, so reviled and loathed in the 21st century, have become everyday facts in modern times. Love, love, love, physical and spiritual! It's not enough to just kiss your children and hug them. But oral stimulation of the genitals of infants by the parents and relatives has resulted in some curious conditioned reflexes. I could write a book about this aspect of mid-22nd century life and probably will.

Legrand comes out of the washroom. Benedictine slaps Chib's face. Chib slaps her back. Gobrinus lifts up a section of the bar and hurtles through the opening, crying, "Poisson! Poisson!"

He collides with Legrand, who lurches into Bela, who screams, whirls, and slaps Legrand, who slaps back. Benedictine empties a glass of P in Chib's face. Howling, he jumps up and swings his fist. Benedictine ducks, and the fist goes over her shoulder into a girl-friend's chest.

Red Hawk leaps up on the table and shouts, "I'm a regular bearcat, half-alligator and half..."

The table, held up in a graviton field, can't bear much weight. It tilts and catapults him into the girls, and all go down. They bite and scratch Red Hawk, and Benedictine squeezes his testicles. He screams, writhes, and hurls Benedictine with his feet onto the top of the table. It has regained its normal height and altitude, but now it flips over again, tossing her to the other side. Legrand, tippytoeing through the crowd on his way to the exit, is knocked down. He loses some front teeth against somebody's knee cap. Spitting blood and teeth, he jumps up and slugs a bystander.

Gobrinus fires off a gun that shoots a tiny very light. It's supposed to blind the brawlers and so bring them to their senses while they're regaining their sight. It hangs in the air and shines like

A STAR OVER BEDLAM

The Police Chief is talking via fido to a man in a public booth. The man has turned off the video and is disguising his voice.

"They're beating the shit out of each other in The Private Universe."

The Chief groans. The Festival has just begun, and They are at it already.

"Thanks. The boys'll be on the way. What's your name? I'd like to recommend you for a Citizen's Medal."

"What! And get the shit knocked out of me, too! I ain't no stoolie; just doing my duty. Besides, I don't like Gobrinus or his customers. They're a bunch of snobs."

The Chief issues orders to the riot squad, leans back, and drinks a beer while he watches the operation on fido. What's the matter with these people, anyway? They're always mad about something.

The sirens scream. Although the bolgani ride electrically driven noiseless tricycles, they're still clinging to the centuries-old tradition of warning the criminals that they're coming. Five trikes pull up before the open door of The Private Universe. The police dismount and confer. Their two-storied cylindrical helmets are black and have scarlet roaches. They wear goggles for some reason although their vehicles can't go over 15 m.p.h. Their jackets are black and fuzzy, like a teddy bear's fur, and huge golden epaulets decorate their shoulders. The shorts are electric-blue and fuzzy; the jackboots, glossy black. They carry electric shock sticks and guns that fire chokegas pellets.

Gobrinus blocks the entrance. Sergeant O'Hara says, "Come on, let us in. No, I don't have a warrant of entry. But I'll get one."

"If you do, I'll sue," Gobrinus says. He smiles. While it is true that government red tape was so tangled he quit trying to acquire a tavern legally, it is also true that the government will protect him in this issue. Invasion of privacy is a tough rap for the police to break.

O'Hara looks inside the doorway at the two bodies on the floor, at those holding their heads and sides and wiping off blood, and at Accipiter, sitting like a vulture dreaming of carrion. One of the bodies gets up on all fours and crawls through between Gobrinus' legs out into the street.

"Sergeant, arrest that man!" Gobrinus says. "He's wearing an illegal fido. I accuse him of invasion of privacy."

O'Hara's face lights up. At least he'll get one arrest to his credit. Legrand is placed in the paddy wagon, which arrives just after the ambulance. Red Hawk is carried out as far as the doorway by his friends. He opens his eyes just as he's being carried on a stretcher to the ambulance and he mutters.

O'Hara leans over him. "What?"

"I fought a bear once with only my knife, and I came out better than with those cunts. I charge them with assault and battery, murder and mayhem."

O'Hara's attempt to get Red Hawk to sign a warrant fails because Red Hawk is now unconscious. He curses. By the time Red Hawk begins feeling better, he'll refuse to sign the warrant. He won't want the girls and their boyfriends laying for him, not if he has any sense at all.

Through the barred window of the paddywagon, Legrand screams, "I'm a gummint agent! You can't arrest me!"

The police get a hurry-up call to go to the front of the Folk Center, where a fight between local youths and Westwood invaders is threatening to become a riot. Benedictine leaves the tavern. Despite several blows in the shoulders and stomach, a kick in the buttocks, and a bang on the head, she shows no sign of losing the fetus.

Chib, half-sad, half-glad, watches her go. He feels a dull grief that the baby is to be denied life. By now he realizes that part of his objection to the abortion is identification with the fetus; he knows what Grandpa thinks he does not know. He realizes that his birth was an accident—lucky or unlucky. If things had gone otherwise, he would not have been born. The thought of his nonexistence—no painting, no friends, no laughter, no hope, no love—horrifies him. His mother, drunkenly negligent about contraception, has had any number of abortions, and he could have been one of them.

Watching Benedictine swagger away (despite her torn clothes), he wonders what he could ever have seen in her. Life with her, even with a child, would have been gritty.

> In the hope-lined nest of the mouth
> Love flies once more, nestles down,
> Coos, flashes feathered glory, dazzles,
> And then flies away, crapping,
> As is the wont of birds,
> To jet-assist the take off.
>
> —Omar Runic

Chib returns to his home, but he still can't get back into his room. He goes to the storeroom. The painting is seven-eights finished but was not completed because he was dissatisfied with it. Now he takes it from the house and carries it to Runic's house, which is in the same clutch as his. Runic is at the Center, but he always leaves his doors open when he's gone. He has equipment which Chib uses to finish the painting, working with a sureness and intensity he lacked the first time he was creating it. He then leaves Runic's house with the huge oval canvas held above his head.

He strides past the pedestals and under their curving branches with the ovoids at their ends. He skirts several small grassy parks with trees, walks beneath more houses, and in ten minutes is nearing the heart of Beverly Hills. Here mercurial Chib sees

ALL IN THE GOLDEN AFTERNOON, THREE LEADEN LADIES

drifting in a canoe on Lake Issus. Maryam bint Yusuf, her mother, and aunt listlessly hold fishing poles and look towards the gay colors, music, and the chattering crowd before the Folk Center. By now the police have broken up the juvenile fight and are standing around to make sure nobody else makes trouble.

The three women are dressed in the somber clothes, completely body-concealing, of the Mohammedan Wahhabi fundamentalist sect. They do not wear veils; not even the Wahhabi now insist on this. Their Egyptian brethren ashore are clad in modern garments, shameful and sinful. Despite which, the ladies stare at them.

Their menfolk are at the edge of the crowd. Bearded and costumed like sheiks in a Foreign Legion fido show, they mutter gargling oaths and hiss at the iniquitous display of female flesh. But they stare.

This small group has come from the zoological preserves of Abyssinia, where they were caught poaching. Their gummint gave them three choices. Imprisonment in a rehabilitation center, where they would be treated until they became good citizens if it took the rest of their lives. Emigration to the megalopolis of Haifa, Israel. Or emigration to Beverly Hills, LA.

What, dwell among the accursed Jews of Israel? They spat and chose Beverly Hills. Alas, Allah had mocked them! They were now surrounded by Finkelsteins, Applebaums, Siegels, Weintraubs, and others of the infidel tribes of Isaac. Even worse, Beverly Hills had no mosque. They either traveled forty kilometers every day to the 16th level, where a mosque was available, or used a private home.

Chib hastens to the edge of the plastic-edged lake and puts down his painting and bows low, whipping off his somewhat battered hat. Maryam smiles at him but loses the smile when the two chaperones reprimand her.

"*Ya kelb! Ya ibn kelb!*" the two shout at him.

Chib grins at them, waves his hat, and says, "Charmed, I'm sure, mesdames! Oh, you lovely ladies remind me of the Three Graces."

He then cries out, "I love you, Maryam! I love you! Thou art like the Rose of Sharon to me! Beautiful, doe-eyed, virginal! A fortress of innocence and strength, filled with a fierce motherhood and utter faithfulness to the one true love! I love thee, thou art the only light in a black sky of dead stars! I cry to you across the void!"

Maryam understands World English, but the wind carries his words away from her. She simpers, and Chib cannot help feeling a momentary repulsion, a flash of anger as if she has somehow betrayed him. Nevertheless, he rallies and shouts, "I invite you to come with me to the showing! You and your mother and aunt will be my guests. You can see my paintings, my soul, and know what kind of man is going to carry you off on his Pegasus, my dove!"

> There is nothing as ridiculous as the verbal outpourings of a young poet in love. Outrageously exaggerated. I laugh. But I am also touched. Old as I am, I remember my first loves, the fires, the torrents of words, lightning-sheathed, ache-winged. Dear lasses, most of you are dead; the rest, withered. I blow you a kiss.
>
> —Grandpa

Maryam's mother stands up in the canoe. For a second, her profile is to Chib, and he sees intimations of the hawk that Maryam will be when she is her mother's age. Maryam now has a gently aquiline face — "the sweep of the sword of love" — Chib has called that nose. Bold but beautiful. However, her mother does look like a dirty old eagle. And her aunt — uneaglish but something of the camel in those features.

Chib suppresses the unfavorable, even treacherous, comparisons. But he cannot suppress the three bearded, robed, and unwashed men who gather around him.

Chib smiles but says, "I don't remember inviting you."

They look blank since rapidly spoken LA English is a hufty-magufty to them. Abu — generic name for any Egyptian in Beverly Hills — rasps an oath so ancient even the pre-Mohammed Meccans knew it. He forms a fist. Another Arab steps towards the painting and draws back a foot as if to kick it.

At this moment, Maryam's mother discovers that it is as dangerous to stand in a canoe as on a camel. It is worse, because the three women cannot swim.

Neither can the middle-aged Arab who attacks Chib, only to find his victim sidestepping and then urging him on into the lake with a foot in the rear. One of the young men rushes Chib; the other starts to kick at the painting. Both halt on hearing the three women scream and on seeing them go over into the water.

Then the two run to the edge of the lake, where they also go into the water, propelled by one of Chib's hands in each of their backs. A bolgan hears the six of them screaming and thrashing around and runs over to Chib. Chib is becoming concerned because Maryam is having trouble staying above the water. Her terror is not faked.

What Chib does not understand is why they are all carrying on so. Their feet must be on the bottom; the surface is below their chins. Despite which, Maryam looks as if she is going to drown. So do the others, but he is not interested in them. He should go in after Maryam. However, if he does, he will have to get a change of clothes before going to the showing.

At this thought, he laughs loudly and then even more loudly as the bolgan goes in after the women. He picks up the painting and walks off laughing. Before he reaches the Center, he sobers.

"Now, how come Grandpa was so right? How does he read me so well? Am I fickle, too shallow? No, I have been too deeply in love too many times. Can I help it if I love Beauty, and the beauties I love do not have enough Beauty? My eye is too demanding; it cancels the urgings of my heart."

THE MASSACRE OF THE INNER SENSE

The entrance hall (one of twelve) which Chib enters was designed by Grandpa Winnegan. The visitor comes into a long curving tube lined with mirrors at various angles. He sees a triangular door at the end of the corridor. The door seems to be too tiny for anybody over nine years old to enter. The illusion makes the visitor feel as if he's walking up the wall as he progresses towards the door. At the end of the tube, the visitor is convinced he's standing on the ceiling.

But the door gets larger as he approaches until it becomes huge. Commentators have guessed that this entrance is the architect's symbolic representation of the gateway to the world of art. One should stand on his head before entering the wonderland of aesthetics.

On going in, the visitor thinks at first that the tremendous room is inside out or reversed. He gets even dizzier. The far wall actually seems the near wall until the visitor gets reorientated. Some people can't adjust and have to get out before they faint or vomit.

On the right hand is a hatrack with a sign: HANG YOUR HEAD HERE. A double pun by Grandpa, who always carries a joke too far for most people. If Grandpa goes beyond the bounds of verbal good taste, his great-great-grandson has overshot the moon in his paintings. Thirty of his latest have been revealed, including the last three of his Dog Series: *Dog Star, Dog Would and Dog Tiered.* Ruskinson and his disciples are threatening to throw up. Luscus and his flock praise, but they're restrained. Luscus has told them to wait until he talks to young Winnegan before they go all-out. The fido men are busy shooting and interviewing both and trying to provoke a quarrel.

The main room of the building is a huge hemisphere with a bright ceiling which runs through the complete spectrum every nine minutes. The floor is a giant chessboard, and in the center of each square is a face, each of a great in the various arts. Michelangelo, Mozart, Balzac, Zeuxis, Beethoven, Li Po, Twain, Dostoyevsky, Farmisto, Mbuzi, Cupel, Krishnagurti, etc. Ten squares are left faceless so that future generations may add their own nominees for immortality.

The lower part of the wall is painted with murals depicting significant events in the lives of the artists. Against the curving wall are nine stages, one for each of the Muses. On a console above each stage is a giant statue of the presiding goddess. They are naked and have overripe figures: huge-breasted, broad-hipped, sturdy-legged, as if the sculptor thought of them as Earth goddesses, not refined intellectual types.

The faces are basically structured like the smooth placid faces of classical Greek statues, but they have an unsettling expression around the mouths and eyes. The lips are smiling but seem ready to break into a snarl. The eyes are deep and menacing. DON'T SELL ME OUT, they say. IF YOU DO...

A transparent plastic hemisphere extends over each stage and has acoustic properties which keep people who are not beneath the shell from hearing the sounds emanating from the stage and vice versa.

Chib makes his way through the noisy crowd towards the stage of Polyhymnia, the Muse who includes painting in her province. He passes the stage on which Benedictine is standing and pouring her lead heart out in an alchemy of golden notes. She sees Chib and manages somehow to glare at him and at the same time to keep smiling at her audience. Chib ignores her but observes that she has replaced the dress ripped in the tavern. He sees also the many policemen stationed around the building. The crowd does not seem in an explosive mood. Indeed, it seems happy, if boisterous. But the police know how deceptive this can be. One spark...

Chib goes by the stage of Calliope, where Omar Runic is extemporizing. He comes to Polyhymnia's, nods at Rex Luscus, who waves at him, and sets his painting on the stage. It is titled *The Massacre of the Innocents* (subtitle: *Dog in the Manger*).

The painting depicts a stable.

The stable is a grotto with curiously shaped stalactites. The light that breaks — or fractures — through the cave is Chib's red. It penetrates every object, doubles its strength, and then rays out jaggedly. The viewer, moving from side to side to get a complete look, can actually see the many levels of light as he moves, and thus he catches glimpses of the figures under the exterior figures.

The cows, sheep, and horses are in stalls at the end of the cave. Some are looking with horror at Mary and the infant. Others have their mouths open, evidently trying to warn Mary. Chib has used the legend that the animals in the manger were able to talk to each other the night Christ was born.

Joseph, a tired old man, so slumped he seems back-boneless, is in a corner. He wears two horns, but each has a halo, so it's all right.

Mary's back is to the bed of straw on which the infant is supposed to be. From a trapdoor in the floor of the cave, a man is reaching to place a huge egg on the straw bed. He is in a cave beneath the cave and is dressed in modern clothes, has a boozy expression, and, like Joseph, slumps as if invertebrate. Behind him a grossly fat woman, looking remarkably like Chib's mother, has the baby, which the man passed on to her before putting the foundling egg on the straw bed.

The baby has an exquisitely beautiful face and is suffused with a white glow from his halo. The woman has removed the halo from his head and is using the sharp edge to butcher the baby.

Chib has a deep knowledge of anatomy, since he has dissected many corpses while getting his Ph.D. in art at Beverly Hills U. The body of the infant is not unnaturally elongated, as so many of Chib's figures are. It is more than photographic; it seems to be an actual baby. Its viscera is unraveled through a large bloody hole.

The onlookers are struck in their viscera as if this were not a painting but a real infant, slashed and disemboweled, found on their doorsteps as they left home.

The egg has a semitransparent shell. In its murky yolk floats a hideous little devil, horns, hooves, tail. Its blurred features resemble a combination of Henry Ford's and Uncle Sam's. When the viewers shift to one side or the other, the faces of others appear: prominents in the development of modern society.

The window is crowded with wild animals that have come to adore but have stayed to scream soundlessly in horror. The beasts in the foreground are those that have been exterminated by man or survive only in zoos and natural preserves. The dodo, the blue whale, the passenger pigeon, the quagga, the gorilla, orangutan, polar bear, cougar, lion, tiger, grizzly bear, California condor, kangaroo, wombat, rhinoceros, bald eagle.

Behind them are other animals and, on a hill, the dark crouching shapes of the Tasmanian aborigine and Haitian Indian.

"What is your considered opinion of this rather remarkable painting, Doctor Luscus?" a fido interviewer asks.

Luscus smiles and says, "I'll have a considered judgment in a few minutes. Perhaps you'd better talk to Doctor Ruskinson first. He seems to have made up his mind at once. Fools and angels, you know."

Ruskinson's red face and scream of fury are transmitted over the fido.

"The shit heard around the world!" Chib says loudly.

"INSULT! SPITTLE! PLASTIC DUNG! A BLOW IN THE FACE OF ART AND A KICK IN THE BUTT FOR HUMANITY! INSULT! INSULT!"

"Why is it such an insult, Doctor Ruskinson?" the fido man says. "Because it mocks the Christian faith, and also the Panamorite faith? It doesn't seem to me it does that. It seems to me that Winnegan is trying to say that men have perverted Christianity, maybe all religions, all ideals, for their own greedy self-destructive purposes, that man is basically a killer and a perverter. At least, that's what I get out of it, although of course I'm only a simple layman, and..."

"Let the critics make the analysis, young man!" Ruskinson snaps. "Do you have a double Ph.D., one in psychiatry and one in art? Have you been certified as a critic by the government?

"Winnegan, who has no talent whatsoever, let alone this genius that various self-deluded blowhards prate about, this abomination from Beverly Hills, presents his junk—actually a mishmash which has attracted attention solely because of a new technique that any electronic technician could invent—I am enraged that a mere gimmick, a trifling novelty, can not only fool certain sectors of the public but highly educated and federally certified critics such as Doctor Luscus here—although there will always be scholarly asses who bray so loudly, pompously, and obscurely that..."

"Isn't it true," the fido man says, "that many painters we now call great, Van Gogh for one, were condemned or ignored by their contemporary critics? And..."

The fido man, skilled in provoking anger for the benefit of his viewers, pauses. Ruskinson swells, his head a bloodvessel just before aneurysm.

"I'm no ignorant layman!" he screams. "I can't help it that there have been Luscuses in the past! I know what I'm talking about! Winnegan is only a micrometeorite in the heaven of Art, not fit to shine the shoes of the great luminaries of painting. His reputation has been pumped up by a certain clique so it can shine in the reflected glory, the hyenas, biting the hand that feeds them, like mad dogs..."

"Aren't you mixing your metaphors a little bit?" the fido man says.

Luscus takes Chib's hand tenderly and draws him to one side where they're out of fido range.

"Darling Chib," he coos, "now is the time to declare yourself. You know how vastly I love you, not only as an artist but for yourself. It must be impossible for you to resist any longer the deeply sympathetic vibrations that leap unhindered between us. God, if you only knew how I dreamed of you, my glorious godlike Chib, with..."

"If you think I'm going to say yes because you have the power to make or break my reputation, to deny me the grant, you're wrong," Chib says. He jerks his hand away.

Luscus' good eye glares. He says, "Do you find me repulsive? Surely it can't be on moral grounds..."

"It's the principle of the thing," Chib says. "Even if I were in love with you, which I'm not, I wouldn't let you make love to me. I want to he judged on my merit alone, that only. Come to think of it, I don't give a damn about anybody's judgment. I don't want to hear praise or blame from you or anybody. Look at my paintings and talk to each other, you jackals. But don't try to make me agree with your little images of me."

THE ONLY GOOD CRITIC IS A DEAD CRITIC

Omar Runic has left his dais and now stands before Chib's paintings. He places one hand on his naked left chest, on which is tattooed the face of Herman Melville, Homer occupying the other place of honor on his right breast. He shouts loudly, his black eyes like furnace doors blown out by explosion. As has happened before, he is seized with inspiration derived from Chib's paintings.

> "Call me Ahab, not Ishmael.
> For I have hooked the Leviathan.
> I am the wild ass's colt born to a man.
> Lo, my eye has seen it all!
> My bosom is like wine that has no vent.
> I am a sea with doors, but the doors are stuck.
> Watch out! The skin will burst; the doors will break.

> "You are Nimrod, I say to my friend, Chib.
> And now is the hour when God says to his angels,
> If this is what he can do as a beginning, then
> Nothing is impossible for him.
> He will be blowing his horn before
> The ramparts of Heaven and shouting for
> The Moon as hostage, the Virgin as wife,
> And demanding a cut on the profits
> From the Great Whore of Babylon."

"Stop that son of a bitch!" the Festival Director shouts. "He'll cause a riot like he did last year!"

The bolgani begin to move in. Chib watches Luscus, who is talking to the fido man. Chib can't hear Luscus, but he's sure Luscus is not saying complimentary things about him.

> "Melville wrote of me long before I was born.
> I'm the man who wants to comprehend
> The Universe but comprehend on my terms.
> I am Ahab whose hate must pierce, shatter,
> All impediment of Time, Space, or Subject
> Mortality and hurl my fierce
> Incandescence into the Womb of Creation,
> Disturbing in its Lair whatever Force or
> Unknown Thing-in-Itself crouches there,
> Remote, removed, unrevealed."

The Director gestures at the police to remove Runic. Ruskinson is still shouting, although the cameras are pointing at Runic or Luscus. One of the Young Radishes, Huga Wells-Erb Heinsturbury, the science-fiction authoress, is shaking with hysteria generated by Runic's voice and with a lust for revenge. She is sneaking up on a *Time* fido man. *Time* has long ago ceased to be a magazine, since there are no magazines, but became a government-supported communications bureau. *Time* is an example of Uncle Sam's left-hand, right-hand, hands-off policy of providing communications bureaus with all they need and at the same time permitting the bureau executives to determine the bureau policies. Thus, government provision and free speech are united. This is fine, in theory, anyway.

Time has revived several of its original policies, that is, truth and objectivity must be sacrificed for the sake of a witticism and science-fiction must be put down. *Time* has sneered at every one of Heinsturbury's works, and so she is out to get some personal satisfaction for the hurt caused by the unfair reviews.

> "*Quid nunc? Cui bono?*
> Time? Space? Substance? Accident?
> When you die—Hell? Nirvana?
> Nothing is nothing to think about.
> The canons of philosophy boom.
> Their projectiles are duds.
> The ammo heaps of theology blow up,
> Set off by the saboteur Reason.
> Call me Ephraim, for I was halted
> At the Ford of God and could not tongue
> The sibilance to let me pass.
> Well, I can't pronounce shibboleth,
> But I can say shit!"

Huga Wells-Erb Heinsturbury kicks the *Time* fido man in the balls. He throws up his hands, and the football-shaped, football-sized camera sails from his hands and strikes a youth on the head. The youth is a Young Radish, Ludwig Euterpe Mahlzart. He is smoldering with rage because of the damnation of his tone poem, *Jetting the Stuff of Future Hells,* and the camera is the extra fuel needed to make him blaze up uncontrollably. He punches the chief musical critic in his fat belly.

Huga, not the *Time* man, is screaming with pain. Her bare toes have struck the hard plastic armor with which the *Time* man, recipient of many such a kick, protects his genitals. Huga hops around on one foot while holding the injured foot in her hands. She twirls into a girl, and there is a chain effect. A man falls against the *Time* man, who is stooping over to pick up his camera.

"Ahaaa!" Huga screams and tears off the *Time* man's helmet and straddles him and beats him over the head with the optical end of the camera. Since the solid-state camera is still working, it is sending to billions of viewers some very intriguing, if dizzying, pictures. Blood obscures one side of the picture, but not so much that the viewers are wholly cheated. And then they get another novel shot as the camera flies into the air again, turning over and over.

A bolgan has shoved his shock-stick against her back, causing her to stiffen and propel the camera in a high arc behind her. Huga's current lover grapples with the bolgan; they roll on the floor; a Westwood juvenile picks up the shock-stick and has a fine time goosing the adults around him until a local youth jumps him.

"Riots are the opium of the people," the Police Chief groans. He calls in all units and puts in a call to the Chief of Police of Westwood, who is, however, having his own troubles.

Runic beats his breast, and howls.

> "Sir, I exist! And don't tell me,
> As you did Crane, that that creates
> No obligation in you towards me.
> I am a man; I am unique.
> I've thrown the Bread out the window,
> Pissed in the Wine, pulled the plug
> From the bottom of the Ark, cut the Tree
> For firewood, and if there were a Holy
> Ghost, I'd goose him.
> But I know that it all does not mean
> A God damned thing.
> That nothing means nothing,
> That is is is and not-is not is is-not
> That a rose is a rose is a
> That we are here and will not be
> And that is all we can know!"

Ruskinson sees Chib coming towards him, squawks, and tries to escape. Chib seizes the canvas of *Dogmas from a Dog* and batters Ruskinson over the head with it. Luscus protests in horror, not because of the damage done to Ruskinson but because the painting might be damaged. Chib turns around and batters Luscus in the stomach with the oval's edge.

"The earth lurches like a ship going down,
Its back almost broken by the flood of
Excrement from the heavens and the deeps,
What God in His terrible munificence
Has granted on hearing Ahab cry,
Bullshit! Bullshit!

"I weep to think that this is Man
And this his end. But wait!
On the crest of the flood, a three-master
Of antique shape. The Flying Dutchman!
And Ahab is astride a ship's deck once more.
Laugh, you Fates, and mock, you Norns!
For I am Ahab and I am Man,
And though I cannot break a hole
through the wall of What Seems
To grab a handful of What Is,
Yet, I will keep on punching.
And I and my crew will not give up,
Though the timbers split beneath our feet
And we sink to become indistinguishable
From the general excrement.

"For a moment that will burn on the
Eye of God forever, Ahab stands
Outlined against the blaze of Orion,
Fist clenched, a bloody phallus,
Like Zeus exhibiting the trophy of
The unmanning of his father Cronus.
And then he and his crew and ship
Dip and hurtle headlong over
The edge of the world.
And from what I hear, they are still
F
a
l
l
I
n
g"

Chib is shocked into a quivering mass by a jolt from a bolgan's electrical riot stick. While he is recovering, he hears his Grandpa's voice issuing from the transceiver in his hat.

"Chib, come quick! Accipiter has broken in and is trying to get through the door of my room!"

Chib gets up and fights and shoves his way to the exit. When he arrives, panting, at his home he finds that the door to Grandpa's room has been opened. The IRB men and electronic technicians are standing in the hallway. Chib bursts into Grandpa's room. Accipiter is standing in its middle and is quivering and pale. Nervous stone. He sees Chib and shrinks back, saying, "It wasn't my fault. I had to break in. It was the only way I could find out for sure. It wasn't my fault; I didn't touch him."

Chib's throat is closing in on itself. He cannot speak. He kneels down and takes Grandpa's hand. Grandpa has a slight smile on his blue lips. Once and for all, he has eluded Accipiter. In his hand is the latest sheet of his Ms.:

THROUGH BALAKLAVAS OF HATE, THEY CHARGE TOWARDS GOD

For most of my life, I have seen only a truly devout few and a great majority of truly indifferent. But there is a new spirit abroad. So many young men and women have revived; not a love for God, but a violent antipathy towards Him. This excites and restores me. Youths like my grandson and Runic shout blasphemies and so worship Him. If they did not believe, they would never think about Him. I now have some confidence in the future.

TO THE STICKS VIA THE STYX

Dressed in black, Chib and his mother go down the tube entrance to level 13B. It's luminous-walled, spacious, and the fare is free. Chib tells the ticket-fido his destination. Behind the wall, the protein computer, no larger than a human brain, calculates. A coded ticket slides out of a slot. Chib takes the ticket, and they go to the bay, a great incurve, where he sticks the ticket into a slot. Another ticket protrudes, and a mechanical voice repeats the information on the ticket in World and LA English, in case they can't read.

Gondolas shoot into the bay and decelerate to a stop. Wheelless, they float in a continually rebalancing graviton field. Sections of the bay slide back to make ports for the gondolas. Passengers step into the cages designated for them. The cages move forward; their doors open automatically. The passengers step into the gondolas. They sit down and wait while the safety meshmold closes over them. From the recess of the chassis, transparent plastic curves rise and meet to form a dome.

Automatically timed, monitored by redundant protein computers for safety, the gondolas wait until the coast is clear. On receiving the go-ahead, they move slowly out of the bay to the tube. They pause while getting another affirmation, trebly checked in microseconds. Then they move swiftly into the tube.

Whoosh! Whoosh! Other gondolas pass them. The tube glows yellowly as if filled with electrified gas. The gondola accelerates rapidly. A few are still passing it, but Chib's speeds up and soon none can catch up with it. The round posterior of a gondola ahead is a glimmering quarry that will not be caught until it slows before mooring at its destined bay. There are not many gondolas in the tube. Despite a 100-million population, there is little traffic on the north-south route. Most LAers stay in the self-sufficient walls of their clutches. There is more traffic on the east-west tubes, since a small percentage prefer the public ocean beaches to the municipality swimming pools.

The vehicle screams southward. After a few minutes, the tube begins to slope down, and suddenly it is at a 45-degree angle to the horizontal. They flash by level after level.

Through the transparent walls, Chib glimpses the people and architecture of other cities. Level 8, Long Beach, is interesting. Its homes look like two cut-quartz pie plates, one on top of another, open end on open end, and the unit mounted on a column of carved figures, the exit-entrance ramp a flying buttress.

At level 3A, the tube straightens out. Now the gondola races past establishments the sight of which causes Mama to shut her eyes. Chib squeezes his mother's hand and thinks of the half-brother and cousin who are behind the yellowish plastic. This level contains fifteen percent of the population, the retarded, the incurable insane, the too-ugly, the monstrous, the senile aged. They swarm here, the vacant or twisted faces pressed against the tube wall to watch the pretty cars float by.

♦ ♦ ♦

"Humanitarian" medical science keeps alive the babies that *should* — by Nature's imperative — have died. Ever since the 20th century, humans with defective genes have been saved from death. Hence, the continual spreading of these genes. The tragic thing is that science can now detect and correct defective genes in the ovum and sperm.

Theoretically, all human beings could be blessed with totally healthy bodies and physically perfect brains. But the rub is that we don't have near enough doctors and facilities to keep up with the births. This despite the ever decreasing birth rate.

Medical science keeps people living so long that senility strikes. So, more and more slobbering mindless decrepits. And also an accelerating addition of the mentally addled. There are therapies and drugs to restore most of them to "normalcy," but not enough doctors and facilities. Some day there may be, but that doesn't help the contemporary unfortunate.

What to do now? The ancient Greeks placed defective babies in the fields to die. The Eskimos shipped out their old people on ice floes. Should we gas our abnormal infants and seniles? Sometimes, I think it's the merciful thing to do. But I can't ask somebody else to pull the switch when I won't.

> **I would shoot the first man to reach for it.**
> **—from Grandpa's** *Private Ejaculations*

The gondola approaches one of the rare intersections. Its passengers see down the broad-mouthed tube to their right. An express flies towards them; it looms. Collision course. They know better, but they can't keep from gripping the mesh, gritting their teeth, and bracing their legs. Mama gives a small shriek. The flier hurtles over them and disappears, the flapping scream of air a soul on its way to underworld judgment.

The tube dips again until it levels out on 1. They see the ground below and the massive self-adjusting pillars supporting the megalopolis. They whiz by over a little town, quaint, early 21st century LA preserved as a museum, one of many beneath the cube.

Fifteen minutes after embarking, the Winnegans reach the end of the line. An elevator takes them to the ground, where they enter a big black limousine. This is furnished by a private-enterprise mortuary, since Uncle Sam or the LA government will pay for cremation but not for burial. The Church no longer insists on interment, leaving it to the religionists to choose between being wind-blown ashes or underground corpses.

The sun is halfway towards the zenith. Mama begins to have trouble breathing and her arms and neck redden and swell. The three times she's been outside the walls, she's been attacked with this allergy despite the air conditioning of the limousine. Chib pats her hand while they're riding over a roughly patched road. The archaic eighty-year-old, fuel-cell-powered, electric-motor-driven vehicle is, however, rough-riding only by comparison with the gondola. It covers the ten kilometers to the cemetery speedily, stopping once to let deer cross the road.

Father Fellini greets them. He is distressed because he is forced to tell them that the Church feels that Grandpa has committed sacrilege. To substitute another man's body for his corpse, to have mass said over it, to have it buried in sacred ground is to blaspheme. Moreover, Grandpa died an unrepentant criminal. At least, to the knowledge of the Church, he made no contrition just before he died.

Chib expects this refusal. St. Mary's of BH-14 has declined to perform services for Grandpa within its walls. But Grandpa has often told Chib that he wants to be buried beside his ancestors, and Chib is determined that Grandpa will get his wish.

Chib says, "I'll bury him myself! Right on the edge of the graveyard!"

"You can't do that!" the priest, mortuary officials, and a federal agent say simultaneously.

"The Hell I can't! Where's the shovel?"

It is then that he sees the thin dark face and falciform nose of Accipiter. The agent is supervising the digging up of Grandpa's (first) coffin. Nearby are at least fifty fido men shooting with their minicameras, the transceivers floating a few decameters near them. Grandpa is getting full coverage, as befits the Last Of The Billionaires and The Greatest Criminal Of The Century.

Fido interviewer: "Mr. Accipiter, could we have a few words from you? I'm not exaggerating when I say that there are probably at least ten billion people watching this historic event. After all, even the grade-school kids know of Win-again Winnegan.

"How do you feel about this? You've been on the case for 26 years. The successful conclusion must give you great satisfaction."

Accipiter, unsmiling as the essence of diorite: "Well actually, I've not devoted full time to this case. Only about three years of accumulative time. But since I've spent at least several days each month on it, you might say I've been on Winnegan's trail for 26 years."

Interviewer: "It's been said that the ending of this case also means the end of the IRB. If we've not been misinformed, the IRB was only kept functioning because of Winnegan. You had other business, of course, during this time, but the tracking down of counterfeiters and gamblers who don't report their income has been turned over to other bureaus. Is this true? If so, what do you plan to do?"

Accipiter, voice flashing a crystal of emotion: "Yes, the IRB is being disbanded. But not until after the case against Winnegan's granddaughter and her son is finished. They harbored him and are, therefore, accessories after the fact.

"In fact, almost the entire population of Beverly Hills, level 14, should be on trial. I know, but can't prove it as yet, that everybody, including the municipal Chief of Police, was well aware that Winnegan was hiding in that house. Even Winnegan's priest knew it, since Winnegan frequently went to mass and to confession. His priest claims that he urged Winnegan to turn himself in and also refused to give him absolution unless he did so.

"But Winnegan, a hardened 'mouse' — I mean, criminal, if ever I saw one, refused to follow the priest's urgings. He claimed that he had not committed a crime, that, believe it or not, Uncle Sam was the criminal. Imagine the effrontery, the depravity, of the man!"

Interviewer: "Surely you don't plan to arrest the entire population of Beverly Hills 14?"

Accipiter: "I have been advised not to."

Interviewer: "Do you plan on retiring after this case is wound up?"

Accipiter: "No. I intend to transfer to the Greater LA Homicide Bureau. Murder for profit hardly exists any more, but there are still crimes of passion, thank God!"

Interviewer: "Of course, if young Winnegan should win his case against you — he has charged you with invasion of domestic privacy, illegal housebreaking, and directly causing his great-great-grandfather's death — then you won't be able to work for the Homicide Bureau or any police department."

Accipiter, flashing several crystals of emotion: "It's no wonder we law enforcers have such a hard time operating effectively! Sometimes, not only the majority of citizens seem to be on the law-breaker's side but my own employers…"

Interviewer: "Would you care to complete that statement? I'm sure your employers are watching this channel. No? I understand that Winnegan's trial and yours are, for some reason, scheduled to take place *at the same time.* How do you plan to be present at both trials? Heh, heh! Some fido-casters are calling you The Simultaneous Man!"

Accipiter, face darkening: "Some idiot clerk did that! He incorrectly fed the data into the legal computer. And he, or somebody, turned off the error-override circuit, and the computer burned up. The clerk is suspected of deliberately making the error — by me anyway, and let the idiot sue me if he wishes — anyway, there have been too many cases like this and…"

Interviewer: "Would you mind summing up the course of this case for our viewers' benefit? Just the highlights, please."

Accipiter: "Well, ah, as you know, fifty years ago all large private-enterprise businesses had become government bureaus. All except the building construction firm, the Finnegan Fifty-three States Company, of which the president was Finn Finnegan. He was the father of the man who is to be buried — somewhere — today.

"Also, all unions except the largest, the construction union, were dissolved or were government unions. Actually, the company and its union were one, because all employees got ninety-five per cent of the money, distributed more or less equally among them. Old Finnegan was both the company president and union business agent-secretary.

"By hook or crook, mainly by crook, I believe, the firm-union had resisted the inevitable absorption. There were investigations into Finnegan's methods: coercion and blackmail of U.S. Senators and even U.S. Supreme Court Justices. Nothing was, however, proved."

Interviewer: "For the benefit of our viewers who may be a little hazy on their history, even fifty years ago money was used only for the purchase of nonguaranteed items. Its other use, as today, was as an index of prestige and social esteem. At one time, the government was thinking of getting rid of currency entirely, but a study revealed that it had great psychological value. The income tax was also kept, although the government had no use for money, because the size of a man's tax determined prestige and also because it enabled the government to remove a large amount of currency from circulation."

Accipiter: "Anyway, when old Finnegan died, the federal government renewed its pressure to incorporate the construction workers and the company officials as civil servants. But young Finnegan proved to be as foxy and vicious as his old man. I don't suggest, of course, that the fact that his uncle was President of the U.S. at that time had anything to do with young Finnegan's success."

Interviewer: "Young Finnegan was seventy years old when his father died."

Accipiter: "During this struggle, which went on for many years, Finnegan decided to rename himself Winnegan. It's a pun on Win Again. He seems to have had a childish, even imbecilic, delight in puns, which, frankly, I don't understand. Puns I mean."

Interviewer: "For the benefit of our non-American viewers, who may not know of our national custom of Naming Day...this was originated by the Panamorites. When a citizen comes of age, he may at any time thereafter take a new name, one which he believes to be appropriate to his temperament or goal in life. I might point out that Uncle

Sam, who's been unfairly accused of trying to impose conformity upon his citizens, encourages this individualistic approach to life. This despite the increased recordkeeping required on the government's part.

I might also point out something else of interest. The government claimed that Grandpa Winnegan was mentally incompetent. My listeners will pardon me, I hope, if I take up a moment of your time to explain the basis of Uncle Sam's assertion. Now, for the benefit of those among you who are unacquainted with an early 20th-century classic, *Finnegan's Wake,* despite your government's wish for you to have a free lifelong education, the author, James Joyce, derived the title from an old vaudeville song."

(Half-fadeout while a monitor briefly explains "vaudeville.")

"The song was about Tim Finnegan, an Irish hod carrier who fell off a ladder while drunk and was supposedly killed. During the Irish wake held for Finnegan, the corpse is accidentally splashed with whiskey. Finnegan, feeling the touch of the whiskey, the 'water of life,' sits up in his coffin and then climbs out to drink and dance with the mourners.

"Grandpa Winnegan always claimed that the vaudeville song was based on reality, you can't keep a good man down, and that the original Tim Finnegan was his ancestor. This preposterous statement was used by the government in its suit against Winnegan.

"However, Winnegan produced documents to substantiate his assertion. Later—too late—the documents were proved to be forgeries."

Accipiter: "The government's case against Winnegan was strengthened by the rank and file's sympathy with the government. Citizens were complaining that the business-union was undemocratic and discriminatory. The officials and workers were getting relatively high wages, but many citizens had to be contented with their guaranteed income. So, Winnegan was brought to trial and accused, justly, of course, of various crimes, among which were subversion of democracy.

"Seeing the inevitable, Winnegan capped his criminal career. He somehow managed to steal 20 billion dollars from the federal deposit vault. This sum, by the way, was equal to half the currency than existing in Greater LA. Winnegan disappeared with the money, which he had not only stolen but had not paid income tax on. Unforgivable. I don't know why so many people have glamorized this villain's feat. Why, I've even seen fido shows with him as the hero, thinly disguised under another name, of course."

Interviewer: "Yes, folks, Winnegan committed the Crime Of The Age. And, although he has finally been located, and is to be buried today — somewhere — the case is not completely closed. The federal government says it is. But where is the money, the 20 billion dollars?"

Accipiter: "Actually, the money has no value now except as collector's items. Shortly after the theft, the government called in all currency and then issued new bills that could not be mistaken for the old. The government had been wanting to do something like this for a long time, anyway, because it believed that there was too much currency, and it only reissued half the amount taken in.

"I'd like very much to know where the money is. I won't rest until I do. I'll hunt it down if I have to do it on my own time."

Interviewer: "You may have plenty of time to do that if young Winnegan wins his case. Well, folks, as most of you may know, Winnegan was found dead in a lower level of San Francisco about a year after he disappeared. His grand-daughter identified the body, and the fingerprints, earprints, retinaprints, teethprints, blood-type, hair-type, and a dozen other identity prints matched out."

Chib, who has been listening, thinks that Grandpa must have spent several millions of the stolen money arranging this. He does not know, but he suspects that a research lab somewhere in the world grew the duplicate in a biotank.

This happened two years after Chib was born. When Chib was five, his grandpa showed up. Without letting Mama know he was back, he moved in. Only Chib was his confidant. It was, of course, impossible for Grandpa to go completely unnoticed by Mama, yet she now insisted that she had never seen him. Chib thought that this was to avoid prosecution for being an accessory after the crime. He was not sure. Perhaps she had blocked off his "visitations" from the rest of her mind. For her it would be easy, since she never knew whether today was Tuesday or Thursday and could not tell you what year it was.

Chib ignores the mortuarians, who want to know what to do with the body. He walks over to the grave. The top of the ovoid coffin is visible now, with the long elephantlike snout of the digging machine sonically crumbling the dirt and then sucking it up. Accipiter, breaking through his lifelong control, is smiling at the fidomen and rubbing his hands.

"Dance a little, you son of a bitch," Chib says, his anger the only block to the tears and the wail building up in him.

The area around the coffin is cleared to make room for the grappling arms of the machine. These descend, hook under, and lift the black, irradiated-plastic, mocksilver-arabesqued coffin up and out and onto the grass. Chib, seeing the IRB men begin to open the coffin, starts to say something but closes his mouth. He watches intently, his knees bent as if getting ready to jump. The fidomen close in, their eyeball-shaped cameras pointing at the group around the coffin.

Groaning, the lid rises. There is a big bang. Dense dark smoke billows. Accipiter and his men, blackened, eyes wide and white, coughing, stagger out of the cloud. The fidomen are running every which way or stooping to pick up their cameras. Those who were standing far enough back can see that the explosion took place at the bottom of the grave. Only Chib knows that the raising of the coffin lid has activated the detonating device in the grave.

He is also the first to look up into the sky at the projectile soaring from the grave because only he expected it. The rocket climbs up to five hundred feet while the fidomen train their cameras on it. It bursts apart and from it a ribbon unfolds between two round objects. The objects expand to become balloons while the ribbon becomes a huge banner.

On it, in big black letters, are the words

WINNEGAN'S FAKE!

Twenty billions of dollars buried beneath the supposed bottom of the grave burn furiously. Some bills, blown up in the geyser of fireworks, are carried by the wind while IRB men, fidomen, mortuary officials, and municipality officials chase them.

Mama is stunned.

Accipiter looks as if he is having a stroke.

Chib cries and then laughs and rolls on the ground.

Grandpa has again screwed Uncle Sam and has also pulled his greatest pun where all the world can see it.

"Oh, you old man!" Chib sobs between laughing fits. "Oh, you old man! How I love you!"

While he is rolling on the ground again, roaring so hard his ribs hurt, he feels a paper in his hand. He stops laughing and gets on his knees and calls after the man who gave it to him. The man says, "I was paid by your grandfather to hand it to you when he was buried."

Chib reads.

♦ ♦ ♦

I hope nobody was hurt, not even the IRB men.

Final advice from the Wise Old Man In The Cave. Tear loose. Leave LA. Leave the country. Go to Egypt. Let your mother ride the purple wage on her own. She can do it if she practices thrift and self-denial. If she can't, that's not your fault.

You are fortunate indeed to have been born with talent, if not genius, and to be strong enough to want to rip out the umbilical cord. So do it. Go to Egypt. Steep yourself in the ancient culture. Stand before the Sphinx. Ask her (actually, it's a he) the Question.

Then visit one of the zoological preserves south of the Nile. Live for a while in a reasonable facsimile of Nature as she was before mankind dishonored and disfigured her. There, where Homo Sapiens(?) evolved from the killer ape, absorb the spirit of that ancient place and time.

You've been painting with your penis, which I'm afraid was more stiffened with bile than with passion for life. Learn to paint with your heart. Only thus will you become great and true.

Paint.

Then, go wherever you want to go. I'll be with you as long as you're alive to remember me. To quote Runic, "I'll be the Northern Lights of your soul."

Hold fast to the belief that there will be others to love you just as much as I did or even more. What is more important, you must love them as much as they love you.

Can you do this?

Don't Wash the Carats:
♦ ♦ ♦ ♦ ♦ ♦ ♦ ♦ ♦ ♦ ♦ ♦ A Polytropical Paramyth

The knife slices the skin. The saw rips into bone. Gray dust flies. The plumber's helper (the surgeon is economical) clamps its vacuum onto the plug of bone. Ploop! Out comes the section of skull. The masked doctor, Van Mesgeluk, directs a beam of light into the cavern of cranium.

He swears a large oath by Hippocrates, Aesculapius, and the Mayo Brothers. The patient doesn't have a brain tumor. He's got a diamond.

The assistant surgeon, Beinschneider, peers into the well and, after him, the nurses.

"Amazing!" Van Mesgeluk says. "The diamond's not in the rough. It's cut!"

"Looks like a 58-facet brilliant, 127.1 carats," says Beinschneider, who has a brother-in-law in the jewelry trade. He sways the light at the end of the drop cord back and forth. Stars shine; shadows run.

"Of course, it's half buried. Maybe the lower part isn't diamond. Even so..."

"Is he married?" a nurse says.

Van Mesgeluk rolls his eyes. "Miss Lustig, don't you ever think of anything but marriage?"

"Everything reminds me of wedding bells," she replies, thrusting out her hips.

"Shall we remove the growth?" Beinschneider says.

"It's malignant," Van Mesgeluk says. "Of course, we remove it."

He thrusts and parries with a fire and skill that bring cries of admiration and a clapping of hands from the nurses and even cause Beinschneider to groan a bravo, not unmingled with jealousy. Van Mesgeluk then starts to insert the tongs but pulls them back when the first lightning bolt flashes beneath and across the opening in the skull. There is a small but sharp crack and, very faint, the roll of thunder.

"Looks like rain," Beinschneider says. "One of my brothers-in-law is a meteorologist."

"No. It's heat lightning," Van Mesgeluk says.

"With thunder?" says Beinschneider. He eyes the diamond with a lust his wife would give diamonds for. His mouth waters; his scalp turns cold. Who owns the jewel? The patient? He has no rights under this roof. Finders keepers? Eminent domain? Internal Revenue Service?

"It's mathematically improbable, this phenomenon," he says. "What's California law say about mineral rights in a case like this?"

"You can't stake out a claim!" Van Mesgeluk roars. "My God, this is a human being, not a piece of land!"

More lightning cracks whitely across the opening, and there is a rumble as of a bowling ball on its way to a strike.

"I said it wasn't heat lightning," Van Mesgeluk growls.

Beinschneider is speechless.

"No wonder the e.e.g. machine burned up when we were diagnosing him," Van Mesgeluk says. "There must be several thousand volts, maybe a hundred thousand, playing around down there. But I don't detect much warmth. Is the brain a heat sink?"

"You shouldn't have fired that technician because the machine burned up," Beinschneider says. "It wasn't her fault, after all."

"She jumped out of her apartment window the next day," Nurse Lustig says reproachfully. "I wept like a broken faucet at her funeral. And almost got engaged to the undertaker." Lustig rolls her hips.

"Broke every bone in her body, yet there wasn't a single break in her skin," Van Mesgeluk says. "Remarkable phenomenon."

"She was a human being, not a phenomenon!" Beinschneider says.

"But psychotic," Van Mesgeluk replies. "Besides, that's my line. She was thirty-three years old but hadn't had a period in ten years."

"It was that plastic intrauterine device," Beinschneider says. "It was clogged with dust. Which was bad enough, but the dust was radioactive. All those tests..."

"Yes," the chief surgeon says. "Proof enough of her psychosis. I did the autopsy, you know. It broke my heart to cut into that skin. Beautiful. Like Carrara marble. In fact, I snapped the knife at the first pass. Had to call in an expert from Italy. He had a diamond-tipped chisel. The hospital raised hell about the expense, and Blue Cross refused to pay."

"Maybe she was making a diamond," says Nurse Lustig. "All that tension and nervous energy had to go somewhere."

"I always wondered where the radioactivity came from," Van Mesgeluk says. "Please confine your remarks to the business at hand, Miss Lustig. Leave the medical opinions to your superiors."

He peers into the hole. Somewhere between heaven of skull and earth of brain, on the horizon, lightning flickers.

"Maybe we ought to call in a geologist. Beinschneider, you know anything about electronics?"

"I got a brother-in-law who runs a radio and TV store."

"Good. Hook up a step-down transformer to the probe, please. Wouldn't want to burn up another machine."

"An e.e.g. now?" Beinschneider says. "It'd take too long to get a transformer. My brother-in-law lives clear across town. Besides, he'd charge double if he had to reopen the store at this time of the evening."

"Discharge him, anyway," the chief surgeon says. "Ground the voltage. Very well. We'll get that growth out before it kills him and worry about scientific research later."

He puts on two extra pairs of gloves.

"Do you think he'll grow another?" Nurse Lustig says. "He's not a bad-looking guy. I can tell he'd be simpatico."

"How the hell would I know?" says Van Mesgeluk. "I may be a doctor, but I'm not quite God."

"God who?" says Beinschneider, the orthodox atheist. He drops the ground wire into the hole; blue sparks spurt out. Van Mesgeluk lifts out the diamond with the tongs. Nurse Lustig takes it from him and begins to wash it off with tap water.

"Let's call in your brother-in-law," Van Mesgeluk says. "The jewel merchant, I mean."

"He's in Amsterdam. But I could phone him. However, he'd insist on splitting the fee, you know."

"He doesn't even have a degree!" Van Mesgeluk cries. "But call him. How is he on legal aspects of mineralogy?"

"Not bad. But I don't think he'll come. Actually, the jewel business is just a front. He gets his big bread by smuggling in chocolate-covered LSD drops."

"Is that ethical?"

"It's top-quality Dutch chocolate," Beinschneider says stiffly.

"Sorry. I think I'll put in a plastic window over the hole. We can observe any regrowth."

"Do you think it's psychosomatic in origin?"

"Everything is, even the sex urge. Ask Miss Lustig."

The patient opens his eyes. "I had a dream," he says. "This dirty old man with a long white beard..."

"A typical archetype," Van Mesgeluk says. "Symbol of the wisdom of the unconscious. A warning..."

"…his name was Plato," the patient says. "He was the illegitimate son of Socrates. Plato, the old man, staggers out of a dark cave at one end of which is a bright klieg light. He's holding a huge diamond in his hand; his fingernails are broken and dirty. The old man cries, 'The Ideal is Physical! The Universal is the Specific Concrete! Carbon, actually. Eureka! I'm rich! I'll buy all of Athens, invest in apartment buildings, Great Basin, COMSAT!

"'Screw the mind!' the old man screams. 'It's all mine!'"

"Would you care to dream about King Midas?" Van Mesgeluk says.

Nurse Lustig shrieks. A lump of sloppy grayish matter is in her hands.

"The water changed it back into a tumor!"

"Beinschneider, cancel that call to Amsterdam!"

"Maybe he'll have a relapse," Beinschneider says.

Nurse Lustig turns savagely upon the patient. "The engagement's off!"

"I don't think you loved the real me," the patient says, "whoever you are. Anyway, I'm glad you changed your mind. My last wife left me, but we haven't been divorced yet. I got enough trouble without a bigamy charge.

"She took off with my surgeon for parts unknown just after my hemorrhoid operation. I never found out why."

THE JUNGLE ROT KID ON THE NOD
by
William Burroughs

If William Burroughs instead of Edgar Rice Burroughs
had written the Tarzan novels...

Foreword

Tapes cut and respliced at random by Brachiate Bruce, the old mainliner chimp, the Kid's asshole buddy, cool blue in the orgone box from
the speech in Parliament of Lord Greystoke alias The Jungle Rot Kid, a
full house, SRO, the Kid really packing them in.

— Capitalistic pricks! Don't send me no more foreign aid! You cor-
rupting my simple black folks, they driving around the old plantation
way down on the Zambezi River in air-conditioned Cadillacs, shooting horse, flapping ubangi at me...Bwana him not in the cole cole
ground but him sure as shit gonna be soon. Them M-16s, tanks, mor-
tars, flamethrowers coming up the jungle trail, Ole Mao Charley promised us!

Lords, Ladies, Third Sex! I tole you about apeomorphine but you
dont lissen! You got too much invested in the Mafia and General Motors, I say you gotta kick the money habit too. Get them green things
offen your back...nothing to lose but your chains that is stocks, bonds,
castles, Rollses, whores, soft toilet paper, connection with The Man...it
a long long way to the jungle but it worth it, build up your muscle and
character cut/

...you call me here at my own expense to degrade humiliate me
strip me of loincloth and ancient honored title! You hate me cause you
hung up on civilization and I never been hooked. You over a barrel
with smog freeways TV oily beaches taxes inflation frozen dinners time-
clocks carcinogens neckties all that shit. Call me noble savage...me tell
you how it is where its at with my personal tarzanic *purusharta*...
involves kissing off *dharma* and *artha* and getting a fix on *moksha* through
kama...

Old Lord Bromley-Rimmer who wear a merkin on his bald head and got pecker and balls look like dried-up grapes on top a huge hairy cut-in fold-out thing it disgust you to see it, he grip young Lord Materfutter's crotch and say — Dearie what kinda gibberish that, Swahili, what?

Young Lord Materfutter say — Bajove, some kinda African cricket doncha know what?

...them fuckin Ayrabs run off with my Jane again...intersolar communist venusian bankers plot...so it back to the jungle again, hit the arboreal trail, through the middle tearass, dig Numa the lion, the lost civilizations kick, tell my troubles to Sam Tantor alias The Long Dong Kid. Old Sam always writing amendments to the protocols of the elders of mars, dipping his trunk in the blood of innocent bystanders, writing amendments in the sand with blood and no one could read what he had written there selah

Me, I'm only fuckin free man in the world...live in state of anarchy, up trees...every kid and lotsa grown-ups (so-called) dream of the Big Tree Fix, of swinging on vines, freedom, live by the knife and unwritten code of the jungle...

Ole Morphodite Lord Bromley-Rimmer say — Dearie, that Anarchy, that one a them new African nations what?

The Jungle Rot Kid bellowing in the House of Lords like he calling ole Sam Tantor to come running help him outta his mess, he really laying it on them blueblood pricks.

...I got *satyagraha* in the ole original Sanskrit sense of course up the ass, you fat fruits. I quit. So long. Back to the Dark Continent...them sheiks of the desert run off with Jane again...blood will flow...

Fadeout. Lord Materfutter's face phantom of erection wheezing paregoric breath. Dig that leopardskin jockstrap what price glory what? cut/

This here extracted from John Clayton's diary which he write in French God only know why...*Sacre bleu! Nom d'un con!* Alice she dead, who gonna blow me now? The kid screaming his head off, he sure don't look like black-haired gray-eyed fine-chiseled featured scion of noble British family which come over with Willie the Bastard and his squarehead-frog goons on the Anglo-Saxon Lark. No more milk for him no more ass for me, carry me back to old Norfolk / / double cut

The Gorilla Thing fumbling at the lock on the door of old log cabin which John Clayton built hisself. Eyes stabbing through the window. Red as two diamonds in a catamite's ass. John Clayton, he rush out with a big axe, gonna chop me some anthropoid wood.

Big hairy paws strong as hold of pusher on old junkie whirl Clayton around. Stinking breath. Must smoke banana peels. *Whoo! Whoo!* Gorilla Express dingdonging up black tunnel of my rectum. Piles burst like rotten tomatoes, sighing softly. Death come. And come. And come. Blazing bloody orgasms. Not a bad way to go…but you cant touch my inviolate white soul…too late to make a deal with the Gorilla Thing? Give him my title, Jaguar, moated castle, ole faithful family retainer he go down on you, opera box…*ma tante de pisse*…who take care of the baby, carry on family name? *Vive la bourgerie!* cut/

Twenty years later give take a couple, the Jungle Rot Kid trail the killer of Big Ape Mama what snatch him from cradle and raise him as her own with discipline security warm memory of hairy teats hot unpasteurized milk…the Kid swinging big on vines from tree to tree, fastern hot baboonshit through a tin horn. Ant hordes blitzkrieg him like agenbite of intwat, red insect-things which is exteriorized thoughts of the Monster Ant-Mother of the Crab Nebula in secret war to take over this small planet, this Peoria Earth.

Monkey on his back, Nkima, eat the red insect-things, wipe out trillions with flanking bowel movement, Ant-Mother close up galactic shop for the day…

The Kid drop his noose around the black-assed motherkiller and haul him up by the neck into the tree in front of God and local citizens which is called gomangani in ape vernacular.

—You gone too far this time the Kid say as he core out the motherkillers asshole with fathers old hunting knife and bugger him old Turkish custom while the motherkiller rockin and rollin in death agony.

Heavy metal Congo jissom ejaculate catherinewheeling all over local gomangani, they say—Looka that!

Old junkie witch doctor coughing his lungs out in sick gray African morning, shuffling through silver dust of old kraal.

—You say my son's dead, kilt by the Kid?

Jungle drums beat like aged wino's temples morning after.

Get Whitey!

The Kid sometime known as Genocide John really liquidate them dumbshit gomangani. Sure is a shame to waste all that black gash the Kid say but it the code of the jungle. Noblesse obleege.

The locals say—We dont haffa put up with this shit and they split. The Kid dont have no fun nomore and this chimp ass mighty hairy not to mention chimp habit of crapping when having orgasm. Then along come Jane alias Baltimore Blondie, she on the lam from Rudolph

Rassendale type snarling — You marry me Jane else I foreclose on your
father's ass.

The Kid rescue Jane and they make the domestic scene big, go to
Europe on The Civilized Caper but the Kid find out fast that the code
of the jungle conflict with local ordinances. The fuzz say you cant go
around putting a full-nelson on them criminals and breakin their necks
even if they did assault you they got civil rights too. The Kid's picture
hang on post office and police station walls everywhere, he known as
Archetype Archie and by the Paris fuzz as *La Magnifique Merde* — 50,000
francs dead or alive. With the heat moving in, the Kid and Baltimore
Blondie cut out for the tree house.

Along come La sometime known as Sacrifice Sal elsewhere as Dis-
embowelment Daisy. She queen of Opar, ruler of hairy little men-things
of the hidden colony of ancient Atlantis, the Kid always dig the lost
cities kick. So the Kid split with Jane for awhile to ball La.

— Along come them fuckin Ayrabs again and abduct Jane,
gangbang her...she aint been worth a shit since...cost me all the jewels
and golden ingots I heisted offa Opar to get rid of her clap, syph, yaws,
crabs, pyorrhea, double-barreled dysentery, busted rectum, split ure-
thra, torn nostrils, pierced eardrums, bruised kidneys, nymphomania,
old hashish habit, and things too disgusting to mention...

Along come The Rumble To End All Rumbles 1914 style, and them
fuckin Huns abduct Jane...they got preying-mantis eyes with insect
lust. Black anti-orgone Horbigerian Weltanschauung, they take orders
from green venusians who telepath through von Hindenburg.

— *Ja Wohl!* bark Leutnant Herrlipp von Dreckfinger at his Kolonel,
Bombastus von Arschangst. Ve use die Baltimore snatch to trap der
gottverdammerungt Jungle Rot Kid, dot pseudu-Aryan *Oberaffen-
mensch*, unt ve kill him unt den all Afrika iss ours! Drei cheers for Der
Kaiser unt die Krupp Familie!

The Kid balling La again but he drop her like old junkie drop pants
for a shot of horse, he track down the Hun, it the code of the jungle.

Cool blue orgone bubbles sift down from evening sky, the sinking
sun a bloody kotex which spread stinking scarlet gashworms over the
big dungball of Earth. Night move in like fuzz with Black Maria. Mysterious sounds of tropical wilds...Numa roar, wild boars grunt like
they constipated, parrots with sick pukegreen feathers and yellow eyes
like old goofball bum Panama 1910 cry *Rache!*

Hun blood flow, kraut necks crack like cinnamon sticks, the Kid
put his foot on dead ass of slain Teuton and give the victory cry of the
bull ape, it even scare the shit outta Numa King of the Beasts fadeout

The Kid and his mate live in the old tree house now…surohc lakcaj fo mhtyhr ot ffo kcaj* chimps, Numa roar, Sheeta the panther cough like an old junkie. Jane alias The Baltimore Bitch nag, squawk, whine about them mosquitoes tsetse flies ant-things hyenas and them uppity gomangani moved into the neighborhood, they'll turn a decent jungle into slums in three days, I aint prejudiced ya unnerstand some a my best friends are Waziris, whynt ya ever take me out to dinner, Nairobi only a thousand miles away, they really swingin there for chrissakes and cut/

…trees chopped down for the saw mills, animals kilt off, rivers stiff stinking with dugout-sized tapewormy turds, broken gin bottles, contraceptive jelly and all them disgusting things snatches use, detergents, cigarette filters…and the great apes shipped off to USA zoos, they send telegram: SOUTHERN CALIFORNIA CLIMATE AND WELFARE PROGRAM SIMPLY FABULOUS STOP NO TROUBLE GETTING A FIX STOP CLOSE TO TIAJUANA STOP WHAT PRICE FREEDOM INDIVIDUALITY EXISTENTIAL PHILOSOPHY CRAP STOP

…Opar a tourist trap, La running the native-art made-in-Japan concession and you cant turn around without rubbing sparks off black asses.

The African drag really got the Kid down now…Jane's voice and the jungle noises glimmering off like a comet leaving Earth forever for the cold interstellar abysms…

The Kid never move a muscle staring at his big toe, thinking of nothing — wouldn't you? — not even La's diamond-studded snatch, he off the woman kick, off the everything kick, fulla horse, on the nod, lower spine ten degrees below absolute zero like he got a direct connection with The Liquid Hydrogen Man at Cape Kennedy…

The Kid ride with a one-way ticket on the Hegelian Express thesis antithesis synthesis, sucking in them cool blue orgone bubbles and sucking off the Eternal Absolute…

*Old Brachiate Bruce splice in tape backward here.

The president of the U.S.A. sat at the desk of the mayor of Upper Metropolitan Los Angeles, Level 1. There was no question of where the mayor was to sit. Before the office of mayor could be filled, the electorate had to move into the city.

The huge room was filled with U.S. cabinet heads and bureau chiefs, senators, state governors, industrial and educational magnates, union presidents, and several state GIP presidents. Most of them were watching the TV screens covering one part of the curving wall.

Nobody looked through the big window behind the President, even though this gave a view of half of the city. Outside the municipal building, the sky was blue with a few fleecy clouds. The midsummer sun was just past the zenith, yet the breeze was cool; it was 73°F everywhere in the city. Of the 200,000 visitors, at least one-third were collected around tourguides. Most of the hand-carried football-sized TV cameras of the reporters were focused at that moment on one man.

Government spieler: "Ladies 'n gentlemen, you've been personally conducted through most of this city and you now know almost as much as if you'd stayed home and watched it on TV. You've seen everything but the interior of the houses, the inside of your future homes. You've been amazed at what Uncle Sam, and the state of California, built here, a Utopia, an Emerald City of Oz, with you as the Wizard..."

Heckler (a large black woman with an M.A. in Elementary School Electronic Transference): "The houses look more like the eggs that Dorothy used to frighten the Nome King with!"

Spieler (managing to glare and smile at the same time): "Lady, you've been shooting your mouth off so much, you must be an agent for the Anti-Bodies! You didn't take the pauper's oath; you took the peeper's oath!"

Heckler (bridling): "I'll sue you for defamation of character and public ridicule!"

Spieler (running his gaze up and down her whale-like figure): "Sue, sue, sooie! No wonder you're so sensitive about eggs, lady. There's something ovoid about you!"

The crowd laughed. The President snorted disgustedly and spoke into a disc strapped to his wrist. A man in the crowd, the message relayed through his ear plug, spoke into his wrist transmitter, but the spieler gestured as if to say, "This is my show! Jump in the lake if you don't like it!"

Spieler: "You've seen the artificial lake in the center of the city with the municipal and other buildings around it. The Folk Art Center, the Folk Recreation Center, the hospital, university, research center, and the PANDORA, the people's all-necessities depot of regulated abundance. You've been delighted and amazed with the fairyland of goodies that Uncle Sam, and the State of California, offers you free. Necessities and luxuries, too, since *Luxury Is A Necessity*, to quote the FBC. You want anything — anything! — you go to the PANDORA, press some buttons, and presto! you're rich beyond your dreams!"

Heckler: "When the lid to Pandora's box was opened, all the evils in the world flew out, and..."

Spieler: "No interruptions, lady! We're on a strict time schedule..."

Heckler: "Why? We're not going anyplace!"

Spieler: "I'll tell you where you can go, lady."

Heckler: "But..."

Spieler: "But me no buts, lady! You know, you ought to go on a diet!"

Heckler (struggling to control her temper): "Don't get personal, big mouth! I'm big, all right, and I got a wallop, too, remember that. Now, Pandora's box..."

The spieler made a vulgar remark, at which the crowd laughed. The heckler shouted but could not be heard above the noise.

The President shifted uneasily. Kingbrook, the 82-year-old senator from New York, harumphed and said, "The things they permit nowadays in public media. Really, it's disgusting..."

Some of the screens on the wall of the mayor's office showed various parts of the interior of the city. One screen displayed a view from a helicopter flying on the oceanside exterior of Upper Metropolitan LA. It was far enough away to get the entire structure in its camera, including the hundred self-adjusting cylinders that supported the Brobdingnagian plastic cube and the telescoping elevator shafts dangling from the central underbase. Beneath the shadow of box and legs was the central section of the old city and the jagged sprawl of the rest of Los Angeles and surrounding cities.

The President stabbed towards the screen with a cigarette and said, "Screen 24, gentlemen. The dark past below. The misery of a disrupted ant colony. Above it, the bright complex of the future. The chance for everyone to realize the full potentiality as a human being."

Spieler: "Before I conduct you into this house, which is internally just like every other private residence..."

Heckler: "Infernally, you mean. They all look just alike on the outside, too."

Spieler: "Lady, you're arousing my righteous wrath. Now, folks, you noticed that all the buildings, municipal and private, are constructed like eggs. This futuristic design was adopted because the egg shape, according to the latest theory, is that of the universe. No corners, all curving, infinity within a confined space, if you follow me."

Heckler: "I don't!"

Spieler: "Take off a little weight, lady, and you'll be in shape to keep up with the rest of us. The ovoid form gives you a feeling of unbounded space yet of security-closeness. When you get inside..."

Every house was a great smooth white plastic egg lifted 18.28 meters above the floor of the city by a thick truncated-cone support. (Offscreen commentators explained that 18.18 meters was 60 feet, for the benefit of older viewers who could not adjust to the new system of measurement.) On two sides of the cone were stairs ending at a horizontal door on the lower side of the ovoid. These opened automatically to permit entrance. Also, a door opened in the cone base, and an elevator inside lifted the sick or crippled or, as the spieler put it, "the just plain lazy, everybody's got a guaranteed right to be lazy." The hollow base also housed several electrical carts for transportation around the city.

The President saw Kierson, the Detroit automobile magnate, frown at the carts. The auto industry had shifted entirely from internal combustion motors to electrical and nuclear power ten years ago, and now Kierson saw the doom of these. The President made a mental note to pacify and reassure him on this point later.

Spieler: "...*Variety Within Unity*, folks. You've heard a lot about that on FBC, and these houses are an example. In reply to the lady's anxiety about the houses all looking alike, every home owner can paint the outside of his house to express his individuality. Anything goes. From reproductions of Rembrandt to psychedelic dreams to dirty words, if you got the guts. Everything's free, including speech..."

Heckler: "They'll look like a bunch of Easter eggs!"

Spieler: "Lady, Uncle Sam *is* The Big Easter Bunny!"

The spieler took the group into the house, and the cameramen went into the atrium, kitchen, and the ten rooms to show the viewers just what the citizens-to-be were getting for nothing.

"For nothing!" Senator Kingbrook growled. "The taxpayers are paying through the nose, through every orifice, with their sweat and blood for this!"

The President said, mildly, "They won't have to in the future, as I'll explain."

"You don't have to explain anything to any of us," Kingbrook said. "We all know all about the economy of abundance versus the economy of scarcity. And about your plans for the transitional stage, which you call ORE, *obverse-reverse* economy, but which I call *schizophrenic horrors in tremens!*"

The President smiled and said, "You'll have your say, Senator."

The men and women in the room were silent for a while as they watched the spieler extol the splendors and virtues of the house with its soundproof walls, the atrium with its pool, the workshop with machinery for crafts, the storeroom, the bedroom-studios, TV in every room, retractable and inflatable furniture, air-conditioning, microfilm library, and so on.

Government shill: "This is fabulous! A hell of a lot better than any noisy rat-ridden dump on the ground!"

Spieler (quoting an FBC slogan): "*Happy and free as the birds in the air!* That's why everybody calls this Bird City and why the citizens are known as freebirds! Everything first class! Everything free!"

Heckler: "Except freedom to live where you want to in the type of house you want!"

Spieler: "Lady, unless you're a millionaire, you won't be able to get a house on the ground that isn't just like every other house. And then you'd have to worry about it being burned down. Lady, you'd gripe if you was hung with a new rope!"

The group went outside where the spieler pointed out that, though they were three hectometers above ground, they had trees and grass in small parks. If they wanted to fish or boat, they could use the lake in the municipal-building area.

Shill: "Man, this is living!"

Spieler: "The dome above the city looks just like the sky outside. The sun is an electronic reproduction; its progress exactly coincides with that of the real sun. Only, you don't have to worry about it getting too cold or too hot in here or about it raining. We even got birds in here."

Heckler: "What about the robins? Come springtime, how're they going to get inside without a pass?"

Spieler: "Lady, you got a big mouth! Whyn't you..."

The President rose from his chair. Kingbrook's face was wrinkled, fissured, and folded with old age. The red of his anger made his features look like hot lava on a volcano slope just after an eruption. His rich rumble pushed against the eardrums of those in the room as if they were in a pressure chamber.

"A brave new concentration camp, gentlemen! Fifty billion dollars worth to house 50,000 people! The great bankruptopolis of the future! I estimate it'll cost one trillion dollars just to enclose this state's population in these glorified chicken runs!"

"Not if ORE is put into effect," the President said. He held up his hand to indicate silence and said, "I'd like to hear Guildman, gentlemen. Then we can have our conferences."

Senator Beaucamp of Mississippi muttered, "One trillion dollars! That would house, feed, and educate the entire population of my state for twenty years!"

The President signalled to cut off all screens except the FBC channel. The private network commentators were also speaking, but the federal commentator was the important one. His pitch was being imitated — if reluctantly — by the private networks. Enough pressure and threats had been applied to make them wary of going all-out against the President. Although the mass media had been restrained, the speech of private persons had not been repressed. For one thing, the public needed a safety valve. Occasionally, a private speaker was given a chance to express himself on TV and radio. And so, a cavalry charge of invective had been and was being hurled at the President. He had been denounced as an ultra-reactionary, a degenerate liberal, a Communist, a Fascist, a vulture, a pig, a Puritan, a pervert, a Hitler, etc., and had been hung in absentia so many times that an enterprising manufacturer of effigies had made a small fortune — though taxes made it even smaller.

From cavalry to Calvary, he thought. All charges admitted. All charges denied. I am human, and that takes in everything. Even the accusation of fanaticism. I know that what I'm doing is right, or, at least, the only known way. When the Four Horsemen ride, the countercharge cannot be led by a self-doubter.

The voice of the Great Guildman, as he was pleased to be called, throbbed through the room. Chief FBC commentator, bureau executive, Ph.D. in Mass Communications, G-90 rating, one who spoke with authority, whose personal voltage was turned full-on, who could, some said, have talked God into keeping Adam and Eve in the garden.

"...cries out! The people, the suffering earth itself, cry out! The air is poisoned! The water is poisoned! The soil is poisoned! Mankind is poisoned with the excess of his genius for survival! The wide walls of the Earth have become narrowed! Man, swelling like a tumor with uncontrolled growth, kills the body that gave him birth! He is squeezing himself into an insane mold which crushes his life out, crushes all hope for an abundant life, security, peace, quiet, fulfillment, dignity…"

The audience, tuning in on forty channels, was well aware of this; he was painting a picture the oils of which had been squeezed from their own pain. And so Guildman did not tarry overlong at these points. He spoke briefly of the dying economy of scarcity, obsolete in the middle 1900's but seeming vigorous, like a sick man with a fatal disease who keeps going on larger and larger shots of drugs and on placebos. Then he splashed bright colors over the canvas of the future.

Guildman went on about the population expansion, automation, the ever-growing permanently depressed class and its riots and insurrections, the ever-decreasing and ever-overburdened taxpayers with their strikes and riots, the Beverly Hills Massacre, the misery, crime, anger, etc.

The President repressed an impulse to squirm. There would be plenty of blacks and grays in The Golden World (the President's own catch-phrase). Utopia could never exist. The structure of human society, in every respect, had a built-in instability, which meant that there would always be a certain amount of suffering and maladjustment. There were always victims of change.

But that could not be helped. And it was a good thing that change was the unchanging characteristic of society. Otherwise, stagnation, rigidity, and loss of hope for improvement would result.

Beaucamp leaned close to the President and said softly, "Plenty of people have pointed out that the economy of abundance eventually means the death of capitalism. You've never commented on this, but you can't keep silent much longer."

"When I do speak," the President said, "I'll point out that EOA also means the death of socialism and communism. Besides, there's nothing sacred in an economic system, except to those who confuse money with religion. Systems are made for man, not vice versa."

Kingbrook rose from his sofa, his bones cracking, and walked stiffly towards the President.

"You've rammed through this project despite the opposition of the majority of taxpayers! You used methods that were not only unconstitutional, sir! I know for a fact that criminal tactics were used, blackmail and intimidation, sir! But you will go no more on your Caesar's road! This project has beggared our once wealthy nation, and we are not going to build any more of your follies! Your grandiose—and wicked — Golden World will be as tarnished as brass, as green as fool's gold, by the time that I am through with you! Don't underestimate me and my colleagues, sir!"

"I know of your plans to impeach me," the President said with a slight smile. "Now, Senators Beaucamp and Kingbrook, and you, Governor Corrigan, would you step into the mayor's apartment? I'd like to have a few words — I hope they're few — with you."

Kingbrook, breathing heavily, said, "My mind is made up, Mr. President. I know what's wrong and what's right for our country. If you have any veiled threats or insidious proposals, make them in public, sir! In this room, before these gentlemen!"

The President looked at the embarrassed faces, the stony, the hostile, the gleeful, and then glanced at his wristwatch. He said, "I only ask five minutes."

He continued, "I'm not slighting any of you. I intend to talk to all of you in groups selected because of relevant subjects. Three to five minutes apiece will let us complete our business before the post-dedication speeches. Gentlemen!" And he turned and strode through the door.

A few seconds passed, and then the three, stiff-faced, stiffbacked walked in.

"Sit down or stand as you please," the President said.

There was a silence. Kingbrook lit a cigar and took a chair. Corrigan hesitated and then sat near Kingbrook. Beaucamp remained standing. The President stood before them.

He said, "You've seen the people who toured this city. They're the prospective citizens. What is their outstanding common characteristic?"

Kingbrook snorted and said something under his breath. Beaucamp glared at him and said, "I didn't hear your words, but I know what you said! Mr. President, I intend to speak loudly and clearly about this arrogant discrimination! I had one of my men run the list of accepted citizens through a computer, and he reports that the citizens will be 100 percent Negro! And 7/8ths are welfares!"

"The other eighth are doctors, technicians, teachers, and other professionals," the President said. "All volunteers. There, by the way, goes the argument that no one will work if he doesn't have to. These people will be living in this city and getting no money for their labor. We had to turn down many volunteers because there was no need for them."

"Especially since the government has been using public funds to brainwash us with the Great-Love-and-Service-for-Humanity campaign for twenty years," Kingbrook said.

"I never heard you making any speeches knocking love or service," the President said. "However, there is another motive which caused so many to offer their services. Money may die out, but the desire for prestige won't. The wish for prestige is at least as old as mankind itself and maybe older."

"I can't believe that no whites asked to live here," Beaucamp said.

"The rule was, first apply, first accepted," the President said. "The whole procedure was computer-run, and the application blanks contained no reference to race."

Corrigan said, "You know that computers have been gimmicked or their operators bribed."

The President said, "I am sure that an investigation would uncover nothing crooked."

"The gyps," Corrigan said, then stopped at Beaucamp's glare. "I mean, the guaranteed income people, or welfares as we called them when I was a kid, well, the GIP whites will be screaming discrimination."

"The whites could have volunteered," the President said.

Beaucamp's lip was curled. "Somebody spread the word. Of course, that would have nothing to do with lack of Caucasian applications."

Kingbrook rumbled like a volcano preparing to erupt. He said, "What're we arguing about this for? This...Bird City...was built over an all-colored section. So why shouldn't its citizens be colored? Let's stick to the point. You want to build more cities just like this, Mr. President, extend them outwards from this until you have one solid megalopolis on stilts extending from Santa Barbara to Long Beach. But you can't build here or in other states without absolutely bankrupting the country. So you want to get us to back your legislative proposals for your so-called ORE. That is, split the economy of the nation in half. One half will continue operating just as before; that half will be made up of private-enterprise industries and of the taxpayers who own or work for these industries. This half will continue to buy and sell and use money as it has always done.

"But the other half will be composed of GIP's, living in cities like this, and the government will take care of their every need. The government will do this by automating the mines, farms, and industries it now owns or plans on obtaining. It will not use money anywhere in its operations, and the entire process of input-output will be a closed circuit. Everybody in ORE will be GIP personnel, even the federal and state government service, except, of course, that the federal, legislative, and executive branches will maintain their proper jurisdiction."

"That *sounds* great," Corrigan said. "The ultimate result, or so you've *said*, Mr. President, is to relieve the taxpayer of his crushing burden and to give the GIP a position in society in which he will no longer be considered by others as a parasite. It sounds appealing. But there are many of us who aren't fooled by your fine talk."

"I'm not trying to fool anybody," the President said.

Corrigan said, angrily, "It's obvious what the end result will be! When the taxpayer sees the GIP living like a king without turning a hand while he has to work his tail off, he's going to want the same deal. And those who refuse to give up won't have enough money to back their stand because the GIP won't be spending any money. The small businessmen who live off their sales to the GIP will go under. And the larger businesses will, too. Eventually, the businessman and his employees will fold their fiscal and pecuniary tents and go to live in your everything-free cornucopias!

"So, if we're seduced by your beautiful scheme for a half-and-half economy, we'll take the first step into the quicksand. After that, it'll be too late to back out. Down we go!"

"I'd say, *Up we go,*" the President said. "So! It's All-or-None, as far as you're concerned? And you vote for None! Well, gentlemen, over one-half of the nation is saying All because that's the only way to go and they've nothing to lose and everything to gain. If you kill the switchover legislation in Congress, I'll see that the issues are submitted to the people for their yea or nay. But that would take too much time, and time is vital. Time is what I'm buying. Or I should say, trading."

Beaucamp said, "Mister President, you didn't point out the racial composition of the city just to pass the time."

The President began pacing back and forth before them. He said, "The civil rights revolution was born about the same time that you and I, Mr. Beaucamp, were born. Yet, it's still far from achieving its goals. In some aspects, it's regressed. It was tragic that the Negroes began to get the education and political power they needed for advancement just as automation began to bloom. The Negro found that there were only jobs for the professionals and the skilled. The unskilled were shut out. This happened to the untrained white, too, and competition for work between the unskilled white and black became bitter. Bloodily bitter, as the past few years have shown us."

"We know what's been going on, Mr. President," Beaucamp said.

"Yes. Well, it's true isn't it, that the black as a rule, doesn't particularly care to associate or live with the whites? He just wants the same things whites have. But at the present rate of progress, it'll take a hundred years or more before he gets them. In fact, he may never do so if the present economy continues."

Kingbrook rumbled, "The point, Mr. President!"

The President stopped pacing. He looked hard at them and said, "But in an economy of abundance, in this type of city, he—the Negro—will have everything the whites have. He will have a high standard of living, a true democracy, color-free justice. He'll have his own judges, police, legislators. If he doesn't care to, he doesn't ever have to have any personal contact with whites."

Kingbrook's cigar sagged. Beaucamp sucked in his breath. Corrigan jumped up from his chair.

Beaucamp said, "That's ghettoism!"

"Not in the original sense," the President said. "The truth now, Mr. Beaucamp. Don't your people prefer to live with their own kind? Where they'll be free of that shadow, that wall, always between white and colored in this country?"

Beaucamp said, "Not to have to put up with honkeys! Excuse the expression, sir. It slipped out. You know we would! But..."

"No one will be forbidden to live in any community he chooses. There won't be any discrimination on the federal level. Those in the government, military, or Nature rehabilitation service will have equal opportunity. But, given the choice..."

The President turned to Kingbrook and Corrigan. "Publicly, you two have always stood for integration. You would have committed political suicide, otherwise. But I know your private opinions. You have also been strong states-righters. No secret about that. So, when the economy of abundance is in full swing, the states will become self-sufficient. They won't depend on federal funds."

"Because there'll be no dependence on money?" Corrigan said. "Because there'll be no money? Because money will be as extinct as the dodo?"

The ridges on Kingbrook's face shifted as if they were the gray backs of an elephant herd milling around to catch a strange scent. He said, "I'm not blasphemous. But now I think I know how Christ felt when tempted by Satan."

He stopped, realizing that he had made a Freudian slip.

"And you're not Christ and I'm not Satan," he said hurriedly. "We're just human beings trying to find a mutually agreeable way out of this mess."

Beaucamp said, "We're horse traders. And the horse is the future. A dream. Or a nightmare."

The President looked at his watch and said, "What about it, Mr. Beaucamp?"

"What can I trade? A dream of an end to contempt, dislike, hatred, treachery, oppression. A dream of the shadow gone, the wall down. Now you offer me abundance, dignity, and joy — if my people stay within the plastic walls."

"I don't know what will develop after the walls of the cities have been built," the President said. "But there is nothing evil about self-segregation, if it's not compulsive. It's done all the time by human beings of every type. If it weren't, you wouldn't have social classes, clubs, etc. And if, after our citizens are given the best in housing and food, luxuries, a free lifelong education, a wide spectrum of recreations, everything within reason, if they still go to Hell, then we might as well give up on the species."

"A man needs incentive; he needs work. By the sweat of his brow..." Kingbrook said.

Kingbrook was too old, the President thought. He was half stone, and the stone thought stone thoughts and spoke stone words. The President looked out the big window. Perhaps it had been a mistake to build such a "futuristic" city. It would be difficult enough for the new citizens to adjust. Perhaps the dome of Bird City should have contained buildings resembling those they now lived in. Later, more radical structures could have been introduced.

As it was, the ovoid shape was supposed to give a sense of security, a feeling of return-to-the-womb and also to suggest a rebirth. Just now, they looked like so many space capsules ready to take off into the blue the moment the button was pressed.

But this city, and those that would be added to it, meant a sharp break with the past, and any break always caused some pain.

He turned when someone coughed behind him. Senator Kingbrook was standing, his hand on his chest. The senator was going to make a speech.

The President looked at his watch and shook his head. Kingbrook smiled as if the smile hurt him, and he dropped his hand.

"It's yes, Mr. President. I'll back you all the way. And the impeachment proceedings will be dropped, of course. But..."

"I don't want to be rude," the President said. "But you can save your justifications for your constituents."

Beaucamp said, "I say yes. Only..."

"No ifs, ands, or buts."

"No. Only..."

"And you, Governor Corrigan?" the President said.

Corrigan said, "All of us are going along with you for reasons that shouldn't be considered — from the viewpoint of ideals. But then, who really ever has? I say yes. But..."

"No speeches, please," the President said. He smiled slightly. "Unless I make them. Your motives don't really matter, gentlemen, as long as your decisions are for the good of the American public. Which they are. And for the good of the world, too, because all other nations are going to follow our example. As I said, this means the death of capitalism, but it also means the death of socialism and communism, too."

He looked at his watch again. "I thank you, gentlemen."

They looked as if they would like to continue talking, but they left. There was a delay of a few seconds before the next group entered.

He felt weary, even though he knew that he would win out. The years ahead would be times of trouble, of crises, of pain and agony, of successes and failures. At least, mankind would no longer be drifting towards anarchy. Man would be deliberately shaping — reshaping — his society, turning topsy-turvy an ancient and obsolete economy, good enough in its time but no longer applicable. At the same time, he would be tearing down the old cities and restoring Nature to something of its pristine condition, healing savage wounds inflicted by senseless selfish men in the past, cleansing the air, the poisoned rivers and lakes, growing new forests, permitting the wild creatures to flourish in their redeemed land. Man, the greedy savage child, had stripped the earth, killed the wild, fouled his own nest.

His anger, he suddenly realized, had been to divert him from that other feeling. Somehow, he had betrayed an ideal. He could not define the betrayal, because he knew that he was doing what had to be done and that that way was the only way. But he, and Kingbrook, Corrigan, and Beaucamp, had also felt this. He had seen it on their faces, like ectoplasm escaping the grasp of their minds.

A man had to be realistic. To gain one thing, you had to give up another. Life — the universe — was give and take, input and output, energy surrendered to conquer energy.

In short, politics. Compromises.

The door slid into the recess in the walls. Five men single-filed in. The President weighed each in the balance, anticipating his arguments and visualizing the bait which he would grab even if he saw the hook.

He said, "Gentlemen, be seated if you wish."

He looked at his watch and began to talk.

♦ ♦ ♦ The Sliced-Crosswise Only-on-Tuesday World

Getting into Wednesday was almost impossible.

Tom Pym had thought about living on other days of the week. Almost everybody with any imagination did. There were even TV shows speculating on this. Tom Pym had even acted in two of these. But he had no genuine desire to move out of his own world. Then his house burned down.

This was on the last day of the eight days of spring. He awoke to look out the door at the ashes and the firemen. A man in a white asbestos suit motioned for him to stay inside. After fifteen minutes, another man in a suit gestured that it was safe. He pressed the button by the door, and it swung open. He sank down in the ashes to his ankles; they were a trifle warm under the inch-thick coat of water-soaked crust.

There was no need to ask what had happened, but he did, anyway.

The fireman said, "A short-circuit, I suppose. Actually, we don't know. It started shortly after midnight, between the time that Monday quit and we took over."

Tom Pym thought that it must be strange to be a fireman or a policeman. Their hours were so different, even though they were still limited by the walls of midnight.

By then the others were stepping out of their stoners or "coffins" as they were often called. That left sixty still occupied.

They were due for work at 08:00. The problem of getting new clothes and a place to live would have to be put off until off-hours, because the TV studio where they worked was behind in the big special it was due to put on in 144 days.

They ate breakfast at an emergency center. Tom Pym asked a grip if he knew of any place he could stay. Though the government would find one for him, it might not look very hard for a convenient place.

The grip told him about a house only six blocks from his former house. A makeup man had died, and as far as he knew the vacancy had not been filled. Tom got onto the phone at once, since he wasn't needed at that moment, but the office wouldn't be open until ten, as the recording informed him. The recording was a very pretty girl with red hair, tourmaline eyes, and a very sexy voice. Tom would have been more impressed if he had not known her. She had played in some small parts in two of his shows, and the maddening voice was not hers. Neither was the color of her eyes.

At noon he called again, got through after a ten-minute wait, and asked Mrs. Bellefield if she would put through a request for him. Mrs. Bellefield reprimanded him for not having phoned sooner; she was not sure that anything could be done today. He tried to tell her his circumstances and then gave up. Bureaucrats! That evening he went to a public emergency place, slept for the required four hours while the inductive field speeded up his dreaming, woke up, and got into the upright cylinder of eternium. He stood for ten seconds, gazing out through the transparent door at other cylinders with their still figures, and then he pressed the button. Approximately fifteen seconds later he became unconscious.

He had to spend three more nights in the public stoner. Three days of fall were gone; only five left. Not that that mattered in California so much. When he had lived in Chicago, winter was like a white blanket being shaken by a madwoman. Spring was a green explosion. Summer was a bright roar and a hot breath. Fall was the topple of a drunken jester in garish motley.

The fourth day, he received notice that he could move into the very house he had picked. This surprised and pleased him. He knew of a dozen who had spent a whole year — forty-eight days or so — in a public station while waiting. He moved in the fifth day with three days of spring to enjoy. But he would have to use up his two days off to shop for clothes, bring in groceries and other goods, and get acquainted with his housemates. Sometimes, he wished he had not been born with the compulsion to act. TV'ers worked five days at a stretch, sometimes six, while a plumber, for instance, only put in three days out of seven.

The house was as large as the other, and the six extra blocks to walk would be good for him. It held eight people per day, counting himself. He moved in that evening, introduced himself, and got Mabel Curta, who worked as a secretary for a producer, to fill him in on the household routine. After he made sure that his stoner had been moved into the stoner room, he could relax somewhat.

Mabel Curta had accompanied him into the stoner room, since she had appointed herself his guide. She was a short, overly curved woman of about thirty-five (Tuesday time). She had been divorced three times, and marriage was no more for her unless, of course, Mr. Right came along. Tom was between marriages himself, but he did not tell her so.

"We'll take a look at your bedroom," Mabel said. "It's small but it's soundproofed, thank God."

He started after her, then stopped. She looked back through the doorway and said, "What is it?"

"This girl..."

There were sixty-three of the tall gray eternium cylinders. He was looking through the door of the nearest at the girl within.

"Wow! Really beautiful!"

If Mabel felt any jealousy, she suppressed it.

"Yes, isn't she!"

The girl had long, black, slightly curly hair, a face that could have launched him a thousand times times a thousand times, a figure that had enough but not too much, and long legs. Her eyes were open; in the dim light they looked a purplish-blue. She wore a thin silvery dress.

The plate by the top of the door gave her vital data. Jennie Marlowe. Born 2031 A.D., San Marino, California. She would be twenty-four years old. Actress. Unmarried. Wednesday's child.

"What's the matter?" Mabel said.

"Nothing."

How could he tell her that he felt sick in his stomach from a desire that could never be satisfied? Sick from beauty?

For will in us is over-ruled by fate.
Who ever loved, that loved not at first sight?

"What?" Mabel said, and then, after laughing, "You must be kidding?"

She wasn't angry. She realized that Jennie Marlowe was no more competition than if she were dead. She was right. Better for him to busy himself with the living of this world. Mabel wasn't too bad, cuddly, really, and, after a few drinks, rather stimulating.

They went downstairs afterward after 18:00 to the TV room. Most of the others were there, too. Some had their ear plugs in; some were looking at the screen but talking. The newscast was on, of course. Everybody was filling up on what had happened last Tuesday and today. The Speaker of the House was retiring after his term was up. His days of usefulness were over and his recent ill health showed no signs of disappearing. There was a shot of the family graveyard in Mississippi with the pedestal reserved for him. When science someday learned how to rejuvenate, he would come out of stonerment.

"That'll be the day!" Mabel said. She squirmed on his lap.

"Oh, I think they'll crack it," he said. "They're already on the track; they've succeeded in stopping the aging of rabbits."

"I don't mean that," she said. "Sure, they'll find out how to rejuvenate people. But then what? You think they're going to bring them all back? With all the people they got now and then they'll double, maybe triple, maybe quadruple, the population? You think they won't just leave them standing there?" She giggled, and said, "What would the pigeons do without them?"

He squeezed her waist. At the same time, he had a vision of himself squeezing *that* girl's waist. Hers would be soft enough but with no hint of fat.

Forget about her. Think of now. Watch the news.

A Mrs. Wilder had stabbed her husband and then herself with a kitchen knife. Both had been stoned immediately after the police arrived, and they had been taken to the hospital. An investigation of a work slowdown in the county government offices was taking place. The complaints were that Monday's people were not setting up the computers for Tuesday's. The case was being referred to the proper authorities of both days. The Ganymede base reported that the Great Red Spot of Jupiter was emitting weak but definite pulses that did not seem to be random.

The last five minutes of the program was a precis devoted to outstanding events of the other days. Mrs. Cuthmar, the housemother, turned the channel to a situation comedy with no protests from anybody.

Tom left the room, after telling Mabel that he was going to bed early — alone, and to sleep. He had a hard day tomorrow.

He tiptoed down the hall and the stairs and into the stoner room. The lights were soft, there were many shadows, and it was quiet. The sixty-three cylinders were like ancient granite columns of an underground chamber of a buried city. Fifty-five faces were white blurs behind the clear metal. Some had their eyes open; most had closed them while waiting for the field radiated from the machine in the base. He looked through Jennie Marlowe's door. He felt sick again. Out of his reach; never for him. Wednesday was only a day away. No, it was only a little less than four and a half hours away.

He touched the door. It was slick and only a little cold. She stared at him. Her right forearm was bent to hold the strap of a large purse. When the door opened, she would step out, ready to go. Some people took their showers and fixed their faces as soon as they got up from their sleep and then went directly into the stoner. When the field was automatically radiated at 05:00, they stepped out a minute later, ready for the day.

He would like to step out of his "coffin," too, at the same time.

But he was barred by Wednesday.

He turned away. He was acting like a sixteen-year-old kid. He had been sixteen about one hundred and six years ago, not that that made any difference. Physiologically, he was thirty.

As he started up to the second floor, he almost turned around and went back for another look. But he took himself by his neckcollar and pulled himself up to his room. There he decided he would get to sleep at once. Perhaps he would dream about her. If dreams were wish-fulfillments, they would bring her to him. It still had not been "proved" that dreams always expressed wishes, but it had been proved that man deprived of dreaming did go mad. And so the somniums radiated a field that put man into a state in which he got all the sleep, and all the dreams, that he needed within a four-hour period. Then he was awakened and a little later went into the stoner where the field suspended all atomic and subatomic activity. He would remain in that state forever unless the activating field came on.

He slept, and Jennie Marlowe did not come to him. Or, if she did, he did not remember. He awoke, washed his face, went down eagerly to the stoner, where he found the entire household standing around, getting in one last smoke, talking, laughing. Then they would step into their cylinders, and a silence like that at the heart of a mountain would fall.

He had often wondered what would happen if he did not go into the stoner. How would he feel? Would he be panicked? All his life, he had known only Tuesdays. Would Wednesday rush at him, roaring, like a tidal wave? Pick him up and hurl him against the reefs of a strange time?

What if he made some excuse and went back upstairs and did not go back down until the field had come on? By then, he could not enter. The door to his cylinder would not open again until the proper time. He could still run down to the public emergency stoners only three blocks away. But if he stayed in his room, waiting for Wednesday?

Such things happened. If the breaker of the law did not have a reasonable excuse, he was put on trial. It was a felony second only to murder to "break time," and the unexcused were stoned. All felons; sane or insane, were stoned. Or *mañanaed*, as some said. The *mañanaed* criminal waited in immobility and unconsciousness, preserved unharmed until science had techniques to cure the insane, the neurotic, the criminal, the sick. *Mañana*.

"What was it like in Wednesday?" Tom had asked a man who had been unavoidably left behind because of an accident.

"How would I know? I was knocked out except for about fifteen minutes. I was in the same city, and I had never seen the faces of the ambulance men, of course, but then I've never seen them here. They stonered me and left me in the hospital for Tuesday to take care of."

He must have it bad, he thought. Bad. Even to think of such a thing was crazy. Getting into Wednesday was almost impossible. Almost. But it could be done. It would take time and patience, but it could be done.

He stood in front of his stoner for a moment. The others said, "See you! So long! Next Tuesday!" Mabel called, "Good night, lover!"

"Good night," he muttered.

"What?" she shouted.

"Good night!"

He glanced at the beautiful face behind the door. Then he smiled. He had been afraid that she might hear him say good night to a woman who called him lover.

He had ten minutes yet. The intercom alarms were whooping. Get going, everybody! Time to take the six-day trip! Run! Remember the penalties!

He remembered, but he wanted to leave a message. The recorder was on a table. He activated it, and said, "Dear *Miss* Jennie Marlowe. My name is Tom Pym, and my stoner is next to yours. I am an actor, too; in fact, I work at the same studio as you. I know this is presumptuous of me, but I have never seen anybody so beautiful. Do you have a talent to match your beauty? I would like to see some run-offs of your shows. Would you please leave some in room five? I'm sure the occupant won't mind. Yours, Tom Pym."

He ran it back. It was certainly bald enough, and that might be just what was needed. Too flowery or too pressing would have made her leery. He had commented on her beauty twice but not overstressed it. And the appeal to her pride in her acting would be difficult to resist. Nobody knew better than he about that.

He whistled a little on his way to the cylinder. Inside, he pressed the button and looked at his watch. Five minutes to midnight. The light on the huge screen above the computer in the police station would not be flashing for him. Ten minutes from now, Wednesday's police would step out of their stoners in the precinct station, and they would take over their duties.

There was a ten-minute hiatus between the two days in the police station. All hell could break loose in these few minutes and it sometimes did. But a price had to be paid to maintain the walls of time.

He opened his eyes. His knees sagged a little and his head bent. The activation was a million microseconds fast — from eternium to flesh and blood almost instantaneously and the heart never knew that it had been stopped for such a long time. Even so, there was a little delay in the muscles' response to a standing position.

He pressed the button, opened the door, and it was as if his button had launched the day. Mabel had made herself up last night so that she looked dawn-fresh. He complimented her and she smiled happily. But he told her he would meet her for breakfast. Halfway up the staircase, he stopped, and waited until the hall was empty. Then he sneaked back down and into the stoner room. He turned on the recorder.

A voice, husky but also melodious, said, "Dear Mister Pym. I've had a few messages from other days. It was fun to talk back and forth across the abyss between the worlds, if you don't mind my exaggerating a little. But there is really no sense in it, once the novelty has worn off. If you become interested in the other person, you're frustrating yourself. That person can only be a voice in a recorder and a cold waxy face in a metal coffin. I wax poetic. Pardon me. If the person doesn't interest you, why continue to communicate? There is no sense in either case. And I *may* be beautiful. Anyway, I thank you for the compliment, but I am also sensible.

"I should have just not bothered to reply. But I want to be nice; I didn't want to hurt your feelings. So please don't leave any more messages."

He waited while silence was played. Maybe she was pausing for effect. Now would come a chuckle or a low honey-throated laugh, and she would say, "However, I don't like to disappoint my public. The run-offs are in your room."

The silence stretched out. He turned off the machine and went to the dining room for breakfast.

Siesta time at work was from 14:40 to 14:45. He lay down on the bunk and pressed the button. Within a minute he was asleep. He did dream of Jennie this time; she was a white shimmering figure solidifying out of the darkness and floating toward him. She was even more beautiful than she had been in her stoner.

The shooting ran overtime that afternoon so that he got home just in time for supper. Even the studio would not dare keep a man past his supper hour, especially since the studio was authorized to serve food only at noon.

He had time to look at Jennie for a minute before Mrs. Cuthmar's voice screeched over the intercom. As he walked down the hall, he thought, "I'm getting barnacled on her. It's ridiculous. I'm a grown man. Maybe…maybe I should see a psycher."

Sure, make your petition, and wait until a psycher has time for you. Say about three hundred days from now, if you are lucky. And if the psycher doesn't work out for you, then petition for another, and wait six hundred days.

Petition. He slowed down. Petition. What about a request, not to see a psycher, but to move? Why not? What did he have to lose? It would probably be turned down, but he could at least try.

Even obtaining a form for the request was not easy. He spent two nonwork days standing in line at the Center City Bureau before he got the proper forms. The first time, he was handed the wrong form and had to start all over again. There was no line set aside for those who wanted to change their days. There were not enough who wished to do this to justify such a line. So he had to queue up before the Miscellaneous Office counter of the Mobility Section of the Vital Exchange Department of the Interchange and Cross Transfer Bureau. None of these titles had anything to do with emigration to another day.

When he got his form the second time, he refused to move from the office window until he had checked the number of the form and asked the clerk to double-check. He ignored the cries and the mutterings behind him. Then he went to one side of the vast room and stood in line before the punch machines. After two hours, he got to sit down at a small rolltop desk-shaped machine, above which was a large screen. He inserted the form into the slot, looked at the projection of the form, and punched buttons to mark the proper spaces opposite the proper questions. After that, all he had to do was to drop the form into a slot and hope it did not get lost. Or hope he would not have to go through the same procedure because he had improperly punched the form.

That evening, he put his head against the hard metal and murmured to the rigid face behind the door, "I must really love you to go through all this. And you don't even know it. And, worse, if you did, you might not care one bit."

To prove to himself that he had kept his gray stuff, he went out with Mabel that evening to a party given by Sol Voremwolf, a producer. Voremwolf had just passed a civil service examination giving him an A-13 rating. This meant that, in time, with some luck and the proper pull, he would become an executive vice-president of the studio.

The party was a qualified success. Tom and Mabel returned about half an hour before stoner time. Tom had managed to refrain from too many blowminds and liquor, so he was not tempted by Mabel. Even so, he knew that when he became unstonered, he would be half-loaded and he'd have to take some dreadful counteractives. He would look and feel like hell at work, since he had missed his sleep.

He put Mabel off with an excuse, and went down to the stoner room ahead of the others. Not that that would do him any good if he wanted to get stonered early. The stoners only activated within narrow time limits.

He leaned against the cylinder and patted the door. "I tried not to think about you all evening. I wanted to be fair to Mabel, it's not fair to go out with her and think about you all the time."

All's fair in love...

                       •

He left another message for her, then wiped it out. What was the use? Besides, he knew that his speech was a little thick. He wanted to appear at his best for her.

Why should he? What did she care for him?

The answer was, he did care, and there was no reason or logic connected with it. He loved this forbidden, untouchable, faraway-in-time, yet-so-near woman.

Mabel had come in silently. She said, "You're sick!"

Tom jumped away. Now why had he done that? He had nothing to be ashamed of. Then why was he so angry with her? His embarrassment was understandable but his anger was not.

Mabel laughed at him, and he was glad. Now he could snarl at her. He did so, and she turned away and walked out. But she was back in a few minutes with the others. It would soon be midnight.

By then he was standing inside the cylinder. A few seconds later, he left it, pushed Jennie's backward on its wheels, and pushed his around so that it faced hers. He went back in, pressed the button, and stood there. The double doors only slightly distorted his view. But she seemed even more removed in distance, in time, and in unattainability.

Three days later, well into winter, he received a letter. The box inside the entrance hall buzzed just as he entered the front door. He went back and waited until the letter was printed and had dropped out from the slot. It was the reply to his request to move to Wednesday.

Denied. Reason: he had no reasonable reason to move.

That was true. But he could not give his real motive. It would have been even less impressive than the one he had given. He had punched the box opposite No. 12. REASON: TO GET INTO AN ENVIRONMENT WHERE MY TALENTS WILL BE MORE LIKELY TO BE ENCOURAGED.

He cursed and he raged. It was his human, his civil right to move into any day he pleased. That is, it should be his right. What if a move did cause much effort? What if it required a transfer of his I.D. and all the records connected with him from the moment of his birth? What if...?

He could rage all he wanted to, but it would not change a thing. He was stuck in the world of Tuesday.

Not yet, he muttered. Not yet. Fortunately, there is no limit to the number of requests I can make in my own day. I'll send out another. They think they can wear me out, huh? Well, I'll wear them out. Man against the machine. Man against the system. Man against the bureaucracy and the hard cold rules.

Winter's twenty days had sped by. Spring's eight days rocketed by. It was summer again. On the second day of the twelve days of summer, he received a reply to his second request.

It was neither a denial nor an acceptance. It stated that if he thought he would be better off psychologically in Wednesday because his astrologer said so, then he would have to get a psycher's critique of the astrologer's analysis. Tom Pym jumped into the air and clicked his sandaled heels together. Thank God that he lived in an age that did not classify astrologers as charlatans! The people — the masses — had protested that astrology was a necessity and that it should be legalized and honored. So laws were passed, and because of that, Tom Pym had a chance.

He went down to the stoner room and kissed the door of the cylinder and told Jennie Marlowe the good news. She did not respond, though he thought he saw her eyes brighten just a little. That was, of course, only his imagination, but he liked his imagination.

Getting a psycher for a consultation and getting through the three sessions took another year, another forty-eight days. Doctor Sigmund Traurig was a friend of Doctor Stelhela, the astrologer, and so that made things easier for Tom.

"I've studied Doctor Stelhela's chart carefully and analyzed carefully your obsession for this woman," he said. "I agree with Doctor Stelhela that you will always be unhappy in Tuesday, but I don't quite agree with him that you will be happier in Wednesday. However, you have this thing going for this Miss Marlowe, so I think you should go to Wednesday. But only if you sign papers agreeing to see a psycher there for extended therapy."

Only later did Tom Pym realize that Doctor Traurig might have wanted to get rid of him because he had too many patients. But that was an uncharitable thought.

He had to wait while the proper papers were transmitted to Wednesday's authorities. His battle was only half-won. The other officials could turn him down. And if he did get to his goal, then what? She could reject him without giving him a second chance.

It was unthinkable, but she could.

He caressed the door and then pressed his lips against it.

"Pygmalion could at least touch Galatea," he said. "Surely the gods — the big dumb bureaucrats — will take pity on me, who can't even touch you. Surely."

The psycher had said that he was incapable of a true and lasting bond with a woman, as so many men were in this world of easy-come-easy-go liaisons. He had fallen in love with Jennie Marlowe for several reasons. She may have resembled somebody he had loved when he was very young. His mother, perhaps? No? Well, never mind. He would find out in Wednesday — perhaps. The deep, the important, truth was that he loved Miss Marlowe because she could never reject him, kick him out, or become tiresome, complain, weep, yell, insult, and so forth. He loved her because she was unattainable and silent.

"I love her as Achilles must have loved Helen when he saw her on top of the walls of Troy," Tom said.

"I wasn't aware that Achilles was ever in love with Helen of Troy," Doctor Traurig said drily.

"Homer never said so, but I *know* that he must have been! Who could see her and *not* love her?"

"How the hell would I know? I never saw her! If I had suspected these delusions would intensify…

"I am a poet!" Tom said.

"Overimaginative, you mean! Hmmm. She must be a douser! I don't have anything particular to do this evening. I'll tell you what…my curiosity is aroused…I'll come down to your place tonight and take a look at this fabulous beauty, your Helen of Troy."

Doctor Traurig appeared immediately after supper, and Tom Pym ushered him down the hall and into the stoner room at the rear of the big house as if he were a guide conducting a famous critic to a just-discovered Rembrandt.

The doctor stood for a long time in front of the cylinder. He hmmmed several times and checked her vital-data plate several times. Then he turned and said, "I see what you mean, Mr. Pym. Very well. I'll give the go-ahead."

"Ain't she something?" Tom said on the porch. "She's out of this world, literally and figuratively, of course."

"Very beautiful. But I believe that you are facing a great disappointment, perhaps heartbreak, perhaps, who knows, even madness, much as I hate to use that unscientific term."

"I'll take the chance," Tom said. "I know I sound nuts, but where would we be if it weren't for nuts? Look at the man who invented the wheel, at Columbus, at James Watt, at the Wright brothers, at Pasteur, you name them."

"You can scarcely compare these pioneers of science with their passion for truth with you and your desire to marry a woman. But, as I have observed, she is strikingly beautiful. Still, that makes me exceedingly cautious. Why isn't she married? What's wrong with her?"

"For all I know, she may have been married a dozen times!" Tom said. "The point is, she isn't now. Maybe she's disappointed and she's sworn to wait until the right man comes along. Maybe..."

"There's no maybe about it, you're neurotic," Traurig said. "But I actually believe that it would be more dangerous for you not to go to Wednesday than it would be to go."

"Then you'll say yes!" Tom said, grabbing the doctor's hand and shaking it.

"Perhaps. I have some doubts."

The doctor had a faraway look. Tom laughed and released the hand and slapped the doctor on the shoulder. "Admit it! You were really struck by her! You'd have to be dead not to!"

"She's all right," the doctor said. "But you must think this over. If you do go there and she turns you down, you might go off the deep end, much as I hate to use such a poetical term."

"No, I won't. I wouldn't be a bit the worse off. Better off, in fact. I'll at least get to see her in the flesh."

Spring and summer zipped by. Then, a morning he would never forget, the letter of acceptance. With it, instructions on how to get to Wednesday. These were simple enough. He was to make sure that the technicians came to his stoner sometime during the day and readjusted the timer within the base. He could not figure out why he could not just stay out of the stoner and let Wednesday catch up to him, but by now he was past trying to fathom the bureaucratic mind.

He did not intend to tell anyone at the house, mainly because of Mabel. But Mabel found out from someone at the studio. She wept when she saw him at supper time, and she ran upstairs to her room. He felt badly, but he did not follow to console her.

That evening, his heart beating hard, he opened the door to his stoner. The others had found out by then; he had been unable to keep the business to himself. Actually, he was glad that he had told them. They seemed happy for him, and they brought in drinks and had many rounds of toasts. Finally, Mabel came downstairs, wiping her eyes, and she said she wished him luck, too. She had known that he was not really in love with her. But she did wish someone would fall in love with her just by looking inside her stoner.

When she found out that he had gone to see Doctor Traurig, she said, "He's a very influential man. Sol Voremwolf had him for his analyst. He says he's even got influence on other days. He edits the *Psyche Crosscurrents,* you know, one of the few periodicals read by other people."

Other, of course, meant those who lived in Wednesdays through Mondays.

Tom said he was glad he had gotten Traurig. Perhaps he had used his influence to get the Wednesday authorities to push through his request so swiftly. The walls between the worlds were seldom broken, but it was suspected that the very influential did it when they pleased.

Now, quivering, he stood before Jennie's cylinder again. The last time, he thought, that I'll see her stonered. Next time, she'll be warm, colorful, touchable flesh.

"*Ave atque vale!*" he said aloud. The others cheered. Mabel said, "How corny!" They thought he was addressing them, and perhaps he had included them.

He stepped inside the cylinder, closed the door, and pressed the button. He would keep his eyes open, so that...

And today was Wednesday. Though the view was exactly the same, it was like being on Mars.

He pushed open the door and stepped out. The seven people had faces he knew and names he had read on their plates. But he did not know them.

He started to say hello, and then he stopped.

Jennie Marlowe's cylinder was gone.

He seized the nearest man by the arm.

"Where's Jennie Marlowe?"

"Let go. You're hurting me. She's gone. To Tuesday."

"*Tuesday! Tuesday?*"

"Sure. She'd been trying to get out of here for a long time. She had something about this day being unlucky for her. She was unhappy, that's for sure. Just two days ago, she said her application had finally been accepted. Apparently, some Tuesday psycher had used his influence. He came down and saw her in her stoner and that was it, brother."

The walls and the people and the stoners seemed to be distorted. Time was bending itself this way and that. He wasn't in Wednesday; he wasn't in Tuesday. He wasn't in *any* day. He was stuck inside himself at some crazy date that should never have existed.

"She can't do that!"

"Oh, no! She just did that!"

"But...you can't transfer more than once!"

"That's her problem."

It was his, too.

"I should never have brought him down to look at her!" Tom said. "The swine! The unethical swine!"

Tom Pym stood there for a long time, and then he went into the kitchen. It was the same environment, if you discounted the people. Later, he went to the studio and got a part in a situation play which was, really, just like all those in Tuesday. He watched the newscaster that night. The President of the U.S.A. had a different name and face, but the words of his speech could have been those of Tuesday's President. He was introduced to a secretary of a producer; her name wasn't Mabel, but it might as well have been.

The difference here was that Jennie was gone, and oh, what a world of difference it made to him.

June 1, 1980

It is now 11:00 P.M., and I am afraid to go to bed. I am not alone. The whole world is afraid of sleep.

This morning I got up at 6:30 A.M., as I do every Wednesday. While I shaved and showered, I considered the case of the state of Illinois against Joseph Lankers, accused of murder. It was beginning to stink as if it were a three-day-old fish. My star witness would undoubtedly be charged with perjury.

I dressed, went downstairs, and kissed Carole good morning. She poured me a cup of coffee and said, "The paper's late."

That put me in a bad temper. I need both coffee and the morning newspaper to get me started.

Twice during breakfast, I left the table to look outside. Neither paper nor newsboy had appeared.

At seven, Carole went upstairs to wake up Mike and Tom, aged ten and eight respectively. Saturdays and Sundays they rise early even though I'd like them to stay in bed so their horsing around won't wake me. School days they have to be dragged out.

The third time I looked out of the door, Joe Gale, the paperboy, was next door. My paper lay on the stoop.

I felt disorientated, as if I'd walked into the wrong courtroom or the judge had given my client, a shoplifter, a life sentence. I was out of phase with the world. This couldn't be Sunday. So what was the Sunday issue, bright in its covering of the colored comic section, doing here? Today was Wednesday.

I stepped out to pick it up and saw old Mrs. Douglas, my neighbor to the left. She was looking at the front page of her paper as if she could not believe it.

The world rearranged itself into the correct lines of polarization. My thin panic dwindled into nothing. I thought, the *Star* has really goofed this time. That's what comes from depending so much on a computer to put it together. One little short circuit, and Wednesday's paper comes out in Sunday's format.

The *Star*'s night shift must have decided to let it go through; it was too late for them to rectify the error.

I said, "Good morning, Mrs. Douglas! Tell me, what day is it?"

"The twenty-eighth of May," she said. "I think..."

I walked out into the yard and shouted after Joe. Reluctantly, he wheeled his bike around.

"What is this?" I said, shaking the paper at him. "Did the *Star* screw up?"

"I don't know, Mr. Franham," he said. "None of us knows, honest to God."

By "us" he must have meant the other boys he met in the morning at the paper drop.

"We all thought it was Wednesday. That's why I'm late. We couldn't understand what was happening, so we talked a long time and then Bill Ambers called the office. Gates, he's the circulation manager, was just as bongo as we was."

"Were," I said.

"What?" he said.

"We *were*, not was, just as bongo, whatever that means," I said.

"For God's sake, Mr. Franham, who cares!" he said.

"Some of us still do," I said. "All right, what did Gates say?"

"He was upset as hell," Joe said. "He said heads were gonna roll. The night staff had fallen asleep for a couple of hours, and some joker had diddled up the computers, or..."

"That's all it is?" I said. I felt relieved.

When I went inside, I got out the papers for the last four days from the cycler. I sat down on the sofa and scanned them.

I didn't remember reading them. I didn't remember the past four days at all!

Wednesday's headline was: MYSTERIOUS OBJECT ORBITS EARTH.

I did remember Tuesday's articles, which stated that the big round object was heading for a point between the Earth and the moon. It had been detected three weeks ago when it was passing through the so-called asteroid belt. It was at that time traveling approximately 57,000 kilometers per hour, relative to the sun. Then it had slowed down, had changed course several times, and it became obvious that, unless it changed course again, it was going to come near Earth.

By the time it was eleven million miles away, the radars had defined its size and shape, though not its material composition. It was perfectly spherical and exactly half a kilometer in diameter. It did not reflect much light. Since it had altered its path so often, it had to be artificial. Strange hands, or strange somethings, had built it.

I remembered the panic and the many wild articles in the papers and magazines and the TV specials made overnight to discuss its implications.

It had failed to make any response whatever to the radio and laser signals sent from Earth. Many scientists said that it probably contained no living passengers. It had to be of interstellar origin. The sentient beings of some planet circling some star had sent it out equipped with automatic equipment of some sort. No being could live long enough to travel between the stars. It would take over four years to get from the nearest star to Earth even if the object could travel at the speed of light, and that was impossible. Even one-sixteenth the speed of light seemed incredible because of the vast energy requirements. No, this thing had been launched with only electromechanical devices as passengers, had attained its top speed, turned off its power, and coasted until it came within the outer reaches of our solar system.

According to the experts, it must be unable to land on Earth because of its size and weight. It was probably just a surveying vessel, and after it had taken some photographs and made some radar/laser sweeps, it would proceed to wherever it was supposed to go, probably back to an orbit around its home planet.

2

Last Wednesday night, the president had told us that we had nothing to fear. And he'd tried to end on an optimistic note. At least, that's what Wednesday's paper said. The beings who had sent The Ball must be more advanced than we, and they must have many good things to give us. And we might be able to make beneficial contributions to them. Like what? I thought.

Some photographs of The Ball, taken from one of the manned orbiting laboratories, were on the second page. It looked just like a giant black billiard ball. One TV comic had suggested that the other side might bear a big white 8. I may have thought that this was funny last Wednesday, but I didn't think so now. It seemed highly probable to me that The Ball was connected with the four-days' loss of memory. How, I had no idea.

I turned on the 7:30 news channels, but they weren't much help except in telling us that the same thing had happened to everybody all over the world. Even those in the deepest diamond mines or submarines had been affected. The president was in conference, but he'd be making a statement over the networks sometime today. Meantime, it was known that no radiation of any sort had been detected emanating from The Ball. There was no evidence whatsoever that the object had caused the loss of memory. Or, as the jargon-crazy casters were already calling it, "memloss."

I'm a lawyer, and I like to think logically, not only about what has happened but what might happen. So I extrapolated on the basis of what little evidence, or data, there was.

On the first of June, a Sunday, we woke up with all memory of May 31 back through May 28 completely gone. We had thought that yesterday was the twenty-seventh and that this morning was that of the twenty-eighth.

If The Ball had caused this, why had it only taken four days of our memory? I didn't know. Nobody knew. But perhaps The Ball, its devices, that is, were limited in scope. Perhaps they couldn't strip off more than four days of memory at a time from everybody on Earth.

Postulate that this is the case. Then, what if the same thing happens tomorrow? We'll wake up tomorrow, June 2, with all memory of yesterday, June 1, and three more days of May, the twenty-seventh through the twenty-fifth, gone. Eight days in one solid stretch.

And if this ghastly thing should occur the following day, June 3, we'll lose another four days. All memory of June 2 will have disappeared. With it will go the memory of three more days, from May twenty-fourth through the twenty-second. Twelve days in all from June 2 backward!

And the next day? June 3 lost, too, along with May 21 through May 19. Sixteen days of a total blank. And the next day? And the next?

No, it's too hideous, and too fantastic, to think about.

While we were watching TV, Carole and the boys besieged me with questions. She was frantic. The boys seemed to be enjoying the mystery. They'd awakened expecting to go to school, and now they were having a holiday.

To all their questions, I said, "I don't know. Nobody knows."

I wasn't going to frighten them with my extrapolations. Besides, I didn't believe them myself.

"You'd better call up your office and tell them you can't come in today," Carole said. "Surely Judge Payne'll call off the session today."

"Carole, it's Sunday, not Wednesday, remember?" I said.

She cried for a minute. After she'd wiped away the tears, she said, "That's just it! I *don't* remember! My God, what's happening?"

The newscasters also reported that the White House was flooded with telegrams and phone calls demanding that rockets with H-bomb warheads be launched against The Ball. The specials, which came on after the news, were devoted to The Ball. These had various authorities, scientists, military men, ministers, and a few science-fiction authors. None of them radiated confidence, but they were all temperate in their approach to the problem. I suppose they had been picked for their level-headedness. The networks had screened out the hotheads and the crackpots. They didn't want to be generating any more hysteria.

But Anel Robertson, a fundamentalist faith healer with a powerful radio/TV station of his own, had already declared that The Ball was a judgment of God on a sinful planet. It was The Destroying Angel. I knew that because Mrs. Douglas, no fanatic but certainly a zealot, had phoned me and told me to dial him in. Robertson had been speaking for an hour, she said, and he was going to talk all day.

She sounded frightened, and yet, beneath the fear was a note of joy. Obviously, she didn't think that she was going to be among the goats when the last days arrived. She'd be right in there with the whitest of the sheep. My curiosity finally overcame my repugnance for Robertson. I dialed the correct number but got nothing except a pattern. Later today, I found out his station had been shut down for some infraction of FCC regulations. At least, that was the explanation given on the news, but I suspected that the government regarded him as a hysteria monger.

At eleven, Carole reminded me that it was Sunday and that if we didn't hurry, we'd miss church.

The Forrest Hill Presbyterian has a good attendance, but its huge parking lot has always been adequate. This morning, we had to park two blocks up the street and walk to church. Every seat was filled. We had to stand in the anteroom near the front door. The crowd stank of fear. Their faces were pale and set; their eyes, big. The air conditioning labored unsuccessfully to carry away the heat and humidity of the packed and sweating bodies. The choir was loud but quavering; their "Rock of Ages" was crumbling.

Dr. Boynton would have prepared his sermon on Saturday afternoon, as he always did. But today he spoke impromptu. Perhaps, he said, this loss of memory *had* been caused by The Ball. Perhaps there were living beings in it who had taken four days away from us, not as a hostile move but merely to demonstrate their immense powers. There was no reason to anticipate that we would suffer another loss of memory. These beings merely wanted to show us that we were hopelessly inferior in science and that we could not launch a successful attack against them.

"What the hell's he doing?" I thought. "Is he trying to scare us to death?"

Boynton hastened then to say that beings with such powers, of such obvious advancement, would not, could not, be hostile. They would be on too high an ethical plane for such evil things as war, unless they were attacked, of course. They would regard us as beings who had not yet progressed to their level but had the potentiality, the God-given potentiality, to be brought up to a high level. He was sure that, when they made contact with us, they would tell us that all was for the best.

They would tell us that we must, like it or not, become true Christians. At least, we must all, Buddhists, Moslems and so forth, become Christian in spirit, whatever our religion or lack thereof. They would teach us how to live as brothers and sisters, how to be happy, how to truly love. Assuredly, God had sent The Ball, since nothing happened without His knowledge and consent. He had sent these beings, whoever they were, not as Destroying Angels but as Sharers of Peace, Love and Prosperity.

That last, with the big P, seemed to settle down most of the congregation. Boynton had not forgotten that most of his flock were of the big-business and professional classes. Nor had he forgotten that, inscribed on the arch above the church entrance was, THEY SHALL PROSPER WHO LOVE THEE.

3

We poured out into a bright warm June afternoon. I looked up into the sky but could see no Ball, of course. The news media had said that, despite its great distance from Earth, it was circling Earth every sixty-five minutes. It wasn't in a free fall orbit. It was applying continuous power to keep it on its path, although there were no detectable emanations of energy from it.

The memory loss had occurred all over the world between 1:00 A.M. and 2:00 A.M. Central Standard Time. Those who were not already asleep fell asleep for a minimum of an hour. This had, of course, caused hundreds of thousands of accidents. Planes not on automatic pilot had crashed, trains had collided or been derailed, ships had sunk, and more than two hundred thousand had been killed or seriously injured. At least a million vehicle drivers and passengers had been injured. The ambulance and hospital services had found it impossible to handle the situation. The fact that their personnel had been asleep for at least an hour and that it had taken them some time to recover from their confusion on awakening had aggravated the situation considerably. Many had died who might have lived if immediate service had been available.

There were many fires, too, the largest of which were still raging in Tokyo, Athens, Naples, Harlem, and Baltimore.

I thought, Would beings on a high ethical plane have put us to sleep knowing that so many people would be killed and badly hurt?

One curious item was about two rangers who had been thinning a herd of elephants in Kenya. While sleeping, they had been trampled to death. Whatever it is that's causing this, it's very specific. Only human beings are affected.

The optimism, which Boynton had given us in the church, melted in the sun. Many must have been thinking, as I was, that if Boynton's words were prophetic, we were helpless. Whatever the things in The Ball, whether living or mechanical, decided to do for us, or to us, we were no longer masters of our own fate. Some of them must have been thinking about what the technologically superior whites had done to various aboriginal cultures. All in the name of progress and God.

But this would be, must be, different, I thought. Boynton must be right. Surely such an advanced people would not be as we were. Even we are not what we were in the bad old days. We have learned.

But then an advanced technology does not necessarily accompany an advanced ethics.

"Or whatever," I murmured.

"What did you say, dear?" Carole said.

I said, "Nothing," and shook her hand off my arm. She had clung to it tightly all through the services, as if I were the rock of the ages. I walked over to Judge Payne, who's sixty years old but looked this morning as if he were eighty. The many broken veins on his face were red, but underneath them was a grayishness.

I said hello and then asked him if things would be normal tomorrow. He didn't seem to know what I was getting at, so I said, "The trial will start on time tomorrow?"

"Oh, yes, the trial," he said. "Of course, Mark."

He laughed whinnyingly and said, "Provided that we all haven't forgotten today when we wake up tomorrow."

That seemed incredible, and I told him so.

"It's not law school that makes good lawyers," he said. "It's experience. And experience tells us that the same damned thing, with some trifling variations, occurs over and over, day after day. So what makes you think this evil thing won't happen again? And if it does, how're you going to learn from it when you can't remember it?"

I had no logical argument, and he didn't want to talk any more. He grabbed his wife by the arm, and they waded through the crowd as if they thought they were going to step in a sinkhole and drown in a sea of bodies.

This evening, I decided to record on tape what's happened today. Now I lay me down to sleep, I pray the Lord my memory to keep, if I forget while I sleep...

Most of the rest of today, I've spent before the TV. Carole wasted hours trying to get through the lines to her friends for phone conversations. Three-fourths of the time, she got a busy signal. There were bulletins on the TV asking people not to use the phone except for emergencies, but she paid no attention to it until eight o'clock. A TV bulletin, for the sixth time in an hour, asked that the lines be kept open. About twenty fires had broken out over the town, and the firemen couldn't be informed of them because of the tie-up. Calls to hospitals had been similarly blocked.

I told Carole to knock it off, and we quarreled. Our suppressed hysteria broke loose, and the boys retreated upstairs to their room behind a closed door. Eventually, Carole started crying and threw herself into my arms, and then I cried. We kissed and made up. The boys came down looking as if we had failed them, which we had. For them, it was no longer a fun-adventure from some science-fiction story.

Mike said, "Dad, could you help me go over my arithmetic lessons?"

I didn't feel like it, but I wanted to make it up to him for that savage scene. I said sure and then, when I saw what he had to do, I said, "But all this? What's the matter with your teacher? I never saw so much..."

I stopped. Of course, he had forgotten all he'd learned in the last three days of school. He had to do his lessons all over again.

This took us until eleven, though we might have gone faster if I hadn't insisted on watching the news every half-hour for at least ten minutes. A full thirty minutes were used listening to the president, who came on at 9:30. He had nothing to add to what the newsmen had said except that, within thirty days, The Ball would be completely dealt with—one way or another. If it didn't make some response to our signals within two days, then we would send up a four-man expedition, which would explore The Ball.

If it can get inside, I thought.

If, however, The Ball should commit any more hostile acts, then the United States would immediately launch, in conjunction with other nations, rockets armed with H-bombs.

Meanwhile, would we all join the president in an interdenominational prayer?

We certainly would.

At eleven, we put the kids to bed. Tom went to sleep before we were out of the room. But about half an hour later, as I passed their door, I heard a low voice from the TV. I didn't say anything to Mike, even if he did have to go to school next day.

At twelve, I made the first part of this tape.

But here it is, one minute to one o'clock in the morning. If the same thing happens tonight as happened yesterday, then the nightside hemisphere will be affected first. People in the time zone which bisects the South and North Atlantic oceans and covers the eastern half of Greenland, will fall asleep. Just in case it does happen again, all airplanes have been grounded. Right now, the TV is showing the bridge and the salon of the trans-Atlantic liner *Pax*. It's five o'clock there, but the salon is crowded. The passengers are wearing party hats and confetti, and balloons are floating everywhere. I don't know what they could be celebrating. The captain said a little while ago that the ship's on automatic, but he doesn't expect a repetition of last night. The interviewer said that the governments of the dayside nations have not been successful keeping people home. We've been getting shots from everywhere, the sirens are wailing all over the world, but, except for the totalitarian nations, the streets of the daytime world are filled with cars. The damned fools just didn't believe it would happen again.

Back to the bridge and the salon of the ship. My God! They *are* falling asleep!

The announcers are repeating warnings. Everybody lie down so they won't get hurt by falling. Make sure all home appliances, which might cause fires, are turned off. And so on and so on.

I'm sitting in a chair with a tilted back. Carole is on the sofa.

Now I'm on the sofa. Carole just said she wanted to be holding on to me when this horrible thing comes.

The announcers are getting hysterical. In a few minutes, New York will be hit. The eastern half of South America is under. The central section is going under.

4

True date: June 2, 1980. Subjective date: May 25, 1980

My God! How many times have I said, "My God!" in the last two days?

I awoke on the sofa beside Carole and Mike. The clock indicated three in the morning. Chris Turner was on the TV. I didn't know what he was talking about. All I could understand was that he was trying to reassure his viewers that everything was all right and that everything would be explained shortly.

What was I doing on the sofa? I'd gone to bed about eleven the night of May 24, a Saturday. Carole and I had had a little quarrel because I'd spent all day working on the Lankers case, and she said that I'd promised to take her to see *Nova Express*. And so I had—if I finished work before eight, which I obviously had not done. So what were we doing on the sofa, where had Mike come from, and what did Turner mean by saying that today was June 2?

The tape recorder was on the table near me, but it didn't occur to me to turn it on.

I shook Carole awake, and we confusedly asked each other what had happened. Finally, Turner's insistent voice got our attention, and he explained the situation for about the fifth time so far. Later, he said that an alarm clock placed by his ear had awakened him at two-thirty.

Carole made some coffee, and we drank four cups apiece. We talked wildly, with occasional breaks to listen to Turner, before we became half-convinced that we had indeed lost all memory of the last eight days. Mike slept on through it, and finally I carried him up to his bed. His TV was still on. Nate Frobisher, Mike's favorite spieler, was talking hysterically. I turned him off and went back downstairs. I figured out later that Mike had gotten scared and come downstairs to sit with us.

Dawn found us rereading the papers from May 24 through June 1. It was like getting news from Mars. Carole took a tranquilizer to quiet herself down, but I preferred Wild Turkey. After she'd seen me down six ounces, Carole said I should lay off the bourbon. I wouldn't be fit to go to work. I told her that if she thought anybody'd be working today, she was out of her mind.

At seven, I went out to pick up the paper. It wasn't there. At a quarter to eight, Joe delivered it. I tried to talk to him, but he wouldn't stop. All he said, as he pedaled away, was, "It ain't Saturday!"

I went back in. The entire front page was devoted to The Ball and this morning's events up to four o'clock. Part of the paper had been set up before one o'clock. According to a notice at the bottom of the page, the staff had awakened about three. It took them an hour to straighten themselves out, and then they'd gotten together the latest news and made up the front page and some of section C. They'd have never made it when they did if it wasn't for the computer, which printed justified lines from voice input.

Despite what I'd said earlier, I decided to go to work. First, I had to straighten the boys out. At ten, they went off to school. It seemed to me that it was useless for them to do so. But they were eager to talk with their classmates about this situation. To tell the truth, I wanted to get down to the office and the courthouse for the same reason. I wanted to talk this over with my colleagues. Staying home all day with Carole seemed a waste of time. We just kept saying the same thing over and over again.

Carole didn't want me to leave. She was too frightened to stay home by herself. Both our parents are dead, but she does have a sister who lives in Hannah, a small town nearby. I told her it'd do her good to get out of the house. And I just had to get to the courthouse. I couldn't find out what was happening there because the phone lines were tied up.

When I went outside to get into my car, Carole ran down after me. Her long blonde hair was straggling; she had big bags under her eyes; she looked like a witch.

"Mark! Mark!" she said.

I took my finger off the starter button and said, "What is it?"

"I know you'll think I'm crazy, Mark," she said. "But I'm about to fall apart!"

"Who isn't?" I said.

"Mark," she said, "what if I go out to my sister's and then forget how to get back? What if I forgot *you*?"

"This thing only happens at night," I said.

"So far!" she screamed. "So far!"

"Honey," I said, "I'll be home early, I promise. If you don't want to go, stay here. Go over and talk to Mrs. Knight. I see her looking out her window. She'll talk your leg off all day."

I didn't tell her to visit any of her close friends, because she didn't have any. Her best friend had died of cancer last year, and two others with whom she was familiar had moved away.

"If you do go to your sister's," I said, "make a note on a map reminding you where you live and stick it on top of the dashboard where you can see it."

"You son of a bitch," she said. "It isn't funny!"

"I'm not being funny," I said. "I got a feeling..."

"What about?" she said.

"Well, we'll be making notes to ourselves soon. If this keeps up," I said.

I thought I was kidding then. Thinking about it later today I see that that is the only way to get orientated in the morning. Well, not the only way, but it'll have to be the way to get started when you wake up. Put a note where you can't overlook it, and it'll tell you to turn on a recording, which will, in turn, summarize the situation. Then you turn on the TV and get some more information.

I might as well have stayed home. Only half of the courthouse personnel showed up, and they were hopelessly inefficient. Judge Payne wasn't there and never will be. He'd had a fatal stroke at six that morning while listening to the TV. Walter Barbindale, my partner, said that the judge probably would have had a stroke sometime in the near future, anyway. But this situation must certainly have hastened it.

"The stock market's about hit bottom," he said. "One more day of this, and we'll have another world-wide depression. Nineteen twenty-nine won't hold a candle to it. And I can't even get through to my broker to tell him to sell everything."

"If everybody sells, then the market *will* crash," I said.

"Are you hanging onto your stocks?" he said.

"I've been too busy to even think about it," I said. "You might say I forgot."

"That isn't funny," he said.

"That's what my wife said," I answered. "But I'm not trying to be funny, though God knows I could use a good laugh. Well, what're we going to do about Lankers?"

"I went over some of the records," he said. "We haven't got a chance. I tell you, it was a shock finding out, for the second time, mind you, though I don't remember the first, that our star witness is in jail on a perjury charge."

Since all was chaos in the courthouse, it wasn't much use trying to find out who the judge would be for the new trial for Lankers. To tell the truth, I didn't much care. There were far more important things to worry about than the fate of an undoubtedly guilty murderer.

I went to Grover's Rover Bar, which is a block from the courthouse. As an aside, for my reference or for whoever might be listening to this someday, why am I telling myself things I know perfectly well, like the location of Grover's? Maybe it's because I think I might forget them some day.

Grover's, at least, I remembered well, as I should, since I'd been going there ever since it was built, five years ago. The air was thick with tobacco and pot smoke and the odors of pot, beer and booze. And noisy. Everybody was talking fast and loud, which is to be expected in a place filled with members of the legal profession. I bellied up to the bar and bought the D.A. a shot of Wild Turkey. We talked about what we'd done that morning, and then he told me he had to release two burglars that day. They'd been caught and jailed two days before. The arresting officers had, of course, filed their reports. But that wasn't going to be enough when the trial came up. Neither the burglars nor the victims and the officers remembered a thing about the case.

"Also," the D.A. said, "at two-ten this morning, the police got a call from the Black Shadow Tavern on Washington Street. They didn't get there until three-thirty because they were too disorientated to do anything for an hour or more. When they did get to the tavern, they found a dead man. He'd been beaten badly and then stabbed in the stomach. Nobody remembered anything, of course. But from what we could piece together, the dead man must've gotten into a drunken brawl with a person or persons unknown shortly before 1:00 A.M. Thirty people must've witnessed the murder. So we have a murderer or murderers walking the streets today who don't even remember the killing or anything leading up to it."

"They might know they're guilty if they'd been planning it for a long time," I said.

He grinned and said, "But he, or they, won't be telling anybody. No one except the corpse had blood on him nor did anybody have bruised knuckles. Two were arrested for carrying saps, but so what? They'll be out soon, and nobody, but nobody, can prove they used the saps. The knife was still half-sticking in the deceased's belly, and his efforts to pull it out destroyed any fingerprints."

5

We talked and drank a lot, and suddenly it was 6:00 P.M. I was in no condition to drive and had sense enough to know it. I tried calling Carole to come down and get me, but I couldn't get through. At 6:30 and 7:00, I tried again without success. I decided to take a taxi. But after another drink, I tried again and this time got through.

"Where've you been?" she said. "I called your office, but nobody answered. I was thinking about calling the police."

"As if they haven't got enough to do," I said. "When did you get home?"

"You're slurring," she said coldly.

I repeated the question.

"Two hours ago," she said.

"The lines were tied up," I said. "I tried."

"You knew how scared I was, and you didn't even care," she said.

"Can I help it if the D.A. insisted on conducting business at the Rover?" I said. "Besides, I was trying to forget."

"Forget what?" she said.

"Whatever it was I forgot," I said.

"You ass!" she screamed. "Take a taxi!"

The phone clicked off.

She didn't make a scene when I got home. She'd decided to play it cool because of the kids, I suppose. She was drinking gin and tonic when I entered, and she said, in a level voice, "You'll have some coffee. And after a while you can listen to the tape you made yesterday. It's interesting, but spooky."

"What tape?" I said.

"Mike was fooling around with it," she said. "And he found out you'd recorded what happened yesterday."

"That kid!" I said. "He's always snooping around. I told him to leave my stuff alone. Can't a man have any privacy around here?"

"Well, don't say anything to him," she said. "He's upset as it is. Anyway, it's a good thing he did turn it on. Otherwise, you'd have forgotten all about it. I think you should make a daily record."

"So you think it'll happen again?" I said.

She burst into tears. After a moment, I put my arms around her. I felt like crying, too. But she pushed me away, saying, "You stink of rotten whiskey!"

"That's because it's mostly bar whiskey," I said. "I can't afford Wild Turkey at three dollars a shot."

I drank four cups of black coffee and munched on some shrimp dip. As an aside, I can't really afford that, either, since I only make forty-five thousand dollars a year.

When we went to bed, we went to bed. Afterward, Carole said, "I'm sorry, darling, but my heart wasn't really in it."

"That wasn't all," I said.

"You've got a dirty mind," she said. "What I meant was I couldn't stop thinking, even while we were doing it, that it wasn't any good doing it. We won't remember it tomorrow, I thought."

"How many do we really remember?" I said. "Sufficient unto the day is the, uh, good thereof."

"It's a good thing you didn't try to fulfill your childhood dream of becoming a preacher," she said. "You're a born shyster. You'd have made a lousy minister."

"Look," I said, "I remember the especially good ones. And I'll never forget our honeymoon. But we need sleep. We haven't had any to speak of for twenty-four hours. Let's hit the hay and forget everything until tomorrow. In which case..."

She stared at me and then said, "Poor dear, no wonder you're so belligerently flippant! It's a defense against fear!"

I slammed my fist into my palm and shouted, "I know! I know! For God's sake, how long is this going on?"

I went into the bathroom. The face in the mirror looked as if it were trying to flirt with me. The left eye wouldn't stop winking.

When I returned to the bedroom, Carole reminded me that I'd not made today's recording. I didn't want to do it because I was so tired. But the possibility of losing another day's memory spurred me. No, not another day, I thought. If this occurs tomorrow, I'll lose another four days. Tomorrow and the three preceding May 25. I'll wake up June 3 and think it's the morning of the twenty-second.

I'm making this downstairs in my study. I wouldn't want Carole to hear some of my comments.

Until tomorrow then. It's not tomorrow but yesterday that won't come. I'll make a note to myself and stick it in a corner of the case which holds my glasses.

6

True date: June 3, 1980

I woke up thinking that today was my birthday, May 22. I rolled over, saw the piece of paper half-stuck from my glasses case, put on my glasses and read the note.

It didn't enlighten me: I didn't remember writing the note. And why should I go downstairs and turn on the recorder? But I did so.

As I listened to the machine, my heart thudded as if it were a judge's gavel. My voice kept fading in and out. Was I going to faint?

And so half of today was wasted trying to regain twelve days in my mind. I didn't go to the office, and the kids went to school late. And what about the kids in school on the dayside of Earth? If they sleep during their geometry class, say, then they have to go through that class again on the same day. And that shoves the schedule forward, or is it backward, for that day. And then there's the time workers will lose on their jobs. They have to make it up, which means they get out an hour later. Only it takes more than an hour to recover from the confusion and get orientated. What a mess it has been! What a mess it'll be if this keeps on!

At eleven, Carole and I were straightened out enough to go to the supermarket. It was Tuesday, but Carole wanted me to be with her, so I tried to phone in and tell my secretary I'd be absent. The lines were tied up, and I doubt that she was at work. So I said to hell with it.

Our supermarket usually opens at eight. Not today. We had to stand in a long line, which kept getting longer. The doors opened at twelve. The manager, clerks and boys had had just as much trouble as we did unconfusing themselves, of course. Some didn't show at all. And some of the trucks which were to bring fresh stores never appeared.

By the time Carole and I got inside, those ahead of us had cleaned out half the supplies. They had the same idea we had. Load up now so there wouldn't be any standing in line so many times. The fresh milk was all gone, and the powdered milk shelf had one box left. I started for it but some teenager beat me to it. I felt like hitting him, but I didn't, of course.

The prices for everything were being upped by a fourth even as we shopped. Some of the stuff was being marked upward once more while we stood in line at the checkout counter. From the time we entered the line until we pushed out three overflowing carts, four hours had passed.

While Carole put away the groceries, I drove to another supermarket. The line there was a block long; it would be emptied and closed up before I ever got to its doors.

The next two supermarkets and a corner grocery store were just as hopeless. And the three liquor stores I went to were no better. The fourth only had about thirty men in line, so I tried that. When I got inside, all the beer was gone, which didn't bother me any, but the only hard stuff left was a fifth of rotgut. I drank it when I went to college because I couldn't afford anything better. I put the terrible stuff and a half-gallon of cheap muscatel on the counter. Anything was better than nothing, even though the prices had been doubled.

I started to make out the check, but the clerk said, "Sorry, sir. Cash only."

"What?" I said

"Haven't you heard, sir?" he said. "The banks were closed at 2:00 P.M. today."

"The banks are closed?" I said. I sounded stupid even to myself.

"Yes, sir," he said. "By the federal government. It's only temporary, sir, at least that's what the TV said. They'll be reopened after the stock market mess is cleared up."

"But…" I said.

"It's destructed," he said.

"Destroyed," I said automatically. "You mean, it's another Black Friday?"

"It's Tuesday today," he said.

"You're too young to know the reference," I said. And too uneducated, too, I thought.

"The president is going to set up a rationing system," he said. "For The Interim. And price controls, too. Turner said so on TV an hour ago. The president is going to lay it all out at six tonight."

When I came home, I found Carole in front of the TV. She was pale and wide-eyed.

"There's going to be another depression!" she said. "Oh, Mark, what are we going to do?"

"I don't know," I said. "I'm not the president, you know." And I slumped down onto the sofa. I had lost my flippancy.

Neither of us, having been born in 1945, knew what a Depression, with a big capital D, was; that is, we hadn't experienced it personally. But we'd heard our parents, who were kids when it happened, talk about it. Carole's parents had gotten along, though they didn't live well, but my father used to tell me about days when he had nothing but stale bread and turnips to eat and was happy to get them.

The president's TV speech was mostly about the depression, which he claimed would be temporary. At the end of half an hour of optimistic talk, he revealed why he thought the situation wouldn't last. The federal government wasn't going to wait for the sentients in The Ball — if there were any there — to communicate with us. Obviously, The Ball was hostile. So the survey expedition had been canceled. Tomorrow, the USA, the USSR, France, West Germany, Israel, India, Japan and China would send up an armada of rockets tipped with H-bombs. The orbits and the order of battle were determined this morning by computers; one after the other, the missiles would zero in until The Ball was completely destroyed. It would be overkill with a vengeance.

"That ought to bring up the stock market!" I said.

And so, after I've finished recording, to bed. Tomorrow, we'll follow our instructions on the notes, relisten to the tapes, reread certain sections of the newspapers and await the news on the TV. To hell with going to the courthouse; nobody's going to be there anyway.

Oh, yes. With all this confusion and excitement, everybody, myself included, forgot that today was my birthday. Wait a minute! It's *not* my birthday!

True date: June 5, 1980. Subjective date: May 16, 1980

I woke up mad at Carole because of our argument the previous day. Not that of June 4, of course, but our brawl of May 15. We'd been at a party given by the Burlingtons, where I met a beautiful young artist, Roberta Gardner. Carole thought I was paying too much attention to her because she looked like Myrna. Maybe I was. On the other hand, I really was interested in her paintings. It seemed to me that she had a genuine talent. When we got home, Carole tore into me, accused me of still being in love with Myrna. My protests did no good whatsoever. Finally, I told her we might as well get a divorce if she couldn't forgive and forget. She ran crying out of the room and slept on the sofa downstairs.

I don't remember what reconciled us, of course, but we must have worked it out, otherwise we wouldn't still be married.

Anyway, I woke up determined to see a divorce lawyer today. I was sick about what Mike and Tom would have to go through. But it would be better for them to be spared our terrible quarrels. I can remember my reactions when I was an adolescent and overheard my parents fighting. It was a relief, though a sad one, when they separated.

Thinking this, I reached for my glasses. And I found the note. And so another voyage into confusion, disbelief and horror.

Now that the panic has eased off somewhat, May 16 is back in the saddle—somewhat. Carole and I are, in a sense, still in that day, and things are a bit cool.

It's 1:00 P.M. now. We just watched the first rockets take off. Ten of them, one after the other.

It's 1:35 P.M. Via satellite, we watched the Japanese missiles.

We just heard that the Chinese and Russian rockets are being launched. When the other nations send theirs up, there will be thirty-seven in all.

No news at 12:30 A.M., June 5. In this case, no news must be bad news. But what could have happened? The newscasters won't say; they just talk around the subject.

7

True date: June 6, 1980. Subjective date: May 13, 1980

My records say that this morning was just like the other four. Hell.

One o'clock. The president, looking like a sad old man, though he's only forty-four, reported the catastrophe. All thirty-seven rockets were blown up by their own H-bombs about three thousand miles from The Ball. We saw some photographs of them taken from the orbiting labs. They weren't very impressive. No mushroom clouds, of course, and not even much light.

The Ball has weapons we can't hope to match. And if it can activate our H-bombs out in space, it should be able to do the same to those on Earth's surface. My God! It could wipe out all life if it wished to do so!

Near the end of the speech, the president did throw out a line of hope. With a weak smile—he was trying desperately to give us his big vote-winning one—he said that all was not lost by any means. A new plan, called Project Toro, was being drawn up even as he spoke.

Toro was Spanish for bull, I thought, but I didn't say so. Carole and the kids wouldn't have thought it funny, and I didn't think it was so funny myself. Anyway, I thought, maybe it's a Japanese word meaning *victory* or *destruction* or something like that.

Toro, as it turned out, was the name of a small irregularly shaped asteroid about 2.413 kilometers long and 1.609 kilometers wide. Its peculiar orbit had been calculated in 1972 by an L. Danielsson of the Swedish Royal Institute of Technology and a W. H. Ip of the University of California at San Diego. Toro, the president said, was bound into a resonant orbit with the Earth. Each time Toro came near the Earth—"near" was sometimes 12.6 million miles—it got exactly enough energy or "kick" from the Earth to push it on around so that it would come back for another near passage.

But the orbit was unstable, which meant that both Earth and Venus take turns controlling the asteroid. For a few centuries, Earth governs Toro; then Venus takes over. Earth has controlled Toro since A.D. 1580, Venus will take over in 2200. Earth grabs it again in 2350; Venus gets it back in 2800.

I was wondering what all this stuff about this celestial Ping-Pong game was about. Then the president said that it was possible to land rockets on Toro. In fact, the plan called for many shuttles to land there carrying parts of huge rocket motors, which would be assembled on Toro.

When the motors were erected on massive and deep stands, power would be applied to nudge Toro out of its orbit. This would require many trips by many rockets with cargoes of fuel and spare parts for the motors. The motors would burn out a number of times. Eventually, though, the asteroid would be placed in an orbit that would end in a direct collision with The Ball. Toro's millions of tons of hard rock and nickel-steel would destroy The Ball utterly, would turn it into pure energy.

"Yes," I said aloud, "but what's to keep The Ball from just changing its orbit? Its sensors will detect the asteroid; it'll change course; Toro will go on by it, like a train on a track."

This was the next point of the president's speech. The failure of the attack had revealed at least one item of information, or, rather, verified it. The radiation of the H-bombs had blocked off, disrupted, all control and observation of the rockets by radar and laser. In their final approach, the rockets had gone in blind, as it were, unable to be regulated from Earth. But if the bombs did this to our sensors, they must be doing the same to The Ball's.

So, just before Toro's course is altered to send it into its final path, H-bombs will be set off all around The Ball. In effect, it will be enclosed in a sphere of radiation. It will have no sensor capabilities. Nor will The Ball believe that it will have to alter its orbit to dodge Toro. It will have calculated that Toro's orbit won't endanger it. After the radiation fills the space around it, it won't be able to see that Toro is being given a final series of nudges to push it into a collision course.

The project is going to require immense amounts of materials and manpower. The USA can't handle it alone; Toro is going to be a completely international job. What one nation can't provide, the other will.

The president ended with a few words about how Project Toro, plus the situation of memory loss, is going to bring about a radical revision of the economic setup. He's going to announce the outlines of the new structure — not just policy but structure — two days from now. It'll be designed, so he says, to restore prosperity and, not incidentally, rid society of many problems plaguing it since the industrial revolution.

"Yes, but how long will Project Toro take?" I said. "Oh, Lord, how long?"

Six years, the president said, as if he'd heard me. Perhaps longer. Six years!

I didn't tell Carole what I could see coming. But she's no dummy. She could figure out some of the things that were bound to happen in six years, and none of them were good.

I never felt so hopeless in my life, and neither did she. But we do have each other, and so we clung tightly for a while. May 16 isn't forgotten, but it seems so unimportant. Mike and Tom cried, I suppose because they knew that this exhibition of love meant something terrible for all of us. Poor kids! They get upset by our hatreds and then become even more upset by our love.

When we realized what we were doing to them, we tried to be jolly. But we couldn't get them to smile.

True date: middle of 1981. Subjective date: middle of 1977

I'm writing this, since I couldn't get any new tapes today. The shortage is only temporary, I'm told. I could erase part of the old ones and use them, but it'd be like losing a vital part of myself. And God knows I've lost enough.

Old Mrs. Douglas next door is dead. Killed herself, according to my note on the calendar, April 2 of this year. I never would have thought she'd do it. She was such a strong fundamentalist, and these believe as strongly as the Roman Catholics that suicide is well-nigh unforgivable. I suspect that the double shock of her husband's death caused her to take her own life. April 2 of 1976 was the day he died. She had to be hospitalized because of the shock and grief for two weeks after his death. Carole and I had her over to dinner a few times after she came home, and all she could talk about was her dead husband. So I presume that, as she traveled backward to the day of his death, the grief became daily more unbearable. She couldn't face the arrival of the day he died.

Hers is not the only empty house on the block. Jack Bridger killed his wife and his three kids and his mother-in-law and himself last month—according to my records. Nobody knows why, but I suspect that he couldn't stand seeing his three-year-old girl become no more than an idiot. She'd retrogressed to the day of her birth and perhaps beyond. She'd lost her language abilities and could no longer feed herself. Strangely, she could still walk, and her intelligence potential was high. She had the brain of a three-year-old, fully developed, but lacking all postbirth experience. It would have been better if she hadn't been able to walk. Confined to a cradle, she would at least not have had to be watched every minute.

Little Ann's fate is going to be Tom's. He talks like a five-year-old now. And Mike's fate...my fate...Carole's...God! We'll end up like Ann! I can't stand thinking about it.

Poor Carole. She has the toughest job. I'm away part of the day, but she has to take care of what are, in effect, a five-year-old and an eight-year-old, getting younger every day. There is no relief for her, since they're always home. All educational institutions, except for certain research laboratories, are closed.

The president says we're going to convert ninety percent of all industries to cybernation. In fact, anything that can be cybernated will be. They have to be. Almost everything, from the mines to the loading equipment to the railroads and trucks and the unloading equipment and the arrangement and dispersal of the final goods at central distribution points.

Are six years enough to do this?

And who's going to pay for this? Never mind, he says. Money is on its way out. The president is a goddamned radical. He's taking advantage of this situation to put over his own ideas, which he sure as hell never revealed during his campaign for election. Sometimes I wonder who put The Ball up there. But that idea is sheer paranoia. At least, this gigantic WPA project is giving work to those who are able to work. The rest are on, or going to be on, a minimum guaranteed income, and I mean minimum. But the president says that, in time, everybody will have all he needs, and more, in the way of food, housing, schooling, clothing, etc. *He* says! What if Project Toro doesn't work? And what if it does work? Are we then going to return to the old economy? Of course not! It'll be impossible to abandon everything we've worked on; the new establishment will see to that.

I tried to find out where Myrna lived. I'm making this record in my office, so Carole isn't going to get hold of it. I love her — Myrna, I mean — passionately. I hired her two weeks ago and fell headlong, burningly, in love with her. All this was in 1977 of course, but today, inside of *me, is* 1977.

Carole doesn't know about this, of course. According to the letters and notes from Myrna, which I should have destroyed but, thank God; never had the heart to do, Carole didn't find out about Myrna until two years later. At least that's what this letter from Myrna says. She was away visiting her sister then and wrote to me in answer to my letter. A good thing, too, otherwise I wouldn't know what went on then.

My reason tells me to forget about Myrna. And so I will.

I've traveled backward in our affair, from our final bitter parting, to this state, when I was most in love with her. I know this because I've just reread the records of our relationship. It began deteriorating about six months before we split up, but I don't feel those emotions now, of course. And in two weeks I won't feel anything for her. If I don't refer to the records, I won't even know she ever existed.

This thought is intolerable. I have to find her, but I've had no success at all so far. In fourteen days, no, five, since every day ahead takes three more of the past, I'll have no drive to locate her. Because I won't know what I'm missing.

I don't hate Carole. I love her, but with a cool much-married love. Myrna makes me feel like a boy again. I burn exquisitely.

But where is Myrna?

True date: October 30, 1981

I ran into Brackwell Lee, the old mystery story writer today. Like most writers who haven't gone to work for the government propaganda office, he's in a bad way financially. He's surviving on his GMI, but for him there are no more first editions of rare books, new sports cars, Western Reserve or young girls. I stood him three shots of the rotgut which is the only whiskey now served at Grover's and listened to the funny stories he told to pay me for the drinks. But I also had to listen to his tales of woe.

Nobody buys fiction, or, in fact, any long works of any kind anymore. Even if you're a speed reader and go through a whole novel in one day, you have to start all over again the next time you pick it up. TV writing, except for the propaganda shows, is no alternative. The same old shows are shown every day and enjoyed just as much as yesterday or last year. According to my records, I've seen the hilarious pilot movie of the "Soap Opera Blues" series fifty times.

When old Lee talked about how he had been dropped by the young girls, he got obnoxiously weepy. I told him that that didn't say much for him or the girls either. But if he didn't want to be hurt, why didn't he erase those records that noted his rejections?

He didn't want to do that, though he could give me no logical reason why he shouldn't.

"Listen," I said with a sudden drunken inspiration, "why don't you erase the old records and make some new ones? How you laid this and that beautiful young thing. Describe your conquests in detail. You'll think you're the greatest Casanova that ever lived."

"But that wouldn't be true!" he said.

"You, a writer of lies, say that?" I said. "Anyway, you wouldn't know that they weren't the truth."

"Yeah," he said, "but if I get all charged up and come barreling down here to pick up some tail, I'll be rejected and so'll be right back where I was."

"Leave a stern note to yourself to listen to them only late at night, say, an hour before The Ball puts all to sleep. That way, you won't ever get hurt."

George Palmer wandered in then. I asked him how things were doing.

"I'm up to here handling cases for kids who can't get drivers' licenses," he said. "It's true you can teach anybody how to drive in a day, but the lessons are forgotten the next day. Anyway, it's experience that makes a good driver, and…need I explain more? The kids have to have cars, so they drive them regardless. Hence, as you no doubt have forgotten, the traffic accidents and violations are going up and up."

"Is that right?" I said.

"Yeah. There aren't too many in the mornings, since most people don't go to work until noon. However, the new transit system should take care of that when we get it, sometime in 1984 or 5."

"What new transit system?" I said.

"It's been in the papers," he said. "I reread some of last week's this morning. The city of Los Angeles is equipped with a model system now, and it's working so well it's going to be extended throughout Los Angeles County. Eventually, every city of any size in the country'll have it. Nobody'll have to walk more than four blocks to get to a line. It'll cut air pollution by half and the traffic load by three-thirds. Of course, it'll be compulsory; you'll have to show cause to drive a car. And I hate to think about the mess that's going to be, the paperwork, the pile-up in the courts and so forth. But after the way the government handled the L.A. riot, the rest of the country should get in line."

"How will the rest of the country know how the government handled it unless they're told?" I said.

"They'll be told. Every day," he said.

"Eventually, there won't be enough time in the day for the news channels to tell us all we'll need to know," I said. "And even if there were enough time, we'd have to spend all day watching TV. So who's going to get the work done?"

"Each person will have to develop his own viewing specialty," he said. "They'll just have to watch the news that concerns them and ignore the rest."

"And how can they do that if they won't know what concerns them until they've run through everything?" I said. "Day after day."

"I'll buy a drink," he said. "Liquor's good for one thing. It makes you forget what you're afraid not to forget."

8

True date: late 1982. Subjective date: late 1974

She came into my office, and I knew at once that she was going to be more than just another client. I'd been suffering all day from the "mirror syndrome," but the sight of her stabilized me. I forgot the thirty-seven-year-old face my twenty-nine-year-old mind had seen in the bathroom that morning. She is a beautiful woman, only twenty-seven. I had trouble at first listening to her story; all I wanted to do was to look at her. I finally understood that she wanted me to get her husband out of jail on a murder rap. It seemed he'd been in since 1976 (real time). She wanted me to get the case reopened, to use the new plea of rehabilitation by retrogression.

I was supposed to know that, but I had to take a quick look through my resumé before I could tell her what chance she had. Under RBR was the definition of the term and a notation that a number of people had been released because of it. The main idea behind it is that criminals are not the same people they were before they became criminals, if they have lost all memory of the crime. They've traveled backward to goodness, you might say. Of course, RBR doesn't apply to hardened criminals or to someone who'd planned a crime a long time before it was actually committed.

I asked her why she would want to help a man who had killed his mistress in a fit of rage when he'd found her cheating on him?

"I love him," she said.

And I love you, I thought.

She gave me some documents from the big rec bag she carried. I looked through them and said, "But you divorced him in 1977?"

"Yes, he's really my ex-husband," she said. "But I think of him now as my husband."

No need to ask her why.

"I'll study the case," I said. "You make a note to see me tomorrow. Meantime, how about a drink at the Rover bar so we can discuss our strategy?"

That's how it all started—again.

It wasn't until a week later, when I was going over some old recs, that I discovered it was *again*. It made no difference. I love her. I also love Carole, rather, *a* Carole. The one who married me six years ago, that is, six years ago in my memory.

But there is the other Carole, the one existing today, the poor miserable wretch who can't get out of the house until I come home. And I can't come home until late evening because I can't get started to work until about twelve noon. It's true that I could come home earlier than I do if it weren't for Myrna. I try. No use. I have to see Myrna.

I tell myself I'm a bastard, which I am, because Carole and the children need me very much. Tom is ten and acts as if he's two. Mike is a four-year-old in a twelve-year-old body. I come home from Myrna to bedlam every day, according to my records, and every day must be like today.

That I feel both guilt and shame doesn't help. I become enraged; I try to suppress my anger, which is born out of my desperation and helplessness and guilt and shame. But it comes boiling out, and then bedlam becomes hell.

I tell myself that Carole and the kids need a tower of strength now. One who can be calm and reassuring and, above all, loving. One who can handle the thousand tedious and aggravating problems that infest every household in this world of diminishing memory. In short, a hero. Because the real heroes, and heroines, are those who deal heroically with the everyday cares of life, though God knows they've been multiplied enormously. It's not the guy who kills a dragon once in his lifetime and then retires that's a hero. It's the guy who kills cockroaches and rats every day, day after day, and doesn't rest on his laurels until he's an old man, if then.

What am I talking about? Maybe I could handle the problems if it weren't for this memory loss. I can't adjust because I can't ever get used to it. My whole being, body and mind, must get the same high-voltage jolt every morning.

The insurance companies have canceled all policies for anybody under twelve. The government's contemplated taking over these policies but has decided against it. It will, however, pay for the burials, since this service is necessary. I don't really think that many children are being "accidentally" killed because of the insurance money. Most fatalities are obviously just results of neglect or parents going berserk.

I'm getting away from Myrna, trying to, anyway, because I wish to forget my guilt. I love her, but if I didn't see her tomorrow, I'd forget her. But I *will* see her tomorrow. My notes will make sure of that. And each day is, for me, love at first sight. It's a wonderful feeling, and I wish it could go on forever.

If I just had the guts to destroy all reference to her tonight. But I won't. The thought of losing her makes me panic.

9

True date: middle of 1984. Subjective date: middle of 1968

I was surprised that I woke up so early.

Yesterday, Carole and I had been married at noon. We'd driven up to this classy motel near Lake Geneva. We'd spent most of our time in bed after we got there, naturally, though we did get up for dinner and champagne. We finally fell asleep about four in the morning. That was why I hadn't expected to wake up at dawn. I reached over to touch Carole, wondering if she would be too sleepy. But she wasn't there.

She's gone to the bathroom, I thought. I'll catch her on the way back.

Then I sat up, my heart beating as if it had suddenly discovered it was alive. The edges of the room got fuzzy, and then the fuzziness raced in toward me.

The dawn light was filtered by the blinds, but I had seen that the furniture was not familiar. I'd never been in this place before.

I sprang out of bed and did not, of course, notice the note sticking out of my glass case. Why should I? I didn't wear glasses then.

Bellowing, "Carole!" I ran down a long and utterly strange hall and past the bedroom door, which was open, and into the room at the end of the hall. Inside it, I stopped. This was a kids' bedroom: bunks, pennants, slogans, photographs of two young boys, posters and blow-ups of faces I'd never seen, except one of Laurel and Hardy, some science fiction and Tolkien and Tarzan books, some school texts, and a large flat piece of equipment hanging on the wall. I would not have known that it was a TV set if its controls had not made its purpose obvious.

The bunks had not been slept in. The first rays of the sun fell on thick dust on a table.

I ran back down the hall, looked into the bathroom again, though I knew no one was there, saw dirty towels, underwear and socks heaped in a corner, and ran back to my bedroom. The blinds did not let enough light in, so I looked for a light switch on the wall. There wasn't any, though there was a small round plate of brass where the switch should have been. I touched it, and the ceiling lights came on.

Carole's side of the bed had not been slept in.

The mirror over the bureau caught me, drew me and held me. Who was this haggard old man staring out from my twenty-three-year-old self? I had gray hair, big bags under my eyes, thickening and sagging features, and a long scar on my right cheek.

After a while, still dazed and trembling, I picked up a book from the bureau and looked at it. At this close distance, I could just barely make out the title, and, when I opened it, the print was a blur.

I put the book down, *Be Your Own Handyman around Your House,* and proceeded to go through the house from attic to basement. Several times, I whimpered, "Carole! Carole!" Finding no one, I left the house and walked to the house next door and beat on its door. No one answered; no lights came on inside.

I ran to the next house and tried to wake up the people in it. But there weren't any.

A woman in a house across the street shouted at me. I ran to her, babbling. She was about fifty years old and also hysterical. A moment later, a man her age appeared behind her. Neither listened to me; they kept asking me questions, the same questions I was asking them. Then I saw a black and white police car of a model unknown to me come around the corner half a block away. I ran toward it, then stopped. The car was so silent that I knew even in my panic that it was electrically powered. The two cops wore strange uniforms, charcoal gray with white helmets topped by red panaches. Their aluminum badges were in the shape of a spread eagle.

I found out later that the police throughout the country had been federalized. These two were on the night shift and so had had enough time to get reorientated. Even so, one had such a case of the shakes that the other told him to get back into the car and take it easy for a while.

After he got us calmed down, he asked us why we hadn't listened to our tapes.

"What tapes?" we said.

"Where's your bedroom?" he said to the couple.

They led him to it, and he turned on a machine on the bedside table.

"Good morning," a voice said. I recognized it as the husband's. "Don't panic. Stay in bed and listen to me. Listen to everything I say."

The rest was a resumé, by no means short, of the main events since the first day of memory loss. It ended by directing the two to a notebook that would tell them personal things they needed to know, such as where their jobs were, how they could get to them, where the area central distributing stores were, how to use their I.D. cards and so on.

The policeman said, "You have the rec set to turn on at 6:30, but you woke up before then. Happens a lot."

I went back, reluctantly, to the house I'd fled. It was mine, but I felt as if I were a stranger. I ran off my own recs twice. Then I put my glasses on and started to put together my life. The daily rerun of "Narrative of an Old-Young Man Shipwrecked on the Shoals of Time."

I didn't go any place today. Why should I? I had no job. Who needs a lawyer who isn't through law school yet? I did have, I found out, an application in for a position on the police force. The police force was getting bigger and bigger but at the same time was having a large turnover. My recs said that I was to appear at the City Hall for an interview tomorrow.

If I feel tomorrow as I do today, and I will, I probably won't be able to make myself go to the interview. I'm too grief-stricken to do anything but sit and stare or, now and then, get up and pace back and forth, like a sick leopard in a cage made by Time. Even the tranquilizers haven't helped me much.

I have lost my bride the day after we were married. And I love Carole deeply. We were going to live a long happy life and have two children. We would raise them in a house filled with love.

But the recs say that the oldest boy escaped from the house and was killed by a car and Carole, in a fit of anguish and despair, killed the youngest boy and then herself.

They're buried in Springdale Cemetery.

I can't feel a retroactive grief for those strangers called Mike and Tom.

But Carole, lovely laughing Carole, lives in my mind.

Oh, God, why don't I just erase all my recs? Then I'd not have to suffer remorse for all I've done or failed to do. I wouldn't know what a bastard I'd been.

Why don't I do it? Take the past and shed its heartbreaks and its guilts as a snake sheds its skin. Or as the legislature cancels old laws. Press a button, fill the wastebasket, and you're clean and easy again, innocent again. That's the logical thing to do, and I'm a lawyer, dedicated to logic.

Why not? Why not?

But I can't. Maybe I like to suffer. I've liked to inflict suffering, and according to what I understand, those who like to inflict, unconsciously hope to be inflicted upon.

No, that can't be it. At least, not all of it. My main reason for hanging on to the recs is that I don't want to lose my identity. A major part of me, a unique person, is not in the neurons of my mind, where it belongs, but in an electro-mechanical device or in tracings of lead or ink on paper. The protein, the flesh for which I owe, can't hang on to *me*.

I'm becoming less and less, dwindling away, like the wicked witch on whom Dorothy poured water. I'll become a puddle, a wailing voice of hopeless despair, and then…nothing.

God, haven't I suffered enough! I said I owe for the flesh and I'm down in Your books. Why do I have to struggle each day against becoming a dumb brute, a thing without memory? Why not rid myself of the struggle? Press the button, fill the wastebasket, discharge my grief in a chaos of magnetic lines and pulped paper?

Sufficient unto the day is the evil thereof.

I didn't realize, Lord, what that really meant.

10

I will marry Carole in three days. No, I would have. No, I did.

I remember reading a collection of Krazy Kat comic strips when I was twenty-one. One was captioned: COMA REIGNS. Coconing County was in the doldrums, comatose. Nobody, Krazy Kat, Ignatz Mouse, Officer Pupp, nobody had the energy to do anything. Mouse was too lazy even to think about hurling his brickbat. Strange how that sticks in my mind. Strange to think that it won't be long before it becomes forever unstuck.

Coma reigns today over the world.

Except for Project Toro, the TV says. And that is behind schedule. But the Earth, Ignatz Mouse, will not allow itself to forget that it must hurl the brickbat, the asteroid. But where Ignatz expressed his love, in a queer perverted fashion, by banging Kat in the back of the head with his brick, the world is expressing its hatred, and its desperation, by throwing Toro at The Ball.

I did manage today to go downtown to my appointment. I did it only to keep from going mad with grief. I was late, but Chief Moberly seemed to expect that I would be. Almost everybody is, he said. One reason for my tardiness was that I got lost. This residential area was nothing in 1968 but a forest out past the edge of town. I don't have a car, and the house is in the middle of the area, which has many winding streets. I do have a map of the area, which I forgot about. I kept going eastward and finally came to a main thoroughfare. This was Route 98, over which I've traveled many times since I was a child. But the road itself, and the houses along it, were strange. The private airport which should have been across the road was gone, replaced by a number of large industrial buildings.

A big sign near a roofed bench told me to wait there for the RTS bus. One would be along every ten minutes, the sign stated.

I waited an hour. The bus, when it came, was not the fully automated vehicle promised by the sign. It held a sleepy-looking driver and ten nervous passengers. The driver didn't ask me for money, so I didn't offer any. I sat down and watched him with an occasional look out of the window. He didn't have a steering wheel. When he wanted the bus to slow down or stop he pushed a lever forward. To speed it up, he pulled back on the lever. The bus was apparently following a single aluminum rail in the middle of the right-hand lane. My recs told me later that the automatic pilot and door-opening equipment had never been delivered and probably wouldn't be for some years — if ever. The grand plan of cybernating everything possible had failed. There aren't enough people who can provide the know-how or the man-hours. In fact, everything is going to hell.

The police chief, Adam Moberly, is fifty years old and looks as if he's sixty-five. He talked to me for about fifteen minutes and then had me put through a short physical and intelligence test. Three hours after I had walked into the station, I was sworn in. He suggested that I room with two other officers, one of whom was a sixty-year-old veteran, in the hotel across the street from the station. If I had company, I'd get over the morning disorientation more quickly. Besides, the policemen who lived in the central area of the city got preferential treatment in many things, including the rationed supplies.

I refused to move. I couldn't claim that my house was a home to me, but I feel that it's a link to the past, I mean the future, no, I mean the past. Leaving it would be cutting out one more part of me.

True date: late 1984. Subjective date: early 1967

My mother died today. That is, as far as I'm concerned, she did. The days ahead of me are going to be full of anxiety and grief. She took a long time to die. She found out she had cancer two weeks after my father died. So I'll be voyaging backward in sorrow through my mother and then through my father, who was also sick for a long time.

Thank God I won't have to go through every day of that, though. Only a third of them. And these are the last words I'm going to record about their illnesses.

But how can I not record them unless I make a recording reminding me not to do so?

I found out from my recs how I'd gotten this big scar on my face. Myrna's ex-husband slashed me before I laid him out with a big ashtray. He was shipped off this time to a hospital for the criminally insane where he died a few months later in the fire that burned every prisoner in his building. I haven't the faintest idea what happened to Myrna after that. Apparently I decided not to record it.

I feel dead tired tonight, and, according to my recs, every night. It's no wonder, if every day is like today. Fires, murders, suicides, accidents and insane people. Babies up to fourteen years old abandoned. And a police department which is ninety percent composed, in effect, of raw rookies. The victims are taken to hospitals where the nurses are only half-trained, if that, and the doctors are mostly old geezers hauled out of retirement.

I'm going to bed soon even if it's only nine o'clock. I'm so exhausted that even Jayne Mansfield couldn't keep me awake. And I dread tomorrow. Besides the usual reasons for loathing it, I have one which I can hardly stand thinking about.

Tomorrow my memory will have slid past the day I met Carole. I won't remember her at all.

Why do I cry because I'll be relieved of a great sorrow?

11

True date: 1986. Subjective date: 1962

I'm nuts about Jean, and I'm way down because I can't find her. According to my recs, she went to Canada in 1965. Why? We surely didn't fall in and then out of love? Our love would never die. Her parents must've moved to Canada. And so here we both are in 1962, in effect. Halfway in 1962, anyway. Amphibians of time. Is she thinking about me now? Is she unable to think about me, about anything, because she's dead or crazy? Tomorrow I'll start the official wheels grinding. The Canadian government should be able to find her through the

International Information Computer Network, according to the recs. Meanwhile, I burn, though with a low flame. I'm so goddamn tired.

Even Marilyn Monroe couldn't get a rise out of me tonight. But Jean. Yeah, Jean. I see her as seventeen years old, tall, slim but full-busted, with creamy white skin and a high forehead and huge blue eyes and glossy black hair and the most kissable lips ever. And broadcasting sex waves so thick you can see them, like heat waves. Wow!

And so tired old Wow goes to bed.

February 6, 1987

While I was watching TV to get orientated this morning, a news flash interrupted the program. The president of the United States had died of a heart attack a few minutes before.

"My God!" I said. "Old Eisenhower is dead!"

But the picture of the president certainly wasn't that of Eisenhower. And the name was one I never heard, of course.

I can't feel bad for a guy I never knew.

I got to thinking about him, though. Was he as confused every morning as I was? Imagine a guy waking up, thinking he's a senator in Washington and then he finds he's the president? At least, he knows something about running the country. But it's no wonder the old pump conked out. The TV says we've had five prexies, mostly real old guys, in the last seven years. One was shot; one dived out of the White House window onto his head; two had heart attacks; one went crazy and almost caused a war, as if we didn't have grief enough, for crying out loud.

Even after the orientation, I really didn't get it. I guess I'm too dumb for anything to percolate through my dome.

A policeman called and told me I'd better get my ass down to work. I said I didn't feel up to it, besides, why would I want to be a cop? He said that if I didn't show, I might go to jail. So I showed.

True date: late 1988. Subjective date: 1956

Here I am, eleven years old, going on ten.

In one way, that is. The other way, here I am forty-three and going on about sixty. At least, that's what my face looks like to me. Sixty.

This place is just like a prison except some of us get treated like trusties. According to the work chart, I leave through the big iron gates every day at twelve noon with a demolition crew. We tore down five partly burned houses today. The gang chief, old Rogers, says it's just WPA work, whatever that is. Anyway, one of the guys I work with kept looking more and more familiar. Suddenly, I felt like I was going to pass out. I put down my sledge hammer and walked over to him, and I said, "Aren't you Stinky Davis?"

He looked funny and then he said, "Jesus! You're Gabby! Gabby Franham!"

I didn't like his using the Lord's name in vain, but I guess he can be excused.

Nothing would've tasted good the way I felt, but the sandwiches we got for breakfast, lunch and supper tasted like they had a dash of oil in them. Engine oil, I mean. The head honcho, he's eighty if he's a day, says his recs tell him they're derived from petroleum. The oil is converted into a kind of protein and then flavoring and stuff is added. Oil-burgers, they call them.

Tonight, before lights-out, we watched the prez give a speech. He said that, within a month, Project Toro will be finished. One way or the other. And all this memory loss should stop. I can't quite get it even if I was briefed this morning. Men on the moon, unmanned ships on Venus and Mars, all since I was eleven years old. And The Black Ball, the thing from outer space. And now we're pushing asteroids around. Talk about your science fiction!

12

September 4, 1988

Today's the day.

Actually, the big collision'll be tomorrow, ten minutes before 1:00 A.M....but I think of it as today. Toro, going 15,000 miles an hour, will run head-on into The Ball. Maybe.

Here I am again, Mark Franham, recording just in case The Ball does dodge out of the way and I have to depend on my recs. It's 7:00 P.M. and after that raunchy supper of oil-burgers, potato soup and canned carrots, fifty of us gathered around set No. 8. There's a couple of scientists talking now, discussing theories about just what The Ball is and why it's been taking our memories away from us. Old Doctor Charles Presley — any relation to Elvis? — thinks The Ball is some sort of unmanned survey ship. When it finds a planet inhabited by sentient life, sentient means intelligent, it takes specimens. Specimens of the mind, that is. It unpeels people's minds four days' worth at a time, because that's all it's capable of. But it can do it to billions of specimens. It's like it was reading our minds but destroying the mind at the same time. Presley said it was like some sort of Heisenberg principle of the mind. The Ball can't observe our memories closely without disturbing them.

This Ball, Presley says, takes our memories and stores them. And when it's through with us, sucked us dry, it'll take off for another planet circling some far-off star. Someday, it'll return to its home planet, and the scientists there will study the recordings of our minds.

The other scientist, Dr. Marbles — he's still got his, ha! ha! — asked why any species advanced enough to be able to do this could be so callous? Surely, the extees must know what great damage they're doing to us. Wouldn't they be too ethical for this?

Doc Presley says maybe they think of us as animals, they are so far above us. Doc Marbles says that could be. But it could also be that whoever built The Ball have different brains than we do. Their mind-reading ray, or whatever it is, when used on themselves doesn't disturb the memory patterns. But we're different. The extees don't know this, of course. Not now, anyway. When The Ball goes home, and the extees read our minds, they'll be shocked at what they've done to us. But it'll be too late then.

Presley and Marbles got into an argument about how the extees would be able to interpret their recordings. How could they translate our languages when they have no references — I mean, referents? How're they going to translate *chair* and *recs* and *rock and roll* and *yucky* and so on when they don't have anybody to tell them their meanings. Marbles said they wouldn't have just words; they'd have mental images to associate with the words. And so on. Some of the stuff they spouted I didn't understand at all.

I do know one thing, though, and I'm sure those bigdomes do, too. But they wouldn't be allowed to say it over TV because we'd be even more gloomy and hopeless-feeling. That is, what if right now the computers in The Ball are translating our languages, reading our minds, as they're recorded? Then they know all about Project Toro. They'll be ready for the asteroid, destroy it if they have the weapons to do it, or, if they haven't, they'll just move The Ball into a different orbit.

I'm not going to say anything to the other guys about this. Why make them feel worse?

It's ten o'clock now. According to regulations posted up all over the place, it's time to go to bed. But nobody is. Not tonight. You don't sleep when the End of the World may be coming up.

I wish my Mom and Dad were here. I cried this morning when I found they weren't in this dump, and I asked the chief where they were. He said they were working in a city nearby, but they'd be visiting me soon. I think he lied.

Stinky saw me crying, but he didn't say anything. Why should he? I'll bet he's shed a few when he thought nobody was looking, too.

Twelve o'clock. Midnight. Less than an hour to go. Then, the big smash! Or, I hate to think about it, the big flop. We won't be able to see it directly because the skies are cloudy over most of North America. But we've got a system worked out so we can see it on TV. If there's a gigantic flash when the Toro and The Ball collide, that is.

What if there isn't? Then we'll soon be just like those grown-up kids, some of them twenty years old, that they keep locked up in the big building in the northwest corner of this place. Saying nothing but Da Da or Ma Ma, drooling, filling their diapers. If they got diapers, because old Rogers says he heard, today, of course, they don't wear nothing. The nurses come in once a day and hose them and the place down. The nurses don't have time to change and wash diapers and give personal baths. They got enough to do just spoon-feeding them.

Three and a half more hours to go, and I'll be just like them. Unless, before then, I flip, and they put me in that building old Rogers calls the puzzle factory. They're all completely out of their skulls, he says, and even if memloss stops tonight; they won't change any.

Old Rogers says there's fifty million less people in the United States than there were in 1980, according to the recs. And a good thing, too, he says, because it's all we can do to feed what we got.

Come on, Toro! You're our last chance!

If Toro doesn't make it, I'll kill myself! I will! I'm not going to let myself become an idiot. Anyway, by the time I do become one, there won't be enough food to go around for those that do have their minds. I'll be starving to death. I'd rather get it over with now than go through that.

God'll forgive me.

God, You know I want to be a minister of the gospel when I grow up and that I want to help people. I'll marry a good woman, and we'll have children that'll be brought up right. And we'll thank You every day for the good things of life and battle the bad things.

Love, that's what I got, Lord. Love for You and love for Your people. So don't make me hate You. Guide Toro right into The Ball, and get us started on the right path again.

I wish Mom and Dad were here.

Twelve-thirty. In twenty minutes, we'll know.

The TV says the H-bombs are still going off all around The Ball.

The TV says the people on the East Coast are falling asleep. The rays, or whatever The Ball uses, aren't being affected by the H-bomb radiation. But that doesn't mean that its sensors aren't. I pray to God that they are cut off.

Ten minutes to go. Toro's got twenty-five thousand miles to go. Our sensors can't tell whether or not The Ball's still on its original orbit. I hope it is; I hope it is! If it's changed its path, then we're through! Done! Finished! Wiped out!

Five minutes to go; twelve thousand five hundred miles to go.

I can see in my mind's eye The Ball, almost half a mile in diameter, hurtling on its orbit, blind as a bat, I hope and pray, the bombs, the last of the five thousand bombs, flashing, and Toro, a mile and a half long, a mile wide, millions of tons of rock and nickel-steel, charging toward its destined spot.

If it *is* destined.

But space *is* big, and even the Ball and Toro are small compared to all that emptiness out there. What if the mathematics of the scientists is just a little off, or the rocket motors on Toro aren't working just like they're supposed to, and Toro just tears on by The Ball? It's got to meet The Ball at the exact time and place, it's just got to!

I wish the radars and lasers could see what's going on.

Maybe it's better they can't. If we knew that The Ball had changed course…but this way we still got hope.

If Toro misses, I'll kill myself, I swear it.

Two minutes to go. One hundred and twenty seconds. The big room is silent except for kids like me praying or talking quietly into our recs or praying and talking and sobbing.

The TV says the bombs have quit exploding. No more flashes until Toro hits The Ball — if it does. Oh, God, let it hit, let it hit!

The unmanned satellites are going to open their camera lenses at the exact second of impact and take a quick shot. The cameras are encased in lead, the shutters are lead, and the equipment is special, mostly mechanical, not electrical, almost like a human eyeball. If the cameras see the big flash, they'll send an electrical impulse through circuits, also encased in lead, to a mechanism that'll shoot a big thin-shelled ball out. This is crammed with flashpowder, the same stuff photographers use, and mixed with oxygen pellets so the powder will ignite. There's to be three of the biggest flashes you ever saw. Three. Three for Victory.

If Toro misses, then only one flashball'll be set off.

Oh, Lord, don't let it happen!

Planes with automatic pilots'll be cruising above the clouds, and their equipment will see the flashes and transmit them to the ground TV equipment.

One minute to go.

Come on, God!

Don't let it happen, please don't let it happen, that some place way out there, some thousands of years from now, some weird-looking character reads this and finds out to his horror what his people have done to us. Will he feel bad about it? Lot of good that'll do. You, out there, I hate you! God, how I hate you!

Our Father which art in Heaven, fifteen seconds, Hallowed be Thy name, ten seconds, Thy will be done, five seconds, Thy will be done, but if it's thumbs, down, God, why? Why? What did I ever do to You?

The screen's blank! Oh, my God, the screen's blank! What happened? Transmission trouble? Or they're afraid to tell us the truth?

It's on! It's on!

YAAAAAAY!

13

July 4, A.D. 2002

I may erase this. If I have any sense, I will. If I had any sense, I wouldn't make it in the first place.

Independence Day, and we're still under an iron rule. But old Dick the Dictator insists that when there's no longer a need for strict control, the Constitution will be restored, and we'll be a democracy again. He's ninety-five years old and can't last much longer. The vice-president is only eighty, but he's as tough an octogenarian as ever lived. And he's even more of a totalitarian than Dick. And when have men ever voluntarily relinquished power?

I'm one of the elite, so I don't have it so bad. Just being fifty-seven years old makes me a candidate for that class. In addition, I have my Ph.D. in education and I'm a part-time minister. I don't know why I say part-time, since there aren't any full-time ministers outside of the executives of the North American Council of Churches. The People can't afford full-time divines. Everybody has to work at least a ten hours a day. But I'm better off than many. I've been eating fresh beef and pork for three years now. I have a nice house I don't have to share with another family. The house isn't the one my recs say I once owned. The People took it over to pay for back taxes. It did me no good to protest that property taxes had been canceled during The Interim. That, say the People, ended when The Ball was destroyed.

But how could I pay taxes on it when I was only eleven years old, in effect?

I went out this afternoon, it being a holiday, with Leona to Springdale. We put flowers on her parents' and sisters' graves, none of whom she remembers, and on my parents' and Carole's and the children's graves, whom I know only through the recs. I prayed for the forgiveness of Carole and the boys.

Near Carole's grave was Stinky Davis's. Poor fellow, he went berserk the night The Ball was destroyed and had to be put in a padded cell. Still mad, he died five years later.

I sometimes wonder why I didn't go mad, too. The daily shocks and jars of memloss should have made everyone fall apart. But a certain number of us were very tough, tougher than we deserved. Even so, the day-to-day attack by alarm syndromes did its damage. I'm sure that years of life were cut off the hardiest of us. We're the shattered generation. And this is bad for the younger ones, who'll have no older people to lead them in the next ten years or so.

Or is it such a bad thing?

At least, those who were in their early twenties or younger when The Ball was smashed are coming along fine. Leona herself was twenty then. She became one of my students in high school. She's thirty-five physically but only fifteen in what the kids call "intage" or internal age. But since education goes faster for adults, and all those humanities courses have been eliminated, she graduated from high school last June. She still wants to be a doctor of medicine, and God knows we need M.D.'s. She'll be forty before she gets her degree. We're planning on having two children, the maximum allowed, and it's going to be tough raising them while she's in school. But God will see us through.

As we were leaving the cemetery, Margie Oleander, a very pretty girl of twenty-five, approached us. She asked me if she could speak privately to me. Leona didn't like that, but I told her that Margie probably wanted to talk to me about her grades in my geometry class.

Margie did talk somewhat about her troubles with her lessons. But then she began to ask some questions about the political system. Yes, I'd better erase this, and if it weren't for old habits, I'd not be doing this now.

After a few minutes, I became uneasy. She sounded as if she were trying to get me to show some resentment about the current situation.

Is she an agent provocateur or was she testing me for potential membership in the underground?

· Whatever she was doing, she was in dangerous waters. So was I. I told her to ask her political philosophy teacher for answers. She said she'd read the textbook, which is provided by the government. I muttered something about, "Render unto Caesar's what is Caesar's," and walked away.

But she came after me, and asked if I could talk to her in my office tomorrow. I hesitated and then said I would.

I wonder if I would have agreed if she weren't so beautiful?

When we got home, Leona made a scene. She accused me of chasing after the younger girls because she was too old to stimulate me. I told her that I was no senile King David, which she should be well aware of, and she said she's listened to my recs and she knew what kind of man I was. I told her I'd learned from my mistakes. I've gone over the recs of the missing years many times.

"Yes," she said, "you know about them intellectually. But you don't *feel* them!"

Which is true.

I'm outside now and looking up into the night. Up there, out there, loose atoms and molecules float around, cold and alone, debris of the memory records of The Ball, atoms and molecules of what were once incredibly complex patterns, the memories of thirty-two years of the lives of four and a half billion human beings. Forever lost, except in the mind of One.

Oh, Lord, I started all over again as an eleven-year-old. Don't let me make the same mistakes again.

You've given us tomorrow again, but we've very little past to guide us.

Tomorrow I'll be very cool and very professional with Margie. Not too much, of course, since there should be a certain warmth between teacher and pupil.

If only she did not remind me of...whom?

But that's impossible. I can remember nothing from The Interim. Absolutely nothing.

But what if there are different kinds of memory?

♦ ♦ ♦ ♦ ♦ ♦ ♦ ♦ ♦ ♦ ♦ ♦ ♦ After King Kong Fell

The first half of the movie was grim and gray and somewhat tedious. Mr. Howller did not mind. That was, after all, realism. Those times had been grim and gray. Moreover, behind the tediousness was the promise of something vast and horrifying. The creeping pace and the measured ritualistic movements of the actors gave intimations of the workings of the gods. Unhurriedly, but with utmost confidence, the gods were directing events toward the climax.

Mr. Howller had felt that at the age of fifteen, and he felt it now while watching the show on TV at the age of fifty-five. Of course, when he first saw it in 1933, he had known what was coming. Hadn't he lived through some of the events only two years before that?

The old freighter, the *Wanderer*, was nosing blindly through the fog toward the surflike roar of the natives' drums. And then: the commercial. Mr. Howller rose and stepped into the hall and called down the steps loudly enough for Jill to hear him on the front porch. He thought, commercials could be a blessing. They give us time to get into the bathroom or the kitchen, or time to light up a cigarette and decide about continuing to watch this show or go on to that show.

And why couldn't real life have its commercials?

Wouldn't it be something to be grateful for if reality stopped in mid-course while the Big Salesman made His pitch? The car about to smash into you, the bullet on its way to your brain, the first cancer cell about to break loose, the boss reaching for the phone to call you in so he can fire you, the spermatozoon about to be launched toward the ovum, the final insult about to be hurled at the once, and perhaps still, beloved, the final drink of alcohol which would rupture the abused blood vessel, the decision which would lead to the light that would surely fail?

If only you could step out while the commercial interrupted these, think about it, talk about it, and then, returning to the set, switch it to another channel.

But that one is having technical difficulties, and the one after that is a talk show whose guest is the archangel Gabriel himself and after some urging by the host he agrees to blow his trumpet, and...

Jill entered, sat down, and began to munch the cookies and drink the lemonade he had prepared for her. Jill was six and a half years old and beautiful, but then what granddaughter wasn't beautiful? Jill was also unhappy because she had just quarreled with her best friend, Amy, who had stalked off with threats never to see Jill again. Mr. Howller reminded her that this had happened before and that Amy always came back the next day, if not sooner. To take her mind off of Amy, Mr. Howller gave her a brief outline of what had happened in the movie. Jill listened without enthusiasm, but she became excited enough once the movie had resumed. And when Kong was feeling over the edge of the abyss for John Driscoll, played by Bruce Cabot, she got into her grandfather's lap. She gave a little scream and put her hands over her eyes when Kong carried Ann Redman into the jungle (Ann played by Fay Wray).

But by the time Kong lay dead on Fifth Avenue, she was rooting for him, as millions had before her. Mr. Howller squeezed her and kissed her and said, "When your mother was about your age, I took her to see this. And when it was over, she was crying, too."

Jill sniffled and let him dry the tears with his handkerchief. When the Roadrunner cartoon came on, she got off his lap and went back to her cookie-munching. After a while she said, "Grandpa, the coyote falls off the cliff so far you can't even see him. When he hits, the whole earth shakes. But he always comes back, good as new. Why can he fall so far and not get hurt? Why couldn't King Kong fall and be just like new?"

Her grandparents and her mother had explained many times the distinction between a "live" and a "taped" show. It did not seem to make any difference how many times they explained. Somehow, in the years of watching TV, she had gotten the fixed idea that people in "live" shows actually suffered pain, sorrow, and death. The only shows she could endure seeing were those that her elders labeled as "taped." This worried Mr. Howller more than he admitted to his wife and daughter. Jill was a very bright child, but what if too many TV shows at too early an age had done her some irreparable harm? What if, a few years from now, she could easily see, and even define, the distinction between reality and unreality on the screen but deep down in her there was a child that still could not distinguish?

"You know that the Roadrunner is a series of pictures that move. People draw pictures, and people can do anything with pictures. So the Roadrunner is drawn again and again, and he's back in the next show with his wounds all healed and he's ready to make a jackass of himself again."

"A jackass? But he's a coyote."

"Now…"

Mr. Howller stopped. Jill was grinning.

"O.K., now you're pulling my leg."

"But is King Kong alive or is he taped?"

"Taped. Like the Disney I took you to see last week. *Bedknobs and Broomsticks.*"

"Then *King Kong* didn't happen?"

"Oh, yes, it really happened. But this is a movie they made about King Kong after what really happened was all over. So it's not exactly like it really was, and actors took the parts of Ann Redman and Carl Denham and all the others. Except King Kong himself. He was a toy model."

Jill was silent for a minute and then she said, "You mean, there really was a King Kong? How do you know, Grandpa?"

"Because I was there in New York when Kong went on his rampage. I was in the theater when he broke loose, and I was in the crowd that gathered around Kong's body after he fell off the Empire State Building. I was thirteen then, just seven years older than you are now. I was with my parents, and they were visiting my Aunt Thea. She was beautiful, and she had golden hair just like Fay Wray's—I mean, Ann Redman's. She'd married a very rich man, and they had a big apartment high up in the clouds. In the Empire State Building itself."

"High up in the clouds! That must've been fun, Grandpa!"

It would have been, he thought, if there had not been so much tension in that apartment. Uncle Nate and Aunt Thea should have been happy because they were so rich and lived in such a swell place. But they weren't. No one said anything to young Tim Howller, but he felt the suppressed anger, heard the bite of tone, and saw the tightening lips. His aunt and uncle were having trouble of some sort, and his parents were upset by it. But they all tried to pretend everything was as sweet as honey when he was around.

Young Howller had been eager to accept the pretense. He didn't like to think that anybody could be mad at his tall, blonde, and beautiful aunt. He was passionately in love with her; he ached for her in the daytime; at nights he had fantasies about her of which he was ashamed when he awoke. But not for long. She was a thousand times more desirable than Fay Wray or Claudette Colbert or Elissa Landi.

But that night, when they were all going to see the premiere of *The Eighth Wonder of the World,* King Kong himself, young Howller had managed to ignore whatever it was that was bugging his elders. And even they seemed to be having a good time. Uncle Nate, over his parents' weak protests, had purchased orchestra seats for them. These were twenty dollars apiece, big money in Depression days, enough to feed a family for a month. Everybody got all dressed up, and Aunt Thea looked too beautiful to be real. Young Howller was so excited that he thought his heart was going to climb up and out through his throat. For days the newspapers had been full of stories about King Kong — speculations, rather, since Carl Denham wasn't telling them much. And he, Tim Howller, would be one of the lucky few to see the monster first.

Boy, wait until he got back to the kids in seventh grade in Busiris, Illinois! Would their eyes ever pop when he told them all about it!

But his happiness was too good to last. Aunt Thea suddenly said she had a headache and couldn't possibly go. Then she and Uncle Nate went into their bedroom, and even in the front room, three rooms and a hallway distant, young Tim could hear their voices. After a while Uncle Nate, slamming doors behind him, came out. He was red-faced and scowling, but he wasn't going to call the party off. All four of them, very uncomfortable and silent, rode in a taxi to the theater on Times Square. But when they got inside, even Uncle Nate forgot the quarrel or at least he seemed to. There was the big stage with its towering silvery curtains and through the curtains came a vibration of excitement and of delicious danger. And even through the curtains the hot hairy apestink filled the theater.

"Did King Kong get loose just like in the movie?" Jill said.

Mr. Howller started. "What? Oh, yes, he sure did. Just like in the movie."

"Were you scared, Grandpa? Did you run away like everybody else?"

He hesitated. Jill's image of her grandfather had been cast in a heroic mold. To her he was a giant of Herculean strength and perfect courage, her defender and champion. So far he had managed to live up to the image, mainly because the demands she made were not too much for him. In time she would see the cracks and the sawdust oozing out. But she was too young to disillusion now.

"No, I didn't run," he said. "I waited until the theater was cleared of the crowd."

This was true. The big man who'd been sitting in the seat before him had leaped up yelling as Kong began tearing the bars out of his cage, had whirled and jumped over the back of his seat, and his knee had hit young Howller on the jaw. And so young Howller had been stretched out senseless on the floor under the seats while the mob screamed and tore at each other and trampled the fallen.

Later he was glad that he had been knocked out. It gave him a good excuse for not keeping cool, for not acting heroically in the situation. He knew that if he had not been unconscious, he would have been as frenzied as the others, and he would have abandoned his parents, thinking only in his terror of his own salvation. Of course, his parents had deserted him, though they claimed that they had been swept away from him by the mob. This *could* be true; maybe his folks *had* actually tried to get to him. But he had not really thought they had, and for years he had looked down on them because of their flight. When he got older, he realized that he would have done the same thing, and he knew that his contempt for them was really a disguised contempt for himself.

He had awakened with a sore jaw and a headache. The police and the ambulance men were there and starting to take care of the hurt and to haul away the dead. He staggered past them out into the lobby and, not seeing his parents there, went outside. The sidewalks and the streets were plugged with thousands of men, women, and children, on foot and in cars, fleeing northward.

He had not known where Kong was. He should have been able to figure it out, since the frantic mob was leaving the midtown part of Manhattan. But he could think of only two things. Where were his parents? And was Aunt Thea safe? And then he had a third thing to consider. He discovered that he had wet his pants. When he had seen the great ape burst loose, he had wet his pants.

Under the circumstances, he should have paid no attention to this. Certainly no one else did. But he was a very sensitive and shy boy of thirteen, and, for some reason, the need for getting dry underwear and trousers seemed even more important than finding his parents. In retrospect he would tell himself that he would have gone south anyway. But he knew deep down that if his pants had not been wet he might not have dared return to the Empire State Building.

It was impossible to buck the flow of the thousands moving like lava up Broadway. He went east on 43rd Street until he came to Fifth Avenue, where he started southward. There was a crowd to fight against here, too, but it was much smaller than that on Broadway. He was able to thread his way through it, though he often had to go out into the street and dodge the cars. These, fortunately, were not able to move faster than about three miles an hour.

"Many people got impatient because the cars wouldn't go faster," he told Jill, "and they just abandoned them and struck out on foot."

"Wasn't it noisy, Grandpa?"

"Noisy? I've never heard such noise. I think that everyone in Manhattan, except those hiding under their beds, was yelling or talking. And every driver in Manhattan was blowing his car's horn. And then there were the sirens of the fire trucks and police cars and ambulances. Yes, it was noisy."

Several times he tried to stop a fugitive so he could find out what was going on. But even when he did succeed in halting someone for a few seconds, he couldn't make himself heard. By then, as he found out later, the radio had broadcast the news. Kong had chased John Driscoll and Ann Redman out of the theater and across the street to their hotel. They had gone up to Driscoll's room, where they thought they were safe. But Kong had climbed up, using windows as ladder steps, reached into the room, knocked Driscoll out, and grabbed Ann, and had then leaped away with her. He had headed, as Carl Denham figured he would, toward the tallest structure on the island. On King Kong's own island, he lived on the highest point, Skull Mountain, where he was truly monarch of all he surveyed. Here he would climb to the top of the Empire State Building, Manhattan's Skull Mountain.

Tim Howller had not known this, but he was able to infer that Kong had traveled down Fifth Avenue from 38th Street on. He passed a dozen cars with their tops flattened down by the ape's fist or turned over on their sides or tops. He saw three sheet-covered bodies on the sidewalks, and he overheard a policeman telling a reporter that Kong had climbed up several buildings on his way south and reached into windows and pulled people out and thrown them down onto the pavement.

"But you said King Kong was carrying Ann Redman in the crook of his arm, Grandpa," Jill said. "He only had one arm to climb with, Grandpa, so...so wouldn't he fall off the building when he reached in to grab those poor people?"

"A very shrewd observation, my little chickadee," Mr. Howller said, using the W. C. Fields voice that usually sent her into giggles. "But his arms were long enough for him to drape Ann Redman over the arm he used to hang on with while he reached in with the other. And to forestall your next question, even if you had not thought of it, he could turn over an automobile with only one hand."

"But...but why'd he take time out to do that if he wanted to get to the top of the Empire State Building?"

"I don't know why *people* often do the things they do," Mr. Howller said. "So how would I know why an *ape* does the things he does?"

When he was a block away from the Empire State Building, a plane crashed onto the middle of the avenue two blocks behind him and burned furiously. Tim Howller watched it for a few minutes, then he looked upward and saw the red and green lights of the five planes and the silvery bodies slipping in and out of the searchlights.

"Five airplanes, Grandpa? But the movie…"

"Yes, I know. The movie showed about fourteen or fifteen. But the book says that there were six to begin with, and the book is much more accurate. The movie also shows King Kong's last stand taking place in the daylight. But it didn't; it was still nighttime."

The Army Air Force plane must have been going at least 250 mph as it dived down toward the giant ape standing on the top of the observation tower. Kong had put Ann Redman by his feet so he could hang on to the tower with one hand and grab out with the other at the planes. One had come too close, and he had seized the left biplane structure and ripped it off. Given the energy of the plane, his hand should have been torn off, too, or at least he should have been pulled loose from his hold on the tower and gone down with the plane. But he hadn't let loose, and that told something of the enormous strength of that towering body. It also told something of the relative fragility of the biplane.

Young Howller had watched the efforts of the firemen to extinguish the fire and then he had turned back toward the Empire State Building. By then it was all over. All over for King Kong, anyway. It was, in after years, one of Mr. Howller's greatest regrets that he had not seen the monstrous dark body falling through the beams of the searchlights — blackness, then the flash of blackness through the whiteness of the highest beam, blackness, the flash through the next beam, blackness, the flash through the third beam, blackness, the flash through the lowest beam. Dot, dash, dot, dash, Mr. Howller was to think afterward. A code transmitted unconsciously by the great ape and received unconsciously by those who witnessed the fall. Or by those who would hear of it and think about it. Or was he going too far in conceiving this? Wasn't he always looking for codes? And, when he found them, unable to decipher them?

Since he had been thirteen, he had been trying to equate the great falls in man's myths and legends and to find some sort of intelligence in them. The fall of the tower of Babel, of Lucifer, of Vulcan, of Icarus, and, finally, of King Kong. But he wasn't equal to the task; he didn't have the genius to perceive what the falls meant, he couldn't screen out the — to use an electronic term — the "noise." All he could come up with were folk adages. What goes up must come down. The bigger they are, the harder they fall.

"What'd you say, Grandpa?"

"I was thinking out loud, if you can call that thinking," Mr. Howller said.

Young Howller had been one of the first on the scene, and so he got a place in the front of the crowd. He had not completely forgotten his parents or Aunt Thea, but the danger was over, and he could not make himself leave to search for them. And he had even forgotten about his soaked pants. The body was only about thirty feet from him. It lay on its back on the sidewalk, just as in the movie. But the dead Kong did not look as big or as dignified as in the movie. He was spread out more like an apeskin rug than a body, and blood and bowels and their contents had splashed out around him.

After a while Carl Denham, the man responsible for capturing Kong and bringing him to New York, appeared. As in the movie, Denham spoke his classical lines by the body: "It was Beauty. As always, Beauty killed the Beast."

This was the most appropriately dramatic place for the lines to be spoken, of course, and the proper place to end the movie.

But the book had Denham speaking these lines as he leaned over the parapet of the observation tower to look down at Kong on the sidewalk. His only audience was a police sergeant.

Both the book and the movie were true. Or half true. Denham did speak those lines way up on the 102nd floor of the tower. But, showman that he was, he also spoke them when he got down to the sidewalk, where the newsmen could hear them.

Young Howller didn't hear Denham's remarks. He was too far away. Besides, at that moment he felt a tap on his shoulder and heard a man say, "Hey, kid, there's somebody trying to get your attention!"

Young Howller went into his mother's arms and wept for at least a minute. His father reached past his mother and touched him briefly on the forehead, as if blessing him, and then gave his shoulder a squeeze. When he was able to talk, Tim Howller asked his mother what had happened to them. They, as near as they could remember, had been pushed out by the crowd, though they had fought to get to him, and had run up Broadway after they found themselves in the street because King Kong had appeared. They had managed to get back to the theater, had not been able to locate Tim, and had walked back to the Empire State Building.

"What happened to Uncle Nate?" Tim said.

Uncle Nate, his mother said, had caught up with them on Fifth Avenue and just now was trying to get past the police cordon into the building so he could check on Aunt Thea.

"She must be all right!" young Howller said. "The ape climbed up her side of the building, but she could easily get away from him, her apartment's so big!"

"Well, yes," his father had said. "But if she went to bed with her headache, she would've been right next to the window. But don't worry. If she'd been hurt, we'd know it. And maybe she wasn't even home."

Young Tim had asked him what he meant by that, but his father had only shrugged.

The three of them stood in the front line of the crowd, waiting for Uncle Nate to bring news of Aunt Thea, even though they weren't really worried about her, and waiting to see what happened to Kong. Mayor Jimmy Walker showed up and conferred with the officials. Then the governor himself, Franklin Delano Roosevelt, arrived with much noise of siren and motorcycle. A minute later a big black limousine with flashing red lights and a siren pulled up. Standing on the runningboard was a giant with bronze hair and strange-looking gold-flecked eyes. He jumped off the runningboard and strode up to the mayor, governor, and police commissioner and talked briefly with them. Tim Howller asked the man next to him what the giant's name was, but the man replied that he didn't know because he was from out of town also. The giant finished talking and strode up to the crowd, which opened for him as if it were the Red Sea and he were Moses, and he had no trouble at all getting through the police cordon. Tim then asked the man on the right of his parents if he knew the yellow-eyed giant's name. This man, tall and thin, was with a beautiful woman dressed up in an evening gown and a mink coat. He turned his head when Tim called to him and presented a hawklike face and eyes that burned so brightly that Tim wondered if he took dope. Those eyes also told him that here was a man who asked questions, not one who gave answers. Tim didn't repeat his question, and a moment later the man said, in a whispering voice that still carried a long distance, "Come on, Margo. I've work to do." And the two melted into the crowd.

Mr. Howller told Jill about the two men, and she said, "What about them, Grandpa?"

"I don't really know," he said. "Often I've wondered...Well, never mind. Whoever they were, they're irrelevant to what happened to King Kong. But I'll say one thing about New York—you sure see a lot of strange characters there."

Young Howller had expected that the mess would quickly be cleaned up. And it was true that the sanitation department had sent a big truck with a big crane and a number of men with hoses, scoop shovels, and brooms. But a dozen people at least stopped the cleanup almost before it began. Carl Denham wanted no one to touch the body except the taxidermists he had called in. If he couldn't exhibit a live Kong, he would exhibit a dead one. A colonel from Roosevelt Field claimed the body and, when asked why the Air Force wanted it, could not give an explanation. Rather, he refused to give one, and it was not until an hour later that a phone call from the White House forced him to reveal the real reason. A general wanted the skin for a trophy because Kong was the only ape ever shot down in aerial combat.

A lawyer for the owners of the Empire State Building appeared with a claim for possession of the body. His clients wanted reimbursement for the damage done to the building.

A representative of the transit system wanted Kong's body so it could be sold to help pay for the damage the ape had done to the Sixth Avenue Elevated.

The owner of the theater from which Kong had escaped arrived with his lawyer and announced he intended to sue Denham for an amount which would cover the sums he would have to pay to those who were inevitably going to sue him.

The police ordered the body seized as evidence in the trial for involuntary manslaughter and criminal negligence in which Denham and the theater owner would be defendants in due process.

The manslaughter charges were later dropped, but Denham did serve a year before being paroled. On being released, he was killed by a religious fanatic, a native brought back by the second expedition to Kong's island. He was, in fact, the witch doctor. He had murdered Denham because Denham had abducted and slain his god, Kong.

His Majesty's New York consul showed up with papers which proved that Kong's island was in British waters. Therefore, Denham had no right to anything removed from the island without permission of His Majesty's government.

Denham was in a lot of trouble. But the worst blow of all was to come next day. He would be handed notification that he was being sued by Ann Redman. She wanted compensation to the tune of ten million dollars for various physical indignities and injuries suffered during her two abductions by the ape, plus the mental anguish these had caused her. Unfortunately for her, Denham went to prison without a penny in his pocket, and she dropped the suit. Thus, the public never found out exactly what the "physical indignities and injuries" were, but this did not keep it from making many speculations. Ann Redman also sued John Driscoll, though for a different reason. She claimed breach of promise. Driscoll, interviewed by newsmen, made his famous remark that she should have been suing Kong, not him. This convinced most of the public that what it had suspected had indeed happened. Just how it could have been done was difficult to explain, but the public had never lacked wiseacres who would not only attempt the difficult but would not draw back even at the impossible.

Actually, Mr. Howller thought, the deed was not beyond possibility. Take an adult male gorilla who stood six feet high and weighed 350 pounds. According to Swiss zoo director Ernst Lang, he would have a full erection only two inches long. How did Professor Lang know this? Did he enter the cage during a mating and measure the phallus? Not very likely. Even the timid and amiable gorilla would scarcely submit to this type of handling in that kind of situation. Never mind. Professor Lang said it was so, and so it must be. Perhaps he used a telescope with gradations across the lens like those on a submarine's periscope. In any event, until someone entered the cage and slapped down a ruler during the action, Professor Lang's word would have to be taken as the last word.

By mathematical extrapolation, using the square-cube law, a gorilla twenty feet tall would have an erect penis about twenty-one inches long. What the diameter would be was another guess and perhaps a vital one, for Ann Redman anyway. Whatever anyone else thought about the possibility, Kong must have decided that he would never know unless he tried. Just how well he succeeded, only he and his victim knew, since the attempt would have taken place before Driscoll and Denham got to the observation tower and before the searchlight beams centered on their target.

But Ann Redman must have told her lover, John Driscoll, the truth, and he turned out not to be such a strong man after all.

"What're you thinking about, Grandpa?"

Mr. Howller looked at the screen. The Roadrunner had been succeeded by the Pink Panther, who was enduring as much pain and violence as the poor old coyote.

"Nothing," he said. "I'm just watching the Pink Panther with you."

"But you didn't say what happened to King Kong," she said.

"Oh," he said, "we stood around until dawn, and then the big shots finally came to some sort of agreement. The body just couldn't be left there much longer, if for no other reason than that it was blocking traffic. Blocking traffic meant that business would be held up. And lots of people would lose lots of money. And so Kong's body was taken away by the Police Department, though it used the Sanitation Department's crane, and it was kept in an icehouse until its ownership could be thrashed out."

"Poor Kong."

"No," he said, "not poor Kong. He was dead and out of it."

"He went to heaven?"

"As much as anybody," Mr. Howller said.

"But he killed a lot of people, and he carried off that nice girl. Wasn't he bad?"

"No, he wasn't bad. He was an animal, and he didn't know the difference between good and evil. Anyway, even if he'd been human, he would've been doing what any human would have done."

"What do you mean, Grandpa?"

"Well, if you were captured by people only a foot tall and carried off to a far place and put in a cage, wouldn't you try to escape? And if these people tried to put you back in, or got so scared that they tried to kill you right now, wouldn't you step on them?"

"Sure, I'd step on them, Grandpa."

"You'd be justified, too. And King Kong was justified. He was only acting according to the dictates of his instincts."

"What?"

"He was an animal, and so he can't be blamed, no matter what he did. He wasn't evil. It was what happened around Kong that was evil."

"What do you mean?" Jill said.

"He brought out the bad and the good in the people."

But mostly bad, he thought, and he encouraged Jill to forget about Kong and concentrate on the Pink Panther. And as he looked at the screen, he saw it through tears. Even after forty-two years, he thought, tears. This was what the fall of Kong had meant to him.

The crane had hooked the corpse and lifted it up. And there were two flattened-out bodies under Kong; he must have dropped them onto the sidewalk on his way up and then fallen on them from the tower. But how explain the nakedness of the corpses of the man and the woman?

The hair of the woman was long and, in a small area not covered by blood, yellow. And part of her face was recognizable.

Young Tim had not known until then that Uncle Nate had returned from looking for Aunt Thea. Uncle Nate gave a long wailing cry that sounded as if he, too, were falling from the top of the Empire State Building.

A second later young Tim Howller was wailing. But where Uncle Nate's was the cry of betrayal, and perhaps of revenge satisfied, Tim's was both of betrayal and of grief for the death of one he had passionately loved with a thirteen-year-old's love, for one whom the thirteen-year-old in him still loved.

"Grandpa, are there any more King Kongs?"

"No," Mr. Howller said. To say yes would force him to try to explain something that she could not understand. When she got older, she would know that every dawn saw the death of the old Kong and the birth of the new.

♦ ♦ ♦ ♦ ♦ ♦ ♦ ♦ ♦ ♦ The Henry Miller Dawn Patrol

Mrs. Stoss, head night nurse of the Columbia Nursing Manor, looked into the room. Henry Miller added fake snores to the genuine ones of his three roommates. From under a half-closed lid, he could see the face of The Black Eagle behind and to one side of her jowly head. Over her broad shoulder rose a dark hand with curved thumb and forefinger meeting.

Signal: The Bloody Baroness won't be flying much tonight.

After Stoss and the attendant had left, Henry thought about what The Black Eagle had said before bedtime.

"Listen, Ace. Stoss is out to get your ass in a sling. I don't know what's bugging that fat mama, but she's sure burned about you getting all that dried-up pussy. She don't want nobody happy nohow. She's always bitching about this and that. *This* is you. *That* is the three husbands died on her.

"Whatever she wanted from her men, she didn't get it. Maybe she don't know what it was herself. Course, she never mentions fucking. She wouldn't say shit if she had a mouthful. Whatever, Ace, I'm on your side. But if she catches you, can't nobody help you."

An hour before dawn, he awoke. Piss call. His joy stick was as upright and as hard as that in the Spad XIII he'd flown fifty-nine years ago. He clutched it, moved it to left and right, saw the wings dipping in response.

He climbed out of bed and stood blinking before the dresser. On it were two framed photographs. One was of his daughter, poor wretch. Its glass was cracked, damaged when he'd flung it across the room after she'd refused to smuggle in booze for him.

The other photo was of a man standing by a biplane. He was a handsome twenty-year-old, a lieutenant of the Army Air Service, himself. The Spad, *The Bitter Pill*, bore a hat-in-the-ring, the 94th Squadron insignia, on its fuselage. The glass shimmered in the faint light, reflecting his days of glory.

Then he'd been half man, half Spad, a centaur of the blue. Flesh welded to wood, fabric, and metal. Now—seventy-nine, bald head, one-eyed, face like a shell-torn battlefield, false teeth, skinny body in sagging pajamas.

But the Lone Eagle was up and ready for another dawn patrol. He limped to the bathroom, favoring the bad knee, and he pissed. His joy stick, which was also, economically, his Vickers machine gun, became as limp as a cigarette in a latrine. Never mind. It'd be functioning when he closed in on the Hun.

After leaving the bathroom, he opened a dresser drawer and removed a leather fur-lined helmet and a pair of flier's goggles. He put these on and taxied to the hall. No enemy craft were in sight. The stench of shit hung in the air, radiated from several hundred obsolete types. They'd crapped in bed, and now some were awake, shrilling for the attendants to clean them up. Nobody was going to do it, though, until after dawn.

Most of the obsoletes were asleep, and they'd be indifferent if they went all day with shit down to their toes. Or, if they were aware of it, they couldn't move, couldn't talk.

Oh, oh! Here came The White Ghost. Around the corner far down the hall, a woman in a wheelchair had appeared. She was up early, looking for a victim. If she kept on her heading, she'd run into the Von Richthofen of the nursing home. Stoss would rave at her like a sergeant reaming out a dumb recruit.

He returned to his hangar to allow The White Ghost to roll on by him. She was ninety-six, but her fuel line wasn't clogged. A real ace, a sky shark, deadly. If she wasn't so damn ugly, he would have challenged her long ago.

Silently, she wheeled on by. She never talked, just cruised day and night, hoping to catch somebody by surprise. As soon as she passed, he banked left and flew down the hall. Though the pace made his undercarriage hurt, and the Hispaño-Suiza in his chest thumped, he got to his objective on schedule.

This hangar held only two, Harz and Whittaker. Harz was a snoring lump, big as a Zeppelin Staaken bomber. He could take her any time, but it was the sleek tough fighters he was after. Like Whittaker. A widow — weren't they all? — of unadmitted age but to his keen falcon eye about seventy-four. Except for some of the young nurses, the handsomest craft in the place.

Her framework was splendid, though covered by wrinkled fabric. Her motor cowlings were still shapely, considering the date on which the factory had shipped her out. He classified her as a Fokker D-VIIF, the best.

She'd been sociable enough—until the day he'd zoomed by and dropped a note challenging her. From then on, she was as cool and aloof as the Kaiser invited to dinner by a pig farmer. But she had class. She'd not run squealing to The Baroness.

His motor having quit racing, he glided toward her, then stopped. What the hell! Something was crawling under the sheet over her. A giant cockroach? A water bug? No, it was her hand moving over her cockpit. The sheet was fluttering like fabric ripping from the wing of a Nieuport in a too-long, too-hard dive.

Grinning, he climbed over the bar at the foot of the bed and raised the sheet.

♦ ♦ ♦

Whittaker moaned, her 185-horsepower, six-cylinder, in-line, water-cooled BMW IIIa purring. Her fingers were playing with her cockpit instrumentation. *Sacré merde!* The hoity-toity Fokker wouldn't answer his challenge, but she wasn't above a jack-off dogfight, a furtive combat with herself.

Under the sheet, in a darkness like the inside of a night cloud, The Lone Eagle glided. Her widespread legs guided him like landing-strip lights. He was ready for sudden action, an air-raid-siren scream, her fists beating at his head like shrapnel from Archie.

He pushed her hand away, felt no start, heard no protest. He nosedived, the wind screaming through the wing wires and struts, his motor roaring. Then he was zeroed in, firing quick short bursts, what the hell, his tongue was a Vickers machine gun, too.

Now, all caution abandoned, he poured a long, slow stream of fire into her cockpit. The Fokker shuddered and moaned under his blasting. Thank God she wasn't like so many of the Columbia Huns. They weren't too clean; they smelled like the early World War One rotary-engine planes. Castor oil was used then for lubrication, and the poor bastards that breathed it got diarrhea.

Her exhaust pipe was clean and her cockpit was sprayed with some Frenchy-smelling perfume. Tasted like bootleg alky. No time for nostalgia now, though.

Whittaker knew he was present, but she wasn't saying a word to him. Still waters run deep; aces fly high. She'd incorporated him into her fantasy; to her, he wasn't real flesh; he was part of her dreamworld. So what? His Vickers was ready. First, though, a few maneuvers. He crawled on up, grabbed her big round cowlings, chewed on the propeller hubs, then eased the gun into the cockpit. She uttered, softly, lovingly, obscenities and profanities she'd probably not heard until she came to the nursing home.

Now she was tossing him up and down as if he were flying through one air pocket after another, hitting updrafts after each one. Now his Vickers was chattering, eating up the cartridges in the belt, the phosphorus-burning bullets tracing ecstasy across the night sky.

It was too much for the D-VIIF. She gave a loud cry, and her fuel tank ruptured. Shit squirted out over his Vickers and his undercarriage.

Cursing, he zoomed out of the cloud cover, sideslipped from the bed and raced toward the doorway. The Staaken was up now, yelling but not knowing what was going on. Without her glasses, she was as blind as a doughboy in a smoke screen.

The Baroness' voice rose from somewhere around the corner of the hall. Trapped! No, not The Lone Eagle! He plunged into a hangar tenanted by four pilots long past flight duty. Oh, oh! A visitor! That crazy crone Simmons, the eighty-year-old with eczema, was in bed with poor old Osborn. She was on all fours between his skinny legs. She didn't mind that his feet had been cut off in an accident years ago. All she was interested in was his joy stick. She'd taken out her false teeth and put them on the bed behind her.

The other old vets were snoring away. Simmons raised her face, which looked like a dried-up used rubber, and she snarled gummily at him. Osborn was on his back, desperately trying to gain altitude, but he couldn't get off the runway. A real kiwi. Henry slid under the bed. If The Baroness came in here, she might be so mad at the two above him she'd forget to check his hangar. If Simmons kept her trap shut....

Simmons yelled. "You footless old bastard! My Gawd, I'm sick and tired of sucking limp dicks!"

Henry was so startled he raised his head and banged it against the springs. "Oh, shit!"

A long silent minute passed. Then the springs began going up and down. Artillery barrage. So Simmons had managed somehow to unjam the old fart's gun. The Lone Eagle should make a run for it. The Baroness would soon be in Whittaker's hangar. He crawled out and stood up. The three oldsters were still sleeping, toothless jaws gaping like baby birds begging for worms. Worms were all they'd get.

Osborn was still on his back. Simmons was standing up, clutching his left thigh with both hands. *Sacrebleu!* His leg was jammed up to the calf up her cockpit. She was bouncing up and down on it like a toy monkey on a stick, a Sopwith Camel caught in an Archie trap. Osborn was being dragged toward the foot of the bed as each bound carried her backward. Simmons was yelping like a hung-up bitch as each downward movement plunged the stump into her.

He started to take off for Allied territory, then stopped as Simmons screamed. One of her plunges had brought her toes between the false teeth, and they'd closed like a wolf trap. As she fell over the end of the bed, he zoomed out laughing. What next?

♦ ♦ ♦

The only one in the hall was The White Ghost. Here she came, full throttle, grinning like the skull insignia on the great Nungesser's Nieuport. She'd wait until he began to pass her, then...wham!

She tried to turn as he circled her widely, but her machine didn't have the terrific right torque of a Camel. He got behind her, pushed as fast as his damaged undercarriage allowed, and then let loose. Around the corner, Stoss bellowed like the motors of a Gotha bomber.

Just as he reached the other corner, he heard a scream followed by a crash. He couldn't resist peeking around the corner. The Baroness was on her back. The machine was lying on its side, its pilot sprawled by it. The Black Eagle was laughing too hard to help either of them.

Henry took off for home base, put his flying gear into the dresser drawer, and crawled into bed. The Fokker's shit was all over his fuselage, but he'd just have to endure it until things settled down. Anyway, the shit didn't smell as bad as Stoss' breath.

The old Hispano was thumping as if it had sand in its bearings. He couldn't take too many sorties like this one much longer. One of these days, the motor'd give out and he'd go into the final dive. So what? Was there a better way to die? He wasn't like the other old pilots, too tired, sick, or senile to care about anything. He was going to stay in the combat zone until The Biggest Ace downed him.

Not, however, before he knocked The Bloody Baroness flaming out of the skies. He hated her as much as she loathed him...to hell with her. He slid back to September 1918. The Big Push. That month, he'd shot down four planes and had busted two Drache observation balloons.

But October first, as he was firing at a Pfalz D-12, that Kraut fighter had come from nowhere behind him. *The Bitter Pill* was in rags, its fabric was burning, his knee was shattered, and boiling radiator water was scalding his legs. He couldn't take to the silk because that asshole, A.E.F. Commander "Black Jack" Pershing, had forbidden American fliers to carry parachutes.

He'd had to ride the out-of-control ship to the ground while he hoped the fuel tank wouldn't explode. Somehow, he'd managed to sideslip it, putting the fire out, and then he'd leveled out just before he crashed into a small river. The Kraut soldiers who dragged him out thought he was dead. No wonder. His left eye and most of his teeth had been knocked out and he was covered with blood.

It was all downglide from then on. The rest of his life — a crippled carpenter with an ailing wife and four kids. Still, the old joy stick, the trusty Vickers, had functioned splendidly. Though he didn't have as many cartridges in his belts as when he'd flown in the Big One, he had more than some young punks he knew.

His daughter said, "But, Dad! You're getting worse! The day nurse told me you're losing control of your bowels!"

"Horsepoppy! One of my roommates crapped on the floor — must have thought he was home — and I slipped on it. I didn't take a shower right away, because the night nurse gets uptight if she finds me out of bed after taps."

She bit her lip, then said, "Mrs. Stoss says you sneak around at night and...uh...bother the old ladies."

"Any of them complaining?"

"No. But she says most of them are too senile to resist. They don't know what's going on, and those who do are just as bad..."

He chuckled. "Say it. Just as bad as me."

The other patients being visited — patients, hell; geriatric prisoners of war — sat on sofas or wheelchairs in the big lounge. They were chattering away like a bunch of French whores or sitting dull-eyed, slack-jawed, drooling, while their relatives tried to get a rise out of them.

By God, a rise could be gotten out of him. Wouldn't they be surprised if they knew just what kind and how many?

"I wish I *had* let you go to the vets' hospital. There aren't any old women there you could take advantage of."

"You're the one wanted me to come here to Busiris so I wouldn't be so far away from you. So I see you once a month — if I'm lucky.

"And don't give me that crap about sixty miles is a long way to drive. No, I made the right decision, after all, even if it was mainly for your convenience. The vets' hospital is out. If I have to choose between elephants' graveyards..."

"Nurse Stoss says she may have to put you in a room by yourself. Or...uh...restrain you."

"You mean, strap me down in bed? Or stick me in a straitjacket? Bullshit! You forget I broke out of the toughest prison camp the fucking Krauts had, and I was almost a basket case."

"Please, Dad, not so loud! And don't use those filthy words! Listen. It won't be easy, but we can work it out if you'll be nice. You could come home…"

"Are you nuts? Your husband hates me! I'd have to sleep on the living-room sofa! That yapping dog drives me crazy!"

"Shh! You're embarrassing me. Mrs. Stoss says you're out of control. She thinks—"

"She *thinks!* But she's never *seen* me doing anything! She's crazier than you think I am."

He waved at The Black Eagle, who was wheeling Mr. Zhinsky out of the lounge. The Black Eagle grinned. He knew who'd caused the uproar that morning.

"Who's that colored man?"

"The spade of the Spads. He flew double patrol last night because one of those drunken Zeps they call attendants couldn't make it. He often works double shifts to support his family and put two kids through college. He's one of those lazy niggers your redneck husband's always talking about. He's my buddy, flies wing for me."

"What're you talking about?"

"Just my senile ramblings."

She stood up, sniffing, and dabbed at her eyes with a handkerchief. "If only you could be like the others."

"You mean, sit around with my mouth open catching flies and let someone wipe my ass for me? Or sing nonsense songs all day and all night until I've driven those who weren't crazy when they came in out of their minds?

"Not me! I'm not giving up! The fucking Kaiser is going to rue the day Wild Hank enlisted. I'm going to keep on racking up my kills."

"Kills?"

"Just a manner of speaking."

"Listen, Dad. That nurse says she's treated you with all the compassion and care in the world, and—"

"Compassion? Care? That steely-eyed Hun? The scourge of the skies?"

"Don't talk so crazy! I can't stand it!"

"Maybe we just ought to write to each other. That way, you won't have to listen to your husband bitching about the cost of the gas you use getting here."

He rose and limped away, not looking at her but saying loudly, "Next time you come, bring some whiskey! And leave the bullshit at home!"

He passed Mrs. Whittaker, who was talking to a visitor. He winked. She turned as red as Von Richthofen's triplane.

Blushing!

So he hadn't been completely a figure in her dreamworld. She had known that he was real flesh. Also, she hadn't told Stoss the truth about the commotion that morning. The code of the skies was unbroken. Chivalry wasn't dead.

Maybe she was too embarrassed to admit to anyone, even herself, what had happened. Or maybe she thought every woman crapped when she had an orgasm. Maybe her husband had been a kinky shit-eater and she'd believed him when he told her that's how everybody did it. But could anyone be that rotten?

What evil lurked in the hearts of men?

Only God and The Shadow knew.

♦ ♦ ♦

All quiet on the Western Front. No impending Armistice, though. The Baroness had changed her schedule and now went up on patrol every half-hour. The Black Eagle had warned that she had the red ass for him, was loaded for bear, and was as mad as a wildcat with a tied-off dang in mating season.

"The next time she hears a ruckus, she's heading right for your room. If you're not in it, she's got you. That means a lot of extra leg-work for her, and that fat-ass don't like that no way. She hates your guts 'cause you won't lie down and die while you're still living. She isn't getting any ass, but she don't want you to, either. A real bitch in the manger."

Henry stayed in bed, except for piss call, for five nights. The sixth, Stoss went back to her regular schedule. Henry grinned. The Lone Eagle had outwaited The Bloody Baroness.

The seventh day, he had to get into action. He'd been on furlough too long. His control stick was out of control. His Vickers was throbbing with the pressure of the ammo belts. At 0510, sure that The Baroness was at her HQ, he put on his helmet and goggles.

"Contact!"

"Contact!"

Out of the hangar, down the runway, then soaring into the wild blue yonder, heavy with the fumes of senior-citizen shit.

Target: Mrs. Hannover. With that name, she had to be a CL IIIa, the beautiful escort fighter that looked like a one-seater from a distance.

But when an Allied pilot got on its tail, he found himself staring into the red eye of the observer's Parabellum machine gun.

He'd talked to the kid—she was only sixty-five—and he'd found her charming. She did have one functional defect, though. She'd sometimes get a faraway look, as if she were listening to a radio receiver in her head. She quit talking; she didn't even notice when you left.

That was why her children had put her in the nursing home. She was an embarrassment, not to mention that she was rich and they were trying to get her declared incompetent.

At 0513, he came in on a glide path, surveyed the area, found her partner sleeping, and landed in her bed. He was ready to take off, full throttle, if she screamed. Instead, she sighed as if she'd known he was coming, and the dogfight was on.

Not much of a combat though. CL IIIa's *did* fool you.

The only thing that bothered him for a while, aside from the lack of aggressiveness, was that she kept crying out, though softly, "Jim! Oh, Jim! My God, Jim!" But if she thought he was some other ace, what the hell? You didn't have to be properly identified by the enemy before you downed her.

His long leave had fired him up so that he decided to stay for another tangle. It took only fifteen minutes to reload his Vickers with the Hannover's help, though she still thought he was that jerk Jim. But just as he was about to shoot again, he felt a stabbing pain in his exhaust pipe. His scream of anguish mingled with her climactic cry, and he barrel-rolled away and out of the bed. It was a crash landing, but he wasn't structurally damaged. The only repairs he needed were to the fabric on his tail and the mid-parts of his wings. They were scraped raw, but, he was flight-ready.

The White Ghost was in her machine at the foot of the bed and cackling like The Shadow (a famous World War One ace before he took up crime fighting). The cane she carried concealed under the blanket over her legs, a Hotchkiss cannon if ever he saw one, was thrusting at the Hannover. The White Ghost was trying to goose her, too.

He swore. He'd forgotten the first rule of aerial combat. Always make sure the Boche isn't sneaking up on your tail.

As he rose, he groaned. He was damaged worse than he'd thought. He felt as if a Le Prieur rocket had been shoved up him. Damn The White Ghost.

"*Schweinhund!* I'll rendezvous with you some other time!"

He sped from the hangar as fast as a seventy-nine-year-old Spad could go. Though he needed a breather, he had no time for it. Get back to base before The Baroness intercepted him. The worst of it was that his Vickers hadn't used the second load. It was sticking out from his pajamas like a 7.7mm Lewis in the nose of a Handley Page 0/400 bomber. He was proud that it had an independent life. But he wished at that moment that he could control it.

Puffing, he banked left and shot down the runway and into his hangar. He just had time to take the scene in before his wheels slid out from under him and he ground-looped. A roommate, Tyson, was standing there, his stick hanging out, a puddle of piss on the floor before him. And there was The Bloody Baroness, cursing and on her hands and knees. She must have run in to check on him and slipped on the mess.

Collision course. He slammed onto her back and her nose went down. Thump! She didn't get up or even move. She stayed in the same position, her nose on the ground, her wings and undercarriage under her fuselage, her tail up.

"Aha! Gotcha!"

Why not? He was done for. There was going to be one hell of a court-martial. He'd be grounded, strapped, jailed, confined, incarcerated. No more dawn patrols. Ever.

It was the first time he'd used such an unorthodox tactic. But ramming your Vickers up the enemy's exhaust pipe was a sure way to make a kill, even if the authorities frowned on it. Though it meant he would go down, too, make the final fall from the big blue, he would add the ace of aces to his list.

He reached under and seized her huge cowlings — they must weigh half a ton apiece — and began the series of maneuvers, Immelmanns, *chandelles, virages,* you name it, that would end in his victory. The only distraction was from Tyson. His usually leaden eyes brightened, and he sneered.

"You filthy buggerer!"

But he walked to his bed and lay down and soon was snoring.

Just before he emptied all of his 7.65mms, she groaned and showed signs of coming to. Then she began panting and moaning. Maybe she was half unconscious, in a fantasy. Like the Fokker and the Hannover, she was only partly in this, to them, disappointing world. Maybe she really didn't know what was going on. Whatever the case, the Vickers was in her exhaust pipe, and that's where she wanted it. She'd wanted it all her life but had been too inhibited to bring it up from the unconscious and tell her husbands that's what she wanted.

It was this that The Black Eagle, whose daughter was a psychology major, had been hinting at.

He didn't care. Psychology-shmychology. Though his Hispaño was straining so hard it was about to tear itself loose, he was shooting her down. Let the aftermath be an afterbirth for all he cared, let…

◆ ◆ ◆

The Black Eagle came in as Henry Miller, the crazy old ace, the last of the fighter pilots of the Big One to engage the Hun, fell off The Baroness. Henry was dead, no mistaking those glazed eyes and that blue-gray color of skin.

Mrs. Stoss was on all fours, her big bare ass sticking up, her anus pulsing and dripping. She was muttering something.

Was it "More! More! Please! Please!"?

Then she was fully awake, and she was screaming as she heaved herself up, and The Black Eagle was laughing hysterically.

The Lone Eagle's smile was broader than his.

ONE

Tom Mix had fled on Earth from furious wives, maddened bulls, and desperate creditors. He'd fled on foot, on horse, and in cars. But this was the first time, on his native planet or on the Riverworld, that he had fled in a boat.

It sailed down-River and downwind swiftly; rounding a bend with the pursuer about fifty yards behind. Both craft, the large chaser and the small chased were bamboo catamarans. They were well-built vessels, though there wasn't a metal nail in them: double-hulled, fore-and-aft rigged and flourishing spinnakers. The sails were made of bamboo fiber.

The sun had two hours to go before setting. People were grouped by the great mushroom-shaped stones lining the banks. It would be some time before the grailstones would roar and spout blue electricity, energy which would be converted in the cylinders on top of the stones into matter. That is, into the evening meal and also, liquor, tobacco, marijuana, and dreamgum. But they had nothing else to do at this time except to lounge around, talk, and hope something exciting might happen.

They would soon be gratified.

The bend which Mix's boat had rounded revealed that the mile-wide River behind him had suddenly become a three-mile wide lake ahead. There were hundreds of boats there, all filled with fishers who'd set their cylinders on the stones and then put out to augment their regular diet with fish. So many were the craft that Mix suddenly found that there was even less room to maneuver than in the narrower stretch of water behind him.

Tom Mix was at the tiller. Ahead of him on the deck were two other refugees, Bithniah and Yeshua. Both were Hebrew, tied together by blood and religion though separated by twelve hundred years and sixty generations. That made much difference. In some ways Bithniah was less a stranger to Mix than she was to Yeshua; in some ways, Yeshua was closer to Mix than to the woman.

All three, at the moment, shared bruises and contusions given by the same man, Kramer. He wasn't in the boat following their wake, but his men were. If they captured the three, they'd return them to "The Hammer," as Kramer had been called on Earth and was here. If they couldn't take the refugees alive, they'd kill them.

Mix glanced behind him. Every bit of sail on the two-masted catamaran was up. It was slowly gaining on the smaller craft. Mix's boat should have been able to keep its lead, its crew was far lighter, but, during the escape, three spears had gone through the sail. The holes were small, but their effect had accumulated during the chase. In about fifteen minutes the prow of the chaser could be touching the stern of his craft. However, Kramer's men wouldn't try to board from the bow of their boat. They'd come up alongside, throw bone grappling hooks, draw the vessels together, and then swarm over the side.

Ten warriors against three, one a woman, one a man who would run away but who refused on principle to fight, and one a man who'd been in many duels and mass combats but wouldn't last long against such numbers.

People in a fishing boat shouted angrily at him as he took the catamaran too near them. Mix grinned and swept from his head his ten-gallon white hat, made of woven straw fibers painted with a rare pigment. He saluted them with the hat and then donned it. He wore a long white cloak made of towels fastened together with magnetic tabs, a white towel fastened around his waist, and high-heeled cowboy boots of white River-serpent leather. The latter were, in this situation, both an affectation and a handicap. But now that fighting was close, he needed bare feet to get a better grip on the slippery deck.

He called to Yeshua to take over the tiller. His face rigid, unresponsive to Mix's grin, Yeshua hastened to him. He was five feet ten inches tall, exactly Mix's height, but considered tall among the people of his time and place on Earth. His hair was black but with an undercoating which shone reddish in the sun. It was cut just below the nape of the neck. His body was thin but wiry, covered only by a black loincloth; his chest was matted with curly black hair. The face was long and thin, ascetic, that of a beardless scholarly-looking Jewish youth. His eyes were large and dark brown with flecks of green, inherited, he'd said, from Gentile ancestors. The people of his native land, Galilee, were much mixed since it had been both a trade route and a road for invaders for several thousand years.

Yeshua could have been Mix's twin, a double who'd not been eating or sleeping as well as his counterpart. There were slight differences between them. Yeshua's nose was a trifle longer, his lips a little thinner, and Mix had no greenish flecks in his eyes nor red underpigment in his hair. The resemblance was still so great that it took people some time to distinguish between them—as long as they didn't speak.

It was this that had caused Mix to nickname Yeshua as "Handsome."

Now Mix grinned again. He said, "Okay, Handsome. You handle her while I get rid of these."

He sat down and took off his boots, then rose and crossed the deck to drop them and his cloak into a bag hanging from a shroud. When he took over the tiller, he grinned a third time.

"Don't look so grim. We're going to have some fun."

Yeshua spoke in a deep baritone in a heavily accented English.

"Why don't we go ashore? We're far past Kramer's territory now. We can claim sanctuary."

"Claiming's one thing," Mix drawled in a baritone almost as deep. "Getting's another."

"You mean that these people'll be too scared of Kramer to let us take refuge with them?"

"Maybe. Maybe not. I'd just as soon not have to find out. Anyway, if we beach, so will they, and they'll skewer us before the locals can interfere."

"We could run for the hills."

"No. We'll give them a hard time before we take a chance on that. Get back there, help Bithniah with the ropes."

Yeshua and the woman handled the sail while Mix began zigzagging the boat. Glances over his shoulder showed that the pursuer was following his wake. It could have continued on a straight line in the middle of The River, and so gotten ahead of Mix's craft. But its captain was afraid that one of the zigs or zags would turn out to be a straight line, the end of which would terminate at the bank.

Mix gave an order to slacken the sail a little. Bithniah protested.

"They'll catch us sooner!"

Mix said, "They think they will. Do as I say. The crew never argues with the master, and I'm the captain."

He smiled and told her what he hoped to do. She shrugged, indicating that if they were going to be boarded, it might as well be sooner as later. It also hinted that she'd known all along that he was a little mad and this was now doubly confirmed.

Yeshua, however, said, "I won't spill blood."

"I know I can't count on you in a fight," Mix said. "But if you help handle the boat, you're indirectly contributing to bloodshed. Put that in your philosophical pipe and smoke it."

Surprisingly, Yeshua grinned. Or perhaps his reaction wasn't so unexpected. He delighted in Mix's Americanisms, and he also liked to discuss subtleties in ethics. But he was going to be too busy to engage in an argument just now.

Mix looked back again. The fox—the chaser was the fox and he was the rabbit—was now almost on his tail. There was a gap of twenty feet between them, and two men at the bows of the double hull were poised, ready to hurl their spears. However, the rapid rise and fall of the decks beneath them would make an accurate cast very difficult.

Mix shouted to his crew—*some* crew!—and swung the tiller hard over. The prow had been pointed at an angle to the righthand bank of The River. Now it turned away suddenly, the boat leaning, the boom of the sail swinging swiftly. Mix ducked as it sang past his head. Bithniah and Yeshua clung to ropes to keep from being shot off the deck. The righthand hull lifted up, clearing the water for a few seconds.

For a moment, Mix thought the boat was going to capsize. Then it righted and Bithniah and Yeshua were paying out the ropes. Behind him he heard shouting, but he didn't look back. Ahead was more shouting as the crews of two small one-masted fishing boats voiced their anger and fear.

Mix's vessel ran between the two boats in a lane only thirty feet wide. That closed quickly as the two converged. Their steersmen were trying to turn them away, but they had been headed inward on a collision path. Normally, they would have straightened this out, but now the stranger was between them, and its prow was angling toward the boat on the port.

Mix could see the twisted faces of the men and women on this vessel. They were anguished lest his prow crash into their starboard side near their bow. Slowly, it seemed too slowly, the prow of that boat turned. Then its boom began swinging as it was caught in the dead zone.

A woman's voice rose above the others, shrilling an almost unintelligible English at him. A man threw a spear at him, a useless and foolish action but one which would vent some of his anger. The weapon soared within a foot of Mix's head and splashed into the water on the starboard.

Mix glanced back. The pursuer had fallen into the trap. Now, if only he could keep from being caught in his own.

His vessel slid by the boat to port, and the end of its boom almost struck the shrouds of the mast tied to the starboard edge of the deck. And then his boat was by.

Behind him, the shouting and screaming increased. The crash of wood striking wood made him smile. He looked swiftly back. The big catamaran had smashed bows first into the side of the fishing boat on his right. It had turned the much smaller single-hulled bamboo vessel around at right angles to its former course. The crew of both boats had been knocked to the deck, including the steersmen. Three of Kramer's men had gone over the side and were struggling in the water. Count them out. That left seven to deal with.

TWO

The rabbit became a fox; the attacked, the attacker. His craft turned as swiftly as Mix dared take it and began beating against the wind toward the two that had collided. This took some time, but Kramer's vessel was in no shape to countermaneuver. Both it and the fishing boat had stove-in hulls and were settling down slowly. Water was pouring in through the hulls. The captain of the catamaran was gesturing, his mouth open, his voice drowned by all those on his boat and the others, plus the yelling from the many other crafts. His men must have heard him, though, or interpreted his furious signs. They picked themselves up, got their weapons, and started toward the vessel they'd run into. Mix didn't understand why they were going to board it. That would be deserting a sinking ship for another, jumping from the boiling kettle into the fire. Perhaps it was just a reflex, a mindless reaction. They were angry, and they meant to take it out on the nearest available persons.

If so, they were frustrated. The two men and two women on the fisher leaped overboard and began swimming. Another boat sailed toward them to pick them up. Its sail slid down as it neared the swimmers, and men leaned over its side to extend helping hands. Two of Kramer's men, having gotten on the smaller vessel, ran to the other side and heaved spears at the people in the water.

"They must be out of their minds," Mix muttered. "They'll have this whole area at their throats."

That was agreeable to him. He could leave the pursuers to the mercy of the locals. But he didn't intend to. He had a debt to pay. Unlike most debts, this would be a pleasure to discharge.

He told Yeshua to take over the tiller, and he got a war boomerang from the weapons box on the deck. It was two feet long, fashioned by sharp flint from a piece of heavy white oak. One of its ends turned at an angle of 30 degrees. A formidable weapon in the hand of a skilled thrower, it could break a man's arm even if hurled from five hundred feet away.

The weapons box contained three chert-headed axes, four more boomerangs, several oak spear shafts with flint tips, and two leather slings and two bags of sling-stones. Mix braced himself by the box, waited until his boat had drawn up alongside the enemy's on the port side, and he threw the boomerang. The up-and-down movement of the deck made calculation difficult. But the boomerang flew toward its target, the sun flashing off its whirling pale surface and it struck a man in the neck. Despite the noise of voices, Mix faintly heard the crack as the neck broke. The man fell sidewise on the deck; the boomerang slid against the railing.

The dead man's comrades yelled and turned toward Mix. The captain recalled the four men aboard the sinking fisher. They threw clubs and spears, and Mix and his crew dropped flat onto the deck. Some of the missiles bounced off the wood or stuck quivering in it. The nearest, a spear with a fire-hardened wooden point, landed a few inches from Yeshua's ear and slid off into the water.

Mix jumped up, braced himself, and when the starboard side of the craft rolled downward, hurled a spear. It fell short of its mark, the chest of a man, but it pierced his foot. He screamed and yanked the point loose from the deck, but he didn't have courage enough to withdraw it from his foot. He hobbled around the deck, shrilling his pain, until two men got him down and yanked the shaft out. The head was dislodged from the shaft and remained half-sticking out from the top of his foot.

Meanwhile, the second fisher, the one which Mix's boat had almost struck, had come alongside the sinking fisher. Three men leaped onto it and began securing ropes to lash the two boats together. Several rowboats and three canoes came up to the fisher, and their occupants climbed aboard it. Evidently, the locals were angry about the attack and intended to take immediate measures. Mix thought they would have been smarter to have waited until the big catamaran sank and then speared the crew members as they swam. On the other hand, by attacking Kramer's men, they were getting deeply involved. This

could be the start of a war. In which case, the refugees would be welcomed here.

However, a catamaran, because of its two hulls, didn't sink easily.
It might even be able to get away, if not back to its homeport, at least
out of this area. The locals didn't want this to happen.

The enemy captain, seeing what was coming, had ordered his men
to attack. Leading them, he boarded the sinking fisher, crossed it, and
hurled himself at the nearest man on the fisher. A woman whirled a
sling above her head, loosed one end, and the stone smashed into the
captain's solar plexus. He fell on his back, unconscious or dead.

Another of Kramer's warriors fell with a spear sticking through
his arm. His comrade stumbled over him and received the point of a
spear with the full weight of its wielder behind it.

The woman who'd slung the stone staggered backward with a spear
sticking out of her chest and toppled into the water.

Then both sides closed, and there was a melee.

Yeshua brought the catamaran up alongside the portside of
Kramer's while Bithniah and Mix let the sail down and then threw
grappling hooks onto the railing. While Bithniah and Yeshua sweated
to tie the two boats together, Tom Mix used his sling. He had practiced
on land and water for hundreds of hours with this weapon, and so he
worked smoothly with great speed and finesse. He had to wait until
an enemy was separated from the crowd to prevent accidentally hitting a local. Three times he struck his target. One stone caught a man
in the side of his neck. Another hit the base of a spine. The third smashed
a kneecap, and the writhing man was caught and held down by some
locals while a flint knife slashed his jugular.

Mix threw a spear which plunged deep into a man's thigh. Then,
gripping a heavy axe, he leaped onto the catamaran and his axe rose
and fell twice on the backs of heads.

The two enemy survivors tried to dive overboard. Only one made
it. Mix picked up the boomerang from the deck, lifted it to throw at the
bobbing head, then lowered it. Boomerangs were too hard to come by
to waste on someone who was no longer dangerous.

Suddenly, except for the groaning of the wounded and the weeping of a woman, there was silence. Even the onlookers, now coming
swiftly toward the scene of the battle, were voiceless. The bafflers looked
pale and spent. The fire was gone from them.

Mix liked to be dressed for the occasion, and this was one of victory. He returned to his boat, winked at Yeshua and Bithniah, and put
on his boots and cloak. His ten-gallon hat had remained on his head

throughout. He returned to the fisher, removed his hat with a flourish, grinned, and spoke.

"Tom Mix, Esquire, at your service, ladies and gentlemen. My heartfelt thanks for your help, and my apologies for any inconvenience our presence caused you."

The captain of the rescue boat said, "Bare bones o' God, I scarce comprehend your speech. Yet it seems to be somewhat English."

Mix put his hat back on and rolled his eyes as if asking for help from above.

"Still in the seventeenth century! Well, at least I can understand your lingo a little bit."

He spoke more slowly and carefully. "What's your handle, amigo?"

"Handle? Amigo?"

"Your name, friend. And who's your boss? I'd like to offer myself as a mercenary. I need him, and I think he's going to need me."

"John Wickel Stafford is the lord-mayor of New Albion," a woman said. She and the others were looking strangely at him and Yeshua.

He grinned and said, "No, he's not my twin brother, or any sort of brother to me, aside from the kinship that comes from being human. And you know how thin that is. He was born about one thousand eight hundred and eighty years before me. In Palestine. Which is a hell of a long way off from my native Pennsylvania. It's only a trick of fate he resembles me so. A lucky one for him, otherwise he might not've slipped the noose Kramer'd tied around his neck."

Apparently, some of his audience understood some of what he'd said. The trouble was not so much vocabulary, though there were some significant differences, as with the intonation and the pronunciation. Theirs somewhat resembled the speech of some Australians he'd met. God knew what they thought his was like.

"Any of you know Esperanto?" he said.

The captain said, "We've heard of that tongue, sir. It is being taught by some of that new sect, the Church of the Second Chance, or so I understand. So far, though, none has come into this area."

"Too bad. So we'll make do with what we have. My friends and I have had a tough time the last couple of days. We're tired and hungry. I'd like permission to stay in your spread for a few days before we go on down the River. Or maybe join up with you. Do you think your boss, uh, lord-mayor, would object?"

"Far from it, sir," the woman said. "He welcomes good fighting men and women in the hope they'll stay. And he rewards them well. But tell us, those men Kramer's they must be, why were they so hot for your blood? They chased you here yet they knew they were forbidden to come here under pain of death."

"That's a long story, ma'am," Mix said.

He smiled. His smile was very attractive, and he knew it. The woman was pretty, a short blonde with a buxom figure, and possibly she was unattached at the moment or thinking of being so. Certainly, there was nothing shy about her.

"You evidently are acquainted with Kramer the Hammer, Kramer the Burner. These two, Bithniah and Yeshua, were prisoners of his, ripe for the stake because they were heretics, according to his lights, and that's what counts in his land. Also they were Jewish, which made it worse. I got them loose, along with a bunch of others. We three were the only ones made it to a boat. The rest you know."

The captain decided he might as well introduce himself.

"I am Robert Nickard. This woman is Angela Doverton. Be not deceived by her immodest manner, Master Mix. She talks boldly and without regard to her sex, unmindful of her place. She is my wife, though there is neither giving nor taking of marriage in heaven or hell."

Angela smiled and winked at Mix. Fortunately, the eye was turned away from Nickard.

"As for this business of heretics, New Albion does not care—officially, anyway—what the religion of a man or woman be. Or indeed if he be an atheist, though how any could be after having been resurrected from the dead, I cannot understand. We welcome all as citizens, so they be hard-working and dutiful, clean and comparatively sober. We even accept Jews."

"That must be quite a change from when you were alive," Mix said.

Quickly, before Nickard could comment on that, he said, "Where do we report, sir?"

Nickard gave him directions. Mix told his crew to return to their craft. They untied the ropes, retrieved the grappling hooks, hoisted sail, and departed down-River. Not, however, before Mix saw Angela Doverton slip him another wink. He had already decided to steer clear of her, desirable though she was. He didn't believe in making love to another man's mate. On the other hand, if she were to leave Nickard, which seemed likely, then...no, she seemed like a troublemaker. Still...

Behind him the business of getting the two damaged boats in to shore before they sank had begun. The lone survivor of the Kramer force had been pulled out of the water and was being taken, bound, to the shore. Mix wondered what would happen to him, not that he cared.

The woman Bithniah steered the catamaran while Yeshua took care of the ropes. Tom Mix stood in the prow, one hand on a shroud to support himself, his long white cloak flapping. He must seem a strange and dramatic figure to the locals. At least, he hoped so. Wherever he was, if he found drama lacking, he drummed up some.

THREE

As almost everywhere in the never-ending valley, both sides of the River were bordered with plains. These were usually from a mile to a mile and a half wide. They were as unbumpy as the floor of a house but sloped gently toward the foothills. A shortbladed grass that no amount of trampling could kill covered them. Here and there were some trees.

Beyond the plains, the hills started out as mounds twenty feet high and sixty feet broad. As they neared the mountains, they became broader and higher and finally converged. The hills were thick with forest. Eighty out of every hundred were usually the indestructible "irontrees," deep-rooted monsters the bark of which resisted fire and shrugged off the edge of even steel axes — though very few of these existed in this metal-poor world. Beneath the trees grew long-bladed grass and bamboos — some only two feet high, some over a hundred. Unlike every other area he'd been in, this lacked ash and yew trees and so the bow and arrow were seldom seen. Most of the bows were made from the mouth horns of a huge fish, but apparently the people here had not caught many of these. Even the bamboo here wasn't suitable for use as bows.

Beyond the hills, the mountains soared. The lower parts were rugged with small canyons and fissures and little plateaus. At the five-thousand-foot height, the mountains became unbroken cliffs, smooth as glass. Then they climbed straight up for another five thousand feet or leaned outward near the top. They were unclimbable. If a man wished to get to the valley on the other side of them he'd have to follow The River, and that might take him years. The Rivervalley was a world-snake, winding down from the headwaters at the North Pole and around the South Pole and back up the other hemisphere to the mouth at the North Pole.

Or so it was said. Nobody had yet proved it.

In this area, unlike some he'd been in, huge vines encircled the trees and even some of the bamboo stands. From the vines grew perennial flowers of many sizes, shapes, and exhibiting every shade of the spectrum.

For ten thousand miles the Rivervalley would be a silent, frozen explosion of color. Then, just as abruptly as it had started, the trees would resume their unadorned ascetic green.

But this stretch of The River trumpeted a flourish of hue.

A mile from the scene of the battle, Mix ordered that Bithniah steer toward the lefthand bank. Presently, Yeshua lowered the sail, and the catamaran slid its nose up onto a slope of the bank. The three got off, and many hands among the crowd grabbed the hulls and pulled it entirely on land. Men and women surrounded the newcomers and asked many questions. Mix started to answer one from a good-looking woman when he was interrupted by soldiers. These wore fish-leather bone-reinforced helmets and cuirasses, modeled after those used in the time of Charles I and Oliver Cromwell. They carried small round shields of leather-covered oak and long stone-tipped or wooden-ended spears or heavy war-axes or big clubs. Thick fish-leather boots protected their legs to just above the knees.

Their ensign Alfred Regius Swinford, heard Mix's report halfway through. Mix interrupted himself then, saying, "We're hungry. Couldn't we wait until we charge our buckets?"

He gestured at the nearest mushroom-shaped stone, six feet high and several hundred feet broad. The bottoms of the gray cylinders of the bystanders were inserted in the depressions on its top.

"Buckets?" the ensign said. "We name them copias, stranger. Short for cornucopia. Give me your copias. We'll charge them for you, and you can fill your bellies after Lord Stafford's talked to you. I'll see that they're properly identified."

Mix shrugged. He was in no position to argue, though, like everybody else, he was uneasy if his "holy bucket" was out of his sight. The three walked among the soldiers across the plain toward a hill. They went past many one-room bamboo huts. On top of the hill was a larger circular wall of logs. They went through the gateway into a huge yard. The Council House, their destination, was a long triangular log building in the center of the stockade. There were many observation towers and a broad walkway behind the outer walls. The sharp-pointed logs towered above this, but windows and slits for defenders to throw spears or pour out burning fish oil on attackers were plentiful. There were also wooden cranes which could be swung over the walls to dump nets full of large rocks.

Mix saw ten large wooden tanks filled with water and sheds which he supposed held stores of dried fish and acorn bread and weapons.

Out of one of the sheds, though, came men carrying baskets of earth. These would be digging a secret underground tunnel to the outside for escape or for a rear attack on the enemy. It wasn't much of a secret if they allowed strangers to see evidence of it. He felt chilled momentarily. Perhaps no stranger who knew of the tunnel would be allowed to leave.

Mix said nothing. He might as well play dumb, though he doubted that the ensign would think he was that unobservant. No. He should try something, however weak.

"Digging a well," he said. "That's a good idea. If you're besieged, you needn't worry about water."

"Exactly," Swinford said. "We should have dug it a long time ago. But then we were shorthanded for a while."

Mix didn't think that he'd fooled the ensign, but at least he'd tried. By then the sun had reached the peaks of the western mountain range. A moment later it sank, and the valley thundered with the eruption of the copiastones along the banks. Dinner was ready.

Stafford and his council were sitting at a round table of pine on a platform at the far end of the hall. Between this and the entrance was a long rectangular table with many bamboo chairs around it. Trap doors in the ceiling were open to let in the light, but this was fading fast. Pine torches impregnated with fish oil had already been lit and set in brackets on the walls or in stands on the dirt floor. The smoke rose toward the high blackened beams and rafters, and the stench of fish heavied the air. Underlying it was another stink—unwashed human bodies. Mix thought that there might have been an excuse for this uncleanliness in seventeenth-century England, but there was none here. The River was within comfortable walking distance. However, he knew that old habits clung hard, despite which they were changing slowly. With the constant passage of people who came from cultures which did bathe frequently, a sense of cleanliness and the shame associated with uncleanliness were spreading. In ten or fifteen years these Englishmen would be soaping regularly in The River. Well, most of them would be, anyway. There were always persons in every culture who would think that water was for drinking only.

Actually, aside from the offensiveness of body odor and the esthetics of a clean body, there was no reason why they should wash frequently. There were no diseases of the body on the Riverworld. Plenty of diseases of the mind, though.

The ensign halted below the platform and reported to Stafford. The others at the table, twenty in all, stared at the newcomers. Many smoked copia-supplied cigarettes or cigars, unknown to them in their time on Earth when pipes only were used.

Stafford rose from the table to greet his guests courteously. He was a tall man, six feet two inches, broad-shouldered, long-armed, slimly built. His face was long and narrow, his eyebrows very thick and tangled, his eyes gray, his nose long and pointed, his lips thin, his chin out-thrusting and deeply cleft. His brownish hair hung to just below his shoulders and was curled at the ends.

In a pleasant voice thick with a Northern burr — he was a native of Carlisle, near the Scotch border — he asked them to sit at the table. He offered them their choice of wine, whiskey, or liqueur. Mix, knowing that the supply was limited, took the offer as a good sign. Stafford would not be so generous with expensive commodities to those he thought were hostiles. Mix sniffed, smiled at the scent of excellent bourbon, and sipped. He would have liked to pour it down, but this would have meant that his hosts would have to offer him another immediately.

Stafford asked Tom Mix to make his own report. This involved a long tale, during which fires were lit in the two great hearths on each side of the central part of the hall. Mix noticed that some of those bringing in the wood were short, very swarthy Mongolianish men and women. These, he supposed, were from the other side of The River which was occupied by Huns. From what he'd heard, these had been born about the time Attila had invaded Europe, the fifth century A.D. Whether they were slaves or refugees from across The River, he could not know.

Stafford and the others listened to Mix with only a few comments while they drank. Presently, their copias were brought in, and all ate. Tom was pleasantly surprised by this evening's offering of his bucket. It was Mexican: tacos, enchiladas, burritos, a bean salad, and the liquor was tequila with a slice of lemon and some salt. It made him feel more at home, especially when the tobacco turned out to be some slim-twisted dark cigars.

Stafford didn't seem to like the liquor he got. He smelled it, then looked around. Mix interpreted his expression correctly. He said, "Would you like to trade?"

The lord-mayor said, "What is it you have?"

This made for an extended explanation. Stafford had lived when North America was first being colonized by the English, but he knew very little of it. Also, in his time, Mexico was an area conquered by the Spanish, and he had almost no data on it. But after listening to Mix's lengthy exposition, he handed his cup to Mix.

Tom sniffed at it and said, "Well, I don't know what it is, but I ain't afraid of it. Here, try the tequila."

Stafford followed the recommended procedure: the drink at once succeeded by the salt and the lemon.

"Zounds! It feels as if fire were leaping from my ears!"

He sighed and said, "Most strange. But most pleasant and exhilarating. What about yours?"

Mix sipped. "Ah! I don't know what the hell brand it is! But it tastes great, though it's a little gross. Whatever its origin, it's wine—of a sort. Maybe it's what the ancient Babylonians used to push. Maybe it's Egyptian, maybe it's Malayan or early Japanese saki, rice wine. Did the Aztecs have wine? I don't know, but it's powerful stuff, and it's rank yet appealing.

"Tequila is a distilled spirit gotten from the heart-sap of the century or agave plant. Well, here's to international brotherhood, no discrimination against foreign alcohol, and your good health."

"Hear, hear!"

Having his supply from the copia, Stafford ordered a keg of lichen liquor in. This was composed of alcohol distilled from the green-blue lichen that grew on the mountain cliffs and then cut with water, the flavor provided by powdered dried leaves from the tree-vines. After quaffing half a cupful, Stafford said, "I don't know why Kramer's men were so eager to kill you that they dared trespass on my waters."

Speaking carefully and slowly, so that they could understand him easier, Mix began his story. Now and then Stafford nodded to an officer to give Mix another drink. Mix was aware that this generosity was not just based on hospitality. If Stafford got his guest drunk enough, he might, if he were a spy, say something he shouldn't. Mix, however, was a long way from having enough to make him loose-tongued. Moreover, he had nothing to hide. Well, not much.

"How far do you want me to go back in my story?"

Stafford laughed, and his slowly reddening eyes looked merry.

"For the present, omit your Earthly life. And condense it previously to your first meeting with Kramer."

"Well, ever since All Souls' Day"—one of the names for the day on which Earthpeople had first been raised from the dead—"I've been wandering down The River. Though I was born in 1880 A.D. in America and died in 1940, I wasn't resurrected among people of my own time and place. I found myself in an area occupied by fifteenth-century Poles. Across The River were some sort of American Indian pygmies. Until then I hadn't known that such existed, though the Cherokee Indians have legends of them. I know that because I'm part Cherokee myself."

That was a lie, one which a movie studio had originated to glamorize him. But he'd said it so often that he half believed it. It couldn't hurt to spread it on a little.

Stafford belched, and said, "I thought when I first saw you that you had some redskin blood in you."

"My grandfather was a chief of the Cherokees," Mix said. He hoped that his English, Pennsylvania Dutch, and Irish ancestors would forgive him.

"Anyway, I didn't hang around the Poles very long. I wanted to get to some place where I could understand the language. I shook the dust off my feet and took off like a stripe-assed ape."

Stafford laughed and said, "What droll imagery!"

"It didn't take me long to find out there weren't any horses on this world, or any animals except man, earthworms, and fish. So I built me a boat. And I started looking for folks of my own time, hoping I'd run into people I'd known. Or people who'd heard of me. I had some fame during my lifetime; millions knew about me. But I won't go into that now.

"I figured out that if people were strung along The River according to when they'd been born, though there were many exceptions, me being one, the twentieth-century people ought to be near The River's mouth. That, as I found out, wasn't necessarily so. Anyway, I had about ten men and women with me, and we sailed with the wind and the current for, let's see, close to five years. Now and then we'd stop to rest or to work on land."

"Work?"

"As mercenaries. We picked up extra cigarettes, booze, good food. In return, we helped out people that needed helping real bad and had a good cause. Most of the men were veterans of wars on Earth and so were some of the women. I'm a graduate of the Virginia Military Institute..."

Another movie prevarication.

"Virginia I've heard about," Stafford said. "But..."

Tom Mix had to pause in his narrative to ask just how much Stafford knew of history since his death. The Englishman replied that he'd gotten some information from a wandering Albanian who'd died in 1901 and a Persian who'd died in 1897. At least, he supposed they had those dates right. Both had been Moslems, which made it difficult to correlate their calendar with the Christian. Also, neither had known much about world history. One had mentioned that the American colonies had gained their independence after a war. He hadn't known whether or not to believe the man. It was so absurd.

"Canada remained loyal," Mix said. "I see I have a lot to tell you. Anyway, I fought in the Spanish-American War, the Boxer Rebellion, the Philippine Insurrection, and the Boer War. I'll explain what these were later."

Mix had fought in none of these, but what the hell. Anyway, he would have if he'd had a chance to do so. He'd deserted the U.S. cavalry in his second hitch because he wanted to get to the front lines and the damned brass had kept him home.

"A couple of times we were captured by slavers when we landed at some seemingly friendly place. We escaped, but the time came when I was the only one left of the original group. The rest were either killed or quit because they were tired of traveling. My lovely little Egyptian, a daughter of a Pharaoh...well, she was killed, too."

Actually, Miriam was the child of a Cairo shopkeeper and was born sometime in the eighteenth century. But he was a cowboy, and cowboys always embellished the truth a little. Maybe more than a little. Anyway, figuratively, she was a daughter of the Pharaohs. And what counted in this world, as in the last one, was not facts but what people believed were the facts.

He said, "Maybe I'll run into her again someday. The others, too. They could've just as well been re-resurrected down-River as up-River."

He paused, then said, "It's funny. Among the millions, maybe billions of faces I've seen while sailing along, I've not seen one I knew on Earth."

Stafford said, "I met a philosopher who calculated that there could be at least thirty-five billion people along The River."

Mix nodded.

"Yeah, I wouldn't be surprised. But you'd think that in five years just one...well, it's bound to happen someday. So, I built this last boat about five thousand miles back, a year ago. My new crew and I did pretty well until we put in at a small rocky island for a meal. We hadn't used our buckets for some time because we'd heard the people were mighty ornery in that area. But we were tired of eating fish and bamboo shoots and acorn bread from our stores. And we were out of cigarettes and the last booze we'd had had been long gone. We were aching for the good things of life. So, we took a chance ongoing ashore, and we lost. We were brought before the local high muckymuck, Kramer himself, a fat ugly guy from fifteenth-century Germany.

"Like a lot of nuts, and begging your pardon if there's any like him among you, he hadn't accepted the fact that this world isn't near what he thought the afterlife was going to be. He was a bigshot on Earth, a priest, an inquisitor. He'd burned a hell of a lot of men, women, and children after torturing them for the greater glory of God."

Yeshua, sitting near Mix, muttered something. Mix fell silent for a moment. He was not sure that he had not gone too far.

Although he had seen no signs of such, it was possible that Stafford and his people might just be as lunatic in their way as Kramer was in his. During their Terrestrial existence, most of the seventeenth-centurians had had a rock-fast conviction in their religious beliefs. Finding themselves here in the strange place neither heaven nor hell, they had suffered a great shock. Some of them had not yet recovered.

There were those adaptable enough to cast aside their former religion and seek the truth. But too many, like Kramer, had rationalized their environment. Kramer, for instance, maintained that this world was a purgatory. He had been shaken to find that not only Christians but all heathens were here. He had insisted that the teachings of the Church had been misunderstood on Earth. They had been deliberately perverted in their presentation by Satan-inspired priests. But he clearly saw The Truth now.

However, those who did not see the truth as he did must be shown it. Kramer's method of revelation, as on Earth, was the wheel and the fire.

When Mix had been told this, he had not argued with Kramer's theory. On the contrary, he was enthusiastic—outwardly—in offering his services. He did not fear death, because he knew that he would be resurrected twenty-four hours later elsewhere along The River. But he did not want to be stretched on the wheel and then burned.

He waited for his chance to escape.

One evening a group had been seized by Kramer as they stepped off a boat. Mix pitied the captives, for he had witnessed Kramer's means of changing a man's mind. Yet there was nothing he could do for them. If they were stupid enough to refuse to pretend that they agreed with Kramer, they must suffer.

"But this man Yeshua bothered me," Mix said. "In the first place he looked too much like me. Having to see him burn would be like seeing myself in the flames. Moreover, he didn't get a chance to say yes or no. Kramer asked him if he was Jewish. Yeshua said he had been on Earth, but he now had no religion.

"Kramer said he would have given Yeshua a chance to become a convert, that is, believe as Kramer did. This was a lie, but Kramer is a mealymouthed slob who has to find justification for every rotten thing he does. He said that he gave Christians and all heathens a chance to escape the fire—except Jews. They were the ones who'd crucified Jesus, and they should all pay. Besides, a Jew couldn't be trusted. He'd lie to save his own skin.

"The whole boatload was condemned because they were all Jews. Kramer asked where they'd been headed, and Yeshua said they were looking for a place where nobody had ever heard of a Jew. Kramer said there wasn't any such place; God would find them out no matter where they went. Yeshua lost his temper and called Kramer a hypocrite and an anti-Christ. Kramer got madder than hell and told Yeshua he wasn't going to die as quickly as the others.

"About then, I almost got thrown into prison with them. Kramer had noticed how much we looked alike. He asked me if I'd lied to him when I told him I wasn't a Jew. How come I looked like a Jew if I wasn't? Of course, this was the first time he thought of me looking like a Jew, which I don't. If I was darker, I could pass for one of my Cherokee ancestors.

"So I grinned at him, although the sweat was pouring out of me so fast it was trickling down my legs, and I said that he had it backwards. Yeshua looked like a Gentile, that's why he resembled me. I used one of his own remarks to help me; I reminded him he'd said Jewish women were notoriously adulterous. So maybe Yeshua was half-Gentile and didn't know it.

"Kramer gave one of those sickening belly laughs of his; he drools until the spit runs down his chin when he's laughing. And he said I was right. But I knew my days were numbered. He'd get to thinking about my looks later, and he'd decide that I was lying. To hell with that, I thought, I'm getting out tonight.

"But I couldn't get Yeshua off my mind. I decided that I wasn't just going to run like a cur with its tail between its legs. I was going to make Kramer so sick with my memory his pig's belly would ache like a boil every time he thought of me. That night, just as it began to rain, I killed the two guards with my axe and opened the stockade gates. But somebody was awake and gave the alarm. We ran for my boat, had to fight our way to it, and only Yeshua, Bithniah and I got away. Kramer must have given orders that the men who went after us had better not return without our heads. They weren't about to give up."

Stafford said, "God was good enough to give us eternal youth in this beautiful world. We are free from want, hunger, hard labor, and disease. Or should be. Yet men like Kramer want to turn this Garden of Eden into hell. Why? I do not know. One of these days, he'll be marching on us, as he has on the people to the north of his original area. If you would like to help us fight him, welcome!"

"I hate the murdering devil!" Mix said. "I could tell you things...never mind, you must know them."

"To my everlasting shame," Stafford replied. "I must confess that I witnessed many cruelties and injustices on Earth, and I not only did not protest, I encouraged them. I thought that law and order and religion, to be maintained, needed torture and persecution. Yet I was often sickened. So when I found myself in a new world, I determined to start anew. What had been right and necessary on Earth did not have to be so here."

"You're an extraordinary man," Mix said. "Most people have continued to think exactly what they thought on Earth. But I think the Riverworld is slowly changing a lot of them."

FOUR

The food from the copias had been put on wooden plates. Mix, glancing at Yeshua, saw that he had not eaten his meat. Bithniah, catching Mix's look, laughed.

"Even though his mind has renounced the faith of his fathers, his stomach clings to the laws of Moses."

Stafford, not understanding her heavily accented English, asked Mix to translate. Mix told him what she'd said.

Stafford said, "But isn't she Hebrew, too?"

Mix said that she was. Bithniah understood their exchange. She spoke more slowly.

"Yes, I am a Hebrew. But I have abandoned my religion, though, to tell the truth, I was never what you would call devout. Of course, I didn't voice any doubts on Earth. I would've been killed or at least sent into exile. But when we were roaming the desert, I ate anything, clean or unclean, that would fill my belly. I made sure, though, that no one saw me. I suspect others were doing the same. Many, however, would rather starve than put an unclean thing in their mouths and some did starve. The fools!"

She picked up a piece of ham on her plate and, grinning, offered it to Yeshua. He turned his head away with an expression of disgust.

Mix said "For Christ's sake, Yeshua. I've told you time and again that I'll trade my steak for your ham. I don't like to see you go hungry."

"I can't be sure that the cow was slaughtered or prepared correctly," Yeshua said.

"There's no kosher involved. The buckets must somehow convert energy into matter. The power that the bucketstones give off is transformed by a mechanism in the false bottom of the bucket. The transformer is programmed, since there's a different meal every day.

"The scientist that explained all that to me said, though he admitted he was guessing, that there are matrices in the buckets that contain models for certain kinds of matter. They put together the atoms and molecules formed from the energy to make steaks, cigars, what have you. So, there's no slaughter, kosher or unkosher."

"But there must have been an original cow that was killed," Yeshua said. "The beef which was the model for the matrix came from a beast which, presumably, lived and died on Earth. But was it slaughtered in the correct manner?"

"Maybe it was," Mix said. "But the meat I just ate isn't from the cow. It's a reproduction, just matter converted into energy. Properly speaking, it was made by a machine. It has no direct connection with the meat of the beast. If what that scientist said was true, some kind of recording was made of the atomic structure of the piece of beef. I've explained what recordings and atoms are to you. Anyway, the meat in our buckets is untouched by human hands. Or nonhuman, for that matter.

"So, how can it be unclean?"

"That is a question which would occupy rabbis for many centuries," Yeshua said. "And I suppose that even after that long a time they would still disagree. No. The safest way is not to eat it."

"Then be a vegetarian!" Mix said, throwing his hands up. "And go hungry!"

"Still," Yeshua said, "there was a man in my time, one who was considered very wise and who, it was said, talked to God, who did not mind if his disciples sat down with dirty hands at the table if there was no water to wash them or there were mitigating circumstances. He was rebuked by the Pharisees for this, but he knew that the laws of God were made for man and not man for the laws.

"That made good sense then and it makes good sense now. Perhaps I am being overstrict, Pharasaical, more devoted to the letter than to the spirit of the law. Actually, I should pay no attention to the law regarding what is ritually clean and what unclean. I no longer believe in the law.

"But even if I should decide to eat meat, I could not put the flesh of swine in my mouth if I knew what it was. I would vomit it. My stomach has no mind, but it knows what is fit for it. It is a Hebrew stomach, and it is descended from hundreds of generations of such stomachs. The tablets of Moses lie as heavy as a mountain in it."

"Which doesn't keep Bithniah from eating pork and bacon," Mix said.

"Ah! That woman! She is the reincarnation of some abominable pagan!"

"You don't even believe in reincarnation," Bithniah said, and she laughed.

Stafford had understood part of the conversation. He said, eagerly, "Then you, Master Yeshua, lived in the time of Our Lord! Did you know him?"

"As much as I know of any man," Yeshua said.

Everybody at the table began plying him with many questions. Stafford ordered more lichen-liquor brought in.

How long had he known Jesus?

Since his birth.

Was it true that Herod massacred the innocents?

No. Herod wouldn't have had the authority if he had wished to do so. He would have been removed by the Romans and perhaps executed. Moreover, such a deed would have caused a violent revolution. No. That tale, which he had never heard until he came to The Riverworld, was not true. It must be a folk story which had originated after Jesus was dead. Probably, though, it was based on an earlier tale about Isaac.

Then that meant that Jesus, Joseph, and Mary did not flee to Egypt?

They didn't. Why should they?

What about the angel who appeared to Mary and announced that she would give birth though she was a virgin?

How could that be when Jesus had older brothers and sisters, all fathered by Joseph and borne by Mary? Anyway, Mary, whom he knew well, had never said anything about an angel.

Mix, observing that the redness of some faces was not wholly caused by the liquor, leaned close to Yeshua.

"Careful," he whispered. "These guys may have decided that their religion was false, but they still don't like to hear denied what they were taught all their lives was true. And a lot of them are like Kramer. They believe, even if they won't say it, that they're in a kind of purgatory. They're still going to Heaven. This is just a way station."

Yeshua shrugged and said, "Let them kill me. I will rise again elsewhere in a place neither worse nor better than this."

One of the councillors, Nicholas Hyde, began banging his stone mug on the table.

"I don't believe you, Jew!" he bellowed. "If you *are* a Jew! You are lying! What are you doing, trying to create dissension among us with these diabolical lies? Or perhaps you are the *devil?*"

Stafford put his hand on Hyde's arm. "Restrain yourself, dear sir. Your accusations make no sense. Just the other day I heard you say that God was nowhere on The River. If He isn't here, then Satan is also absent. Or is it easier to believe in Old Nick than in the Creator? This man is here as our guest, and as long as he is such, we will treat him courteously."

He turned to Yeshua. "Pray continue."

The questions were many and swift. Finally, Stafford said, "It's getting late. Our guests have gone through much today, and we have much work tomorrow. I'll allow one more."

He looked at a tall distinguished-looking youth who'd been introduced as William Grey.

"Milord, care you to put it?"

Grey stood up somewhat unsteadily.

"Thank you, my lord-mayor. Now, Master Yeshua, were you present when Christ was crucified? And did you see him when he had risen? Or talk to someone reliable who had seen him, perhaps on the road to Emmaus?"

"That is more than one question," Stafford said. "But I'll allow it."

Yeshua was silent for a moment. When he spoke, he did so even more slowly.

"Yes, I was present when he was crucified and when he died. As for events after that, I will testify only to one thing. That is, he did not rise from the dead on Earth. I have no doubt that he rose here, though."

A clamor burst out, Hyde's voice rising above the others and demanding that the lying Jew be thrown out.

Stafford stood up, banging a gavel on the table, and cried, "Please, silence, gentlemen! There will be no more questions."

He gave orders to a Sergeant Channing to conduct the three to their quarters. Then he said, "Master Mix, I will speak with you three in the morning. God gives you a pleasant sleep."

Mix, Yeshua, and Bithniah followed the sergeant, who held a torch, though it was not needed. The night sky, blazing with giant star clusters and luminous gas clouds, cast a brighter light than Earth's full moon. The River sparkled. Mix asked the soldier if they could bathe before retiring. Channing said that they could do so if they hurried. The three walked into the water with their kilt-towels on. When with people who bathed nude, Mix did so also. When with the more modest, he observed their proprieties.

Using soap provided by the copias, they washed the grime and sweat off. Mix watched Bithniah. She was short and dark, full-bosomed, narrow-waisted, and shapely-legged. Her hips, however, were too broad for his tastes, though he was willing to overlook this imperfection. Especially now, when he was full of liquor. She had long, thick, glossy blue-black hair and a pretty face, if you liked long noses, which he did. His fourth wife, Vicky Forde, had had one, and he'd loved her more than any other woman. Bithniah's eyes were huge and dark, and even during the flight they had given Mix some curious glances. He told himself that Yeshua had better watch her closely. She radiated the heat of a female alley cat in mating season.

Yeshua now, he was something different. The only resemblance he had to Mix was physical. He was quiet and withdrawn, except for that one outburst against Kramer, and he seemed to be always thinking of something far away. Despite his silence, he gave the impression of great authority — rather, of a man who had once had it but was now deliberately suppressing it.

Channing said, "You're clean enough. Come on out."

"You know," Mix said to Yeshua, "shortly before I came to Kramer's territory, something puzzling happened to me. A little dark man rushed at me crying out in a foreign tongue. He tried to embrace me; he was weeping and moaning, and he kept repeating a name over and over. I had a hell of a time convincing him he'd made a mistake. Maybe I didn't. He tried to get me to take him along, but I didn't want anything to do with him. He made me nervous, the way he kept on staring at me.

"I forgot about him until just now. I'll bet he thought I was you. Come to think of it, he did say your name quite a few times."

Yeshua came out of his absorption. "Did he say what his name was?"

"I don't know. He tried four or five different languages on me, including English, and I couldn't understand him in any of them. But he did repeat a word more than once. Mattithayah. Mean anything to you?"

Yeshua did not reply. He shivered and draped a long towel over his shoulders. Mix knew that something inside Yeshua was chilling him. The heat of the daytime, which reached an estimated 80° F at high noon (there were no thermometers), faded away slowly. The high humidity of the valley (in this area, anyway) retained the heat until the invariable rains fell a few hours after midnight. Then the temperature dropped swiftly to an estimated 65° F and stayed there until dawn.

Channing led them to their residences. These were two small, square, one-room bamboo huts, the roofs thatched with the huge leaves of the irontree. Inside each was a table, several chairs, and a low bed, all of bamboo. There were also wooden towel racks and a rack for spears and other weapons. A baked-clay nightjar stood in one corner. The floor was a slightly raised bamboo platform. Real class. Most huts had bare earth floors.

Yeshua and Bithniah went into one hut; Mix, into the other. Channing started to say good night, but Mix asked him if he minded talking a little while. To bribe the sergeant, he gave him a cigar from his grail. At one time on Earth Mix had smoked, but he had given up the habit to preserve his image as a "clean-cut" hero for his vast audiences of young moviegoers. Here, he alternated between long stretches of indulgences or abstinences. For the past year, he had laid off tobacco. But he thought it might make the sergeant chummier if he smoked with him. He lit up a cigarette, coughed, and became dizzy for a moment. The tobacco certainly tasted good, though.

Micah Shepstone Channing was a short, muscular, and heavy-boned redhead. He'd been born in 1621 in the village of Havant, Hampshire, where he became a parchment maker. When the civil war broke out, he'd joined the forces against Charles I. Badly wounded at the battle of Naseby, he returned home, resumed his trade, married, had eight children of whom four survived to adulthood, and died of a fever in 1687.

Mix asked him a number of questions. Though his interest was mainly to establish a friendly feeling, he was curious about the man. He liked people in general.

He then went on to other matters, the personalities of the important men of New Albion, the setup of the government, and the relations with neighboring states, especially Kramer's Deusvolens, which the Albions pronounced as Doocevolenz.

During the English Civil War, Stafford had served under the Earl of Manchester. But, losing a hand from an infected wound, he went to live in Sussex and became a beekeeper. In time he became quite prosperous and branched out from honey to general merchandising. Later, he specialized in naval provisions. In 1679 he died during a storm off Dover. He was, Channing said, a good man, a born leader, quite tolerant, and had from the first been instrumental in establishing this state.

"'Twas he who suggested that we do away with titles of nobility or royalty and elect our leaders. He's now serving his second term as lord-mayor."

"Are women allowed to vote?" Mix said.

"They weren't at first, but last year they insisted they get their rights, and after some agitation, they got them. There's no holding them," Channing said, looking somewhat sour. "They can pick up any time they want and leave, since there's little property involved and no children to take care of and blessed little housework or cooking to do. They've become mighty independent."

Anglia, on the south border of New Albion, had a similar system of government, but its elected chief was titled the sheriff. Ormondia, to the north, was inhabited chiefly by those royalists who'd been faithful to Charles I and Charles II during the troubles. They were ruled by James Butler, first Duke of Ormonde, lord-lieutenant of Ireland under Charles I and Charles II, and chancellor of Oxford University.

"It's *milord* and *your grace* in Ormondia," Channing said. "Ye'd think that England had been transplanted from old Earth to The River. Despite which, the titles are mainly honorary, ye might say, since all but the duke are elected, and their council has in it more men born poor but honest and deserving than nobles. What's more, when their women found out ours was getting the vote, they set up a howl and there was nothing His Grace could do but swallow the bitter pill and smile like he was enjoying it."

Though relations between the two tiny states had never been cordial, they were united against Kramer. The main trouble was that their joint military staffs didn't get along too well. The duke didn't like the idea of having to consult the lord-mayor or deferring to him in any way.

"Far as that goes, I don't like it either," Channing said. "There should be one supreme general during a war. This is a case where two heads be not better than one."

The Huns across The River had caused much trouble in the early years, but for some time now they'd been friendly. Actually, only about one-fourth of them were Huns, according to Channing. They'd fought among themselves for so long they'd killed off each other. These had been replaced by people from other places along The River. They spoke a Hunnish pidgin with words from other languages making up a fourth of the vocabulary. The state directly across from New Albion was at the moment ruled by a Sikh, Govind Singh, a very strong military leader.

"As I said," Channing said, "for three hundred miles along here on this side the people resurrected were mainly British of the 1600s. But there's some ten-mile stretches where they aren't. Thirty miles down are some thirteenth-century Cipangese, fierce little slant-eyed yellow bastards. And there's Doocevolenz, which is fourteenth-century and half-German and half-Spanish."

Mix thanked him for the information and then said that he had to turn in. Channing bade him a good night.

FIVE

Mix fell asleep at once. Sometime during the night he dreamed that he was making love to Victoria Forde, his fourth wife, the one woman whom he still loved. Drums and blarings from many fish-bone horns woke him up. He opened his eyes. It was still dark, but its paleness indicated that the sun would soon come up over the mountains. He could see through the open window the graying sky and the fast-fading stars and gas clouds.

He closed his eyes and drew the edge of the double blanket-length towels over his head. Oh, for a little more sleep! But a lifetime of discipline as a cowboy, a movie actor, and a circus star on Earth, and as a mercenary on this world, got him out of bed. Shivering in the cold, he put on a towel-kilt and splashed icy water from a shallow fired-clay basin onto his face. Then he removed the kilt to wash his loins. His dream-Vicky had been as good in bed as the real Vicky.

He ran his hand over his jaw and cheeks. It was a habit he'd never overcome despite the fact that he did not have to shave and never would. All men had been resurrected permanently beardless. Tom didn't know why. Maybe whoever had done it didn't like facial hair. If so, they had no distaste for pubic or armpit hairs. But they had also made sure that hair didn't grow in the ears and nose hairs only grew to a certain length.

The unknowns responsible for the Riverworld had also made certain adjustments in the faces and bodies of some. Women who'd had huge breasts on Earth had wakened from death here to find that their mammaries had been reduced in size. Women with very small breasts had been given "normal"-sized breasts. And no woman had sagging breasts.

Not all were delighted. By no means. There were those who'd liked what they had had. And of course there had been societies in which huge dangling breasts were much admired and others in which the size and shape of the female breast meant nothing at all in terms of beauty or sex. They were just there to provide milk for the babies.

Men with very small penises on Earth here had penises which would not cause ridicule or shame. Mix had never heard any complaints about this. But a man who'd secretly yearned on Earth to be a woman had once, while drunk, poured his grievances into Mix's ear.

Why couldn't the mysterious beings who'd corrected so many physical faults have given him a female body?

"Why didn't you tell them what you wanted?" Mix had said, and he'd laughed. Of course, the man couldn't have informed the Whoevers. He'd died, and then awakened on the banks of The River, and in between he'd been dead.

The man had hit Tom in the eye then and given him a black whopper. Tom had had to knock him out to prevent further injury to himself.

Other deficiencies or deviations from the "normal" had also been corrected. Tom had once met a very handsome, perhaps too handsome Englishman — eighteenth century — who'd been a nobleman. From the groin upward, he'd been perfect, but his legs had been only a foot and a half long. Now he stood six feet two inches high. No complaints from him. But his grotesqueness on Earth had seemingly twisted his character. Though now a beautiful man in body, he was still embittered, savagely cynical, insulting, and, though he was a great "lover," hated women.

Tom had had a run-in with him, too, and broken the limey's nose. After they'd recovered from their injuries, they became friends. Strangely, now that the Englishman's handsomeness was ruined by the flat and askew nose, he'd become a better person. Much of his hatefulness had disappeared.

It was often hard to figure out human beings.

While Tom had been drying himself, he'd been thinking about what the Whoevers had done in the physical area to people. Now he wrapped himself in a cloak made of long towels held together with magnetic tabs inside the cloth, and he picked up a roll of toilet paper. This, too, had been provided by the copias, though there were societies who didn't use it for the intended purpose. He left the hut and walked toward the nearest latrine. This was a ditch over which was a long bamboo hut. It had two entrances. On the horizontal plank above each, a crude figure of a man, full-face, had been incised. The women's crapper was about twenty yards distant from it, and over its entrances crude profiles of women had been cut into the wood.

If the custom of daily bathing was not yet widespread in this area, other sanitation was enforced. Sergeant Channing had informed Mix that no one was allowed to crap just anywhere he or she pleased. (He did not use the word "crap," however, since this had been unknown in the seventeenth century.) Unless there were mitigating circumstances, a person caught defecating outside the public toilets was exiled — after his or her face had been rubbed in the excrement.

Urinating in public was lawful under certain situations, but the urinator must take care to be unobserved if the opposite sex was present.

"But it's a custom more honored in the breach than in the observance," Channing had said, quoting Shakespeare without knowing it. (He'd never heard of the Bard of Avon.) "In the wild lawless time just after the resurrection, people became rather shameless. There was little modesty then, and people, if you'll pardon the phrase, just didn't give a shit. Haw, haw!"

At regular intervals, the latrine deposits were hauled up to the mountains and dropped into a deep and appropriately named canyon.

"But some day it's going to be so high that the wind'll bring the stink down to us. I don't know what we'll do then. Throw it into The River and let the fish eat it, I suppose. That's what those disgusting Huns across The River do."

"Well," Mix had drawled, "that seems to me the sensible way to do it. The turds don't last long. The fish clean them up right away, almost before the stuff hits the water."

"Yes, but then we catch the fish and eat them!"

"It don't affect their taste any," Mix had said. "Listen, you said you lived on a farm for a couple of years, didn't you? Well, then you know that chickens and hogs eat cow and horse flop if they get a chance, and they often do. That didn't affect their taste when they were on the table, did it?"

Channing had grimaced. "It don't seem the same. Anyway, hogs and chickens eat cow manure, and there's a big difference between that and human ordure."

Mix had said, "I wouldn't really know. I never ate either."

He paused. "Say, I got an idea. You know the big earthworms eat human stuff. Why don't you people drag them out of the ground and throw them into the shit pit? They'd get rid of the crap, and the worms'd be as happy as an Irishman with a free bottle of whiskey."

Channing had been amazed. "That's a splendid idea! I wonder why none of us thought of it?"

He'd then complimented Mix on his intelligence. Mix hadn't told him that he'd been through many areas in which his "new" idea was a long-standing practice.

These places, like this one, had been lacking in sulfur. Otherwise, they would have processed nitrate crystals from the excrement and mixed it with charcoal and sulfur to make gunpowder. The explosive was then put into bamboo cases to be used as bombs or warheads for rockets.

Mix went into the latrine shed and sat down on one of the twelve holes. During the short time he was there, he picked up some gossip, mostly about the affair one of the councilmen was having with a major's woman. He also heard a dirty joke he'd never heard before, and he'd thought he'd heard them all on Earth. After washing his hands in a trough connected to a nearby stream, he hastened back to his hut. He picked up his grail and walked forty yards to Yeshua's hut. He'd intended to knock on the door and invite the couple to go with him to the nearest charging stone. But he halted a few paces from the door.

Yeshua and Bithniah were arguing loudly in heavily accented English of the seventeenth century. Mix wondered why they weren't using Hebrew. Later, he would find out that English was the only language they had in common, though they could carry on a very limited conversation in sixteenth-century Andalusian Spanish and fourteenth-century High German. Though Bithniah's native tongue was Hebrew, it was at least twelve hundred years older than Yeshua's. Its grammar was, from Yeshua's viewpoint, archaic, and its vocabulary was loaded with Egyptian loanwords and Hebrew items which had dropped out of the speech long before he was born.

Moreover, though born in Palestine of devout Jewish parents, Yeshua's native tongue was Aramaic. He knew Hebrew mainly as a liturgical tool, though he could read the Torah, the first five books of the Old Testament, with some difficulty.

As it was, Mix had some difficulty in understanding half of what they said. Not only did their Hebrew and Aramaic pronunciations distort their words, they had learned their English in an area occupied by seventeenth-century Yorkshire people, and that accent further bent their speech. But Mix could fill in what he didn't grasp. Usually.

"I'll not go with you to live in the mountains!" Bithniah was shouting. "I don't want to be alone! I hate being alone! I have to have many people around me! I don't want to sit on top of a rock with no one but a walking tomb to talk to! I won't go! I won't go!"

"You're exaggerating, as usual," Yeshua said loudly but much more quietly than Bithniah. "In the first place, you will have to go down to the nearest foothill copiastone three times a day. And you may go down to the bank and talk whenever you feel like it. Also, I don't plan to live up there all the time. Now and then I'll go down to work, probably as a carpenter, but I don't..."

Mix couldn't understand the rest of what the man said even though he spoke almost as loudly as before. He had no trouble comprehending most of Bithniah's words, however.

"I don't know why I stay with you! Certainly, it's not because no one else wants me! I've had plenty of offers, let me tell you! And I've been tempted, very tempted, to accept some!

"I do know why you want me around! Its certainly not because you're in love with my intelligence or my body! If it were, you'd delight in them, you'd be talking to me more and have me on my back far more than you do!

"The only reason you stick with me is that you know that I knew Aharon and Mosheh, and I was with the tribes when we left Egypt and when we invaded Canaan! Your only interest in me is to drain me of all I know about your great and holy hero, Mosheh!"

Mix's ears figuratively stood up. Well, well! Here was a man who'd known Christ, or at least claimed to, living with a woman who'd known Aaron and Moses, or at least claimed to. One or both of them however, could be liars. There were so many along The River. He ought to know. It took one to recognize one, though his lies were mainly just harmless prevarications.

Bithniah screamed, "Let me tell you, Yeshua, Mosheh was a louse! He was always preaching against adultery and against lying with heathen women, but I happen to know what he practiced! Why, he even married one, a Kushi from Midian! And he tried to keep his son from being circumcised!"

"I've heard all that many times before," Yeshua said.

"But you don't really believe I'm telling the truth, do you? You can't accept that what you believed so devoutly all your life is a bunch of lies! Why should I lie? What would I gain by that?"

"You like to torture me, woman."

"Oh, I don't have to lie to do that. There are plenty of other ways! Anyway, it's true that Mosheh not only had many wives, he would take other men's women if he got a chance! I should know; I was one of them. But he was a real man, a bull! Not like you! You can only become a real man when you've taken dreamgum and are out of your mind! What kind of a man is that, I ask you?"

"Peace woman," Yeshua said softly.

"Then don't call me a liar!"

"I have never done that."

"You don't have to! I can see in your eyes, hear in your voice, that you don't believe me!"

"No. Though there are times—most of the time, in fact—when I wish I'd never heard your tales. But great is the truth, no matter how much it hurts."

He continued in Hebrew or Aramaic. The tone of his voice indicated that he was quoting something.

"Stick to English!" Bithniah screamed. "I got so disgusted with the so-called holy men always quoting moral proverbs, and all the time their own sins stank like a sick camel! You sound like them! And you even claim to have been a holy man! Perchance you were! But I think that your devoutness ruined you! I wouldn't know, though! You've never actually told me much about your life! I found out more about you when you were talking to the councilmen than you've ever told me!"

Yeshua's voice, which had been getting lower, suddenly became so soft that Mix couldn't make out a word of it. He glanced at the eastern mountains. A few minutes more, and the sun would clear the peaks. Then the stones would give up their thundering, blazing energy. If they didn't hurry, they'd have to go breakfastless. That is, unless they ate dried fish and acorn bread, the thought of which made him slightly nauseated.

He knocked loudly on the door. The two within fell silent. Bithniah swung the door open violently, but she managed to smile at him as if nothing had occurred.

"Yes, I know. We'll be with you at once."

"Not I," Yeshua said. "I don't feel hungry now."

"That's right!" Bithniah said loudly. "Try to make me feel guilty, blame your upset stomach on me. Well, I'm hungry, and I'm going to eat, and you can sit here and sulk for all I care!"

"No matter what you say, I am going to live in the mountains."

"Go ahead! You must have something to hide! Who's after you? Who are you that you're so afraid of meeting people? Well, I have nothing to hide!"

Bithniah picked up her copia by the handle and stormed out. Mix walked along with her and tried to make pleasant conversation. But she was too angry to cooperate. As it was, they had just come into sight of the nearest mushroom-shaped rock, located between two hills, when blue flames soared up from the top and a roar like a colossal lion's came to them. Bithniah stopped and burst into her native language. Obviously she was cursing. Mix contented himself with one short word.

After she'd quieted down, she said, "Got a smoke?"

"In my hut. But you'll have to pay me back later. I usually trade my cigarettes for liquor."

"Cigarettes? That's your word for pipekins?"

He nodded, and they returned to his hut. Yeshua was not in sight. Mix purposely left his door open. He trusted neither Bithniah nor himself.

Bithniah glanced at the door

"You must think me a fool. Right next door to Yeshua!"

Mix grinned.

"You never lived in Hollywood!"

He gave her a cigarette. She used the lighter that the copia had furnished; a thin metallic box which extended a whitely glowing wire when pressed on the side.

"You must have overheard us," she said. "Both of us were shouting our fool heads off. He's a very difficult man. Sometimes he frightens me, and I don't scare easily. There's something very deep—and very different, almost alien, maybe unhuman about him. Not that he isn't very kind or doesn't understand people. He does, too much so.

"But he seems so aloof most of the time. Sometimes, he laughs very much and he makes me laugh, for he has a wonderful sense of humor. Other times, though, he delivers harsh judgments, so harsh they hurt me because I know that I'm included in the indictment. Now, I don't have any illusions about men or women. I know what they are and what to expect. But I accept this. People are people, although they often pretend to be better than they are. But expect the worst, I say, and you now and then get a pleasant surprise because you don't get the worst."

"That's pretty much my attitude," Mix said. "Even horses aren't predictable, and men are much more complicated. So you can't always tell what a horse or a man's going to do or what's driving him. One thing you can bet on. You're Number One to yourself, but to the other guy, Number One is himself or herself. If somebody acts like you're Number One, and she's sacrificing herself for you, she's just fooling herself."

"You sound as if you'd had some trouble with your wife."

"Wives. That, by the way, is one of the things I like about this world. You don't have to go through any courts or pay any alimony when you split up. You just pick up your bucket, towels, and weapons, and take off. No property settlements, no in-laws, no kids to worry about."

"I bore twelve children," she said. "All but six died before they were two years old. Thank God, I don't have to go through that here."

"Whoever sterilized us knew what he was doing," Mix said. "If we could have kids, this valley'd be jammed tight as a pig-trough at feeding time."

He moved close to her and grinned.

"Anyway, we men still have our guns, even if they're loaded with blanks."

"You can stop where you are," she said, although she was still smiling. "Even if I leave Yeshua, I may not want you. You look too much like him."

"I might show you the difference," he said.

But he moved away from her and picked up a piece of dried fish from his leather bag. Between bites, he asked her about Mosheh.

"Would you get angry or beat me if I told you the truth?" she said.

"No, why should I?"

"Because I've learned to keep my mouth shut about my Earthly life. The first time I told about it, that was less than a year after the Day of the Great Shout, I was badly beaten and thrown into The River. The people who did it were outraged, though I don't know why they should have been. They knew that their religion was false. They had to know that the moment they rose from the dead on this world. But I was lucky not to have been tortured and then burned alive."

"I'd like to hear the real story of the exodus," he said. "It won't bother me that it's not what I learned in Sunday school."

"You promise not to tell anybody else?"

"Cross my heart and hope to fall off Tony."

SIX

She looked blank.

"Is that an oath?"

"As good as any."

She was, she said, born in the land of Goshen, which was in the land of Mizraim, that is, Egypt. Her tribe was that of Levi, and it had come with other tribes of Eber into Mizraim some four hundred years before.

Famine in their own land had driven them there. Besides, Yoseph— in English, Joseph—had invited them to come. He was the vizier of the Pharaoh of Egypt and so was able to get the tribes into the land of plenty just east of the great delta of the Nile.

Mix said, "You mean, the story of Joseph is true? He *was* sold into slavery by his brothers, and he *did* become the Pharaoh's righthand man?"

Bithniah smiled and said, "You must remember that all that happened four hundred years before I was born. It may or may not have been true, but that was the story I was told."

"It's hard for me to believe that a Pharaoh would make a nomadic Hebrew his chief minister. Why wouldn't he choose an Egyptian, a civilized man who'd know all the complicated problems of administering a great nation?"

"I don't know. But the Pharaoh of lower Egypt then, when my ancestors came into Egypt, was not an Egyptian. He was a foreigner, one of those invaders from the deserts whom the English call the Shepherd-kings. They spoke a language much like Hebrew, or so I was told. He would have regarded Joseph as more or less a cousin. One of a kindred people, anyway, and more to be trusted than a native Egyptian. Still, I don't know if the story is true, since I did not see Joseph with my own eyes, of course. But while my people were in Goshen, the people of upper Egypt conquered the shepherd-kings and set up one of their own as Pharaoh of all Egypt."

That, said Bithniah, was when the lot of the sons of Eber and of Jacob began to worsen. They had entered Mizraim as free men, working under contract, but then they became slaves, in effect if not officially.

"Still, it was not so bad until the great Raamses became Pharaoh. He was a mighty warrior and a builder of forts and cities, and the Hebrews were among the many people set to build these."

"Was this Raamses the first or the second?" Mix said.

"I don't know. The Pharaoh before him was named Seti."

"He would have been Raamses II," Mix said. "So *he* was the Pharaoh of the Oppression! And was the man who succeeded him named Merneptah?"

"You pronounce his name strangely, but, yes, it was."

"The Pharaoh of the exodus."

"Yes, the going-forth. We were able to escape our bondage because Mizraim was in turmoil then. The people of the seas, as the English call them, and as they were called in my time, invaded. They were, I hear, beaten back, but during the time of troubles we took the opportunity to flee Mizraim."

"Moses, I mean Mosheh, didn't go to the Pharaoh and demand that his people be allowed to go free?"

"He wouldn't have dared. He would have been tortured and then executed. And many of us would have been slain as an example."

"You've heard of the plagues visited upon the Egyptians by God because of Moses' requests? The Nile turning to blood, the plague of frogs, the slaying of the firstborn male children of all the Egyptians and the marking with blood of the doorposts of the Hebrews so that their sons might be spared?"

She laughed and said, "Not until I came to this world. There was a plague raging throughout the land, but it killed Hebrew as well as Egyptian. My two brothers and a sister died of it; and I was sick with it, but I survived."

Mix questioned her about the religion of the tribes. She said that there was a mixture of religions in the tribes. Her mother had worshipped, among others, El, the chief god that the Hebrews had brought with them when they had entered the land of Goshen. Her father had favored the gods of Egypt, especially Ra. But he had participated in offering sacrifices to El, though these were few. He couldn't afford to pay for many.

She had known Mosheh since she was very young. He was a wild kid (her own words), half-Hebrew, half-Mizraimite. The mixture was nothing unusual. The women slaves were often raped by their masters or gave themselves willingly to get more food and creature comforts. Or sometimes just because they liked to have sexual intercourse. There was even some doubt about whether or not one of her sisters had a Hebrew or an Egyptian father.

There was also some doubt about the identity of Mosheh's father.

"When Mosheh was ten years old he was adopted by an Egyptian priest who'd lost his two sons to a plague. Why would the priest have adopted Mosheh instead of an Egyptian boy unless the priest was Mosheh's father? Mosheh's mother had worked for the priest for a while."

When Mosheh was fifteen, he had returned to the Hebrews and was once again a slave. The story was that his fosterfather had been executed because he was secretly practicing the forbidden religion of Aton, founded by the accursed Pharaoh Akhenaton. But Bithniah suspected that it was because Mosheh was suspected by his father of lying with one of his concubines.

"Didn't he have to flee to Midian later on when he killed an Egyptian overseer of slaves? He is supposed to have murdered the man when he caught him maltreating a Hebrew slave."

Bithniah laughed.

"The truth is probably that the Egyptian caught him with his wife, and Mosheh was forced to kill him to keep from being killed. But he did escape to Midian. Or so he said when he returned some years later under a false name."

"Moses must have been horny as hell," Mix said.

"The kid grows up to be a goat."

On returning with his Midianite wife, Mosheh announced that the sons of Eber had been adopted by a god. This god was Yahweh. The announcement came as a surprise to the Hebrews, most of whom had never heard of Yahweh until then. But Yahweh had spoken from a burning bush to Mosheh, and Mosheh had been charged to lead his people from bondage. He was inspiring and spoke with great authority, he seemed truly to burn as brightly with the light of Yahweh as the burning bush he described.

"What about the parting of the Red Sea and the drowning of Pharaoh and his soldiers when they pursued you Hebrews?"

"Those Hebrews who lived long after we did and wrote those books I've been told about were liars. Or perchance they weren't liars but just believed tales that had been told for many centuries."

"What about the golden calf?"

"You mean the statue of the god that Mosheh's brother Aharon made while Mosheh was on the mountain talking to Yahweh? It was a calf, the Mizraimite god Hapi as a calf. But it wasn't made of gold. It was made of clay. Where would we get gold in that desert?"

"I thought you slaves carried off a lot of loot when you left?"

"We were lucky to have our clothes and our weapons. We left in a hurry, and we didn't want to be burdened down any more than we could help, if the soldiers came after us. Fortunately, the garrisons were undermanned at that time. Many soldiers had been called to the coast to fight against the people of the sea."

"Moses did make the tablets of stone?"

"Yes. But there weren't ten commandments on them. And they were in Egyptian sign-writing. I couldn't read them; three-fourths of us couldn't. Anyway, there wasn't room on the tablets to write out ten commandments in Egyptian signs. And the writing didn't last long. The paint was poor, and the hot winds and the sand soon flaked the paint off."

SEVEN

Mix wanted to keep on questioning her, but a soldier knocked on the doorpost. He said that Stafford wanted to see the three at once. Mix called Yeshua out of his hut, and they followed the soldier to the council hall. Nobody said a word all the way.

Stafford said good morning and asked them if they intended to stay in New Albion.

The three said that they would like to be citizens.

Stafford said, "Very well. But you have to realize that a citizen owes the state certain duties in return for its protection. I'll enumerate these later. Now, what position in the army or navy are you particularly fitted for? If any?"

Mix had already told him what his skills were, but he repeated them. The lord-mayor told him that he would have to start as a private, though his experience qualified him to be a commissioned officer.

"I apologize for this, but it is our policy to start all newcomers at the bottom of the ranks. This prevents unhappiness and jealousy among those who've been here for a long time. However, since you have stone weapons of your own, and these are scarce in this area, I can assign you to the axeman squad. Axemen are treated as elite, as something special. After a few months, you may be promoted to sergeant if you do well, and I'm sure you will."

"That suits me fine," Tom said. "But I can also make boomerangs and instruct your people in throwing them."

Stafford said, "Hmm!" and drummed his fingers on the desk for a moment.

"Since that'll make you a specialist, you deserve to be sergeant immediately. But when you're with the axe squad, you'll still have to take orders from the corporals and sergeants. Let's see. It's an awkward situation. But...I can make you a nonactive sergeant when you're in the squad and an active sergeant when you're in the capacity of boomerang instructor."

"That's a new one on me," Mix said grinning. "Okay."

"What?" Stafford said.

"Okay means 'all right.' It's agreeable with me."

"Oh! Very well. Now, Yeshua, what would you like to do?"

Yeshua said that he had been a carpenter on Earth and had also done considerable work in this field here. In addition, he had learned how to flake stone. Moreover, he had a small supply of flint and chert. The boat they'd fled in happened to have a leather bag full of unworked stone brought down from a distant area.

"Good!" Stafford said. "You can start by working with Mr. Mix. You can help him make boomerangs."

"I'm sorry," Yeshua said. "I can't do that."

Stafford's eyes widened. "Why not?"

"I am under a vow not to shed the blood of any human being nor to take part in any activity which results in the shedding of blood."

"But what about when you were running away? Didn't you fight then?"

"No, I did not."

"You mean that if you'd been captured you would not have defended yourself? You'd have just stood there and allowed yourself to be slain?"

"I would."

Stafford drummed his fingers again while his skin became slowly red. Then he said, "I know little of this Church of the Second Chance, but I have heard some reports that its members refuse to fight. Are you one of them?"

Yeshua shook his head.

"No. My vow is a private one."

"There isn't any such thing," Stafford said. "Once you've told others of your vow, it becomes a public thing. What you mean is that you made this vow to your god."

"I don't believe in gods or a God," Yeshua said in a low but firm voice. "Once I did believe, and I believed very strongly. In fact, it was more than a belief. It was knowledge. I *knew*. But I was wrong.

"Now I believe only in myself. Not because I know myself. No man really knows anything, including himself, or perhaps I should say that no man knows much. But I do know this. That I can make a vow to myself which I will keep."

Stafford gripped the edge of his desk as if he were testing its reality.

"If you don't believe in God, then why make such a vow? What do you care if you shed blood while defending yourself? It would only be natural. And where there is no God, there is no sin. A man may do what he wants to do, no matter how he harms others, and it is right because all things are right or all things are wrong if there is no Upper Law. Human laws do not matter."

"The vow is the only true thing in the world."

Bithniah laughed and said, "He's crazy! You won't get any sense out of him! I think that he refuses to kill to keep from being killed because he wants to be killed! He would like to die, but he doesn't have guts enough to commit suicide! Besides, what good would it do! He'd only be resurrected some other place!"

"Which," Stafford said, "makes your vow meaningless. You can't really kill anybody here. You can put out a person's breath, and he will become a corpse. But twenty-four hours later, he will be a new body, a whole body, though he had been cut into a thousand pieces."

Yeshua shrugged. "That doesn't matter. Not to me, anyway. I have made my vow, and I will not break it."

"Crazy!" Bithniah said.

"You're not intending to start a new religion, are you?" Mix said.

Yeshua looked at Mix as if he were stupid.

"I just said that I don't believe in God."

Stafford sighed. "I don't have time to dispute theology or philosophy with you. This issue is easily disposed of, however. You can leave our state at once, and I mean this very minute. Or you can stay here but as an undercitizen: There are ten such living in New Albion now. They, like you, won't fight, though for different reasons from yours. But they have their duties, their work, just like all citizens. They do not, however, get any of the bonuses given to citizens every three months by the state, the extra cigarettes, liquor, and food. They are required to contribute a certain amount from their copias to the state treasury. And they must work extra shifts as latrine-cleaners. Also, in case of war, they will be kept in a stockade until the war is over. This is so they will not get in the way of the military. Another reason for this is that we can't be sure of their loyalty."

"I agree to this," Yeshua said. "I will build you fishing boats and houses and anything else that is required as long as they are not directly connected with the making of war."

"That isn't always easy to discern," Stafford said. "But, never mind, we can use you."

After they were dismissed and had gone outside, Bithniah stopped Yeshua.

Glaring, she said, "Goodbye, Yeshua. I'm leaving you. I can't endure your insanity any longer."

Yeshua looked even sadder. "I won't argue with you. It will be best if we do separate. I was making you unhappy, and it is not good to thrust one's unhappiness upon another."

"No, you're wrong about that," she said. Tears trickled down her cheeks. "I don't mind sharing unhappiness if I can help relieve it, if I can do something about it. But I can't help you. I tried, and I failed, though I don't blame myself for failing."

Yeshua walked away.

Bithniah said, "Tom, there goes the unhappiest man in the world. I wish I knew why he is so sad and lonely."

Mix glanced at his near-double, walking swiftly away as if he had some place to go, and said, "There but for the grace of God go I."

And he wondered again what strange meeting of genes had resulted in two men, born about one thousand, eight hundred and eighty years apart in lands five thousand miles apart, of totally different ancestry, looking like twins. How many such coincidences had happened during man's existence on Earth?

Bithniah left to report to a woman's labor force. Mix looked up a Captain Hawkins and transmitted Stafford's orders to him. He spent an hour in close-order drill with his company and the rest of the morning practicing mock-fighting with axe and shield and some spear-throwing. That afternoon, he showed some craftsmen how to make boomerangs. In a few days he would be giving instruction in the art of throwing the boomerang.

Several hours before dusk, he was dismissed. After bathing in The River, he returned to his hut. Bithniah was in hers, but Yeshua had left.

"He went up into the mountains," she said. "He said something about purifying himself and meditating."

Mix said, "He can do what he wants with his free time. Well, Bithniah, what about moving in with me? I like you, and I think you like me."

"I'd be tempted if you didn't look so much like Yeshua," she said, smiling.

"I may be his spitting image, but I'm not a gloomy cuss. We'd have fun, and I don't need dreamgum to make love."

"You'd still remind me of him," she said. Suddenly she began weeping, and she ran into her hut.

Mix shrugged and went to the nearest stone to put his copia upon it.

EIGHT

While eating the goodies provided by his copia, holy bucket, miracle pail, grail, or whatever, he struck up a conversation with a pretty but lonely-looking blonde. She was Delores Rambaut, born in Cincinnati, Ohio, in 1945. She'd been living in the state across The River until this

very afternoon. Her hutmate had driven her crazy with his unreason-
able jealousy, and so, after putting up with him for a long time, she'd
fled. Of course she said, she could just have moved out of the hut, but
he was likely to try to kill her.

"How was it living with all those Huns?" he said.

She looked surprised.

"Huns? Those people aren't Huns. They're what we call Scythians.
At least, I think they are. They're mostly a fairly tall white-skinned
people, Caucasians. They were great horsemen on Earth, you know,
and they conquered a wide territory in southern Russia. In the seventh
century B.C., if I remember right what I read about them."

"The people here call them Huns," he said. "Maybe it's just an
insulting term and has no relation to their race or nationality. Or whatever. Anyway, I'm glad you're here. I don't have a mate, and I'm lonely."

She laughed and said, "You're kind of rushing it, aren't you? Tom
Mix, heh? You couldn't be...?"

"The one and only," he said. "And just as horseless as the ancient
Scythians are now."

"I should have known. I saw enough pictures of you when I was a
child. My father was a great admirer of yours. He had a lot of newspaper clippings about you, an autographed photo, and even a movie
poster. *Tom Mix in Arabia.* He said it was the greatest movie you ever
made. In fact, he said it was one of the best movies he ever saw."

"I kind of liked it myself," he said smiling.

"Yes. It was rather sad, though. Oh, I don't mean the movie. I mean
about all your movies. You made...how many?"

"Two hundred and sixty — I think."

"Wow! That many? Anyway, my father said, oh, it was years later,
when he was a very old man, that all of them had disappeared. The
studios didn't have any, and the few still existing were privately owned
and fading fast."

Tom winced, and he said, "*Sic transit gloria mundi.* However, I made
a hell of a lot of money and enjoyed blowing it. So, what the hell!"

Delores had been born five years after he'd rammed his car into a
barricade near Florence on the highway between Tucson and Phoenix.
He'd been traveling as advance agent for a circus and was carrying a
metal suitcase full of money with which to pay bills. As usual, he was
driving fast, ninety miles an hour at the time. He'd seen the warning
on a barrier that the highway was being repaired. But, also as usual,
he'd paid no attention to the sign. One moment, the road was clear.
The next...there was no way he could avoid the crashing into the barricade.

"My father said you died instantly. The suitcase was behind you, and it snapped your neck."

Tom winced again.

"I always was lucky."

"He said the suitcase flew open, and there were thousand-dollar bills flying all over the place. It was a money shower. The workmen didn't pay any attention to you at first. They were running around like chickens with a fox loose in the henhouse, catching the money, stuffing it in their pockets and under their shirts. But they didn't know who you were until later. You got a real big funeral, and you were buried in Forest Lawn Cemetery."

"I had class," he said. "Even if I did die almost broke. Was Victoria Forde, my fourth wife, at the funeral?"

"I don't know. Well, what do you know? I'm eating and talking with a famous movie star!"

Tom had felt hurt that the workers had been more interested in scooping up the money that was whirling like green snowflakes than in finding out whether he was dead or not. But he quickly smiled to himself. If he'd been in their skins, he might have done the same thing. The sight of a thousand-dollar bill blown by the wind was very tempting—to those who didn't earn in ten years what he'd made in a week. He couldn't really blame the slobs.

"They put up a monument at the site of the accident," she said. "My father stopped off to see it when he took us on a vacation trip through the Southwest. I hope knowing that makes you feel better."

"I wish the locals knew what a big shot I was on Earth," he said. "Maybe they'd give me a rank higher than sergeant. But they hadn't heard of movies until they came here, of course, and they can't even visualize them."

After two hours, Delores decided that they'd known each other long enough so that he was no longer rushing it. She accepted his invitation to move into his hut. They had just reached its door when Channing appeared. He'd been sent to summon Mix at once to the lord-mayor.

Stafford was waiting for him in the Council Hall.

"Master Mix, you know so much about Kramer and have such an excellent military background that I'm attaching you to my staff. Don't waste time thanking me.

"My spies in Kramer's land tell me he's getting ready for a big attack. His military and naval forces are completely mobilized, and only a small force is left for defense. But they don't know where the invasion will be. Kramer hasn't told even his staff, as yet. He knows we have spies there just as he has his spies here."

"I hope you still don't suspect that I might be one of his men," Mix said.

Stafford smiled slightly.

"No. My spies have reported that your story is true. You're not a spy unless you're part of a diabolically clever plot to sacrifice a good boat and some fighting men to convince me you're what you claim to be. I doubt it, for Kramer is not the man to let go of Jewish prisoners for any reason whatsoever."

Stafford, Mix learned, had been impressed by the showing of Mix in the fight on The River and by the reports of Mix's superiors. Also, Mix's Earthly military experiences had given Stafford some thought. Tom felt a little guilty then, but it quickly passed. Moreover, Mix knew the topography and the defenses of Deusvolens well. And he had said the night before that the only way to defeat Kramer was to beat him to the punch.

"A curious turn of phrase but clear in its meaning," Stafford had said.

"From what I've heard," Mix said, "Kramer's method of expansion is to leapfrog one state and conquer the one beyond it. After he consolidates his conquest, he squeezes the bypassed area between his two armies. This's fine, but it wouldn't work if the other states would unite against Kramer. They know he's going to gobble them all up eventually. Despite which they're so damned suspicious they don't trust each other. Maybe they got good reason, I don't know. Also, as I understand it, no one state's willing to submit itself to another's general. I guess you know about that.

"I think that if we could deliver one crippling blow, and somehow capture or kill Kramer and his Spanish sidekick, Don Esteban de Falla, we would weaken Deusvolens considerably. Then the other states would come galloping in like Comanches so they could really crush Deusvolens and grab all the loot that's for the grabbing.

"So, my idea is to make a night raid, by boat, of course, a massive one that would catch Kramer with his pants down. We'd burn his fleet and burst in on Kramer and de Falla and cut their throats. Knock off the heads of the state, and the body surrenders. His people would fall apart."

"I've sent assassins after him, and they've failed," Stafford said. "I could try again. If we make enough diversion, they might succeed this time. However, I don't see how we could carry this off. Sailing up-River is slow work, and we couldn't reach Kramer's land while it's still dark if we left at dusk. We'd be observed by his spies long before we got there, most probably when we amassed our boats. Kramer would be ready for us. That would be fatal for us. We have to have surprise."

"Yeah," Mix said. "But you're forgetting the Huns across The River. Oh, by the way, I just found out they're not really Huns, they're ancient Scythians."

"I know that," Stafford said. "They were mistakenly called Huns in the old days because of their savagery and our ignorance. The terminology doesn't matter. Stick to the relevant points."

"Sorry. Well, so far, Kramer has been working on this side of The River only. He's not bothered the Huns. But they aren't dumb, according to what I've just heard."

"Ah, yes, from the woman, Delores Rambaut," Stafford said.

Tom Mix tried to repress his surprise. "You've got spies spying on your own people."

"Not officially. I don't have to appoint people to spy on their own countrymen. There are enough volunteers to come running to me with accounts of everything that goes on here. They're gossips, and they're nuisances. Occasionally, though, they tell me something important."

"Well, what I meant when I said the Huns weren't dumb was that they know that Kramer's going to attack them when he has enough states on this side of The River under his belt. They must know he'll move against them then so he can consolidate this whole area. They know it'll be some years from now, but they know it's coming. So, they might be receptive to some ideas I've been hatching. Here's what we could do."

They talked for another hour. At the end, Stafford said that he'd do what he could to develop Mix's plan. It was a desperate one, in his opinion, chiefly because of the very little time left to carry it out. It meant staying up all night and working hard. Every minute that passed gave Kramer's spies just that much more opportunity to find out what was happening. But it had to be done. He didn't intend to sit passively and wait for Kramer to attack. It was better to take a chance than to let Kramer call the shots. Stafford was beginning to pick up some of Mix's twentieth-century Americanisms.

NINE

Intelligence reported that Kramer was not using his entire force. Though he theoretically had available enough soldiers and sailors to overwhelm both New Albion and Ormondia, in fact he was afraid to withdraw many from his subject states. His garrisons there were composed of a minority of men from Deusvolens and a majority of collaborators in the occupied states. They kept the people terrorized and had built earth and wooden walls on the borders and stationed troops in forts along these. The copias of most citizens were stored in well-guarded places and only passed out during charging times. Anyone who wished to flee either had to steal his copia or kill himself and rise somewhere else on The River with a new copia. The former was almost impossible to do, and the latter course was taken only by the bravest or most desperate.

Nevertheless, if Kramer weakened the garrisons too much, he would have a dozen revolutions at once.

From what Stafford's spies said, Kramer had quietly taken two out of every ten of his soldiers and sailors in the subject states and brought them to Deusvolens and Felipia, the state adjoining his north border. His fleet was stationed along the banks of The River in a long line. But the soldiers and the boats might be amassed at any time during the night. What night was, of course, unknown.

"Kramer's spies know that you and Yeshua and Bithniah are here," Stafford said to Mix. "You think that he'll attack New Albion just to get you three back. I don't believe it. Why should you three be so important to him?"

"Others have escaped him," Mix said, "but never in such a public manner. The news has gotten around, he knows it, and he feels humiliated. Also, he's afraid that others might get the same idea. However, I think that he's been planning to extend his conquests, and we've just stimulated him to act sooner than he'd intended.

"What he'll do, he'll bypass Freedom and Ormondia and attack us. If he takes New Albion, he'll then start his squeeze play."

Messengers had been sent to Ormondia, and the duke and his council had met Stafford and his council at the border. Half the night had been spent in trying to get the duke to agree to join in a surprise attack. The rest of the night and all morning had been taken up in arguing about who the supreme general should be. Finally, Stafford had agreed that Ormonde should be in command. He didn't like to do so, since he thought the duke wasn't as capable as himself. Also, the New Albionians would not be happy about serving under him. But Stafford needed the Ormondians.

Not stopping for even a short nap, Stafford then crossed The River to confer with the rulers of the two "Hunnish" states. Their spies had informed them that Kramer was planning another invasion. They hadn't been much concerned about it, since Kramer had never attacked across The River. Stafford finally convinced them that Kramer would get to them eventually. They bargained, however, for the majority of the loot. Stafford and the duke's agent, Robert Abercrombie, reluctantly agreed to this.

The rest of the day was taken up in making plans for the disposition of the Hunnish boats. There was much trouble about this. Hartashershes and Dherwishawyash, the rulers, argued about who would take precedence in the attack. Mix suggested to Stafford that he suggest to them that the boats carrying the rulers should sail side by side. The two could then land at the same time. From then on it would be every man for himself.

"But all of this may go awry," he said to Mix. "Who knows what Kramer's spies have found out? There may even be some in my own staff or among the Huns. If not, the watchers in the hills will have observed us."

Soldiers in New Albion and Ormondia were scouring the hills, searching for spies. These would be hiding, unable to light signal fires or beat on their relay drums: Some would have slipped through the hunters to carry their information on foot or by boat. That, however, would take time.

Meanwhile, envoys from New Albion had gone to three of the states south of its border. They would attempt to get these to furnish personnel and craft in the attack.

Tom had, by the end of the night, been commissioned a captain. He was supposed to don the leather, bone-reinforced casque and cuirass of the Albionian soldier, but he'd insisted that he keep his cowboy hat. Stafford was too weary to oppose him.

Two days and nights passed. During this time, Mix managed to get some sleep. In the afternoon of the third day, he decided that he'd like to get away from all the bustle and noise. There was so much going on that he could find no quiet place to sleep. He'd go up into the hills and find a silent spot to snooze, if that was possible. There were still search parties there.

First, though, he stopped at Bithniah's to see how she was doing. She was, he found, now living with a man whose mate had been killed during the River-fight. She seemed fairly happy with him. No, she hadn't seen "the crazy monk," Yeshua. Mix told her he'd seen him at a distance now and then. Yeshua had been cutting down some pine trees with a flint axe, but Mix didn't know for what purpose.

On the way to the hills, he ran into Delores. She was on a work party which was hauling logs of the giant bamboo down to the banks.

These were being set up to reinforce the wooden walls lining the waterside of New Albion's border. She looked tired and dirty and not at all happy. It wasn't just the hard labor that made her glare at Mix, however. Not once had they had time or the energy to make love.

Tom grinned at her and called, "Don't worry; dear! We'll get together after this is all over! And I'll make you the happiest woman alive!"

Delores told him what he could do with his hat.

Tom laughed and said, "You'll get over that."

She didn't reply. She bent her back to the rope attached to the log and strained with the other women to get it up over the crest of the hill.

"It'll be all downhill from now on," he said.

"Not for you it won't," she called back.

He laughed again, but, when he turned away, he frowned. It wasn't his fault that she'd been drafted into a work party. And he regretted as much as she, maybe more, that they hadn't had a honeymoon.

The next hill was busy and loud with the ring of stone axes chopping at the huge bamboo plants, the grunting of the choppers, and the shouted orders of the foremen and forewomen. Presently, he was on a still higher hill, only to discover that it, too, was far from conducive to sleep. He continued, knowing that when he got to the mountain itself, he would run into no human beings there. He was getting tired and impatient, though.

He stopped near the top of the last hill to sit down and catch his breath. Here the great irontrees grew closely together, and among them were the tall grasses. He could see no one, but he could hear the axes and the voices faintly. Maybe he should just lie down here. The grass was not soft, and it was itchy, but he was so fatigued that he wouldn't mind that. He'd spread out his cloak and put his hat over his face and pass out quickly into a much-deserved sleep. There were no insects to crawl over him or sting him, no pestiferous ants, flies, or mosquitoes. Nor would any loud bird cries disturb him.

He rose and removed his white cloak and placed it on the grass. The sun's hot rays came down between two irontrees on him; the long grass made a wall around him. Ah!

Stafford might be looking for him right now. If so, it was just too bad.

He stretched out, then decided he'd take his military boots off. His feet were hot and sweating. He sat up and slid one boot from his right foot and started to remove the woven-grass sock. He stopped. Had he heard a rustle in the grass not made by the wind?

His weapons lay by him, a chert tomahawk and a flint knife and a boomerang, all in straps in his belt. He took all three out, laying the boomerang on the cloak, and he held the tomahawk in his right hand and the knife in his left.

The rustling had stopped, but after a minute it resumed. He rose cautiously and looked over the top of the grass. There, twenty feet away, toward the mountain, the grass was bending down, then springing up. For a while he couldn't see the passerby. Either he was shorter than the tall blades or he was bending over.

Then he saw a head rise above the green. It was a man's, dark-skinned, black-haired, and Spanish-featured. That wasn't significant, since there were plenty like him in the area, good citizens all, some of them refugees from Deusvolens and Felipia. The stealthiness of the man, however, indicated that he wasn't behaving like one who belonged here.

He could be a spy who'd eluded the search parties.

The man had been looking toward the mountain, presenting his profile to the watcher. Mix ducked down before the stranger turned his head toward him. He crouched, listening. The rustling had stopped. After a while, it started again. Was the man aware that somebody else was here and so was trying to locate him?

He got down on his knees and put his ear to the ground. Like most valleydwellers, the fellow was probably barefooted or wore sandals. But he might step on a twig, though there weren't too many of those from the bushes. Or he might stumble.

After a minute of intent listening, Mix got up. Now he couldn't even hear the noise of the man's passage. Nor was there any movement of the grass caused by anything except the breeze. Yes! There was! The fellow had resumed walking. The back of his head was moving away from Mix.

He quickly strapped on his belt, fastened his cloak around his neck, and put the boot back on. With his white hat held by the brim in his teeth, the knife in one hand, the tomahawk in the other, he went after the stranger. He did so slowly, however, raising his head now and then above the grass. Inevitably, the followed and the follower looked at each other at the same time.

The man dropped at once. Now that he'd been discovered, Mix saw no reason to duck down. He watched the grass as it waved, betraying the crawler beneath as water disturbed by a swimmer close to the surface. He breasted the grass, striding swiftly toward the telltale passage but ready to disappear himself if the green wake ceased.

Suddenly, the dark man's head popped up. Surprisingly, he placed a finger on his lips. Mix stopped. What in hell was he doing? Then the man pointed beyond Mix. For a second, Mix refused to look. It seemed too much like a trick, but what could the man gain by it? He was too far away to get any advantage by charging when Mix was looking behind him.

Trick or not, Mix had too much curiosity. He turned to look over the territory. And there was the grass moving as if an invisible snake were crawling over it.

He considered the situation quickly. Was that other person an ally of the dark man and sneaking up on himself? No. If he were, the dark man wouldn't be pointing him out. What had happened was that the dark man was an Albionian who had detected a spy. He'd been trailing him when Mix had mistaken him for a spy.

Mix had no time then to think about how he might have killed one of his own people. He dropped down and began approaching the place where the third person was — had been, rather, since by the time he got there the unknown would probably be some place else. Every twelve feet or so he rose to check on the unknown's progress. Now the ripples were moving toward the mountain away from both himself and the dark man. The latter, as indicated by the moving grass, was crawling directly toward where Mix had been.

Tired of this silent and slow play, sure that a sudden and violent action would flush out the quarry, Mix whooped. And he ran through the grass as swiftly as it would allow him.

The afternoon was certainly full of surprises. Two heads shot up where he had expected one. One was blonde, and the other was a redhead. The woman had been in front of the man as they had crawled and crouched and risen briefly like human periscopes, though he hadn't actually seen them coming up to observe.

Mix stopped. If he'd made a mistake about the identity of the first person, could he be doing the same with these two?

He shouted to them, telling them who he was and what he was doing here. The dark man then called out, saying that he was Raimondo de la Reina, a citizen of New Albion. The redhead and the blonde then identified themselves: Eric Simons and Guindilla Tashent, also citizens of the same state.

Mix wanted to laugh at this comedy of errors, but he still wasn't sure. Simons and Tashent might be lying so that the others would let down their guard.

Tom stayed where he was. He said, "What were you two doing here?"

"For God's sake," the man said, "we were making love! But please do not bruit this about. My woman is very jealous, and Guindilla's man would not be very pleased if he heard about this, either!"

"Your secret is safe with me," Mix called.

He turned toward de la Reina, who was walking toward him. "What about you, pard? There isn't any reason to say anything about this, is there? Especially since it makes all of us look like fools?"

There was another problem. The two lovers were probably shirking their duties. This could be serious, a court-martial business, if the authorities learned about it. Mix had no intention of reporting it, but the Spaniard might feel that it must be brought to the attention of the authorities. If he insisted, then Mix couldn't argue with him. Not too strongly, anyway.

He, Simons, and Tashent hadn't moved. De la Reina was plowing through the grass toward him, probably to talk the situation over with him. Or perhaps he thought that the pair wasn't to be trusted. Which made sense, Mix thought. They could be spies who'd invented this tale when found out. Or, more likely, prepared it in case they were discovered.

But Mix didn't really think this was so.

Presently, the Spaniard was a few feet from him. Now Mix could clearly see his features long and narrow, aquiline, a very aristocratic Hispanic face. He was as tall as Mix. Through the bending grass Mix glimpsed a green towel-kilt, a leather belt holding two flint knives, and a tomahawk. One hand was behind his back; the other was empty.

Mix wouldn't allow anybody to get near him who hid one hand. He said, "Stop there, amigo!"

De la Reina did so. He smiled but at the same time looked puzzled. "What's the matter, friend?"

He spoke seventeenth-century English with a heavy foreign accent, and it was possible that he had trouble understanding Mix's twentieth-century American pronunciation. He was given the benefit of the doubt, though not very much.

Tom spoke slowly. "Your hand. The one behind your back. Bring it out. Slowly."

He chanced to look at the others. They were moving toward him, though slowly. They looked scared.

The Spaniard said, "Of course, friend."

And de la Reina was leaping toward him, shouting, the hand now revealed, clutching a flint blade. There were only a few inches showing, but there was enough to slash a jugular vein or a throat. If the Spaniard had been smarter, he could have concealed the entire weapon in his hand and let the hand swing naturally. But he had been afraid to do that.

Tom Mix swung the tomahawk. Its edge cracked against de la Reina's temple. He dropped. The blade fell from his grip.

Tom called to the two. "Stop where you are!"

They looked at each other uneasily, but they halted.

"Hold your hands up," he said. "High above your heads!"

The hands went up as high as they could go. Simons, the redhead, said, "What happened?"

"Get over under that irontree!"

The two started to walk toward the indicated place. An abandoned hut stood under it, but the grass around it had been recently cut. It had grown back to a height of a foot, enabling Mix to see if they carried weapons or not.

He bent down and examined the Spaniard. The fellow was still breathing, though harshly. He might or might not recover, and if he did, he might never have all his wits about him. It would be far better for him if he died, since he was bound to be tortured. That was the fate of all spies in this area who failed to kill themselves when facing inevitable capture. This one would be stretched over a wooden wheel until the ropes on his wrists and ankles pulled his joints apart. If he wouldn't give any worthwhile information or he was thought to be lying, he'd be suspended naked over a low fire and slowly seared.

During his turnings on the spit, he might have one eye or both poked out or an ear sliced off. Should he still refuse to talk, he'd be taken down and cooled off with water. Then his fingernails and toenails might be pulled out or tiny cuts made in his genitals. A hot flint tip might be thrust up his anus. One finger at a time might be severed and the stump immediately thereafter cauterized with a hot rock.

The list of possible tortures was long and didn't bear thinking about by any sensitive imaginative person.

Mix hadn't seen the Albionians put any spies to the question. But he had witnessed some inquisitions while Kramer's prisoner, and so he knew too well the horrors awaiting the Spaniard.

What could this poor devil tell that was worth hearing? Nothing, Mix was sure.

He straightened up to check on Simons and Tashent. They were under the branches of the tree now, standing near the hut.

He stooped and slashed the man's jugular vein. Having made sure that he was dead and having collected the valuable weapons, he walked toward the tree. The fellow would be resurrected in a whole body somewhere along The River far from here. Maybe someday Mix would run into him again, and he could tell him about his act of mercy.

Halfway toward the tree, he halted. From above, somewhere on the mountain, the wild skirling of a bamboo syrinx floated down.

Who could be up there wasting time when everybody was supposed to be working hard? Another pair of lovers, one of whom was entertaining the other with music between couplings? Or was the skirling some sort of signal by a spy? Not very likely, but he had to consider all possibilities.

The blonde and the redhead still had their hands up. Both were naked. The woman certainly had a beautiful body, and her thick pubic hair was just the red-gold that especially excited him. She reminded him of a starlet he'd run around with just after his divorce from Vicky.

"Turn around," he said.

Simons said, "Why?" But he obeyed.

"Okay," Mix said. "You can put your hands down now."

He didn't tell them that he'd once been stabbed by a naked prisoner who'd gripped a knife between the cheeks of his buttocks until he was close to his captor.

"Now, what happened?"

Events had been much as he'd thought. The two had sneaked off from a work party to make love in the grass. While lying in the grass between bouts, getting ready to light up cigarettes, they'd heard the spy walking nearby. Picking up their weapons, they'd started to trail him. They were sure that the stranger was up to no good.

Then they'd seen Mix following de la Reina and were just about to join him when the Spaniard had seen them. He'd been a quick thinker in trying to deceive Mix into believing that they were the spies.

"He might've succeeded if he hadn't tried to kill me at once instead of waiting for a better time," Tom said. "Well, you two get back to your duty."

Guindilla said, "You aren't going to tell anybody about this, are you?"

Tom said, grinning, "Maybe, maybe not. Why?"

"If you keep quiet about this, I could make it worth your while."

Eric Simons snarled, "Guin! You wouldn't, would you?"

She shrugged, causing intriguing ripples.

"What could it hurt? It'd be just this once. You know what'll happen if he turns us in. We'll be put on acorn bread and water for a week, publicly humiliated, and...well, you know how Robert is. He'll beat me, and he'll try to kill you."

"We could just run off," Simons said.

He looked very nasty. "Or would you like to tumble this man, you slut!"

Tom laughed again, and said, "If you got caught while deserting, you'd be executed. Don't worry. I'm not a blackmailer, a lecherous hard-hearted Rudolf Rassendale."

They looked blank. "Rassendale?" Simons said.

"Never mind. You wouldn't know. You two get going. I'm not telling anybody the whole truth. I'll just say I was alone when I discovered the Spaniard. But tell me, who's playing the syrinx up there?"

They said that they had no idea. As they walked away into the grass to retrieve their weapons and clothes, they quarreled loudly. Mix didn't think their passion for each other would survive this incident.

When their wrangling voices faded out, Tom turned to the mountain. Should he go back to the plain and report that he'd killed a spy? Go up the mountain to check out the syrinx player? Or do what he had come here for, that is, sleep?

Curiosity won out. It always did with him.

Telling himself he should have been a cat, one who'd already used up one of his nine lives, he began climbing. There were fissures along the face of the mountain, ledges, little plateaus, and steep narrow paths. Only a mountain goat or a very determined or crazy person would use these to get up the cliff, however. A sensible man would look up it and perhaps admire it, but he'd stay below and loaf or sleep or roll a pretty woman in the grass. Best of all, he'd do all three, not to mention pouring down some good bourbon or whatever his copia gave him in the way of booze.

Sweating despite the shade, he pulled himself over the edge of one of the small plateaus. A building that was more of an enclosed leanto than a hut was in the middle of the tablerock. Beyond it was a small cascade, one of the many waterfalls that presumably originated from unseen snows on top of the mountains. The cascades were another mystery of this planet, which had no seasons and thus should rotate at an unvarying 90 degrees to the ecliptic. If the snows had no thawing period, where did the water come from?

Yeshua was by the waterfall. He was naked and blowing on the pan's pipe and dancing as wildly as one of the goat-footed worshippers of The Great God. Around and around he spun. He leaped high, he skipped, he bent forward and backward, he kicked, he bent his legs, he pirouetted, he swayed. His eyes were closed, and he came perilously close to the edge of the plateau.

Like David dancing after the return of the ark of God, Mix thought. But Yeshua was doing this for as invisible audience.

And he certainly had nothing to celebrate.

Mix was embarrassed. He felt like a window-peeper. He almost decided to retreat and leave Yeshua to whatever was possessing him. But the thought of the difficulty of the climb and the time he had taken made him change his mind.

He called. Yeshua stopped dancing and staggered backward as if an arrow had struck him. Mix walked up to him and saw that he was weeping.

Yeshua turned, kneeled and splashed the icy water from a pool by the side of the cataract, then turned to face Mix. His tears had stopped, but his eyes were wide and wild.

"I was not dancing because I was happy or filled with the glory of God," he said. "On Earth, in the desert by the Dead Sea, I used to dance. No one around but myself and The Father. I was a harp, and His fingers plucked the strings of ecstasy. I was a flute, and He sounded through my body the songs of Heaven.

"But no more. Now I dance because, if I do not, I would scream my anguish until my throat caught fire, and I would leap over the cliff and fall to a longed-for death. What use in that? In this world a man cannot commit suicide. Not permanently. A few hours later, he must face himself and the world again. Fortunately, he does not have to face his god again. There is none left to face."

Mix felt even more embarrassed and awkward.

"Things can't be that bad," he said. "Maybe this world didn't turn out to be what you thought it was going to be. So what? You can't blame yourself for being wrong. Who could possibly have guessed the truth about the unguessable? Anyway, this world has many good things that Earth didn't have. Enjoy them. It's true it's not always a picnic here, but when was it on Earth? At least, you don't have to worry about growing old, there are plenty of good-looking women, you don't have to sit up nights wondering where your next meal is coming from or how you're going to pay your taxes or alimony. Hell, even if there aren't any horses or cars or movies here, I'll take this world anytime! You lose one thing; you gain another."

"You don't understand, my friend," Yeshua said. "Only a man like myself, a man who has seen through the veil that the matter of this physical universe presents, seen the reality beyond, felt the flooding of The Light within..."

He stopped, stared upward, clenched his fists, and uttered a long ululating cry. Mix had heard only one cry like that—in Africa, when a Boer soldier had fallen over a cliff. No, he hadn't really heard any Boer soldier. Once more, he was mixing fantasy with reality. "Mix" was a good name for him.

"Maybe I better go," Mix said. "I know when there's nothing to be done. I'm sorry that—"

"I don't want to be alone!" Yeshua said. "I am a human being; I need to talk and to listen, to see smiles and hear laughter, and know love! But I cannot forgive myself for being...what I was!"

Mix wondered what he was talking about. He turned and started to walk to the edge of the plateau. Yeshua came after him.

"If only I had stayed there with the Sons of Zadok, the Sons of Light! But no! I thought that the world of men and women needed me! The rocks of the desert unrolled before me like a scroll, and I read therein that which must come to pass, and soon, because God was showing me what would be. I left my brothers in their caves and their cells and went to the cities because my brothers and sisters and the little children there must know, so that they would have a chance to save themselves."

"I got to get going," Mix said. "I feel sorry for whatever's riding you, but I can't help you unless I know what it is. And I doubt that I'd be much help then."

"You've been sent to help me! It's no coincidence that you look so much like me and that our paths crossed."

"I'm no brain doctor," Mix said. "Forget it. I can't straighten you out."

Abruptly, Yeshua dropped the hand held out to Mix, and he spoke softly.

"What am I saying? Will I never learn? Of course you haven't been sent. There's Nobody to send you. It's just chance."

"I'll see you later."

He began climbing down. Once he looked upward, and he saw Yeshua's face, his own face, staring down at him. He felt angry then, as if he should have stayed and at least given some encouragement to the man. He could have listened until Yeshua talked himself into feeling better.

By the time he had reached the hills and started walking back, he had a different attitude. He doubted that he could really aid the poor devil.

Yeshua must be half cracked. Certainly he was half baked. And that was a peculiar thing about this world and the resurrection. Everybody else had not only been awakened from the dead with the body of a twenty-five-year-old—except, of course, for those who had died on

Earth before that age — but all who had suffered a mental illness on Earth had been restored mentally whole.

However, as time passed, and the problems of the new world pressed in, many began to sicken again in their minds. There wasn't much schizophrenia; but he understood from talking to a twentieth-centurian that at least three-quarters of schizophrenia had been proved to be due to a physical imbalance and was primarily genetic in origin.

Nevertheless, five years of life in the Rivervalley had produced a number of insane people, though not in the relative proportions known on Earth. And the resurrection had not been successful in converting the majority of the so-called sane to a new viewpoint, a different attitude, one that phased in with reality.

Whatever reality was.

As on Earth, most of humanity was often irrational, though rationalizing, and was impervious to logic it didn't like. Mix had always known the world was half mad and behaved accordingly, usually to his benefit.

Or so he had thought then. Now, since he had time sometimes to contemplate the Terrestrial past, he saw that he had been as half-mad as most people. He hoped he'd learned his lessons, but there were plenty of times when he doubted it. Anyway, except for a few deeds, he'd been able to forgive himself for his sins.

But Yeshua, miserable fellow, could not forgive himself for whatever he had been or had done on Earth.

TEN

After telling Stafford about de la Reina, he went to his hut, and he drank the last of his whiskey, four ounces.

Whoever would have thought that there'd be a dead ringer for Tom Mix, and an ancient Jew at that, for Christ's sake? It was too bad Yeshua hadn't been born at the same time as he had. Yeshua could have made good money as his stand-in.

Despite the noise still swirling around the hut, he managed to sleep well. The rest didn't last long, though. Two hours later, Channing woke him up. Tom told him to shove off. Channing continued to shake his shoulder, then gave up on that method of wakening, and emptied a skin-bucket full of water on his face. Sputtering, swearing, striking out with his fists, Mix came up off the bed. The sergeant ran out of the hut laughing.

The council lasted an hour, and he went back to the hut for some more shut-eye. He was roused momentarily when the copiastones thundered. Fortunately, he'd promised some cigarettes to a man if he'd place Mix's copia for him so he wouldn't go supperless.

Sometime later, Delores came in, set down their copias, and then tried to wake him up for their first, and possibly last, lovemaking. He told her to go away, but she did something that very few men could ignore. Afterward, they ate and then smoked a couple of cigarettes. Since he might not come out of the invasion alive, one coffin nail wouldn't hurt him. Anyway, Delores didn't like smoking alone after being plumbed.

The cigarette, however, made him cough, and he felt dizzy. He swore off again though the tobacco certainly had tasted delicious. A moment later, having forgotten his resolve, he lit up another.

A corporal came after him then. Tom kissed Delores. She cried and said that she was sure she'd never ever see him again.

"I appreciate your sentiments," Tom said. "But they aren't exactly comforting."

The fleets of Anglia and New Cornwall, a neighboring state which had decided at the last minute to join the invasion, were approaching the New Albion shores. Tom, dressed in his ten-gallon hat, cloak vest, kilt, and Wellington boots, got onto the flagship. It was the biggest man-of-war in New Albion, three-masted, carrying ten catapults. Behind it came the other largest boats, four men-of-war. After it trailed twenty frigates, as the two-masters were called, though they looked little like the frigates of Earth. After them came forty cruisers, single-masted but large catamarans. Following them were sixty one-masted war canoes, hollowed out of giant bamboo logs.

The night-sky blazed down on a River in which the traffic of tacking vessels was thick. There were a few unavoidable collisions, but little damage resulted, though they caused a lot of shouting and cursing. The danger increased as the Hunnish, or Scythian, fleets put out. Bull's-eye lanterns burning fish oil signaled everywhere. An observer in the hills would have been reminded of the dance of fireflies on Earth. But if there were any spies left, they didn't light signal fires or beat drums. They were lying low, still hiding from the search parties. All the male soldiers left behind were manning the forts and other important posts. Armed women were beating the hills now.

The miles dropped by slowly. Then the Ormondian fleet sailed out to join them, the duke's flagship in the van. More signals were rayed out.

Just north of Ormondia was the determinedly neutral state of Jacobea. Stafford and Ormonde had debated inviting it to be an ally, but had finally decided against it. There was little chance of its joining, and even if it had, its security couldn't be trusted. Now, as the fleet ventured into Jacobean waters, the cries of sentinels came to it. Its crews saw torchlights flare up, and they heard the booming of the hollow-log and fish-skin drums. The Jacobeans, fearing an invasion, poured out of their huts, their weapons in hand, and began falling into formation.

Up in the hills, signal fires began building up. These were tended by Kramer's spies, which Jacobea allowed to operate unmolested.

However, the clouds were forming in the skies. Fifteen minutes later, they emptied their contents, drowning out the fires. If Stafford's planning went as hoped for, there would be no relay of warning signals to Kramer.

The signal-man on the duke's boat flashed a message to the Jacobeans. It identified the fleets and said that they intended no harm. They were sailing against Kramer, and if Jacobea cared to join them, they'd be welcome.

"They won't do it, of course," Stafford said. He laughed. "But it'll throw them into a frenzy. They won't know what to do, and they'll end up doing nothing. If they follow us into battle, and we lose, God forbid, then Kramer will take his vengeance on them. If we win by God's good will, then they will be in our bad graces, and we might invade them. 'Twould only be justice if we did, and it would serve the scurvy curs right. But we have no desire to bring more sorrow and bloodshed upon this land. They won't know that, though."

"In other words," Mix said, "they won't know whether to shit or go blind."

"What? Oh! I see what you mean. It's a powerful phrase but most distasteful. Just like the excrement you referred to."

Grimacing, he turned away.

Whatever changes the Riverworld had made in Stafford, one had not been a tolerance for obscene language. He no longer believed in the god of the Old and New Testament, though he still used His name, but he reacted as strongly here as on Earth to "dirty" words. Half a Nonconformist still lived within him. Which must give him daily pain, Mix thought, since the ex-royalists and the ex-peasants in this area were not averse to earthy speech.

The boats passed the state just below Deusvolens as the fog rose up from The River and rolled down from the hills on schedule. From then on, the men in the crow's nests above the gray clouds directed the sailing by pulling on ropes. The men handling these on the decks told the steersmen which way to turn the tiller and when to expect the great booms to swing over. It was dangerous navigation, and twice Mix heard the crash of boats colliding.

After what seemed an endless time, the signal was given that Deusvolens had been sighted. At least, they hoped that it was their destination. Sailing so blindly, with the plains as well as The River concealed in fog, they could not be sure.

Shortly before the sky was due to turn pale under the greater blaze of the rising sun, the capital "city" of Fides was sighted. One of the watchmen came down to report.

"There be great lights all over the place. Something's stirring, my lord-mayor."

A moment later there was a cry from aloft.

"Boats! Many boats! They're heading straight for us! Beware, milord!"

Stafford revealed that he could curse as well as any when under great pressure.

"God's wounds! It's Kramer's fleet! The goddamned swine! He's setting out on his own invasion! What damnable timing! May he rot in the devil's ass forever!"

Ahead of them came the clamor of war, men shouting, the blowing of flutes, beating of drums, then, faintly, the sound of great vessels in the vanguard ramming into each other, screams as men fell into the water or were speared, knifed, clubbed, or axed.

Stafford ordered that his craft ignore the Kramerian fleet, if possible and head for Fides. He also commanded that signals be sent by his watchman to the other Albionian boats.

"Let the duke and the Cornishmen and the Huns take care of the enemy on the water!" he said. "We'll storm ashore as planned!"

As the sun cleared the mountains on their left, it disclosed a high earth and rock rampart on top of which was a wall of upright logs extending as far as the eye could see. At its base the fog was a woolen covering, but this would soon be burned away by the sun. There were thousands of helmeted heads behind the wall and above them the heads of thousands of spears. The huge alarm-drums were still booming, the echoes rolling back from the mountain behind it.

Amidst the deafening bruit, the flagship, *Invincible*, pulled up alongside the main gate, just past the end of the piers, and loosed, one by one, great stones from its catapults. These smashed in the main gates. Other boats, in Indian file, came up and loosed their boulders. Some struck too high, some too low. Nevertheless, five other huge holes were breached in the wooden walls and a few defenders smashed.

Instead of turning around to use the catapults on the other sides, a maneuver that would have taken much time, the boats sailed along the banks. They had to tack some to keep from grounding and so being rammed by those behind them. When the flagship had gone far enough to give room for its followers to stop, its sails were dropped, and its bow turned toward shore. Anchors, large stones tied to ropes, dropped into the shallows. At once, the small boats were launched, and since there was no room in them for all those aboard, many soldiers leaped into the water.

They swarmed ashore under a hail of spears, clubs, slingstones, and axes onto the strip of land between the bases of the ramparts and the edge of the banks. They ran toward the smashed gateway, many carrying tall ladders.

Mix was among those in the lead. He saw men fall in front and on both sides of him, but he escaped being struck. After a minute, he was forced to slow his pace. The gateway was still a half mile away; he'd be too tired to fight at once if he ran full speed. The strategy of Stafford and the Council didn't seem so good now. They were losing too many men trying to amass at the breaches for a massive assault. Still, if the plans had gone as hoped, they might have worked quite well. The other fleets were to sail along the walls and throw the big rocks at intervals above and below where Stafford's vessels were. Thus, fifty different breaches could have been stormed and the Deusvolentians would have had to spread out their forces to deal with these.

If only Kramer's fleet hadn't decided to set out just before the big attack came. If only...that was the motto of generals, not to mention the poor devils of soldiers who had to pay for the if-only's.

As he ran he glanced now and then toward The River. The fog was almost gone now. He could see...

The deafening thunder of the copiastones erupting almost made his heart stop. He'd completely forgotten about them. They were inside the earth walls, set within log wells. At least the enemy wasn't going to have time to eat breakfast.

He looked to his right again. Out in The River were at least fifty vessels grappled in pairs, the crews of each trying to board the other. Many others were still maneuvering, trying to run alongside the foe so that they could release missiles: fish-oil firebombs, stones, spears hurled by atlatls, clubs, stones tied to wooden shafts. It was too bad that there hadn't been time to make boomerangs and train men how to use them. They would have been very effective.

He couldn't determine how the battle on the water was going. Two ships were on fire. Whether they were enemy or friend, he didn't know. He saw a big war canoe sink, a hole in its bottom made by a boulder cast by a catapult. A frigate was riding over the stern of a large catamaran. It was too early to say on whom Victory was smiling. She was a treacherous bitch, anyway. Just as you thought you couldn't lose, she slipped in something that resulted in you running like hell to get away from the defeated-suddenly-become-conquerors.

Now the attackers had joined in front of the gateway or before the other breaches. He had to catch his breath, and so did most of the others. However, men who'd landed from boats that had stopped close to these were already storming up the rampart and going through the holes in the walls. Trying to, anyway. Many dead or wounded lay on the slopes and in the entrances. Above them the Kramerians cast spears or hurled stones or poured burning fish oil from leather buckets into down-tilted stone troughs.

Tom cast his spear and had the satisfaction of seeing it plunge into one of the faces, above the pointed ends of the log wall. He pulled his heavy axe from his belt and ran on.

Only so many defenders could get on the walkways behind the walls, and many of these had been struck by spears or large, unworked stones attached to wooden shafts.

On the ground behind the walls would be massed many soldiers, far outnumbering the invaders. At first, they'd crowded across the gateway, but now, as the first wave of Albionians crumbled, the Deusvolentians retreated. They were waiting for the next wave to come through. Then they would spread out, surround them, and close in.

A major shouted for the next charge to begin. Mix was glad that he couldn't be in that. Not unless those ahead of him were so successful that everybody got in.

Stafford, standing near Mix, shouted at the major to hold the attack. Two frigates were coming in. They'd be able to throw their catapults over the anchored ships and over the walls and into the men beyond them. The major couldn't hear him in the din. If he had, he wouldn't have been able to stop. Those behind forced him through the gate. Mix glimpsed him getting a spear in the chest, then he toppled forward out of sight.

Presently, Tom was being forced ahead by those axemen behind him. He fell once over a body, was kicked hard several times, struggled up, and began climbing up the steep slope of earth. Then he was through the gateway, walking over bodies, slipping, catching himself, and he was in a melee.

He fought as well as he could in the press, but he had no sooner engaged a spearman than he was whirled away, and he was fighting somebody else, a short dark man with a leather shield and a spear. Mix battened the man's shield aside with his axe and knocked the spear downward. He brought the axe upward, striking the man on the chin. The fellow reeled back, but something hit Mix's wrist, and he dropped his axe.

Quickly, Tom pulled out his tomahawk with his left hand and leaped on the man, knocking him down. Astride him, he brought the weapon down, splitting the skull between the eyes. He rose, panting. An Albionian staggered back and fell against him, flattening him. He writhed out from under and got to his feet. He wiped away the blood from his eyes, not knowing if it was his or the soldier's who'd fallen over him. Certainly, he hadn't been aware of any head wound.

Panting, he glared around. The battle was going against the invaders. At least a fourth were casualties, and another fourth would soon be. Now was the time for a strategic withdrawal. But between him and the gateway were at least one hundred men, facing inward, their spears thrust out, waiting. The invaders were trapped.

Beyond them, at the other breaches, the fight was still going on. There were, however, so many Kramerians between him and the entrances that he couldn't make out the details.

Stafford, bloody, his helmet knocked off, his eyes wide, gripped his arm.

"We'll have to form men for a charge back through the gateway!"

That was a good idea, but how were they to do it?

Suddenly, by that unexplained but undeniable telepathy that exists among soldiers in combat, all the Albionians came to the same decision. They turned and fled toward those blocking the exit. They were speared in the back as they ran, hurled forward by clubs and axes from behind, or knocked over by weapons from the sides. Stafford tried to marshal them for a disciplined attack. He must have known that it was too late, though he tried valiantly nevertheless. He was bowled over by two men, rose, and fell again. He lay on his back, his mouth open, one eye staring up at the sky. The other was pierced by a spearhead.

Slowly, pulled by the weight of the shaft, his head turned, and his one eye was looking straight at Mix.

Something struck Tom in the back of the head and his knees loosened. He was vaguely aware that he was falling, but he had no idea who he was or where he was, and he had no time to try to figure it all out.

ELEVEN

Tom Mix awoke, and he was sorry that he had.

He was lying on his back, a throbbing pain in the back of his head and a twisting in his stomach. The face looking down was blurry and doubled, wavering in and out. It was long and thin and hatchety, dark, black-eyed, a grim smile showing rows of white teeth in which the two front lower were missing.

Tom groaned. The face belonged to de Falla, Kramer's ramrod. The teeth had been knocked out by Tom himself while making his escape from this very place, Fides. He didn't think he'd be doing a repeat performance.

The Spaniard spoke in excellent, only slightly accented English.

"Welcome to Deusvolens."

Mix forced a smile.

"I don't suppose I bought a return ticket?"

De Falla said, "What?"

Mix said, "Never mind. So what kind of cards are you planning to deal me?"

"Whatever they are, you'll accept them," de Falla said.

"You're in the driver's seat."

He sat up and leaned on one arm. His vision wasn't any better, and the movement made him want to throw up. Unfortunately, his last meal had long been digested. He suffered from the dry heaves, which made the pain in the back of his head even worse.

De Falla looked amused. No doubt, he was.

"Now, my friend, the shoe, as you English say, is on the other foot. Though you don't have any footwear."

He was right. Mix had been stripped of everything. He looked around and saw his hat on a man nearby and beyond that someone wearing his boots. Four men, actually. He must have had a concussion, no slight one. Well, he'd had worse injuries and survived to be better than ever. The chances for living long, though, didn't seem good.

There were bodies everywhere on the ground, none of which was moving or making a sound. He supposed that all but the lightly wounded had been put out of their pain. Not for the sake of mercy but for economy. There was no use wasting food on them.

Someone had pulled the spear out of Stafford's eye.

De Falla said, "There's still a battle on The River. But there's no doubt who'll win now."

Tom didn't ask him who had the upper hand. He wouldn't give him that satisfaction.

The Spaniard gestured to two soldiers. They lifted Mix between them and started to march him across the plain, detouring around corpses. When his legs gave way, they dragged him, but de Falla came running. He told them to get a stretcher. Mix didn't need to ask why he was being so well treated, relatively speaking. He was a special prisoner to be saved for special reasons. He was so sick and weak that, at the moment, he didn't even care about the reasons.

They carried him to where the huts began and down a street and out past the huts to a compound. This was very large, though it held only a few prisoners. The log gate was swung open, and he was taken to an enclosure of upright logs set into the ground. Within this was a small hut. He was in a compound within a compound.

The two soldiers set him down inside the hut and checked on the amount of water in a baked-clay pot, his drinking supply. The nightjar was looked into, and one of the soldiers bellowed out a name. A short, thin worried-looking man ran up and got chewed out for not emptying it. Mix thought that he must indeed be special if such details were being taken care of.

Apparently, the previous occupant had not been so highly regarded. The stench was appalling even though the lid was on the thunder mug.

Seven days passed. Mix became better, his strength waxed, though it did not reach its fullness. Occasionally, he was troubled with recurrences of double vision. His only exercise was walking around the hut, around and around. He ate three times a day but not well. He had identified his copia which had been taken off the flagship by his captives, but he was allowed only half the food it gave and none of the cigarettes or liquor. His guards took these for themselves. Though he had smoked only two cigarettes in the past two years, he now yearned fiercely for more.

Daytime wasn't so bad, but late at night he suffered from the cold and the dampness. Most of all he suffered from not being able to talk to anybody. Unlike most of the guards he'd encountered during a dozen periods of incarceration, these refused to say a single word to him. They even seemed to be reserved with their grunts.

On the morning of the eighth day, Kramer and his victorious forces returned. From what he could overhear of the guards' conversation, New Albion, Ormondia, and Anglia had been conquered. There would be plenty of loot and women for all, including those who had not participated in the invasion.

Tom thought Kramer was celebrating too soon. He still had New Cornwall and the Huns to deal with. But he supposed that the defeat of their navies had made them pull in their necks for a while.

The other prisoners, about fifty, were hustled from their repair work on the ramparts back into the compound. Sounds of jubilation came from the area around the main gateway, drums beating, flutes shrilling, cheering. Kramer came through first—even at this distance Mix recognized the fat body and the piggish features—on a big chair carried by four men. The crowds shouted their greeting and tried to swarm around him but were pushed back by his bodyguard. After him came his staff and then the first of the returned soldiers, all grinning widely.

The chair was deposited in front of Kramer's "palace," a huge log structure on top of a low hill. De Falla came to greet him then, and both made speeches. Mix was too far away to hear what they said.

Some naked prisoners were marched in at spear point and double-stepped to the compound. Among the dirty, bruised, bloodied bunch was Yeshua. He sat down at once with his back to the wall, and his head sank as if he were completely dejected. Tom yelled at him until a man asked him whom he wanted. The man went across the compound and spoke to Yeshua. At first, Tom thought that Yeshua was going to ignore him. He looked at Tom for a moment and then let his head hang again. But after a while he rose, somewhat unsteadily, and walked slowly to the circular enclosure. He looked through the spaces between the logs, his eyes dull. He had been beaten about the face and body.

"Where's Bithniah?" Tom said.

Yeshua looked down again. He said, hollowly, "She was being raped by many men the last I saw of her. She must have died while they were doing it. She'd stopped screaming by the time I was taken to the boat."

Mix gestured at some female prisoners.

"What about them?"

"Kramer said he wanted some alive...to burn."

Mix grunted, and said, "I was afraid that was why they didn't kill me. Kramer's going to get a special revenge out of me."

He didn't add, though he was thinking it, that Yeshua would also be in the "privileged" class. Yeshua must know it, anyway.

He said, "If we start a ruckus, we might force them to kill some of us. If we're lucky, we'll be among the late unlamented."

Yeshua raised his head. His eyes were wild and staring.

"If only a man did not have to live again! If he could be dust forever, his sadness and his agonies dissolved into the soil, eaten by the worms as his flesh is eaten! But no, there's no escape! He is forced to live again! And again! And again! God will permit him no release!"

"God?" Tom said.

"It's just a manner of speech. Old habits die hard."

"It's tough just now," Tom said, "but in between the bad times it's not so bad. Hell, I'm sure that someday all this fighting will stop. Most of it, anyway. It's a time of troubles now. We're still getting straightened out, too many people are behaving like they did on Earth. But the setup's different here. You can't hold a man down. You can't tie him to his job and his house because he carries his own food supply with him and it doesn't take long to build a house. You can enslave him for a while, but he'll either escape or kill himself or make his captors kill him, and he's alive again and free and has another chance for the good life.

"Look here! We can make those buggers kill us now so we don't have to go through all the pain Kramer's figuring to give us. The guards aren't here now. Pull back the bar on the gate and let me out. As you can see, I can't reach through to do it myself. Once I'm out, I'll organize the others, and we'll go out fighting."

Yeshua hesitated, then gripped the big knob at the end of the massive bolt and, straining hard, withdrew it. Mix pushed the heavy gate open and left his prison within a prison.

Though there were no guards within the compound, there were many on the platforms outside the walls and in the towers. These saw Mix leave, but they did not object, which, Tom thought, meant that they knew he had to be released from it soon, anyway. He was just saving them the trouble of opening the gate.

It wouldn't be long before the prisoners would be herded out of the compound.

He called to the others, about sixty, to gather around him.

"Listen, you poor bastards! Kramer's got you marked for torture! He's going to put on a big show, a Roman circus! We're all going to wish soon we were never born, though I guess you know that! So I say we should cheat them! And save ourselves all that pain! Here's what I think we should do!"

His plan seemed wild to them, though mainly because it was unheard of. But it offered escape of a sort which once would not have been regarded as such. It was better than just sitting there like sick sheep waiting to be slain. Their tired eyes took on some life; their exhausted and abused bodies lost their shrunken appearance, swelling up with hope.

Only Yeshua demurred.

"I cannot take a human life."

Tom said, in an exasperated tone, "You won't be doing that! Not in the sense we knew on Earth! You'll be giving your man his life! And saving him from torture!"

A man said, "He doesn't have to take anybody's life. He can volunteer to be one of those that'll die."

"Yeah, that's right," Tom said. "How about it, Yeshua?"

"No. That would make me a collaborator in murder, hence, a murderer, even if the one murdered was myself. Besides, that would be suicide, and I cannot kill myself. That, too, would be a sin, against..."

He bit his lower lip.

"Look!" Tom said. "We don't have time to argue. The guards are getting mighty curious now. First thing you know, they'll be storming in here."

"That is what you want," Yeshua said.

Angrily, Tom cried out, "I don't know what you did or where you were when you were on Earth, but whatever it was or whoever you were, you really haven't changed! I've heard you say you've lost your religion, yet you act like you haven't lost a shred of it! You don't believe in God anymore, yet you were just about to spout off about not going against God! Are you crazy, man?"

"I think I've been crazy all my life," Yeshua said. "But there are some things I will not do. They are against my principles, even though I no longer believe in The Principle."

By then the captain of the guards was shouting at the prisoners, demanding to know what they were up to.

"Forget the mad Jew," a woman said. "Let's get this over with before they get here."

"Line up then," Mix said.

All except Yeshua got into one of two lines in which each person faced another. That was just as well since they were, without him, even-numbered. Opposite Mix was a woman, a brunette whom he vaguely remembered seeing in New Albion. She was pale and trembling but game enough.

He lifted the chamberpot by its rim and said, "You call it."

He swung the brown pot up, loosed it, and watched it turn over and over. Sixty-two pairs of eyes were fastened upon it.

"Open end!" the woman called out loudly but shakily.

The container, turning, fell. It landed on its bottom and cracked in two.

"Don't hesitate!" Tom shouted. "We don't have much time, and you might lose your nerve!"

The woman closed her eyes as Tom stepped up to her and gripped her throat. For a few seconds she held her arms out at right angles to her body. She was attempting to put up no resistance, to make the job easier for him and quicker for her. The will to live was, however, too strong for her. She grabbed his wrists and tried to break his grip. Her eyes opened wide as if she were pleading with him. He squeezed her throat more tightly. She writhed and kicked, driving her knee up between his legs. He bent away though not swiftly enough to avoid getting the knee in the belly.

"Hell, this ain't going to work!" he said.

He released her. Her face was blue by then, and she was gasping. He hit her in the chin, and she dropped onto the ground. Before she could regain consciousness, he was choking her again. It only took a few seconds to still her breath. Wanting to make sure, he held on a little longer.

"You're the lucky one, sister," he said, and he rose.

The people in his line, which had won the toss or lost it, depending upon the viewpoint, were having the same trouble he'd had. Though the other line had agreed beforehand not to fight against their stranglers, most of them had been unable to keep their promise. Some had torn loose and were slugging it out with their would-be killers. A few were running away, pursued. Some were dead, and some were now trying to choke their chokers.

He looked at the big gate. It was swinging open. Behind it was a horde of guards, all armed with spears.

"Stop it!" he roared. "It's too late now! Attack the guards!"

Without waiting to see how many had heard him, he ran toward the first of the spearmen. He yelled to give himself courage and to startle the guards into self-defense. But what did they have to fear from an unarmed, naked, and enfeebled man?

The guards nearest him did, however, raise their spears.

Good! He'd hurl himself onto the points, arms out, catching some in his belly and some in his chest.

But the captain bellowed out an order, and they reversed their weapons. The shafts would be used as clubs.

Nevertheless, he leaped, and he saw the butt end of the spear that would knock him senseless.

TWELVE

When he awoke, he had two pains in his head, the new one far worse than the old. He also was suffering again from diplopia. He sat up and looked around at the blurred scene. There were bodies of the prisoners here and there. Some had been killed by the others, and some had been beaten to death by the guards. Three of the guards lay on the dirt, one dead, the others bleeding. Apparently, some prisoners had wrested the spears away from the guards and gotten some small revenge before being killed.

Yeshua was standing away from the rest of the prisoners, his eyes closed and his mouth moving. He looked as if he were praying, but Mix doubted that he was.

When he looked back, he saw about twenty spearmen marching through the compound gate. Kramer was leading them. Mix watched the short, fat youth with the dark-brown hair and very pale blue eyes walking toward him. His piggish face looked pleased. Probably, Mix thought, he was happy that Mix and Yeshua had not been slain.

Kramer stopped a few feet from Mix. He looked ridiculous, though he must think he made a splendid figure. He wore a crown of oak wood each of the seven points of which sported a round button cut from mussel shells. His upper eyelids were painted blue, an affectation of the males of his land, an affectation which Mix thought was fruity. The upper ends of his black towel-cape were secured around his fat neck with a huge brooch made from copper, an exceedingly rare and expensive metal. On one plump finger was an oak ring in which was set an uncut emerald, also a scarce item. A black towel-kilt was around his paunch, and his knee-length boots were of black fish-leather. In his right hand he held a long shepherd's crook, symbol that he was the protector of his sheep — his people. It also signified that he had been appointed by God for that role.

Behind Kramer were two bloodied and bruised and naked prisoners, whom Mix had not seen before. They were short dark men with Levantine features.

Mix squinted. He was wrong. He did know one of the two. He was Mattithayah, the little man who had mistaken Mix for Yeshua when they had first been Kramer's prisoners.

Kramer pointed at Yeshua and spoke in English.

"Iss zat ze man?"

Mattithayah broke into a storm of unintelligible but recognizable English. Kramer whirled and sent him staggering backward with a blow of his left fist against the jaw. Kramer said something to the other prisoner. This one answered in English as heavily accented as Kramer's, but his native tongue was obviously different.

Then he cried, "Yeshua! Rabbi! We have looked for you for many years! And now *you* are *here*, too!"

He began to weep, and he opened his arms and walked toward Yeshua. A guard banged the butt of his spear on his back, over the kidney area, and the little man groaned and fell on his knees, his face twisted with pain.

Yeshua had looked once at the two men and had groaned. Now he stood with downcast eyes.

Kramer, scowling and muttering, strode up to Yeshua and seized his long hair. He jerked it, forcing Yeshua to raise his head.

"Madman! Anti-Christ!" he shouted. "You'll pay for your blasphemies! Yust ass your two crazedt friendss vill pay!"

Yeshua closed his eyes. His lips moved soundlessly. Kramer struck him in the mouth with the back of his hand, rocking Yeshua's head. Blood flowed from the right corner of Yeshua's lips.

Kramer screamed, "Shpeak, you filt! Do you indeedt claim to be Christ?"

Yeshua opened his eyes, and spoke softly.

"I claim only to be a man named Yeshua, just another son of man. If this Christ of yours did exist and if he were here, he would be horrified, driven to madness with despair, at what had happened on Earth to his teachings after he died."

Kramer, yelling, hit Yeshua alongside the head with his staff. Yeshua fell to his knees and then crumpled forward, his head hitting the earth with a soft thud. Kramer drove the toe of his boot against the fallen man's ribs.

"Renounce your blasphemiess! Recant your Satanic ravingks! You vill escape mush pain in zis worlt if you do, ant you may safe your zoul in the next!"

Yeshua raised his head, but he said nothing until he had regained his breath.

"Do what you will to me, you unclean Gentile."

Kramer shouted, "Shut your dirty mous, you inzane monshter!"

Yeshua grunted as Kramer's boot toe drove into his side again, and he moaned for a little while thereafter.

Kramer, his black cloak flapping after him, strode to Mattithayah and his companion.

"Do you shtill maintain zat zis lunatic iss ze Blessedt Zon of Godt?"

The two were pale beneath their dark skins, and their faces looked as if they were made of melting wax. Neither replied to Kramer.

"Answer me, you svine!" he cried.

He began to beat them with the shepherd's staff. They backed away, their hands up to protect themselves, but they were seized by the guards and kept from retreating.

Yeshua struggled to his feet. Loudly, he said, "He is so savage because he fears that they speak the truth!"

Mix said, "What truth?"

His double vision was increasing, and he felt as if he should vomit. He was beginning to lose interest in everything but himself. God, if only he could die before he was tied to the stake and the wood set afire!

"I've heard that question before," Yeshua said.

Mix didn't know for a moment what Yeshua meant. Then illumination flooded in. Yeshua had thought he'd said, "What *is* truth?"

After Kramer had beaten Mattithayah and his friend into unconsciousness, they were dragged out through the gate by their legs, their heads bumping, their arms trailing along behind their heads. Kramer started to walk toward Yeshua, his staff lifted high as if he intended to give him the same treatment. Mix hoped that he would. Perhaps, in his rage, he'd kill Yeshua now and thus save him from the fire.

The joke would certainly be on Kramer then.

But a sweating, panting man ran through the gate, and he cried out Kramer's name. It was thirty seconds, though, before he caught his wind. He was the bearer of ill news.

Apparently, there were two fleets approaching, one from up-River, one from down-River. Both were enormous. The states to the north of Kramer's and the states to the south of the newly conquered territories had been galvanized into allied action against Kramer, and the Huns across from them had joined them. They finally realized that they must band together and attack Kramer before he moved against them.

Kramer turned pale, and he struck the messenger over the head with his staff. The man fell without a sound.

Kramer was in a bad way. Half of his own fleet had been destroyed in its victory, and the number of his soldiers had been considerably reduced. He wouldn't be ready for a long time to launch another attack nor was he well fitted to withstand an invasion from such a huge force.

He was doomed and he knew it.

Despite Mix's pain and the knowledge of the fire waiting for him, he managed a smile. If Kramer were captured, he would undoubtedly be tortured and then burned alive. It was only just that he should be. Perhaps if Kramer himself felt the awful flames, he might not be so eager to subject others to them when he rose again.

But Mix doubted that.

Kramer shouted orders to his generals and admirals to prepare for the invasion. After they had left, he turned, panting, toward Yeshua. Mix called to him.

"Kramer! If Yeshua is who those two men claim he is, and they've no reason to lie, then what about you? You've tortured and killed for nothing! And you've put your own soul in the gravest jeopardy!"

Kramer reacted as Mix had hoped he would. Screaming, he ran at Mix with the staff raised. Mix saw it come down on him.

Kramer must have pulled his punch. Mix awoke some time later, though not fully. He was upright and tied to a great bamboo stake. Below him was a pile of small bamboo logs and pine needles.

Through the blur, he could see Kramer applying the torch. He hoped that the wind would not blow the smoke away from him. If it rose straight up, then he would die of asphyxiation and would never feel the flames on his feet.

The wood crackled. His luck was not with him. The wind was blowing the smoke away from him. Suddenly, he began coughing. He looked to his right and saw, vaguely, that Yeshua was tied to another stake very near him. Upwind. Good, he thought. Poor old Yeshua will burn, but the smoke from his fire will kill me before I burn.

He began coughing violently. The pains in his head struck him like fists. Vision faded entirely. He fell toward oblivion.

But he heard Yeshua's voice, distorted, far away, like thunder over a distant mountain.

"Father, they *do* know what they're doing!"

God said, "Bring me Cecil B. DeMille."

"Dead or alive?" the angel Gabriel said.

"I want to make him an offer he can't refuse. Can even *I* do this to a dead man?"

"Oh, I see," said Gabriel, who didn't. "It will be done."

And it was.

Cecil Blount DeMille, confused, stood in front of the desk. He didn't like it. He was used to sitting behind the desk while others stood. Considering the circumstances, he wasn't about to protest. The giant, divinely handsome, bearded, pipe-smoking man behind the desk was not one you'd screw around with. However, the gray eyes, though steely, weren't quite those of a Wall Street banker. They held a hint of compassion.

Unable to meet those eyes, DeMille looked at the angel by his side. He'd always thought angels had wings. This one didn't, though he could certainly fly. He'd carried DeMille in his arms up through the stratosphere to a city of gold somewhere between the Earth and the moon. Without a space suit, too.

God, like all great entities, came right to the point.

"This is 1980 A.D. In twenty years it'll be time for The Millennium. The Day of Judgment. The events as depicted in the Book of Revelation or the Apocalypse by St. John the Divine. You know, the seven seals, the four horsemen, the moon dripping blood, Armageddon, and all that."

DeMille wished he'd be invited to sit down. Being dead for twenty-one years, during which he'd not moved a muscle, had tended to weaken him.

"Take a chair," God said. "Gabe, bring the man a brandy." He puffed on his pipe; tiny lightning crackled through the clouds of smoke.

"Here you are, Mr. DeMille," Gabriel said, handing him the liqueur in a cut quartz goblet. "Napoleon 1880."

DeMille knew there wasn't any such thing as a one-hundred-year-old brandy, but he didn't argue. Anyway, the stuff certainly tasted like it was. They really lived up here.

God sighed, and he said, "The main trouble is that not many people really believe in Me any more. So My powers are not what they once were. The old gods, Zeus, Odin, all that bunch, lost their strength and just faded away, like old soldiers, when their worshippers ceased to believe in them.

"So, I just can't handle the end of the world by Myself any more. I need someone with experience, know-how, connections, and a reputation. Somebody people know really existed. You. Unless you know of somebody who's made more Biblical epics than you have."

"That'll be the day," DeMille said. "But what about the unions? They really gave me a hard time, the commie bas...uh, so-and-so's. Are they as strong as ever?"

"You wouldn't believe their clout nowadays. "

DeMille bit his lip, then said, "I want them dissolved. If I only got twenty years to produce this film, I can't be held up by a bunch of goldbrickers."

"No way," God said. "They'd all strike, and we can't afford any delays."

He looked at his big railroad watch. "We're going to be on a very tight schedule."

"Well, I don't know," DeMille said. "You can't get anything done with all their regulations, interunion jealousies, and the featherbedding. And the wages! It's no wonder it's so hard to show a profit. It's too much of a hassle!"

"I can always get D. W. Griffith."

DeMille's face turned red. "You want a grade-B production? No, no, that's all right! I'll do it, I'll do it!"

God smiled and leaned back. "I thought so. By the way, you're not the producer, too; I am. My angels will be the executive producers: They haven't had much to do for several millennia, and the devil makes work for idle hands, you know. Haw, haw! You'll be the chief director, of course. But this is going to be quite a job. You'll have to have at least a hundred thousand assistant directors."

"But...that means training about 99,000 directors!"

"That's the least of our problems. Now you can see why I want to get things going immediately."

DeMille gripped the arms of the chair and said, weakly, "Who's going to finance this?"

God frowned. "That's another problem. My Antagonist has control of all the banks. If worse comes to worse, I could melt down the heavenly city and sell it. But the bottom of the gold market would drop all the way to hell. And I'd have to move to Beverly Hills. You wouldn't believe the smog there or the prices they're asking for houses.

"However, I think I can get the money. Leave that to Me."

◆ ◆ ◆

The men who really owned the American banks sat at a long mahogany table in a huge room in a Manhattan skyscraper. The Chairman of the Board sat at the head. He didn't have the horns, tail, and hooves which legend gave him. Nor did he have an odor of brimstone. More like Brut. He was devilishly handsome and the biggest and best-built man in the room. He looked like he could have been the chief of the angels and in fact once had been. His eyes were evil but no more so than the others at the table, bar one.

The exception, Raphael, sat at the other end of the table. The only detractions from his angelic appearance were his bloodshot eyes. His apartment on the West Side had paper-thin walls, and the swingers' party next door had kept him awake most of the night. Despite his fatigue, he'd been quite effective in presenting the offer from above.

Don Francisco "The Fixer" Fica drank a sixth glass of wine to up his courage, made the sign of the cross, most offensive to the Chairman, gulped, and spoke.

"I'm sorry, Signor, but that's the way the vote went. One hundred percent. It's a purely business proposition, legal, too, and there's no way we won't make a huge profit from it. We're gonna finance the movie, come hell or high water!"

Satan reared up from his chair and slammed a huge but well-manicured fist onto the table. Glasses of vino crashed over; plates half-filled with pasta and spaghetti rattled. All but Raphael paled.

"*Dio motarello! Lecaculi! Cacasotti! Non romperci i coglion!* I'm the Chairman, and I say no, no, no!"

Fica looked at the other heads of the families. Mignotta, Fregna, Stronza, Loffa, Recchione, and Bocchino seemed scared, but each nodded the go-ahead at Fica.

"I'm indeed sorry that you don't see it our way," Fica said. "But I must ask for your resignation."

Only Raphael could meet The Big One's eyes, but business was business. Satan cursed and threatened. Nevertheless, he was stripped of all his shares of stock. He'd walked in the richest man in the world, and he stormed out penniless and an ex-member of the Organization.

Raphael caught up with him as he strode mumbling up Park Avenue.

"You're the father of lies," Raphael said, "so you can easily be a great success as an actor or politician. There's money in both fields. Fame, too. I suggest acting. You've got more friends in Hollywood than anywhere else."

"Are you nuts?" Satan snarled.

"No. Listen. I'm authorized to sign you up for the film on the end of the world. You'll be a lead, get top billing. You'll have to share it with The Son, but we can guarantee you a bigger dressing room than His. You'll be playing yourself, so it ought to be easy work."

Satan laughed so loudly that he cleared the sidewalks for two blocks. The Empire State Building swayed more than it should have in the wind.

"You and your boss must think I'm pretty dumb! Without me the film's a flop. You're up a creek without a paddle. Why should I help you? If I do I end up at the bottom of a flaming pit forever. Bug off!"

Raphael shouted after him, "We can always get Roman Polanski!"

Raphael reported to God, who was taking His ease on His jasper and cornelian throne above which glowed a rainbow.

"He's right, Your Divinity. If he refuses to cooperate, the whole deal's off. No real Satan, no real Apocalypse."

God smiled. "We'll see."

Raphael wanted to ask Him what He had in mind. But an angel appeared with a request that God come to the special effects department. Its technicians were having trouble with the roll-up-the-sky-like-a-scroll machine.

"Schmucks!" God growled. "Do I have to do everything?"

♦ ♦ ♦

Satan moved into a tenement on 121st Street and went on welfare. It wasn't a bad life, not for one who was used to Hell. But two months later, his checks quit coming. There was no unemployment any more. Anyone who was capable of working but wouldn't was out of luck. What had happened was that Central Casting had hired everybody in the world as production workers, stars, bit players, or extras.

Meanwhile, all the advertising agencies in the world had spread the word, good or bad depending upon the viewpoint, that the Bible was true. If you weren't a Christian, and, what was worse, a sincere Christian, you were doomed to perdition.

Raphael shot up to Heaven again.

"My God, You wouldn't believe what's happening! The Christians are repenting of their sins and promising to be good forever and ever, amen! The Jews, Moslems, Hindus, Buddhists, scientologists, animists, you name them, are lining up at the baptismal fonts! What a mess! The atheists have converted, too, and all the communist and Marxian socialist governments have been overthrown!"

"That's nice," God said. "But I'll really believe in the sincerity of the Christian nations when they kick out their present administrations. Down to the local dogcatcher."

"They're doing it!" Raphael shouted. "But maybe You don't understand! This isn't the way things go in the *Book of Revelation!* We'll have to do some very extensive rewriting of the script! Unless You straighten things out!"

God seemed very calm. "The script? How's Ellison coming along with it?"

Of course, God knew everything that was happening, but He pretended sometimes that He didn't. It was His excuse for talking. Just issuing a command every once in a while made for long silences, sometimes lasting for centuries.

He had hired only science-fiction writers to work on the script since they were the only ones with imaginations big enough to handle the job. Besides, they weren't bothered by scientific impossibilities. God loved Ellison, the head writer, because he was the only human he'd met so far who wasn't afraid to argue with Him. Ellison was severely handicapped, however, because he wasn't allowed to use obscenities while in His presence.

"Ellison's going to have a hemorrhage when he finds out about the rewrites," Raphael said. "He gets screaming mad if anyone messes around with his scripts."

"I'll have him up for dinner," God said. "If he gets too obstreperous, I'll toss around a few lightning bolts. If he thinks he was burned before...Well!"

Raphael wanted to question God about the tampering with the book, but just then the head of Budgets came in. The angel beat it. God got very upset when He had to deal with money matters.

♦ ♦ ♦

The head assistant director said, "We got a big problem now, Mr. DeMille. We can't have any Armageddon. Israel's willing to rent the site to us, but where are we going to get the forces of Gog and Magog to fight against the good guys? Everybody's converted. Nobody's willing to fight on the side of anti-Christ and Satan. That means we've got to change the script again. I don't want to be the one to tell Ellison..."

"Do I have to think of everything?" DeMille said. "It's no problem: Just hire actors to play the villains."

"I already thought of that. But they want a bonus. They say they might be persecuted just for *playing* the guys in the black hats. They call it the social-stigma bonus. But the guilds and the unions won't go for it. Equal pay for all extras or no movie and that's that."

DeMille sighed. "It won't make any difference anyway as long as we can't get Satan to play himself."

The assistant nodded. So far, they'd been shooting around the devil's scenes. But they couldn't put it off much longer.

DeMille stood up. "I have to watch the auditions for The Great Whore of Babylon."

The field of 100,000 candidates for the role had been narrowed to a hundred, but from what he'd heard none of these could play the part. They were all good Christians now, no matter what they'd been before, and they just didn't have their hearts in the role. DeMille had intended to cast his brand-new mistress, a starlet, a hot little number — if promises meant anything — one hundred percent right for the part. But just before they went to bed for the first time, he'd gotten a phone call.

"None of this hanky-panky, C.B.," God had said. "You're now a devout worshipper of Me, one of the lost sheep that's found its way back to the fold. So get with it. Otherwise, back to Forest Lawn for you, and I use Griffith."

"But...but I'm Cecil B. DeMille! The rules are O.K. for the common people, but..."

"Throw that scarlet woman out! Shape up or ship out! If you marry her, fine! But remember, there'll be no more divorces!"

DeMille was glum. Eternity was going to be like living forever next door to the Board of Censors.

The next day, his secretary, very excited, buzzed him.

"Mr. DeMille! Satan's here! I don't have him for an appointment, but he says he's always had a long-standing one with you!"

Demoniac laughter bellowed through the intercom.

"C.B., my boy! I've changed my mind! I tried out anonymously for the part, but your shithead assistant said I wasn't the type for the role! So I've come to you! I can start work as soon as we sign the contract!"

The contract, however, was not the one the great director had in mind. Satan, smoking a big cigar, chuckling, cavorting, read the terms.

"And don't worry about signing in your blood. It's unsanitary. Just ink in your John Henry, and all's well that ends in Hell."

"You get my soul," DeMille said weakly.

"It's not much of a bargain for me. But if you don't sign it, you won't get me. Without me, the movie's a bomb. Ask The Producer, He'll tell you how it is."

"I'll call Him now."

"No! Sign now, this very second, or I walk out forever!"

DeMille bowed his head, more in pain than in prayer.

"Now!"

DeMille wrote on the dotted line. There had never been any genuine indecision. After all, he was a film director.

After snickering Satan had left, DeMille punched a phone number. The circuits transmitted this to a station which beamed the pulses up to a satellite which transmitted these directly to the heavenly city. Somehow, he got a wrong number. He hung up quickly when Israfel, the angel of death, answered. The second attempt, he got through.

"Your Divinity, I suppose. You know what I just did? It *was* the only way you could get him to play himself. You understand that, don't You?"

"Yes, but if you're thinking of breaking the contract or getting Me to do it for you, forget it. What kind of an image would I have if I did something unethical like that? But not to worry. He can't get his hooks into your soul until I say so."

Not to worry? DeMille thought. I'm the one who's going to Hell, not Him.

"Speaking of hooks, let Me remind you of a clause in your contract with The Studio. If you ever fall from grace, and I'm not talking about that little bimbo you were going to make your mistress, you'll die. The Mafia isn't the only one that puts out a contract. *Capice?*"

DeMille, sweating and cold, hung up. In a sense, he was already in Hell. All his life with no women except for one wife? It was bad enough to have no variety, but what if whoever he married cut him off, like one of his wives—what was her name?—had done?

Moreover, he couldn't get loaded out of his skull even to forget his marital woes. God, though not prohibiting booze in His Book, had said that moderation in strong liquor was required and no excuses. Well, maybe he could drink beer, however disgustingly plebeian that was.

He wasn't even happy with his work now. He just didn't get the respect he had in the old days. When he chewed out the camerapeople, the grips, the gaffers, the actors, they stormed back at him that he didn't have the proper Christian humility, he was too high and mighty, too arrogant. God would get him if he didn't watch his big fucking mouth.

This left him speechless and quivering. He'd always thought, and acted accordingly, that the director, not God, was God. He remembered telling Charlton Heston that when Heston, who after all was only Moses, had thrown a temper tantrum when he'd stepped in a pile of camel shit during the filming of *The Ten Commandments*.

Was there more to the making of the end-of-the-world than appeared on the surface? Had God seemingly forgiven everybody their sins and lack of faith but was subtly, even insidiously, making everybody pay by suffering? Had He forgiven but not forgotten? Or vice versa?

God marked even the fall of a sparrow, though why the sparrow, a notoriously obnoxious and dirty bird, should be significant in God's eye was beyond DeMille.

He had the uneasy feeling that everything wasn't as simple and as obvious as he'd thought when he'd been untimely ripped from the grave in a sort of Caesarean section and carried off like a nursing baby in Gabriel's arms to the office of The Ultimate Producer.

◆ ◆ ◆

From the *Playboy* Interview feature, December, 1980.

Playboy: Mr. Satan, why did you decide to play yourself after all?

Satan: Damned if I know.

Playboy: The rumors are that you'll be required to wear clothes in the latter-day scenes but that you steadfastly refuse. Are these rumors true?

Satan: Yes indeed. Everybody knows I never wear clothes except when I want to appear among humans without attracting undue attention. If I wear clothes it'd be unrealistic. It'd be phoney, though God knows there are enough fake things in this movie. The Producer says this is going to be a PG picture, not an X-rated. That's why I walked off the set the other day. My lawyers are negotiating with The Studio now about this. But you can bet your ass that I won't go back unless things go my way, the right way. After all, I am an artist, and I have my integrity. Tell me, if you had a prong this size, would you hide it?

Playboy: The Chicago cops would arrest me before I got a block from my pad. I don't know, though, if they'd charge me with indecent exposure or being careless with a natural resource.

Satan: They wouldn't dare arrest me. I got too much on the city administration.

Playboy: That's some whopper. But I thought angels were sexless. You are a fallen angel, aren't you?

Satan: You jerk! What kind of researcher are you? Right there in the Bible, *Genesis* 6:2, it says that the sons of God, that is, the angels, took the daughters of men as wives and had children by them. You think the kids were test tube babies? Also, you dunce, I refer you to *Jude 7* where it's said that the angels, like the Sodomites, committed fornications and followed unnatural lusts.

Playboy: Whew! That brimstone! There's no need getting so hot under the collar, Mr. Satan. I only converted a few years ago. I haven't had much chance to read the Bible.

Satan: I read the Bible every day. All of it. I'm a speedreader, you know.

Playboy: You read the Bible? (Pause.) Hee, hee! Do you read it for the same reason W. C. Fields did when he was dying?

Satan: What's that?

Playboy: Looking for loopholes.

◆ ◆ ◆

DeMille was in a satellite and supervising the camerapeople while they shot the takes from ten miles up. He didn't like at all the terrific pressure he was working under. There was no chance to shoot every scene three or four times to get the best angle. Or to reshoot if the actors blew their lines. And, oh, sweet Jesus, they were blowing them all over the world!

He mopped his bald head. "I don't care what The Producer says! We have to retake at least a thousand scenes. And we've a million miles of film to go yet!"

They were getting close to the end of the breaking-of-the-seven-seals sequences. The Lamb, played by The Producer's Son, had just broken the sixth seal. The violent worldwide earthquake had gone well. The sun-turning-black-as-a-funeral-pall had been a breeze. But the moon-all-red-as-blood had had some color problems. The rushes looked more like Colonel Sanders' orange juice than hemoglobin. In DeMille's opinion the stars-falling-to-earth-like-figs-shaken-down-by-a-gale scenes had been excellent, visually speaking. But everybody knew that the stars were not little blazing stones set in the sky but were colossal balls of atomic fires each of which was many times bigger than Earth. Even one of them, a million miles from Earth, would destroy it. So where was the credibility factor?

"I don't understand you, boss," DeMille's assistant said. "You didn't worry about credibility when you made *The Ten Commandments*. When Heston, I mean, Moses, parted the Red Sea, it was the fakiest thing I ever saw. It must've made unbelievers out of millions of Christians. But the film was a box-office success."

"It was the dancing girls that brought off the whole thing!" DeMille screamed. "Who cares about all that other bullshit when they can see all those beautiful long-legged snatches twirling their veils!"

His secretary floated from her chair. "I quit, you male chauvinistic pig! So me and my sisters are just snatches to you, you baldheaded cunt?"

His hotline to the heavenly city rang. He picked up the phone.

"Watch your language!" The Producer thundered. "If you step out of line too many times, I'll send you back to the grave! And Satan gets you right then and there!"

Chastened but boiling near the danger point, DeMille got back to business, called Art in Hollywood. The sweep of the satellite around Earth included the sky-vanishing-as-a-scroll-is-rolled-up scenes, where every-mountain-and-island-is-removed-from-its-place. If the script had called for a literal removing, the tectonics problem would have been terrific and perhaps impossible. But in this case the special effects departments only had to simulate the scenes.

Even so, the budget was strained. However, The Producer, through his unique abilities, was able to carry these off. Whereas, in the original script, genuine displacements of Greenland, England, Ireland, Japan, and Madagascar had been called for, not to mention thousands of smaller islands, these were only faked.

♦ ♦ ♦

"Your Divinity, I have some bad news," Raphael said.

The Producer was too busy to indulge in talking about something He already knew. Millions of the faithful had backslid and taken up their old sinful ways. They believed that since so many events of the Apocalypse were being faked, God must not be capable of making any really big catastrophes. So, they didn't have anything to worry about.

The Producer, however, had decided that it would not only be good to wipe out some of the wicked but it would strengthen the faithful if they saw that God still had some muscle.

"They'll get the real thing next time," He said. "But we have to give DeMille time to set up his cameras at the right places. And we'll have to have the script rewritten, of course."

Raphael groaned. "Couldn't somebody else tell Ellison? He'll carry on something awful."

"I'll tell him. You look pretty pooped, Rafe. You need a little R&R. Take two weeks off. But don't do it on Earth. Things are going to be very unsettling there for a while."

Raphael, who had a tender heart, said, "Thanks, Boss, I'd just as soon not be around to see it."

The seal was stamped on the foreheads of the faithful, marking them safe from the burning of a third of Earth, the turning of a third of the sea to blood along with the sinking of a third of the ships at sea (which also included the crashing of a third of the airplanes in the air, something St. John had overlooked), the turning of a third of all water to wormwood (a superfluous measure since a third was already thoroughly polluted), the failure of a third of daylight, the release of giant mutant locusts from the abyss, and the release of poison-gas-breathing mutant horses, which slew a third of mankind.

DeMille was delighted. Never had such terrifying scenes been filmed. And these were nothing to the plagues which followed. He had enough film from the cutting room to make a hundred documentaries after the movie was shown. And then he got a call from The Producer.

"It's back to the special effects, my boy."

"But why, Your Divinity? We still have to shoot The-Great-Whore-of-Babylon sequences, the two-Beasts-and-the-marking-of-the-wicked, the Mount-Zion-and-The-Lamb-with-His-one-hundred-and-forty-thousand-good-men-who-haven't-defiled-themselves-with-women, the..."

"Because there aren't any wicked left by now, you dolt! And not too many of the good, either!"

"That couldn't be helped," DeMille said. "Those gas-breathing, scorpion-tailed horses kind of got out of hand. But we just *have* to have the scenes where the rest of mankind that survives the plagues still doesn't abjure its worship of idols and doesn't repent of its murders, sorcery, fornications, and robberies."

"Rewrite the script."

"Ellison will quit for sure this time."

"That's all right. I already have some hack from Peoria lined up to take his place. And cheaper, too."

DeMille took his outfit, one hundred thousand strong, to the heavenly city. Here they shot the war between Satan and his demons and Michael and his angels. This was not in the chronological sequence as written by St. John, but the logistics problems were so tremendous that it was thought best to film these out of order.

Per the rewritten script, Satan and his host were defeated, but a lot of nonbelligerents were casualties, including DeMille's best cameraperson. Moreover, there was a delay in production when Satan insisted that a stuntperson do the part where he was hurled from Heaven to Earth.

"Or use a dummy!" he yelled. "Twenty thousand miles is a hell of along way to fall! If I'm hurt badly I might not be able to finish the movie!"

The screaming match between the director and Satan took place on the edge of the city. The Producer, unnoticed, came up behind Satan and kicked him from the city for the second time in their relationship with utter ruin and furious combustion.

Shrieking, "I'll sue! I'll sue!" Satan fell towards the planet below. He made a fine spectacle in his blazing entrance into the atmosphere, but the people on Earth paid it little attention. They were used to fiery portents in the sky. In fact, they were getting fed up with them.

DeMille screamed and danced around and jumped up and down. Only the presence of The Producer kept him from using foul and abusive language.

"We didn't get it on camera! Now we'll have to shoot it over!"

"His contract calls for only one fall," God said. "You'd better shoot the War-between-The-Faithful-and-True-Rider-against-the-beast-and-the-false-prophet while he recovers."

"What'll I do about the fall?" DeMille moaned.

"Fake it," The Producer said, and He went back to His office.

♦ ♦ ♦

Per the script, an angel came down from Heaven and bound up the badly injured and burned and groaning Satan with a chain and threw him into the abyss, the Grand Canyon. Then he shut and sealed it over him (what a terrific sequence that was!) so that Satan might seduce the nations no more until a thousand years had passed.

A few years later the devil's writhings caused a volcano to form above him, and the Environmental Protection Agency filed suit against Celestial Productions, Inc. because of the resultant pollution of the atmosphere.

Then God, very powerful now that only believers existed on Earth, performed the first resurrection. In this, only the martyrs were raised. And Earth, which had had much elbow room because of the recent wars and plagues, was suddenly crowded again.

Part I was finished except for the reshooting of some scenes, the dubbing in of voice and background noise, and the synchronization of the music, which was done by the cherubim and seraphim (all now unionized).

The great night of the premiere in a newly built theater in Hollywood, six million capacity, arrived. DeMille got a standing ovation after it was over. But *Time* and *Newsweek* and *The Manchester Guardian* panned the movie.

"There are some people who may go to Hell after all," God growled.

DeMille didn't care about that. The film was a box-office success, grossing ten billion dollars in the first six months. And when he considered the reruns in theaters and the TV rights...well, had anyone ever done better?

He had a thousand more years to live. That seemed like a long time. Now. But...what would happen to him when Satan was released to seduce the nations again? According to John the Divine's book, there'd be another worldwide battle. Then Satan, defeated, would be cast into the lake of fire and sulphur in the abyss.

(He'd be allowed to keep his Oscar, however.)

Would God let Satan, per the contract DeMille had signed with the devil, take DeMille with him into the abyss? Or would He keep him safe long enough to finish directing Part II? After Satan was buried for good, there'd be a second resurrection and a judging of those raised from the dead. The goats, the bad guys, would be hurled into the pit to keep Satan company. DeMille should be with the saved, the sheep, because he had been born again. But there was that contract with The Tempter.

DeMille arranged a conference with The Producer. Ostensibly, it was about Part II, but DeMille managed to bring up the subject which really interested him.

"I can't break your contract with him," God said.

"But I only signed it so that You'd be sure to get Satan for the role. It was a self-sacrifice. Greater love hath no man and all that. Doesn't that count for anything?"

"Let's discuss the shooting of the new Heaven and the new Earth sequences."

At least I'm not going to be put into Hell until the movie is done, DeMille thought. But after that? He couldn't endure thinking about it.

"It's going to be a terrible technical problem," God said, interrupting DeMille's gloomy thoughts. "When the second resurrection takes place, there won't be even Standing Room Only on Earth. That's why I'm dissolving the old Earth and making a new one. But I can't just duplicate the old Earth. The problem of Lebensraum would still remain. Now, what I'm contemplating is a Dyson sphere."

"What's that?"

"A scheme by a 20th-century mathematician to break up the giant planet Jupiter into large pieces and set them in orbit at the distance of Earth from the sun. The surfaces of the pieces would provide room for a population enormously larger than Earth's. It's a Godlike concept."

"What a documentary its filming would be!" DeMille said. "Of course, if we could write some love interest in it, we could make a he...pardon me, a heaven of a good story!"

God looked at his big railroad watch.

"I have another appointment, C.B. The conference is over."

DeMille said good-bye and walked dejectedly towards the door. He still hadn't gotten an answer about his ultimate fate. God was stringing him along. He felt that he wouldn't know until the last minute what was going to happen to him. He'd be suffering a thousand years of uncertainty, of mental torture. His life would be a cliffhanger. Will God relent? Or will He save the hero at the very last second?

"C.B.," God said.

DeMille spun around, his heart thudding, his knees turned to water. Was this it? The fatal finale? Had God, in His mysterious and subtle way, decided for some reason that there'd be no Continued In Next Chapter for him? It didn't seem likely, but then The Producer had never promised that He'd use him as the director of Part II nor had He signed a contract with him. Maybe, like so many temperamental producers, He'd suddenly concluded that DeMille wasn't the right one for the job. Which meant that He could arrange it so that his ex-director would be thrown now, right this minute, into the lake of fire.

God said, "I can't break your contract with Satan. So..."

"Yes?"

DeMille's voice sounded to him as if he were speaking very far away.

"Satan can't have your soul until you die."

"Yes?"

His voice was only a trickle of sound, a last few drops of water from a clogged drainpipe.

"So, if you don't die, and that, of course, depends upon your behavior, Satan can't ever have your soul."

God smiled and said, "See you in eternity."

This day, for Charlie Roth, would always be the Day of the Locust.

Twenty-nine years old, a Welfare Department employee, he was now an agent of its new branch, the General Office of Special Restitution. Every workday had been a bad day since he had entered the WD. But in times to come, he would liken today to tree destruction wrought in a few hours by the sky-blackening and all-devouring swarms of the desert locust, *Schistocerca gregaria*.

Charlie Roth, attaché case filled with sterilization authorization forms, walked up a staircase in Building 13 of the Newstreet Housing Authority. He was headed toward the apartment of Riches Dott, unmarried mother of many. For the moment, his guilt and tension were gone. His mind was on Laura, the seventh child of Riches Dott. Laura was the only one of the fifteen children for whom he now had any hope. An older brother who had a high IQ and an intense but low ambition was a lifer in Joliet Penitentiary. An older sister had had a remarkable mathematical talent, long ago whisked away in the smoke of crack and snark.

Advising and aiding Laura was not part of his official mission. But perhaps he could be someone to talk to who really cared about her. He would give her money out of his own shallow pocket if that would make firmer a resolve that must be shaking despite her strong will.

Yet he himself might need help soon. Big help.

Ever since his wife, five months pregnant, had left him, he had been getting more and more easily angered. But their separation was only a lesser part of the steam-hot wrath he could just barely control. The larger part troubled him whether he was sleeping or awake.

His mind was like a water strider. One of those bugs (family Gerridae) that walked on the still waters of ponds. Its specially modified back legs skimmed the surface tension, that single layer of molecules that was a skin on the pond to the strider. The legs of his mind, an arthopod Jesus that had suddenly lost its faith in its powers, were poking now and then through the skin.

"I'm going to sink and then drown! I wanted to save all these wretches because I loved them! Now I hate them!"

Here he was, God help him, a would-be entomologist who could not master chemistry and mathematics. He had given up his goal before he even got his M.A. A man who loves the study of bugs, what does he do when he can't do that?

He becomes a social worker.

As he turned onto the landing, he heard quick-paced footsteps above him. He paused, and Laura Dott appeared. She smiled when she saw him, said, "Hello, Mr. Roth," and clattered down the steps toward him. She was in the uniform of a waitress at a local fast-food restaurant. Just turned eighteen, Laura had been removed from her mother's welfare dependency roll. Though still living with her mother, she was making straight A's in high school and working five days a week from 4:00 P.M. until midnight, minimum wage.

She had always been an honor student. How she could have done that while living in the pressure-cooker pandemonium of her mother's apartment, Charlie did not understand. Equally mysterious was how she had managed to stay unpregnant, drug-free, and sane. Some other youths in this area had done the same, but their mother wasn't Riches.

"Hi, Laura," he said. "I'd like to talk to you."

She went past him, her head turned toward him. She was slim and long-legged, and her skin was as close to black as brown could get. She flashed a beautiful smile with teeth white and regular but long and thick.

"Busy, busy, busy, Mr. Roth. If it's important, see me during my mid-break, eight o'clock. Sorry."

She was gone. Charlie sighed and went on up the steps. At the top he saw Amin Ketcher coming down the hall from the staircase at the opposite end. He reached the door of Mrs. Dott's apartment before Charlie got there, and leaned against the wall by the door.

If he was waiting for Laura, he was too late. Probably held up completing a deal: crack, zoomers, blasters, and snark. The bastard. She's told him time and again to get lost. He's street-smart and shadow-elusive, but a loser: at twenty, the known father of twelve children, boasting of it, yet not giving a penny to support them.

So far he had refused to sign the form authorizing his sterilization. Why should he? He had the cash for a fleet of new cars. Moreover, the ability to knock up a horde of teenagers was, to him, one of the main proofs of his manhood. But they had been pushovers. He wanted Laura Dott because she had only contempt and disgust for him, though she knew better than to insult him verbally.

Charlie strode down the hall. "Hey, a Charlie Charlie," Ketcher said. "The General Office of Special Reestituutiion man. The white gooser."

He inclined his handsome copper-colored face to look down on Charlie's six feet from his six feet six inches. His oil-dripping kinky hair was cut in the current "castle" style: high crenellated walls and six-inch-high turrets. A silver-banded plastic nosebone, huge gold earrings, and a ticktacktoe diagram, the symbol of his gang, cut by a razor into each cheek, gave him the barbaric appearance he desired. He wore a sequined purple jacket and jeans overlaid with battery-powered electric lights and neon-tube rock slogans. These flashed on and off while the yang-n-yin music of the EAT SHIT AND LIVE band played from a hundred microphone-buttons on his garments.

The enormous pupils of his glistening black eyes could have been caused by belladonna, used by many youths. But his faint gunpowdery odor told Charlie that he was on snark. The latest designer drug, its effects and chemical traces vanished within five minutes after being used. The narcs had to test a suspect on the spot to get the evidence to convict the user. That was possible only if a van carrying the heavy and intricate test equipment was at once available.

Also, every tiny bag of snark held two easily breakable vials. If the carrier was caught by the police and he had enough time, he threw the bag against anything hard. Bag, snark, and vials went up in a microexplosion. No drug residue was left.

Charlie passed by Ketcher and stopped in front of the door. He could hear the blast of the TV set and the yelling of children through the door. Something crashed loudly, and Riches's high-pitched voice drilled through the plastic.

"I swear, Milton, you knock that chair over again, I slap you sillier'n you already be!"

The doorbell had long been out of order. Charlie knocked hard three times on the door.

"Old fat-ass Riches ain't going to sign," Ketcher said. "You wasting your breath. Or you waiting till Laura come home from school? You wasting your time there, too, Charlie. She ain't interested in no small white dongs."

"You paleolithic atavism!" Charlie said, snarling. "You've been harassing Laura long enough to know she'd sooner screw an ape with diarrhea than you. Anyway, you mush-brained marker, she isn't going to be around much longer. She'll be getting out of this shithole and away from corpse worms like you. Very, very soon, I promise you."

Ketcher stepped closer to Charlie. His enormous eyes were as empty of intelligence as a wasp's.

"What that mean, paley...whatever? You making a racial remark, you blue-eyed shithead? I turn your skinny ass in to the Gooser Office. And what you mean, Laura gonna be gone?"

Charlie regretted losing his cool, and so warning Ketcher that Laura would soon be out of his reach.

The door started to swing open. The TV roared, and the children's voices shrilled like a horde of cicadas.

"You're extinct," Charlie said. "A fly in amber still kicking because you don't know you're dead. Laura'd sooner eat a live cockroach than let you get into her pants."

He stepped through the doorway and closed it while Ketcher yelled,"I'll cut you when you come out, you white motherfucker!"

Sure you'll cut me, Charlie thought. You know I just have to use Riches's phone, and the troops stationed down on the corner will be up here. If they find the knife on you, you go straight to a prison work camp.

Though often in the family room, Charlie had now been admitted only because Riches had not heard his knock. One of the ten children living there had happened to be close to the door. He was optimist enough at the age of six to take the chocolate bar Charlie offered and not wonder what it was going to cost him later. But he slid the bar inside his urine-yellowed jockey shorts, his only garment, before his siblings caught sight of it.

Mrs. Dott answered his greeting with a scowl, and then stared straight at the screen.

Charlie, sighing, pulled three stapled sheets from his attaché case. This visit, he was required only to read to her Paragraph 3 from Form WD-GOSSR C-6392-T. Though he knew that Riches probably could not hear his voice above the blaring commercial or the shouting and screaming children, he did not care.

"'...available to all American citizens (see Paragraph 5 for age, mental, and physical exceptions and restrictions) REGARDLESS OF RACE, GENDER OR RELIGION. Guaranteed free: any new 100% American-made automobile, motorcycle, or pickup truck with 100 gallons of gasoline or diesel oil or alcohol, ten quarts of motor oil, a year's license plate, one year's warranty (see Paragraph 4.d for exceptions) and casualty insurance (see Paragraph 4.e for exceptions and restrictions)....'"

Before he could get to the section dealing with the freedom of the government from lawsuits, Riches shrilled, "I told you time and again! Ain't nobody gonna mess around with my body!"

She settled back in the stained, torn, and broken-springed sofa. Riches looks like a huge queen bee swollen with eggs, Charlie thought.

Despite the anger twisting her face, her gaze was fixed on the soap opera unfolding its story as slowly as the wings of a just-molted dragonfly.

Holy humping Jesus! Charlie thought. She's borne sixteen children. Had clap three times. Syph twice. It's a miracle she's escaped AIDS. She doesn't really understand the connection between sexual intercourse and venereal disease, though it's often been explained to her. All those babies have drained the calcium from her bones, spiders sucking out the juice, leaving her toothless and with a widow's hump.

Don't mess around with her body?

Though he wasn't going to change her mind, he had to make his request this final time, then report the failure. The big praying-mantis eyes of Junkers, his boss, would get deadlier and colder. He'd shout, "How you expect this office to keep up its quotas if you piss out on me?"

"Mrs. Dott," Charlie said, "all but six in this building have signed up, and I'm sure most of those will eventually come through. You're forty-five. The cutoff date is forty-six. Why throw all that money away? Chances are high you can't have any more babies, anyway."

Suddenly she looked smug and sly. Patting her anthill stomach, she said, "You think I be too old to have any more? Wrong, Charlie. Got me another. She got one, too."

She pointed at thirteen-year-old Crystal, watching TV.

Her smile became even slier. "The law say Crystal can't sign up with you goosers 'less I say she can till she fifteen. No way!"

She did not look at him as he walked away. Nor did she seem to notice that he was lingering by the door. The dusty wall mirror showed his light red hair and pale and grim face. The dark circles around his eyes looked like Sioux smoke rings signaling for help. His guts hurt as if wasp larvae had hatched inside him and were eating their way out.

Why? What he was doing was rational and humanitarian. It was not just for the good of the people as a whole, though it was that, too. It was also for the good of the people at whom the missions were directed, and it involved no force or cruelty, none that was apparent, anyway.

He saw a cockroach, *Blatta orientalis,* inevitable companion of dirt and colleague of poverty, scuttle out from beneath an end of Riches's sofa. It seized a potato-chip fragment and shot back into the darkness under the sofa.

The piece contained an antifertility drug harmless to humans. Charlie thought that 99.9 percent of the cockroaches might be made infertile. But 0.1 percent would survive because they had mutated to resist the drug. From that would come billions.

He went into the hallway. Ketcher was alone with a youth, an obvious customer. Seeing Charlie, both went down the stairs. A faint acrid odor like battlefield smoke hung in the hall. Charlie felt as if he had gone through a firefight. He was trembling slightly. The hallway with its garbage cans, its dusty light bulbs, and its hot, unmoving air seemed to shift a little. Somewhat dizzy, he leaned against the scabrous, once-green wall for support.

What he was doing was for the best. How many times had he told himself that? The welfare recipients were in an economic-social elevator, its cables cut, falling faster and faster, nothing but disaster at the bottom for them — and for all citizens, since what happens to a part always affects the whole. At the same time, their numbers were increasing geometrically, far out of proportion to the rest of the population. Misery, hopelessness, disease, malnutrition, violence, and deep ignorance were also expanding.

The Ronn-Eagan legislation had not passed without vehement, and even violent, opposition, especially from some religious groups. But the nonreligious reaction to the excesses of the last three decades of the previous century was very strong. And though the law had made already burdensome taxes much heavier, it did promise an eventual lightening of the tax load and a large reduction in the welfare populations. But the vehicle-making, insurance, and petroleum industries, and the businesses dependent on these, were booming.

Someday the welfare problem (which also encompassed a part of the crime-drug problem) would be a small one. Why, then, did he have these dreams in which he strode down a very narrow and twilit hallway with no end? The doors ahead of him were open, but he slammed them shut as he passed.

"Charlie Roth! A ghost among spooks!"

Only Rex Bessey used that greeting. He climbed up from the staircase on which Charlie ascended. His face was a full, dark moon. Then another moon, checked black and white, the vest covering his huge paunch, rose above the steps. He smiled as he limped toward Charlie.

"I got more than today's quota. Those rednecks go apeshit over pickups. How you doing, Charlie?"

"Wasted too much time on Riches Dott, a hopeless case."

"That asshole Junkers thought he was screwing us when he gave me the white area and you the black," Rex said. "But when I remind those Neanderthal rednecks I played tackle for the Bears until I wrecked my leg, they get friendly. That makes me one of the good old boys even if I am a fucking nigger. What helps, I give them a few beers to soften them up."

His attaché case clinked when he shook it.

"Why don't you carry some beer, too?"

"Principles," Charlie said.

Rex laughed loudly. "Sure! You practicing genocide, and you got principles?"

Charlie did not get angry. Once, when drunk, Rex had admitted that he fully agreed with the sterilization policy. He hated his job, but he wouldn't like any work unless it brought in big money.

"This Laura Dott you'd like to rescue," he had once said. "She might make it, but only because she's very smart and strong. What about her brothers and sisters? They were born not so smart or so strong. Why should they have to live in the bottom of the shitpool just because they aren't superhuman? If they were given the environment your average upper-level poor people have...well, why go on? We've been through this before. End of lecture. Have another drink?"

Now he said, "Let's hoist a few at Big Pete's."

"The quota."

"That's Junkers's, not the GOOSR's. Why should we sweat and grunt and crap golden turds so that black-assed bastard can get promotion faster? I knew him when he was extorting lunch money from the little kids in sixth grade. He tried that once with me, and I kicked him in the balls. He hates my guts for that, but he isn't going to fire me. He knows I'll tell how he got his job, which he isn't qualified for, and he'll be out on his ass. Forget his quota."

Charlie had heard all this before. He said, "O.K."

Shortly before five, their eyes tending toward the glassy, they walked into the office. Junkers was not there. Charlie faxed his reports and went home to his apartment on High Street. It was one of seven semi-sleazy units in a once-magnificent mansion built by a whiskey baron in 1910. He could look down from his bathroom window at his domain of work, that part of Hell that did not border on the Styx, but on the Illinois River.

The small, dead-aired, and close-pressing apartment rooms rang with his footsteps as if they were great high-ceilinged palace halls. After his wife left him, he had been able to endure the apartment only when he was asleep. Now nightmares swarmed over him like carrion flies.

While his CD player poured out Mahler's *The Song of the Earth*, he ate a TV dinner. Then, sitting on the sofa, staring at the blank set, he slowly drank a tall glassful of medium-priced bourbon. Before he drowsed away, he set the alarm. Its loud ring startled him from — thank God! — a dreamless sleep. Beethoven's Fifth was just starting its loud knocking at the door of destiny.

After a shower he looked out the window. The darkness was thick enough that lights were beginning to be turned on. For him, there was only one glow in the Southside of the city: Laura's, a firefly (family Lampyridae) winking above a night-struck meadow.

Twenty minutes later, his hangover only slowly receding, he drove away in his beat-up and run-down car. (Maybe he should get sterilized and have a new car for the first time in his life.) Ten minutes later he was in the Newstreet HPA area. He would not have ventured there alone after dark, but the green-capped Special Police and steel-helmeted Emergency Reserve troops stationed on various street corners ensured a sort of safety. An FDA-unit van passed Charlie on the other side of the street. Black, mournful faces looked out from behind the barred windows.

The shiny new cars were bumper to bumper in the streets, parked on the sidewalks and jammed into open lots between houses.

Charlie's car turned into the alley back of Tchaka's Fast Food Emporium. A young black, his neon-tubed garments glowing, leaned against the wall by the side entrance. When he saw Charlie's car, he shut the door and stepped inside. He was "Slick" Ramsey, one of Ketcher's gang. He looked furtive, but that did not mean much down here.

Unable to find a parking space in the alley, Charlie drove slowly around the block. Before he was halfway, he realized — he jumped as if stung by a bee — that the kids on their work break always stood in the alley, talking and horsing around. But they had not been there.

He brought the car screeching around the corner and into the alley. His headlights spotlighted Ramsey's shiny, sweaty face sticking out from the doorway. Ramsey quickly shut the door. Charlie stopped the car by the door and was out of the car before it had quit rocking. He knew, he just knew, that Ketcher, inflamed with snark, his cool burned away when he found out that Laura would soon be out of his reach, was no longer waiting to get what he just had to have.

Ramsey and another youth caught Charlie by the arms as he burst into the dimly lit hallway. A third, John "Welcome Wagon" Penney, came toward him with a knife in his hand. Charlie screamed and kicked out. His foot slammed into Penney's hand, and the blade dropped.

Twisting and turning, stomping on the feet of the two holding him, he broke loose and was down the hall and through the doorway from which Penney had come. Still screaming, he plunged into a large, well-lit storeroom. The workers were huddled in a corner, four of the gang standing guard, holding knives. One worker was down on her knees, vomiting, but several of her fellows were grinning and cheering Ketcher.

At the opposite corner, Laura, naked, was on her back on the floor with Ketcher, fully dressed, on top of her. Charlie saw her face, bloodied, her mouth fallen open like a corpse's, her eyes wide and glazed. Her outspread arms were pinned to the ground by the heavy feet of two gang members.

Silent, all stared at Charlie except Ketcher and Laura. He was savagely biting her nose while pumping away.

Charlie got to Ketcher before the others unfroze. No longer yelling, the others silent, the only sounds the slap of his shoes and those of the pursuers from the hall, he charged. No one got in his way, and he slammed his hands against the pockets of Ketcher's jacket. The vials within the bags broke; the two chemicals mingled; the bags popped like firecrackers; the brief spurts of flame from them looked like flaming gas jets.

Ketcher screamed while struggling to tear off his jacket.

The two standing on Laura's arms jumped at Charlie and grabbed him. Still silent, Charlie slapped at their pockets. There was more popping, and they let loose of him and tried to get rid of the clothes before they burned to death.

The workers ran yelling out of the storeroom. Some of the gang followed them. Two ran at Charlie, their knives waving. By then Ketcher's jacket was on the floor, but he was rolling in agony on the concrete, and seemingly unaware as yet that Charlie was here. Charlie snatched up the smoking and flaming jacket and thrust it into the face of the nearest knife fighter.

He had become a fire in a wind, whirling, slapping jacket pockets, staggering back when a blade went through his left biceps, grabbing a wrist when his cheek was sliced, and twisting the wrist until it cracked. Only because he acted like a crazy man and was as elusive as a gnat did he escape death.

When he saw Ketcher—his ribs, his shoulders, the front of his thighs, and one side of his face bright red with burns, again on top of Laura, but now slamming her head repeatedly into the concrete floor, blood spreading out below her, her mouth slack and open, her eyes shattered glass—Charlie truly became crazy.

Ketcher's only thought now seemed to be to kill Laura. It was as if he blamed her for the burns.

The rest of his gang had run out of the storeroom. They knew that the cops and the troops would soon be here.

Coughing from the smoke, Charlie ran toward Ketcher and Laura. Suddenly Ketcher sat back. His breath cracked. His chest heaved. But he looked at his work with what seemed to be satisfaction. Where the blood on Laura's face did not conceal it, her deep brown skin was underlayered with gray.

Ketcher rose, and Charlie turned. Ketcher started, and his eyes widened.

"You, you done this?" he said. "The white gooser?"

He half-turned and looked down at Laura.

"The uppity bitch is dead. I had her; she ain't gonna get away."

Charlie stopped and picked up a knife.

Ketcher turned back toward him. "I killed the bitch. I'll kill you, too, Charlie Charlie."

Charlie screamed. According to what he was told, he was still screaming when the cops came. He did not remember.

If he was screaming until his throat was raw for days afterward, it was because he was giving vent to all the futility and despair and suffering and the sense of being imprisoned, straitjacketed, chained, which he felt for himself and which the cesspool dwellers he worked for felt far more keenly than he. And it was for Laura, whose drive and brains might have freed her, given her some freedom, anyway. No one raised here ever really got free of it.

He did not remember stabbing Ketcher many times. Vaguely, he did recall a blurred vision of Ketcher on his back, his arms and legs up in the air and kicking like a dying water beetle. Charlie was told that blood had covered him, Ketcher, and Laura like liquid shrouds. His informant, a black cop, had not been trying to impress him. Born here, she had seen worse when she was in diapers.

When discharged from the mental ward of the hospital five months later, Charlie had no job and did not look for one. In what seemed a short time, he was on welfare.

The irony was doubled when Rex Bessey came to ask him if he wished to sign up for sterilization.

"I'm really embarrassed," Rex said. "But it's my job."

Charlie smiled. "Don't I know. But I'm not going to sign. My wife — you know Blanche — called me yesterday. She just had a baby girl. We're going to get together again. It may not work out, but we're trying for the sake of the baby, for ours, too. I got hope now, Rex. I'm on welfare, but I won't be forever. My situation's different. I wasn't raised on pub-lic aid, handicapped by my environment from birth, and I don't have two strikes against me because I'm black. I can make it. I will make it."

Rex got a beer and sat down. He said, "You've been so sunk in hopeless apathy, your friends just gave up. You know I was the last to quit coming around. You just wouldn't stop your dismal talk about Laura. I did my best, but I couldn't cheer you up. I'm sorry, I just couldn't take you anymore."

Charlie waved his hand. "I don't blame you. But I'm better. I know I'll make it. My wife's phone call, well, soon as I hung up, something seemed to turn over. How can I describe it? I'll try. Listen, insects thrive as a species mainly because they breed so wondrously. Kill all but two, and in less than a year, there are 10 billion. It's nature's way; God's, if you prefer. People aren't insects, but nature doesn't seem to care about the individual human or insect being killed, or even millions being wiped out. Laura Dott was one of the unlucky ones, and that's the way it is.

"But I'm human. I do what insects can't do. I care; I hurt; I mourn; I grieve: But I wasn't doing what most humans do. Healing, getting over the hurt as time did its work, accepting this world for what it is. Nor was I trying to do my little bit to make the world just a little better. I gave up even that after Laura died."

Charlie fell silent until Rex said, "And?"

"Blanche and I were discussing what to name the baby. Blanche's mother was named Laura, and she wanted to name the baby Laura. I was so struck with the coincidence, I couldn't talk for a minute."

Rex leaned forward in the chair, his huge hand squeezing the sides of the beer can together.

"You mean?"

"One Laura down, one Laura to go."

MICHAEL CROTEAU

In Joe Lansdale's heartfelt introduction to this book, he managed to express, in less than 1,500 printed words, what I have been trying to say on the Internet for the last ten years. Philip José Farmer is perhaps the most wildly imaginative writer in a field built on the furthest reaches of the imagination. He is considered by most of his peers to be a giant, yet precious few of his books are in print.

Thankfully I have been given a much easier task than Joe; I don't need to try to tell you what makes Phil special, I just need to ponder this question: Is this collection "The Best" of Philip José Farmer? Given the restrictions put on this project — no novels, short stories only, and keeping it under 600 pages, I'd say it comes pretty close. It is certainly more ambitious than the "best of" type collections that have come before it.

During the 1950s, Phil was being noticed for his novellas, novelettes and short stories. Since the 1960s, most science fiction readers have discovered him through his longer works, mainly the World of Tiers and Riverworld Series. His Tarzan and Doc Savage "biographies" as well as novels based on these and other pulp characters introduced him to an ever-widening audience, as did his novels based on the characters of authors such as Herman Melville, Jules Verne, Kurt Vonnegut, Jr., and Frank Baum. However, as Joe Lansdale points out and as this book will almost certainly prove, Phil's most remarkable, but somehow overshadowed, work is his shorter fiction.

Phil's first Hugo Award, as Best New Talent for 1952, was won on the strength of "The Lovers" and "Sail On! Sail On!" Both are included in this collection. He won his second Hugo Award, this one for best Novella of 1967, for "Riders of the Purple Wage." This was Phil's contribution to the legendary anthology *Dangerous Visions*, and is also included in this collection. "Riders" was also nominated for the Nebula award, as was the story "After King Kong Fell" which, you guessed it, is also included here.

Speaking of nominees, four more of his stories have been nominated for the Hugo award, "The Alley Man," "My Sister's Brother,"

"The Day of the Great Shout" and "Sketches among the Ruins of my Mind." Three of these four are included in this volume, the only one missing is "The Day of the Great Shout," which was essentially the first half of the Hugo award winning novel *To Your Scattered Bodies Go*.

The remaining handpicked stories in this collection have all stood the test of time. All have been reprinted in anthologies and/or (mostly and) collected in other Farmer collections.

While most of Phil's diehard fans could certainly decry that one of their personal favorites is missing from this collection, the blame lies entirely with the mass and diversity of Phil's work. Even at nearly 600 pages, some gems had to be left out. I believe that this volume, like all the stories in it, will stand up well over time and will be considered an important book in the Farmer canon. Perhaps, like the novels mentioned above, this will be the book that is most instrumental in introducing future generations to Philip José Farmer and his remarkable imagination.

One final thought…as I asked Joe Lansdale after reading his introduction—Just what is it about Philip José Farmer that makes him adored by his fellow science fiction writers, perhaps even more than he is by his fans? That alone should tell you something about him.

Michael Croteau, webmaster of www.pjfarmer.com
The Official Philip José Farmer Home Page